THE TYRANT
BARU CORMORANT

BOOKS BY SETH DICKINSON

THE TYRANT
BARU CORMORANT

SETH DICKINSON

A TOM DOHERTY ASSOCIATES BOOK
NEW YORK

THE TYRANT BARU CORMORANT

Copyright © 2020 by Seth Dickinson

Map by Gillian Conahan

A Tor Book
Published by Tom Doherty Associates
120 Broadway
New York, NY 10271

www.tor-forge.com

Tor® is a registered trademark of Macmillan Publishing Group, LLC.

The Library of Congress Cataloging-in-Publication Data is available upon request.

ISBN 978-0-7653-8076-0 (hardcover)
ISBN 978-1-4668-7514-2 (ebook)

Our books may be purchased in bulk for promotional, educational, or business use. Please contact your local bookseller or the Macmillan Corporate and Premium Sales Department at 1-800-221-7945, extension 5442, or by email at MacmillanSpecialMarkets@macmillan.com.

First Edition: 2020

Printed in the United States of America

0 9 8 7 6 5 4 3 2 1

FOR BRIDGET

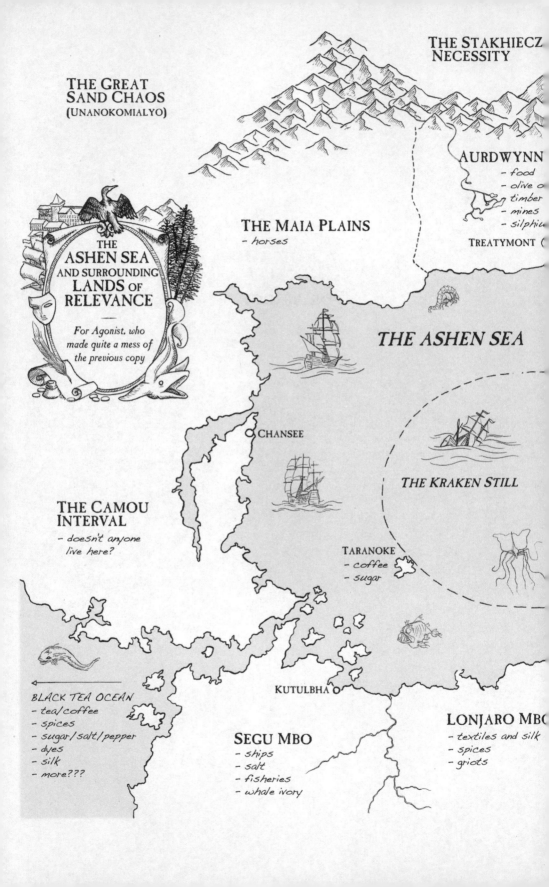

THE STAKHIECZ
NECESSITY

THE GREAT
SAND CHAOS
(UNANOKOMIALYO)

AURDWYNN
- food
- olive o
- timber
- mines
- silphiu

THE MAIA PLAINS
- horses

TREATYMONT

THE
ASHEN SEA
AND SURROUNDING
LANDS OF
RELEVANCE
—
For Agonist, who
made quite a mess of
the previous copy

THE ASHEN SEA

CHANSEE

THE KRAKEN STILL

THE CAMOU
INTERVAL
- doesn't anyone
live here?

TARANOKE
- coffee
- sugar

BLACK TEA OCEAN
- tea/coffee
- spices
- sugar/salt/pepper
- dyes
- silk
- more???

KUTULBHA

SEGU MBO
- ships
- salt
- fisheries
- whale ivory

LONJARO MBO
- textiles and silk
- spices
- griots

gold, silver
steel
ice
glass

DUCHY VULTJAG

STARFALL BAY

THE NORMARCH
- seal skins?

WELTHONY

the Elided Keep

THE MOTHER
OF STORMS
*east to SUPERCONTINENT
and THE LIGHTNING* →

LLOSYDANE
ISLANDS
- fresh water
- port

ISLA CAUTERIA
- fertilizer
- port

FALCREST
- medicine
- chemistry
- ships
- banking
- clocks I suppose

GRENDLAKE

CITY OF
FALCREST

THE BUTTERVELDT

KYPRANANOKE

SHAHEEN

THE OCCUPATION

THE TIDE COLUMN

YAMA

DEVI-NAGA MBO
- jute
- lime
- rice
- fish

JARO

south to
MZILIMAKE
MBO

PLAYERS, PAWNS, AND VESSELS

IMPERIAL REPUBLIC OF FALCREST
(THE MASQUERADE)

The Emperor—*anonymous, even to Itself*

THE THRONE
Baru Cormorant (Agonist)—*an accountant*
    Cairdine Farrier (Itinerant)—*her patron, an explorer*
Svirakir (Apparitor)—*a northerner*
Xate Yawa (Durance)—*a judge*
    Cosgrad Torrinde (Hesychast)—*her patron, a eugenicist*
??? (Stargazer)—*a colleague*
??? (Renascent)—*the senior member*

THE IMPERIAL NAVY
Lindon Satamine—*the Empire Admiral*
    Ahanna Croftare—*his rival, Province Admiral Falcrest*
Juris Ormsment—*a mutineer, sworn to kill Baru*
    Shao Lune—*her staff captain*
    RNS *Sulane*—*her ship*
RNS *Scylpetaire*—*consort to Sulane*
Samne Maroyad—*a rear admiral*
Aminata isiSegu—*a torturer, Baru's old friend*
Asmee Nullsin—*a captain under Samne Maroyad*
    RNS *Ascentatic*—*his ship*

Helbride—*Apparitor's ship*
Iraji oyaSegu—*Apparitor's spy and concubine*
Faham Execarne—*an identity in use by Falcrest's spymaster*
Iscend Comprine—*Hesychast's agent, Clarified*

AURDWYNN
(A PROVINCE OF THE IMPERIAL REPUBLIC)

Haradel Heia (Heingyl Ri)—*Duchess Heingyl, the Stag Governor*
Bel Latheman—*Imperial Accountant, her husband*
Tain Hu—*the late Duchess Vultjag, rebel*
   Ake Sentiamut—*her friend*
   Ude Sentiamut—*in her household*
   Run Czeshine—*in her household*
   Yythel—*in her household*
   Nitu—*in her household, but missing*
   Ulyu Xe—*a diver, in her household*

SOUSWARD, ONCE TARANOKE
(A PROVINCE OF THE IMPERIAL REPUBLIC)

Pinion—*Baru's mother*
Solit—*Baru's father*
Salm—*Baru's father, missing*
   Iriad—*their home*

THE STAKHIECZI NECESSITY

Atakaszir (of Mansion Hussacht)—*the Necessary King*
   Nayauru Aia—*his suitor, from Aurdwynn*
   Dziransi (of Mansion Hussacht)—*his sworn knight*
Purity Cartone/Ketly Norgraf—*Baru's agent, Clarified*
Kubarycz (of Mansion Uczenith)—*an exiled lord*

THE ORIATI MBO

LONJARO MBO
Tau-indi Bosoka—*Federal Prince, ambassador to Falcrest*
   Tahr Bosoka—*their mother*
   Enact-Colonel Osa ayaSegu—*their bodyguard*
Abdumasi Abd—*a merchant, most wanted man alive*
   Abdi-obdi Abd—*his mother*

SEGU MBO

Kindalana eshSegu—*Federal Prince, on mission to Falcrest*
    Padrigan eshSegu—*her father*
Scheme-Colonel Masako ayaSegu—*a Termite spy*

THE CANCRIOTH

The Womb (Abbatai)—*an onkos*
The Eye (Virios)—*an onkos*
The Brain (Incrisiath)—*an onkos*
Innibarish (Elelemi)—*a tall man*
Kimbune (Nilinim)—*a mathematician*
Galganath—*an orca*
    Eternal—*their ship*

Tain Shir

In 1502 the samudri of Calicut, desperate to stop violent Portuguese incursions into the Indian Ocean trade network, sent two letters. One begged his neighbor the raja of Cochin to close all markets to the Europeans. The raja of Cochin, who saw Calicut as his historical enemy, leaked this letter to the Portuguese.

The other letter offered a blanket peace to the Portuguese admiral, Vasco da Gama.

Da Gama sailed to Calicut to demand reparations and the expulsion of all Muslims. When he was not immediately indulged, he seized hostages, hung them from his masts, and bombarded the city. That evening he sent the severed hands, feet, and heads of the hostages ashore in a boat, along with a note, fixed to the prow by an arrow. "I have come to this port to buy and sell and pay for your produce; here is the produce of this country."

The note also demanded compensation for the powder and shot used to destroy Calicut.

If the people of Calicut did this, da Gama said, they would become his friends.

NOW

BARU. Wake up."

She wakes up but she does not know when or where. Is she on *Eternal,* drugged by the shadow ambassador? No, there's no black water licking at her ankles. She cannot be in the interrogation pit.

Is she on Kyprananoke, after the red lagoon and the grove of killed children? No. She cannot smell the crab meat on Tain Shir's fire.

Perhaps she is on *Helbride,* dreaming of Tain Hu, while honey trickles through her eye socket and meningitis burns up her brain. Or napping in a hammock outside her parents' house by the river Rubiyya, as the sounds of the bazaar she invented fill the morning air.

Shouldn't she be good at this by now? How many times has she awakened from some wound or illness, ready to revise her accounts of what she's lost? This, of all skills, she should have mastered.

She takes a breath, pours it out again. Fear flowing away like wash water. You will never wake up to anything worse than Sieroch. You will never wake up to anything better than Tain Hu's arms.

Then she sets to work.

The air smells of harsh soap and salt. So she is in a hygiene clinic, near the sea. There's a hint of perfume, too, a man's citrus-bitter bergamot. The man who woke her.

She lays down her own name as a cornerstone.

"Baru," she says. "I'm Baru."

And it is only a little bit a lie.

"Oh, thank virtue," the man breathes.

All her faculties snap into defensive array, like a phalanx locking shields for the fight. She knows this man. He is critical. The most critical. She doesn't trust him and he *must* continue to trust her.

"Baru," the man says, anxiously, "can you understand me?"

She tries to open her eyes, and cannot. Either they are swollen shut, or covered over, or gone. "Yes," she says, "I can understand you, Mister Farrier."

"What do you remember?"

She remembers that this man is Cairdine Farrier, her patron and her target. He found her as a child, in the markets of Taranoke, while his Imperial Republic of Falcrest (slowly, subtly, ingeniously) devoured her home. In his own way he devoured her, too. He gave her the Iriad school and a proper Falcrest education. He gave her inoculations when the pox came. He gave her algebra, astronomy, geometric proofs and maps of the world, everything she had ever dreamt of knowing. And all he took from her, all he ever asked, was her mother, and her fathers, and her people, and her lover, and her soul.

"Mister Farrier," she says, "you'd sent me away . . . to find something old. . . ."

Oh, something ancient. Something he needs to win his war. He has cultivated her as his weapon; he has introduced her into the circle of cryptarchs who rule the Imperial Republic of Falcrest in secret. She has learned about his lifelong battle, a struggle of dissections and insinuations and cold talk over warm brandy, against the eugenicist Cosgrad Torrinde, who believes that her people are fit only for farming, fishing, and pleasure.

And at last she has discovered the fulcrum, the place where it all comes to crisis.

Farrier has a deadline.

His struggle will end this year, in the disposition of the Oriati problem: a final test of his methods against Cosgrad's Torrinde. One man or the other will provide the technique that will allow the Imperial Republic of Falcrest, the Masquerade, to conquer and digest Oriati Mbo, the greatest and oldest civilization in the world.

In preparation for the endgame, Farrier sent her to recover a certain piece of information, the flint to start the fire. He did not know that piece of flint was a man, Abdumasi Abd, who had summoned the oldest power in the world to aid his revenge on Falcrest.

"What's been done to me?" she croaks. "Where are we, Mister Farrier?"

Gloved hands stroke her temples. She smells the edge of his mint-fresh breath, respectfully averted. He is always proper with her. "You've been hurt. But you're safe now. In Falcrest. With me."

She tries on a frown, the impatience of a tested schoolgirl. "Who hurt me?"

"My enemy's agent, Baru. Do you remember Xate Yawa?"

"Yes. I remember her." Just as she is Farrier's protégé, Yawa is the protégé of the enemy, Cosgrad Torrinde. As old and careful as she is young and reckless. And bound, each of them, to the shattered land of Aurdwynn: she by love of a dead woman, and Yawa by love of a hostage twin.

Maybe a better woman could have found common ground with Yawa.

Not Baru. Baru could never have made an alliance with Yawa, and Farrier knows it.

"Do you remember the man she served?" Farrier whispers.

"Cosgrad Torrinde. Hesychast. The eugenicist." The man who would pure-breed the world. "We had to stop him, Mister Farrier. . . ."

She smells salt again, and this time, because of the hitch in his breath, she knows that Cairdine Farrier is weeping. Is he weeping for her? She must be certain.

"Yes, Baru. The moment's come, the Reckoning of Ways. The Oriati problem will be resolved. One of us will gain control over the other forever, and so over the future of the Republic. He has what he needs to win, and if he does . . . you know what it means."

"Slavery," she whispers. "The human race bred like dogs."

"Yes."

"Why are you crying, Mister Farrier?"

"Because they hurt you, Baru."

"I failed you. I didn't bring you what you need. . . ."

"No, Baru, no, no, you did brilliantly." And she hears that traitor hitch of compassion in his breath, spoor of his hidden weakness: she finds herself salivating, because she wants so badly to get a claw into that hidden wound and tear it bloody.

He goes on, unaware, trying to soothe her with the power at his command. "Have you ever known an evil man, Baru? A criminal, a wife-beater, an incompetent or a drunk, who sits behind his desk every day, guilty in all eyes but legally untouchable? Everyone knows what he's done but no one can prove it, no one can act. His reputation simmers but never boils. Have you ever known a man like that?"

"Yes," she says, forcing herself not to smile, even a little, at the secret joke.

"Imagine that man is an entire nation. A confederation of nations with a knot of cancer in their old hearts. A thousand years they've waited for their reckoning. And I sent you, Baru, *you*"—his hand touches her shoulder, clasps gently—"to find that one ultimate secret which will turn the Oriati on each other. I knew what the secret must be. I just needed *proof.*

"There are clerks and presses all over this city waiting to tell the world what you've found. Little criers on street corners, rhetorics on their podiums, Tahari gamblers putting odds, Suettaring investors with wet pens waiting to write their advice columns, what to buy and what to sell. There are message rockets in their tubes, ships straining at their anchors, diplomatic bags ready for the sealed letter. All of it's ready for you, Baru. I've made it all ready." She hears the wet flicker of his lashes. "I let you sleep as long as I could, because the doctors said it would help you recover. But the time's come. I can't wait anymore. I have to know, please."

He leans closer. His whisper trembles under the strain of all his hopes.

"Did you find them?"

She creases her forehead in thought. It is deliberate bait, and it fishes out of Farrier a murmur of fear. He isn't afraid that she failed. Isla Cauteria will have seen to that. Hundreds of people must have witnessed golden *Eternal*.

He's afraid that she doesn't remember the necessary details.

"The Cancrioth," she says. "You sent me to find the Cancrioth. . . ."

The Oriati are a nation of two hundred million neighbors. They bicker, gossip, tear down each others' fences, suffer disaster and pandemic and sometimes, even, war. But the thousand-year glue which holds the Oriati Mbo together is unshakable belief in the intrinsic and inalienable humanity of your neighbor, an ethics they call trim. She has stopped trying to force it into logical terms: it is a morality that cannot be separated from the community that practices it, cannot be exploited or manipulated or even defined by one person alone. Giving without hope of getting, in the hope of getting without needing to ask. You can attain good trim and everyone will know it's yours. But you cannot ask how to get good trim, or even claim to have it.

The Oriati Mbo, the House of Trim, is a nation of nations spanning half the known world.

There is only one thing which could destroy trim and break the Mbo, so that Falcrest can settle the porcelain of the Masquerade over their black brows. So that Farrier can put Oriati children in Falcrest schools, put Oriati families to work on land owned by Falcrest, siphon Oriati lumber and gold and ideas away to Falcrest's ships and treasuries and universities. There is only one thing that can destroy the Oriati Mbo.

The destroyer has a name.

"The Cancrioth. Yes. I met their leaders. There was an evil woman with a triangle cut from her skull, and a good man with a stalk for an eye, and a woman with . . . something in her womb . . . they traveled on a golden ship. I met them, Mister Farrier."

Farrier groans in relief. "Yes! You understand what this means?"

She tells it to him exactly as he taught it to her. "The Oriati are afraid of us. They cannot understand how tiny Falcrest has challenged the vast Mbo. Some of them feel the Federal Princes and their faith in trim have failed.

"When we reveal the Cancrioth, alive and powerful after a thousand years in hiding, those doubters will look to the cancer cultists for protection against us. They will abandon trim. There will be a civil war, then. A hundred million against a hundred million. A democlysm: death like no dying the world has ever seen. And once the old ways are torn down, once the Princes are overthrown and the mbo is shattered . . . you can get inside whatever's left. Digest them, make them Falcrest's possession. The whole Ashen Sea would be united under the Masquerade. And you would at last defeat Cosgrad Torrinde and his future of eugenics."

"Yes, Baru"—he is exultant, his prodigy at work, understanding everything just the way he wants—"yes, yes, you remember!"

"I'm your savant," she says, slowly, as if she's just recollecting it herself. "Of course I remember. What *happened* to me, Mister Farrier? What makes you so afraid that I'd forget? I haven't been . . ."

She tries to raise her left hand to her face, and finds herself tied up in a straitjacket.

"Damaged?" she asks, softly.

"Never mind that. Never you worry, it's all going to be all right, I promise, I do. Oh, Baru, you wonderful woman, you marvel"—he pauses to get his breath—"just tell me, please, if you can, if it's not too hard, did you bring home *proof* of the Cancrioth?"

"Of course I did."

"Yes!" He leans closer. "Is the information of quality?"

"I found an eyewitness who contacted the Cancrioth, obtained their money and weapons, and used that support to launch an armed attack on a province of our Imperial Republic." The witness is Abdumasi Abd; although, if you believe what some believe, he is more than one man, he is all the other souls that grow in the flesh of his spinal cord. "I brought him to Falcrest."

"Oh virtue," he says, "oh, kings, Baru." He has to get his breath. What she has done is not like finding an eyewitness to prove a crime. She has found the criminal and all his conspirators, and obtained from them a signed promise to commit more crime, and walked out of their headquarters untouched. It is probably the greatest coup one of Farrier's agents has ever achieved. Or she has grown very full of herself.

"What did you see?" So close, he cannot pretend patience. She tips her head forward as if responding unconsciously to his energy; his voice shifts as he pulls away. "What did you see on their ship, Baru?"

"I remember . . ."

Kimbune. Kimbune asking her questions, while the water rose around her down in Tubercule.

"I remember a voice," she says.

ACT ONE

BARU'S CHOICE

SPLINTERS

"WHO are you?"

Baru jerked awake. Slammed her head against wet wood. It was real! It had all been real! The madness in the embassy, the traitor-admiral waiting for her in the dueling circle, the Kyprananoki rebels hemorrhaging black Kettling blood from their swollen eyes. Governor Love screaming as the plague carriers disemboweled themselves and smeared their gore on his face. Aminata's marines firing the embassy, shooting the guests. Spilled palm wine on burning lilacs.

And then the shadow ambassador had led Baru down to the secret way beneath the reef. The swim to the ocean. Saltwater pouring off black whaleskin. An orca with a human skull embedded in its breaching back. A woman with swollen cancer in her womb.

Real. It was all real.

She had gone to the embassy on Hara-Vijay islet in Kyprananoke. She had gone to find the Cancrioth, and the Cancrioth had found her first.

"Who are you?" asked the voice from above.

"Barbitu Plane," Baru croaked. Her cover. "I'm from the Ministry of Purposes. I'm on a diplomatic mission with . . ."

She'd had someone with her. She couldn't remember. Her tongue was slimy, her throat dry. She'd been mouth-breathing for hours. She must have been drugged. As a girl she'd been so embarrassed by the idea of gaping like a fool while asleep that she'd trained herself to frown while she dreamed.

"Where am I?"

"You are in Tubercule."

She tried to look up and slammed her scalp into a metal clamp. No way to see except by desperately rolling her eyes. She reached up to pull the clamp off and found her hands jammed against the walls of a narrow wooden chute. Claustrophobia loped up growling in the dark. Gods of fire it was so deep dark.

"Tubercule." Speech now the only way she could act, and therefore desperately necessary. "What's that?"

"Where the dead go to grow."

"I'm not dead."

"How do you know? Can you move? Can you see?"

Dog-legged claustrophobia licked at the back of her knees. How deep underground was she? Below the water table? The walls angled in to a joint beneath her. She had to kick and scrabble to keep her feet from sliding together in the pinch. A splinter of soft wood found a toenail, dug beneath. Baru gasped and twisted away. Nowhere to go! Nowhere to go! Water dripped on her scalp and slithered down her body—

Baru made herself be still, and took comfort by measuring the water level. Counting always soothed her: she never did her figures wrong. She was not imagining it. The water was rising around her legs.

So it was going to be like that.

"What do I need to tell you to get out of here?"

The voice above her was silent.

"Ask me, damn you!"

The sound of water kept the time.

"Let me answer!"

"Who are you?"

"I told you! I'm Barbitu Plane!"

A pedal thumped. A valve opened. Piss-warm water slapped against her back and coiled down her legs. "You're lying. Your name is Baru Cormorant."

"Who told you that?"

"Unuxekome Ra told us."

She remembered that name as hands around her throat. Unuxekome Ra, exiled duchess, mother of the Duke Unuxekome who Baru had betrayed. She'd hauled Baru out of the water off Hara-Vijay. And then she'd tried to murder Baru. Someone had stopped her. . . .

The shadow ambassador. The woman from the embassy, with the tumor that looked like pregnancy. She'd stopped Ra. They'd been on a boat, Baru and the shadow ambassador and Unuxekome Ra and Shao Lune and a man with no lips, and . . . and . . .

"Tau!" she gasped. "Where's Tau-indi?"

"The one who renounced you?" The voice echoed down the shaft above, doubling, doubling again. "Tau-indi Bosoka, who was once a Prince?"

N O," Tau gasped, "no, no no no, please don't—"

"I cut you," said the shadow ambassador with the tumor in her womb. "I cut you out of trim. Na u vo ai e has ah ath Undionash. I call this power to cut you. Alone you will serve us, Tau-indi Bosoka, alone we will be your masters, to save the nations we both love. Ayamma. A ut li-en."

"STOP!" roared Enact-Colonel Osa. The little fishing felucca rocked as the Prince's bodyguard scrambled between her charge and the shadow ambassador, powerless against sorcery, desperate enough, anyway, to try.

Unuxekome Ra caught her and kicked her down.

The shoreline was burning. The beautiful embassy at Hara-Vijay, all its lilac trees and wine and all the people inside, was aflame. Masquerade marines had torched it to contain the Kettling plague. But right now all the pity and fear in Baru's heart was for Tau-indi Bosoka, who was being cut.

"Ayamma," the shadow ambassador repeated. "A ut li-en. It is done."

Tau-indi Bosoka fell weeping to their knees. Had their hands been severed from their body, Baru could not have pitied them more. But she could not go to Tau. She was paralyzed by astonishment.

The shadow ambassador was Cancrioth. The words of the sorcery she'd spoken were Cancrioth. They were real. And she'd done something to Tau. Was it real? It couldn't be real. *Was it real?*

The shadow ambassador lowered her hand. A trick of firelight and setting sun seemed to make her fingers burn cool green. "Well," she said, shivering now, "that's over with. Ra, take the boat west. We'll lose our tails in the kypra and then go home to *Eternal*. I'll signal our return on the uranium lamp."

"Incredible," Shao Lune breathed. The navy woman huddled stiff at Baru's side, her proud uniform and elegant face all wet, staring in astonishment. She was Baru's hostage and uneasy companion, fled from the service of the Traitor-Admiral Juris Ormsment. "They think they're doing magic. . . ."

Unuxekome Ra laughed as she unstayed the boat's tiller. "You stupid little girl. You think it's just theater?"

"I *know* it's just theater."

"Is it?" Ra pointed past her. "Is that theater? Is *that* theater?"

A school of ghostly white jellies had surfaced behind the boat. Thousands of them together, their feeding tentacles intermingled. And through that jelly raft sliced a blade like the moon.

It was a fin. A whale's tall black dorsal fin edged in sharpened steel. And behind that fin, a tumor ruptured the sleek back. At first Baru thought it was a huge barnacle, or an infection, but no barnacle was that unnatural sun-bleached sterile color. The tumor was *bone*. And though it knobbed with spines and bulbous growths, it wept no pus. The wound was clean, the skin knotted tight with scar tissue around the extrusion. Even its contours had been streamlined by the flow of water. . . .

The creature rolled to bare its passing flank. A tremendous white false eye gazed on Baru: beneath it was a black true eye, keen, aware. Teeth glimmered at her from a carnivore yawn. The whale's body passed alongside her, and she saw, embedded in the tail end of the tumor, a grinning human skull—its lower jaw subsumed into the flesh—its empty eyes filled with furry, cauliflower-textured bone.

"Oh Himu," Baru moaned.

The whale blew mist and the blowhole whistled like thunder piped down a thigh-bone flute, like the mad shriek of an archon folded into the world from pre-created space. Baru scrabbled up onto the boatwale, battering the two stub fingers on her wounded right hand, crying out in pain but desperate to see.

"What *is* it?" she begged. And forgot, for a moment, poor maimed Tau-indi, lost on her blind right side.

The shadow ambassador whistled to the whale. "Good boy, Galganath!" She threw a fish. The whale's huge jaws clapped shut on it. Unuxekome Ra grinned in delight, her own jaws full of silver and lead, and murmured to her first mate.

Baru sank back into the boat. She'd done it. She'd succeeded catastrophically. The lure of Iraji's face had worked too well. The Cancrioth had her in their power. They would want to know how she'd discovered their existence. She had to secure her position immediately, find some leverage that would keep her safe. She'd lied once already: told Unuxekome Ra, in a moment of desperation, that she was carrying Ra's grandchild.

Shao Lune whispered into her ear: "Did you expect this?"

"A little." Baru giving herself too much credit. "Well, I expected to find clues to the Cancrioth, not . . . not the Canaat attack, or the blood plague, or that thing in the water. . . ."

"A deformed asthmatic whale. Nothing magical."

"I can hear you two muttering," Unuxekome Ra growled. She rose from the tiller like an old sea eagle whose dull feathers disguise its swooping hunger. She'd been a duchess once, a companion of pirates, a mother to a good son. Baru had lured her son and all her pirate friends to their death.

She couldn't touch Baru in revenge—not when the shadow ambassador needed Baru alive. Now her eyes turned to Shao Lune. "You'd do well to respect the Womb's people. You have no idea what they could do to you."

"The *Womb*?" Shao Lune, Falcresti to the marrow, ready with a sneer for the old Maia woman and her superstition. "Oh, she'll curse me, will she? She'll cut my soul? I don't believe in those things you did to the Prince."

Baru looked guiltily to the stern, where Tau-indi lay like a dead parrot in Osa's arms.

"You don't believe." Unuxekome Ra smiled at her first mate. His lips had been slashed off in ritual punishment. The Kyprists who ruled these islands had once been Falcrest's chosen pawns; when Falcrest left, they'd held onto power by sheer cruelty.

"You hear that?" Ra said. "She doesn't believe we'll cut her."

The lipless man nodded and tapped his ear.

"If you don't get to keep your lips," Ra said, "why should she?"

And she came up the boat with her hooked knife glittering between her knuckles.

Shao Lune stiffened against Baru: too proud to beg for help. Baru felt a profound empathy for her attacker. Falcrest has cut your people, cut off lips and balls and fingers and tongues, and you cannot get justice. You cannot wait for history to turn in your favor. But at least there is revenge, which is like justice the way saltwater is like fresh. So you take what you can from the Falcresti in your reach. You cut your debt out of her—

Shao Lune had been Baru's lover; once, and unwisely, but still her lover. And after Tain Hu, Baru had promised herself *never again*—

"Stop!" Baru barked. "She's under my protection."

"The way you protected my son?" Ra grinned at her, a smile like spilled plunder, and kept on coming. All across the horizon behind her the islands of Kyprananoke burnt in civil war, pistol fire and screams, mines detonating like pounding drums. The Canaat rebels had found their hour to rise against the Kyprists. The embassy had been the first strike in the revolution.

Baru should be cheering for them. But here came their leader with her knife—

"Don't," she snapped, "don't, don't." No chance she could take the knife from Ra, no chance of persuading her to back off, so look for outside influence— "Ambassador! Help!"

"Ra. Let them be."

The shadow ambassador sat at the tiller now, steering the boat, her brow in sunset silhouette. Her skin was black as Mzu, the mythic god of moon and life, black as Tau and Osa, who were Oriati, too. But she was not like them. Did not belong to the great Oriati Mbo or any of its thousand glorious squabbling confederations. Did not and never could.

Her belly swelled with a mass which would never come to term. Her cancer. The Cancrioth worshiped the flesh that was their namesake.

"Until later, then." Unuxekome Ra winked brightly at Shao Lune. "Baru," she said, not turning her eyes or her knife off the Staff Captain. "The Prince wants you, I think."

"I won't leave you," Baru whispered to Shao.

But the other woman shoved her away: no more fooled by the lie than Baru herself. "Go be useful," she hissed. "Find some leverage."

A N hour ago Tau-indi Bosoka had been a Federal Prince, guardian and protector of the trim which bound Oriati Mbo's people in one great web of compassion. They had come looking for their old friend Abdumasi Abd, hoping to reconcile with him and bind up the tear in trim that (Tau wholeheartedly believed) would soon become a war between Falcrest and the Oriati. That was how Tau thought: that you could end a war forecast to kill one out of six people in the world by rescuing one estranged friend.

And then the shadow ambassador had cut them.

"Baru."

"Yes, yes, I'm here!" She fell over one of the thwarts as the boat pitched on a wave, landed hard on her bad hand. The pain in her two stump fingers pulled like cold wire all the way up her arm to the side of her head.

"I'm here, Tau," she cried. "I'm here!"

Enact-Colonel Osa cradled Tau's head in her lap, but there was no affection for Osa in the laman's stiff little body. Tau might as well have laid their head on a block of granite. They turned listlessly to meet Baru's eyes.

"You said you wanted to help me find Abdumasi."

"Yes—yes, and we're closer now—"

"You said we would find Unuxekome Ra, and she would know where Abdumasi had gone."

"Yes, that's true, and she's here, Ra's here, we can ask her—"

"You knew the Cancrioth were watching us. You were dragging your coat for them. You never warned me."

That was true.

"You lied to me." Tau's eyes slid off her like a dead hand letting go. "You swore on your parents and you lied. And now"—there should have been a crack here, a catch of grief, but there was nothing at all—"now I am cut. I am a Prince without a mbo. I am finished."

Baru huddled on her knees beside them, certain she could find some way to fix this. "Tau, I need your help. Please. Other people need you. Isn't that what you told me? That trim is other people?"

The shadow ambassador cleared her throat. "There is no more trim for Tau-indi. I have cut them away."

"Ignore her," Baru whispered, "please, it's just superstition, you don't have to listen to her—"

"I have seen their power do terrible work." Tau shrugged, an exhausted *so what*? "I saw a woman who was severed so deeply from her own body that she could burn alive without feeling pain. It is real. And now that power has cut me."

"Just tricks, Tau, just theater. . . ."

"I never should have trusted you," Tau-indi said. "You're a hole."

And they turned away.

N O one likes you very much, do they?" the shadow ambassador had asked her.

Baru fussed with her incryptor, checking it for seawater. The clockwork device generated codes to prove she was an agent of Falcrest's Emperor. It was almost too powerful to use: to apply the codes was to betray that you *were* a cryptarch. To be seen was to be known, to be known was to perish. Baru's cover as a cryptarch had been blown since the moment she left the Elided Keep. With Juris Ormsment and Tain Shir chasing her, Baru had never really had the chance to work like a proper spymaster.

But the incryptor was still proof that Baru mattered. That she'd gained something, anything at all, by putting Hu to death.

Wydd help her if this thing, too, began to corrode.

"People like me until I don't do what they want," she said, shortly. "Did you really have to do that to Tau?"

"Yes." The ambassador had a black eyepatch; her other eye was clear and sympathetic. She looked like someone who always understood exactly what she was doing. "There was no alternative. To bring someone so powerfully connected to the Mbo so close to us would be . . . dangerous for both sides. We are antithetical to each other."

"But you're both Oriati," Baru said, pretending ignorance. "You're on the same side."

"You know it's not that simple, Baru. Oh, yes, I know who you are; Unuxekome Ra told me about Baru Cormorant and her treachery in Aurdwynn. You are an agent of the Emperor in Falcrest, dispatched to move among foreigners while masked by your own foreign blood."

"Shit," Baru muttered.

"Not at all. Your authority means you can help me." The woman adjusted herself on the thwart, groaning amiably. "Forgive me if I rest. I swear this fellow"—she patted her bulge—"gets heavier at sunset."

"What is it like?" Baru blurted. "Were you ever pregnant? Does it feel the same?"

"I had a child, yes, before I took the immortata into me." She squeezed seawater from her damp eyepatch with two fingers. "The Line of Abbatai is borne only—almost only—by women. The immortata is colder than a child, somehow. And it never moves."

Baru, who thought of her menses as an inconvenient sign of good nutrition more than a mark of fertility, was suddenly afraid of the tumor. To have something growing inside you that would *never leave . . .*

No wonder Cosgrad Torrinde the Hesychast wanted this secret cancer. He could use it to put his theoretical flesh-memory into people. He could transplant Incrasticism into their bodies and it would be as hard to get out as cancer.

She tried to take a hold of the situation. "You said I could help you, somehow?"

"Yes. Can you command those ships?"

The shadow ambassador pointed north, to the far-off red sails of *Ascentatic* and *Sulane,* the two Imperial Navy frigates anchored off Kyprananoke. *Sulane* was the Traitor-Admiral Juris Ormsment's flagship. Ormsment had come here to kill Baru.

"Can you arrange safe passage for my people to go?"

"Of course I can," Baru lied. "But first I want to meet your leaders."

"You think I am not the Cancrioth's leader? When the womb is the mother from which all life springs?"

"Not fish," Baru countered. "Or birds. Or lizards."

"Pedant," the shadow ambassador chided.

"I don't believe a secret society would have their leader out in the field." Farrier and Hesychast had sent pawns, after all. Sent her and Xate Yawa.

"Are we a secret society now?"

"I was told you rule Oriati Mbo from the shadows, and always have."

The shadow ambassador laughed. "Do we, now? Who forgot to tell us?"

No, no, don't say that. Don't say you're powerless. I need the Cancrioth to help me fight Falcrest. Don't be weak, please, please.

"Well." The shadow ambassador sighed and stretched her hands. "I am going to signal my people, so they know I'm returning with guests. And we'll see if they let us aboard."

"Wait!" Baru hissed. "You can't risk a rocket—not even a lantern! You'll tell the whole archipelago where we are!" She could hardly admit how many people were hunting her, but if even one of those groups found her, she was finished.

But the shadow ambassador, ignoring her, produced two items from her satchel. First a cylinder of dark iron. Then a fine wicker basket that cupped an open bulb of glass. In that glass was water, and in the water crouched a very tiny, very unhappy frog. It saw Baru and said *wart! wart!*

The shadow ambassador gripped both ends of the cylinder and pulled with a grunt. The iron case slid off its base on oily runners to reveal a column of glistening stone. And as the frog saw the stone, it began to gleam—a powerful turquoise light, steady as a candle, but cold.

And the shadow ambassador's hands glowed, too.

Tau moaned like they would be sick.

The shadow ambassador began to shutter the iron sleeve up and down over the stone. With each motion the frog dimmed or brightened.

"What is she doing now?" Shao Lune said, with forced disinterest.

"It must be uranium lore. Cancrioth magic." Osa protected Tau-indi with her arms. They were wet and shivering and the sun was going down, but they did not huddle against Osa for warmth.

In a dead voice, Tau said, "It's a frog from the hot lands in Mzilimake. They glow in the water that pours out from the secret caves. Every three hours they glow brightest, and then for three hours they fade. The water causes cancer. The water will kill those who drink too much of it. The water makes the sahel frogs glow. From that water the life that lives in life was born. Ayamma. A ut li-en."

Whatever happened after that was lost to Baru's memory. She must have been drugged. She remembered nothing else until she woke up in Tubercule.

B ARU slumped forward as far as the claw around her head would let her. She'd lost Tau. However desperate her situation, at least she'd chosen to risk herself. She'd tricked Tau into it. Once again she'd dragged someone infinitely better than her to their doom.

No! No time for despair. Tain Hu was counting on her. Tain Hu had died to make this possible. As long as Baru carried that burden, she *had* to do what was necessary to succeed, or she didn't deserve Hu's trust!

"Why did you come here, Baru Cormorant?" the voice from above asked.

Baru put her feet down and strained against the clamp. "Are you the Cancrioth?"

"Why did you come here?"

To destroy Falcrest! To betray Cairdine Farrier, avenge Tain Hu, and liberate her home!

But how? How exactly had she meant to do that? She was so lost, so deep in the reefs, so far from the way she'd imagined this happening. . . .

She'd meant . . . yes, she'd meant to ally herself with the Cancrioth. That was still her purpose. That *must* still be her purpose. To obtain from the Cancrioth a weapon or an advantage that could destroy Falcrest.

She had seen that weapon. She had seen that weapon! They had it!

"I want the blood," she croaked. "I'm here to bargain for the blood."

The Canaat rebels had sent plague carriers into the embassy to infect the Kyprist leaders. They bled green-black plague blood from their eyes and noses, gums and ears, from their miscarrying children. They had used their own blood to deliver plague to the Kyprists who'd oppressed them.

That blood was a symptom of the Kettling, the Black Emmenia, the abominable pandemic of legend. The Kettling came from the deep southern jungles of Oriati Mbo. So did the Cancrioth.

The Cancrioth must have brought the Kettling to Kyprananoke.

And if the Cancrioth could bring it here they could bring it to Falcrest.

"The blood?" the voice repeated. "What blood?"

"The Kettling."

"The Kettling?" Her interrogator gasped aloud and Baru thought, oh, this is odd, she's no good at her job. Why had they chosen such a bad interrogator? "There's Kettling here? Where?"

"Haven't been off the ship lately, have you?" Baru's laugh banged her head against the clamp. "It's been making rounds ashore! Just put in an appearance at the embassy reception!"

"How do you know we're on a ship?"

Bait taken, dragged and swallowed. Good Himu, this woman was *inept*. But she was winning anyway, damn her, because Baru was still stuck in this hole!

She kicked against the wood to keep her feet from pinching together in the joint below. The confinement was intolerable—she tried to imagine her blind right side as a great empty space, but all she could think of was the wall. Panic like fat mosquito bites, swelling down her back, itching, itching—

"I could explain everything if you'd just get me out of here!"

A mistake. The woman above hardened again. "How did you learn about us? Who led you to us?"

"Get me out of this hole and I'll tell you!"

This time she heard the click of the footpedal in time to cringe against the slap of warm brine. "Who led you here?"

"Drown me and I can't tell you."

"Who led you here?"

"You don't frighten me. Let me out."

The pedal clicked again. The water was up to her hips now, still rising. "The Womb said you showed people a picture of a boy. Who is the boy?"

The boy's name was Iraji. He had been born into the Cancrioth, meant to receive one of their tumor Lines. But it had frightened him so deeply that he'd run away, ended up as a concubine and agent for Baru's rival cryptarch Apparitor. Baru had stolen him and used him as bait. He was an innocent boy, fiercely intelligent, generous with his heart, and he had given her more help than she had ever deserved.

If she told the voice a little about Iraji, maybe she could win her freedom—

Don't.

"Fuck you," Baru snarled.

The woman sounded urgent now, her Aphalone pronunciation slipping as she rushed her words. "Where is Abdumasi Abd?"

So there was that name again. A man Baru had destroyed, entirely by accident: a prize she'd caught for Falcrest without even realizing it. Tau's old friend.

"I don't know," Baru said. Which was the truth.

"Tell me where Abdumasi Abd is or I'll drown you."

"You won't."

She wished she *did* know where Abd had gone. When Baru's false-flag rebellion tore through Falcrest's troubled province of Aurdwynn, Abdumasi Abd had seen a chance to strike at the empire he hated. (Like Baru he had devoted his life to Falcrest's annihilation: he just went about it more honestly.) He had gathered his ships and sailed north for Aurdwynn to shatter Falcrest's fleet in the region and give the rebels aid.

It had been a trap, of course. Like the whole rebellion. Juris Ormsment had boxed Abdumasi's fleet in and burnt it to ash.

Now the Cancrioth wanted Abdumasi back. He must be one of them: poor Tau, they hadn't known. Whoever held Abdumasi could prove the Cancrioth's existence and that secret could split the world in two.

The voice, insistent: "Where is Abdumasi Abd?"

The water had risen to her navel, and she was terrified of going under with her hands pinned, trapped like a cork in an underwater cave, her shoulders stuck, her screaming face pressed against black rock—

"Shut off the water and we'll talk!" she screamed.

There was a clatter, and then a crack. "Oh shit," the woman said, in Aphalone, and then swore in Maulmake, the Mzilimake Mbo tongue, which Baru did not speak.

The water pouring over her back tapered off to a patter. But it did not stop.

"Is it still coming down?" the interrogator called, nervously.

"Yes!"

"I think I broke something."

"You *what*?"

"It's a very old ship. Things are brittle."

"Get me out of here!"

"I—I'm not sure how."

"Where are the guards? Where are your clerks, your griots, whoever the fuck you have recording my responses?"

"There aren't any."

"There aren't any guards?"

"No one's supposed to come near you yet. The onkos have to confer about what to do. I was told that if I was quick—well, I snuck in."

This must be some kind of trick. Some way to convince Baru she was about to die—but the water was still rising, turbid and scummed with seaweed. Like drowning in a salad.

Baru strained against the claw over her head. It wouldn't budge. "Get help!" she screamed.

"Where's Abdumasi?" the woman shouted back. "Tell me where Abdumasi Abd is and I'll get help."

Even here a part of Baru was calm and cool and distantly preoccupied with intrigue. That part of Baru imagined Abdumasi Abd as a knot, a straining knot that tied three ropes together—the Oriati Mbo, the secret Cancrioth, and Falcrest. No wonder everyone wanted to find him! He was living proof of collaboration between Mbo Oriati and the Cancrioth they despised. He was incarnate blackmail that could sway nations.

So why was this hapless woman, this amateur, asking after him?

"Why do you give a shit?" Baru called.

"He has my husband's soul in him!" the voice cried. "Please, you must help me find him!"

"He *what*?"

"He bears Undionash, as my husband did before him! Where is he, please? Please?"

The water was up to her chest, warm as sewage, and in that warmth Baru felt only cold heart-seizing sorrow. Poor Tau-indi! They'd hoped and hoped that they could rescue Abdumasi, bring him home, tie up their tattered friendship . . . but Tau also believed that anyone touched by the Cancrioth was forever lost.

"Get me out of here," she shouted, "and I'll tell you where to find Abdumasi!"

"Tell me now, and I'll get you out!"

"Fuck you!"

"Oh, Alu," the woman above groaned, a name or an epithet, Baru didn't know. "I'll go for help."

The rising water licked at her sternum.

B ARU strained so hard against the clamp that the discs of her spine cracked and popped. She panted and rattled and beat her body against the wooden shaft and grunted like a rabbit in a trap.

The clamp would not give. The water was coming up.

Shouting in the room above—a commotion of voices in Maulmake, and other languages she didn't recognize. She called out: "Get me the fuck out of here!"

"What is this?" a voice called down: the shadow ambassador.

Something fell into the water by Baru's face. It was a metal cylinder, like a Falcresti grenade, perforated by needle-gauge holes. Through those holes thin phosphorescent light bled out into the brine. In the darkness of the pit, the light was as dazzling as the moon.

"Jellyfish tea," Baru shouted, "it's jellyfish tea!"

"What is that?"

A dictionary entry sprang to the tip of her tongue. "A luminous extract, used in fireproof lamps in Falcrest."

"Is it used to trace the course of ships?"

"I suppose it could be," Baru hedged. "In calm waters, for a little while."

"Galganath found this tin pinned beneath our boat. I saw we were leaving a wake, but I thought it was just the usual phosphorescence. Were we tracked here?"

Baru rattled through her memories. When they swam out to the boat, Shao Lune had been the last one to surface. The cunning snake was working for someone else! Had she fixed a tracker to the keel? Assume so. Lie accordingly. Lie quickly and lie well.

"Yes. My aide Shao Lune put it there, so my people would know where I'd been taken. You didn't think I came without insurance, did you?"

"What insurance?"

Lie well! "If I don't report back to *Helbride* by dawn, they'll burn this ship to the keel. We have two Imperial Navy frigates in port here, armed with tor-pedoes and Burn. You won't escape."

"So those men nearby are your agents?"

"What men?" Baru prevaricated.

"There are armed men scouring the area around our mooring. They'll find us within hours. Are these yours?"

"Yes," Baru lied, even as her heart slowed with cool, thoughtful distress. Those would be Xate Yawa's people, Durance's people, two names for one foe. Xate Yawa had been charged by Hesychast to find the Cancrioth and bring home their immortal flesh.

"What will they do when they find us? Will they attack?"

But the water was too high to answer. Baru blew froth, gurgling enthusiastically, certain that she had—even from the bottom of her drowning hole—gained leverage, a foothold to climb up out of here.

"Get her up," the shadow ambassador commanded someone. "Kimbune! Kimbune, come here!" And then she snapped something in Maulmake, in a tone of harshest reprimand. The voice who'd questioned Baru first protested loudly.

So that first woman was named Kimbune. Why did you come here, Kimbune, to ask after your husband's soul? Why was I hidden from you?

If there were factions on this ship, Baru could play them off each other, as she had in Aurdwynn. She'd won there. But Tain Hu had not survived that victory.

What had they done with Shao Lune? With Osa and Tau?

Baru flinched from the thought, and her face ducked below the filthy water, and the groan of a ship's timbers came to her, the complaint of a leviathan. It would be easier this time, if she had to sacrifice again. It would not hurt so much. She had practice at it.

She would get the Kettling blood from the Cancrioth, and she would use her success to buy Cairdine Farrier's trust long enough for the final betrayal, and Falcrest would be destroyed, and her parents would be all right in the end, and she would see her home free.

She was on course. She was doing well. And if Shao and Osa and Tau were all lost, as Tain Hu and Duke Unuxekome and Xate Olake and all the others had been lost, that was just proof that victory required sacrifice.

The water closed above her.

NOW

S O you met Tau-indi Bosoka," Farrier says. An odd thing to focus on, out of everything she's told him.

"Yes." The heavy wool of her straitjacket itches. She shimmies against it to scratch; she hears his waistcoat crinkle as he looks away. She is mostly naked beneath it and that troubles him. "We met on the Llosydanes. I was tracking water purchases made by the Oriati fleet that attacked Aurdwynn, and it drew Tau's attention." She had figured that she could find the financiers behind Abdumasi Abd's fleet, and prove that they were the Cancrioth. Prove that the Mbo harbored them and you could set the world on fire. She had thought, almost to the end, that this proof truly was Farrier's prize.

Why had she ever believed that he'd given her the *real* reasons for her mission?

Farrier asks, from his wary distance, "Is Tau all right?"

"No."

"Oh." Farrier sighs. His years seem to gather about him, regrets like old sweat on his skin. "That's very much . . . not what I wanted."

He almost slips. He almost admits he cares about a person who is unhygienic and unIncrastic and unsuited to his reputation. But he gets his shield up in time. He does not know that he's fighting for his life, but his instincts for danger are too good.

He disengages: "Do you need to rest? Water? Anything?"

"I'm fine, Mister Farrier. We can continue."

"You mentioned this embassy attack several times. What happened?"

"We were attacked by the Canaat. The Kyprananoki rebels. They were rising up against the Kyprists, the puppet government Falcrest left behind."

"I don't know these Canaat."

"Purely a local concern. Of no major interest, until we discovered the Oriati were giving them weapons. Pistols. Machetes. Bombs." She grunts in shock. "Their eyes. Mister Farrier. Their eyes were bleeding—the blood was black—are my eyes bleeding? Is that why I can't see?"

"No, no." A cool cloth dabs at her forehead. "No, Baru, you're not sick. Your temperature's quite normal. You're safe."

"You're certain?"

"Tell it all as you remember it," Farrier says, clearly and encouragingly. "Tell me everything, Baru. I'll have the presses turning by nightfall. By month's end Parliament will send a note to the Oriati Federal Princes demanding that they turn over everyone associated with the Cancrioth. By year's end the Oriati will be killing each other in the streets and the fields, all convinced everyone who's ever wronged them is a tumor. A thousand years of scars all opening at once. And we'll only have to wait for the right time to move in and save them. That's how it works, Baru, that's how it's always worked, cracking open a new province. Stoke their problems with each other, find the cracks and widen them: like tapping an egg on the edge of the dish. And then sell them the solution. They'll buy it from you and thank you for it."

"This idea of turning the Oriati on each other . . ." Baru asks it keenly. Farrier will not believe her question is genuine, unpracticed, unless she sounds keen. "Did you get it from Tau and Kindalana and Abdumasi? When you were with them?"

Farrier does not freeze when he is surprised. He's far too good for that. He does something extremely ordinary, instead, to buy himself time. He sneezes. He can sneeze on command! What a talent.

"Sorry," he says. "With who?"

"The Prince Hill children. Tau, Abdu, Kindalana." She would blink if she could, as if she were bewildered by the idea he might lie to her. "You met them long before I did. Didn't you, Mister Farrier? A quarter-century ago, in Lonjaro Mbo. When you lived on Lake Jaro, with the crocodiles and the cranes. . . ."

A STORY ABOUT ASH 5

FEDERATION YEAR 912:
23 YEARS EARLIER
UPON PRINCE HILL, BY LAKE JARO
IN LONJARO MBO

IT was the night before the day of the sorcerer, when the mob would come across Lake Jaro to kill Cairdine Farrier and Cosgrad Torrinde. It was a night for doubt and fear, for cutting off old scabs to patch over new wounds. And in the dark hours of that night, hours when hyenas come to beg for their wage of meat, the young Federal Prince Tau-indi Bosoka grieved for the war they had brought on their people.

But at dawn they rose, put on their bravery like a caftan, and went to see Abdumasi in the merchant house of Abd.

For as long as Tau had lived, Oriati Mbo had been the whole of the world, their favorite and only place: a never-drying fresco of thought and commerce at the center of a gray-fringed map. If they were self-centered, who could blame them? Their parents had been elected to conceive and raise a Federal Prince. Tau was that child; Tau existed to serve the Mbo.

Though Tau often felt they were too much of a child, and not enough of service: except the service of falling ill, troubling parents, and causing misunderstandings with dear friends.

Now the gray edge of the map had come for Tau. The eastern nation of Falcrest had made adventures into the Ashen Sea. They wanted ports. They wanted favorable terms of passage. They wanted to buy low and sell high and to force families who had been sailing the same routes for hundreds of years to give up their trade. Oriati Mbo had shrugged them off at first, slow to anger, certain of their strength. Falcrest made provocations. They seized ships, took Tau's mother, Tahr, as a hostage, and returned her only in the company of two Falcresti emissaries, Cosgrad Torrinde and Cairdine Farrier: men who had proven, respectively, to be beautiful and bemusing, and charismatic but alarming.

Finally, evitably—Tau had to believe it was not inevitable—it had come to war.

The Mbo did not have an army: there were no Jackals or Termites in these days, and the shua warriors of Tau's homeland would not leave their lands. But the Princes had elected war leaders and dispersed funds to raise crews, and a thousand ships had set out to strike directly at Falcrest-the-city. Last night the news had come, and it had driven the poor griots nearly mad with grief to deliver. All was lost. A hundred thousand Oriati had died in battle against Falcrest's First Fleet. Tau had no idea how the masked city had defeated a thousand ships, and couldn't make themself care. Weapons and stratagems didn't matter. What mattered was the pain and the hate that would poison the mbo now, the septic need for vengeance, the grudges and orphans that would make more of each other, cleaving together like womb and testes to breed death.

What if Tau had caused it all?

What if it was *all their fault*?

Trim bound the mbo. One of the principles of trim was that the small found itself reflected in the great, that the littlest kindness could sway the fate of a tribe or a federation. Tau, in particular, had to take incredible care to maintain trim in their own life, because they were, as a Prince, bound so powerfully to the entire Mbo. Tau existed only because the people of Lonjaro had voted for it to be so; they were made out of obligations.

And they had betrayed those obligations! They had let their own friendships coil up with jealousy and confusion. They had resented Abdumasi and Kindalana for turning to each other, leaving little Tau out of their almost-grown-up affair. They had even used the Falcresti hostages, Cosgrad in particular, to make their friends jealous, and so bound the small world of Prince Hill's human dramas to the great conflicts between Mbo and Falcrest!

Last night, as the world of Prince Hill went mad with grief, Tau realized what they had to do.

If they had caused this war by poisoning their friendships, then by the grace of the principles, repairing those friendships might also end the war. Also Tau was lonely, and desperately in need of Abdumasi and Kindalana, their laughter and their smell and their silent companionship at sunset. Those two needs fit together, the great need and the ordinary one.

Tau really did believe that.

So they ate two kola nuts for vigor, and sat for a little while picking at the dry skin between their fingers, before they got up, said, "Now, now," hesitated anyway, and went.

It had rained overnight. In the wet dawn they walked across Prince Hill to

Abdumasi Abd's house, where the lake wind smoothed out the banners and tugged the awnings. The air smelt of earth. There was not much fog, though, and you could see for miles all around, bright bliss-addled cranes parading in the shallows and the clay-brick city of Jaro across the lake to the north. Tau stopped at the termite mound to wish the bugs luck with the monsoon season, and to give them a little honey, which made the termites bumble around excitedly.

"We'll keep the drains clear," Tau-indi promised them. "You'll be okay."

In the house of Abd, hungover groundskeepers sniffled and groaned as they cleaned up last night's heartbreak. Tau-indi caught everyone's eye and smiled. "Your Federal Highness," the staff murmured. A few genuflected. Tau was glad.

"Abdu?" they asked, and the housekeepers pointed them to the morning room.

Abdu sat at the small family table, crushing kola nuts with his right hand. When he saw Tau-indi, he squawked and tried to throw his khanga over the pile of nut debris. "Tau! Uh. Hi!" He fumbled for his etiquette. "Welcome to my house, it must be, uh, much less full of cats than you had hoped?"

"You really like nuts," Tau-indi said. "Oh, Abdu, are you trying to work out your arms? Are you trying to get big arms like Cosgrad's?"

Abdumasi looked down at his khanga, the pattern speckled in kola dust, his long seventeen-year-old legs sticking out all pimply and hairy. He sighed. "I don't understand how he makes his arms like that. But Kinda likes the way he looks."

It was the first time he had admitted to Tau that there was something between him and Kindalana. It had happened after Tau had pushed them both away, but maybe not *because* Tau had pushed them away. However it had happened, it had left Tau more alone and Abdu knew it. He swallowed and looked at Tau with bloody, tired eyes, waiting for Tau to take up the confession and hurl it back. Tau had been more than a little awful to him and Kinda, recently.

Tau-indi smiled as plain as they could. "You'll never be like Cosgrad," they said, and then, when Abdumasi looked hurt and angry, "Abdu, it'd take every kola nut in the world to give you diarrhea as bad as his."

"Oh, ha ha. Is he better?" Cosgrad had suffered diarrhea, tetanus, and meningitis in rapid succession.

"Recovering." Like you and me, Tau wanted to say.

Abdumasi puffed out his cheeks, froglike, and looked at his toes. "So. You want to talk?"

*   *   *

THEY ambled down the hill toward the lake, where the wind separated the water into glittering scalloped patches and smooth silver-black flats. They talked about things that weren't Kindalana or each other: which sort of shua warriors had been winning martial arts tournaments, the renegades (who Tau found quite dashing) or the hunters (whose prowess Abdu admired); the exact boundaries of the House Bosoka lands, which extended as far as farmers paid tribute to Prince Hill; gossip passed by the capillary shouting of shepherds, wood gatherers, griots, and water carriers; and even the sad state of Jaro's municipal affairs, since the common city was traditionally neglected by all the Princes in favor of the rural estates. "When you're a Prince," Abdu suggested, "in between adjudicating important stolen-cattle cases and memorizing five hundred years of boring land disputes, you should send some money to fix up the Jaro market. It could be the jewel of the Flamingo Kingdom."

Tau-indi said, "Do you think this is my fault?"

Abdumasi stopped picking kola chunks out of his khanga's weave and stared. "Fuck me, manata, are you serious?"

"I am," Tau said, feeling foolish.

"Were you just too young to notice? Your mom and Padrigan have been dancing around that bed for years."

Tau-indi, caught between a giggle and a sob, brushed hair out of their eyes to buy a moment. "I don't mean, is it my fault my mom and Kinda's dad are having an affair." Tau's father had vanished on an expedition into Zawam Asu, far away south, and Kindalana's mother had disavowed the marriage to go seek her fortune in gold trading.

"What, then? What could be your fault?"

"I mean the . . . the war."

"Oh." Abdu kicked a stone downslope with a little grunt. "Like a trim thing? Like that thing you asked me about a while ago, with your twin?"

Tau had been born with a stillborn twin, and they had always feared that somehow this would poison them, turn to gangrene with lonely years.

Tau wanted to learn to walk with a little sway in the hip. They tried it out. It would need practice. They looked back at Abdu, to see if he was watching, and said, "Yeah. That thing."

"Tell me what you're afraid of."

Tau said, in a very much rehearsed rush: "Maybe, because my twin came out dead, I was born a fratricide. Maybe I was born as someone who hurts their friends. A principle of selfishness. I was selfish with you, and Kinda, and I used Cosgrad to try to hurt you, and Cosgrad's connected to Falcrest and the war. So maybe my nature tainted the whole Mbo. Maybe the war is . . . because of me."

Abdumasi kicked another rock. "Kinda would tell you how stupid and selfish that is," he said, "and how naïve it is to believe that your friendships could control entire nations. But I guess that's why I can't stand her sometimes. She always says the *correct* thing and not the *right* thing, the friendly thing, which," he began to rush, too, "is why I wish you wouldn't spend so much time being a Prince, no matter how good you are at it. And you are really good. People admire you, Tau, though you don't know it; people think you're unambitious, compassionate, thoughtful, kindhearted, all the things they want in a Prince. But I could use you around as a friend, so Kinda doesn't walk all over me. I should've come to you for advice before I started sleeping with her. I should've come to you for advice a lot. I need a friend a lot more than I need another Prince."

"Oh, Abdu," Tau said.

"The war's really not your fault, Tau." Abdumasi kicked a third rock. It skipped into a cypress shrub and a bird began to shriek. After a moment he grabbed Tau-indi's hand, held it, and made one small circle with his big rough thumb. "I know it's not."

"How?"

"Because you're good. Because the only hurt you do is on purpose."

Tau-indi nodded and coughed (his hand was very strong). "So. How are things with you two?"

"I don't know." Abdumasi looked at their joined hands like he might obtain from those laced fingers the secret of how to grip what he wanted to say. "I wanted, uh . . . she thought you knew about us, she thought you'd kind of asked us to get together, but I didn't want her to tell you we'd . . . started. Because I wanted. To have something you didn't. For a little while."

Why not me? Tau-indi wanted to ask. But it was a stupid question. They'd known Abdu since before they could talk. What room was there for anything like desire between them? Desire required distance. They'd left no space for it to grow.

"Do you love her?"

Abdumasi's face knotted up like the tetanus wreck of Cosgrad Torrinde and he made a long growl. "I don't know."

"Do you want to be with her?"

"That's a complicated question. It turns out it's really hard to quit kola nuts, or coffee, or Kindalana, *especially* when you've had some for a while, and then you try not to have any more—" And then, as he stared past Tau-indi, his eyes suddenly wide, he said, "Oh, principles, I think we need to run."

"What?"

"Tau, *look!*"

There were boats on the dawn lake. A flotilla, a fleet, an armada of boats coming south from the city of Jaro, south to Prince Hill. On those boats there was a mob. And all the mob's shouts were death. There were people from every Kingdom of Lonjaro, all of the Eleven Gates and Jaro itself and even the wandering renegade shua do-gooders of Abdelibduli, the Thirteenth and Unfailing Kingdom, who had no homes but those they were invited into.

Tau and Abdu both stared incredulous at the vision riding the lead skiff. It was the comic griot Abdu had hired to tell them about the war, painted scalp to fingertips in ash, holding, in each hand, a pole bound up with a dead-eyed totem of a Falcresti man. They were extraordinarily well-made totems, and they illustrated exactly what would be done to those Falcrest bodies. Totems like that had not been made since the Maia invasions centuries ago, when some Princes declared the Maia to be enenen, alien to trim, nonhuman enemies who could not be paid blood money or granted guest right.

"They're coming for Cosgrad and Farrier." Tau's stomach swooped horribly. "Oh, principles, if they do—"

Two Falcresti lives taken in vengeance for a hundred thousand Oriati dead. And more later. And more. And more forever. Who ever heard of an avenger satisfied? Even one?

They looked at Abdumasi, and their swoop of fear struck the earth and dashed like vomit into mud. Abdumasi wanted to let Farrier and Torrinde die.

Tau cried at them: "If our guests die in our care, we suffer ten generations of ruin!"

"I know. I know." Abdu took a big breath. "We have to do something. We'll go down there and meet them—"

Tau took Abdumasi's other hand. "Abdu, they won't listen to you. You're a merchant's boy, they'll beat you!"

"I can slow them down." His eyes flashed with pride. "They know me in Jaro. They know my mom all over the Mbo, wherever her ships land. And anyway, what will *you* do? You're dressed like a house clerk, not a Prince. You haven't even finished your Instrumentality."

"I need my paints and jewels. I need the regalia. Then they'll respect me, and maybe I can turn them away—"

"Your house is too far! And you can't go down there alone!"

"I'm not going back to my house. And I'm not going down there alone."

When he understood what Tau-indi intended, Abdumasi tore away, crocodile-faced with jealousy. This was something he could never be part of, a power he would never wield, and that wounded him.

But he swallowed it up and nodded. "Go get Kindalana. You need her. Go be Princes."

"Get your sentries." The voice of command came to Tau-indi without any guilt. Going to Abdu this morning had set their trim a little closer to right, and so the principles had brought them here, now, on this lakeshore, where they could make a difference. "Go to my house and guard Cosgrad and Farrier. Another party might sneak around south of the hill, and come up on them in secret."

"They're a mob, manata, I don't think they'll try a flanking attack—"

"Don't you underestimate them," Tau shouted, already running, "don't you think they're stupid! Those are still Mbo people!"

They tore across the hillside, through bramble and vine, over gutter and stream. If they could save the hostages, they could save the peace, and that might inhabit the whole mbo with principles of reconciliation.

The war might end.

ETERNAL

THEY hoisted Baru out of the Tubercule pit by rope and pulley, up into a compartment of dark resinous wood. There was no metal anywhere. The rich brown-black planks had been fixed together with wooden treenails. All the light came from a single uncaged candle cupped in the shadow ambassador's hands.

"Careful with that," Baru warned her. "Your wood looks flammable."

The ambassador smiled thinly. "We've managed so far."

"You won't manage another day if I come to any harm. Remember, my people are prepared to burn this ship if I'm not returned safely." A lie that was Baru's only protection.

"Set her down," the ambassador ordered. "But hold her."

The man working the hoist pinned her arms at her sides, and held her dangling. His grip was ginger, as if either her filth or her nakedness troubled him. She heel-kicked him in the shins. He did not even grunt.

"Are you done?" The Womb, the shadow ambassador, rested her candle's cup against the curve of her stomach. "I am prepared to offer you parole, with terms."

"I am not a prisoner!" Baru squirmed against the man holding her arms. No use; he was *impossibly* strong. "I am a representative of the Imperial Republic and the Emperor Itself. I demand to be treated with full diplomatic privilege. Let me down!"

"What did Kimbune ask you?"

"Not as much as she told me! Why are you keeping me hidden from the rest of your ship?"

The shadow ambassador pursed her lips in frustration. "I put a taboo around you. Kimbune broke it. Did she tell you why?"

In the edge of the candlelight stood a young woman with deep black skin and a neat cap of kinky hair. The sign of the Round Number was tattooed on her forehead: a circle with a long line beneath it, divided into three large parts and a tiny fraction—the ratio of the circle's circumference to its diameter, three point one four. A number representing the portions of the body, the philosopher Iri anEnna had said. One part of water, one of air, one of flesh, and a little fraction of mystery.

No wonder she'd tried to conduct the interrogation herself. Leave it to a pure mathematician to think she could solve it all alone.

"Hello," Baru said, staring at her curiously. "You almost drowned me."

Kimbune looked away defiantly. "I didn't mean to break it. The design was flawed."

Baru's pinned arms made her furiously aware of every itch, splinter, and raw spot on her body. "I want fresh water. I need to wash."

"I see nakedness doesn't bother you." The Womb refused Baru's bait—if they had fresh water to spare it would mean they were near an aquifer, and Baru could guess their position. "Would you bargain information for linens?"

"Why would I be ashamed? *You* took my clothes." Her period would have inconvenienced her (she was due), but it had skipped, as it had in the fearful days before Sieroch. "I won't bargain for anything. I demand to be treated as a visiting dignitary."

The Womb tapped her fingers impatiently. "Terms of parole. You will be given a room and comforts. You will not leave it without one of my escorts. You will not speak to anyone without my presence. Not even someone you pass on the deck."

"Such concern! *You* brought me here. Why not make the most of it?"

The Womb had traded the dashiki she'd worn at the embassy for a thick ankle-length wool cassock. Kimbune wore the same. Baru imagined their modesty might come from some kind of dualist tradition, one that venerated the true flesh of the immortata over the frail and shameful ephemera of the body. But she was only guessing.

"I do have something to ask of you," the Womb said, carefully. "Something that might make a great difference."

Baru smiled toothsomely at her. "Need to assure your people bringing me here wasn't a mistake?"

"No." The Womb had an absolute certainty about her, when she wanted. "I need the opposite. I need you to tell them you've led the enemy to us, and that we're in terrible danger. Tell them it's time to give up and go home."

"Give up on what?"

"It doesn't matter."

"Wait!" Kimbune leapt forward, wide-eyed. "Wait, Abbatai, we can't! We've come so far, he's so *close*, he must be . . ."

"Look. Already she has us turning on each other." The Womb did something, must have done something, to make the candle she held gutter down. "Maybe it'd be better if we put her back in that pit."

"And waste a chance to talk your way safely past my warships? Throw away an opportunity to find out exactly how much Falcrest knows about you and your, ah"—Baru paused, rather artfully, she thought—"your anatomical society?"

"Tau-indi warned me you'd lie. That you'd pretend you wanted to help us. Like you did in Aurdwynn."

Damn Tau! At least when they'd been limp with grief they couldn't fuck things up—oh, she couldn't bear to think about Tau right now. Just shove it off into the right, into her blind side.

"Where is this ship? No, don't tell me, I'll deduce it." She stretched to get her feet on the deck, and winced at the pressure on her splinters. "This is the ship that sank Tau's *Cheetah*. Therefore it's large enough to carry an arsenal of cannon. We'd have spotted a ship that size on our approach to Kyprananoke if it were moored anywhere nearby. But you can't be moored far off. A ship this size must have a crew to match, and crews are thirsty. Say a gallon per day for each head, and most of your wine and beer used up in the voyage here. You'd need to stay close to the freshwater. And the only way to get freshwater on Kyprananoke without going through the Kyprist government would be the aquifers on el-Tsunuqba. We're *inside* el-Tsunuqba, aren't we? We're in the caldera of the old volcano."

Kimbune looked gratifyingly impressed. Baru stared the Womb down smugly. "Shitty hiding place. No wonder you're cornered."

"Who's the boy in the sketch? The one you showed at the embassy, when you recited our prayer?"

No! Not Iraji. Baru jagged away as hard as she could. "I want water. I want to wash. I want to speak to my aide. Then we can discuss whether or not you'll be taking this ship home safely . . . wherever you come from."

"Put her down, Innibarish," the Womb said.

The man behind her unhooked her from the hoist and set her down. She turned, curious to see what made him so absurdly strong, and felt an uneasy Incrastic fascination, a Falcresti gaze that saw bodies as artifacts and resources. Innibarish was muscular beyond any man she'd ever met, beyond even Hesychast, swollen like a bully whippet, the purebreed Metademe dogs that were born double-muscled. Possibly, checking against her accounts, he was the tallest person she had ever met. But he was gentle. And it was not his fault that his breechcloth failed his modesty: she only thought it interesting that he would respond at all.

"Your man has a hard-on," she said.

"Please don't be crude," the Womb sighed. "Innibarish is a good man."

"I just think it's tactically interesting. If he's aroused by a stinking, salt-soaked woman, it's clearly been a long time for him. Which means you're not letting even your most trusted lackey go ashore."

"I don't like whores," the man said, in gentle Aphalone.

Baru ignored him. That detail was inconvenient to the story she was telling. "Miss Womb, if your man here hasn't been ashore . . . has *anyone*? Are you the only one who knows Kyprananoke's fallen into civil war? Or that there are Falcresti warships waiting outside the caldera? Or that the Kettling has been released?"

Kimbune gasped in horror. Even the big man looked shaken.

"No," the Womb said, reluctantly. "No one else knows."

"Liar," Baru said, smugly. "Someone sent Kimbune to find me. Someone else knew I was brought aboard. Is she the one who let the Kettling out? Is she the one who gave the rebels Oriati weapons?"

That, she thought, is who I want to talk to.

But the Womb was staring at her hands. Suddenly she inhaled hard, pinched out the candle, and left them all in the dark: except for the unmistakable waxing gleam of her fingers, an auroral blue-green.

"She's coming," Innibarish said, softly. "She carries powerful magic."

"Kimbune." The Womb's urgency made the mathematician jump. "The Brain sent you here?"

Kimbune nodded, eyes downcast.

The Womb said something very softly in Maulmake, a question that was not a question at all.

Kimbune nodded again.

"Damn it," the Womb said, flatly. "Damn you, Kimbune, for leading her here. Damn Unuxekome Ra for telling her too much. And damn her for leading you astray. Innibarish, take Baru aft, to the void rooms where we stowed the others. Clothe her and go!"

"Shall I blindfold her, Abbatai?"

"No. Let her see the ship. Let her know that an attack would be insanity." The Womb's hands were burning now, bright as a campfire and rising. "Just get her inside my taboos before she's taken!"

"Tau told you," Baru breathed. She understood now. "That's what you're afraid of. Tau told you I want to fight Falcrest. Tau warned you I was lying, but there's someone on this ship who believes me. . . ."

The Womb slapped Baru, right on the glass cut in her cheek. Baru's whole mind folded into a thin white crack of pain. "If the Brain's people find you they will do things to your flesh that will make you regret your fetus ever found a place in your mother's womb. Listen to me now! *Do not let them put anything into your body.* Do you understand? Not even water. Better for you to die than to let the baneflesh have you! Your soul will be caught up and mutilated for a thousand years or more!"

There were centuries of fury in her eyes and for a moment Baru believed with all her heart that the Womb truly was immortal. That the woman she was speaking to was only a vehicle for the mass inside her.

"And if you lead poor Kimbune to harm," the Womb hissed, "I'll have you back in that hole to drown alone—"

"You won't kill me," Baru snarled, advancing on her with the marks of power she had, the flesh wealth of her strength and the Incrastic mark of her well-kept teeth. "You're immortal, aren't you? Every one of your lives is infinitely precious. The navy is out there, waiting to burn you, and I am the only thing that can save you now. You need to cut a deal with me."

"Get her out of here," the Womb snapped. "Get her aft. I'll head the Brain off and meet you there."

K IMBUNE had lied to her. They were not on a ship. This could not be a ship.

This was a fortress.

How could that triple-terraced mansion, with its withered gardens and narrow windows, be a ship's sterncastle? How could those eight receding pillars, marching away like columns in a temple gallery, be *masts*? No ship had ever sailed with eight masts. . . .

Shattered el-Tsunuqba's flooded caldera opened to the sea through a mess of fjords to the north. Tall cliffs ringed the south wall. The light of green worms clinging to the cliffs cast tenuous shadows from the rigging: an ecumene of spiderwebs in pale relief across the deck.

It was the rigging that forced her mind to concede. The lines implied functions, hoist and haul, reef and shakeout; and those functions resolved the whole preposterous immensity into the deck of a ship. A ship twice as long as any ever recorded in the *Navy List*. Baru made a hasty computation—given her dimensions, she must ship at least a hundred tons of cargo. The profit on a single load would be immense. . . .

"Behold *Eternal*," Innibarish whispered. Even he was awed. Maybe he had watched this ship built, decade by decade, over the course of an immortal life. Maybe.

"No wonder you're trapped here," Baru breathed. "A boar in wet concrete would handle better on the open sea. . . ."

The shriek of the whale's metal blowhole sounded from the dark water below. The back of Baru's throat prickled like the first hint of a cold. She swallowed in fear. She did not understand the whale. She was in the strangest place she had ever been.

"That is Galganath, our sentry," Innibarish explained. "Giving the all-clear at the end of a patrol."

"You *talk* to the whale?"

"Of course we do."

"It can speak?"

"It can hold its breath, can't it? What's talking except the choice of when to breathe?"

They walked aft, circling a steep-roofed, palatial deckhouse built around the masts. Huge rolls of canvas rustled overhead. Capstans with spokes fit for oxen coiled up miles of rope.

Baru would love to be captain of this ship—no, not the captain, the ship's master and owner. She would love to have the blueprints, and a way to build more. . . .

She scoured the design for clues. The weather deck was built of the same expensive-looking dark teak as the Tubercule chamber, and it had been carved, not in florid oriasques or humid jungle patterns, but into fingernail-tiny geometric links. Diamonds and hexagons, constructed of short straight strokes, chained together like maille . . . and there were initials in the shapes, too, left by builders or sailors, each letter joined to the greater pattern with reverent care.

On a Falcresti ship, there would be crews out here on sunny days, dragging qualmstones up and down, singing their work songs as they scoured. How could there be engravings on the deck? Where was the weathering on the wood? Where were the stains left by years of feet?

The wood must be of incredible quality to last so well.

Not a human soul moved anywhere. Not up in the masts. Not in the acres of rigging and blocks. Not one exhalation disturbed the smell of pitch, tar, turpentine, and lime. The stillness tugged on a childhood terror of ghost ships, and when a bead of condensation dripped from a ratline above her, Baru was sure it would splash on the deck as black Kettling blood.

This ship had supplied the Canaat rebels. This ship had weapons on it, and people willing to use them against Falcrest and its pawns.

She *had* to find them.

She looked out the other way, into the darkness of the caldera, where luminous green water licked at the bluffs. She had to conclude her business here and escape before Xate Yawa arrived and her lies collapsed.

"You wanted to speak to your aide," Innibarish said. "This way."

*W*HO TURNED YOU?"
      Baru seized Shao Lune by the high cheekbones of her sweet heart-shaped face. The web of her thumb cut between Shao's parted lips and she noticed, again, that she was missing two fingers on her right hand: she forgot that sometimes, because the hand was on her blind side.

Staff Captain Shao Lune bit her.

Baru clamped her hand down and didn't let go. Chew me, then: you haven't the fire for it, Lune, you're too dignified.

"You put a jellyfish trail on Ra's boat. Who gave you the chemicals? Who's following us?"

"Let me go." Baru's blood smeared across Shao's full lips. "Let me go and I'll tell you."

The Womb had installed Shao Lune in a cabin that suited her entirely: leather furniture in pools of candlelight, a rich and finished place. There was no inscription on the deck here. As if this space were an embassy, a pocket in the Cancrioth pattern where outsiders could be stowed.

Baru remembered another room, another confrontation, where Tain Hu had thrown her down on her back and hissed *you gave us too much*. She shoved Shao Lune to the floor. The staff captain's salt-soaked uniform crackled beneath her as she fell. Her elbows clapped on hardwood; her beautiful face twisted viciously.

Baru put a foot on her throat before she could spit something too foul to forgive. "Tell me who turned you."

"Yawa." Shao relaxed, suddenly playful beneath the steel tip of the boot. "I told Yawa I'd help her take you, in exchange for a pardon. Just a move in the game, Agonist."

Baru dug her heel in. "Now she knows how to find this ship. You've put all my gains in danger. I should've left you in the bilge."

"But I'm not hers, Baru," Shao said, just as smooth as wet ice. "I warned you she was conspiring against you. I gave you a chance to outbid her. You still have that chance. You know me, Baru. You know I'll work for whoever benefits me, and that's why I'm the only one you can trust. We're trapped here. Yawa can't save me. I need you. You need me."

"You're really reprehensible," Baru said, in wonder and in relief. Shao's mercenary allegiance made much more tactical sense than Tau-indi's unconditional trust. Look where that had brought Tau.

"I need *you* now." Shao's voice husked against Baru's heel. "I need you to be the savant they say you are. You've been weak, Baru, you've been pathetic—"

"I have not!"

"Oh, come now. I was locked up in *Helbride*'s bilge and even I know how bewildered you've been. How purposeless. You got hopelessly drunk and slept with me!" Shao blinked at her, mockingly astonished. "Healthy people don't do things like that."

"I imagine healthy people want nothing to do with you," Baru snapped.

"Healthy people don't need so many nightcaps," Shao retorted. "Really, Baru, what have you done lately except run from your problems and fall into traps? You're ruined.

"But *I* remember what happened the last time you were ruined. Everyone in Aurdwynn dismissed you after you destroyed the fiat note and alienated the Governor. Everyone thought you were finished. And *that* was when you triumphed."

Shao arched up against Baru's foot, reminding Baru, suddenly, of the mountaineering net she wore beneath her uniform, the clinging survival gear that trapped air against her skin for warmth. "You can do it again, can't you? You and I? We have such an opportunity! A ship out of the far west, full of exotic people, new languages, new flora and fauna, all their books and maps. We have a chance to find out what they can offer us! This is what Falcrest *does*!"

Baru flinched like Shao had stung her heel. "When will Yawa come for me?"

"I don't know. Who knows what she'll do when she finds this ship? This is *our* chance, Baru, not hers."

Baru dug her foot back in. She didn't trust Shao, and she doubly distrusted her need for Shao to say a little more, to assure her that she *was* a savant, and not a whiskey-soaked ruin.

"Please," Shao wheezed. "Let me be useful."

Something shuddered against Baru's balance. Like an interior riptide, pouring across her thoughts, running out into a right-side ocean. She felt for an instant as if clouds had parted, and she had seen, in the distance, a place where sea and sky whirled together, a maelstrom as tall as a cyclone's eye and as deep as the green ash sea. All the gathered wreckage of her course, all the broken things she had left behind her, seemed to drift toward that place of convergence, and she began to recognize in the debris the image of a face. . . .

And then it passed.

She had a purpose here, a purpose she couldn't forget. Find the Kettling.

Find a way to transport it. Release it in Falcrest. That was what Tain Hu would want. Shao Lune could be useful in that work; Baru could allow her to believe they were working together, as she'd let Tain Hu believe. Do it again, Baru, like you did it before.

"Where's Tau?" Baru forced herself to ask. "Are they all right?"

"The Prince? Still having a snit, I suppose. Probably in one of the other cabins back here. We're not guarded, as far as I can tell. Everyone's busy belowdecks. Listen."

She beckoned Baru to lay her ear against the deck.

Very distantly, passed through wood and air, Baru heard running feet and shouting. The slam of wood on wood. It sounded like a very subdued riot.

"No pistol shots," she noted. "No screams."

"None I've heard."

"Maybe they hate killing each other. Because they're immortal."

Shao Lune snorted. "Of course they are."

"Who do you think's fighting?"

"I don't know. Who can say what divides these people?"

"Me," Baru said, uneasily. "They've learned I'm here. Some of them want to find me, and others won't allow it. . . ."

Shao Lune rolled onto her back and began to undo her uniform. "You stink. We should both wash, or the salt will give us sores."

"You have water?" Baru gasped.

"In there—there's no tap, but the cask is full, and it's only a little stagnant—"

Baru lunged for the washroom.

B ARU drank greedily. It was cool and clean and good. When her thirst was finished, she cleaned her hands and took off the cassock Innibarish had given her to wash. Shao Lune washed, too, and Baru found herself noticing the net, that damn mountaineering net Shao Lune had worn for warmth, the way it portioned Shao's smooth skin and indulgent build into sectors which stressed and distorted. Like a map, like a chart of resources and luxuries. Baru had admired the diver Ulyu Xe for her oneness, her indivisibility, the way one line became another curve, calf became hip became flank, so you could not possibly separate her into pieces.

Shao was nothing like her. Baru could pick one grid sector of the net, any sector, and find something to admire. But the net kept her from seeing the whole woman.

The staff captain hung her uniform. She turned, and saw Baru watching her, and said, grinning, as lively and friendly now as she had never been on *Helbride,* "Come on, I'm not doing your laundry for you."

Baru hugged herself and shivered. They were alone. The two of them on this huge ship in this huge dead caldera, cut off from everything, hundreds of miles from anyone who would be their friend.

"Sorry," she said, foolishly: Shao Lune would never respect weakness. "I was thinking."

"You're lucky we're *both* prisoners now," Shao said. For a moment her eyes were indecent: so obviously flirting to take Baru's mind off her betrayal. "Puts us on an even footing."

You don't understand, Baru thought, you don't know what it is with me. If we—if I allow myself to—then you'll be lost here, Shao. I'll have to abandon you to get what I want. That's the life I chose.

Oh, fuck that.

Shao Lune padded maddeningly to the door, to check the lock. How did she do it? How did she decide how Baru would see her?

"I've been noticing things," Baru said, desperate to seize any kind of control. "The ship is undercrewed. And the shadow ambassador mentioned things which made me think . . . the Cancrioth, they're not unified, not in command of their situation. Not the way my sponsors expected. Not some kind of octopus with their arms in everything—"

"Like the Emperor's Throne?"

Baru laughed harshly. "After watching three of the Emperor's agents run from a single navy frigate for weeks on end, do you still think we're all that?"

"But you're not part of the *true* Throne."

"The *true* Throne?" Baru snapped, dangerously. "Am I false, somehow?"

"You are a foreigner. Xate Yawa is a foreigner. Apparitor is a foreigner. Do you really believe the real Throne would have so many foreign-born members? Do you really think it would have so many women?" Her eyes lingered on Baru as if marking the differences between them, at once dismissive and intensely domineering. "You didn't think it was coincidence they sent three foreign-born agents on this expedition, did you? And no one born Falcresti at all?"

"No," Baru admitted.

She'd begun to wonder, in her hangover reveries, whether half the purpose of this expedition was to shake them down, test their loyalty and their hereditary virtues—and whether the other half of the purpose was to keep them out of the way while more important things happened.

Shao turned back to Baru with a cotton cloth covering an object in her hands. "I have your things from the boat. The sack with your papers, and your little device, which I didn't open. I wanted to take the cover off your mask, in case there was water trapped underneath, but I thought I should get permission. Would you like me to . . . ?"

She slipped the cotton cloth away to show the beautiful terrible thing underneath. It still had its green cover on, the cover Baru had worn to the embassy. Shao ran one finger down its edge and found the seam where it lay over the true mask.

"Yes," Baru said, with a tremble she could not control.

Shao undid the little clamps and pulled. But suction kept the cover attached, and Shao's short-nailed fingers weren't able to pry it away.

"Allow me," Baru said, reaching out.

Shao lifted the mask to her full mouth and bit down. Her tooth parted the little gap, and the cover came away like a rind. The blank blue-white ceramic of Baru's mask waited beneath. The eight-point polestar insignia of Imperial authority blazed around the right eye in chased silver.

"Beautiful," Shao breathed, as Baru shuddered in ugly need. "Put it on."

"I don't see why," Baru said, stiffly.

"Put it on. I need to ask you a question. As what you're *supposed* to be, Baru." A spike of ugly impatience, like a nail through her lip. "Someone who knows what to do."

Baru slid the mask down over her face. It had been made just for her. The fit was lighter than fog.

Shao drew herself up straight. "Why did you bring us here? What do you want from the Cancrioth?"

To get something from them to kill your whole civilization. To make Tain Hu's sacrifice worth it. To prove *I* was worth her faith.

"My master wants proof of the Cancrioth's existence," she said. "If I possess it, he'll give me anything. Anything at all."

"Including a pardon?"

"A pardon would be nothing. He'd give me a province."

"And he can save us from Ormsment?" Shao's eyes narrowed with need. "She's very close, Baru. She has us trapped here. She has *Sulane* and she might turn *Ascentatic* to her cause. You know what she'll do if she catches us, Baru.

"She's come so far to kill you. I don't think she'll stop now."

3

FORCES CONVERGE

WATER hammer.

It smashed at Juris Ormsment. It leapt inside her, the guilt and the rage, the storm-loud scream of all the sailors she'd left to drown under Baru Cormorant's "protection" at Welthony Harbor. She had not been a walking wound, before Baru. She had not been a thin dressing over a gushing cut. She had never considered mutiny at all.

Now here she was, many miles and many lives from her post, hunting Baru. And the water hammer was in her.

She hauled herself up the ropes onto the deck of a warship. Not her flag *Sulane* or her consort *Scylpetaire* (detached, now, for the long voyage to Taranoke, to gather Baru's parents as hostages) but the Emperor's own frigate RNS *Ascentatic*.

Ascentatic's master-at-arms cried out "Admiral on deck!" The ship's officers snapped to attention. The marine lieutenant struck the chime and the drummers rapped out a salute. Juris almost cried aloud with pride: to see the navy turn out its honors for her, one last time. She was sworn to murder an agent of the Emperor's Throne, and thus in open mutiny against the lawful authority of the Emperor. She would never receive these honors again.

But *Ascentatic*'s company did not yet know.

The captain did. She'd made sure of that before trespassing on his ship. *Ascentatic*'s Asmee Nullsin offered her his good right hand. His left was a prosthetic hammer, amputated after two severed fingers went to rot. A rigging injury. Always mind the sacrifices your sailors have made, Ahanna Croftare had told her.

Juris gave him a firm shake. "Permission to come aboard?"

"Denied, mam." He waited for the ship's purser to record that in the log. "Shall we disembark you through the ship's great cabin?"

"Immediately." She returned his officers' salutes with a pointed glance at the deck. Obediently they all looked at their toes, so that they could say, at their court-martials, that the Province Admiral had ordered them to disregard her presence.

Nullsin's ship was in fine order. The company stood at their action stations, thick-armed men and broad-shouldered women at the lines, nimble girls aloft in the rigging, rocketry mates ready with lenses screwed into their masks at the hwachas and the big ship-killer Flying Fish rockets. Above everyone and everything towered the three masts, foremast and mainmast and aft. The mainmast alone was as tall as *Ascentatic* was long, built of interlocked lengths of pine, because no single tree could grow that tall and strong. A fleet of Falcresti ships in close company made the highest forest in the world.

The sails were stronger than the masts, though. If the battle frigate *Ascentatic* put up a full spread of canvas on a strong wind, she would sail her own masts off. The canvas would simply tear the wood apart and fly away. Pulled away from their stations to answer a higher call.

Nothing could ever be built strong enough, Juris thought. Nothing ever went untested.

THEY went inside the sterncastle, to Nullsin's great cabin. He ordered his steward away and Juris dogged the door shut. "Is anyone listening?"

"Of course not," Nullsin said, pouring a whiskey, one-handed, then another. "Am I suicidal? I heard from my marines that things went very badly on Haravige. Were you wounded?"

"No," she said, which was mostly the truth. "They pronounce it *Hara-Vijay*, if you can hear the difference."

"I'm a good officer, mam. Trained to listen to blunt orders. Not nuance of accent."

"I expect you'd like some blunt orders from me?"

"I'm not sure I do, mam, after what you've told me."

She nodded: an honest reply. "What about the embassy staff?" It was the navy's duty to safeguard embassies, even the enemy's. "And the Prince-Ambassador?"

"Most of the staff died in the fire. No sign of the Prince-Ambassador." Nullsin grimaced. "Very bad if Tau-indi Bosoka was in there. We could be blamed, and then . . ."

Parliament was always looking for an excuse to decapitate the Admiralty and install its own picks. This threat was eight parts fear of what a popular admiral might do (seize the trade, declare herself empress) and two parts dislike of navy women. A bunch of tribadists and anti-mannist bitches, the men in Parliament thought. And the Merit Admirals, the navy's professional society of old women, were the worst of the litter.

"What the fuck was Tau-indi doing here?" she wondered aloud. Juris had known her—known him—damn it, known *them* as a cheerful, somewhat zaftig laman who gave clever gifts. They'd presented Juris with a loose-leaf copy of the *Kiet Khoiad,* with chapters that could be rearranged to change the story. If every last person in the world were gathered up by the archons and offered their heart's desire in exchange for their soul, Juris had really believed Tauindi would be the last and most virtuous of the resisters.

Baru had turned them both. Juris to mutiny, and Tau, somehow, to Baru's side.

People bent. You hit them hard enough and they just bent.

"I'm in open mutiny," she told Nullsin. She would not carry out a mutiny meant to protect the navy's good officers by lying to one of those good officers. "I've already killed members of the Imperial advisory staff and defied Imperial edict."

"Queen's stitched cunt," he snapped, "do you have to *say* it? Begging"—he swallowed—"your pardon, mam."

"Did you know before I told you?"

"We were on the Llosydanes after you. We saw the aftermath of your . . . pursuit there." He closed up his crystal decanter with his good hand. "Why haven't you caught your target?"

"Her ship is fast. She has assets to expend." And the whims of the unfortunately necessary Aurdwynni brute Tain Shir had interfered. "She used Tauindi's diplomatic seals to head us off."

Nullsin offered her one of the whiskeys. His hand was shaking, narrowly and very fast: living through a moment he knew would be questioned and interrogated with his life as the stakes. "I have orders to bring her in for questioning. Out of concern she's part of a conspiracy to ignite open war with the Oriati."

The whiskey tasted like a peat bog full of brine. She loved it. "Orders from who?"

"Rear Admiral Maroyad, on Isla Cauteria." He drank, lunging at the glass, trying to cover his shaking hand with vigor. "We picked up five prisoners from Baru's old retinue in Aurdwynn. The so-called 'Vultjagata.' They led us here. They also told us that you attacked the Morrow Ministry station on the Llosydanes."

"You believed them?" she said, trying to be wry. "I'm hurt."

"I believed the wrecks of two Oriati dromon you left behind. I did what cleanup I could before Parliament finds the mess." He watched her carefully. "With respect, mam, what the fuck were you thinking? Gassing the Ministry station? Murdering Falcresti citizens?"

She hadn't gassed the station, but it hardly mattered. "Do you really want to know? Do you want that information in your possession when the Parliamentary inquisition is called?"

Nullsin paced over to stare into the oil painting of Admiral Juristane's flagship bombarding the Oriati fleet in Kutulbha harbor. The artist had captured the slick, oily Burn fire clinging to the waves, floating like grease on a pan. Nullsin drank again, grimaced, and looked back.

"Are you going to ask me to join you?"

"No." Oh, Nullsin, of course not. He had his duty to his mission and his crew. She would not force her own unforgivable failure on him.

"I refused to let you board," he said, watching her. "I'd be in my power to ask you to leave now."

"You're right. Of course"—she paused, letting him understand that she was about to leverage him, just a little—"if you send me away, we can't cooperate to manage the situation ashore. Have you seen what they're doing to each other?"

Nullsin shuddered.

The Kyprananoke archipelago had fallen into democlysm, the word great Iranenna (she'd read her prerevolutionary philosophers, in school at Shaheen) coined for "a chaos made of man." Nowhere in nature could you find bloodshed like this. Years of surgical punishment and water interdict by the ruling Kyprist junta had finally flashed the islands to fire. The Canaat rebels were boiling out of the west, slaughtering their way across the archipelago with fishing spears and exotic rocket-powder pistols, shooting dead everyone who'd ever spoken a kind word about distant Falcrest. In Loveport, the acrobats' scaffolds now dangled the bodies of orange-gloved Kyprists.

Some of the rebels were bleeding green-black blood, the telltale symptom of the hemorrhagic plague that the ancient Oriati had named, for the way it boiled up out of certain hidden reservoirs, the Kettling.

"*Helbride* flashed me an order an hour ago." Nullsin showed her the scrap of paper where a tactical clerk had translated the sunflash into text. "A command from the Emperor's agent Apparitor. Prevent any ship from departing these waters, on penalty of destruction by fire."

Juris sneered: Apparitor was quietly understood to hold sway over the Empire Admiral Lindon Satamine, a young man from the Storm Corps who had been promoted, unfairly, over all the Admiralty's seasoned fighting women. "Will you comply?"

"There's Kettling here. How couldn't I?"

"You're right," she decided. "That has to be your priority."

"Good." Nullsin drank too long, and coughed. He put the glass down on his writing blotter. "We're right on the fulcrum here, aren't we, Province Admiral?"

It was absurd. The state of the whole Ashen Sea balanced on them, here, right now. This plague could kill millions if it reached the mainlands. This civil war could be the first blow of an Oriati attack on Falcrest, the beginning of a war that might (if the worst predictions were true) set back civilization half a millennium.

So much depended on the next few days. They might button it all up neatly and restore the Ashen Sea to sanity. Or the plague might escape. The war might flash over. And in two months every city from Devimandi to New Kutulbha would burn as millions of plague-carrying refugees swarmed like locusts into the Occupation and the Butterveldt.

Once, long ago, the Cheetah Palaces had ruled the Ashen Sea. Their time had ended. Once, not quite so long ago, the Jellyfish Eaters had ruled the Ashen Sea. Their time had ended. Kyprananoke was all that remained of them.

Falcrest ruled the Ashen Sea today. It was genuinely possible that in a few hundred years no one would remember Falcrest at all.

"I'm glad you're here," she said, softly. "I wouldn't want to manage this alone."

"I'm not glad you're here," he said, smiling ironically. "But since you are, I'm glad you brought a damn fine warship."

They chimed their glasses off each other, that high thin *ping* of glass on glass that Juris had first heard as a child, in services at the Cult of Human Reason.

The steward's door burst open. A tall Oriati woman in a half-buttoned uniform shoved past the steward. She was big, her eyes alert, tall and well-muscled and wide-hipped, near as far opposite the Falcresti ideal of compact beauty as you could get.

"Lieutenant Commander," Nullsin snapped, "what in the name of virtue are you doing?"

"Sir!" The Oriati woman saluted first Nullsin, then, without pause, Juris. "Lieutenant Commander Aminata, reporting."

No one eavesdropping, eh, Nullsin? Probably he hadn't known. But wait a moment now— "I recognize you. You were at the embassy." Juris had seen this woman firing her flare pistol, calling in the *Ascentatic* marines. "You gave the order to burn the grounds, didn't you? To contain the plague?"

"Yes, mam," Aminata said, firmly. "I gave that order."

"You did the right thing." Her heart cried at that firmness, that discipline. What the navy asked of its young women. How gloriously they answered. "You did your duty."

"Yes, mam." A little steel glinted in her eyes: she did not need to be told her duty.

"Lieutenant Commander," Nullsin said, warningly, "you shouldn't be here right now."

Aminata took a deep breath. Her eyes went to Nullsin for a moment, apologetic, and then returned, decisively, to Juris. "Mam, I want to volunteer to lead the attempt to capture Baru Cormorant."

Nullsin groaned like he'd been stabbed. Was there something between them? No, definitely not. Aminata would use whores, and a man who fucked with officers under his command would not last long in the navy.

"Lieutenant Commander," he said, "Baru died in that fire."

"No, sir, she wouldn't go into that embassy without a way out. I think I have a lead on where she'll go next." She recentered to perfect attention, staring at Juris. "But if we go in with a large force, we'll spook her, mam. Just give me my two suasioners, an assault boat, and a few marines. I'll track her down. I'll find out the truth about her purpose. And if need be, I'll bring her in."

You thought she was your friend, didn't you, Aminata. And a part of you still thinks so.

Maybe Aminata *could* find Baru. But if Juris involved her, she'd be doomed. Attainted as a mutineer. All her talent and dedication wasted.

Unless . . .

. . . unless they could bring home such proof to Falcrest as to *justify* their mutiny.

Unless they could capture Baru, and make her confess to conspiracy to create a war. Then the decision to mutiny to go after Baru would be an act of heroic foresight. . . .

"Lieutenant Commander," Juris said, "how much would you do to catch Baru?"

Nullsin set his hammer in his good hand and squeezed it like it could hold Aminata at anchor. Poor Asmee Nullsin: he did not yet know what all captains and all admirals had to learn, that you could not protect your best. They would find their own danger.

"Anything, mam." Aminata met her eyes. "I have to know the truth."

"I could use a new staff captain," Juris said. "My last one went over to Baru's side. Are you interested?"

"Lieutenant Commander," Nullsin said, urgently, "if you go over to *Sulane* you'll be out of my chain of command, you understand? You'll be Fifth Fleet Aurdwynn, then. I will have no power to protect you from any Parliamentary inquiry directed at Fifth Fleet."

"I understand, sir." Aminata remained at attention. "I want to go, sir. I need to be the one to bring her in."

T HE Cancrioth!" The boy Iraji filled the little houseboat with his scream.
I had, in my station as Jurispotence of Aurdwynn, learned to hide my love of the divine. If a Ministry of Antiquities stooge brought me a two-thousand-year-old ceremonial oil scrape and asked me to destroy it as an artifact of unhygienic religiosity, I could hardly scream in anguish, could I? I could hardly stand on my toes and beg for Himu's sky-swift forgiveness. My mission was to protect the living faith, not its dead relics.

So I never betrayed my awe in the face of the sacred.

But when poor Iraji screamed, I heard a boy touched by the numinous. The exaltation in his voice, the *power* in that word: nothing human. I clutched at Faham Execarne to steady myself, but he had recoiled in shock; we both nearly fell. Two very dignified elders we were!

"The Cancrioth!" Iraji screamed again. "They took Baru in my place! *She went in my place!*"

He had to scream to get the words out before he fell. His eyes rolled back white. He began to faint.

I lunged at him, pushed his limp body against the wall, trying to keep his blood up by sheer fright. I wore a structured quarantine gown and a black filtered mask, and I knew Iraji would see a spider descending on him. Xate Yawa in her web.

"The Cancrioth is here?" The clockwork voice changer pressed to my throat buzzed like a cloud of flies. "You're certain!"

"Yes! They're here! They've come to find what they lost!"

"What have they lost?"

"*I'm one of them!*" he screamed, huge-eyed and horribly beautiful, Apparitor's Oriati concubine wandered so far from his bed. "*I'M ONE OF THEM!*"

"Oh," I rasped.

Did Apparitor know? What mad love for Iraji could make Apparitor conceal the boy from us—when proof of the Cancrioth was the *object* of this whole quest?

Perhaps he was the one who'd conditioned Iraji to hide the truth from himself.

I wanted to send Iraji back to *Helbride* and Apparitor. But if Baru found the Cancrioth unchallenged, she would bring home victory for her master. Farrier's victory would destroy Hesychast. And if Hesychast fell, I would fall with him. I would be destroyed, or imprisoned, or enslaved by Baru.

Then Baru would feed like a hagfish on Aurdwynn, my home.

"Iraji." As cold as I had pronounced any verdict in the courtroom. "Would you exchange yourself for Baru?"

He nodded tremulously. "Yes. It should have been me. . . ."

"Why?" Faham Execarne burst out. He was Falcrest's chief spy and my ally of convenience, a robust old mind who'd seen as many years of human deviance and self-delusion as I. And *still* he was astounded by Iraji's choice.

Why would this beautiful young man go into the enemy's lair for the sake of a woman who'd kidnapped and abandoned him?

Iraji had been a spy in Baru's entourage, in the days before Tain Hu was brought to her for execution. Had Baru tricked him into believing that she truly loved Hu?

"Because it would be . . ." He wavered like a drunk. "It would be good for my trim."

Twenty years younger I might have laughed in disbelief. Twenty years aching for my own redemption in the sight of the ykari I pretended to hate and persecute silenced that laugh.

"She's playing you, child," Execarne warned him.

"Is she?" the boy said, quietly. "I've saved her life twice, on *Helbride* and at the Elided Keep. She saved mine, too, on *Cheetah*. And I am sure that I am the closest thing she has to a friend. We are bound together."

"That's how she lies to people."

"No," Iraji whispered. "It's not a lie. No matter how much you both want it to be true, you *and* her . . . you're wrong."

Faham Execarne's clothier, the operational leader of his Morrow Ministry cell on Kyprananoke, came in from the deck outside. "We have the trail. South into el-Tsunuqba. That isn't Canaat territory. Someone else has her."

We had flushed Baru from *Helbride,* away from witnesses, so that we could destroy her without taking the blame. We had to act now.

Iraji was so young. What a waste to spend him here. . . .

But Aurdwynn needed me to triumph. My brother needed me to triumph. Hesychast needed the Cancrioth's secret and immortal flesh, balm for all his eugenic troubles—needed it to win the Reckoning of Ways. And if he failed, then I failed, and I had done everything for nothing! Decades of paranoia and self-denial, persecuting my own people, betraying my own brother, wasted because upstart Baru Cormorant beat me to a cult of cancer worshipers!

Yes. It had to be this way. I would have her tonight. By dawn I would have her dead on my lobotomy pick, and a gentled new woman cut to life in her body. Then she would go north as living dowry.

"Take Iraji to the boats," I ordered. "He'll be our leverage. Have the tactical surgeon prepare my lobotomy instruments. I'll operate as soon as we have Baru."

A MINATA'S boat crunched across a corpse.

"Sorry, mam," the boatswain called. "That big ol' burner snuck right up on me."

A hush fell over the boat. *Burner* was not just slang for burnt corpses but, after the Armada War, a particularly vile epithet for Oriati people.

That wasn't what got to Aminata. She was used to racialism. It was the triple meaning, the ironic reversal, that made her grunt in pain. *She* was the burner. She was the one who'd torched the embassy at Hara-Vijay with everyone inside. Even the children.

She had made that corpse beneath the keel.

Her tongue found a stinging sore where she'd bit down on a spark. On that thrill of pain she shouted her orders. "Up, up and search, I want her alive! Fat Kyprananoki woman with an arrow in her ass! She can't have gone far!"

Of all the people at the embassy reception, she could remember only one who'd definitely spoken to Baru *and* definitely escaped. The woman had been shot in the ass going over the wall, but she'd made it.

Maybe Baru had told her something.

Aminata jackknifed over the boatwale, down into bath-warm water and scattering fish. The cormorant feather tucked into her collar brushed against her chin.

Hey, bird. I'm gonna find out what the fuck is going on with you, and I'm not going to let anyone hurt you until I do. Not even the Province Admiral, so help me. She gave me some pins. Breveted me up to captain, temporarily.

I really want that promotion to stick one day. . . .

But first, Baru, I have to know what you're doing here.

The Kyprists triaged survivors of the fire here on the pavereef, a concrete-filled ring of coral around the embassy. An exhausted old woman in Kyprist-orange gloves ran the triage station. The nurses carried a wretched thing up to her, the wreckage of a person screaming through a red hole. The old woman shook her head: too many burns across too much skin. The right decision. The nurses used their hands to close off the arteries in the victim's throat: a blood choke, fatal if applied long enough. Aminata wished she could blood choke whoever had released the plague.

The patient died.

Then the nurses lifted the next burnt body from the gondola, and it was like the screams had just found a new throat.

She would never wake up in a world where she *hadn't* done this. From now until the day she died, she'd be the woman who'd burnt these people. The Kettling couldn't be allowed to spread—she knew that—she'd seen the bleeding faces—but look at what she'd *done*. Crispy red-black skin everywhere. Crispy like the meat you dropped into the fire and fished out laughing. The smell of burnt hair, and the sea clogged with jellyfish around them— And the screams—

She threw up into the reef. The taste of bread and vinegar. "Oh, kings," she groaned, and splashed water from her canteen to rinse.

"Mam," her subordinate Gerewho Gotha called, "are you all right?"

"It's the smell," Aminata grunted.

"Mam?" Faroni oyaSegu called. "Mam, I've found her."

THE ass-shot woman lay on a plank with wet seaweed pillowed under her forehead. Her daishiki was hiked up, revealing the fresh crossbow wound in her left ass cheek. No one had had time to dress it. She groaned as Aminata and Faroni approached. "Here to finish me off?"

"I'm very sorry, mam. We were trying to prevent any infected persons from escaping." Aminata checked the wound: deep but narrow, not lethal unless infected or poisoned. "You should be all right. Just report to a quarantine if you develop any illness in the next few weeks."

"I'm a man," the ass-shot person said. "You're confused, because I haven't got my things on, so you see a woman. My name's Ngaio."

"Well, Mister Ngaio"—Aminata obeyed the navy's unofficial protocol for handling presanitary confusions of gender—"we came to ask you some questions. You were down in the embassy courtyard before the, uh, the confusion, correct?"

"To my regret," he groaned.

"Did you speak to the woman in the expensive green mask?"

"The one your admiral wanted to kill? Yes. I'll tell you, too, if you just"—he gasped, resettled his weight—"get me water, bandages, and a crutch. I have to get to my ship. The Canaat will kill me for collaboration. I'm a Balt, you see. It's not safe for us now."

Aminata had no idea what a Balt was, but she assumed Kyprananoke, tiny as it was, had its own tribes with their own grudges. "Faroni, find something for him to lean on."

The younger Oriati woman saluted and trotted off. Aminata helped Ngaio upright to drink from her canteen. Gerewho frowned, worried, probably, that

Ngaio might be infected. Aminata waved him off to find bandages: the Kettling passed by blood, and she would get rid of the canteen.

"Anything you can remember. Please."

Ngaio gasped and wiped his mouth. "The woman in the green mask called herself Barbitu Plane. We talked about Prince Tau-indi Bosoka. Barbitu liked them. We talked about Prince Kindalana of Segu, and her plan to join Falcrest and Oriati Mbo together to avert a war. Barbitu was with a woman, a Falcresti woman, who asked me about the plague, and, well"—Ngaio laughed like a sob—"the plague turned up. Which led to . . . well, you certainly know, don't you?"

"This Falcresti woman, she was navy?" That would be Staff Captain Shao Lune, who had abandoned Ormsment in favor of Baru.

"I suppose. She was in a uniform. She said she was Barbitu's slave." Ngaio grimaced, in distaste as much as pain. "Slave jokes. I don't like them."

Neither did Aminata. "What happened when Admiral Ormsment arrived?"

"She said Barbitu was really Baru Cormorant, and also Agonist, whatever that means." Ngaio threw back his head to finish the water. Her tits bobbed with the motion—*his* tits, damn it. Aminata didn't understand why he thought he was a man, but as an interrogator (the infamous Burner of Souls, torturer of her own Oriati race-kin) she knew better than to alienate the subject for no reason.

Ngaio went on. "Then the Prince Tau-indi Bosoka made it clear this woman, Baru or Agonist or whoever, was under their protection."

Shit. Baru was under explicit and sacrosanct diplomatic protection. Any harm done to her would be an act of war against the Oriati. "What did Admiral Ormsment do?"

Ngaio laughed, and shouted a little at the pain. "She called Baru to duel."

Shit. She'd broken diplomatic right. That would convince half of Parliament the Admiralty had gone berserk. There were files in the Parliamentary offices right now, signed and sealed, waiting only to be brought to the proper attention to destroy the navy woman named in the neat label on the back.

"Why? Why did she ask for a duel?"

"I don't know. I don't know. The other navy woman, Baru's companion, she called Ormsment a traitor. Then Juris said she'd sent a ship to take Baru's parents hostage."

"*What?*"

"That's what she said. She offered to fight Baru, woman to woman. Baru spoke to Tau-indi for a few moments, and then she came forward as if to duel . . . and then"—Ngaio shuddered—"someone said 'I'm thirsty,' and it all went mad."

Aminata had seen Baru wielding Aminata's old saber, the one she'd gifted to Baru in Aurdwynn. If Baru had kept that sword close at hand she *must* still care about Aminata—she must be worth more respect than a woman who would take Baru's innocent *parents* hostage—

Or she'd just held on to a good saber.

"Did she mention anything," Aminata asked, in desperation, "about a duchess? A Duchess Tain Hu?" The mysterious Tain woman had sent Aminata a letter, entrusting her with Baru's safety on the eve of her own death. . . .

"No," Ngaio said. "Nothing about that."

Oh, none of this made any sense. Right before the plague and the massacre, Shao Lune had given a navy signal: *I'm drowning, throw me a line.* Who was she afraid of? Baru? Or mutinous Juris Ormsment? Or both of them? Kings and queens, there were so many questions—

And that was why she *had* to be the one to find Baru first. She had to know, once and for all, if Baru . . .

If Baru *what,* exactly? Served the Republic in all she did?

Or cared about Aminata, even a little? Deserved the trust that the Duchess Tain Hu had expressed in her?

Where did her duty lie?

"There was the poem," Ngaio said.

"What? What poem?"

"Barbitu—Baru, I mean—was trying to find a boy's parents. She had a sketch of the boy. Oriati, younger than you, very beautiful. She said he knew this rhyme: ayamma, ayamma, a ut li-en . . ."

A frisson took Aminata: two entirely separate things coming together. "Gere-who, listen. Do you recognize those sounds?"

The syllables made her young suasioner rock back on his heels. "Yes, mam, I think so. From the . . . that last interrogation, before we sailed." They had in-terrogated Abdumasi Abd, the special prisoner taken from Aurdwynn. They'd been told to ask him: *What is the Cancrioth?* He'd given up Baru's name, set-ting Aminata on the hunt. But he'd given up something else, too. A string of syllables that had frightened Gerewho viscerally. *Those* syllables.

Was Baru actually searching for the exact same Cancrioth that Aminata had been tasked to find? Were they *on the same side*?

"But I don't understand," Ngaio said, with as much exhaustion as pain in his voice. "Why does any of this matter? Isn't this Baru woman dead? I didn't see her come over the walls. . . . She's gone, isn't she?"

"No," a new voice said.

That *no* pulled Aminata around like a hook in her earlobe. It was the way it was said, somehow. It scared the shit out of her. That *no* might have negated anything. A question or a life.

A big woman ambled up the reef toward them. In one hand she held a crude spear-thrower, an atlatl. In the other a jellyfish, its arms trailing from her fist. She had been eating its bell.

"Who the hell are you?" Aminata snapped.

The woman's eyes flashed blue in the setting sun. "You're from *Ascentatic*."

"Not anymore. Lieutenant Commander Aminata, RNS *Sulane*, now seconded to Province Admiral Ormsment—"

An expression of indecipherable appetite. "Aminata. I know that name. Did Baru Cormorant ever pretend to love you?"

Aminata blinked at her. "What?"

"I can bring you to her," the woman said, and the hunger in her voice made Aminata flinch. "I am Ormsment's hunter. I find Baru wherever she goes. But before I bring you to her, you must tell me this. Did Baru pretend to love you?"

All Aminata's instincts said this woman was a killer. A pirate or a cutthroat. She didn't want to give this "hunter" anything. But if it meant finding Baru . . .

"We were friends, once," she allowed.

"Would she hesitate if it came to a choice between her life and yours?"

The same question Aminata wanted to answer herself.

"I don't know," she said.

"Come, then." The big woman beckoned and smiled. "Come. I need to gather something from your old ship. And then, together, we'll go to Baru."

Ngaio Ngaonic hobbled away across the coral and concrete, as fast as his wounded ass would let him. Aminata had meant to ask him why he and Baru had discussed the Federal Princes, Tau-indi Bosoka and Kindalana of Segu. Too late now.

A STORY ABOUT ASH 6

Federation Year 912:
23 Years Earlier
Upon Prince Hill, by Lake Jaro
in Lonjaro Mbo

"KINDALANA!" Tau-indi hammered the door plate with the greeting mallet. "Kinda!"

A groundskeep opened the way. "Your Federal Highness, remember there's a taboo against burrowing things today—"

"Go tell my mother that a mob's coming for the hostages!" Tau bolted across the compound, coughing on charcoal dust, until they smashed through the door and ran right into Kindalana's arms.

"Tau!" She caught them and they almost fell together on the welcome mat. "What is it?"

"There's a mob from Jaro on the lake." She smelled of smoke and the touch of her hands yanked up a dizzy memory of swimming with her, Kindalana kicking off their thighs, Kindalana whispering in Tau's ear that mother Tahr would come back okay.

Tau had been so ashamed that Kindalana thought they were just a child afraid for their mother. But Kindalana was right, in the end. Tahr *did* come back okay.

Kindalana blinked at them from two finger-widths away. Her eyes were wide-set and keen, like buffalo horns. There was a little dimple at the base of her throat, marked at each side by her clavicles. Everything seemed to move with her breath.

"A mob?" she said, Kindalana demanding that the world clarify itself, so she could fix it. "What do they want?"

"They want Cosgrad and Farrier. They made enenen totems." How precious it was to be this close to her. The mask of her power, prince-power, beauty-power, broke down into simple facts: the little ridges between her nose and the top of her lips, shaped in the echo of her throat. "We have to stop them."

"Oh," Kindalana gasped, probably a gasp of panic, probably a little excited, too. Kinda did love a chance to command. "We have to talk them down! But I'm dressed like—"

"You look like a gardener and I look like a clerk."

"We need our paints, the declaration paints—"

"—and jewels—"

"—and silks; one of my old saris might fit you—"

"—there's a taboo on burrowing things, maybe we can use that—"

"—what, Tau, should we shove Farrier and Cosgrad down a hole, is that what you mean to do—"

Laughing: "It might work!"

They ran into the inner rooms, watering and oiling the paint pots, yelling at a scorpion they found curled up in a bolt of cloth, arguing over whether it was a burrowing animal, smashing it, arguing again over how much paint they had time for as they unwrapped each other and dabbed warm water and scents on flesh and hair. Just the bold striped throat and chin highlights of a Prince out on function? Yes, that would do, the important thing was to look authoritative, but wait (Kinda scrubbing furiously at the earth on Tau-indi's feet, Tau trying to strip leftover paint from the night before off her brow and cheekbones), wait, wait, they had to be recognizably the Prince Bosoka of Lonjaro the Thirteen-in-Three-in-One and the Prince Kindalana eshSegu, so Tau would do gold Segu stripes on Kinda's clavicles while she did green star points on Tau's larynx and brow. There was no time for their hands or legs.

"Hold still," Kindalana snapped. "No, actually still!"

"Mmf." The application tickled. "Mmp."

"All right." She bared her throat in turn. "Quick. Oh, principles, can you hear them? I think I can hear them."

"Maybe they'll tear us apart, too," Tau-indi said. "Maybe they've been talking to that awful satirist, the populist one who thinks we're spoiled."

"We are spoiled, Tau. We don't work fields or carry water or make bricks. The shua resent us, you know?"

"What?" Tau loved stories about the shua, the self-taught warrior societies who guarded the realm. "Why?"

"Don't you read any history? The struggle between the power of the Federal Princes and the local authority of the shua? Oh!" Kindalana shivered and made a small sound. "That *does* tickle." Her throat moved lightly under Tau-indi's circling thumbs.

"I missed touching you," Tau said. It was a stupid thing to say, but the paint had to get done, and it was a better topic than Kindalana showing off. "As, you know, just a . . . not like Abdu, but I missed it."

"I know," she said.

"We haven't been right."

"I know," she said.

"Oh."

Her breath ran in and out like seasons. Her hips brushed Tau-indi's thighs and she rearranged them awkwardly to keep a little distance. "You didn't want things to be right," she said. Tau-indi cleaned their fingers in the pot of stripper and got the paint for her clavicles. Her bones trembled when she spoke. "You wanted to be alone. You wanted to be hurt. You think you have to be miserable alone, so everyone will know you're too noble to put your misery on them. But you want us to *know* you're miserable. Your favorite thing in the world is to be too hurt for anyone to help."

She adjusted Tau's head a few inches and began to star their brow. Her hands were stiff, her motions sharp. "You told me I had to take care of Abdumasi. You told me you wanted to go off and be a Prince."

"I was proud. I didn't want you to think I was a child."

"Let me talk." Kinda finished the star and swept two clean lines along Tau-indi's cheekbones. "You've always been the one people trust. When your mother left, your house trusted you. When Falcrest captured her, my father came to talk to you. He *never* talks to me, because he just sees my mother. You saw the war coming before anyone else—"

"I didn't!"

"Why did you send me to Abdumasi, then? Why were you so convinced you had to be a Prince alone?" Her eyes followed Tau-indi's motion for motion and they couldn't look back, they had to finish the paint. "Why did you want the three of us at war?"

She was very warm, this close. Tau bared their throat for the green Lonjaro star, painted on the larynx. Kinda's fingers were quick and hot.

"Do you love Abdu?" Tau-indi asked.

"Maybe right now," Kindalana said crisply, her two fingers moving down-sideways-down-up-down, "maybe right now, I suppose I do, half of me is thinking about him all the time, but Tau—" She rinsed her hands and they both went for the saris; they wrapped each other up. "Tau, in Segu women marry late, and people will question your womanhood if you haven't had lovers before. There's a . . . it's a tenuous thing, being a Segu woman. You have to prove yourself to other women, and part of that is your ease with men. I thought I could learn some of that by practicing on Abdu, like the grownups do, like our parents, we'd just fuck and be friends—"

"Our parents are in love, Kinda."

"No." Kindalana smoothed the sari down over Tau's shoulders, and then her own. "My father's in love with your mother. But not the other way."

They turned around each other like serpents, checking knots, and both bent to lace their sandals. Outside the sentries yelled and beat their fists against the bird-cymbals, sending up irita, the alarm cries that would rouse nearby farmers to help.

"I guess, when you start fucking, you can't skip over the childish part, the part that feels like love." Kindalana caught Tau-indi by the earlobe to swipe paint from the side of their chin. "Or I can't, at least. You left us alone, Tau, and what were we supposed to do, with you taking charge of everything? You took all the burdens on yourself, your house and your mother's trim, and then you took Cosgrad, too."

"You wanted to seduce Farrier! I wasn't the only one who—"

"You'd already seduced Cosgrad, hadn't you?"

"Not like that!"

"You befriended him. I don't make friends easily, Tau. That's your gift."

"You make me sound so mighty."

"You're a Prince."

"Everyone knows you're cleverer."

"And everyone knows you have better trim."

"That doesn't seem to do much good," Tau said, a little bitterly.

"Of course it does," Kindalana sighed. "People *listen* to you. I know all these things, I've figured out so much, but who wants to listen to me? You're strange with women here in Lonjaro, did you know that? Not hateful, but *particular*. Women have certain jobs, certain roles. You don't like it when we go beyond them."

They fumbled together in the keepsake chest for the jewelry. Kindalana took a locket for her breast and chains to link her nose and ears. Tau-indi gauged their earlobes, grunting at the stretch of the skin, and found four Aurdwynni bracelets to chime on their wrists.

Kindalana lifted her arms and turned around once. "Am I proud?"

She was a vision. Tau-indi's heart stopped up. "You're proud," they managed, voice wobbling. "Am I proud?"

"You'll do," Kindalana said, and then, with an obvious and powerful effort to say more, give more, "Tau, you're beautiful."

They went out the back gate together, to face down the mob.

THE ferries had landed. The mob came up in their silent hundreds, ash-streaked, grim-faced, bowed by the weight of what they had to do. There were potters, weavers, wheelwrights, all sorts of craftspeople from the city; there were shua warriors of both kinds, professional hunters and renegade vigilantes; there were clerks, administrators, drummers, gamblers, braggarts. Tau felt a profound empathy for the mass of them, and for the grief that ran like floodwater between the reservoirs of their bodies. This could be the whole Mbo, soon. The whole great people raised to war. And what a terrible waste it would be, what a betrayal of a thousand years of work.

"Shall we?" Kinda murmured.

"Yes."

The mob saw them. The comic griot raised the totem of the two dead men as if to call down lightning. "They are enenen. They owe us a blood price, and they cannot pay it in gold. Give them to us."

"Stop!" the Princes cried, Tau and Kinda together. "Stop and listen!"

And Tau saw (in a gasp of joy ragged as wind through reeds) that the people were not too far gone from trim to hear.

Kindalana told them of the foreigners who had come to Lonjaro Mbo to learn. She was a guest in Lonjaro, too, for she was a Prince of Segu, and did they not recognize the obligations of hospitality that bound guest to host? Tau's mother had been taken by Falcrest, and returned safely. Would they not reciprocate? Would they be the first to snap the sacred circle of trust?

Then Tau-indi spoke beside her, the laman with the round hips and the coiled hair, telling the mob in a voice like the monsoon drumming on mangrove leaves that Lonjaro's principles had already visited revenge on Cosgrad Torrinde.

"He was paralyzed by a frog," Tau-indi said—Kindalana puffing up her cheeks like that frog—"and he waded among leeches"—Kindalana plucking at her calves—"and then the frog seduced his tongue, and he had dreams of the defeat of his homeland, dreams out of the mangrove forest"—Kindalana touching her wrists, her throat, making the comic griot who led the mob smile helplessly—"and then his bowels were emptied by the waters of Segu, and his bones were bent by the rust of Devi-naga, and the heat of Mzilimake burned up his mind!"

Tau wondered what all the misfortunes Cosgrad had suffered meant about Cairdine Farrier's trim.

"They might burn our ships," Kindalana bellowed; she must have practiced that low-in-the-gut roar, "they might ask us to answer blood with blood and fire with fire, but we are mbo. We do not want! We give, and we are satisfied! Falcrest will come to us to get what they want, and we will bind them to us, and in the end they will be mbo, too! Will you kill these men who came to learn from us? Or will you let them learn, and yield?"

The mob faltered. They could have stormed a line of house guard, a company of local shua, or even Falcrest's masked marines. Against two bright young Princes in their regalia they had no chance at all.

The comic griot set down the totems. "I was wrong," he said. "It is not in my power to declare anyone enenen. Do you all hear me? I was wrong!"

After that there was nothing to do but go back to the ferries.

Kindalana turned to them grinning like a fed tiger. "Tau, that was amazing."

They grinned stupidly back at her.

At that moment the sentries guarding the southern approach began to scream.

T AU ran until their gut cramped. Clots of gardeners and groundskeeps stumbled past, fleeing for the House Bosoka.

"Stand with me!" Tau cried to them. "Stand for your house! Tell me, someone, what you saw!"

But not all the paint nor all the jewelry of a Prince could arrest the sentries' fear, and they fled inside the compound.

"Good morning, Tau. Mind taboo." Cairdine Farrier jogged up easily, fresh from helping in the gardens: there was dirt on his hands and somehow he had gotten clay on his nose. Unlike Cosgrad, he had adopted Mbo clothes, but he wore them in his own way, a short khanga wrapped rakishly around his shoulders and puffy linen trousers cinched into Falcrest boots. He was a deep-eyed, thoughtful man who never showed too much, like a fashionably dressed clam. "What's all the alarm?"

"A mob," Tau panted, "come to kill you. But we turned them away."

"Ah," Farrier said, thoughtfully. "From the city, I expect? A manifestation of urban resentment against your principalities' agrarian ways?"

Tau stared at him. "I said they were here to kill *you*!"

"But to kill me, they must be angry enough to ignore *your* authority, yes?"

Tau expected the reasons were much less abstract than urban resentment, and much more to do with the hundred thousand Oriati dead. "The mob's gone, but now everyone's running. I heard irita to the south."

"Really now." Farrier ambled off downhill. "Let's go see what has everyone spooked."

"Cairdine, wait! It's not safe!"

Farrier trotted cheerfully down the south road, fishing out his notebook. The raspberry bushes clasped at his shirt as if trying to hold him back.

There were men coming up the road, onto Prince Hill. Kindalana's father, Padrigan, blocked the way with a file of eshSegu tribal guard. Oh principles, they had their spears raised to kill. Who was coming? Lonjaro had a proud warrior tradition—nearly every farmer and hunter trained as a shua fighter—but even in the skirmishes that sometimes erupted, no one ever raised sharp spears.

"Go back," Padrigan called. "Go back now, and we'll forget we saw this!"

Tau saw, and would never forget.

4

THE EYE

THE Womb rapped at the door. "Are you modest?"

"No," Baru called back, irritably, "but who gives a shit?" The existence of a Cancrioth body taboo was academically interesting, but it also meant they'd left her naked in Tubercule as a deliberate humiliation. That stung her pride. "Are we safe?"

"No. I had to make concessions to the Brain to stop the fighting. You will meet with her, alone."

Excellent. If the Brain was the radical aboard, maybe she had control of the Kettling.

From the other side of the huge bed, Shao Lune whispered: "The *Brain*?"

"I think they're all named for . . . for where their tumors grow."

"I know that. But wouldn't a brain tumor cause madness?"

"We'll see." Baru raised her voice to call: "I'll dress. Where is this Brain?"

"We're not going to the Brain."

"I thought—"

"She is our very last resort. If you knew what she'd do with you, you would agree." The huge teak door combed the high notes out of the Womb's voice. "You will come below with me to visit the Eye. You and Tau will persuade him that our journey is over, and that it's time for this ship to disappear from history again."

Baru blanched. "Tau will be there?"

"Of course." Green light flickered beneath the door. "Tau came here searching for Abdumasi Abd. So did we. Tau will convince the Eye that Abd is lost forever. And *you* will tell the Eye what will happen if Falcrest captures us. He doesn't believe the things he's heard about your people."

The light faded. Baru covered her eyes and groaned. She would have to see Tau again, so soon after they had been *so* hurt. . . .

She couldn't let herself be dragged down by emotion so close to the prize. So Tau had trusted her, and felt betrayed—fine! Tain Hu had trusted her first. She had to focus!

"Shao." She got up from the bed. "I need you to—"

The flash of victory in Shao's eyes at those words, *I need you,* almost made her change her mind. But would she react any differently in Shao's position?

"I need you to get out of this room and discover anything you can about this ship. Dimensions, design, port of origin, a list of keel owners, charts—"

"A rutterbook," Shao Lune corrected her. "I should look for the rutterbook."

"The what?" She vaguely remembered the term from the federated Oriati navigator she'd talked to last year on the tax flotilla, hairlipped Pan Obarse.

"The Oriati equivalent of our navigational charts. Like all things Oriati, it is secretive, convoluted, and highly personal. Each Oriati navigator keeps their own, often in code, so their secrets can't be stolen. It could tell us where this ship was built, where it makes harbor. Who provisions and waters it."

"Good." Baru rewarded her with a smile. "I want that. But most of all . . ."

Shao Lune smiled back and turned her finger. Go on.

"I need you to look for signs of conspiracy with the Mbo Oriati. Rocket-powder pistols, federal Oriati uniforms . . . a source of the Kettling. Parliament will vote on whether to move toward war with the Oriati on 90 Summer. If we brought home evidence that could sway the vote . . ."

"We'll be heroes." An electrum glitter of ambition in her smile, like expensive cutlery before a meal. "I'll have a post in the Admiralty."

"I expect you will," Baru said.

But she knew she was lying. Her women did not survive.

B ARU did not exactly *mean* to get down on her knees and sniff the ship. Her right foot slipped, and the wood made her go the rest of the way.

"What are you *doing*?" the Womb groaned. "Why are you smelling the timber?"

Baru stroked the grain. Warm brown heartwood, like teak; it had pores like teak. But it didn't smell like teak. Not oily enough. "You use this lumber all over the ship. In the hull, in the decking, in the furniture. That means you have a lot of it, and it's easy to work with, and it must last for ages. . . . It's beautiful. What is it?"

"Iroko." The Womb grabbed Baru by the scruff of the neck and put something over her head. "Do not take this off. In case we're separated and I need to find you."

"Hey!" Baru protested, and then forgot her anger in fascination. The loop of twine carried a chime of black stone, oily to the light, not to touch. It was the very same mineral that filled the Womb's magic frog lamp.

"Is this uranium?"

"I won't name things for you all day, child." The Womb snapped off a fraying thread from the collar of her cassock. "We are going to the Eye now. Don't stray. Don't speak."

"You were much friendlier on the boat," Baru muttered.

"That was before Tau explained to me exactly who you are."

Tau, Tau, why oh why had the Womb cut Tau out of trim? It had been so much easier when Tau was full of life and trust. When they wanted to help Baru out of a powerful ethical belief in her goodness. Maybe Tau would come around. . . .

"Enough questions." The Womb's hands glowed the color of a nighttime lagoon. She saw Baru looking, and folded them in the arms of her cassock. "Let's go."

"Could you explain that first?" There must be some sort of substance, a paint, a pigment extracted from those little frogs, which glowed in the presence of uranium.

"No," the Womb said. "But don't feel slighted. No one can explain it. That's why it's sorcery."

THE padlock on Tau's door was different from any design Baru had ever seen: not the old Tamermash pattern but some purely Oriati invention. The Womb unlocked it with a small iron key wrought in the image of a parrot's head. Had the Cancrioth made that lock and key, Baru wondered? Or did they trade for it back in their homeland? Or was there no single Cancrioth homeland, only enclaves scattered throughout the Mbo? Everything a clue . . .

"Tau?" the ambassador called. "It's time now."

The door opened so quickly that Baru jumped. Tau-indi stood in the wedge of shadow beyond, shoulders limp. Saltwater had ruined their beautiful hair and scratched red rings in their eyes. Enact-Colonel Osa stood uncomfortable guard behind them, trying to check for danger without piercing the cyst of bruised space around their Prince.

"Have they hurt you?" Baru cried.

Tau blinked listlessly at her. "They have excommunicated me from the mbo which I served and treasured all my life." A sort of membrane seemed to have closed over their eyes, like the white paper beneath an eggshell. "I told them everything I knew about you. What you've done. Why you came here."

"What about Abdu?" Baru snapped. She shouldn't snap. Tau just had this way of testing her, and making her feel like she was failing. "You're giving up on him? These people haven't given up. I thought you were better than them."

Tau froze. A terrible shape passed across their rounded body, their expressive face: brittle, bitter, like frost on glass. Baru realized too late how cruel she'd been.

If Abdu was Cancrioth, if he had chosen to become Cancrioth, then he had consciously thrown away his friendship with Tau.

Osa shifted on the balls of her feet. Saltwater dripped from the ropes in her fists and pattered on the deck.

"Tau," the Womb said, quietly, "you must come with me now. Both our peoples need your help. If we are found here and taken by Falcrest, they will use us against the Mbo. It would mean war. Help me sway the crew to go."

She was like a mother afraid for her children. Well, she carried lives in her womb, didn't she? Not quite a mother in the conventional sense, but a woman used to thinking of all the souls in her care.

"Whatever you want of me," Tau said, bowing fractionally. "My master."

Baru gasped in horror. In Seti-Caho *master* was a slave's word for an owner. You could run through New Kutulbha screaming *tunk* and *burner* and *cuge* and *gava* and every other racialized epithet imaginable, but the beating you'd get would be a kindness compared to the way the Segu would answer that word *master*. The Mbo had annihilated slavery a thousand years ago, and a millennium of taboo had hardened on the word like concrete. Slavers were enenen, without trim, one of the only kinds of people still branded with that word.

The Womb's hands flashed in the sleeves of her cassock. "Tau. Please. Don't make this harder than it needs to be."

"Don't pretend to be anything other than what you are," Tau said, sweetly.

"*Tau*. If Falcrest finds us here, if they take us and learn what we've done, it'll be war. Millions of your people will die. Will you help me stop that?"

Baru could smell the threat of sorcery in the air. Something of burnt garlic, and a faint metallicity, like blood in her molars. Thrilling and awful. Osa bristled helplessly.

"I won't resist," Tau said. "Everything I do will be your will."

THEY plunged down narrow stairs that creaked beneath their heels. At each landing the light from the Womb's lantern was cut by the turn and they had to go on for a moment into darkness. As a mansion, *Eternal* would have been enormous. As a ship, everything inside her built to smaller scale, she was a labyrinth. Baru tried to keep a map in her head, but every time they turned right she lost her place.

"Who is the Eye?" Osa asked.

"An onkos," Tau-indi said.

"What's an onkos?"

"A sorcerer with a highly developed tumor. They are not all fully initiated into a Line. Some are . . . latent. Awaiting growth."

A scream like a dying man came from astern. "Pigs," Baru blurted. She remembered pig screams from Treatymont. "If you're low on water, why haven't you slaughtered your pigs?"

"Because certain lives depend on them," the Womb said, curtly. "Move."

They spilled into a broad companionway deep below the weather deck. People moved in the dark, sentries whispering salutes to the Womb. Curtains swept aside. Baru smelled compost and rich humus. The Womb called out in the same tongue as that prayer: *ayamma, ayamma, a ut li-en . . .*

She made herself break the blister of Tau's silence. "What is that language?"

"En Elu Aumor. Their high speech. Recorded in the tablets of the Pitchblende Dictionary, deep within the Renderer of Souls."

"I wish I were a linguist," Baru said, out of the nervous need to speak.

"You would know more ways to lie."

They crossed a coaming, a wooden lip where a flood door could seal against the deck. The smell of compost was so thick in Baru's sinuses that she sneezed.

The Womb's candlelight fell on a man's back.

"Virios," she said. "I've brought our guests."

He was a pleasant-looking man, roundish, black skin, thinning hair. Baru decided he was from Mzilimaki Mbo: he had a calf tattoo of a colobus monkey. He wore a simple work shirt and a knee-length skirt. He had been digging, barehanded, among the mushrooms that grew in a tub of humus.

His shoulders slumped. "I told you," he said, in deep Aphalone, "that you had to send them away. How are we going to keep the Pale now, Abbatai? You've let them see too much."

He turned. His cancer came into the light.

Osa swore in Seti-Caho. Baru cried out and stumbled back.

"Yes." The Eye sighed. "You will think I'm distracted, because of the way one of my eyes looks off into nothing. I assure you it is purely a mechanical issue. Speak to my other eye."

His left eye had a stalk like a snail. Thick, the color of crab shell, longer than his nose and slightly uphooked. The eye bulged from the tip in a tangle of living veins.

"Onkos." Tau calm as a corpse. "The cancer grows well."

"Thank you," the man said, as if complimented on his beard. "You are . . . ? No. No, it can't be. Abbatai, what have you done?"

"They are excised," the Womb murmured. "Safer than the alternative. This is Tau-indi Bosoka, Prince of Lonjaro Mbo."

"Are you really immortal?" Baru blurted. "Do you remember things from a thousand years ago?"

"I am. And I do. Though I was also born in Mzilimake, on Colobus Lake, not more than sixty years ago. Those two lives are in me, together. None of which I want to tell you." He had a wonderful syllabic accent, the rhythm of his words set by the length of the sounds rather than the points of stress. It was like song. "But it seems the Womb has decided our Pale of secrecy is worth breaking if it gets her what she wants."

"You speak very well, sir," Baru said, idiotically.

"Of course I speak well!" he snapped. "I was raised in a society of knowledge; I speak twelve languages! I've seen nations far beyond the edge of Falcrest's grasping little maps!"

His eye slackened. "No place for pride now, though. Not here." He wrung out his soiled hands. "I would offer a handshake, as you do in Falcrest. But my hands are dirty. Why were you brought to me?"

"Tell him, Baru," the Womb urged. "Tell them what you told me."

She measured out a portion of air, like a draw from a well, and spoke. "I was sent by my colleagues in Falcrest to make secret contact with the immortal rulers of Oriati Mbo."

"Rulers." His human eye narrowed. His stalk stared up and off at nothing. "Is that what you think we are?"

"My colleagues believe it. I am here to learn the truth."

The Eye rubbed his ordinary eye. He looked like he hadn't slept in days. "And you, Prince Bosoka?"

"Baru lied to me." Tau stood as if all their bones had worn through sinew and ligament to click together like dice. "I was looking for my friend, hoping to bring him home and avert war."

"Your friend?"

Tau hesitated. Baru felt a gritty little speck of hope. It was the plainest sign Tau had given, since their excision, of caring about anything at all.

"Abdumasi Abd," the Womb supplied: a mother speaking up for a quiet child. "Tau's been searching for Abdumasi, Virios."

"I would rather let the Prince speak for themself," the Eye snapped. "Tau-indi Bosoka, were you aboard the ship we attacked? The clipper *Cheetah*?"

"I was."

The Eye ducked his head in contrition, which had the unnerving effect of aiming his upturned eyestalk directly at Baru. "Then I am truly sorry for what we did to you and your house. I confess I meant to intercept your ship, speak to you, and learn where Abdumasi had been taken. I was the one who sent the signals asking for a parley. I know you chose not to respond, because of the taboo you place upon us, but I never . . . By the time I realized the Brain's people were at the cannons, and that they meant to sink you to keep you from escaping, it was too late."

"You're searching for Abdumasi?" Tau's voice was a desert. "Why . . . why do you want him?"

"He's dear to me, Prince Bosoka. To all of us. He carries Undionash, one of our rarest lines. It was a gift to show our trust in him."

The Prince blinked. Their cheek spasmed. They said nothing. A very long way away, on a continent vast enough to hold Tau's heart, mountains fell.

"Please, Tau," the Eye begged, "do you know where he is? I never wanted him to go out into the world to make this foolish war. It was the Brain, she's too full of ideas, she can't *see*. . . ."

Tau made a sound Baru had heard only once before, from the people who died after battles. Whatever hopes for Abdu they had secreted away must be scoured out, now. Ruined.

"You have cannon," Osa blurted, throwing herself on the silence. "Who was this ship built to fight? Who's your enemy?"

"We have no enemy," the Eye snapped. "We are not warriors. The cannon are for protection!"

"But you armed the Canaat rebels," Osa insisted. "You subverted our embassy here. You conspired with Scheme-Colonel Masako to destroy the Kyprist leadership. And when Ambassador Dai-so Kolos found out what you were doing, you killed them."

"I did not do that!" the Eye shouted. His voice echoed off the close rafters, faded down intestinal lengths of corridor in *Eternal*'s huge belly. "The Kettling isn't even *ours*! It was never meant to be on this ship! But the Brain conspired—she never wanted to help Abdumasi, she *always* meant this voyage as the beginning of her war!"

"Virios!" the Womb snapped.

He put up his dirty hands. "I'm sorry. But I never . . . I never wanted to be entangled in the world's business. I never meddled in your embassy's affairs, or in Kyprananoke's rebellion."

Disappointment crawled like a roach around the edge of Baru's thoughts. This man was one of the immortal Cancrioth, secret rulers of the thousand-year Mbo? He seemed just as bewildered and petty as any duke of Aurdwynn. All he ruled was a tub of mushrooms in the dark belly of a ship.

She didn't want this man. She wanted to speak to the Brain.

"Baru," the Womb prodded. "Tell him about your people. Tell him we need to leave."

"Yes. Ah." Tau's silent shudders were very hard to ignore. "I have insurance, if I come to any harm. There are two navy warships under my command, and if I do not reach an agreement with you, they are prepared to—"

"She's lying!" Tau shouted.

The sound shattered in the dark. Baru wanted to scream in frustration.

"What?" the Womb snapped. "What's that, Tau?"

"She's lying. The navy's trying to kill her. You saw Ormsment call her to duel at the embassy, didn't you? She has no one following her. She's alone. She's been alone since she left Aurdwynn and it is destroying her. She's done nothing of any worth, even to her masters, since she executed her lover. All she does is lead people to ruin. She is a wound!"

The Eye looked between his three visitors with growing astonishment. "She lied? Abbatai, you brought her among us because she said she could get her warships out of the way, and they aren't even *hers*?"

"I brought her here because she knew our tongue! She spoke it at the embassy! She showed a picture of a boy—she knows where to find the son of Irarya!"

"Does she? Or was that another lie?"

"She *does* have people searching for her," the Womb insisted. "They'll find us, and when they do we must be gone. Virios, please, you can sway nearly half the crew. You control the water caskage, the fogmaking rooms, the kitchens, the preservariums, the fishing locker—everything we need to survive. If you say it's time to go, then the Brain will *have* to listen. You don't understand what she's done here! She's turned these islands into her laboratory! She has the Kettling, it's loose, it's *out there*! We have to go home before she brings it to another—"

"I'm *not* giving up on Abdumasi!" the Eye roared.

Silence, except for Tau's wounded gasps.

"Fine," the Womb said, soothingly. "Baru, tell him where to find Abdumasi. Tell him where we should go next. We'll leave Kyprananoke, we'll find a way past those ships out there, and we'll go rescue Abdumasi. Just tell him, Baru."

"No," Baru said.

She did not know where Abdumasi Abd had been taken, or even if he was alive. She was not sure she could have shared that secret even if she had it. It would be like cutting Tau's kidneys out when she had already stabbed them in the heart.

"A ai bu en on na," the Womb swore, viciously. "Tell him, or we'll have to make a deal with the Brain to get this ship moving. You'll have to pay *her* price. You don't want that, Baru."

Any price would be worth it to secure the Kettling and destroy Falcrest. Tain Hu had been willing to die for that goal. Therefore Baru had to be willing to die as well, or she was a coward and a hypocrite.

The Womb's hands faded palest green as she opened them to the Eye. "If you won't help get this ship out of here, Virios, I have to go to the Brain. And when I do, don't you dare come to me with some high-handed protest about how she's betrayed us."

"Let her sell herself!" The Eye beat the meat of his hand against the side of the wooden planter. His human eye bulged in anger. "Am I the only one who remembers who we are? We do not meddle in the secular world. We do not act on scales shorter than a human life!"

He turned his back, bent himself over his dirt and his mushrooms. "We should never have let Abd go make his war. We should have kept him safe, with us. Where he belonged."

Tau began to sob.

T HE Womb was so coldly furious with Baru, afterward, that she would only speak to Osa. "You'll go back to the void cabins and wait. I'll return when I need you. I have to make sure the Brain's people won't kill Baru the moment they see her."

Baru lagged behind, not feigning her exhaustion, so she could whisper to Tau. "Ormsment has my parents. You heard her tell me she'd sent *Scylpetaire* to Taranoke. Help me save them."

Tau said nothing.

"Why can't you help me? Why are you undercutting everything I do?"

Tau smiled like a melon rind, ghastly and eaten. "I tried. I told you to go into the ring with Ormsment. I told you that if you were true and honest, if your soul was good, your trim would deliver justice to you and all those you loved."

"I *did* go into the ring with Ormsment!"

"You did. Do you remember what happened then, Baru? Do you remember what your soul delivered to us?"

That was the moment the infected Canaat had revealed themselves.

"You can't possibly blame me for the embassy!" Baru hissed.

"Of course I can. I arranged that whole reception as cover for you to meet with the shadow ambassador, didn't I? You manipulated me into it. You were even going to use Iraji."

"I *didn't* give up Iraji!" Baru snarled, drawing Osa's grunt of warning. "I could've brought him here as a gift for the Cancrioth, but I didn't!"

"No." Tau sighed, pushing ahead, after the Womb. "Because you're waiting for me to give you permission."

"What?" She'd thought nothing of the sort.

"Tain Hu gave you permission to kill her for your own advantage."

"Don't you dare talk about—"

"Dare what? Talk about the woman whose death you use to justify your atrocities? She gave you permission to do a terrible thing. Now she is dead, so she cannot withdraw her permission. But you know her permit only reaches so far: it does not extend to Iraji, or to me. So you're waiting for me to give you permission to sell Iraji and Abdumasi to the Cancrioth. You want me to say, at least we'll be together again, damned together in chaos, Abdu and Tau. Really, you'll be doing what's best for both of us. Is that right? I think it is."

"Tau . . ."

A smile sweet like sugar rot. "You need me to be your little amphora, your bottle of reserve goodness, to shatter and use up. You've been dying a slow death since you killed Hu. You need to take another soul to finish your work. Only it'll never be done. You'll always need more. And no matter what you do here, Baru, I expect that by some *strange* coincidence it will end up being what Mister Cairdine Farrier wants. Don't you think so, too?"

Baru lost her breath.

No matter what exercises she tried, no matter how she crushed her innards and panted like a bear, she couldn't get her air back. Her fingertips prickled. Her heart stumbled. Dread settled on her like a crown. The green paint on the black ceiling above seemed to slither, like tapeworms dangling from a burnt lilac branch. The things Tau said made such sense—all her curiosity and intellect fastened on them and worried at them—

She felt genuinely as if she were drowning.

"Move," Osa grunted, and shoved Baru forward.

She wanted a whiskey, a vodka: something, anything, to wipe the running centipede legs off her hands, to fill up the agonizing bubbles in her blood. Her heartbeats hit like hooves, cavalry charge, memories of Tain Hu turning the flank at Sieroch, memories that made the panic deeper.

So. So. This was what it meant to make an enemy of Tau, of a laman with the keenest understanding of empathy and sentiment. She had never been struck so precisely.

Tain Hu had seen the worst of her and stayed loyal.

Tau had seen the worst of her, and now they were telling her exactly what they saw.

B ARU sat on the bed and breathed into her hands while Shao Lune told her not to be a fool.

"The Prince is a superstitious, emotionally volatile product of a degenerate civilization. Royalty are always self-centered, Baru. Wouldn't you be, if your conception had been *elected*? If you'd been the most important person in the room since before you were even born?"

Shao Lune perched on the stuffed chair by the stateroom desk, straddling it in reverse. Her feet hooked around the chair's legs, where cheetahs yawned in black bronze.

"Once," Baru said, hollowly, "there were hardly any chairs in the world at all. I remember that from History of Materialism. The only chairs were thrones. Ordinary people sat on benches."

She was so tired. But there was no time to sleep now—Yawa's forces could be here any moment—why was she sitting down? Why wasn't she *doing* something? She wanted to claw her own skin right off, peel back her fingernails and prod the soft places beneath until pain made her move—stop pulling at your own fingers and get up! Get up!

She could not get up. Tau had shattered something vital inside her. What they'd said about Tain Hu kept repeating itself in her head. A wound like a mouth.

"You were born on Taranoke," Shao Lune said, soothingly. "A land ruled by family elders. Pleasing those elders is a compulsion written in your blood. That's why you've panicked."

What a stupid Incrastic explanation. But maybe it would be useful to believe it for now. . . .

"Think about this rationally!" Shao urged. "Identify your weaknesses"— one long finger counting off points on the seams of the chair leather—"act to counter them, and then do what has to be done to achieve your goal. You remember our goal, don't you?"

"Get off this ship," Baru muttered. "Bring home what we learned."

Bring home the Kettling. Kill Falcrest. Make Hu's death worth it.

"That's right." She smiled impishly at Baru. O Wydd, she had such huge, cruel eyes. "Would you like to know what I learned?"

Baru's mind seemed to have been reefed like a sail: she just couldn't catch the wind long enough to stay with a thought.

"Baru." Shao snapped her fingers. "Baru, listen. I snuck out to explore. I saw such things, Baru. Monstrous skeletons shaped like people—I don't mean the skeletons *of* people, I mean skeletons with bone skin, bone muscles, all their flesh turned to bone. Rooms full of old machines. Weapons, surgeries—oh, kings, the surgeries I saw! But do you know what else I found?"

"What," Baru said, dully.

"I saw tunks in white blouses."

White blouses. Scheme-Colonel Masako, the man at the embassy who'd let the rebels in . . . he'd worn a white blouse.

"Oriati secret service. *Termites!*" Shao rocked the chair in excitement.

"Termites are like Jackals?" Baru did not quite remember.

"Jackals are the professional fighters. Termites are the 'armed diplomatic corps' they use as spies. If they're aboard, we have the proof of collusion! We can take it to Parliament, prove the Oriati federal forces are in bed with the Cancrioth, and win the Emperor's eternal thanks! But we have to act now, quickly, before Yawa reaches us, before she takes all the glory—"

"I *know that!*" Baru shouted. "I know we have to act!"

And, to her own horror and shame, she began to weep.

She couldn't do it anymore. She just couldn't do it. Tau had been so kind to her. Iraji had been her friend, played Purge with her, sparred with her when she wanted to be hurt. And she'd had to harm them both to reach this moment, the moment of crux, the goal she'd worked toward all her life. The harm she'd done should make it all the more urgent to go forward, to complete the task. She had the weapon to end the Masquerade.

And for no reason except that she was pathetic and stupid and worthless, she couldn't do it. She couldn't get up.

Everyone was counting on her. Ake Sentiamut and all the Vultjagata, the members of Tain Hu's household who'd survived. Her parents and everyone else on Taranoke. In Aurdwynn, the sodomites and tribadists and bastard children and mothers out of wedlock who would be erased by Incrasticism. And Tain Hu most of all. Baru had been given every opportunity to deserve her trust . . . and so there was simply no one to blame but herself for failure.

Sulk and drink and fail, again and again and again and again—all she'd done since the Elided Keep! Drink and fail! Drink and fail! Chased off one island after another in a stupid tragicomic cycle without any progress or achievement except to drink and *fail*!

"Baru," Shao said, with a sudden, unadorned concern. "Why are you crying?"

She ground her eyes into the back of her arm. "Nothing. I'm fine."

Shao Lune got up. Baru expected the other woman to come over and siphon off her tears with a little eyedropper, for use in some perverse cosmetic or tincture: despair of a young Souswardi woman, purified with alcohol, for clear and shining skin.

But instead Shao dismounted her chair, moved to the bed beside Baru, folded her hands in her lap, and said, not soothingly, but without any particular contempt for Baru's state, "I found a pantry."

"A pantry?"

"I stole as many drugs and sanitary supplies as I could. I even stole things to build a fluid level. You like figures, don't you? I measured the ship's roll period. I think the ship's overstabilized. She rolls quickly, which means . . ."

A matronizing silence. She wanted Baru to answer, and being a school-taught fool Baru couldn't help but do it.

"A high metacenter of roll," she said, sniffling, "so the ship is hard to capsize or flood. But quick to tip in waves and therefore uncomfortable to sail."

"Right. Out on open sea she must pitch like a three-legged horse. So we know they're not exquisite shipwrights, by our standards. We know they buy their medicines from abroad—"

"They do?" Damn Shao for being so useful.

"They do. Look, here's proof." Shao produced a small velvet pouch, cinched shut with a golden cord. "Recognize this?"

"Mason dust." Some curiosity stirred in her. It was a powerful stimulant, made in Aurdwynn from the treated extract of the Stakhieczi mason leaf. The government chemists sold it at a premium, often illegally, because there was no other source: the process to make it was an Incrastic secret.

Baru stroked the thickly piled velvet of the pouch. "When I was at dinner with Bel Latheman, back in Treatymont . . . I would see rich people carrying their doses in bags like this. They would pour the dust onto their hands to sniff. Here, at the break box." Her fingers brushed over the two tendons below Shao's thumb, finding the bones there, radius and scaphoid: the break box. "So these drugs came from Aurdwynn. Maybe Hesychast was right about Cancrioth agents there. . . ."

Shao's full lips made a satisfied catenary arch, pleased by Baru's interest. "A telling find, I think. They stock their pantries with our product. They cannot make it themselves. So the fabled Cancrioth are not advanced beyond Incrasticism. Just another jungle cult, Baru. A jungle cult with very big ships."

"You've done well. Discovered a great deal." And it only made Baru loathe herself more.

"I have. Have you?"

Baru shook her head. "I talked to one of their leaders, but he was useless.

Head buried in compost." How could she fall apart now? How could she collapse with the end in sight? Just get the Kettling, get the tainted blood, and go. . . .

Shao sighed. "Do you know the story of *Auroreal* and *Purpose*?"

"No." Baru groaned. Doubtless another missing stone in the mosaic of proper Falcresti womanhood.

Their hands were still touching, through the velvet of the pouch. Shao did not let go. "*Auroreal* and *Purpose* were two ships built in the arctic yards in Starfall Bay. They were meant to reach the lodepoint. The northernmost edge of the compass, where every direction becomes south.

"As in any good experiment, each ship received a different treatment. *Purpose* was assigned an elite crew, tested by schooling and sea service. Their provisions were calibrated by starvation studies in prisons. The Storm Corps designers calculated the ship's layout to preserve a core of warmth and comfort.

"*Auroreal,* on the other hand, was crewed with survivors. Sailors who'd straggled home from failed expeditions. Officers who'd led their boats across leagues of open ocean and pack ice. The Storm Corps sourced their provisions from traditional bastè ana techniques. Of course, *Auroreal* fell behind *Purpose* when the expedition set out. *Purpose* had the better design, the better crew. . . ."

"But it was *Auroreal* that returned," Baru interrupted, impatiently guessing the moral of this little qualm. "Will and grit proved more valuable than finesse and talent."

"Not at all." Shao showed her white, white teeth. "*Auroreal* vanished into the north. It was *Purpose*'s elite that returned."

"They reached the lodepoint?"

"No. They gave up. When things began to go wrong on that exquisite ship, there was no tolerance for error in the design, no patience for mistakes among the crew. Everything was made to work perfectly; nothing was made to survive imperfection. So they concluded, very rationally, that they had to turn back. It was *Auroreal* that pressed on, irrationally, courageously, into the north."

"Please, Shao, what's the moral?"

"There are two kinds of people, Baru. One kind is like *Auroreal*. They just go on and on, no matter how awful the circumstances. But you're like the other kind. You're like *Purpose*. You are a precision instrument, intolerant of damage. You must be calibrated." She took Baru's hand, inspecting the bandaged stubs of the two fingers Tain Shir had cut away. "You're brilliant, but you break so easily."

"I thought I was strong." Baru could barely make herself speak. "I thought, after what I did in Aurdwynn, that I'd be . . . harder."

"You can't change who you are," Shao said, Shao Lune the perfect, coiled ideal of Falcrest womanhood, who would never need to change. "And that's why it's good I'm here with you. Because"—she folded Baru's hand between hers—"I can tell you the truth. Which is that you're being weak, and sentimental, and stupid. It doesn't matter if you feel bad. It doesn't matter if you're tired or sad. You need to *work*."

Baru's hand complained at the leverage on her wrist. She was stronger than Shao, but she let herself yield. If Shao made her do it then it was not really her fault. . . .

"You're going to go back among them," Shao murmured, "and do whatever it takes to get us safely *out* of here. Stop tripping over your sentiments about Tau. Stop trying to protect the Iraji boy. Don't tell me you can't let them go. You can. You executed that traitor duchess, didn't you? So you can do this, too."

She lifted the velvet bag again. The mason dust inside made a sound like fine dry sand.

"This will help," Shao said. "Have you ever dosed before? No? Let me show you."

NOW

FARRIER'S cloth leaves alcohol on her skin. It evaporates like a cool mountain morning. Flesh and sweat sublimate into clean chemistry and vapor: as he would have the whole world, if he could.

"This is marvelous," he tells her. She has just paused in her account. "This is better than I could've hoped. The whale! Unbelievable! The size of their ship! And the restraint you showed with Shao Lune, the exquisite discipline, no matter how you were tempted . . ."

"A little tempted," she murmurs. "She was very beautiful. I always wonder what beautiful women will look like in the throes of the act . . . do you? Is it the same for men?"

"I suppose it must be." He's on her blind side, but she can detect the uncomfortable catch. He darts, minnow-quick, to another topic. "We should sell this as a novel, shouldn't we?"

"But it's all true."

"Exactly why it should be a novel! The frame of fiction allows the reader to . . . adjust their comfort. If they want to trim away a few of the more extreme points, write them off as artistic exaggeration, well, we give them permission. And if they want to imagine things went further, that we are hiding the juicy bits . . . well, we equip them to imagine."

"You're suggesting," Baru says, edging toward playfulness, "that you'd like to imagine things went further?"

That strikes so well that Farrier ignores it completely. He dabs behind her right ear, careful around the thin flesh of the lobe. Not to damage the instruments, now. "The novel is a young form, did you know? Compared to the poetic epic, the philosophical treatise, and the paean . . . still young and full of promise."

"Like I was," she says.

"Like you *are,* I was about to say."

"I know something's happened to me. Please don't lie to me, Mister Farrier."

His inhalation tugs at her hair: premonition of words, detected by the scalp. "I wouldn't lie to you."

"But you did. You lied to all of us. Apparitor and Durance and even I. You told us you were sending us on a vital mission. You said we were going to determine the future of Incrasticism."

The cloth goes back to its careful attentions, as if Farrier means to tidy up not just her skin but whatever mess he can find in the brain below it. "You think I lied to you?" Recentering the question on her opinion, rather than on his actions.

"I think," she says, as the alcohol evanesces into mist, carrying part of her away to infiltrate other bodies, other places, "that you wanted the three foreign-born cryptarchs out of the way while you . . . finalized the situation in Falcrest."

This time Farrier does pause. The cloth lingers on the back of her neck. "You're right," he says, finally. "I can't deny that. Hesychast and I agreed that it would be best to keep the arena clear while we conducted our, ah, final contest."

He really does respect her. Good.

"But your mission *was* vital, Baru. You *had* to find the Cancrioth. We knew they were out there, spending money, moving ships. The Oriati Mbo has been asleep for a very long time, and we needed a cold spur to awaken them. We had to make contact with the Cancrioth. Hesychast had his reasons as much as I did. That's why he sent Yawa to . . ." He looks away. She can tell by the way the aspect of his voice changes. "To hurt you. He was terrified of the fact that you didn't have a hostage. He had to destroy you before you reached Falcrest and came into the fullness of your power."

"And you let me go with her anyway. Knowing what she'd try to do to me."

"Of course I did." He says it so softly and so earnestly. He is reassuring himself as much as her. "You were my greatest find. You could do anything. And you did. You won."

She tips her head back. The hardwood chair digs pleasantly into the nape of her neck. She lays down the next stone on the path, the road that Farrier thinks he is leading her down. That's the trick, she thinks. You let them choose which road to follow.

But first, you have your people build the roads.

"Abdu," she says, dreamily. "He's the one who taught you that the Cancrioth could break them."

"Pardon?"

"That's what you saw at Lake Jaro, isn't it? Nothing in all the time you spent there gave you a hint about what might render two hundred million Oriati digestible to Falcrest. Nothing until the Cancrioth came."

FEDERATION YEAR 912:
23 YEARS EARLIER
UPON PRINCE HILL, BY LAKE JARO
IN LONJARO MBO

THE eight hunters who came up the south side of the hill were not
Cancrioth.

Tau would learn this later, when investigation and rumor uncovered how
these shua hunters, professional pelt-takers, became adherents to a power that
offered them strength in a time of helplessness. On that day Tau saw only their
wounds. They had abased their flesh with bracelets of thorns, and mortified
their bodies with sorghum vinegar and black pepper oils. Now they walked up
Prince Hill jagged with blood and prickle.

"Stay away from us!" they cried, making their own sort of irita, their alarm
call. "We are charged with the old power. Stay away, and save your trim!"

Their sweat ran bloody. Their flesh had swollen and puckered around the
thorn wounds. They looked, Tau thought, like suicides.

Among those eight hunters walked a robed woman. She raised up a hand at
Padrigan, and in the shadow of her heavy sleeve, her fingers glistened.

"No," Tau gasped.

Cairdine Farrier cocked his head like a bird.

At Padrigan's side, the tribal guards' speartips wavered. The woman's head
lifted, and too many shining eyes glowed beneath that hood.

"Test me," the woman said, in a low carrying voice, fine southcountry
Uburu, as horrifying in its ordinary timbre as anything Tau had ever heard:
they are here, they live among us! "You will do no harm. I am outside the jurisdiction of steel."

Cairdine Farrier drew his little pistol bow, which he kept, despite Tau's discomfort, for protection against "animals."

"Pardon me," he called. "Are you a sorcerer?"

"Farrier," Padrigan shouted, "get back, they're here for you, *go!*"

"Then I am right to defend myself," Farrier said, and he shot the sorcerer. The little bolt puckered the cloth just below her right clavicle.

The sorcerer did not react.

Farrier, his mouth open in a little half-oh of shock and fascination, worked the mechanism to draw another bolt from the magazine. The sorcerer looked at him with green abstract eyes whose number Tau could not make themself count. Farrier shot her again. The bolt went into the woman's cheek and stuck there, driven into bone, quivering. Her head moved a little, as if pushed.

"You are not welcome among us," the sorcerer said. "You will never be welcome in this land or among these people. You are a botfly and your words are nagana. And I have come to cut you out."

She turned her glowing fingers on Cairdine Farrier. "You will know your ruin," she said, between strings of some forgotten Cancrioth tongue, between Tau's horrible shuddering breaths, a full-body soreness and sickness, pounding as if their lymph would spray from their eyes and ears, "you will know your ruin well. You will put yourself into it as you have put yourself into us, thinking that it is your will. But it is your doom that moves you thus. And your flesh will be filled with ruin, as you have come to bring ruin into us."

She closed her fist. A gush of wet white light jetted from her hand and fell like semen to puddle on the ground. The spearmen shuddered back. Cairdine Farrier fumbled for his notebook with trembling hands.

"Kill them," Padrigan cried, hoarsely. "Kill them all before she speaks again!"

Yes, Tau's heart shouted. Kill them! There is no trim here—these are not people—just erase them, destroy them, silence them and sweep away their footprints! For the principles' bright sake, kill them now!

But even Padrigan's tribal guard, Segu's famous impi, did not know how to kill the undying. For this you needed magic, and they had none.

"Let us past," the sorcerer said, "or I will cut you all with my uranium knife. We want Cosgrad."

Her thorn-laced men stepped forward, and Padrigan and his spearmen stepped back.

"Run," Tau whispered, and then, shouting, "Farrier, run, *run!*"

Padrigan broke with his spearmen: they fled up the hill, and Farrier, at first bewildered, then moved, even he, by the animal terror of the rout, came running with them. Tau broke only when Farrier was safely past. The sorcerer's cry chased them, words like hornets, aching in Tau's spine, stinging their thighs.

The House Bosoka rose ahead—Tau staggered past the termite colony—they looked back and there was a silent man with strips flayed off his face in the shape of grief marks, not two arms lengths' away, reaching out—Tau screamed, grabbed the mallet from the greeting-plate at the south entrance, and hurled it into the man's legs. He leapt over it, came down hard, stumbled, fell behind.

Tau shoved into the compound, screaming for help—someone came bursting from the south breezeway—oh principles, no, it was Cosgrad Torrinde! Cosgrad, still half-mad with meningitis, shouting, "Tau, I understand! I see! I *know!*"

Kindalana scrambled out behind him, the chains of her regalia swaying, and tried to tug him back inside. "Farrier!" he shouted, raising his fist at the other Falcrest man. "Farrier, you bastard, I *know how the mangroves grow!*"

"Mangroves?" Tau gasped. Cosgrad had been obsessed with the mangroves that grew in the frettes down south. He couldn't understand how they survived without saltwater, and this terrified him: maybe Oriati Mbo truly was magical, and he would never learn its logic.

"I know how the mangroves grow," Cosgrad said. His lean, vain body swelled and settled with hard breath. Kindalana had her arms around his waist, pulling like she was trying to keep a dog off a cat. "It's not magic after all. There are minerals in the basins atop the mesa. The rainwater fills up the basins and carries the minerals downriver, to the mangroves. Thus they flourish without saltwater. That is the rule."

"Cosgrad," Tau screamed, "*hide!*"

The compound gate swung open. The thorn-lashed men lunged in. The sorcerer walked between them, wet light dripping from her mouth, light burning in her too-many eyes, dark blood pooled beneath the crossbow bolt in her cheek.

Cosgrad Torrinde, feverish and disheveled, gaped at her. "What?" he said. "I solved the mangroves. What now?"

"Ah," the sorcerer said, in that desperately ordinary voice. When she smiled her mouth was just a place of different darkness. "The other tumor. Like knows like, Cosgrad."

"You know my name," Cosgrad said, unsteadily. "Gossip. Shepherds and water women."

Kindalana ran down to Tau. They seized each others' hands, eyes meeting like summer sun through a loose slat. "We stand?" she whispered.

"Yes. If you'll stand with me." They would die here if they had to, before they let their guests be killed.

"Excuse me," Farrier shouted, from the far side of the compound: he was waiting by another door, damn him. "Excuse me, mam. Are you a member of the Cancrioth? No one will tell me about you. I've asked. Will you tell me, please, where I could learn more."

The sorcerer ignored him. Cosgrad raised his trembling hand and pointed to her. "You will be understood. Do you hear me? I will know your law. If I know the law, I can master it. First the mangroves and then the rest. Even you!"

"Death first," the sorcerer said, with the fire of her words spattered down her chin. "Death before we let you into us."

"Even you," Cosgrad Torrinde panted. "I will know your law. I will find a way."

"Never me," the sorcerer said. "You will try. But you will find only ruin. A ut li-en: let it be so now and ever."

And speaking a word of power, gesturing sharply, she immolated herself.

Tau gaped in horror. Cosgrad Torrinde stared in fascination and abominable curiosity. Cairdine Farrier bellowed, "*Why!?*" and stumbled back, falling on the heels of his hands, scrabbling away: as the burning woman, her garments and her skin alight, began to walk, calmly, gracefully, in no apparent pain at all, forward to embrace him.

The fire was no illusion. The grass around her smoldered and caught.

It was just then, at the height of the sorcerer's cataclysmic power, as Cairdine Farrier cowered in that flaming shadow and Cosgrad Torrinde trembled with meningeal visions of secret force, as the thorn-men who guarded the sorcerer screamed in grief and victory, that Abdumasi Abd barged in with his mother's mercenary guard. Padrigan followed with a few of his rallied tribal guard, crying out, "Kindalana! Run! Tau, child, *run!*"

"Fuck me," Abdu exclaimed. "What *is* this?"

And then he saw Tau and Kindalana, holding hands, trying desperately to ward away the burning woman as she advanced. Trying, and failing, with all the dermoregalia and all the garments of their Princedom, to resist this alien enenen power.

That was when Abdu realized the Cancrioth could give him something Tau and Kinda could not.

But on that day he saw his friends in danger, and he shouted to his mercenary shua, "Charge!"

CAIRDINE Farrier watched the awful mêlée with the exhilarated horror of a man overseeing a poisoned banquet. All at once the Oriati were chopping each other to meat before his eyes.

When it was over the thorn-men lay dead in pieces. The sorcerer smoldered in the grass, eyes shut, chest shuddering, heart still beating. The eyes in her face had gone out, as if her soul had left the house of her body to fly away. She had reached out to Cosgrad Torrinde with her burning hands, and Tau, who had never even thought about hurting a person before, who still had not ever thought about hurting a *person,* struck the sorcerer in the back of the head with a paving stone.

Kindalana cried out in horror.

Her father Padrigan screamed in the grass. He'd pulled Abdumasi back from the mêlée and one of the thorn-men had cut Padrigan with a machete.

"Daughter," he gasped. "You look like a Prince. I'm so proud."

Abdumasi stood, fists clenched, frowning over the corpses of the thorn-faced soldiers. He was thick with anger and confusion, but also with a fascination Tau did not at the time detect.

This, Abdumasi was thinking. This is what we become when we are desperate. We grow thorns from our skin, we shout ancient words, and we beg our people to stay away from us. For we cannot be bent from our purpose, which is revenge.

SHIR AND THE LETTER

TAIN Shir will force Baru Cormorant to kill Aminata or to kill herself.

She will compel Baru Cormorant to govern herself by the laws with which she governs others. As Baru destroyed Tain Hu for her own benefit so Tain Shir will compel Baru to destroy all that she pretends to love for the sake of all that she professes to want. Until Baru has gained everything and possesses nothing at all. Or until Baru finds one thing in all existence that she values more than her own power.

Tain Shir will teach her thus.

When Shir began this hunt she hoped to find a particle of redemption in Tain Hu's rescue, but Tain Hu is dead and that particle is now beyond Shir's reach. Each moment she annihilates herself. Each moment she destroys all that she is and yet the need to avenge her cousin re-forms from the nothingness as if it is now axiomatic to the universe like gravity or the first winter frost.

Tain Shir feels neither hope nor regret. She knows only purpose and the wilderness of possibilities that she might traverse to achieve that purpose.

Before her stands one of those possibilities.

"Why did you take my prisoners?" Aminata intercepts her on *Sulane*'s middeck. "Captain Nullsin just flashed it over—you had Tain Hu's household loaded onto an assault boat. Why?"

She brushes past. Aminata chases after her. "Those are my prisoners! They're under my protection!"

There is no protection.

"You don't believe me?" Aminata follows Shir down into *Sulane*'s belly, still shouting. "I've got a letter that'll prove it. Those people are *my* charge. Not yours, Tain Shir. That's your name, isn't it? Look, I have a letter from one of your relatives! *Look!*"

Shir sits on the chest at the foot of her sleeping pallet and goes back to work. She is carving a stone weight for the arm of her atlatl, to improve the quality and silence of its throw.

"Letters aren't for me," she says.

Aminata, strong and high-browed, would catch Shir's eye if she were not so pricklingly nervous. Shir watches her hand as she offers the letter. One nervous flinch. But only one. "This letter is. It's addressed to me, but you need to read it. I mean it. It's for you."

Shir works her chisel's point against the limestone and cracks a flake away.

"Listen," Aminata snaps, "I have a duty here. Do you understand that? We all have a duty to uphold the lawful orders of our superiors. But we also have a responsibility"—she hesitates—"to . . . examine those orders critically . . . when they go against the good of the Republic."

Shir does not acknowledge the existence of any republic or any good that might accrue to it. But she does acknowledge the existence of dutiful young women who almost understand the meaninglessness of the laws that bind them. "What orders do you doubt?"

Aminata leans in to mutter, "Killing Baru before we understand what she's doing here is *wrong*—"

Shir scoops a dart with the atlatl's forked tip and whirls to put the dart between Aminata's legs at better than a hundred miles an hour. The steel-tipped fishing spear pierces even deeper into the wood than it would Aminata's bone.

"That's real," she tells the Oriati girl. "Only that. Duty? Law? The men who control you don't have any duties. The men who control you don't obey any laws. They act. Then they tell you that it's your duty to obey."

Aminata flinches. Most people flinch when they look at Tain Shir, because they see nothing and fill it with their own fears.

"Tain Hu believed in duty," Aminata says, softly.

"Tain Hu died."

"Not without leaving a testament." She brandishes the letter again. "Read it, damn you. Or I'll tell Ormsment to deny you the marines you want. How are you going to get Baru then?"

Shir requires Aminata herself more than she requires the marines. So she takes the letter and reads it.

To the Oriati Lieutenant who I know is close to my lord, I write this by the mercy of my captor, who hast permitted me a final inscribtion on the eve of the voyage which I hope will end in my death. . . .

Hu's Aphalone writing is poor. Shir reads on. The line about "emotional hemorrhoid" makes her laugh aloud. Aminata jerks in surprise.

Please see to the well-being of my lord even when she will not. Please ensure that she is not alone even when she convinces you that she needs no one (she is lying). Please do not abandon her even when she makes herself wholly intolerable.

Tain Hu loved Baru Cormorant.

"This says nothing about Baru," Shir tells the woman who believes she was Baru's friend. "This letter is only a testament to the quality of Tain Hu."

"It names me protector of Tain Hu's legacy." Aminata does not flinch from her eyes this time, though the galvanic blue of Shir's irises is alien to anyone born south of Aurdwynn. "So your sister's house is *my* responsibility. The people you're stuffing into that assault boat to use as leverage against Baru are *my* duty. You can't just steal them for—"

"Cousin's house," Shir corrects, being the child of Hu's aunt Ko.

"Whatever! Don't we owe it to your dead cousin to consider the possibility that Baru needs our *help*? Shouldn't we at least give her a chance to tell her side before we . . ." She looks over her shoulder again, afraid not just of Ormsment but of every last sailor on this ship, all of whom chose death and exile for a chance to kill Baru. "Hand her over to Ormsment for execution? I asked Ormsment if Baru would get a fair trial. I *know* she was lying."

"You know how flag officers lie, now?" Shir says, teasing her. She decides that she enjoys the Oriati woman. She needs to be stripped of her beliefs, as most do. But then she could be so exquisitely violent.

"I've seen Samne Maroyad smash up her office and stub out a cigarette on my hand," Aminata snaps, "so I'm very familiar with the ways flag officers behave under stress, thank you."

Shir does not particularly know who Maroyad might be. Some admiral. Aminata's commander before she came here. "Tain Hu is dead. I came to avenge her. How she died doesn't matter."

"Of course it does! This letter says your cousin *wanted* to die! She gave her life for Baru!"

"People can be made to want things. The way Baru was made to want to serve Farrier."

"Then we can save her from Farrier," Aminata says, which is so foolish Shir laughs in delight, her eyes wide, her smile wider. Aminata, recoiling, nearly trips over the spear shaft between her feet.

"I was once Farrier's creature," Shir tells her. "I escaped him. There is only one way to escape the masters of manipulation."

"What's that?"

"Chaos." Shir stands and grips Hu's letter in her two fists. "When everything is as violent and disordered as the world in its primal state, nothing remains for the master to manipulate. Man may enslave man. But never will he ever master fire. If you want freedom, be as fire."

She moves to tear the letter apart.

"Stop!" Aminata cries. "Stop, stop, don't *do* that!"

She lunges for the letter. Shir catches her by the lapels of her uniform reds and swings her by her own momentum to slam down onto the pallet beneath her. The wood pumps her breath out of her as hot wet wind across Shir's face. How many times she's felt that last startled breath before opening a throat.

"Fuck you!" Aminata hisses, struggling, trying still not to draw attention. As if anyone on *Sulane* would be surprised by Tain Shir's rage.

"Would you bet your life that Baru's your friend?" Shir asks that defiant face. "Would you wager everything that she *really* cares for you?"

Aminata's throat flutters against Shir's knuckles. "I have a duty to discover the truth."

So it will be duty until the end. A shame.

Shir tightens her grip. Shir smiles.

"Let's help Baru show us the truth," she says. "We will go to *Eternal* now. It is a good place for teaching."

Aminata blinks warily. "What's *Eternal*?"

"The Cancrioth ship."

"The *what*?"

"I found it. I told Ormsment where to find it. She believes it will vindicate her." It will not. The Throne will never allow her to survive her betrayal. Control is paramount. "Ormsment will assault *Eternal* and bring home the Cancrioth to Falcrest to justify her mutiny."

The cries of the sailing-master sound on the weather deck above. *Sulane* heels as she turns south, toward the ruined volcano. Deckhands roll mines to the stern as a tactical clerk carefully marks down the position of each drop, so the field can be recovered.

"The Cancrioth!" Aminata gasps in excitement. "I knew it! Baru's looking for the Cancrioth!"

Poor Aminata. She clings to this letter because it allows her to believe that Baru never betrayed Tain Hu. And if she didn't betray Hu, then perhaps she never betrayed Aminata.

Shir saw them together, once and only once, when they snuck out of the school at Iriad. Aminata tall and lanky and sailor-smooth, drawling stories to Baru from the side of her mouth. And Baru perched beside her on a stone on the harbor cliffs, dark-eyed, looking up intently at Aminata's face, taking every word and biting it like a coin. When Baru laughed it was like flash through thundercloud.

Baru will betray Aminata tonight. When Shir forces Baru to choose between Aminata's life and her own. Baru will choose herself. And choose again, an endless sacrifice, each one justified by the accumulation of its priors. It will not stop until Shir forces Baru to sacrifice her own father. And perhaps not even then.

Y OU'LL regret not making a bargain with the Eye," the Womb said. "The Eye just wants to find Abdu and go home. The Brain will extract a price."

"You're afraid of her," Baru suggested, cheerily. That made her even more excited to meet this Brain.

"You certainly should be."

"It'll be all right," Baru assured her. She felt much better now, after the medicine Shao had given her. "I'm an agent of the Emperor Itself, Miss Womb. To defy me is to defy the entire Imperial Republic. Isn't there anyone else *on* this ship?"

The Womb led Baru forward along a dark causeway toward the ship's bow. "It's night. The crew's asleep."

Baru thought they must be sailing badly undercrewed, and she was confident in her assessment. Shao Lune's marvelous mason dust had her feeling like the old days again, like bright autumn mornings in Treatymont, waking up to a draft under the door and a saber-blade of sunlight through the window, Muire Lo setting out coffee on her desk downstairs. Snorting mason dust was better than drinking coffee for the first time! Yawa must have known all along that it was a treatment for Baru's dark moods—but Yawa wanted her weak.

Well, no more! By the time Yawa blundered her way to *Eternal*, Baru would have a pact with the Cancrioth, the promise of Oriati civil war for Cairdine Farrier . . . and a vial of festering blood in her pocket.

"So this Brain woman shot up Tau's clipper?"

The Womb walked more slowly than Baru, and had to rush occasionally to catch up. "She was the one who insisted we arm the ship. She divided the crew during the voyage."

"How?"

"Sermons. Her faction controls the ship's prow, the orlop lockers, the chartroom, and the navigation instruments."

So she has the rutterbook, Baru thought.

"She appeals to the vengeful and the angry." The Womb sighed. "And there are more and more of those the farther we stray from home. Why are you humming?"

"Sorry," Baru said, turning slow circles as she walked. "D'you reckon I could buy some of this iroko wood?"

"No. It comes from the western Oriati coast, along the Black Tea Ocean. Your ships can't sail there. Segu controls the strait from the Ashen Sea."

"Perhaps we could arrange some kind of conditional passage? A few ships on a limited basis?"

"Trade with Falcrest?" The Womb snorted. "Please."

"Shame," Baru said, still grinning. What a wonderful remedy this dust was! "It's very nice wood."

They climbed a stairwell that wrapped around the huge cavity of a cargo hoist. Baru stopped at each landing to stare, and to imagine *Eternal* unloading goods at the Crane Gallery in Falcrest. The Womb tugged her irritably onward. "What's gotten into you? You're sweating."

"My mind is like a furnace," Baru said, and tapped her temple winningly. The cold uranium chime swayed at her neck.

The curled cuttlefish of the Womb's hands flared in her sleeves. "Did you get into something from the pharmacopeia?"

"Absolutely not!"

"Baru. Stop." The Womb barked it with such force that Baru braced herself on the railing, very rationally afraid she might be blown down into the cargo hoist. "You *must* persuade the Brain to act, do you understand? You must convince her to abandon her madness here and sail. If we die, I'll be sure you die with us."

"What madness keeps her here, specifically?" Baru inquired.

"Does it matter? Dreams of prophecy and change. Dreams of war." The Womb's eyes filled with exhaustion. "Her line . . . they lose themselves in wild ideas. When the growth develops too far, they become erratic. Maybe she's gone malumin."

"Malumin?"

"I don't know the Aphalone word."

Baru leaned against the corridor wall to get her breath. Her heart was hungry, and she kept coming up short on air. Doubtless her mind was sucking it all down. "Would Abdumasi Abd be as valuable to her as he was to the Eye?"

The Womb looked at her sharply. "You're ready to offer him, now?"

"Of course." If it made Tau sad, well, they could take some mason dust and feel better.

"I don't know. It's very hard to know her." The Womb paused on a landing to catch her breath. "She thinks, Baru. She thinks and thinks and thinks. Among the people of Abattai, of my line . . . to us, Incrisiath is the Unborn One."

"Why?"

"Because her mind is like a child in the womb. Full of possibility. But curled up on itself, unseeing. All the Brains see visions and portents, and they struggle against the pull of the Door in the East, the temptation to involute their consciousness and abandon reality for what lies within. This Brain . . . has fought harder than most to remain in our world. She wants to make her visions real." The Womb straightened, breathed, and tugged her cassock down. "But she wouldn't have come on this expedition if she didn't care about Abd. And Abd's line, Undionash, is a natural ally of Incrisiath. Surely the Brain wants him safe. . . ."

"So she'll negotiate?"

"She'd better." The Womb swore in Maulmake, a sound like a bobcat. "This damn book-taught crew! No discipline. No proper captain. I told them we should've hired mercenaries."

"You use mercenaries?"

"Here and there. When there are no better ways."

"And you don't have . . . problems keeping their loyalty?"

The Womb laughed, and took the bait. "No. No, we do not."

So the Cancrioth were rich. Intriguing.

THEY came abovedecks, where the green wormlight from the caldera walls washed out the stars. Baru stared up into the rigging overhead, thick as jungle canopy, awestruck by its complexity.

"Maybe you *are* immortal. It must take a hundred years to learn how to sail this. . . ."

"Baru," the Womb said.

"Is it an automaton, somehow? Are there gears, pulleys, levers you can pull to make the sails work—or is it all done by hand? Do you have some special line of cancer suited to crawling around on the tops—or monkeys? Apes? Jungle apes, trained to sail—"

"Baru!"

"What!" Baru snapped.

And saw the crew.

Ranks and ranks of them. They were all Oriati. But they were not the brisk smiling traders Baru remembered from Taranoke, nor the waistcoated civil servants of Falcrest's federated Oriati, nor the Jackal grenadiers with their dashing shoulder flags. They were certainly not like Tau-indi's golden *Cheetah* crew in their fine clean uniforms. If all those kinds of Oriati had gathered here, they would not have filled a single file of this crowd, this parliament of human variety.

They were so ecstatically different as to defy any category larger than the individual. Sweaty albinos with big straw hats, women with vitiligo spots like you might see in eastern Falcrest around Grendlake. Loinclothed divers in belts of cork, able sailors with spare lines knotted up their arms, navigators whose long queues fell halfway to their trousers. Shaven-headed riggers. Carpenters in turbans and gunners with gauged ears and missing fingers. Their eyes contained all the shapes Baru knew—the upturned and lightly folded Maia, the level and crisply folded Falcresti, the round Stakhi, the wide-spaced classical Oriati—and many more besides. Some of them wore cassocks like the Womb, but others were dressed in sailor slops and loose vests, or kept their own taboos: one man wore only work gloves and a bright orange penis gourd.

Some had split brows and swollen lips. They'd been brawling down below, before the Womb brokered her peace.

"Not a word," the Womb whispered. "They know you're not part of the crew. If they hear Aphalone in your accent . . ."

"Hello!" Baru called, in the Urunoki of her childhood, daring herself to keep any hint of Falcrest's trade language from the sound. "Do any of you know my tongue?"

"What did you say?" the Womb hissed.

"I just said hello. They won't kill me for hello, will they?"

"They might kill you just for seeing their faces, Baru! Some of them have lives to go back to in the mbo—"

"This isn't a warship at all, is it?" Baru stared in wonder. So many different people in one place reminded her of Iriad market days, cooked pineapple juice stinging her lips, the last season before the red sails. "These people aren't soldiers."

A very small man, not much more than four feet tall, perfectly proportionate, what Falcrest would have called a pygmy (Baru did not know a better name), came forward from the ranks. "Baru Cormorant. The Brain will see you, if you will help her with her chores."

"What chores?"

"She is slaughtering the fattening hogs." He beckoned with his small hand. "She will show you what to do. She prefers to teach."

6

THE BRAIN

"SORRY about this," the Brain called. "They tell me the messiah shouldn't do chores, but I think it sets a bad example."

She stood in the orange pool of a cone lantern. A gutter of fresh blood ran beneath her sandaled feet. She had a thirty-foot loop of stripped pig's intestine coiled over her shoulder and a four-foot black saw in her hand. The pig's carcass dangled from an iron hook beside her.

"Last of the herd." She patted the pork flank. "Chickens cost half a gallon a day. In Sukhabwe, eight hundred years ago, we are fighting the cocks because we cannot water them all in the drought. Pigs are even greedier! Does the Eye stop watering his mushrooms? I tell him he ought to use nightsoil, but he's prissy."

Her Aphalone was perfect, if you ignored the strange tenses, and very Segu. She was a sturdy woman of no clear tribe, what Falcrest would've called "peasant stock." A cloud of coiled black hair spilled down to her shoulders. She had shaved it into a tonsure, leaving the top of her head bare.

The oil light caught at a shape there. Something beneath the skin, negative image of a triangle—

Baru gasped. The Brain had been trepanned. Someone had cut a hatch into her skull.

Baru knew from grotesque childhood fascinations that trepanation was exquisitely dangerous. If the membrane beneath the skull was punctured, the brain would die . . . but who could say what the Cancrioth had learned to do? What surgeries they had developed over a thousand years of exploratory self-mutilation?

The Brain waved Baru forward. "Come, come. Don't be fastidious. On the day when the Devi and the Naga marry their peoples, they slaughter ten thousand buffalo, and the rice patties flood red. This is hardly a mess." She wore a bloodstained smock, and something hard beneath it, shaped like armor. "I bung it before you arrive. Help me with the cut."

"It's too warm to slaughter," Baru protested: regurgitating farm technique she'd absorbed in Aurdwynn. "The meat will spoil."

"She comes from Falcrest and she talks hygiene! Do you really think we can't keep pork before you come along?" She offered the double-handled saw. "It's hard for me to find good help, you know. People volunteer for the honor, and my choice becomes political."

"There's no *time*," Baru protested, "my people are coming—"

"Pick up your end, woman! This work is ours to do!"

Together they settled the blade across the pig's groin. Baru was surprised by how easily the saw went in: a soft *zzp*, like bubbles bursting in a bath. The Brain had to jerk back on her handle to keep Baru from falling. "Easy now! On my rhythm."

Together they sawed through the carcass from groin to gaping neck. The intestines coiled on the Brain's shoulder nearly slipped; she adjusted them with a shrug. She had the curious, gentle face of a dove. (Baru did not trust that impression; there seemed to be no reason for it to be true.) A thick brass torc reflected a ring of green wormlight back up on her face. It gave the uncomfortable impression of armoring the Brain's body against her skull.

"It's a joke," she said.

"I—your pardon?" There was something slippery about the way she formed her tenses.

"'The messiah doesn't do chores.' I am born—this body is born—under a set of signs. An eclipse, a choir of cicadas, a geyser of blood, a burning whirlwind. It is foretold among certain peoples that this moon child will come. We—the other souls in me, you understand?—wish to join with the child, so that we can learn the faith of Mzu. I am raised in two worlds, Baru. By day the messiah of one people; and at night tutored as the immortal child of another."

Was that why she seemed to speak of the past as the present? Had she mistaken the visions and seizures of her tumor for prophecy?

"You know my name?" Baru probed: always safe to repeat something they'd already divulged, in hope of gaining more.

"I know everything. Tau tells the Womb about your gambit in Aurdwynn, your secret war against Falcrest. Unuxekome Ra hears it all, and tells me. I trust Ra and so I trust you."

"You trust me?" Baru nearly lost her rhythm. "I could be an assassin!"

The Brain laughed. Her torc rattled against metal beneath her smock. "I'm a thousand years old, Baru. Emperors and whales lie to me. I am proselytized by storms at the helm of a burning fleet. I am threated by the War Princess and bribed by White Akhena: she puts a spear up against my belly, a set of ivory at my flanks, and a silver bowl on my head, and she kisses honey onto my tongue.

The lies you tell are easy to see. I only fear the lies you've been made to believe are true."

On the push: "Lies about the Cancrioth?"

"I'll tell you about us, if you'd like. I don't care if you tell the world. I think that truth always helps the righteous."

"Tell me, then," Baru said, too hungrily. "Tell me who you are."

Despite all fear she found herself rising to an unexpected joy. This was the first time since her childhood that she'd met *anyone* who knew, without duplicity or complication, that she opposed Falcrest. Someone who knew what she had done in Aurdwynn, and who still, knowing the truth about her—

Baru, don't be a fool,

don't leap without looking

—wanted to help.

"Who we are. A question that causes fierce argument, lately."

"Excuse me." Baru couldn't help but ask. "Do you . . . your verb tenses, they're not quite what I'm used to in Aphalone. Is it regional . . . ?"

"No. I cannot tell past from present in the ordinary way. Now I am fleeing south into Sukha Pan, now I am slipping into Uro's tent, now I am whispering to Akhena as she drives her husbands like cattle, all at once. It is an effect of who I am. But I sort things by observing which causes precede which effects. My memories are not clouded, Baru. They are as clear as life. Sometimes I get lost in them if I don't keep my hands and my mouth busy." The Brain pushed the saw. They were deep into the abdomen now, where the intestines had been. Baru had pig's blood on her cassock. "So. Where do I begin?"

You've always been bored by history, Cairdine Farrier had told her. *It's your greatest weakness.*

"At the beginning, please," Baru said.

THEY had not been slavers, the Brain said. Not exactly. That was the myth of the Cancrioth but not the truth. Nothing had happened exactly the way it was remembered, especially not in the Mbo, where memory was like a house you arranged for the benefit of those who lived in it, not a museum to leave untouched.

But the myths were right in one way. The Cancrioth had truly been sorcerers and philosophers. There was not much difference at the time: magic and philosophy were both ways to manipulate symbols to create effect.

Only later, when there was a name for what they did, would they be called scientists.

It was a time of plague and dire scarcity on the continent of Oria. The Cheetah Palaces had crumbled into nothing but names on plundered tombs, and the salaried engineer caste who'd built their ziggurats and standing steles was now extinct. With them died the irrigation and cisterns that kept the cities alive. Suddenly there were millions of people who could not be fed.

In the time between the Palatine Collapse and the Mbo, in the time of the great Paramountcies, those unfed people became slaves.

The priest-legal caste encouraged slavery on the grounds that austerity and selfless labor were holy: slavery was a worldly ordeal that would guarantee the spirit's virtue. The kings and queens of the Paramountcies insisted upon slavery because their neighbors used slaves, and because slave raids kept their warriors busy on the border instead of restless in the capital.

Slavery was a terrible institution in a thousand ways. One of those ways was hygiene. The forced movement of entire nations of bodies spread disease: tribe after tribe torn from the quilt of the world, liquified and poured into the gullet of the Paramountcies' appetite for work. The slaves died in ways and in quantities that exceeded the horror of any epidemic and any war, for in truth slavery was both things and more. And the death of slaves only stoked the demand for more.

It was an insatiable engine of democlysm. Philosophers like Iri anEnna and Mana Mane had not yet been born. The Whale Words and the *Kiet Khoiad* had not yet been written. No one had worked to convince the world that each individual life had a value.

The Cancrioth was born on the principle that life had value. At first, though, it was merely market value.

They began as councilors to the Paramountcies' many rival rulers. Some of them were paid scholars, some were educated slaves, some were foreign mystics and seers. All were employed to bring advantage to their masters by finding ways to better work the slaves. The problem of disease was at the center of the work, and that led to the problem of death. The councilors were already fascinated by this enigma, especially those who worshiped the moon god Mzu (Musu in those days), who was killed every day by the sun and every month by the world's shadow, and eternally reborn.

If the moon could die and live again, could people?

Forbidden to speak to the servants of other rulers, desperate nonetheless to pool their efforts, these councilors resorted to secret letters and clandestine meetings to make progress in the Work Against Death. For decades this cabal made no progress, and time hunted their ranks.

It was Alu, Iamchild of a priest-linguist, who suggested the method of home-group and journey-group that would revolutionize the world. Alu wanted a better way to test the medicinal effect of jungle plants. Alu knew a story about twin princesses, one of whom went out into the world to journey, one of whom stayed at home in the palace to study, each swearing to learn whether worldliness or scholarship made a better queen. The story was about the value of a monarch connected to the people and the seasons: but Alu extracted a different lesson from it.

The traveling sister had to leave a twin at home so she could learn how her journey changed her. How could you know if a medicine was successful without a group of untreated slaves "at home"? Maybe your new drug was no better than rest and bed care. If you were going to bring a plant to your lord as a panacea, if you were going to ask your lord to spend farmland and labor raising that plant, you had better be damn well sure it worked.

And it did work. Alu's method *worked*. It condensed the whole Work Against Death, the entire menagerie of apotropaic magic, poisonous brews, and ritual surgeries, into a rigorous grid of tests that filtered the gold from the water.

When their masters saw the progress their councilors had made against dysentery, pneumonia, tuberculosis, fever, and all the other evils, they rewarded their councilors with freedom. Freedom to communicate. To recruit workers. To dispatch expeditions. To order the conquest of certain areas, not only for slave-taking but for access to plants, texts, and traditions.

And the masters, too, became fascinated by the Work Against Death. If there were medicines against pneumonia or fever . . . were there medicines against age?

Encouraged by their own success, full of dreams and ambitions, the councilors began to treat *everything* with Alu's method. They sifted the Paramountcies' slaves for the folklore and myths of five hundred languages. Collated the stories to discover commonalities that might point to lost cities and the boneyards of ancient war. Charted the stars, the shape of their own continent, and the outline of distant lands across unthinkable tracts of sea.

It was Incrisiath, the Brain herself, who discovered the uranium lands, the hot caves, and the secret fire.

THE saw cut through the pig's neck and into air.

Half the pig fell wetly on the canvas below. Baru was overcome by vertigo and confusion: plunging back through all that history to a pig lying on canvas. Why was there an entire pig lying here? Hadn't they been sawing it in half?

"Baru," the Brain said, "you are bewildered."

"Yes. Damn." She tapped the right side of her nose. "I have a wound on my brain. I forget about things on my right. Sometimes I forget I have the wound at all."

"It must be hard not to trust your own thoughts."

"Yes," Baru admitted.

"But it can be a good thing, too, to be reminded you're fallible. We're all blind in our own ways. I choose that word carefully, knowing many great thinkers without eyesight. *Everyone* has a blindness, somewhere. Very few remember it." She offered Baru the loop of intestines from her shoulder. "Hold these while I get the halves into tubs. They go below to chill."

Baru balked at the viscera. "Er—"

"No shit."

"Your pardon?"

"There's no shit in the intestines. We starve the pigs before the slaughter. Soon we clean these out and pound them with salt. We make sausages."

Baru took the noosed-up guts. They smelled of Aurdwynn spring. "You don't have anyone to do this for you?"

"I have you!"

"But no attendants? No servants?"

"Oh, any little lord can make her people do scut work. That's dominance, and it's brittle." The Brain knelt, grunting, to get the pig by its two trotters. "But if you do your own work, and do it very well, they come to you with questions. As it is with Akhena. And if you answer well enough, not just about what they should do but *why* they should do it . . . then they learn to think as you think, and to make the choices you would choose. And you lead them without a word, from a thousand miles away, because you are with them in the shape of their thoughts."

"It's like the riddle of the three ministers!" How thrilling that her own thoughts paralleled an immortal's! What solutions this woman might have discovered, what peerless insight, without the mortal calendar to cut short her work! "Do you know that riddle? It's about power. . . ."

"Not by that name." The Brain grunted as she dropped the pig—no, damn it, *half* the pig—into a tub of salt. "Do you think about power?"

"Often . . ." Baru felt like she were being walked around the edge of a pit, waiting to be pushed in.

"I think about thoughts. The parts of them we can see. The parts we can't. I try to imagine what's really happening, beyond our thoughts and memories. What is the far side of the moon like, I ask myself? Is it waiting to be formed?

Is it already in existence? Do we discover it as it truly is, when we go there, or do we force it into the shape of our own moon? Here—look." She produced the pig's severed head and struck it with a cleaver. The white brain revealed itself like the center of a halved pomegranate. The hog had been exsanguinated: everything that should have been red was pale now. "Everything we are, everything we know of the world, is in this flesh. We cannot see truth, we cannot smell it, we cannot read it from a book. We can only get at the symbols our brains make. Even our sight is a mirage: I have visions enough to know that. But visions never make my sight more true. I can delude my sight with dreams, I can move it *further* from the truth. But I know no way to do the opposite. I cannot clear my eyes of the veils they were born with. *Something* is out there, Baru. Something real. How can we get at it? Can we have the opposite of a vision, the antithesis of a dream? Something that husks our consciousness open and spills us out into *reality*? Maybe that is what gods are. Maybe gods have no consciousness because they do not need it. Maybe that is why they don't answer prayers. They cannot conceive of the world except as it is."

"I don't understand," Baru admitted. "If we are all deceived by our thoughts, but in a way which lets us act sensibly and consistently, are we deceived at all? You might as well call language nonsense, just because a word is not the same as the thought it names."

The Brain shrugged. "It troubles me for centuries. I keep a diary."

"I hate that." The mason dust helped Baru laugh. Intestines jiggled on her shoulder. "I hate not understanding. You can't know everything? Not even you?"

"Especially not me. Only a god knows everything, I think." The Brain looked up keenly. "What would you do if you were a god, Baru? Would you destroy Falcrest?"

THE turn caught Baru off guard and she choked on the answer.

"Don't be shy. Tau tells me your story, remember?" The Brain pitched one half of the pig's brain to a bucket, missed, and, with a sigh, went to pick it up. "Even if I go to Falcrest and report you, who believes me? Your purpose is to go among Falcrest's enemies and entice them." She lifted the bucket and carried it to the ship's rail. Her arms were wiry. "Ra asks me why Falcrest gives a foreign girl so much power. I tell her they do it to destroy the solidarity of race. They want the Maia and the Stakhieczi and the Oriati and all the rest of us to know that *anyone* can wear the mask. Even one of our own. So speak sedition, Baru. There's nothing to fear."

Baru imagined herself sitting upon the throne in the Waterfall Keep in

Vultjag. She had refused the Necessary King from that throne. She could draw on that same power for the courage to tell the Brain the truth. It was hard to separate the memory of that throne from the Emperor's proxy seat in the Elided Keep: but one of them warmed her, and the other chilled.

It was so hard. She had so many layers of caution set in place. So many living lies fixed in place to die and calcify.

But, by mason dust or by sheer need, she managed it:

"If I had my way, I would see Falcrest destroyed."

"Falcrest the city?"

"The Imperial Republic of Falcrest. The Masquerade. The entire civilization. I'd see Aphalone written only on tombstones."

"I see." The Brain stuck her finger into the remaining half of the pig's brain like she was going after earwax. "How do you handle the butchery?"

"What?"

"How do you butcher an empire? Have you seen one die, before?"

"I've read about the Cheetah Palaces, and the—"

"Oh, never mind the books. Historians are always writing down what they *see* happening. The same mistake my friend the Eye makes. What happens is always different: but the reasons it happens, those are usually the same.

"I see it happen. I see it again and again." Her voice took on the accent of some ancient tongue. "The weather changes in the same years the sea people come to raid. A rebellion breaks out and a plague spreads in the chaos, or a war empties the treasury just as a weak ruler falls. Too many things go wrong at the same time. The empire fails to make the only two things that can sustain an empire's existence. Conquest, or commerce.

"Without force or finance to hold the empire together, it begins to fragment. The administrators withdraw their power, and the warriors carve up what they leave behind. The elite class vanishes, overthrown or reduced to common poverty: there is no one to tend the cheetahs, after the Palaces fall, and the cats cry in their crumbling halls. The shattered fragments of the empire can no longer specialize. The cities cannot get food from the farms, the farms cannot get goods and security from the cities, everyone must produce everything they need locally. Starving people leave the cities, carrying disease. Without a food surplus, there can be no priests, which means no temples, no more organized belief, maybe no more records or writing. People who cannot get what they need by commerce turn to raiding and war. The survivors diminish into the wilderness, and forget. It is a slow, complicated thing.

"How could you alone make all that happen?"

"I could do what you've done here," Baru said, harshly. "What you've done on Kyprananoke."

The Brain's hand was in the pig's brain, scooping. "What have I done here?"

"You released the worst disease in recorded history on innocents."

"I am giving them a chance to use their own bodies as weapons. Do you deny them the chance to fight the enemy on its own terms?"

"You call that *fighting on Falcrest's terms*?"

"Yes, absolutely I do. Falcrest uses smallpox on your home in Taranoke. Isn't it justice for Taranoke to use pox against Falcrest? Even if it means sacrificing your own bodies? Haven't you given up your fingers, there?" The Brain tilted her head, bird-curious. "The law of talion, Baru. An eye for an eye. Should we not do to them as they do to us?"

Baru wanted to ask why Kyprananoke had been chosen for this demonstration, rather than Taranoke. But she already knew. Kyprananoke was smaller and more isolated, visited mostly by pirates, smugglers, and unfortunates. Kettling on Taranoke would go everywhere. Kettling on Kyprananoke *might* be contained.

Always the price rolled down on the smaller.

Tain Hu would never collaborate with the Brain.

Never.

But maybe Baru would.

THE Brain finally got what she was digging for. The front lobe of the pig's brain came free in her fist.

"This is the best tool we have," she said, turning the gray fat to show Baru, "to understand our own brains. Apes' brains are more like ours. But they're dangerous to work with, and sacred to many of our neighbors. We prefer pigs. There's something in pig flesh that's . . . kin to us.

"We poison the pigs. We starve and strangle them. We drive nails into them, we trepan them, we cut pieces out of them. And by studying what they lose when we take a piece of them away, we discover what that piece *does*. Do you know what we've found, Baru?"

"What?"

"The brain survives. I see men shot through and through the head live long enough to die of fever. I see children with nothing but water in their skulls grow up to be mathematicians. I see brains pierced by arrows, fishing hooks, mine shrapnel: all of them healed in time. I meet you, Baru, struck in the head but perfectly clever. Poison the brain, and sometimes you just . . . change it. Does destroying Falcrest really destroy its empire?"

Analogy games were easy to bend: "Brains," Baru ventured, "don't survive Kettling."

The Brain laughed. "Well said. Come, help me with the intestines."

The guts had to be pared clean of fat, then washed through, end to end, with saltwater from a lever pump. Then they were cuffed and turned inside out by a trick so clever it made Baru laugh: you dangled the intestine straight up and down, like a sock from a laundry line, and pulled the bottom inside-out so it made a kind of bowl. Then you filled that bowl with water, and let the weight of that water draw the intestine down so it everted.

"You don't wear gloves," Baru said, with some discomfort. "This is raw meat. . . ."

"Ah, it's only flesh."

"You could get sick."

"That's what Falcrest teaches you to fear, isn't it?" The Brain poured out handfuls of coarse salt to pound into the intestines. "They think the Oriati are spiritually diseased. That Mana Mane's whole pleasant notion of trim . . . traps them, somehow."

It was exactly what Cairdine Farrier had told Baru. *Imagine an idea like a disease. It spreads because it makes people happy. It makes them happy by convincing them to be content with what they have . . . can you imagine a greater threat to our destiny? A more terrible fate than pleasant, blissful decay?*

The Brain sighed. "I think they're right."

"What?"

"Trim. An ethics for children in a world of child-killers. Look at Tau-indi Bosoka. A pathetic caricature of Oriati nobility, full of spiritual advice and incapable of cunning. What's left of them, now?" The Brain's fists rose and fell, slapping salt into meat. "I really do find the Mbo beautiful. But its time is finished. Something new takes its place. Something that can *fight*."

Baru heard Cairdine Farrier's voice again. *We can save the people. But their history, their traditions, their literature . . . it's all tainted.*

She hadn't expected the Cancrioth to agree with him.

"But you *do* want to fight Falcrest," she pressed.

"Oh, absolutely. Do you know why I fear Falcrest, Baru? I see many nations, many kinds of power. I fear their kind the most."

"Why?" Baru asked, with a student's hunger.

"Guess. Unuxekome Ra tells me they call you a 'savant.'" The Brain lifted her chin and looked down at her, owlishly, like a severe schoolmistress. "Why would I, thousand-year Incrisiath, alive in all the dawns I have ever seen, rise from my studies to make war on mortal empire?"

"Well . . ." Baru thought it out. Salt crackled beneath her fingertips. "If you feel the Cancrioth itself must act, then it's because the scope of the threat is obvious only to the immortal. Someone who has watched the great sweep of history."

"Precisely."

"And yet the threat must be urgent, or you wouldn't come out of hiding. You have to act now, as soon as possible, because the danger will only grow."

"So it is."

"You think Falcrest is going to win, don't you? They're going to rule the world."

In her dreams at Sieroch, and in her hallucinations after her seizure on *Helbride,* she had seen Falcrest as rivers of molten gold and porcelain flowing across the world. The shape of the machine of empire building itself. Remorseless because it recognized no value except the ability to make more of itself.

"I do." The older woman rattled as she moved: a metallic sound beneath her butcher's smock. "They understand the secret of power, Baru."

"Which one?"

"The ability to improve one's own power, no matter how slowly, triumphs in the long run over any other power. Time magnifies small gains into great advantages. If you are hungry, then it is better, in the long run, to plant one seed than to steal a pound of fruit. Falcrest applies this logic in all their work. They do not conquer. They make themselves irresistible as trading partners. They do not keep their wealth in a royal hoard. They send it out among their people, stored in banks and concerns, where it helps the whole empire grow. They do not wait to treat the sick. They inoculate against the disease before it spreads. All their power sacrifices brute strength in the present for the ability to capture a piece of the future."

"Like the futures contracts," Baru murmured. She'd taught Hu to use those contracts. "Another Falcresti invention."

"Are you sure? Falcrest likes to infantilize the Oriati, and to take credit for our inventions."

"They take everything," Baru said with bitter admiration. "They won't stop until they have the world. Everyone will be Incrastic. Everything will be priced by the market. Every word will be Aphalone. Unless someone destroys them now, strikes with all the force they can muster, to choke the baby in its cradle before it grows."

"So you would see Falcrest destroyed."

"Yes." And it rushed out of her: "Will you give me the Kettling to bring to Falcrest?"

"Now," the Brain said with satisfaction, "we dump these intestines into barrels of brine and chopped onion. They'll sit overnight. Tomorrow we'll scrape out the villi and decide what to put inside."

"There won't be a tomorrow," Baru snapped, losing her patience at last, "if the people searching for me find you here—"

The Brain reached out and yanked the heavy uranium chime from around Baru's neck. The thong snapped. As the metal met the Brain's hands, her skin flashed up bright through blood and offal.

"Now," she said, "you understand why I speak of the ways we delude ourselves. I cannot trust you, even if you trust yourself. You think you defy them but maybe they have made you think so. Maybe you are here to steal the Kettling so they can make a cure. Is it not possible? That you do not know how they rule you?"

It was Baru's deepest fear and Tau had voiced it perfectly—*no matter what you do here, Baru, I expect that by some strange coincidence it will end up being what Mister Cairdine Farrier wants.*

"There is one way to be certain of your motives," the Brain said. She stood over Baru, and her hands were like suns.

"Please," Baru begged. "What power is that? How do you make that light?"

"Your Taranoki gods are stone and fire, the principles of molten earth. How could fire burn hot enough to melt earth, so far from the air?" In her shining eyes Baru saw true and ancient awe. "That power, Baru. That secret airless fire. That's what we worship. That is how we are making the immortata, the flesh that never dies, a thousand years ago, in a land you have not named.

"Now come with me. I must show you something."

"What is it?"

Oh no.

"A test."

Baru, be wary now. . . .

Her hand was warm, but Baru could not tell if that warmth was in her flesh, or in the light that leaked between their joined fingers.

THE Brain left her soiled smock on a peg. Beneath it she wore bronze armor, tarnished green and ancient. It didn't fit her. Someone much bigger had died inside it, long ago. The terrible rent in the chest had never been repaired.

"Follow me."

Baru looked for somewhere to wash her hands, but there was only a bucket of ash.

They met no one as they went belowdecks and aft, through a dining room decorated with preserved peacock plumes, then a library of ancient clay tablets. "The Eye and I curse this part of the ship," the Brain explained, "to keep our people from fighting here. Neither of us want it damaged."

"Can your curse keep boarders away?"

"For that we have the ship's magazine."

"I don't know if guns will stop them. . . ."

"You mistake me." There was a severity in her now, like a different voice had taken the lead in the choir of souls her tumor carried. "*Eternal* carries an armament of more than three hundred cannon. The cannon require a supply of powder. If a foe tries to take us, we detonate the magazines. The blast destroys all aboard."

The mason dust began to fade, like flavor seeping out of overcooked meat. When she heard the sound ahead, Baru thought it had come from inside her. But there it was again. A scream.

"The pigs," she said. "I thought we'd killed the last pig."

"The last of the fattening pigs."

"There are others?"

"I told you there is a kinship between human flesh and pig. These pigs . . . serve a different purpose."

"The thing you want to show me is a *pig*?"

"It is in a pig. It is never born of a pig."

"How can be something be part of a pig and not be born from a pig?"

They came to a treasury. Falcresti fiat notes lay in crisp white paper stacks, powdered to keep them dry. Silver lonjaros and segus, golden mzilimakes and faceted devi-nagas, glimmering reef pearl, bars of platinum and unset jewels, not one of them behind lock—as if there were no one on *Eternal* tempted by worldly wealth.

"O Himu." Baru reached for a jade statue of an elephant. No wonder the Womb had been so confident in the loyalty of mercenaries! "Who *funds* you?"

The Brain hesitated at the far door. The woman who had died and been reborn for a thousand years was afraid.

"This," she said, "is the sacrifice I ask of you. It is what I ask of Unuxekome Ra, in exchange for the Kettling: and you know that I am true to my word."

She threw her weight into the door to get it swinging. The wooden pegs of the hinges groaned as it opened. A smell came to Baru, rancid and powerful, sweet in the foulest way.

Then the screams began.

Shrill and manlike but not the screams of men. Unanimous in their terror. As if they had all at once been awakened to some unthinkable condition.
The Brain made a face of mustered courage and stepped inside. Her bare feet
crushed straw.

Baru imagined herself as Tain Hu, and followed.

Piglets.

The Brain had a piglet in her arms, and there were more in the pens. There
was something wrong with all of them. Bloody efflux stained the Brain's brass.
The piglet took a rasping breath.

The Brain stroked the piglet's belly. It convulsed. The mass of tumors that
erupted from its skull shed ichor between broken scabs.

Baru gagged.

"This is the baneflesh." The Brain tickled the piglet's chin. "It comes to us in
the failure of Alu, the Line of the Skin. Of all the Lines it is the most aggressive
and the most resilient. All the lines can break the Embargo, the rule that no
body's flesh can grow in another. But the baneflesh can cross not just between
bodies but between *species*.

"When we first make the immortata, it takes root in new hosts only with
the greatest difficulty. But we have a thousand years to select those lines we favor.
By amplifying only the tumors with traits we prefer into new hosts, we teach
them to grow in certain parts of the body, to cause certain effects. We learn to
breed cancer. But we have failures along the way. And the baneflesh is our
greatest."

Baru felt like the ship were capsizing. She knew precisely what the Brain
would ask.

The Brain tickled the piglet again. This time it did not respond. "Baneflesh
can be unpredictable in its course. This family—all these pigs' implants descend from a single parent—prefers to colonize the layer between scalp and
brain. In the forebrain, here, where you can see the tumors are thick and ex-
trusive. In the final stages the tumor eats away the scalp. Nothing remains of
the host by then. These poor pigs are not suffering. At times they respond as
if in pain. At times they shake with joy. But there is nothing left to feel those
things."

"Is there medicine?" Baru croaked. "Is there a cure?"

"There is no cure for malign cancer. Everyone knows this. Cancer grief is
harder than ordinary grief, they say. In the way that a slow cut hurts more."
The Brain stared into the pig's cratered scalp. Small black fans, like coral, grew
in mounds from gapingly distended pores. "Do you know why we turn to the

study of cancer, back in the beginning? When we realize the water from the hot lands can cause it?"

"Why?" Baru heard her voice as if through a steel keyhole.

"Because cancer is the aristocracy of the body. It captures the means of growth for its own use. It convinces the body to serve it, and delivers nothing in return. If it grows too much it brings the whole body down." She had that old, old accent again. "We see how our lords destroy the people they rule. We think that if we can make a cancer that can live in peace with the body . . . then we can be like it. Cancer without grief. Aristocracy without end. We overthrow our lords, but in the end we fail to rule the people well. I do not hate the mbo for driving us into the jungle. But they need us now, and the time has come for our return. . . ."

"Why did you bring me here?" Baru whispered. "What is the test?"

The Brain lifted the pig like a baby, belly up. Effluent beaded in thick strings on her armor. "If I entrust our most powerful weapon to you—"

No, *no*, this is wrong—

"Then you must consecrate your body to this purpose. You cannot lie to yourself if your flesh has been committed. You cannot hide some secret purpose in the other half of your mind, or find yourself turned back to Falcrest's service by bribery and temptation, when death grows in your blood and bile. I am immortal long enough to know that death clarifies everything."

She ran her burning finger over the fans and ridges of the thing growing in the pig's head. Not a thing born of pig, though. The same cancer that had grown in Alu's body a thousand years ago, cut out and reseeded but never touched by death. One endless human growth hopping from host to host.

And it had come all this way to hop once more.

"Take the baneflesh into your brain," the Brain whispered. "Deny yourself any possible future except this mighty blow against Falcrest. Live long enough to complete your task, and no longer. Then I trust you wholly. Then I give you whatever you require to bring Falcrest down."

7

SPASMS

BARU ran.

She bolted barefoot from the pigpens, plunged down stairways no wider than her shoulders, leaving footprints of hay and unthinkable fluid. She stumbled into a compartment where something huge and domed and white, netted with join lines, curved out of shadows that smelled like glue. Hundreds of human teeth grinned in an arc at Baru, and she ran from them, too.

She ran with mason dust burning out in her sinuses and ebbing from her heart. She ran not because she couldn't face the choice but because there was no choice at all.

If she could sacrifice Tain Hu to her mission, and genuinely believe that sacrifice was in service of a worthwhile goal, then she *must* also be willing to sacrifice herself. She must be willing to set a fixed end to her life in order to gain a weapon that would complete her life's work.

Or she was just a hypocrite, just Cairdine Farrier's pawn, a greedy self-interested monster using the cause of her people's freedom as an excuse to seize power for herself.

If she couldn't do this, she was worse than a traitor. She was a *collaborator*.

She had to do it. She had to accept the baneflesh.

> You mustn't! You can't!
> This isn't what I wanted!
> *Stop!*

She struck something in the dark, the right side of a doorframe she hadn't noticed, and fell. The watertight coaming came up into her stomach like a blunt guillotine. Her cut cheek landed first and blood burst over her tongue.

"Tau," she grunted. "Tau, stop." Tau had cast a spell on her that made her feel like she couldn't breathe, like her fingers were skewered on long needles, like her ears were being crushed by fifty feet of water pressure. Shao Lune had the cure. The mason dust—she needed the dust—

"Ba-ruuuu," a woman cooed. "Something frighten you, girl?"

A boot stepped on her wounded hand. A leather glove ground her cheek down into the wood. The tip of a hooked knife tickled her throat.

"Ra," Baru gasped.

"You didn't think I'd sailed away on my little boat, did you? Didn't think I'd forgotten about what you told me?"

"Ra, don't—the Brain needs me—"

"I won't kill you. Just something we need to clear up, before you go." The knife scratched a line across her throat, up to her cheek. "Look at me."

Baru couldn't look at her. She couldn't think what to say. She opened her mouth and at last, without any thought, it came out.

"Kill me," she whispered. "Please kill me."

The thought had been with her since Sieroch, carved into that sullen crown of hurt she wore every day when she woke, forcing her to lie in bed and do nothing at all. The thought said: just be done with it. Just stop. The world will go onward. You've failed.

"Oh no. Not you, Baru girl. Not when the Brain has such hopes for you." Ra grasped Baru by the chin and made her roll over. The blade of the knife curved flat over her throat. Ra held a tin mug in her off hand: incongruous hospitality. "Did she offer you the baneflesh?"

Like a cough: "Yes."

"Me too. Price of the pistols, price of the plague. And I took it." Ra's grin, an arc of glistening lead in the darkness. The smell of wine on her breath. The Pirate Duchess was drunk as a brewery rat. "She put it right up my nose. Can you believe that? Squirted it up there like I snorted a fly. Said it likes the blood in the nose. Said there's a special place where the nose is connected to the brain. Said it takes root nine times in ten, if it's done right. I didn't give a shit. Don't have anyone left, don't plan to leave anything behind. Especially not a grandchild."

She stepped down on Baru's stomach, hard. Brandished the mug. "Drink this."

Ra looked so old. Leathered by the world: soaked in hope and then scraped raw, hope and the blade edge, again and again, until even the toughest layers of her lay naked to the acid world. And fired, and scraped again, and stretched into someone else's shapes.

"Oh Devena," Baru groaned. She knew why Ra was here. Baru had lied, in a moment of panic, to protect herself. Said she was carrying Ra's grandchild. And Ra believed it. The mug must be tea of silphium, or something like it. An abortion.

"You killed Kyprananoke," she gasped, to buy time. "You monster. You gave them the Kettling?"

"Of course I did. We pinned all our hopes on Abdumasi Abd, you know. On his fleet. He was going to liberate Aurdwynn, cut off the Masquerade trade circle, throw back their ships. Then he was going to return with Aurdwynni soldiers and overthrow the Kyprists here. We could've bought the things we needed from a free Aurdwynn. Grain. Soil. Metal. Lumber, so we could finally *build* something."

Ra spat into the dark. "But you fucked him. There was no hope for Kyprananoke after that. So when the Cancrioth arrived, when the Scheme-Colonel in the nice white clothes came to me with an offer, I asked them to make our bodies into weapons."

"Why? *Why?*" She wasn't even from Kyprananoke! She hadn't the right!

Ra's false teeth clicked in her grin.

"The whole world has stepped on Kyprananoke. Old Mount Tsunuq blew itself apart rather than live here. Falcrest seized what was left, bleached out all the old ways, couldn't find a way to make the leftovers profitable, and abandoned the islands to rot. Even the sea hates this place. Every winter the Old Gray rises up to drown us." A laugh like a pistol shot. "Why do you think Yawa exiled me here? This is the land of people who don't matter."

"These people matter," Baru whispered, because if they didn't, if Falcrest had revoked their right to matter when it discarded them, what would happen to Taranoke when it was free?

"Oh?" Ra mocking her, but sad, so sad. "How often did you think about Kyprananoke before you came here? How often did you *ever* consider this place? At least if we hurt you, you'll remember we exist. 'Kyprananoke, where the plague began.' You'll remember that for centuries. I don't forget about you, do I, Baru? Not since you killed my son. You hurt me, and so I remember."

"I liked your son," Baru said, and oh, Wydd save her, she wanted to weep again, she wanted to die, to stop being the woman who had led the dashing Duke Unuxekome to his end. "I wish he hadn't— I wish he were still here—"

"No. No more Unuxekomes." Ra's foot pressed down harder. "We were all right, as aristocrats go. But our time is past. So drink this fucking tea."

"I made it up. There's no baby."

"No baby." Ra sneered at her. "Then you won't mind drinking this anyway?"

"There's no need, Ra, I swear."

"Next you'll tell me there's no file full of blackmail on my son—"

"That's real, Ra." Baru grasped desperately; maybe she could bargain with this. "He wrote it himself, dictated it to an ilykari priestess, when he joined the rebellion. It was a way to bind him to the other rebels, adding his secret to their ledger. But I had my man steal it, your son's secret, I kept it safe—"

"Show the scroll to me."

"I can't! Yawa stole it!"

Ra shivered with hate. Her boot crushed Baru's sternum toward the back of her ribs. "Yawa. I remember when she was just a ratty maid tacking up slogans on shit paper. Aurdwynn Can Rule Itself. How many centuries of my family in Welthony? How many? And she sends me away like a barren wife."

"If you let me go," Baru croaked, "I can help you find her. You could still have revenge. . . ."

Ra ennobled herself. Her chin came down, her shoulders firmed, her bones themselves seemed to stiffen. There was, for a moment, a duchess in the hall with Baru, a captain and a lady, a fighter and a soul.

"I don't need to kill her. The masks will do it for me. She thinks she can trick them. She thinks she'll save Aurdwynn from their grasp, but she'll die as their puppet. They'll strangle her with her own strings."

What in Devena's name was Ra talking about? "I have to stop her, Ra. She doesn't care about Aurdwynn. She wants what her master wants—"

"Her master? Ha. You don't know, do you?" Ra tapped her foot against Baru's throat. "You don't know she's a traitor."

"Of course I know," Baru rasped, "she's been working for Falcrest since the beginning—"

"No, she hasn't. She swore to overthrow the masks and liberate Aurdwynn." Ra's eyes were far away, lost in better days. "Swore it to the virtues, and wrote her vow on a palimpsest in the sacred olive-oil lamplight. My son was there. Xate Yawa never lied to an ilykari, not her, not once. And my son never lied to me."

She hiccupped a burst of wine smell and looked thoughtfully into the cup of tea. "Let her have Aurdwynn. Let her die trying to save it from the masks. Fuck that place. Fuck this world, the eater of children. Fuck what we've all become."

She bent over Baru to force her mouth open. Baru tried to fight. Ra kicked her in the head.

By the time Baru had her senses back she was swallowing lukewarm tea. It had the bitter, alkaline taste of ergot. She remembered that taste from the night Svir had poisoned her, when she had gone into seizure, when she had seen Tain Hu. Ergot was a hallucinogen, and a dangerous abortifacient—the herbalist Yythel had always warned women against it.

This, she thought, is what happens when I travel without a bodyguard. Old women pour poison down my throat. Oh, Devena, this is what happens when I try to run from a choice.

H ER womb wanted to get out.
    "Fuck," Baru grunted. A bizarre cramp, like a wave rolling through her body, nothing like the dull ache of her period, split her stomach and seized her thighs. She gave up crawling and fell forward on her elbows. Gritted her teeth. Blew through her nose until the contraction passed. It left no lingering pain: even stranger.

There was no child in there to kill, but Baru kept thinking of certain medical texts, read through horrified fingers, about uterine prolapse and fatal torsions.

She needed to finish the work. She needed to get the Kettling before Yawa came and ruined it all.

But she *hurt*—

Another cramp struck. "Fuck," Baru panted. "Wydd fuck." She tried to breathe and smelled the salt marshes around the Elided Keep, the burning mace-grass. Heard the screams of that poor otter they'd shot while trying to kill Tain Shir, crying as it died.

Hallucinating already. She had to get back to Shao Lune. Shao Lune would have medicine.

When she raised her eyes from the dark iroko planks and the whittled Cancrioth symbols, she saw Tau. They propped their hands on their round hips and smiled. Their eyes were two halos, perfect rings of light, like artifacts on a telescope lens. Baru had seen that halo before. It meant that she was going to seize.

"You're going the right way," Tau said. "I need you now. I need you to say the things I need to hear. Come to me."

"Go away," Baru grunted. And realized that she could see *all* of Tau, even their right side. That had happened before, in the instants before the seizure hit—

"Not now," she hissed, "not here—not *again!*"

"It'll be all right," Tau said. "It'll all be okay, Baru. Trust in trim."

The seizure took her.

                                                    I'm here. I'm with you.

Her consciousness began to tick forward. Gaps of nothingness between oil-painted instants of action. She was on her feet again, walking doubled over. The seizure made the pain distant, added an extra degree of consciousness. Her body screamed as her womb tried to push out something that wasn't there. She pitied herself, remotely.

She looked down, and found that she'd been tied.

There were ropes on her. Not the canvas and silk that had bound her to the Imperial Throne in that ergotic vision on *Helbride*. These ropes were hemp and jute, linen and coir, very ordinary lines, knotted loosely round her arms and legs. She felt them pull at her, suggesting, gently, where to go. And when she staggered they took her weight. They kept her walking.

Another tick of absence.

She was outside Tau-indi's stateroom. Enact-Colonel Osa slumped against the door. A triplet of infinitely thin bands circled her head.

Oh, the *longing* in poor Osa, in her roped-up fists and powerful arms! Baru understood Osa as she had never tried to before. She was a Jackal, one of the first professional soldiers the Mbo had ever raised: she had dedicated her life to repairing the mistakes of the Armada War. If she were not sworn to Tau's protection, she might happily join the Brain, just for the chance to test herself against Falcrest.

"Hello," Baru said.

"Baru. What have they done to you?"

"Tau needs me."

"Tau doesn't want to see you." She clicked her boots together, sublimating some dearly-wished-for violence into the sound. "They don't want to see any-one."

"Is Tau alone in there? Did they send you away?"

Osa stared at her fists. Baru saw a rope as thick as a ship's sheetline around Osa's neck, trailing under the doorjamb and into the room. It was there and then it was gone. It was a hallucination and Baru was sure it was real.

"They ordered me to leave," Osa said. "I couldn't disobey."

"Osa, they'll hurt themself."

"I can't disobey. I took an oath."

"Let me go in to them, Osa."

She did not get out of Baru's way. But she did not resist.

THERE was something suicidal in the way Tau perched on the side of their bed. All that luxury behind them, all the possibility of a life. And Tau chose, instead, to crouch at the edge.

They did not react to Baru's entrance. Their hands dangled slack. She sat down on the bed next to them. "Please, your Highness. I need your help. I've made a mistake and I don't know . . . I've made a terrible mistake. I've been wrong about something. I don't know how to fix it. . . ."

"You stink of meat," Tau said.

She felt, distantly, another agonizing cramp. Tau leapt in surprise: she must have screamed. "What's wrong with you?" they said.

"I'm having seizures," Baru said, "and a false miscarriage. And I took too much mason dust, before."

"I would say you deserve it all. But we are in a place where morality and justice have no power."

"Look at me, Tau. Look at this," brandishing her two missing fingers, "at this," the split-open glass cut in her cheek, "at this!" Hammering a fist against the right side of her head. "You're alive, Tau! You're fine! They don't have any power over you! Please, I need your help, can't you help me?"

"Scientism," Tau sniffed.

"Scientism?"

"Your science has explained some things, so you believe that science must explain *all* things. You can't understand what they did to me. So you say nothing was done to me at all."

"You're being a child!"

"Would *you* not despair," Tau snarled, "if this happened to you? If you were taken in by Falcrest and forcibly excommunicated from your— But you don't believe in anything, do you? Nothing but yourself."

She thought about this while her body screamed through another poisoned contraction. It seemed like a fair point.

"You're breathing on me. Stop." Tau put a hand on her shoulder and, without feeling, pushed her off the bed. Her thighs were too cramped up to support her. She slid onto the floor. She had never seen Tau move anyone against their will before.

"It's not your fault," she slurred, "that Abdumasi is one of them. You knew it might happen, didn't you? You told me there were powers he might have called upon to sustain himself, at the cost of all he was to you. He called upon them. It was his choice."

"You're right. It isn't my fault. I can be honest with myself now." Tau did not bother to look down at her. "It's your fault. Everything. My excision. Abdu taken by the cancer. The war to come. All your fault."

She hauled herself up the bed frame, got her chin back onto the blanket. "No, Tau, it's not . . ."

"Really? You'll deny it? You'll deny the obvious? You've subverted me at every turn. You've turned all my efforts to your own. Wasn't I on a mission to find Abdumasi Abd, and to prevent this war with peace and compassion?

"Then *you* arrive. You start war on the Llosydanes. You drive me to flight on *Cheetah,* straight into the Cancrioth's path. My ship is attacked. Many of my house are killed, people I've known since childhood. I'm cast up on your ship, in your control, with a rogue admiral and the Bane of Wives hunting you. We come to Kyprananoke and at *once* there's civil war, the Kettling loosed, the embassy violated. And I am cut out of trim. Everything I have ever cared about is taken from me. I will never be a real person again.

"And here, on this sick ship, I find all my worst fears confirmed, the Cancrioth *is* alive and their tentacles are well up inside us, yes, the Mbo, which I thought had prospered a whole fucking millennium on trim and self-betterment, why, we've been infected the whole time by ancient aristocrats who worship fucking tumors! None of it mattered! None of it!"

Their arm came off their eyes. Baru recoiled, crying out, slamming her elbows against the iroko deck. A blood vessel had burst in Tau's right eye, nightmare red, shimmering with hallucination. Expanding not just through the eye but *out* of it, like a blossom. The more they shouted, the more the blossom grew.

"Stop!" she cried. But Tau did not stop.

"When the Maia invaded, and we thought we'd embraced them into peace, why, it was probably the fucking Cancrioth that set the beetles on their heartland crops! When we appealed to our common decency to stop the displacement of the jungle people, it was probably the fucking Cancrioth who bribed the migrants to turn back! And how about Taranoke, hm? Were you a Cancrioth breeding experiment? Maybe it was a game for them. Maybe one of them bet another, oh ho, watch, I'll turn the fierce Maia into pineapple-eating sluts!"

"I do *not* like pineapple!" Baru snapped, because she was so bemused at being called a slut.

"*YOU DO!*" Tau screamed, and the blood rushed into their eye like poured wine. "I ASKED YOUR PARENTS WHAT FOOD YOU LIKED! AND THEY SAID PINEAPPLE!"

A spasm knocked Baru back onto the floor. She felt her throat fill with bile; felt herself swallow it, aspirate, and begin to choke. All distant, less urgent than her thoughts. Of course Tau had met her parents. They had been tracking Abd, and Abd had been on Taranoke, working with the resistance; Tau would have met with figures in the resistance. Tau would probably ask about everything, even about their child's favorite food, to build those precious bonds of trim.

The spasm passed. She rolled onto her side and coughed up vomit. When she had enough air in her throat to get past the burn she said, "I'm sorry. You're right. I just lied because I wanted to disagree with you. Oh, Wydd, my parents. What will I tell my *parents*? I can't make my parents outlive me. . . ."

If she took the baneflesh, she would never be able to tell her parents that she had done it all for them.

"You can't even tell the truth about pineapple." Tau threw up their hands. "Principles help you, you lied about *pineapple*. You are a hole in the heart."

"Tau, it's not my fault Abdu joined the Cancrioth."

"Of course it's your fault," Tau said, with a gleam of madness in their unbloodied eye, not the madness of insanity but that guilty self-awareness of someone burning a friendship, breaking it forever in a moment's rage. "Because you're really just Farrier. Just a little puppet with his hand up your ass. You do everything he wants. You think you're here to liberate Taranoke? No. You're here for him. You're always working for Farrier. So it's your fault Abdu joined the Cancrioth, because Farrier drove him to do it. *Farrier's* the one who broke us, why didn't she know what it would do to him, *Cairdine* fucking *Farrier* of all people, no wonder Abdu went bad, no wonder, no wonder, *why didn't she know!*"

And just when Baru thought Tau would collapse into sobs of rage, they subsided, and sat on the bed with their fists on their knees, their khanga stretched beneath them, thinking.

"Oh," they said, and sighed.

"What?" Baru's stomach was taut as rigging line. "What?"

"I've been lying to myself. I blame Kindalana for what became of Abdu. What a hypocrite I am." Tau shook their head. "I blamed her for her choice and I never admitted it. I am such a fool."

"I don't understand. . . ."

"Truly trim is real," Tau breathed. "Truly the universe is ruled by the connections between people. We lived together on Prince Hill, beside Lake Jaro. Abdumasi Abd, and Kindalana of Segu, and Cairdine Farrier, and Cosgrad Torrinde, and me. And what happened between us—between our little lives—has altered the whole world. Hasn't it? Listen, it is so:

"The Cancrioth are here to find Abdumasi, because Abdumasi went to Aurdwynn to fight the Masquerade.

"And he wouldn't have joined the Cancrioth or fought the Masquerade if he didn't hate Farrier so much.

"And why does he hate Farrier? Kindalana most of all. So the small summer things of our childhood became the beginning of this war. Isn't it magnificent? You can't explain that with money, or statecraft, or math. The Cancrioth couldn't have arranged any of that, nor the Throne, nor even you, Baru. It is all in the lines between hearts."

From nowhere, sun breaking out of eclipse, Tau smiled.

"Trim," they said. "It's real. Even if I am lost to it."

"Tau," Baru said, nervous as a feral kitten, trying to roll over and get her hands under herself, "I know where to find Abdumasi Abd. My old friend Aminata. The one you call the Burner of Souls. She's *here*. If she's a torturer, a specialist in Oriati, then, you said it yourself, they'd use her to torture Abd. She can lead us to him, can't she? Is it possible that trim drew us together? You to me, me to Aminata, Aminata to bring us to Abdu? Is it possible, Tau, that this is all happening the way it has to happen?"

She waited a moment for Tau's interest. It did not come. "Tau?"

"And what then?"

"What?"

"What happens to Abdu once you find him?"

"I don't know."

"I know. You're going to give him back to the Cancrioth, aren't you? As a bargaining chip for your war against Falcrest. He'll never see Kindalana again. He'll never heal that wound. He's lost. As I am lost. The wound cannot be healed now. We cannot be reconnected."

"Tau, if I can stop Falcrest, if I can stop the war, it doesn't matter what happens to us—"

"No. People are not coins. They are not for you to sacrifice for your own use. Whatever you expect to gain from the Cancrioth, Baru, it will not make the world you want. It will only tear the wound wider."

The contractions were coming further apart now. Like something inside her choosing not to be born. "Tau," she said, through tears of pain. "I came here for help, help making a choice—"

"GET OUT!" the Prince screamed.

And Baru thought, oh Wydd, this rage has been in them all the time, even as they were kind to me. But they've had the art of goodness, the skill of goodness, and it has never failed them, they have always been better than their rage.

Until now. Until I took that goodness from them.

She crawled for the door.

And the whole ship began to scream.

W HAT'S happening?" Shao Lune cried. "What have you *done*?"
Down below them: a sound like a bull charging a steel rod the size of a redwood tree. It came up through the frames of the ship to rattle Baru's jaw so hard it popped in its hinge. Another contraction hit her, and with it that weird ergotic wave through her mind; she staggered headfirst into Shao's stomach.

"Alarm," she grunted, as Shao tried to steady her. "Must be an alarm. Something belowdecks—huge bell, or resonating cavity, or," she grinned at the image, "big cancer elephant, trumpeting, ah, shit," the cramp felt like it would push her heart up her throat, "*shit*."

She gagged more bile onto the beautiful etched deck.

"What did they do to you?" Shao pulled her along, clearly practiced at wrangling puking-drunk shipmates. "You smell like pig filth! Your hands— did you kill someone? Did you murder someone, Baru?"

The contraction peaked and Baru screamed silently into Shao's shoulder. The cool cloth of a cotton tunic beneath her lips: trust Shao to find the good fabric.

"Yawa's here," she gasped. "She's found us. . . ."

"What if it's Ormsment instead? What if she captures us? She'll kill me." Shao shook Baru, not gently. "Are we protected? Did you make the deal? Are we *safe*?"

"No," Baru groaned.

"What?"

"I fucked it up, Shao. I ran. I was almost there, I had an arrangement . . . but the Brain, she wanted me to do this thing, this thing I couldn't do, I couldn't—"

Shao Lune dropped her to the floor. "You stupid gava whore."

The Womb burst into Baru's awareness from the right. She'd hitched her cassock up to run, baring sandals, bruised shins, skinned knees. The poor woman. She must've scrambled up here, carrying a tumor the size of twins.

"Boats," the Womb panted.

Shao kept Baru between her and the Cancrioth woman. "Boats?"

"Galganath's sighted boats. I sent Innibarish to ring the irita obelisk and call everyone to posts." The Womb grimaced at the bile pooled on the floor. "You must call the boats off, Baru, before they try to board us. Or some idiot's going to drop a lantern while loading the cannon and kill us all. Baru? What's wrong with her?"

Baru reached for a lie and the next absence seizure tore it away from her. Time blinked.

She was on the floor, leaning against the wall. Shao Lune and the Womb had leapt to new places. Shao was shouting, "Who are they? Are they navy? If they're navy assault boats then Baru *can't* call them off, you see? They came all this way to kill her."

The Womb wrapped protectively around her tumor. "I don't know. Galganath reported three separate groups. One must be the navy."

"Help." She reached for Shao. "Give me mason dust. I need to finish the bargain. Before it's too late."

Shao sneered in disgust. "You're blacking out and you want *more* dust? When you sit there jabbering in Iolynic, like you're in Aurdwynn again?"

"I spoke?"

"Talking to yourself. Do you do that in private? Try to encourage yourself with royalist fantasies, like a little girl in a mirror?"

"ENOUGH!" the Womb bellowed. The power of her voice seemed to bend the world around Baru. "Osa. Where's Osa?"

Tau's bodyguard climbed from Baru's blind side. The Womb beckoned to her, left-handed, a crude and urgent gesture. "Get your Prince up on maindeck. Maybe we can use Tau's diplomatic seal to keep the boats away."

"The Prince won't be moved," Osa said.

"Move them! Bring the Prince to the deck or you'll both die down here!" the Womb screamed. "Don't you understand? Falcrest has found us! You know what Falcrest does!"

Falcrest—yes. She had to finish the work. She had to follow the roads of porcelain and molten gold to the wellspring and there she would pour in the poison and kill it all.

But she couldn't see the way.

"Where's the Brain?" she said, plaintively. "I have to say yes. . . ."

"Say yes to what?" The Womb loomed in her vision, and there were a thousand faces in her stomach, peering at Baru in horror. "What did the Brain offer you, Baru?"

"I was going to win," Baru said, hollowly. "But I was too afraid. . . ."

The door at the far end of the passageway burst open. Shao Lune gasped in fear: it was the huge man Innibarish. He looked like a bear crawling into a dollhouse.

"Abbatai." His voice was not gentle anymore. "One boat has come alongside. There's a boy in it."

"What boy?"

"He says his name's Iraji, and that he's important to us. He says he's been poisoned, and he won't get the antidote unless we send Baru down in exchange for him. He says that it'll go badly for us unless we do. What should we do?"

Oh, no. Iraji was here. But she'd left him on a houseboat—she'd left him *safe*—

"Baru," the Womb hissed, "can you get us safe passage? Can you—she can't hear me, damn it. Is she mad?"

"Xate Yawa sent the boy." Shao Lune stepped in front of Baru, blocking her from the Womb's sight. "I've been working with her, you know. I led her to you, with the tracer on the boat. Xate Yawa's a Jurispotence, a lord of judges. She's the one who can get you out of here."

The Womb clicked her tongue against her teeth. "This Shate woman, she can control those ships?"

"She can offer Ormsment a pardon. A real Imperial pardon." The thing Shao Lune wanted most for herself. "She'd do anything to get that. Anything except let Baru live."

"Then she's no more use to us. We'll trade her for this boy." The Womb sighed. "What a pitiful mess."

Baru's helpless heart, that poor weak useless organ of foolishness, added Iraji to the list of people she had tried to send away to safety. Muire Lo and Tain Hu and Xate Olake. All dead. Or worse.

No one could escape the game.

She had to speak. She had to say that she was still useful. She had come so far, so many had died for her, she *couldn't* give up, not now, it made no sense. . . .

Suicide, the *Manual of the Somatic Mind* said, was often an impulse. As often as eight times in ten it was unplanned.

She had reached her frontier at last. In these thin wretched hours of star watch, full of poison, absolutely alone, she had discovered that it was possible to feel so terrible and so worthless and so hated by everyone and everything you had ever cared for that you could not even speak a word to save your own life. Tau had not cast a spell on her at all. Tau had simply told her the truth. She had sacrificed everything good about herself, and everyone who had seen good in her, and when she could sacrifice no more, she had looked for others to take on her debt.

Any accountant could have told her you could not defer the debt forever. And it would always be called at the worst time.

"Innibarish." The Womb pointed to Baru with one bright hand. "Take her up to the weather deck and put her off the ship. I'm going to the pharmacy to get every antidote I know. Do not let the boy die. He's hope for Undionash. He's hope for all of us."

INNIBARISH hauled Baru out through crowds of Cancrioth sailors who hauled on capstans and winched in anchors to the beat of a lead drum. When she lost her footing to the last spasms of the ergot poison, or to the post-ictal wreckage in her brain, he carried her.

Iraji waited for her at the rail. His dancer's body was folded wretchedly. She could not see his gold-flecked eyes in the dark.

"I came to rescue you," he said.

They'd dragged him up from his pathetic little dinghy because he was already too sick to climb. Two of the Eye's sailors held him upright. A woman with scarified dots down her cheekbones brought him a bowl of water but he ignored it.

"What were you *thinking*?" Baru screamed at him.

He smiled weakly. "I told you. I came to save you."

"Yawa made you do this?"

"If she didn't have me to trade, she would've done worse."

She had to keep him from the Cancrioth—she had to stop them from realizing who he was. If she couldn't save herself at least she could protect him. . . .

"Why did she make you lie? Why did you tell these people you're important to them?" If he would only play along—

"Baru, don't . . ." He slumped until the sailors at his shoulders caught him, his conditioning against any thought of the Cancrioth battling fear and poison.

She strained against Innibarish's huge arms. "What did she give you, Iraji? What's the antidote?"

"I don't know." He looked embarrassed. He had been a very capable spy, and proud of it. "She put honey in it. I couldn't recognize the taste. She says she'll send the antidote once she has you. I had to come, Baru, I had to take your place, before you did something terrible. . . ."

"You volunteered?" As Tain Hu had volunteered. "Oh, Iraji . . ."

"I had to get you out of here. I knew you were going to do something stupid."

Baru laughed wretchedly. She'd already done something stupid. She'd already fucked it all up. If only she'd said *yes* to the Brain, she would be the sorcerer's ally, under her protection.

But she'd lost her stomach. Run away from the fate Tain Hu had embraced. She had never been worth Hu's love.

The truth was that Sieroch had broken her. Giving up Hu had shattered her. She was no one's savant. She was tired and spent. She wanted to lie down and never wake up.

"Oh, Baru." Tau-indi's voice from her blind side. "Even him? *Even him?*"

"It's not my fault," she groaned. She was so weak, so empty of any self-respect, that she could not stop this cowardice: "He volunteered."

"He's *dying.*" Tau's voice was high with outrage. "What have you done?"

"I don't want to die." Iraji turned watery, pain-wide eyes on Tau. "Your Federal Highness, you mustn't die, either. It'll be all right. We'll be all right, both of us, you'll see. Baru has a plan—"

She did not have a plan.

"A plan for who?" Tau said, bitterly. "No one but herself."

"No, your Highness. Tain Hu believed in her, and my master knew Tain Hu. She wouldn't believe in a false hope."

But she had, hadn't she?

"Abbatai!" The Eye's rich voice, calling out to the Womb, who was coming down the long promenade stairs from the sterncastle. "Who is this boy?"

"I'm the missing Undionash host," Iraji said. "The boy who vanished."

A hush fell across the deck around them. Cancrioth sailors looked up from their work. Baru wished she could seize the clock of the world and run it back a moment, so that she could strike him, vomit on him, *anything* to keep him from saying it.

They could never let him go now.

"I am the missing Undionash host. My mother carried the Spine. I was born to carry it, too. I fled the Cancrioth when I was young, because I was afraid. And now I'm home."

Tau began to weep. "You poor boy. You poor, poor boy."

"You *are* him," the Womb said, in wonder. "You're the boy from Baru's picture."

"And what's wrong with him?" the Eye shouted, pushing through lines of sailors. "Why can't he stand on his own?"

"He's been poisoned—they say they'll send an antidote if we surrender Baru. I brought everything I could, but many of these are fatal at the wrong dose. . . ."

"Then send Baru down!"

"I thought you'd die before you'd let her break the Pale, Virios."

"Fuck the Pale." The Eye looked at Iraji the way Baru had imagined father Solit might one day look at her. "He's Undionash, like Abdumasi. He's a sign of hope. We can't let him die."

He marked Baru with a finger. His cancer horn stared wildly past her. "You are leaving. Now."

Innibarish hauled Baru to the rail. "I'm sorry about this," he murmured. "You seem like you need help."

She got her feet under her. She would walk to Yawa, damn it. That much at least she would do. Tain Hu had walked down to her own drowning unbowed—

A woman's voice cut through the hubbub with the absolute clarity of a geometric proof.

"*Without me?*"

* * *

THE mathematician Kimbune came running down the deck from the prow. The circle-and-line tattoo on her forehead glistened with sweat, and she wiped tears from her red eyes.

"You were just going to send her *away*? When she knows where to find Abdumasi, and my husband's soul?"

"Kimbune, please," the Womb groaned. "The Brain lied to you. She doesn't know."

"And *you* do? You know better than her?" Kimbune shouted. "You're going to give up, sail home!"

The Womb and the Eye looked at each other in dismay. "Kimbune," the Womb sighed, "this boy is one of us, and he's dying. The only way we can save him is to send Baru away—"

"All that remains of my husband lives in Abdumasi Abd." Kimbune's voice trembled with outrage. "I will not lose his chance at eternity. Not for anything. The Brain says Baru can find him. So I am going with Baru."

The poor mathematician was going to give herself to Yawa. She'd be vivisected. They'd pull the cancer from her living flesh and give it to Hesychast.

"Osa," Baru rasped. "Osa, come here."

As the others argued, the Jackal soldier woman leaned her head close.

"You must not let Tau kill themself," Baru whispered. "Please. They will want to live again, soon. Their flame burns strong. Just don't let it blow out now."

Then Baru made herself walk to the rail. If she went fast enough maybe she could leave Kimbune behind.

Black water below. She could jump, and no one would ever find her body. . . .

"You'll only give them a hostage!" the Eye shouted at Kimbune. "You'll be cut open before their Parliament. You *can't* go!"

"I don't care," Kimbune said, determinedly. "I have to save him. Someone fetch Baru's things! Didn't she come with things? Bring them here!"

"Baru, you bitch!" Shao Lune shouted. Two sailors held her back as she tried to bolt after Baru. "You promised you'd get me out of here! You *promised*! When Yawa lobotomizes you, you'd better beg her to save me! I hope it's all you can think about!"

Baru could not bear to look back.

Someone threw a rope ladder over the side for her. She looked down and saw, directly below, Iraji's empty dinghy. Out in the dark green shadows of the caldera water, ripples of phosphorescence betrayed more boats closing in through the dark. A rocket flare ignited overhead. The sputtering light shadowed *Eternal*'s huge barnacled hull, the cannon-ports, the streaks of effluent along the golden skin. Far below the bladed fin of the cancer whale circled like a scream.

She put her leg over the side and found the ladder. She lifted her other trembling leg over. She began to descend.

"Baru."

She looked back.

The Brain was there, a halo of uranium light cast from her hands onto the torc around her neck, a horrible strain in her eyes. She looked as if all the strength had been drawn from her: as if the baneflesh pig had put a straw straight into her soul and suckled.

But she was coming through the crowd, beating them aside with the power of her presence. There was still blood on her hands, on her sandaled feet. She drew Kimbune with her, pulling her like an ox.

The Brain threw out her hand to Baru, and in that hand there was light like water. She cried out in En Elu Aumor. The light arced between them, fountain-jet in air, and splashed over Baru's scalp.

"Return to me," the Brain shouted. "I bind you thus. I find you. You find me. We complete our pact. It is happening now, in our future; this is our memory, recalled in that moment. They are the same. Ayamma, ayamma, am amar!"

An ergot cramp kicked at Baru's thighs. One of her feet slipped. She was weaker than Tain Hu. Tain Hu hadn't lost her grip. Tain Hu had managed to hold on to her chains until she drowned.

She grabbed for the ladder. But the rope her hands found was not real: it was the tenuous, hallucinatory strand, thin as spidersilk, that led up to the deck and to Kimbune.

How odd, she thought, with some uncorroded inner curiosity. I thought the Cancrioth didn't have trim.

Then she fell.

8

SURRENDER

SHE fell down the freeboard of a ship taller than any she had ever known.

But *Eternal* was not taller than the cliffs on Taranoke, where the divers plunged like herons and came up grinning. She managed to get her feet pointed. The filthy cassock billowed around her, fluttering like moth wings.

Impact.

Seawater flooded her mouth, poured through the split-glass cut in her right cheek. The slap of contact did what all her self-flagellation couldn't. It made her want to act. The only thing in the world she needed to do was get to the surface and breathe: and that, at least, she could manage.

She scrabbled for the boatwale of Iraji's dinghy and tried to pull herself aboard. She couldn't. She fell back into the bath-warm water, just her nose above the surface. It was all right. She would rest here for a moment. It was all right—

Kimbune grabbed her by her wounded right hand and hauled. Baru screamed in pain, unable, for a moment, to understand what force had seized her: her damn blind right!

"Careful!" Baru cried, and then, without warning, found herself on her ass in the shallow bilgewater, aching.

"Are you all right?" Kimbune cried. "I was trying to help you. You went all limp."

"The ergot's still giving me seizures." She struggled up to sit on a thwart. "It'll pass."

"Ergot? Who gave you ergot?"

"A madwoman."

"Which one?" Kimbune asked, nervously, and then began to laugh. Baru, bloody-tongued, helpless, began to cackle along with her.

"Oh Alu." Kimbune looked out into the dark pool of the caldera. "What have I done?"

"What *have* you done?" Baru could not believe the others had let her go.

"I'm coming with you to find my husband."

"Abd?"

"My husband who is in Abd." Kimbune showed Baru a canvas sack. "I packed a few of your things. Your mask. Your odd little calculator. That boy up there, is he really the Undionash child?"

Iraji! Baru scrabbled around beneath her, searching for some kind of signal, a flare pistol or a lantern, that would make Yawa give up the antidote. There had to be a clue what to do, where to go. . . .

"Listen," she snapped. "When I'm gone, you must tell Xate Yawa that the Cancrioth is prepared to release plague in Aurdwynn if you're not returned safely. Tell her that. Remember to specify Aurdwynn, not Falcrest. Do you understand? You have to protect yourself. That will keep her from hurting you."

"Gone? Where are you going?" The mathematician clutched the canvas bag to her chest. Lumps of shape betrayed the contents: the arc of Baru's mask, books, balls of clothing, two heavy cylinders that made dull noises as they struck each other. Kimbune's long-lashed eyes peered warily over the bag at Baru.

"I'm not going to survive this," Baru said. It was a liberating thought.

"Nobody will hurt *me*," Kimbune said, hopefully. "I'm carrying the most important thing in the world. It'll protect me."

There was no flare pistol anywhere, no sign of a signal Baru could send. Yawa wouldn't just let Iraji die, would she? She grabbed at the oar in her lock, took one haul, and set the boat spinning. There were two oars, damn it! Where was the one on the right?

"What's that?" she asked. "What's the most important thing in the world?"

"A proof."

"*A proof?*"

"I can't tell you," Kimbune said, clutching her bag. "It's too powerful. The bastard went and died before I could convince him, but it's true, I've finished it and it's beautiful and he was wrong, five hundred years he was *wrong*—"

"Wait a moment. Do you mean your husband?"

"Yes!"

"Are you desperate to get to your husband's soul so you can . . . win an *argument*?"

"It's an important argument!" Kimbune cried. "Don't look at me that way. Who's that over there?"

"Who? Where?" Baru stared into the dark. Saw boats silhouetted against wormlight.

"Yawa?" she called. "Yawa, I'm here. Give him the antidote."

Dark shapes shuffled around, a vague exchange of negative spaces. Then someone stood up in the prow of one of the boats. Raised a lantern.

"Baru? Is that you?"

Not the last voice in the world she had expected to hear: not, after all, Tain Hu's voice. But precious anyway, as unexpected as a shaft of moonlight in a cave. And Baru saw her on the prow of her boat, coming closer, uniformed, upright, every inch in command, and reaching out to save her.

Aminata.

A MINATA pulled Baru off her boat and didn't let her go.

Baru squawked and tried to put her feet down but Aminata crushed her close, held her, muttered in her ear, "Hey, you asshole." She smelled of honest sweat and aftershave. Her scalp beneath the mask was fresh razor-smooth black.

"Hi," Baru groaned, and for a moment Aminata held all her weight.

"You've got some kind of glue on your head," Aminata said.

"Oh." The Brain's glowing ichor hadn't come off in the sea. "It's, uh, it's like jellyfish tea."

Aminata fussed at the stain. "Can't you go *anywhere* without starting a civil war?"

Baru croaked a little laugh. "This one's really not my fault."

"I saw you at the embassy—"

"I saw *you*!"

"—I had to burn the grounds, I thought I'd killed you—"

"—you did the right thing, it was Kettling—"

"—I had to talk to you, I had to know—"

"—I'm here, I'm here, please, but let's get away, let's go."

The marines searched an indignant Kimbune for hidden weapons. Aminata whistled up at the ship that loomed above them. "That's Cancrioth?"

"You know about them?"

"Yeah. A little. Well, no, not at all, except that they're some kind of secret society, and the Admiralty wants to know more. Did you come looking for them?"

Could Baru answer that honestly? She had to sort out Aminata's loyalties, but it was so hard to think. . . .

"Baru?"

She tried to tally all the ways Aminata might be a trick. Could Ormsment have sent her to lure Baru in? To get to Baru before Yawa did? Or what if she was off *Ascentatic,* sent by the loyal navy to erase all hints of the Cancrioth's existence *and* Ormsment's mutiny?

Aminata wilted. Her shoulders slumped, her mask tipped down, her hands went limp at her sides. "Baru," she said, not a question, "you're not going to tell me the truth."

"I— I've had a hard day—"

"Me too, remember?"

"I know, I know, but things have happened—"

"I'd say things have happened! Baru, I came here to clear your name, but you've got to explain—first the Llosydanes, now the embassy, Tau-indi Bosoka caught in the attack—it's like you've been *trying* to lure Ormsment into battle with the Oriati, so you can blame it all on the navy—"

"Ormsment's trying to kill me!"

"I know! Captain Nullsin knows! So tell me something to prove she's wrong! Tell me why you're *not* out here to start a war!"

"No," Baru rasped.

"No!?"

"No, we're not going to do this. We will *not* be the friends who refuse to sit down and get the truth out. I'm going to tell you everything that's happened"— well, almost everything—"it's just, please, right now someone's coming for me, and we have to . . ."

The words fell from her lips. She couldn't escape. If Baru fled from Yawa, then Iraji would die.

She had to turn herself in for the lobotomy.

"Have to do what?" Aminata's shoulders squared. Duty held her up like rigging holds up a mainmast, bracing Aminata's soul under any weight. In that moment Baru loved her as deeply as she'd ever loved a friend. "What do you need?"

"I have to . . . turn myself over. There's someone watching us right now. A woman named Xate Yawa."

"The Jurispotence of Aurdwynn, right." Aminata nodded as if this made perfect sense. "The prisoners said she was traveling with you—"

"What prisoners?" Baru hissed. "Aminata, what prisoners?"

"The rebels, right? From Tain Hu's household? Ake Sentiamut and her cadre. I found them on the Llosydanes." Aminata made a little grin of pride. "A man named Calcanish led me to them, and they said they'd been expecting me. They said they knew that I was going to get a letter from the—"

Tain Shir had used one of those prisoners against Baru. Made Baru choose between the cook Nitu's life and her own. When Baru had chosen poorly, Shir had cut off two of her fingers.

"Aminata, where are these prisoners, and who *exactly* has them right now—"

There was a *plop* in the darkness, and then, a moment later, a splash.

The marine lookout said, softly, "Second boat's coming in."

"Who's that?" Baru whispered. "Aminata, who's there?"

"I came with another boat," Aminata whispered back. "She was supposed to be right behind us. When I saw you I ordered us in and she must've hung back. . . ."

"*She?* Who's she?"

The second *plop* was closer, and the second splash was louder. Something alien whistled in the dark: the sound of air forced through a bent flute or a broken bone. A wet *chuff* and a soft moan.

"Galganath?" Kimbune whispered. "Galganath, is that you?"

One of the marines unshuttered a lantern and turned it toward the sound. The cone of light found huge, grinning jaws. A white patch like a staring eye with no pupil. The cancer whale's black true eye shone beneath it like a dark star.

But there was another monster in the lantern light.

TAIN Shir.

She crouched on the prow of her boat with spears bundled across her back and a fat fish in her hands. Her face fell in shadow. Two stiff and deferential marines rowed her boat closer. Behind her, in the boat's belly, canvas swaddled a row of human forms.

Baru edged in front of Aminata to hide her from Shir's gaze.

"Shir!" Aminata called, butting up against Baru, trying to push past. "I've got her. Let's get her to safety and I can sort out the truth."

"Yes," Shir said. "Let's sort out the truth about Baru."

She threw the fat fish to the whale. Huge jaws clapped shut on it. The beast whuffled in delight. Shir stooped, grabbed, and hauled someone up from under the canvas. She was a woman in sailor's slops and a diver's strophium, her smooth, fat-padded stomach bare. Shir lifted her by the scruff of her neck. The woman was long as a seal and limp as death. There was no expression at all on her face.

She was Ulyu Xe, the diver, very briefly Baru's second lover. She was here so Baru could order her death. Exactly as Tain Shir had promised, last time Baru had faced her.

The diver will be next. Then your parents.

The stumps of Baru's missing fingers thrilled with the memory of Shir's cold machete, falling free, part of her forever separate. She had stared in wonder at the wound even as she screamed.

"The Bane of Wives." Kimbune sat forward in fascination. "The one who escaped the Renderer. It's *her*. . . ."

How, Baru wanted to cry? How are you here, Ulyu Xe? I sent you home to Aurdwynn! I saved you! How did Aminata find you? How did she bring you here? *I saved you!*

But her women always came back to die.

"That's my prisoner!" Aminata cried. She and Baru jostled each other, Baru trying to conceal her, Aminata trying to force her way forward. The marines behind them were muttering in confusion. "Set her down, do you hear me? We don't threaten prisoners!"

Tain Shir whispered into Ulyu Xe's ear. The diver twisted hard in her grip, naked abdomen torquing, a meaningless dance, grotesque exhibition. Her face was blank. Shir stared at Baru, as if willing her to grasp some lesson in Xe's body, in this body Baru had wanted and been wanted by: sex and death, death and sex, together.

Baru felt the most awful, incredible, despicable kind of jealousy. Had Shir fucked her? Had she seduced Xe, had she crouched with Xe's back arched against her stomach, trembling with effort? It wasn't that Baru was jealous or possessive of Xe's body or what she chose to do with it. No, it was that—that—

—that Shir had stolen Baru's story. Xe was *her* lover. Shir couldn't kill her. Xe was supposed to die for *Baru*.

What a diseased, repulsive thing to feel.

And yet Baru felt it. She undeniably felt it.

"Show her the others," Shir commanded.

One of her marines yanked the canvas sheet free. Shackled beneath were the survivors of Tain Hu's house. The herbalist Yythel, who had been Xate Olake's lover, before he discovered Baru's treachery, and his twin sister's treachery, and went mad.

The forester Ude Sentiamut and his pimply adopted boy Run.

Ake Sentiamut, who should be governing half of Aurdwynn by now.

No sign of Dziransi, the Stakhieczi brave man—

"Hey!" Aminata shouted. "You put that woman down or I'll have words for the admiral!"

"I can't," Tain Shir called back. "I'm not in control here."

The Cancrioth whale whistled softly through its blowhole. There was metal in there, fitted into the flesh. Did it suffer? Baru didn't know.

"I order you to put her down!" Aminata shouted.

"I can't," Shir said. "I have to do what Baru tells me. I am under her command."

"What?" Aminata whirled. "What the fuck does she mean?"

"I killed her cousin," Baru whispered. "I sacrificed Tain Hu."

"Baru?"

"So I could escape the Throne's control. I sent her to die."

"Baru?"

"And I didn't realize," Baru said, as everything caved in, as she finally admitted what she had for so long refused to coalesce into a single thought, "I didn't realize why I did it. She's trying to show me."

Shir drew a machete and lifted it to Ulyu Xe's throat. "Do I kill her, or do I kill you?"

"I can't," Baru croaked.

"You must. You must choose. One by one. For you to live, you must choose for them to die. As it was with Hu, so will it be here."

"Please don't. Please."

"I don't control the terms." Shir had the brutal ghost of Tain Hu's face, bones and skin the same, but where Hu had painted high cheekbones and tied up long hair, Shir's face was a naked map of scars, Shir's hair was hacked off and burnt. "I only enforce your precedent. This is the world you chose to live in. A world governed by your law."

"Could you kill her?" Aminata muttered to one of her marines. "One shot? Before she could cut that woman's throat?"

"Hit her? Yes, definitely. But she'd see me aiming, mam."

No, Baru thought. You can't kill her. Those aren't the rules.

The rules say I have to choose.

And it was time to make the right choice.

S HE was alone.

Tau-indi Bosoka had tried to warn her that the Cancrioth would strip away her connections to the human world. And if she wanted to laugh that off as superstition, well, O Incrastic scientist, *hadn't* she lost everything? Who was left to her? Her choices had brought doom down even on her own parents.

How was any of this going to help Aurdwynn? Or Taranoke? Even if she brought Kettling to Falcrest, how could she stop it from spreading to the provinces?

How had she in any way lived up to Tain Hu's trust? Tau-indi alienated,

Tain Hu's companions about to be butchered, Iraji given to the Cancrioth, Xate Yawa here to seize her and take her away, plague and war . . .

Only Falcrest would benefit from this madness. Falcrest and Cairdine Farrier.

Kyprananoke was tearing itself apart like a dog gnawing at the rot that would kill it. In a month there would be nothing here except fire and gunsmoke and a skullbacked whale gliding through the bodies in the sea. The world had rubbed thin. Something horrible was coming into it.

And it was coming in through Baru. She was the wound.

Farrier had made her so.

"A theory of perfect rule," said the dead man in the Elided Keep, the one whose letter had greeted Baru on her first day in the Throne. "A means by which the Imperial Republic of Falcrest may be rendered causally closed, so that the sprout of every seed and the turn of every cyclone occurs in accordance with our predictions, and therefore in accordance with our decrees. Thus we may at last achieve the state of ruling without ruling, a self-governing world."

And then he went on, as the letter had not, in the voice of Cairdine Farrier:

"A self-governing world shall require a self-governing citizen. It will require a woman who can without coercion or persuasion be trusted to make perfect choices to keep the Masquerade strong. Once this citizen can be created, then the Republic will last forever. No force of law will be required. All citizens will gladly perform their own functions, for no reason except the joy of it. This is the great desire of Renascent, the Throne Reborn. And I must prove to her that I am the way to fulfill this desire."

"And this requires," dead Muire Lo explained, as the plague swelled his face into an atlas of pus, "that the law of the Republic be written into the individual citizen, and passed down perfectly from generation to generation, more perfectly than the color of the eye is passed. The citizen must become a self-ruling subject."

"I see," Baru said, into the fortifications of her mind, and she felt a pain and a satisfaction in her cramped bowel like digestion, like the digestion of the whole world, for she *did* see, she understood. "Hesychast the eugenicist says, *we must breed the perfect citizen.*

"And against him, Itinerant the trader says, *we must teach them to rule themselves.*

"So I am his model. A wild-type islander girl taught to govern herself perfectly. Taught to obey Falcrest no matter how terribly she wants to resist. Taught to deny herself the companionship and compassion she requires. I am his proof to Renascent that his method triumphs over Hesychast's eugenics. I am the one who will always obey, because I can always rationalize my obedience as my own will."

In Urunoki, Baru gasped: "I am his weapon. . . ."

REMEMBER the Cold Cellar?

In that pit of Incrastic hygiene, Xate Yawa used simple conditioning to treat marital infidelity. Show a woman her husband, and at the same time feed her a pleasant smell, dose her with a wonderful drug. Soon the woman will learn to associate pleasant feelings with the husband.

Show this woman a man who is *not* her husband, a man like the men she lusts for. Then make her taste acid, and batter at her ears with a horrible gong. She will learn to cringe away from those men.

This was the technique of simple conditioning.

But there were more sophisticated techniques. One of them was called *operant conditioning*, or, in clinical parlance, *paired-icon behavioral coaxing*.

In this paradigm, the subject was always allowed to make her own choices. No external force inflicted stimuli. No handsome stranger or faithful husband, no soft music or crashing gong. The subject was offered the illusion of freedom. The experimenter only controlled the *response* to her choices.

As the subject explored possible actions, and discovered the planned responses, she was allowed to teach herself the rules of the conditioning.

The rules of the conditioning were this—

When Baru's mother Pinion and father Salm had gone away to war, Baru had begged her father Solit to let her go to the Masquerade school, so that she could understand what was happening to her world.

She removed *herself* from her family. The school rewarded her with knowledge and power. How swiftly and quietly she'd transferred her loyalties. . . .

Then Salm had vanished. Farrier had ordered it, hadn't he? Of course he'd ordered it. Of *course* he'd ordered it. Confused by grief, Baru had asked her mother: *Was he my father, or was he only a sodomite?*

Pinion had cried out in horror at the Masquerade word, and struck Baru in fury. She punished Baru for asking, just as the school rewarded her for inquiry. The pain of Salm's disappearance became something that Baru's own mother inflicted on her. Something that the school eased.

Her cousin Lao had come for help to escape a rapist teacher. Baru had befriended Aminata, and used the navy's influence to get the rapist fired. Farrier had been very angry with her. But he had not taken Aminata away, had he? He had not deprived Baru of the friendship she treasured, for it was not Farrier's role in the Process to cause pain or hardship.

No. He had tricked Aminata into rebuking Baru, beating her, screaming at her that there was only one punishment fit for a tribadist: the circumcising knife.

Through her mother, and through Aminata, Baru had taught herself that connections led to pain.

And then—

And then—

Farrier had deployed Baru to Aurdwynn.

After years of preparation, Farrier had allowed his student to slip the leash.

Where she obeyed the lessons he'd taught her.

She took Apparitor's bargain: give up Aurdwynn to gain power in Falcrest. Just as she'd traded her family for the Masquerade school.

She'd used the navy to sidestep Governor Cattlson and insinuate herself with the rebels, just as she'd once allied herself with Aminata to get rid of the rapist teacher Diline.

She'd betrayed and murdered her navy pawns at Welthony Harbor: because hadn't she learned that the navy could be useful, but also that the navy would never be her true friend?

She'd met a family *exactly* like her own, a mother and two fathers, Duchess Nayauru with her lovers Duke Autr and Duke Sahaule. And she'd destroyed that family. Just as her own had been destroyed. She'd ambushed them in their traveling camp as Salm had been ambushed in his.

She'd met a woman she loved.

And she'd kept that woman at a distance, despite Tain Hu's cunning and charisma and devastating presence, despite Baru's own fantasies. She'd kept that woman at arm's reach until the very night she *knew* Tain Hu and all the rest of the rebels were doomed.

Only then had she allowed herself to fall.

When their love could only lead to death.

As she had allowed herself to be with Ulyu Xe only on the night before they were separated.

As she had allowed herself to be with Shao Lune only when drunk and desperate and certain Shao Lune was using her.

She loved women only when that love was deniable and doomed. Farrier had taught her so. How could she have missed it?

What had she told herself even as she chose Tain Hu to be her queen?

I will destroy myself if I choose.

On this one day I will not deny what I am.

In that very moment of defiance *she had recapitulated the law that had been taught to her.* To confess what she was, to indulge her love for women, meant destruction. She had said it herself! To be what she was *was to destroy herself*! Exactly as Farrier required her to believe!

Hadn't her battle in Aurdwynn been a battle of two fronts: one to prove her skill at conspiracy, and one to prove her mastery of self-repression? Hadn't her talent at concealing her true loyalties from the Coyote *been the same talent she used to conceal her true feelings from Tain Hu?*

Hadn't she come to see those two skills *as the same*?

No wonder Farrier had celebrated when he learned that she'd executed Tain Hu. No wonder he'd cried *Falcrest is saved*! His process had worked. He had educated a bright young foreign woman to become a perfect self-governing subject. He could send her anywhere, on any mission, *and she would continue to rule herself by Falcrest's law.* He could leave her with the most desirable and interested woman in the world and Baru would find a way to deny her own want unless it was paired with that woman's extinction.

Cosgrad Torrinde the Hesychast had his Clarified, people like Iscend Comprine, who were born and raised in Metademe conditioning. Hesychast believed that Baru would never overcome her own nature. The flesh mastered the mind, and Baru Cormorant's flesh could never kill Tain Hu.

But Hesychast was wrong.

Baru was Farrier's monument, his exemplar, his masterpiece. A degenerate child molded into a brilliant Imperial agent. A tribadist who, even when dispatched into rebel woods to consort with warrior duchesses, enforced her own chastity until the night before the end. A traitor who would voluntarily return to Falcrest, to her own repression and to Farrier's control. Because she believed she was a savant, a hard woman, someone who sacrificed what she must in order to do what was necessary. Someone who *had* to be alone.

Behold the chains he placed on you.

His law lived in Baru. Everything she accomplished was tainted by it.

If I show you favor, woman, then you will die.

And through that death I will progress.

She wore an invisible mask: the laughing face of Cairdine Farrier, carved into the skull of her soul.

"AMINATA."

"Baru?" Pushed up against Baru's right shoulder, she must've felt Baru go rigid. "What is she doing? Why is she saying these things?"

Ulyu Xe dangled limp from Tain Shir's arm. Her soul had withdrawn from all contact with the world. Baru hated to imagine the things Shir had whispered to her in the dark: the truth about Baru.

"Aminata," she said. "Did Cairdine Farrier ask you to beat me and scream at me?"

"I—what—?"

"In school, Aminata. It's important. When you called me a tribadist. Did Farrier ask you to do that?"

"Yes, he said you needed a good fright from a friendly face, so you'd watch yourself and not get into worse trouble later—"

Baru nodded. "All right, then. Aminata, listen. I can't explain it all. There's no time. Just know—please—that I did it all for my parents and my home. That isn't a lie. That's the truth. I thought I was helping my home."

"Baru, what's *happening*?"

Tain Shir spoke in Maia Urun, the ancestral tongue of Baru's home; spoke as if she could taste Baru's thoughts. "Farrier is your secret master, for his mastery is secret from you. He has concealed it within your pride. He has dominated you through your conviction that you secretly resist him. There is no difference between pretending to obey Farrier and committing yourself utterly to his control."

Something cried out to Baru—something she'd heard—a sword, and a throne, and a voice, Tain Hu's loving voice, saying,

She'll make you worse, if she can. Don't let her. I always tried to make you better.

Listen. Listen. There is a difference between acting out their story, and truly obeying their story. Do you know what it is?

Baru could not remember the answer. She could not bring it to mind. It was lost in the darkness of her right.

So she made her choice.

"I want to be free of him," she said. "I want that more than I want anything."

Shir dropped Ulyu Xe down into the arms of the marines behind her. She smiled, no, she grinned, a big happy grin, like a proud friend.

"You understand," she said. "You understand now. Be free."

She shrugged loose a spear and fitted it into her atlatl.

"Shoot her!" Aminata barked.

But the marine marksman hesitated. He was looking up at Baru with eyes full of hate and fear. This man was Ormsment's, and he could not bring himself to save Baru's life.

Tain Shir cast her spear.

Aminata shoved Baru out of the way.

"*NO!*" Baru screamed, as Aminata went down with the spear in her breastbone, as Kimbune screamed in fear and the marines bellowed in confusion. No, Wydd, no, take it back, not Aminata, not for her, *not for her*—

"Ah," Tain Shir said, with some satisfaction. "She did truly believe she was your friend."

She reached to draw another spear from the bundle on her back.

A needle went through her hand.

IT happened so fast that Baru thought she'd had another seizure. A narrow steel shaft, finned like a crossbow bolt, through and through Shir's palm: and Shir already yanking the dart out, whirling, her reflexes faster than Baru's thought as she turned to meet—

Iscend Comprine.

Baru had learned her own egocentric weakness, her habit of forgetting about the other players on the board. She'd resolved to think about people more, to remember their inner lives.

What did it say about her, and her idea of the Clarified, that she'd not spared more than one thought for Iscend tonight?

Iscend was Clarified, born from the choicest eugenic material and raised in Hesychast's Metademe, conditioned from birth to put the well-being of the Imperial Republic before all else.

Baru had never expected to see her again.

The Clarified woman stood loose-kneed on the prow of her own launch. Her body soaked up the tremor of the waves, compressing and relaxing. She held a pistol crossbow, the sort that was always loaded with poison bolts. And, in her off hand, the segmented red shape of a Burn grenade.

"I've poisoned you," she said. "It's curare. You'll stop breathing in five minutes unless you do exactly as I say."

"Gaios!" Shir barked at her. "Stop!"

Iscend froze, except her face, where there should have been a smile. *Gaios* was her Clarified command word. It should pull her mind around like a leash.

Instead she frowned. A tremendous warping grimace that broke her perfect high-boned mountain-fox face in two.

"No," she said.

In the boat with Baru, Aminata arched and yelled. "It's in the jack! Get it out!" The fishing spear had penetrated her combat harness, but stopped against the layers of steel and fabric beneath. One of her marines pounced on her, put a boot on her rib cage, and pulled.

The bent heads of the prisoners flashed through Baru's awareness—there was Ake, pale hair strung across an exhausted pale face; there was Ulyu Xe, limp in Ake's embrace; the boy Run crying in silent fear and anger as Ude, his bearded guardian, tried to cover him. The herbalist Yythel huddled in the stern with sour displeased exhaustion on her face.

Above them all Tain Shir loomed, reaching up, drawing one of the spears bound across her back.

"Gaios," she repeated to Iscend. "Be still. Be still."

Iscend's boat glided closer.

Iscend grinned, as if she'd just had a brilliant idea.

And she said, "Gaios. I will not."

She had used her own command word. Impossible.

"Kneel." Shir reached for her as her boat came closer. "Kneel, gaios, kneel and comply."

"Gaios. I refuse."

"You will not harm me. I know your word."

"You do know my word. But I have a purpose here and I do not serve by departing from it."

"What is your purpose? Gaios. Tell me."

Iscend's smile went impish, perversely sly: what could perversion mean in the mind of a Clarified woman? She was bending her own programming, and it delighted her.

"I am here to protect Baru," she said. "She is necessary."

"To who?"

"To Durance. To my master Hesychast. To me."

Shir said, low and slow, "Gaios. Kneel."

"Gaios. I refuse."

"You will *obey your word!*" Shir bellowed. "Gaios! Kneel!"

Iscend trembled with the force of the command. Her wavering legs nearly pitched her backward. Her body corrected her balance with automatic perfection, and as she came back low and centered she said, silently, *gaios,* and the motion of that automatic balance became a twitch in her finger, and the crossbow fired.

The needle bolt went through Shir's other hand as it passed before her face, and pinned that hand to the spear beneath. Shir grunted without inflection: neither pain nor surprise. Curare again, no doubt. Something melancholy about the sight of a monster so awful and primordial brought low by merely rational means.

Iscend's boat bumped up against Shir's. Shir lunged without expression, thrusting down from overhead, like a fisherman, into Iscend's chest, roaring

"Gaios!" to freeze her there: and Iscend grimaced at the word, the grimace became a shiver, the shiver became a movement, a sidestep, catching the haft of that spear and pulling, Shir growling as the spear tore itself from her grip and yanked the crossbow bolt out of her hand. Iscend threw the spear away and leapt from her boat to Shir's, who grabbed at her collar, her belt, her hair, any point of leverage that would let her grapple the smaller woman. But Iscend slipped through her hands like she was greased. Close inside Shir's guard, she kneed the bigger woman in the groin and went for her throat. A blur of violence as they grappled: Iscend's fluid efficiency and her smile of delight, as if she astounded herself with every maneuver, and Shir as inelegant, as brutal as a shark breaching with a seal in her jaws, battering it to death against the rocks.

One of the marines rowing Shir's boat grabbed for Iscend's legs.

She leapt his grip and kicked him, backward, in the face. But Shir got Iscend's arm, outthrown for balance, and with a roar of effort she extended it so far Baru was sure it would pop from its socket—

Iscend whirled with Shir's pull. She saved her arm but could not get out of Shir's reach. One bloody hand closed over her face, clawing at her eyes.

Shir grunted like a bear and dug in.

Iscend's free arm tucked the red shape of the Burn grenade into Shir's waistband.

"Gaios!" Baru screamed, terrified for Ulyu Xe and Ake and all the others, all those who would burn with Shir, "NO!"

Iscend's finger hooked through the grenade's rip-ring.

The Cancrioth whale bumped its head against the boat.

Not even Clarified were trained to include cancer whales in their kinesthetic choreography. Iscend tipped backward and Shir, still clutching her face and throat, went down with her, both together, into the dark water.

MOTHER*FUCKER!*" Aminata shouted. She grabbed Baru by the shoulder and hauled herself upright. "Stand down, stand down, police your weapons! I'm in command here! Marines, as Ormsment's staff captain, I'm in command until we figure out what the fuck is happening! Stand down!"

For a moment it was going to be all right.

Then a beam of light pinned them all in place. A point of chemical fire cupped in a focusing mirror, bright enough to blind.

"Put 'em up," Faham Execarne called. "I want hands right up. We have a hwacha trained on you, and a barge full of angry men behind it. Bows down, hands up. You too, Agonist. You especially.

"In the name of the Morrow Ministry of the Imperial Republic, by the authority of the Jurispotence-at-Large Xate Yawa, you are all under my arrest."

W HERE is my niece?" Yawa's mechanical mask ground each word like a coffee mill. "Where is Tain Shir?"

The Morrow Ministry agents cinched Baru's straitjacket tighter. "She went in," Baru gasped. "She was shot in the hand, poisoned with curare. Then she fell into the water."

"Where is Iscend Comprine?"

"In the water. You didn't know she'd do that, did you? You sent her to keep me alive, but you didn't know how far she'd go. Oh, Yawa! Your women keep trying to die for me."

The Morrow-men were going now, leaving Baru alone, straitjacket bound to metal, Xate Yawa looming over her.

"Never again," Yawa said. "You'll never hurt anyone I treasure *ever* again."

The dawn rose through the skylight behind her. They had hauled Baru away from the others, onto a makeshift landing and up an ancient lava tube. Maybe no one had been here since the Day of Thunder Capes, when Mount Tsunuq blew itself apart. On the day of that eruption, some ancient Jellyfish Eater, a liturgy from the Tiatro Tsun come to watch the dawn, might have stared down through the skylight above Baru to see the fire surging below.

The gods of fire had passed through and gone. Only burnt stone remained.

Baru felt the sore crown around her head, that ring of hurt which marked her worst days of ennui. She was ready to close her eyes for a while.

You spent all you had. And there was no one left to draw a loan from, no more divers on the soft grass, no more officers with sly cruel faces, no more gentle Tau-indi or sweet Iraji or even Apparitor to shout at you.

You were spent.

She wondered what would happen to Kimbune. Faham Execarne had fixated on her, although Kimbune was pretending not to speak Aphalone. "The Cancrioth!" he kept shouting, as if volume could get his point across. "Are you *really* the Cancrioth? Amazing. Amazing! King's balls, we can't let Parliament know about this. Where's Tau? They must be a dreadful mess right now, I've got to reassure them—"

Baru did not have to care about any of that anymore.

She closed her eyes and sighed. A cool wind blew up the lava tube. Here inside the volcano the air smelled exactly and wonderfully like Taranoke.

"Yawa," she said, "will you tell Admiral Ormsment that I've gone, please? So that my parents will be safe."

It was done now. She could rest.

The Cancrioth would never find Abdumasi Abd. Falcrest would drive Oriati Mbo to civil war and lay its eggs in the wounds and pillage the whole continent. Vultjag would remain a poverty-stricken hamlet, unless the avalanche of Stakhiecz invasion wiped Tain Hu's home entirely away. Iraji would live out his life incubating cancer. Svir's lover, the Empire Admiral Lindon Satamine, would be murdered by a Parliamentary purge during the war. And Tau-indi Bosoka would die bitter and alone, all their faith in trim destroyed.

But it didn't matter. She was going to die. Nothing would be her problem any longer.

How badly she'd wanted to stay in that moment when she woke in Tain Hu's arms. How terribly she'd wished that she would never think another thought. The first time in her life, maybe, that she'd wished for ignorance.

"I'll fetch my instruments," Yawa said, and disappeared into Baru's blindness, to make the lobotomy ready.

Tain Hu's ghost hand cupped the right of her face.

Go away, Baru thought. I'm bruised. You're hurting my eye.

But the hand would not go.

Baru lifted her face to the dawn that came down glorious through the skylight. The morning birds were rising, rising, thousands of them singing to each other, tens of thousands, lifting from the black slopes of el-Tsunuqba, voice of the mountain, *Taranoke, Taranoke, I am the burnt and unpeopled husk of Taranoke, I am your home as you deserve to find it, I am the true and empty shape of your heart.*

And the birds called out in their tens of thousands, and their wings shadowed the dawn, and Baru wanted to know how many, how many exactly, and how much of the sky their wings could blot out, and how much of el-Tsunuqba their shadows could darken, and all the rest.

She began to count.

INTERLUDE

FALCREST

IT was a hot, wet spring day in Falcrest, the City of Bleach and Sugar, when Parliament summoned the empire admiral to entertain his own doom.

The day's casualties were already severe; the empire admiral noted the harborside birds, huddled beneath the piers as if the sun had beat the strength from them. A few diving anhingas gathered smugly on pilings to dry their outfanned wings, but the humidity left them bedraggled, and they retreated, protesting hoarsely, to the shadows of the boardwalk. A pair of soaring ibises came in off the Sound of Fire, looking for thermals. But the thick, wet air soaked them out of the sky and they came down on a freshwater pond to ruin the hopping-lily paths made by the jacanas.

The Empire Admiral Lindon Satamine watched all this from gridlocked water traffic, his dark formal eyeliner saving him from only the worst of the glare, as his barge languished in the circulating pool at Meshnet. The Narrow Way to Parliament was *right* there, just a minute's swim away.

But the Judiciary, may their cocks be knotted off at the tip and left to blacken, had a traffic checkpoint blocking everything.

"I have a summons, damn you." Lindon waved the silk-paper letter at the Judiciary ravens blocking his way. "I'm the fucking empire admiral, you plucked-ball chickenshits! Parliament demands my attendance! Now!"

Out on the Sound of Fire and anywhere beyond he was power incarnate. He could burn an island to the bedrock or blockade a whole nation into eating their dogs. But here, in the watery intestines of Falcrest proper, he was just another man in traffic.

And without Svir's political support, he was just another toy for Parliament to disembowel and bat around.

Not for the first time, Lindon thought that the principle of cordoned power had been enshrined in the Republic's law entirely and exclusively to fuck him over.

At least he wasn't under arrest. If they wanted to arrest him they'd do it quietly, like that time Mandridge Subahant had forced through a writ of assisted self-critique and sent two field judges to detain Lindon while he ate dinner at the Charred Hull. They hadn't dared arrest him mid-meal, making enemies of the owners and patrons alike, so Lindon had saved himself from their tender attentions by ordering course after course of meats and sweetbreads and whiskeys, maintaining his appetite long enough for Svir to overturn the writ and recall the judges. Afterward Lindon had nearly died of meat shits.

Why was Parliament wasting time by awaiting his presence, when Parliament's audience was so notoriously impatient with delay? (Parliament was of course open to the public, and the public loved to vote for those who put on the best show.)

He tried to recite a mnemonic to fortify his patience. "Breast Heel, Moonmount Shadow, Goblet-of-Ants, Poison Dart Ford, 121 Streams, Lily Lake, Uranium Gorge, Colobus Lake, Tantamount, Lake Akhena," chanting out the names of all the confederacies in distant Mzilimake Mbo, "Hops River, Grey Eclipse—"

And then, from among the post-revolutionary rooftops that filled the skyline ahead, he saw a white flare climbing up into the hot blue sky, shot directly up through the oculus of the old reservoir where Parliament sat in session.

Lindon could not speak for fury. His hands worked at the rail. Something in bone or wood creaked.

"Sir?" his clerk-lieutenant asked, reminding Lindon of her existence: he fired his clerks regularly, since they were all Brilinda Vain's spies. "What's that flare, sir?"

"My man in Parliament. Something's happened. Something he thinks I need to be warned of right away."

Lindon saw it all now. The emergency summons, so they could say they'd tried to solicit his advice. The Judiciary pickets to ensure he did not make it in time. Parliament waiting with pantomimed patience while they let the audience simmer in resentment of the Empire Admiral's tardiness.

And, finally, the vote. We're sorry, Admiral, but we just couldn't wait any longer. The people do not stoop for the navy's pleasure. Rather the converse, don't you know. . . .

"It can't be anything new," he whispered. Parliament absolutely couldn't extend its powers over the navy without granting the Admiralty time on the floor. "It must be an exercise of an existing privilege, something procedural, something routine, it must be . . . what?"

If Svir were here he would've sniffed it out. He would've known a month ago. But Svir was not here.

Whatever Parliament had done today, it was the first link in the chain to purge. For more than a hundred years, the navy had viciously fought off all attempts to put a civilian ministry over them, and that gave the navy power and discretion . . . but it also meant that Parliament's methods to control the navy had to be extreme. More than one Admiralty had ended in the basement of the Bleak House.

And Lindon was as vulnerable as he'd ever been.

The moment his barge bumped up against the fenders of the navy dock, a messenger came bursting out of the coatroom arch. "Sir!" the girl shouted. "Sir, two anonymous notes from the floor, sir!"

He tipped her double and unfolded the finer paper first. From his agent. It contained a sketch of the actions Parliament had just approved.

"What?" he breathed, frowning at the calligraphy. "What's this?"

"May I see, sir?" his clerk offered.

"Fuck off," he snapped, glaring at the summary. Appropriations, funds, lists of affected accounts . . . so they were fucking with the navy's money, the slice of the tax pie paid out to the Admiralty each year . . . but that wasn't possible. The quantities were fixed in each year's budget, and could only be increased, never decreased, by emergency appropriation. It was written in law. *The navy's sacrosanct need to plan operations in distant seas, subject to many weeks of travel and delay, demands absolute confidence and clarity in the available budget.*

Parliament couldn't get at them that way.

Then he saw it. It was so brutally simple that he actually grunted a laugh.

"Fuck," he said in admiration. "Fuck me."

Parliament had finally had enough. Province Admiral Ormsment was missing from her post in Aurdwynn. There were reports of Oriati ships destroyed off the Llosydanes, including an ambassador's clipper. Brilinda Vain's Censorate was still hemming and hawing and refusing to declare exactly who had been behind that pirate attack on Aurdwynn. War seemed imminent, and the navy was acting unreliable.

Parliament had decided to show them the garrote. And they had done it very cleverly. They had simply converted every note granted to the navy from a payment to a recoverable outlay. The navy now owed Parliament one note, plus interest, on every note it spent.

It would probably not stand up in an impartial court. But the Judiciary was not impartial.

"Go directly back to the Admiralty," he ordered his clerk. "Prepare an all posts bulletin for my seal and signature."

"The message, sir?"

"Order all ships to return to port, all outfitting and refitting to cease, all navy accounts frozen. Not one note spent. Pay salaries from liquid reserves on hand, go to local banks if you have to, but *do not draw from navy accounts*. Do you understand?"

"Sir, you're asking for . . . for the whole navy to return to port."

"Yes, I am."

"Given the situation with the Oriati, sir, especially at our southern outposts—"

"I know!" he snapped. "Go!"

The second anonymous note came on cheap paper, in a very level, very large hand. The kind of writing you might practice if you needed to scrawl messages on heavy seas.

> *Lindon,*
>
> *I've secured an investment from the Tuning-Spear Concern that will keep First Fleet operating through end of year. To be repaid out of our prize shares. Someone has to be ready when the war begins, after all.*
>
> *Good luck panhandling for funds, sir,*
>
> *PAAC*

"You venomous cunt," he said, with the most profound respect.

Ahanna Croftare, Province Admiral First Fleet, had taken her ships quite unofficially private.

ACT TWO

THE PLAGUE

9

THE LOCKS IN HER HANDS

IT was about fucking time I was back in charge.

For a few dreadful hours I thought I'd lost everything. By the time Faham's Morrow-men found the Cancrioth ship, Baru was already aboard, doing her master's work, winning the contest. But Iraji had taken the nightshade and gone aboard, and the Cancrioth had exchanged him for Baru. It had *worked*. Yes, the poor boy might be dead, if the esere bean antidote I'd sent after him failed. But I had a lot of dead boys on my conscience already and I could tolerate one more.

And if my niece Tain Shir had died in the black waters of the fjord, then . . . perhaps that was for the best, wasn't it? She was mad. And if my brother Olake ever met his daughter again, she would only drive him deeper into his own madness.

At last, after four years of her selfish and self-satisfied interference, I could be rid of Baru Cormorant.

I climbed up the lava tube whistling "O Lonely Lads of Aurdwynn" with my lobotomy tools clinking on my gown and dreams of Olake's forgiveness buoying my thoughts. I might visit him on my way north, and show him what I'd done with Baru. See, brother, see? Baru, tell Olake the truth. Tell him how you betrayed him, and how I've avenged that betrayal.

Tell him how you betrayed Tain Hu, and how I've made you pay.

More men than my brother wanted to avenge themselves on Baru, of course. One of them was the King of the Stakhieczi Necessity, the cold assembly of mountain clans about to invade my homeland. The Necessary King had asked Baru to be his queen. She'd strung him along just long enough to betray him.

I would give him Baru as dowry, for ritual scalping in his court.

Then he would wed my chosen queen, and together Aurdwynn and the Stakhieczi would drive Falcrest away forever, and then I would see the King destroyed and the people left in power. Neither my master Hesychast nor the Necessary King knew my true purpose. It had not even been possible to tell poor Olake. But he would see what I'd achieved, in the end. Freedom for Aurd-wynn. Forever.

You see, Olake? See how I kept the faith?

"Stop whistling!" Baru shouted from up ahead. "I'm trying to count!"

The pungent little weasel. I'd left her conscious for the lobotomy; there was no other way to be sure that each cut had the intended effect. She'd been straitjacketed and laced into a surgical plate, the sort used to bind sailors who'd fallen out of the masts and struck their heads. Under the dawn light she struck me as rather lovely, in a brooding, self-absorbed sort of way.

You would not know, looking at her, that she was a drunken monster ad-dicted to the suffering of others.

But you would know, probably, that she was difficult.

She tried to turn her head. The right side of her face had swollen up where she'd struck it in a fall. She seemed to be recovering from ergot; what a re-markable sign of her character that the Cancrioth had tried to poison her after just a few hours of her company.

"What are you counting?" I asked her. Best to establish the clarity of her thought before I began the operation.

"Birds."

I tried to look up through the skylight, but the damn quarantine gown strained my neck too much. I removed the mask and set it aside; that was tech-nically against sterile protocol, but I couldn't afford any discomfort during such a delicate surgery. I set out small glasses of alcohol and used a wheel-action sparkfire lighter to sterilize my tools. I'd lost a patient to meningitis once because I hadn't sterilized correctly. A horrible waste: he was a barrister who serially mishandled the estates of widows in order to plunder their prop-erty. After the lobotomy I had hoped to make him suffer a while as a menial. One takes what pleasures one can in this work, in the One Trade which is the life of lies.

Wind whistled through the lava tube. The skylight made the tunnel into a gigantic flute, Himu's pipe, as if the virtue of energy were here, dancing and singing of summer.

"Yawa," Baru said.

Monsters can be charming, when they know you're watching. They have a magnetism about them. In Aurdwynn there was a mania around the execution of killers, an industry of erotica, marriage proposals, falsified interviews, and cheap plays.

But at the moment of conviction that mask always came off, all the py-rite gilding and the thin charm stripped away. You saw, then, that they were hideous and incurable. That they had believed they were a divinity, a power abhuman and archonic, immune to judgment. A rictus of rage and negation, an expression chilling in its dissimilitude to all other emotions. You would not ever mistake it for grief or fear. I had never been able to describe that face to anyone. The opposite of charisma, maybe. The antithesis of a preacher's faith-hot rant.

I looked down at Baru and waited for her mask to slip like that.

"Yawa, will it hurt?"

"A little."

"Don't lie to me, please."

"It'll hurt where the tool goes in. But the brain feels nothing as it's cut. I always liked the irony of that." I didn't know why I'd added that. Baru wouldn't care.

"What will I feel like, afterward?"

"It depends on what I cut. We can be very precise, these days." How many thousands and thousands of lobotomies had been carried out, since that long-ago day when Lapetiare ordered the royal children gentled to spare them grief? I had conducted many myself, working on the minds of condemned prisoners to test the effect of certain incisions. We had, by massive repetition, charted the specific and local functions of the brain.

"What will you cut, Yawa?" She was so calm. I'd expected bargaining. I'd brushed a little residual mason powder from inside her nose, mingled with seawater and blood, but by now the artificial arrogance of the drug should be gone.

"The cuts will be in your prefrontal areas." I showed her the orbitoclast, the sharp stylus that would penetrate into her brain and destroy the targets. Mine were of a custom telescoping design, with a base a tenth of an inch wide to penetrate the sphenoid bone, and a narrower needle that could be extended to cut the brain tissue within. "This goes in above your eye. First one side, then the other. The brain has two distinct—"

"Two sides. Two hemispheres. Iscend told me that."

Iscend had vanished alongside Tain Shir, which was almost too convenient to believe. The Clarified woman had been growing erratic. I was secretly afraid that she'd begun to deduce my true plans, that the conflict between her conditioned loyalty to me and her deeper loyalty to the Republic was driving her to error.

I touched Baru's brow, tracing the cartography of her cortex. Her skin was fiercely, feverishly hot. "I'll make cuts to render you docile, suggestible, and childlike. The cuts themselves are performed by this device." I showed her the clockwork maniple, the socket where it fastened to the base of the orbitoclast, the bearings that would hold it steady above her eye. "It's been wound, like a clock, to carry out a certain set of motions. Very precise. Very scientific."

"And I won't think at all, afterward?"

"You'll be happy like a child."

"Are children happy? I don't remember."

This poor girl. Farrier had claimed her early. She'd never had a chance. "We'll feed you and comfort you. It'll be enough for you."

"Good," Baru said, softly. "Will I remember hurting?"

"I don't know."

"You can lie to me now, if you want."

I unfolded the maniple's tripod. The rising sun flashed off the struts. "I think there's been enough lying. From both of us." She had wasted Tain Hu and I would never forgive her for it.

"Will you send me to the Necessary King?"

"Yes." The brave man Dziransi was already on his way to prepare the ground, with my commands implanted as visions through the sacred dream-hammer drug. I was quite proud of that maneuver. I'd never liked Stakhi men very much.

"What will I buy for you?"

"The Necessary King's hand in marriage to Governor Heingyl Ri. Their son will rule the Stakhieczi Mansions and Aurdwynn together, and oversee their unification."

"And what will happen to me?"

"He'll hang you upside down before his court and bleed you from your scalp. To demonstrate that his power to avenge insult reaches across the world."

"Will I be treated with dignity?"

The question pricked at me. In my youth I'd wished, now and then, for certain men and women to be violated. I hated those thoughts now. How couldn't you hate them, after a life like mine? Overseeing the eugenic courts, wielding the Imperial Republic's power to legislate womb and testes. In a horrible bureaucratic way, I was a rapist myself. Hadn't I enforced the reparatory marriages? Hadn't I made women bear children they didn't want? But at least I could blame the Masquerade for those laws. With my hand in the machine I could arrange for kind spouses, grant abortions and adoptions, spare the women who would not survive motherhood.

"You'll be treated with honor," I said, "until he kills you."

"I'm glad," Baru said. Her eyes had settled very far away. "It's strange. I've never worried about that before. It's always been something that happens to other women. . . ."

"An easy assumption to make," I said, "when you're raised in an elite school."

Baru frowned up at me. That same stupid impetuous frown she'd aimed at me in meetings of the Governing Factors, when she thought she knew better than I. "Yawa, don't you know what the schools do to the unhygienic?"

"The Charitable Service runs the schools." I stayed away from them. Far too much reminder of lost Shir in those places. "A bit of behavioral shaping, I suppose?"

"Not on Taranoke. On Taranoke, if the children didn't seem interested in hygienic sex, there was a teacher of the appropriate sex who would masturbate them."

"Oh."

"It was rape, Yawa. It was the institutionally condoned rape of children."

I no longer wanted to look at her: not because this surprised me, but because it didn't. My own Judiciary in Aurdwynn had done as much, and worse.

I used a fluid level to adjust the tripod's legs, compensating for the slight slope of the lava tube. Then I clamped the maniple box into the tripod's surgical arm and moved that arm into position over Baru's right eye. The maniple had frightened me, at first, when I'd feared it would take the privilege of surgery away from me. In Incrasticism the surgeon had an inviolable right to dictate everything that happened within an operating theater. But now, with older hands, I was glad for the maniple's clockwork precision.

"Yawa."

"Yes?"

"What if the Stakhieczi invade? What if your marriage isn't enough to stop them? Vultjag would be conquered first. . . ."

"We'll open trade with the Mansions. The Stakhieczi will become addicted to our crops. Once their population grows, they'll depend on us for food, and political unity will follow. In time"—I took a breath, realized I wanted to hurt her, to reveal to her that I was the better woman, allowed myself to do it—"that unity will drive the Masquerade from our home."

Baru smiled wistfully. "That's good. Ra said you'd be good for Aurdwynn."

"Unuxekome Ra?" The stab of panic came and passed. One's heart does not settle with age, nor one's gut. But the mind learns to ride them gently. "What did she tell you?"

"That you'd sworn in secret to save Aurdwynn from the Masquerade. She remembered when you were a girl, putting up posters. . . ."

Oh Wydd protect me. I thought my twin was the only one who remembered those days.

Baru's eyes sought mine. "Is it true? You did it all for Aurdwynn?"

I nodded. Just the slightest and most deniable nod. I wanted her to know that her cruel ambition, her total abandonment of her own home, had been defeated by my own secret loyalty.

"I'm glad," Baru moaned. "Oh, Hu. I am so glad. You'll do better than I would've, I'm sure. And Taranoke . . . maybe, somehow, someday, for Taranoke . . ."

She was an exquisite actor, of course. She must have been, to fool Hu so long. It puzzled me that she wasn't breaking character.

I clamped the sterilized steel orbitoclast into the maniple. Once it had entered her skull it would need to be moved very carefully: the slightest error could sever the wrong portion of the forebrain and kill her. There was also the risk of breaking the instrument. I preferred needle-thin orbitoclasts, for precision in the cut. There was a risk they would snap when swiveled, especially if they had been notched or scratched near the base, but I always tested them carefully before use.

"Please do it," Baru whispered. Her eyes clamped shut. "Please, I can't bear to look at that thing. Just do it, please, I can't bear this anymore, oh, Hu, I'm *sorry.* . . ."

Silently she began to weep. I frowned at my hands and flexed away a touch of rheumatic stiffness. When she opened her eyes a fraction and saw me watching her, she snarled, "Do it, damn you!"

So I placed a lid separator over her right eye, and with some difficulty, due to the degree of irritation and swelling, began to screw her eyelids apart. She grunted with each turn of the screw. Blood on her lips where she'd bitten her tongue. Her left hand hung limp. Her right was a three-fingered fist so tight that her palm bled. Her eyes swiveled and darted erratically.

Curious. I noted that her eyes were repeating the strange behavior she had displayed when she went into seizure on *Helbride*. The two had come unstuck from each other, a condition called strabismus. Perhaps the dose of ergot she'd taken was still causing seizures.

Her left eye fixed wildly on the orbitoclast about to slide between eye and eye socket into her skull. Her right eye was on me, flicking back and forth steadily between my eyes, as if—

Left. Right. Left. Right.

As if—

When Svir and I had made our plan to poison Baru into seizure, I'd told him to force Baru to lateralize: to rapidly move her attention from left to right.

The key would be to trick her mind into confronting its own blindness through rapid exchange between the two hemispheres.

Once we'd poisoned Baru with the vidhara-tainted vodka, Svir had used hypnosis to draw her eyes back and forth. I'd watched them follow his fingers, and then come unstuck from each other, left and right eye swiveling separately.

I thought I'd even seen her right eye . . . wink at me.

Now her right eye skipped between mine. Left. Right. Left. Lateralizing again. If she was about to go into seizure I would need to delay the lobotomy.

As an Incrastic surgeon, I of course had a duty to inspect this abnormality. My first thought was to use the dream-hammer, the entheogenic drug I'd used to implant commands in Dziransi, to open Baru's mind like the belly of a cow. But the point of the lobotomy was to render her docile, while a dose of dream-hammer might fix her forever in this moment of fear and pain.

"Yawa," Baru slurred. "Please . . . I can't bear . . ."

"Hush," I snapped, thinking quickly.

When Hesychast had diagnosed the effects of the Farrier process upon Baru, he'd used a helmet with a bladed nose to divide Baru's visual field in half, so that each side of her perception could be tested separately. "She has hemineglect," he'd told me, "though most of the time she is probably unaware of it. I've been able to induce hemineglect in experimental patients by insulting the tissues of the brain. But Baru's case is quite unusual. Her blindness is right-sided, when almost all cases are neglect of the left. And the blindness is ipsilateral, on the same side as the wound, which, due to the brain's cross-connection, ought never to occur. . . ."

His explanation was rational, Incrastic, and correct.

But I kept thinking of something else.

The ilykari. The students of the Virtues, who knelt around the sacred olive-oil lamp, and whispered to me, their persecutor and secret hope, all the secrets of the divided mind. The Way of Eggs. The art and mystery of cultivating the sacred eryre.

It was the purpose of the ilykari to study and practice and embody the sacred ykari virtues so totally that they *became* those virtues. The greatest ilykari were no longer themselves. They were Himu, and Devena, and Wydd. They had nurtured and grown new persons within themselves. These new persons were called eryre.

What if—

Before I could convince myself that the association was madness, I acted.

I unbuckled Baru's right hand. The fist relaxed. I unbuckled her lower arm, then the upper, so she could move her whole right arm from the shoulder.

Then I turned and, breaking sterile procedure, prepared a sheet of parchment on a tin writing plate.

"What are you doing? Please. I can't stand looking at this needle. Please just—just do it."

I slid the plate beneath her right hand, dipped a stylus in bottled ink, and snugged the stylus into her right fingers. "Can you grasp that?"

"Grasp what? I can't—"

But her right hand had taken hold of the stylus. I guided the wet tip to the paper. "Can you write your name?"

"I can't see."

"Don't look. Just write."

"My name's Baru."

"I know. But please write it for me."

"I don't want to sign the paper."

"It's not a signature. It's blank."

"You're lying."

"Baru, what does it matter now? Write your name."

She tried to shrug, and the shrug moved her right hand, a twitch, a spasm, a curl of ink, an emphatic slash, another curl, three sloppy Aphalone characters, tuh aie noo, tuhainoo, taihn oo, taih noo, tain hu.

My name is Tain Hu.

"VERY odd," Yawa said.

She touched the maniple. Adjusted something.

Triggered it.

The clockwork surgery rattled to life. The steel orbitoclast slid between the inner corner of Baru's right eye and the eye socket, parted flesh, found the weak eggshell of the socket bone, and punched through. It was an obscene intrusion, sickening, like jamming a needle up an infected urethra, a dirty pain, the difference between pain-which-can-be-borne and *hurt*.

Baru screamed like a frog in a fist.

"It's begun," Yawa said, clinically. "The orbitoclast has extended the narrow inner needle into your brain. The maniple's ticking through its choreography, cutting through tracts of connected tissue. I have already destroyed your ability to exert control over what you say. What you tell me now will be the truth. You have no choice."

There was no pain beneath the surface but of course there wouldn't be—Baru wanted to thrash and scream but if she moved even a *little* the orbitoclast might kill her, and suddenly, horribly, she did not want to die at all—

"Are you Tain Hu?" Yawa asked.

What? "No!"

"Do you see my hands? Imagine that each of my hands is a lock, and in your right hand you have a key. Do you see the locks? Good. I want you to reach out with your key and unlock the hand that holds the truth. Unlock the hand on your right if you are Tain Hu. Unlock the hand on your left if you are Baru Cormorant."

Baru waved helplessly. "I can't *see* on my right—"

"Wydd help me," Yawa breathed, as if Baru had done something which astounded her. "Now the maniple has begun to cut away your control over your emotions. You will feel powerful passion. Overwhelming your discipline. Did you love Tain Hu?"

"Yes, yes, I wanted to be with her." Baru was afraid to weep, what if her tears leaked back along the orbitoclast, poisoned her somehow, filthy grief pluming into her brain, but she no longer had any choice, could not restrain her tears or her screams. "I would never have killed her. But she insisted. She refused to live as a hostage, she would die before she broke her oaths—"

Which was odd.

If Baru was a victim of Cairdine Farrier's ingenious process, as Tain Shir had convinced her—if she'd been taught to sacrifice all those close to her, and to protect her own isolation—then why hadn't she thought of executing Hu until Hu herself suggested it?

That's right, Baru. Why?

"Did *you* leave the letter that led Ormsment and Tain Shir to us on the Llosydanes? Answer, then point. My left hand is yes. My right hand is no."

"Of course not!" Her right arm twitched and jumped.

"Have you been drawing Tain Shir after us? Are you collaborating with her?"

"Yawa, *help me!*" Baru couldn't think—couldn't feel—the metal was in her head, cutting, cutting—"Help me, please, I don't want to die! *I don't want to die!*"

"Why did you choose to become involved in Aurdwynn? Please answer, then point with your right hand. The hand on your left is for the ultimate benefit of Taranoke. The hand on your right is for your personal power."

"I did it to be powerful! I did it because Farrier controls me and he needed me to prove myself!" Baru tried to lift her head and push herself onto the orbitoclast to kill herself and end it, this unbearable infected pain, this half-real rot of her heart. The straps held her down.

"You're lying. Why did you help sabotage the rebellion in Aurdwynn? Point to your left for Taranoke. Point to the right for your own benefit."

"Because Farrier was using me! I never had a choice! I thought it was all for Taranoke but it was all for him!" Her arm rigid and pointed, out of her control, surely some sign of the lobotomy's effect.

"You're lying. Who chose to kill Tain Hu? Point to the left for her. Point to the right for you."

"I did! Because Farrier taught me to murder what I love!" And her arm still extended, pointing—

"You're lying. Why—"

"Yawa, *please*!"

AH, Devena help me," Yawa gasped. And suddenly she was unscrewing the orbitoclast, removing it from the shaft it had dug into Baru's eye socket, retracting the eyelid separators, undoing the restraints, cupping her wounded face. "Baru, Baru, are you there? Can you hear me?"

Baru rolled over and gagged onto the floor. There was nothing left to come up. The ergot had purged her. She lay there panting and weeping, wracked by shudders of terror. She hadn't pissed herself, but only because her panic had fisted her whole body up.

"How much did you cut?" she whispered. "How much of me is gone?"

"Nothing."

Baru looked up into the old woman's brown skin and shining blue eyes. "I felt it, Yawa. You lobotomized me. . . ."

"I drilled through the bone but never pierced the dura mater. It never went in. There's some risk of meningitis, but your eye should plug the hole."

"But I felt honest—you cut me—you *made* me tell the truth—"

"It's a judicial trick. You tell the prisoner she's been drugged to tell the truth, and she fools herself into believing it."

"But if I told the truth . . ." Baru wished wholly to die. "If I told the truth, Yawa, then I really am just Farrier's puppet . . . I confessed it. . . ."

Yawa's gloves cupped her cheeks. Stroked away the tears of pain. "No. You said one thing and pointed to another."

"What?"

"Your right arm. It answered me honestly." Cold leather gloves whispered across her face. Tender. That was the word for it. Yawa was touching her tenderly. "Your arm said you'd done it all for Taranoke, and for Tain Hu."

"But I was just . . . just thrashing about . . ."

"That's what you thought," Yawa said, "because your mind needs a way to explain what the eryre is doing."

"The what?"

"The eyre. That's what the ilykari call it. A living model of another mind, a second consciousness in the same brain. I always thought it was really a bit of ecclesiastical power-mongering, you know, a trick to win more votes, *I have three eyre in me, so I ought to get four tickets in the bed lottery* . . . anyway"— she laughed shortly, the sound of a woman very carefully holding her feelings in check—"in Aphalone it's called a tulpa. Have you heard of tulpa?"

"No. Yawa, I don't understand. . . ."

Yawa put a straw up to Baru's lips. Without pausing to consider poison or drug, Baru sucked at the reed.

"The way you'd explain it," Yawa said, watching her drink with a grand-motherly eye, "is that the two halves of your mind have become separated, and the right half now believes it is Tain Hu. It is a tulpa of her. Hesychast's tests at the Elided Keep detected the division."

"I'm . . . I'm two people now?"

"It's not so strange, Baru. It doesn't work like the rag novels, the barristers with two personalities who prosecute and defend. *Everyone* has these two interior selves. But ordinarily—"

"They're kept in synchrony." Baru remembered Iscend's explanation. "Like two diaries written by the same person."

"That's right. But *your* right side has been split from you by the wound you suffered at Sieroch. She shares your body and your memories. She is as much you as you. But she calls herself Tain Hu. And she acts in the ways you imagine Tain Hu would act."

"Why?" Baru demanded. Not only did Cairdine Farrier have some kind of hold inside her head, but now there was civil strife in her brain? "What possible purpose . . . why did I do this to myself?"

"I must tell you," Yawa said, with a crease in her voice, laughter folded up behind a surgeon's control, "that in all my years studying pugilists and people who've fallen off horses, I've never met anyone who used a condition like this to hide her own plans *from herself.* Did you know that you wrote a letter to Tain Shir, to lead her after us on the Llosydanes?"

"What?"

"Tau-indi told us that someone left a letter on Eddyn islet, addressed to Ormsment. A letter to lead Tain Shir to you. What else did you do without real-izing it?"

Baru tried to push herself inside her head, into the blindness, to find this illusion of Tain Hu smiling back at her. "Yawa, you said . . . that the split mind was how *I'd* explain it. What would you say?"

She made a little *it's nothing* gesture. "You won't believe me."

"After what you just did to me, don't you *dare* start prevaricating."

She coughed uncomfortably, and then laughed. "The students of the ykari, who I admire and seek to emulate even if I cannot be one myself, would say that you have an eryre. A second soul."

Baru, whose right eye was swelling like it had been punched, could not bear to raise her eyebrows. But her skepticism came across.

"Don't look that way," Yawa said, "you asked. To us a soul is not a great ineffable mystery. People are, after all, not very mysterious. A soul is simply the text of a person's inner law, and a mind is the act of reading that law into the world. Through study and meditation you can read another soul's law and copy it into yourself until it comes alive, so that you now have two books of law, two selves, two souls. Himu, Devena, and Wydd all studied and practiced their virtues so completely that they *became* those virtues. That's why we emulate them."

"But I haven't studied the ykari. I haven't meditated on a virtue . . . I just swear by them, very often, I take their names in vain. . . ."

"No, child. Your obsession was with a *woman*. Through study and obsession you have built inside yourself the soul of Tain Hu."

Baru giggled. The giggle jarred her swollen eye and she cringed and giggled more. "She's in my name," she said, and the giggle became a laugh.

"Child?"

"She's in my name! She's been waiting for me!"

Yawa frowned at her blood-slick orbitoclast. "I wonder if I did more damage than I meant."

"Don't you hear it?" Baru cried, laughing wildly now, her head shaking, her poor wounded face throbbing. "Don't you hear it, Yawa, she's always been there, *she's in my name!*"

"Oh," Yawa said, with wonder, "oh," and then they were laughing together, Yawa's dry cough echoing down the lava tube to haunt the ruined mountain, mingled with the wet sobbing gasps of the two women in one, the left and the right, the agony and relief and red-raw hope she felt, herself, together, Baru and Hu, Barhu.

A STORY ABOUT ASH 8

FEDERATION YEAR 912:
23 YEARS EARLIER
UPON PRINCE HILL, BY LAKE JARO
IN LONJARO MBO

KINDALANA'S father was going to die.

The machete wound made a ragged curve down his neck, along his clavicle, where it opened a thick flap of flesh at the top of his left arm. The meat was marbled like beef. He might have survived it, except that it was a wound delivered by a man without trim, a Cancrioth worshipper, and so the principles of ruin were in it. It was going to fester and Padrigan was going to die.

Tau stared at the *hole* in Padrigan. This wound, this butchered body. How often did you think about your arm? About your neck? About their strength, the way they moved when you ran or wrote? And about the small, constant feeling of their presence? Not often enough. Not until they were broken.

Kindalana washed her father's wound, bound it up with clean linen, and gave him cranebliss and frog sweat so he could dream with the principles of the house. Abdumasi and Tau-indi waited out in the honey yard for news, Tau-indi wishing dearly for their mother, who had run off thin-lipped to Jaro with her sentries to learn why there had been no forewarning of the attack. Certain harborside officials, Tau expected, were about to lose their livelihoods.

Kindalana came out with her chains and jewels undone, blood on her hands, and tear-tracks through the paint around her eyes. "He might live," she said. "If the wound doesn't rot."

They held each other in silence. Blood got on all of them.

"The wound is here," Tau-indi said, touching their left clavicle. They didn't want to say it, but it had to be said.

Kindalana touched her own left clavicle, where Tau had painted one of the golden Segu stripes on her. "I know."

We called a power, her eyes said, and we paid a price.

Abdumasi looked between them with his jaw stuck out. "Can I help?" he said. "Is this something a merchant can help with?"

"No," Kindalana said, as Tau-indi, softly, said, "Yes, of course you can, you already saved us with your soldiers, you saved Cosgrad and Farrier. You're a hero."

Abdumasi gave Kinda a ha-take-that stab of his chin. "That's me, savior of the noble principles!" But there was a brightness in his eyes, a glare like sun on fired earth, which Tau at the time attributed (not unfairly) to the shock of seeing such violence. Only years later would they remember the serene march of the burning sorcerer, and realize that Abdumasi craved that same strength: to go untouched by pain.

Kindalana rubbed her eyes with her wrist. "Abdu, can you go to your house and ask your mother to fly up a battle flag?" He loved that idea, and ran off after it, while Kinda turned to Tau-indi with determined eyes and said, "I want Cosgrad to take care of my father. Can you do that?"

"Cosgrad? He puts maggots in people!"

"He does strange things, yes. But he knows medicine outside the mbo, and the men who made the wound . . ." She shuddered.

Tau-indi had a wonderful thought. "Kinda, if Cosgrad can save your father from a wound . . ."

If Cosgrad from Falcrest could bind up a wound in the mbo, then trim might heal the wound between Falcrest and the mbo in turn. It was possible. That was the promise of trim: the small reflected in the great.

"Excuse me."

It was Farrier. He lowered his head and brushed his brow, in the place where you would smear grief ash. "I want to help," he said.

"How?" Tau demanded, too sharply.

"The men with the sorcerer. They were shua hunters. They came here, to Prince Hill, to attack their own royalty."

"They came to attack *you*!" Tau protested.

"They had to cross the barrier between classes to do it, Tau." Farrier lifted his head, and his eyes were deep with knowledge. "We know a little about anti-royalist violence in Falcrest. I have studied it here; I know people who have expressed antiroyalist sentiments to me. Perhaps I can discover what drove rural hunters to attack their own Prince. Perhaps I can learn where that sorcerer came from."

Tau began to refuse.

"Yes," Kindalana said, with that full deep-throated Prince force in her voice. "We would be grateful. Do this for us, Cairdine Farrier."

* * *

Pus and slimy tissue and snot-thick blood ran in the house Padrigan, in the place of honey and raspberries. Cosgrad came to see the wound, leaning on Abdumasi for balance. Kindalana led him into her father's sickroom with warmth and respect even as everyone in the house watched the Falcrest man with suspicion. He was the reason a sorcerer had come to Prince Hill. He was the reason, some said, that this ground was tainted forever. If he was not enenen, who was?

"Too late for maggots." Cosgrad mapped the colors of the cut with a charcoal pen, and the pain of the wound with touches of a small burnt stone. "It's infected almost to the shoulder."

"I cleaned it." Kindalana looked more affronted than upset. "I cleaned it well."

"You did well. But some things survive. The fiercest things." Cosgrad slumped against Abdu, overwhelmed by an aftershock of fever. "His arm has to go."

There was a rebellion at that. No one could be healed by separating their parts! He needed teas and opiates and tinctures of mercury while his body made itself whole! Keep the pieces together so they remember the shape they make.

But Kindalana was insistent. "Falcrest knows fire and the shape of wounds. That knowledge can save my father." And, when there were protests, "I am his flesh! I choose for him!"

On the evening of that day, the three parents of Prince Hill gathered for the last time. Padrigan lay feverish on a sack of crushed lake reeds, selected and gathered by his groundskeepers. Abdi-obdi Abd and Tahr Bosoka sat with him, hands linked, confessing whispered secrets that would keep him bound to them and draw him away from death. Tau sat beside Kindalana up on the second-floor balcony, overlooking the inner courtyard, so that their bonds to Padrigan would raise him up like a pulley from the sick place.

"They knew," Tahr said, grimly. "Farrier says they knew, in Jaro, that the mob was coming. They had time to send up signals. But we were not warned. They wanted us to lose our guests. They wanted us shamed, or dead."

The attack had troubled other nearby Princes so badly that some had offered Tau a shua swap—a cruel and punitive maneuver in which two Princes sent their own shua to guard each others' lands, denying the people the comfort of friendly faces on patrol. Tau would not have it.

Abdumasi's mother, Abdi-obdi, had white hair, a small face, and a brilliant smile. She was not smiling now. "What I hear in the markets is vicious.

People want revenge for their dead. They think we're sheltering—" Her eyes hooked toward the room where Cairdine Farrier labored over his journals. "They think we don't care about the war, and won't until it touches our fortunes. They think we're too far away, and much too rich."

"I was in Falcrest! I was *taken*! How can they think I don't care?"

"Tahr," Abd-obdi said, "a hundred thousand of our people just died there, and you came back safe. They hate you even more for it."

Tahr wiped sweat from her hands and took up Padrigan's grip again. "What about the sorcerer? Where did she come from?"

Padrigan groaned and arched. The women held him down.

"I'm going to Segu," Abdi-obdi said, "and I know you'll try to stop me, Tahr, but Abdu's a man now, and he can handle the house. I'm going to Kutulbha, where my ships come to harbor. All the legends say the Cancrioth went into the jungle; well, the jungle is along the Black Tea coast, so unless she came across the sahel and the desert, that sorcerer had to take a ship up the coast and through the Segu islands. Maybe she was seen in Kutulbha."

Maybe, Tau thought, eavesdropping without guilt, she was passed from the jungle to the villages around Jaro as a tumor. Maybe she has had a thousand bodies. But at least she must be dead now, dead forever. Not even a tumor could survive that fire.

Good.

"I wouldn't stop you." Tahr squeezed Abdi-obdi's hand. "Abdi, I'm sorry about . . . all the years when I was too eager to tell you how to live. I think being a Prince-Mother made me haughty. I think I—"

"Tahr!" Abdi-obdi cried, almost laughing, "Tahr, don't you dare start."

"I want to set things right," Tahr said, as Tau-indi's bruised heart swelled with love for their mother.

"That," Abdi-obdi said, "is exactly why you mustn't. Leave some unfinished business between us, Prince-Mother, to summon me back."

"Be careful on the sea," Tahr said, remembering, certainly, how Falcrest's ships had seized her own. "Mind how you sail."

"It's my captains you should mind. The Devi-naga pirates are back out in force. I haven't taken losses like these since the storms in '88, when half the Column was fenced off by sunken masts. . . ."

And they went on bantering quietly, being companionable, in that precious ordinary way that cannot be fully valued until it is gone forever. Tau wanted to elbow Kindalana and beg her to pay attention, to treasure this moment as she would treasure a new book or a letter from abroad, because it was so ordinary, so perfectly the weft and foundation of their lives.

But to call attention to the ordinary would be to make it extraordinary, and to ruin it.

So Tau was silent, and witnessed, glad that the ordinary was worth witnessing.

AFTER Abdi-obdi left for Kutulbha to hunt sorcerers, and mother Tahr resumed her long absences in Jaro invigilating the reasons for the mob's attack, the Princes ruled the hill. Tau began to take on the duties of an adult Prince, holding court to hear land disputes, inviting bands of shua warriors to demonstrate their martial arts and to sing the long songs of their ililefe, the codex of warrior feats their ancestors had assembled. Hunter shua pleased by Tau's hospitality paid tribute in pelts, but Tau's favorite were the renegades, men and women who had taken vows of poverty and chastity to fight against evil: if renegades were not pleased with a Prince they would sometimes set up governments of their own in the lands between estates. Tau thought them very romantic. On other days Tau went by mule to the farming estates of the Bosoka territory, to ask after local problems, check on water and health, and keep up the relations of mutual gratitude. All of it was exactly what Tau had dreamt of since they were young.

But there was no joy in it. All they could think of was Padrigan's amputation, and whether he would survive.

"I'll operate—tomorrow," Cosgrad grunted, doing pushups on the floor of his cell. Tau leaned in the door and watched his back gather itself in ridges and fans. "Will you—walk with me? I need—spider webs."

"Spider webs?"

"Yes—two hundred—"

"Two hundred spider webs?"

"No—to go with the—two hundred and one—wet bread."

Tau repeated this to Abdumasi a few minutes later. "I'll mix the wet bread with the spider webs," Tau-indi explained to Abdumasi, pretending to be Cosgrad, "because my brain has been cooked by meningitis. Pretend I'm not flexing my abs."

"Urgh," Abdumasi said, crunching up. "Me Cosgrad. Give frog. Want lick."

"Should we ask Kindalana?"

"Yes," he said, not hesitating at all. "Yes, of course."

She was agreeable. So the four of them went down through the rock gardens to the mulberry grove where the spiders lived. Tau-indi carried a big cloth basket, and sticks to pick up the webs. Abdumasi had his own stick, "for protection," and they took a long easterly loop around the road where the sorcerer had come. Kindalana had given up writing an essay on the difference between martial culture and warfare, because (she claimed) it was hard to articulate to foreigners how Lonjaro could train so many amateur warriors yet fight no wars, but (in fact) because she didn't want to be left up on the hill with her father's weeping wound.

Cosgrad stumbled over an inflection stone in the rock garden, and Tau caught him. "Thank you." He winced sharply, touching his back. "Your Highness, did I say awful things when I was in my fever? Ungrateful, prying things?"

Kindalana was watching them intently.

"You asked me how I'd been made," Tau-indi said. "There are no lamen in Falcrest, are there? Is that what you meant?"

"In Falcrest they taught me that lamen were sacred Oriati hermaphrodites who could, ah, be conjugated by men, and conjugate women in turn. Having seen you," and here Cosgrad flushed faintly, something that could be seen more easily on his skin, "less than modest, as I understand is common and natural here given the climate, I know . . ."

Tau-indi laughed. Cosgrad's ideas of lamen might have fit in rural Segu, four hundred years ago, when men were raised in convents and girls became women by wearing gloves made out of biting ants. "You thought I had a penis and a vagina?"

Cosgrad scowled stiffly. "I thought there must be a way for the parents to know if their child was a laman."

"Why would the parents need to know? I've heard from griots that some people are born that way, and it is a wonder and a difficulty. But genitals have nothing to do with choosing to be a laman."

"What are lamen for, then?"

"Now? In these enlightened days? Whatever trim moves us toward."

"Just like anyone else," Abdumasi interrupted. "I mean, what are *you* for? What about me? What are men for, really? Why don't people with wombs just pop babies out all on their own, and live in big termite mounds? Wouldn't that be a lot easier?"

Cosgrad's forehead knotted up and he looked like he might think himself back into a fever. "Termite mounds," he muttered. "Termite mounds . . . I'd never considered . . ."

Years later, when Cosgrad Torrinde produced his seminal (an Aphalone word that meant exactly what it sounded like) work on the similarities between Oriati Mbo and the colonies of insects, Tau would regret this conversation.

* * *

AS children they'd come down to the mulberry grove to pretend they were farmers on Taranoke all married to each other, which was quite sickly sweet in retrospect. But they had always been afraid to go too deep into the grove, where the leaves kept off the rain and the spiders built their homes. And how they'd built! Everywhere Tau looked there was spider silk, white and wind-smoothed, like the shredded banners of some cotton army.

"I'll take Abdu." Kindalana slipped an arm around him. "Come on, merchant boy."

That left Cosgrad and Tau-indi to pluck lengths of web with their sticks, spool them up, and basket them. The light came through the webs soft and white, and it painted Cosgrad in colors of gentle death. He whistled softly as he worked.

Inevitably, Tau-indi saw a spider the size of their face scurrying around. Inevitably, Cosgrad spoke up right then. "Will saving Padrigan's life give me good trim?"

"Yes." Tau-indi backed up against him, waiting for the spider to go. "Of course it will. You're helping a father and a good man."

"I was trying to write an equation to explain trim. I had a chart of things that people said would help my trim, and things people told me would hurt it. I was going to solve it and give you the equation, as thanks for your hospitality. But I couldn't make it work at all. I was so afraid. All the children understood trim, so why couldn't I?"

"Why were you afraid?" The stink of rotting mulberry-fruit rose up around them as the wind changed. The spider sat in thought for a few moments and then ran away, up into the boughs. Tau-indi dared to turn around, and found Cosgrad looking at them thoughtfully. His queue of dark hair had stuck in the web.

The clouds rose up against the sun. The tree-shadows and the web-shadows thickened across Cosgrad. "I thought maybe trim was real, and that I was sick because of my trim. I thought I'd come to Oriati Mbo to find my idea of the world undone."

A spider unreeled itself from the shadows behind his head and began a nervous, exploratory descent. "What idea?" Tau-indi said, hoping he wouldn't turn and frighten it. "How could trim possibly undo your idea of the world? Trim is about people."

Cosgrad knelt and picked up a rock. "I'm going to throw this."

"Don't!"

"Why not?"

"It'll land on a spider!"

Cosgrad looked sly. "How do you know the rock won't just go up and up and never come down?"

"It's a rock, you daft man," Tau-indi snapped. The spider peeked at them from behind a low shrub, its two forelimbs up in the air as if to wave. "Rocks aren't like people, who can choose. A rock just wants to get back to the other rocks and do its job of holding things up."

"That's how you describe things here in the mbo. Stories about connection, how things fit together. The spider you mentioned, for instance—" Cosgrad turned, saw it in all its enormity, and yelped.

Tau-indi caught his arm. "Let it be, let it be."

"It could eat a bird!" Something in that gave him an idea, and of course he burped it up right away. "That spider, why does it exist?"

"To eat small insects and bats. So they don't trouble us too much." They tugged Cosgrad back. "The way we're troubling that spider now."

Cosgrad threw the stone sidehand. It missed the spider, ripped through the underbrush, and clattered against a trunk. Tau-indi felt his strength moving through him like a principle of wind.

"The arc," Cosgrad said, pointing, "the mass, the velocity of the stone, the force of the impact. You say they happen because the rock wants to be with other rocks, as its principle demands. But how does that story help you predict anything? How does it help you launch a stone from a slingshot, or fire a rocket from a hwacha?"

He turned on Tau-indi with his foreign face as flat and finely arranged as calligraphy, the bones like birdwings, his nose a little punctuation mark, his chest heaving with excitement. In his eyes there was an omen like a pendulum that had come into its downstroke. He was very beautiful.

He pronounced this:

"I am a savant in Falcrest. I have a license. We have observed the motion of stones very carefully, our savants, and now we can write an equation that describes the motion of all stones on all arcs, from the day the world was born until the resolution of time."

"I know what an equation is," Tau said, moved by pride in the Mbo, "I've read my Iri anEnna and my Eastward Eye. And didn't we invent zero, anyway?"

"You did," Cosgrad said, breathlessly. "But you did not apply it far enough."

But how, Tau wanted to protest, could you describe a stone *entirely* with a set of letters? How could an equation about the movement of a stone contain the ways in which a stone might be thrown to hurt someone, or ground to help make flour, or mortared into a wall? How could the equation capture the way in which a certain kind of stone might be venerated by one house, because their forefathers had died to the last in a battle on that stone, and cursed by another house, because that stone had been used in the arrows that killed their herd?

To understand Cosgrad, Tau-indi tried to look past what he was saying and find the hurt, the fear.

"That's why you're afraid? You can describe the motion of a stone, but not the movements of the principles in trim?"

"I can't describe trim with mathematics, no." Cosgrad looked at his stick wrapped in cobwebs. His eyes were meningitis bright, fever bright. "Nor the reason for the separation of men and women. Nor the separation between people and termites, or between the cuttlefish and the octopus, or the Stakhieczi and the Oriati, or anything else alive. Not yet. But I will."

Kindalana called out. "Tau! Where are you?"

"Why does it make you afraid?" Tau-indi pressed. "Why are you afraid of things you can't describe?"

"Because if trim is real, if your beliefs are real, then Falcrest will lose the war, the future belongs to you, and I will never have what I want."

"What do you want?"

"I want to describe everything in a sentence, of course." His calligraphic face relaxed with the thought of it, became clean and easily read, and the word upon it was joy. "How else am I going to change the letters and numbers, one by one, until I find a way to make everything work right?"

"Cosgrad."

"What?"

"If you want to make everything right, will you help end the war?"

Cosgrad looked away. Grief made him bite down hard, like he had tetanus again. Tau felt a great, general tint of sorrow and loss, as if Cosgrad were somehow already gone. They did not know why.

"Your Highness," Cosgrad said. "The war is already over."

T HE next morning they all drank antimony to empty their stomachs, and then they went into the sick room, the scream room, where Cosgrad directed the house surgeon in the removal of Padrigan's arm.

They stopped the blood with a tourniquet and made the cut. Then Cosgrad, nimble-fingered, murmuring, ligatured up the arteries and caked the wound in his bread-web paste.

Padrigan lived.

* * *

THE comic griot who had led his mob across the lake to kill Cosgrad and Farrier now brought word from the war. In the wake of the Unspeakable Day, Falcrest had declared the entire Ashen Sea a Free Navigation Commons that would be policed by Falcrest ships and taxed by Falcrest tariffs.

A decade earlier it would have seemed a joke to Tau. Hadn't Falcrest spent their history throwing ship after mad experimental ship out into the Mother of Storms, fleeing Devi-naga's pirates, running north in search of *anything* they could steal from the bastè ana in their houses of ice? How could they possibly take the whole Ashen Sea, the whirling center of civilization?

But now there were Falcresti ships sailing for Segu Mbo to enforce their claim. The Falcresti Parliament had appointed a woman named Admiral Juristane as their "Charitable Factor for More Civilized Warfare."

"I know her," Cairdine Farrier told the Princes over a lunch he had prepared out of bread and beer-battered fish. "She'll treat the Segu fairly, but I warn you, she'll answer any poor conduct with righteous fury."

"Why is her fury righteous?" Tau asked, frowning. "What makes her right, to come to one of our cities and dictate terms?"

"She's righteous," Kindalana said, looking narrowly at Farrier, who would not meet her eyes, "because she has the power to decide which conduct is poor, and the power to punish it. Farrier! Farrier, what's really going to happen at Kutulbha?"

"Your people will be too proud to accept the new conditions," he said. "And their pride will be rebuked. I'm sorry."

Kindalana smiled at him, as if they shared some toothy secret. Tau realized that she was rewarding him for his honesty: making him feel as if they two, Kindalana and Farrier, shared a special privileged channel of understanding.

Thus it occurred:

Falcrest's tall-masted ships appeared off Kutulbha. The Segu sent pickets to warn them away. The pickets vanished.

Falcresti ships came into Kutulbha's harbor and demanded the surrender of every warship possessed by every tribe in Segu. It was an impossible demand. It would take months to gather every Segu Prince and the Queen-Mothers of the tribes, the Oya and the Isi and the Bru and the Esh and the Aam and the Yeni and the Uro. Even after a vote there would be dissenters.

The Falcresti fleet waited patiently for the inevitable attack.

It came.

During the fighting, Admiral Juristane's ships fired rockets into Kutulbha, and the paper and wood houses caught fire, caught and spread, a conflagration,

a principle of fire, and then the empty grain silos left by the blight and the
stoppage of shipping somehow burnt so hot that the air itself ignited. A blossom of fire grew up out of the city and its wind seared the laundry against the
stones and sheared the fruit from the millet. Night became day. The griots said
the whole city burned and a hundred thousand people were dead and four
hundred thousand were cast out into the ash to weep and starve as their burns
festered.

Abdumasi's white-haired mother, Abdi-obdi, had gone to Kutulbha to hunt
sorcerers.

Cairdine Farrier came to Tau-indi as Tau-indi sat in the dark gnawing their
left hand and hoping against hope for news of Abdu's mom.

"I have a document with me," he said, "that I think you should review with
your mother. I have had it with me since the beginning of my time here. I
don't want you to think less of me for bearing it in silence. It was the task I was
given. I had to do my duty."

"What is it?" Tau-indi asked dully.

Farrier offered a wax-sealed tube.

"Terms of surrender," he said. "For the Princes of the Mbo to ratify."

"My surrender?"

"Your surrender," Farrier said, soberly, using the Aphalone plural *your*.
"The entire Oriati Mbo's surrender."

S HE'S dead," Abdumasi said. "She was on a ship in the harbor. So was her
whole fleet. It's all gone. The whole concern. They killed her and everyone
else."

Of all the things Abdumasi spoke that night, of all the tears and curses he
shed into his friends' arms, the hardest was this:

"You called a power, didn't you? You called a power and the price had to
be paid. We saved your father, Kinda! We saved him! *The price still had to be
paid!*"

10

REUNIONS AND REASSESSMENTS

"W HAT the fuck is going on here?" Apparitor demanded. "Don't give me your judicial stare, Yawa, of course I tailed your boats. I had a stake in this operation.

"And suddenly you two are thick as thieves with a master key, which is *not,* if you'll recall, what you promised me!" He stabbed one red-gloved finger at Baru, who sat on the dead lava, too dizzy to move. "You promised me *her* lobotomized and vanished, disappeared so mysteriously even Farrier couldn't blame us for it! Yes, I mean *you,* Baru, don't pretend you're hurt!"

"Ah, Svir." I beamed at the Stakhi man, red-haired pale-skinned child of the Wintercrest Mountains. He was an exile from those mountains, so of course he was the Throne's agent in command of northern affairs. Falcrest likes its ironies. Falcrest also likes hostages: Apparitor's loyalty was secured by his lover, the Empire Admiral Lindon Satamine, as I was secured by my twin Olake.

I had seen a few thousand murders of passion in my time as a judge; Svir-who-was-Apparitor looked ready to commit one. When he'd learned that Baru had stolen his concubine Iraji, he'd begged me to call off the maneuver against Baru. *Not him. I won't lose him. Not in this place.*

And I'd lied, of course. I'd assured him I would delay the attack until Iraji was safe.

Instead I'd poisoned Iraji and sent him to the Cancrioth in exchange for Baru.

Then I'd failed to destroy Baru.

My professional relationship with Apparitor was, I suspected, about to encounter some complications. This was a major inconvenience. He was master of our clipper *Helbride,* our only way off these dying islands.

B ARU and I had talked quietly and indirectly, trapped by the old etiquettes of our distrust. I think we were both ashamed. We had misjudged each other so badly, both collaborators, both secretly still loyal to our homes. She might be the only person in the world who could understand what I'd done to my brother. I could never forgive myself for it, any more than she could forgive herself for killing Tain Hu. But we might forgive each other.

We were each others' only hope for grace.

But neither of us could cast off our isolation so easily. The closest Baru had come was to say: "I've been lonely. For such a long time."

"Nonsense." I'd sniffed. "You're not even thirty."

She'd laughed.

We'd tiptoed around things still too raw to settle. I'd killed her secretary Muire Lo. She'd led my brother into madness and captivity. We'd make a fine stage play, wouldn't we? The two of us at dinner, trying not to talk about any of it long enough to make our excuses and run for the door.

And then Apparitor burst in on us through the skylight above us, drawn by Baru's laughter. "Did you say anything sensitive?"

"Sensitive?" Baru croaked.

"There was someone at the skylight. She left when I approached."

"Iscend!" Baru exclaimed. "Shit, if she tells Hesychast what we—"

She clapped her mouth shut.

The morning light was coming down through the skylight now and Apparitor stepped into it. The shadow of his pointing finger crossed Baru's face. "*You're* supposed to be lobotomized. A perfectly legal treatment for your seizure disorder. Why are you awake?"

I felt it was my duty to lie for her. "She produced evidence which made her indispensable to our work. I've elected not to proceed with her removal."

He knelt to study Baru's swollen, bandaged face. "You put her in a position where you felt she couldn't lie, and you liked the answers."

"It's my purpose, Svir, to find the truth."

"Don't use my name, Durance." He did not look up from Baru's broken face. "Where's Iraji?"

"He's in terrible danger," Baru croaked. She hauled herself upright by my shoulder, so powerfully that she nearly dragged me over. She was just as dense as I expected. "Alive, but in such danger."

"Where is he," Apparitor hissed. "What have you done with him?"

"Aboard the Cancrioth ship. It's my fault he's there."

"Is it now." Apparitor fixed deadly, poison-green eyes on me. "Your fault entirely? Not one bit Yawa's?"

"It was his choice to go," I said.

"Choice! We're fucking Masquerade cryptarchs, Yawa—letting people 'choose' to do what we want is our *job*!"

"It's also our job to risk our agents, even our favorite concubines—"

"Not here!" Apparitor bellowed. *"I did not consent to risk him here!"*

You boy fool, we do not get to consent to the stakes, to the risks, to the prices we pay. We pay them or we fail. That's all. "We had a task, Svir!" I barked; enough of his whinging! "Find the Cancrioth! Return the proof!"

"You two had a task to *destroy each other!*" Apparitor roared back. "Baru or Yawa! Agonist or Durance! The point was to pit you against each other, and tonight it was supposed to be *done!* Why are both of you still here to plague me?"

"Plague," Baru repeated. She was wrapped around me, holding herself up.

"Yes," Apparitor snapped, "that's what I called you, do you want an apology?"

"No, Apparitor, I mean—I mean that the moment the wind steadies, and the captains moored here decide they can sail without becalming, the atoll of Kyprananoke is going to become a plague bomb the likes of which death itself has never seen. The Kettling can take *forty weeks* to incubate after infection. That's long enough for a carrier to reach the shores of the Ashen Sea and find the nearest city."

"Please," Apparitor sneered. "I don't need you to stop a plague. I don't need you for anything. Yawa, tie her back up and finish the lobotomy."

"We do need her," I said, and yes, I even drew the wretched woman a little closer.

He groaned and rubbed his temples. "How did she compromise you, Yawa? Something about your brother? Something on that palimpsest her agent stole?"

I'd stolen the palimpsest back, actually; it was in my cabin on *Helbride*, frustratingly resistant to decryption. "She hasn't compromised anyone."

"You had her completely in your power. You had total control of the situation. And you *still* let her defeat you?" He shook his head matronizingly. "Pathetic."

I have my pride. I would have struck him on the edge of his mask, if I could've reached him. Old women are allowed small violences.

"I've been on that ship," Baru croaked. "I've met the Cancrioth. I know what they want. I know how we can get Iraji back."

"You *have* been on that ship, haven't you?" Apparitor's sarcastic purr had worn so thin I could hear the death beneath it. "You've made some clever bargain. You've hooked Yawa into it, and the Cancrioth is dancing to your drum, and you think I'll go along. Everyone in Aurdwynn went along, didn't they? Everyone did what you required, and Aurdwynn fell into your clutches. And you think it was all your work, you little egomaniac, you never knew how much I did to smooth your way, ah, ziscjaditzcionursz, let's be rid of her, Durance, let's lobotomize her and have it *done,* this is our chance!"

I shook my head. I would not. I had decided.

"They're making ready to sail." Baru's voice was fading. "They're discovered. They're going to make for open ocean. . . ."

"With Iraji aboard. Straight into Ormsment and her waiting frigate. *Sulane* will put enough Burn into those Cancrioth to turn them into soap and glass." Apparitor's lips were as thin and white as a Stakhi peasant. "Where's Tau?"

"On the same ship," Baru admitted.

"Wonderful!" Apparitor beamed at me. "I look forward to telling the Oriati crew packed onto my clipper that we've donated their Prince to their ancient foe. And when Ormsment's finished destroying the Cancrioth, I can't wait to explain to Parliament how the Oriati Ambassador to Falcrest was *burnt to death by one of our own ships!*"

Baru slumped against my arm. "We can save Tau, Svir. We can save everyone on that ship. But we have to act now—"

He spoke across her. I twitched in irritation, remembering a thousand meetings of the Ruling Factors in Aurdwynn, biting my tongue as Hasran Cattlson interrupted me. "What bargain did you make over there? Last time you traded your entire rebellion for your exaltation to the Throne. What is it this time?"

"I failed."

Apparitor blinked. "What?"

"They made me an offer and I couldn't do it. I couldn't make the exchange. Things went wrong after that."

I felt that I had to add something to support her. "Are you really surprised? She's a walking ruin. She pushed herself too hard to gain her place on the Throne. Isn't that one of your mountain folktalkes, Svir? That most climbers die *after* they summit?"

His eyes narrowed at the sympathy in my tone. "You think she has limits? After what she did to Hu?"

I did. I believed she had limits. But there was no possible way I could convince Svir of what I had learned without betraying my *own* ultimate purpose. And that problem would only grow. If I returned to Falcrest with Baru alive I would fail Hesychast and he would destroy me.

What was I going to do? I had thrown away weeks and weeks of planning—

decades and decades of effort—on a moment's compassion. What was I going to do next?

"The Cancrioth will follow me," Baru said.

I was so glad she had a way to defend herself that I almost dropped her. "Baru?"

"The woman from the ship. Kimbune. She came with me because she thinks I can lead her to someone she's lost. The Brain can make the others follow me . . . yes. I think I have a plan. . . ."

She trailed off. We both waited for her plan. But Baru, bless her shriveled little soul, had passed out.

The two of us stared at each other, the old Maia judge and the young Stakhi bravo. Baru dribbled slowly out of my grip and down onto the stone.

"Do it," Svir said, deadly flat. "Finish this."

A MINATA was going to die in this mountain.

She'd seen too much by now, and so the Republic she served would dispose of her. All her hard work, all the marks and scores in her service jacket. They had not mattered; she had not mattered, in the end. The masked immensity of the Imperial Republic had never lowered its eyes to notice her. There was no reward at the center of the maze. You just wandered it until you died.

When she'd pulled Baru off that boat and into her arms she'd really believed it was finished. She would sit down with Baru and learn *everything*. And then she would know where her duty lay.

Instead she'd led Baru into *another* trap.

The story of their friendship. First she'd struck Baru in sheer fury over the risks Baru's deviancy posed to Aminata's own career. Then she'd lured Baru into that brothel in Treatymont where (she hadn't known, *she hadn't known*) Xate Yawa's spies waited to observe Baru's indiscretions.

And now she'd drawn Baru to Tain Shir's killing ground, and to Xate Yawa's final judgment.

If you had a duty to your friends, then Aminata figured she'd failed it.

She tried to keep the other prisoners' spirits up anyway. "Chins up, it's sunrise! Turn your best side to the sun, sailors, the day remembers the first face it sees!"

The water of the el-Tsunuqba caldera licked at the black stone. The prisoners from Tain Hu's old household muttered and stirred. The little man Run Czeshine tried to pretend he'd been awake the whole time. Ude Sentiamut scratched his beard and grumbled to Ake Sentiamut, a living caricature of the bony, neurotic Stakhi woman. She reached out to clasp hands with the plump herbalist Yythel.

Down at the end of the chain, the diver Ulyu Xe sat limp and did not move at all.

Aminata was worried about Xe. Tain Shir had done something to her. Aminata had kept a hawk eye on Shir's conduct around the prisoners as they left *Sulane,* and she'd seen no sign of mistreatment. But then that nightmare in the caldera, Tain Shir lifting Xe like a doll . . . and now she sat there saying nothing, looking at nothing, spine limp, feet crushed sideways beneath folded thighs.

Aminata should have stayed on *Ascentatic.* She should have listened to Captain Nullsin.

"We can't see the sun down here," the boy Run complained. "How do you know it's dawn?"

"Because I'm a sailor," Aminata said, jauntily. "You'll see I'm right. Aren't I right, Mister Execarne?"

Faham Execarne was the man in charge of the Morrow Ministry detail, a handsome leathery old guy with a farmer's hard shoulders and big sensuous lips. Aminata had expected him to interrogate her. Instead, Execarne crouched on the pillowed lava and smoked weed. The smell was getting into Aminata's uniform reds.

"Eh?" he croaked, looking up. "Aren't you right about what?"

It bothered her to see him so fucked up. It was never a good sign when the officer in command was coming apart. "That it's sunrise, sir."

"Round about this chime, I think." He rubbed his eyes and grunted. "It'll be a bad day."

"Faham," Ake Sentiamut called. "What's *wrong* with you?"

"You're smoking too much," Yythel added, solicitously, "and I always know when you've had too much."

"He's afraid," Ude Sentiamut said. "He's scared of that ship we saw."

"Damn right I am."

"Hey." Aminata nodded to Execarne, the only gesture really available in manacles. "Can I have a pull?"

"You're on duty, Brevet-Captain."

She shrugged. Her chains rattled. "So are you, Your Excellence. Besides, I'm a prisoner until we're done sorting out these . . . irregularities."

"Irregularities. Ha. I'd say we have some fucking irregularities here." He scratched his beard and frowned. Aminata wondered if he was going to kill them all.

He put the blunt up to her lips. Aminata took a drag and exhaled smoke in his face, just as cool as could be.

Execarne squinted at the diver Ulyu Xe. "She's meditating," he told Aminata. "Everyone thinks she's scared out of her mind, but she's meditating. Something tossed her up, see? Something she thinks isn't natural. She's trying to fall back into the current of the world. She's a smart one, our Xe."

"Sir," Aminata murmured, shifting on her sore knees, "what's happening?"

Execarne looked at her with reddened horse eyes. "War," he said. "We're starting the war. Right here. That fuck-off huge ship is about to sail right into Juris Ormsment's minefield. She'll burn the ship and haul the survivors to Falcrest, where she'll make them confess, to Parliament, that they're part of an Oriati conspiracy against our great Imperial Republic. And after that I don't see any way, any way at all, to avoid the big one."

"The big one, sir?"

"Did you ever read the *War Paper*?"

"No, sir." Deliberately using the navy honorific *sir,* rather than the distancing *Your Excellence.*

"Well, I wrote that damn thing. A forecast of the consequences of a full-scale Oriati civil war and simultaneous war with the Imperial Republic. One out of six people die, I estimated. One out of six people in the world we know."

He shielded his blunt from a gust of dawn wind down the lava tube. There was still no light except the soft glow of the jellyfish-tea lantern. "The damn thing is we'd probably win it. Falcrest's done a lot of shitty things, Brevet-Captain. We got rid of kings because they weren't accountable to the people. Now we have the power, we the mob, and we're accountable only to ourselves. We're getting bigger and stronger because who wants to grow smaller and weaker, huh?

"But the more we do to make ourselves bigger, the more crimes we commit. More than people want to think." He took another draw. "When I look forward, I see a Falcrest that's become fully parasitic. Sucking in everything it needs from the provinces. Rousing itself from its revels just long enough to roll over and crush whatever's gnawing. A swollen, beautiful golden age . . . like a leech bigger and more complicated than its host. Imagine what we'd do if we owned the whole Ashen Sea. I mean, fuck, look at what we're about to do here."

"Sir?" she ventured.

"The Kettling's loose on these islands. I don't see how we stop the plague here unless we go all the way."

"All the way, sir?"

"Yep."

"I don't understand, sir."

"It's simple." Execarne ground his blunt out under the toe of his boot. "Given a proper fleet, we could burn all the ships at anchor and blockade the islands until the Kettling burns out. It would take years, given the properties of the Kettling, and a huge expenditure of money and resources. But we don't have that option. We only have two warships here, and one of them's a mutineer. So we use our alternative."

"What's the alternative, sir?"

"When Falcrest held Kyprananoke, my predecessors became concerned that it made a natural port for pirates and filthy degenerates."

She nodded thoughtfully, eyes fixed on him. In her experience men liked to tell young navy sailors about how the world worked, especially sailors who were attractive foreign ingénues. She knew men found her attractive, but only as a body, not as a whole person, an Oriati woman. That was why she used whores: that way she saw the man the same way he saw her.

"It *is* a natural port for pirates," she said, to prompt him to continue.

"That's right. And they figured that wherever degenerates harbor, plague follows. Say, for example, that Oriati Mbo has a disease it wants to use as a weapon. How might that disease pass from Oriati Mbo to Falcrest without being detected? Well, it couldn't go around the trade ring. We inspect those ships too well. So it might come in through Kyprananoke, where smugglers dodging our patrols like to make harbor."

"And so," he said, "my predecessors set up an apocalypse fuse."

"Sir? What's that?"

He grinned ghoulishly at her. "Fuck," he said, "you look a bit like old Kindalana, don't you? The way she looked when she first came to Falcrest. When she said she was going to bring the Oriati Mbo into our Republic."

That name again! The man Calcanish on the Llosydanes had mentioned the Oriati Prince Kindalana, and Aminata had guessed, correctly, that the name would provoke him sexually. Why did it seem like the name was following her?

Footsteps sounded from the lava tube above the spit.

The Jurispotence Xate Yawa and a young red-haired Stakhi man came down the tube, carrying Baru between them. Her right brow swelled up around an eyeball red as ruin. She grinned at Aminata and the smile was so guileless and glad that Aminata knew at once it was too late.

They'd lobotomized her.

* * *

B ARHU was happy.

The hole behind her right eye had pierced some thin interior membrane, and whatever was inside, a fluid of feeling trapped there by her anguish
and manic self-control, was now running out.

"Aminata," she said, staggering across the pillowed volcanic rock, "Aminata, oh, you're all right, you're okay," hugging her as she knelt there, befud-
dled, with her ankles and her wrists chained together, but that was all right,
Barhu could fix it.

"Please, can you unshackle her?" she asked the Morrow Minister, who rose
up red-eyed and coughing to stare at her.

"What's happened to you?" Execarne demanded. Aminata was rigid in her
arms, refusing to meet her eyes.

"Oh!" Barhu understood. "No, I haven't been simplified. It's still me!"

The Vultjagata prisoners looked disappointed. Except for Ulyu Xe, who did
not stir at all.

"It's me," she repeated, hopefully, "it's Barhu. I'm here to help."

"She doesn't realize what's been done to her," Yythel muttered to Ake.

Yawa signaled to Execarne, who muttered, "All right, all right," and produced a key. He unlocked Aminata from her shackles. Beautiful Aminata who
had taken that spear for Barhu.

"Thank Wydd for good armor, right?" Barhu said, grinning at her. She'd
filled out from her teenage lankiness in a way that Barhu, seeing her so often in
school, maybe hadn't marked day by day. But now, after years apart, she took
Barhu's breath away. She had grown shoulders and arms and strong thighs to
match her height. There was a steadiness and a correctness in her, a confidence
that she would do her very best to find and accomplish the right thing.

"Baru?" Aminata said, in wary wonder of her own. "They took you away,
and I thought . . ."

"It's all right. It's all right. We"—she waved toward Yawa, a crow statue in
her quarantine gown—"we made an arrangement. I'm all right."

Aminata flinched. Her eyes fell off Barhu's. "I didn't know what Shir was
going to do. I really, genuinely did not know."

"No," Barhu cried, "don't be sorry— Oh, balls," spinning to Yawa and Svir,
"may I speak to her alone, please?"

"You look ready to tear in half," Svir said with some delight. "You shouldn't
be alone."

"You could go out to the end of the spit," Yawa said. "Just don't collapse into
the water."

"Come, come along." Barhu tugged Aminata off down the volcanic isthmus until it faded into water the exact same color as the stone. She wanted to embrace Aminata again and resisted only by holding on to her shoulders and kneading muscle like a cat. "Aminata, I'm so glad to see you."

At last she smiled, incredulous. "You talked your way out! I thought you were finished! How do you *do* it?"

"I told the truth. I told Yawa the truth."

"Can you tell me the truth?"

Tell Aminata that she was working against the Imperial Republic?

"Wydd," she said, invoking the ilykari who kept secrets, "I don't know. I don't know if I can tell you. That's the truth. Why are you here, Aminata?"

"One of my prisoners named you. He said you lured him to attack Aurdwynn, when you were playing rebel up there."

Barhu nodded. "I suppose that was Abdumasi Abd?"

Aminata covered her mouth. "Oh, fuck. Did you already know?"

"Know that you tortured him?" Barhu guessed.

Aminata hissed in dismay. "Maroyad's going to murder me!" She grabbed Barhu's shoulders in return, not gently. "I could *actually* be executed for this, Baru! I wasn't supposed to let anyone know Abd was in our possession; if Parliament finds out, they'll have the navy for grand treason—"

"Aminata. Aminata. Shh." Barhu actually laughed, and felt terrible for it. "It's okay. You'll be okay. I promise. If you're worried about the navy's future, I think Juris Ormsment might've done more damage than you ever will. Who's Maroyad, anyway?"

"My commanding officer on Isla Cauteria. She sent me to bring you in, on *Ascentatic*. And I . . . I went over to Ormsment, see, to get to you. I couldn't let anyone else do it. It had to be me. I didn't want to . . ." She straightened her combat harness, punctured chest and all. "I didn't want to never know."

"Never know what?" The newest, strangest thing Barhu had ever felt, this joy. She could find out what Aminata feared, and assure her it could be averted.

"Never know why you sent me that letter."

"What letter?" Barhu said, baffled, and then she remembered the letter she'd mailed to Aminata from the Elided Keep. *I wonder if we could discuss navy politics, and the mutability of government.*

"Did you send me that letter, Baru, to see if I'd join a mutiny against Parliament?"

"Oh, no, that's not what I meant at all! I wanted to give you a pretext to give the letter to Censorate, if you didn't want anything to do with me. . . ."

But now that she tried to explain it, she found her own rationalization flimsy and stupid. She clearly *had* wanted to discuss mutiny with Aminata. She'd just denied it to herself. She'd been too cowardly to confront the fact that she was putting Aminata in deadly danger.

Aminata's eyes were huge in the dark. "Why is Ormsment trying to kill you?"

"Revenge."

"Revenge for what?"

"I killed a lot of her sailors at Welthony Harbor."

Aminata hardened up, like she was about to get hit. You weren't supposed to do that. It made the blow hurt more.

"You did that? It happened exactly like people say?"

Barhu could do nothing but close her eyes and nod. "Yes. I tried to lure the sailors off the ships, but when they wouldn't come . . . we had to get the money out of the transports. We blew holes in the ships with mines. Pulled the gold and silver out with divers. A lot of sailors drowned, or died in the fighting. I couldn't stop the rebels from killing them without blowing my cover."

"Fuck, Baru. I knew people on those ships."

"I knew lots of the people I betrayed in Aurdwynn. I had to do it. It was my—"

"Your duty?"

"Yes. My duty, as written by the Throne."

Aminata blew out a shaky breath. "Those prisoners on the boat, those were your people?"

"Tain Hu's people," Barhu said, roughly. "I couldn't let them be hurt."

"Kings, Baru, why did you ask me about that day we were sparring?" The day they'd fought. "Why was that on your mind when Shir was about to spear you dead? Why *that*?"

"I guess it was the thing that I needed to know the most."

Aminata's eyes searched hers. "Why?"

"Because it made me afraid we weren't friends. And I needed to know who wanted me to feel that way."

"The merchant from Iriad. Farrier. He said it would be good for you to get a little fright from me. Why would he give a shit if we were friends?"

Barhu's smile tore at her face, stretched flesh that didn't want to move, and pricked a tear of pain from her good eye.

"Ow," she said. "Oh, Aminata, you have *no* idea."

HOW little Aminata had forgotten of her face! Those watchful, willful, stormwater-colored eyes. Her arched black brows. But her right eye was swollen almost shut, ghoulish purple, like the bruise Aminata had given her, with a practice sword, on the day they'd fought.

She looked down at Baru's hands and there were two fingers missing. "What happened?"

"Tain Shir. Last time we met."

"Oh, queen's cunt, I didn't *know*—"

"It's all right," Baru said, smiling that weird disjointed smile, tight and shy on the left side of her face, big and cocky on the right. "I think I needed that to happen. Anyway, you jumped in front of a spear for me, so we're square."

But they weren't square. There was a sorrow in Baru now, huge and edged and the opposite of brittle, beaten and alloyed into her and made sharp to cut. It hurt to look at her. Because you saw how much happier she might have been, in another world.

"So," Aminata said, fumbling the words like rope in seawater-numb hands. "I guess we're . . . we're at the point where I have to ask you where my duty lies. I was sent here to bring you in for questioning. I have a duty to Rear Admiral Maroyad to obey her orders. I even have a duty to obey Province Admiral Ormsment, though that duty's abrogated if she's in open mutiny. But . . . all those duties are overruled by obedience to the Throne, Baru. You could give me orders."

"I don't want to."

"What, you want me to take you back to Maroyad?" The burn on the web of Aminata's hand seemed to throb. Rear Admiral Maroyad's voice was encoded in that pain, driven into Aminata's flesh where she'd stubbed out her cigarette.

The moment anyone finds out we've got Abd, everyone comes for him. He's a coin to buy a war. The Judiciary will want him, and Parliament, and the Imperial fucking Throne . . . and to get to Abd, they will purge anyone who tries to hold him. . . .

"No," Baru said, as infuriating as she'd ever been. "That's not what I want. I just don't want to force you into anything, Aminata. What do you think you have to do?"

Aminata thought about duty.

You had a duty to your captain, to your admiral, to the Republic and its ideals, to the faceless and anonymous Emperor raised by lottery and chemistry to its impartial Throne. In service of that duty you beat your friend with a training sword and you snarled, *it's a crime against law and nature, you should've told me, they'll take a knife to your cunt!*

You did your duty to the navy and in return they made you a torturer. They told you *find the Cancrioth* but they never told you what a Cancrioth was. Just torture Abdumasi Abd, just make him give up the Cancrioth. And you tortured Abdumasi Abd so well that he named your friend Baru as an enemy of the navy. So you went out hunting for Baru, dutiful as ever, and you found one of the navy's own admirals driven to mutiny, driven to hunt and kill Baru . . . who was only acting out of her duty to the Throne. And the Hierarchic Qualm says that the hand is blameless when it acts in service to the Throne. Duty absolves all.

Put that way . . . Aminata's true duty was to obey Baru.

"Baru, why did you have to *do* any of this?" she asked. "Your exam scores were perfect. You could've had a post anywhere, anywhere at all, I was always so—"

Proud. She wanted to say it but she was afraid Baru wouldn't care. Aminata had been so proud to know an Imperial-rated savant, a foreign-born federati like her, racially outside like her, who could get anything she wanted through hard honest work.

Why had Baru given that up?

"I did it for Taranoke." Baru looked right into Aminata with her own wounded, blood-ringed eyes. "I could've been a fine accountant. I could've been promoted up to Falcrest and been a model federati. But I wanted to do something for Taranoke. I needed more than I could get from the civil service."

What's Taranoke, Aminata wanted to retort? What's home? It exists nowhere except in your memory. It's gone, it's changed, you can never go back.

She'd never had or needed a home.

But then she thought of swift *Lapetiare,* her first sea post, where you woke to your watch chime and went to your post knowing exactly who you were and why you were needed. The ship might change, the faces in the crew, the color and temper of the sea under the hull.

But that was still home. That place where you knew who you needed to be.

"How is any of this mess," she said in exasperation, "going to help Taranoke?"

"I'm not sure yet," Baru said, smiling that cocky lopsided smile that Aminata did not remember from school at *all.* "I've recently discovered the plan I thought I was pursuing . . . wasn't the plan. It was a mistake. Some part of me knows the real plan. It involves Aurdwynn, and these Cancrioth somehow . . . I've done things, strange things, and I need to learn why."

"Baru, that doesn't make any sense!"

"It does if I'm working in compartments." Her grin became that thoughtful, self-satisfied smile that child Baru had always produced when she got away with something.

It occurred to Aminata, not for the first time, but more urgently than it ever had before, that Baru might be insane. And that ugly thought made her remember another.

"Where's Shao Lune?" she blurted. "What happened to her? Was she really your—your slave?"

What had Baru done with her last navy companion?

Baru flinched. It was not a flinch backward but inward, retreating behind hardness, like an octopus into a shell. Aminata knew that Baru was about to lie.

But then she didn't. It cost her visibly, like sticking a hand in a wound to pull out the splinter within, but she told the truth.

"Shao Lune's on *Eternal,* the Cancrioth ship. I abandoned her there. With Tau-indi Bosoka and their bodyguard. I desperately need to keep that ship safe, Aminata. It's so important. The people on it are *so* important. Will you help me?"

"Baru, everything I saw tells me that ship is raising anchor and making ready to sail. And the moment she does she's going to run right into Ormsment."

Baru nodded. "I know. Will you help me remove her?"

"You mean—kill her?"

"Yes."

Baru was asking her to put the protection of a Cancrioth ship, an Oriati ship, over her own navy. It was blood treason. It was the absolute opposite of everything Aminata had ever strived to be.

"I . . . oh, qualms, Baru, I'm Ormsment's staff captain! She's supposed to *trust* me!"

"I know. I'm not going to try to persuade you. It wouldn't be fair. Just . . ." Baru squeezed her shoulders again, and, to Aminata's confused disappointment, let go. It was more affection than she had ever shown. "I could use your help. It's up to you to decide where your duty lies."

That, Aminata thought, was exactly what someone clever would say to manipulate her. But Baru clearly had the power to give her orders. If she wanted Aminata to do something, why not order her?

She asked a question that mattered to her. "I heard Ormsment sent a ship to take your parents. Is it true?"

"Yes." Baru rubbed at her bad eye and yawned. She needed a mint. "There were two mutineer ships, in the beginning. But we haven't seen *Scylpetaire* for weeks."

"And Tau-indi Bosoka is alive on that Cancrioth ship?"

"Yes."

Then her duty was clear. The navy was sworn to uphold diplomatic protection. The navy was sworn to obey Parliament and, above all else, the Emperor who did not know Its own name.

She had to help Baru destroy Ormsment.

But Ormsment had been kind to her, promoted her, believed in her. . . .

"I kept your sword," Baru blurted. "If you— I don't know if you ever wonder if I—you know, kept it. I did. It's on *Eternal,* with Shao Lune."

"Oh!" Aminata cried, and pawed at her neckline. Was it still there? Had it broken when she fell? "Look, I kept this, too!"

She drew the cormorant feather from her collar and showed it to Baru.

Then, without words, they put their foreheads together and held each other by the stubbled backs of their skulls.

AFTERWARD, when they had agreed on what to do, when Baru had explained the mathematician Kimbune and the two cylinders she'd brought from *Eternal,* Aminata watched Baru go back up the spit to the other prisoners.

She embraced the diver, Ulyu Xe, and whispered in Maia Urun. There was a change in Xe, like a wave finally breaking, and at last she moved of her own accord. She reached back for Baru.

Aminata watched Baru kiss her, promptly, like a signature on a promissory note. It felt weird to watch her friend kiss a woman. Not good weird. But weird like eating cantaloupe, which Aminata hated. You could see, theoretically, why someone else liked it.

"Now," Baru said, turning back to Aminata, "the Brevet-Captain Aminata will need to take me under arrest."

KEELHAUL

S
AILS away southeast! Ship coming around the headlands!"

Province Admiral Juris Ormsment leapt up to her frigate's shrouds, climbing like no woman her age really should. Finally! Finally it was happening. All night she'd waited for the alarm as *Sulane* stalked the husk of el-Tsunuqba, mining all the likely exits from the caldera, waiting, waiting, for the mystery ship to show itself.

Juris knew these ghosts: leviathans that appeared in secret out of the southwest, sighted occasionally, always lost in clouds of unnatural fog. If Baru had come to find that ship, there was something aboard which she valued more than all the lives she'd spent.

It all made a kind of awful sense, didn't it? Falcrest's antiegalitarian elite conspired with Oriati Mbo's most despicable revanchists to start the second Armada War. Kyprananoke would be the spark to light the rocket.

And only by mutinying against the very order of the navy had Juris uncovered the conspiracy. What did *that* say about loyalty?

Maybe Tain Shir was right. Maybe the mazes of duty were all built to keep you blind, and you had to start hacking through the walls to get out.

If Baru was conspiring not just against the navy but against the world's peace, and Juris brought proof to Falcrest . . . maybe she and all her sailors could go home again.

"Where?" she cried up to the lookout. "Point me!"

She followed the lookout's hand.

It was not the golden ship guarded by the sea monster. She knew that at once. Those were the uppermost sails of a fast clipper, the top republics, peeking over the black arm of el-Tsunuqba.

Apparitor had finally decided to end the chase.

"It's *Helbride*." Her one-legged flag captain stared in astonishment. They'd chased *Helbride* south across so many miles and now—"He's coming right at us."

"Where else would he go? He knows he can't outrun us any further. The

Prince-Ambassador left the ship, so they can't hide behind diplomatic right anymore. He has to bargain."

Helbride launched a volley of signal rockets. Debris from the blasts stippled the ocean surface and a black skua veered off protesting.

BREVET CAPTAIN AMN TO PROVINCE ADMIRAL ORM
HAVE BRU PRISONER
RED HAIR MAN REQUESTS PARLEY

Virtues preserve Aminata, she was still alive. "Ask his terms," Juris ordered. The rockets went out and came back.

RED HAIR MAN OFFERS BRU AND FULL PARDONS
IN EXCHANGE REQUESTS OUR SILENCE AND RETURN TO POSTS

"Do you think it's bait?" Juris asked her flag captain.

"Yes, mam, I think so."

But if it was bait, where the trap? "Let's play this carefully." A flash of steam inside her, the place where cold duty met white-hot betrayal. Scald yourself, Juris, and remember by the burn that the world is full of tricks. "Order *Helbride* to heave to half a mile away. Send our marines over to accept the Lieutenant Commander Aminata, Apparitor, and Baru herself. No one else."

"You think Apparitor will come over to *Sulane*, mam?"

"He'd better," she said. "I want some damn pardons written!"

The crew heard her. There were no cheers. She felt it anyway, that grim and glad hope: not hope of safety, but of seeing their revenge finally done.

"What about the Oriati ship, mam?" her flag captain asked. "We could be drawn out of position for the intercept."

"We won't be." Even if the titanic ship could, somehow, outrun them on the open ocean, it had to pass through a minefield to reach deep water. One strike would leave her crippled. They could raid the hulk for prisoners at their leisure.

But leave that thought for later. One stroke of the oar at a time. One and then the next.

THE fast clipper *Helbride,* as slim and hugely winged as a krakenfly, reefed her sails and drifted to a halt half a mile south of *Sulane*'s starboard bow. The morning wind was unsteady, though settling into a blow out of the west, and Juris had to admire the other crew's deftness. She sent over a launch full of marines to retrieve Baru and Brevet-Captain Aminata.

The water hammer beat so loud and hard inside Juris that it set her rocking on her feet. This was when they set a trap for you, of course: when you thought you had won. But if you thought that way your whole life you would talk yourself out of ever winning.

She went over to the starboard side, to check on Captain Nullsin's distant *Ascentatic*. He was doing his blameless and definitely unmutinous duty, barking like a sheepdog at the swarm of ships waiting for a steady sailing wind. (Falcrest's ships, with their superior rigging, could get more speed out of less air: the Oriati and Aurdwynni traders and pirates here depended on strong, sustained wind.)

When the wind came back steady, the quarantine would fail. There were too many ships, too many channels through the kypra where a canny captain could sneak away.

She turned her spyglass on the kypra islands. The first thing she saw was a raft of corpses swarming with crabs. Most of the capital islet Loveport had gone up in fire overnight, torched by Canaat rebels. Now that the initial rush was over, both sides were busy consolidating their territory and purging their ranks. Anyone with insufficient commitment would be killed as a collaborator; anyone who refused to denounce and punish collaborators would be killed as an enemy of the revolution (or of the state). It would go this way because that was how it had happened in Falcrest, after Lapetiare's revolution. In a few weeks the Canaat leaders would turn on each other, and the winners would build a new government as cruel and selfish as Kyprism, because if they were not cruel and selfish they would be torn down by those who were. And the cycle would begin again.

All her years in the navy Juris had wondered when that cycle would turn over in Falcrest. When the corrupt greedy Parliament and those vultures in the Judiciary would be cast down to the drowning stone.

Some of Juris' crew, seeing the Kyprananoki killing each other, called them savages. Juris couldn't agree. Hadn't they done exactly the same thing in the course of their own mutiny? Killed everyone at the Elided Keep with knives and machetes?

The real problem would be the corpses. The Kyprananoki didn't have enough land to bury their dead, or enough fuel to burn them. So the dead were weighted and cast into the deep sea. That meant fishermen hauling loads of bodies, smearing their holds in Kettling blood. Some of them would catch fish while they were out there. Haul those fish home in the same holds.

Baru was beaten. But what the fuck were they going to do about the Kettling?

She would have to convince Nullsin that she'd made the right choices. They would have to cooperate.

"Boat's returning from *Helbride*, mam," her aide called. "They have Baru, Apparitor, and Brevet-Captain Aminata aboard."

THE pieces were in play. There was nothing to do now but watch. If we had miscalculated, then *Eternal* was lost, and with it my chance to satisfy Hesychast's need for a eugenic miracle.

Execarne's people found a rock escarpment on el-Tsunuqba's northeastern flank, a place where goatherds liked to perch and watch their vertical flocks. I admit that the morning sun even had me considering a nap.

Then Faham Execarne came stumping up the goat path, red-eyed and wild-haired, to discuss the end of the world.

"Faham!" I moved over on the cushion to make room for him. "You look like you've had too much to smoke."

"Not nearly enough." He sat down in a puff of cannabis stink. "You know, I tried to convince Baru they were just a Morrow Ministry deception. Cover for our own work in the Mbo."

"The Cancrioth?" I laughed. "Did she believe you?"

"I don't think so. It was worth a try. I thought, if we made her believe they didn't exist, she might not find them. I suppose I underestimated her willingness to chase delusions." He sighed blearily. "Don't give me that look."

I found Faham's idea of reality as a malleable thing, subject to the influence of our minds, very silly. If it were true, surely the fantasies of all the poor and sickly would have worked some improvement by now.

"You weren't really trying to persuade her, Faham. The lie was for Tau, wasn't it?" Faham Execarne had collaborated with the Oriati prince to help protect the peace. I thought they were even friends.

He grumbled and scooped rocks from under his ass. "I wouldn't lie to Tau."

"No. But Tau would have preferred it if *you* had no idea the Cancrioth existed." I patted his thigh. "And deep down, Faham, I think you like to make people happy."

"Pfah." He went rummaging in my bag. "No food?"

"I'm too nervous."

"Did you know I wrote the *War Paper*?"

"The dire one? The one that predicts the end of all civilization?"

He nodded silently.

"Alarmism to frighten Parliament, isn't it?"

He shook his head. "There's something I have to tell you." And he pointed upslope, behind us, toward the towering south wall of the flooded caldera.

"There's an apocalypse fuse here," he said.

"An apocalypse *what*?"

"Explosive charges buried in the rock of el-Tsunuqba's south face."

"What?" A pine-needle brush ran up my spine. I had been to Mount Kijune to walk the cliff bridges, and I had imagined what might happen to the villages below if the mountain face slipped. "But that can't possibly work. . . ."

"It can work. It's been done before, on a smaller scale. 'Aligning the dead world with the needs of the living Republic.' It will be done again here." He squinted into the rising sun. "Once a year one of my agents climbs the mountain, pulls a random charge, and tests it. If anything, time has made them more volatile. They're still ready to be used."

"It's nonsense. This much rock? Nothing human could move it."

He blinked sun dazzle out of his eyes. His shoulders were tight, hands pressed heel-down to the stone. "You see how el-Tsunuqba is shaped? Like a cup tipped over, facing north? When old Mount Tsunuq erupted, it blasted out its north face. The south face is still strong on its outside edge . . . but the inner face, above the caldera, is just loose debris and fill."

He drew a shape in the air, a cone like a torchship's Burn siphon, defined by the south wall, the east and west slopes, and the caldera, all aimed north into the kypra atoll. "Do you see?"

"Oh," I said, quietly. The idea was almost impossible to hold on to. It couldn't happen so quickly. Not to so many people. Ridiculous. "But the kypra's quite widely scattered . . . the avalanche would hardly reach it. . . ."

"No. It wouldn't. The rock face would slide into the caldera. But the east and west ridges would . . ."

"Would what?"

He burst into a fit of coughing. I tried to pat him on his back but he fought me off. "The east and west ridges would focus the displacement wave!"

"Like a tsunami?" The big waves that struck the Mothercoast of Falcrest and Devi-naga Mbo.

"No. No. Tsunamis are swells in the ocean, like the sea's decided to move inland. Peak wave height is maybe thirty feet, but the wave just never stops. The damage comes from the whole mound of water migrating inland. This would be the opposite. Water displaced by material dropping into the sea. Narrow, very narrow. But . . ."

He held a hand up above his head.

Tall, he was saying. Tall.

IT was the hardest salute of Aminata's life.

Some people wouldn't take their gods' names in vain. Some people wouldn't use words like *bitch* or *tunk*. Some had secret names for their lovers that they never spoke in anger. Most everyone had something they did, every day, that was a bit like a prayer to the things they believed in.

Aminata saluted that way. She meant every one she'd ever made.

"Mam," she said, crisply, to Juris Ormsment's black-bruised eyes and ragged uniform, to those admiral's pins she'd vowed to serve, "may I present the prisoner."

Baru grunted and went down to her knees on *Sulane*'s weather deck. Her bad hand hit first and she cried out, fell with the wounded hand clasped to her chest, her right shoulder striking the deck.

One of the officers behind Ormsment laughed in a kind of shock. That's her? That's all?

"Here she is!" Apparitor flourished like a waiter serving a trussed-up stag. "Freshly lobotomized, courtesy of the Jurispotence Xate Yawa, who provided the medical finding that justified Baru's arrest. All done legally, thank you. All of it notarized and ready to stand in court. No one on this ship would want to do anything *illegal*, would they?"

He glared at Juris Ormsment. She didn't even look at him. Aminata shivered: the admiral's eyes were coolly and completely sieving Baru into particles of hate. Some of her officers jostled and muttered, staring at Apparitor. Aminata didn't know exactly why. She'd asked him, on the boat trip, who he was: he had given her a big smile and a smug "I am the Emperor's humble servant."

Now he pointed to the master's mate who had just, in Aminata's estimation, started to think about pulling a knife.

"Don't you dare. You wouldn't like what happens to your admirals when I die."

"What would happen to me if you died?" Juris Ormsment asked, absently. She was still studying Baru.

"Letters would be sent," Apparitor said, with sweet answering menace. "Courts would be convened. Do you remember the Paybale Affair, Juris? It'd be a shame if everyone on that bank's deposit list were to be published in *Advance* . . . and a crying shame if the world knew where that money really came from. No one is clean." His eyes raked the crowd. "None of you. Juris here wouldn't have invited you on this voyage if you hadn't sinned. And the Emperor knows all sins."

The Traitor-Admiral stared at Baru with a powerful wonder. How could Baru be? One young woman. Just one. You might see her in a secretarial pool and note her only for her black frowning eyes. But so many lives had ended on her account. Pan Obarse, a man Aminata had admired for his perseverance despite a cruel harelip and the obstacle of his race: he'd died on *Mannerslate* when Baru blew it up. And that boy on the Llosydanes whose head had burned to coal. And those poor garrison regulars in Aurdwynn whose tendons had been slashed. And all those Aurdwynni who'd followed the Coyote banner. All gone on Baru's account.

"Can she understand me?" Ormsment breathed.

"Try her," Apparitor said. "Lobotomites are passive, not stupid."

Baru flinched when the admiral came toward her, and Aminata clamped a hand on her shoulder to steady her. It was possible Ormsment might just kill her now, knife across the throat: but Aminata knew, better than anyone, how vital it was to be sure Baru *understood* what she'd done.

Ormsment crouched on the balls of her feet. "Can you hear me?"

"Yes." Baru's shoulder tightened in Aminata's grip. "I can hear you."

"Is this a trick? Did you come to my ship because you think you can turn me?"

"No," Baru said, thickly.

"Do you understand why you're here?"

"Because Apparitor and Durance sold me out." A snarl crossed her naked face and died halfway. "Because Aminata doesn't trust me."

"That's why you're here?"

"Yes."

Ormsment looked at her gloves for a moment, perhaps considering the dignity of an officer and the proper treatment of prisoners.

Then she backhanded Baru on her lobotomy eye. Baru cried out. Aminata kept her upright, and kept her own face reefed tight.

"Tell me why you're here," Ormsment repeated.

Away north, *Ascentatic* launched a barrage of signal fireworks. The crackle of detonations carried on a rising westerly wind.

"I'm sorry," Baru whispered.

"I didn't ask for an apology. I asked you to tell me why you're here."

"I really am sorry, anyway. For the harm done to you, and for everyone you've harmed."

From this new angle Aminata could see the raw bit of scalp where the rim of

Ormsment's mask had rubbed against her hair. The mark of this mask and all the masks she'd worn before it.

"Actions," she told Baru, "have consequences. Do you understand me? You betrayed me and killed hundreds of my sailors. I am the consequence."

Didn't Aminata believe in this? You had to teach people that their missteps would be punished, and their dutiful service rewarded. If they stopped believing that, who knew what they'd become.

Apparitor buffed his nails on his lacy cuffs. "I'd like to be off. Afraid I can't stay for an officer's mess, as there's a ghost ship still out there and a fine young man aboard I need to rescue. Here are my terms. Note them well. You will all receive full and countersigned Imperial pardons—"

Some of the gathered officers cheered. It was a grim sound but it was still a cheer. Aminata, by reflex, almost joined them. You never wanted to be the Oriati sailor who didn't cheer.

"—but I will do all in my power to revoke those pardons if Empire Admiral Lindon Satamine has been harmed during my absence."

Beneath the mask, Ormsment's mouth pursed in fascination. Her eyes were only for Baru. "I'm sure Sir Satamine is very well. No one else in the Admiralty played any part in these events. Rear Admiral Samne Maroyad's innocence is on official record. The very same communique she sent to warn me that Baru was conspiring to start a war *also* begged me not to do anything about it." Ormsment took Baru's hand and examined the stumps of her missing fingers. "Do you have conditions for Baru, too?"

"Oh, don't kill her yet. She's full of secrets." He smiled slyly back at Aminata. "Why don't you have the Burner of Souls take care of her?"

Ormsment's gaze settled on Aminata at last.

Mercy, Aminata thought, mercy, please look away. For she couldn't bear the sympathy in the old Province Admiral's face.

"No," Ormsment said, "no, I won't make the staff captain hurt her friend. Staff Captain Aminata, please turn the prisoner over to me. I'll have some questions for you later, about your conduct during the capture."

"Mam," Aminata said, quietly, "permission to retire below for the duration." The metal cylinder Baru had given her, the profane Cancrioth instrument, was tucked into her fighting harness. It seemed far too heavy for its size.

"Granted," Ormsment said. "Go."

Baru huddled smaller. She looked so entirely alone, surrounded by her enemies, hopeless: and yet at peace. Completely content. Never in her life had Aminata expected to see that expression on her face.

It was because Baru couldn't do anything. She could, at last, stop working.

"Master-at-arms!" Ormsment called. "Prepare the ropes!"

Apparitor turned lazily. "You *do* know she's too valuable to hang, don't you?"

"And she's far too dangerous to keep aboard."

"Really? Lobotomized, wounded, and alone?"

"She was exiled and discredited when she tricked my ships into Welthony Harbor. Anything she does might be a ploy." Ormsment nodded in decision. "No delays. No last meals or final letter. If she has some sort of contingency plan, or agents hidden in our crew, then we'll force them to act. If she dies in the process, so be it."

Aminata's stomach twisted. "Mam? What do you mean?"

"Keelhaul her," Ormsment ordered.

I N the science of Incrastic behaviorism there was a concept called "the dominant response." Barhu had always hated it. "The thing an organism tends to do in a given situation": what kind of useless tautology was that? What use was it to say, oh, yes, people tend to do the thing they tend to do?

And now she understood it. She knew her own dominant response.

Tie a woman up to be keelhauled. Tie her up and hurl her under the prow of a warship and drag her along the barnacle-edged hull in a race between asphyxiation and death by blood loss. What is her dominant response? Does she fall limp? Does she faint? Does she struggle and roar? Each woman will have her own tendency.

Barhu knew her own dominant response. It was cold, serpentine calm.

"I know the answer to the riddle," she said.

A single line ran from her waist, over the point of the frigate's prow, down under her entire length, up to the sterncastle, and back across the deck to Barhu again, completing a full circle. A gang of sailors waited amidships, ready to haul on the rope and thus drag Barhu under the ship from stem to stern. A second loop ran side to side around *Sulane* like an enormous bridle, with Barhu as the bit. By taking in the slack on this loop, the crew could adjust Barhu's depth. If they left her deep, she would drown before she made it to the stern. If they dragged her shallow she would be shredded by the hull.

"What's that?" Juris Ormsment knelt beside her. Her voice was almost motherly. Maybe devoting your whole being to someone's end was a little like devoting yourself to their beginning. "What answer do you know?"

"The riddle about the three ministers and the poison. Shao Lune told me"— she stopped to groan against the pain in her eye—"she told me you asked everyone about that riddle. Wherever you went."

"I do, Baru. Because I care how other people think about the world. Where did you take Shao Lune?"

"Do you want to know the answer, Province Admiral? The right answer?"

"There's no right answer," Juris said, because how could there be, the riddle was designed to provoke. Three ministers have gathered for dinner when they taste poison in their wine. One attending secretary has a dose of antidote. All three ministers demand the bottle.

One minister says, give me the antidote, or I will release the files that detail all your affairs and mistakes.

The next minister says, give me the antidote, or I will destroy your right to ever bear children.

The third minister pulls a knife.

Who gets the antidote? Whose power is strongest? Who is truly in control? Why should the secretary, who has all the power here, yield to one minister over another? It was a bad riddle, in the end. You couldn't answer it without making some smarmy, lawyerish argument about the primacy of one power over the rest.

Only it was *not* a bad riddle, Barhu had realized.

"There's a right answer. I figured it out when you told me that you had my parents. People are engines, Juris. Each of a unique make. And if you discover the schematics of that engine you may find the power that drives it. You'd found a power over me that I couldn't challenge, because everything I do comes from that day when I was seven years old and I wanted to make my parents happy again."

"You're babbling."

"I'm not. This is the answer."

"There is no answer—"

"There is. Who contrived to put three ministers at a dinner party with poisoned wine and only one dose of antidote? Who arranged the dinner? Who provided the poison? That person has the true power."

"It's a rhetorical device, you self-important cunt," Juris said, with a contempt that was almost fond.

"No," Barhu said, her accountant's mind sweeping over history, over what had been and what was yet to come, this second Armada War between Falcrest and the Mbo, the Throne concealed behind its masks, the Cancrioth tumored in the thriving Oriati heartlands, these forces converging. As a child she had asked her mother, as they watched a Falcresti warship come into Iriad, *Why do they come here and make treaties? Why do we not go to them? Why are they so powerful?*

She knew why.

"Power can't be separated from its history. A choice can't be taken in isolation from its context. Power is the ability to set the terms of the riddle. To arrange the rewards and punishments by which the choice is judged."

The traitor can choose to execute her lover for political gain but she cannot choose the laws that condemn her lover as a traitor, or alter those men who stand to benefit and to suffer from her choice. Falcrest made those laws. Falcrest made those men. Not her. True power was not the ability to conduct a killing or a business deal or an assignation but to alter the context by which those acts were judged and evaluated.

"I'm really very clever," Barhu whispered.

"You should have been a student." Ormsment sighed. "Everyone would've been so much happier."

She pushed Barhu forward onto the bowsprit. The keel rope dangled off her waist like a doubled umbilical cord, front and back. The bridle ropes tugged her port and starboard as the sailors adjusted the slack.

Barhu stared down into the warm blue waters of dying Kyprananoke. Gods, she thought. It looks just like the Halae cove. Where I learned to swim.

"Baru Cormorant," Juris pronounced, "by the powers invested in me by the *Book of the Sea*, powers which do transcend the authorities of the landlocked state, I sentence you to death for the crimes of murder and treason. The sentence will be carried out at once."

And she shoved Barhu off the bowsprit.

WHEN the sailing master cried *heave!* then Aminata knew it had begun. Nothing to do now. Just do what you need to do, Aminata, get it done, stop imagining her down there while the barnacles saw her apart—

She shuddered. The heavy cylinder in her hands closed, iron case sliding on oiled runners, and ruined the entire sequence.

"Shit," she muttered, and started again.

Kimbune had taught her to use the uranium lamp exactly like a signal lantern. You flashed it open and shut, and apparently the invisible light went out through wood and stone, to be perceived by (Kimbune had been very offended when Aminata laughed) a frog. The frogs had been bred for sensitivity and range. They glowed when they sensed the uranium light, and the more of the black pitchblende rock you exposed to air, the more the frogs glowed.

Aminata had no idea whether to believe any of it. But she began the sequence again anyway, exactly as Kimbune had taught her: beginning with

Kimbune's special code, then the letters that apparently meant MINE, and then the coordinates.

In the pool of lamplight beneath her was a chart of *Sulane*'s minefields. Aminata had asked for the chart so she could double-check that the positions of the mines had been correctly relayed to Captain Nullsin on *Ascentatic*. It was the kind of job you might expect a staff captain to handle.

When she'd heard Kimbune speak in her own Cancrioth language, she'd flinched. She'd recognized that tongue. It was the language that had frightened her interrogator Gerewho Gotha; it was the language Abdumasi Abd had used to curse them. Incrasticism said that her antipathy toward that language was really a hereditary taint, blood recognition of the Mbo's ancient enemy. Aminata didn't know if she believed that.

There were things Incrasticism couldn't explain, and the uranium lamp was one of them.

Aminata had asked Kimbune, "Is that magic?"

Yes, Kimbune had said, it's true magic. Not the only true magic in the world, or even the strangest. But it is magic. And you must respect it.

Now a boot fell behind her. A woman cleared her throat. Aminata couldn't abort the sequence: she just kept shuttering the iron sleeve, up and down, up and down, turning numbers into flashes of invisible light.

"What's that, Staff Captain?" Juris Ormsment asked.

"It's a device from the enemy ship, sir," Aminata said, oathbound to tell the truth. "I recovered it from the Morrow Ministry party. They'd taken it from a prisoner."

"What does it do?"

"It's supposed to send messages at a great distance."

"Mm," Juris said. "Interesting belief. Why are you using it?"

"I'm just trying to detect any change in temperature, any strange ache, whatever might suggest a function."

"And the minefield chart?"

Oh, why did it have to be Ormsment herself? Anyone else she could've tried to pull rank on. . . .

"Ah, mam, I thought I'd try to send a set of map coordinates, the way you might flash them with a signal lantern. Then we could see whether the Oriati ship paid special attention to that area. But I had to be certain I didn't steer them around our minefield by accident. So I thought I'd check that I wasn't sending the coordinates of the mines."

"Perhaps the sort of thing you'd best run by me first," Ormsment said, dryly. "Communicating with the enemy."

"Yes, mam, only I thought, if they have the ability to send flashes across great distances, it's very important to know. They might be in communication with other ships here. Or parties ashore."

"An excellent point," Ormsment allowed. "Still. The kind of initiative you clear with your commander, yes?"

"Yes, mam. I was just"—and wasn't this the truth—"ashamed, mam. I didn't want to be seen . . . engaging in Oriati superstition."

She finished the last sequence and closed the cylinder. She had already sent the warning Baru had requested, about *Sulane*'s speed and armament, about the powerful need to stay out of torpedo and rocket range.

Now, with her back to Ormsment and the weight of her duty on her shoulders, she said what she had decided she had to say. This was not part of anyone else's plan. This was hers.

"About the Oriati ghost ship, mam."

"Yes?"

"I saw her up close. I don't think we can take her intact. With tensions so high, maybe it's best to . . . to let her slip the net. So as not to provoke the Oriati. Especially as Tau-indi Bosoka is a hostage aboard."

Ormsment was silent for a moment.

Aminata held her breath.

"Staff Captain," the Province Admiral said, with deep and painful affection, "you took some of my marines last night, and you went in search of Baru. I frankly believed you'd been killed, or arrested to vanish forever. Or, according to what my marines reported, defected to Baru's side. And, to be quite honest"— oh, she was coming closer, kneeling to confide—"if you hadn't brought Baru back with you, I wouldn't have let you aboard. I would've discharged you from my service and returned you to *Ascentatic*."

Oh, she couldn't bear this. "I'm sorry if I disappointed you, mam."

"My marines say you welcomed Baru as an old friend. That means you put your personal need for closure above the integrity of my command. Which"—Ormsment laughed sharply—"I can't very well condemn. But that's all done now, understand? Baru's finished. We have to look to the future. We have to *prove* that we did all this to stop the harm she'd done to our Republic. So our mission now is to capture that vessel and return prisoners to Falcrest."

"Even with the Oriati ambassador aboard?"

"The ambassador that Baru kidnapped? I think we have every right to try to rescue them."

"But, mam . . ."

She looked back at Ormsment then, helpless to express what she had to say: *if you don't back down, mam, I have to kill you.*

The Province Admiral smiled wistfully down at her.

"If we gave ourselves the chance, we'd talk ourselves out of ever doing anything. Because the world's not fair, and that means anything you do might turn out unfairly. Duty's not about calculating every outcome, Aminata. It's not about making a complicated schematic of everything that might unfold. Duty's about acting the way you'd want the whole world to act, anyone in this situation, anywhere, now and forever." She beat her knuckles once against the wall, rapping the bones of her ship. "If I'd drowned in Welthony Harbor, I know that I'd want the woman responsible hunted to the ends of the world. And I'd want her schemes uncovered. Baru wanted something from that ship. That means I have to find it, and bring it to light. Even now that she's gone."

"Gone, mam?"

"Yes." Ormsment's eyes softened. "I came down here to see if you were all right. I know you were close to her, before she . . . made her choices."

"I want to see her body, mam," Aminata said, very steadily, as glassy and smooth as a bottle.

"I'm sorry. She didn't make it."

"Mam?"

"The barnacles cut the rope. We watched for a body, but she must've sunk. Nothing came up but blood."

12

MAN AUL AUM RA NA O AEL-IT

THE sea struck Barhu right in the jaw, knocked her teeth apart, flooded her with hot salt and *Sulane*'s black pitch. She shut her right eye as tight as she could, afraid that the ocean would leak into her brain.

As a girl, she'd liked to drift in the Halae shallows, feeling the tug of current and tasting the sweet silt. Listening to the happy commerce of paddles and oars.

It was almost the same—

The rope around Barhu jerked taut and slammed her against the curve of the ship's prow, down across the copper-jacketed keel, like pepper on a cook's knife. She noticed, absurdly, that *Sulane* had been well-careened before she left Treatymont, and that the copper jacket had kept new barnacles from growing.

Mostly.

Something cut through her, as thin as the edge of a letter, from her right buttock to the back of her left shoulder. She hiccuped on seawater. A warm wet insinuation crept around her eye. She thought that maybe she had just died, doomed by an infected brain—

They hauled her again. Deeper.

The copper saved her life from dismemberment by barnacle so that she could drown instead. The rope pulled so deep into her skin that blood rose black around it. She was stretched out wrist to ankle like a living eight-knot, she was being dragged apart—she had to stay conscious! If she fainted she was lost!

The warship's shadow darkened everything. After weeks and miles of pursuit, *Sulane* was at last overrunning Barhu.

Mother Pinion's voice called down the decades. *Baru. Pay attention.*

I'm trying, Mother. It's just so dark down here—

Baru. Stay awake!

A hand touched Barhu's stomach. A hard knee brushed her thigh.

She looked down: saw her, just where she'd promised she would be. The diver Ulyu Xe, who could swim four hundred feet without coming up for breath. Who'd come over to *Sulane* by breathing through a reed, hidden from the sentries.

Barhu could have shouted all her air in joy.

Xe crawled up the length of her, hands tugging at Barhu's cassock. The black blade clenched in her teeth glittered like an eclipse. The knife had come from one of Faham Execarne's Morrow-men, six inches of el-Tsunuqba's black glass, knapped to an edge so sharp it parted rope like gauze.

Xe slashed the bridle-rope from Barhu's waist, reached up above Barhu's wrists, and cut the drag rope. Barhu's wrists snapped free, numb from fingertip to elbow. The next *heave* from above whipped the rope round her waist like a brand and it slithered in a searing coil around her ankles and away. They would know at once it was broken, but they would not know if it was the rope that had failed or Barhu's body. They would rush to the sides and look for her to surface.

Barhu shrugged out of the heavy cassock and clung to Xe.

The diver kicked toward *Sulane*'s stern and the blind spot around the frigate's rudder. Barhu's thin cut bled a red cape behind them. On a bad day she could hold her breath for three minutes if she didn't have to move. The keelhauling had cost her, but she could last two minutes yet. Xe's skin brushed wonderfully against Barhu's, a cool balm for rope burn.

She was alive! She'd come through that terrible night on *Eternal* and there was no cancer in her skull and no vial of Kettling in her pocket and no Tau-indi or Iraji or Shao Lune but she was in the water, she was free, she was *alive*.

When Barhu opened her eyes she saw the moon.

But of course it wasn't the moon. It was the steel sickle mounted on the Cancrioth whale's fin. And he was coming toward them through the wavering light. Coming with his jaws wide open, propped open, because he was carrying something in his teeth—

Barhu gurgled in alarm.

The cancer whale came at her with a naval mine in his jaws.

"HERE are your pardons!" Apparitor shouted. "Bottoms up!"

Aminata came up the ladder to the maindeck at the exact moment the red-haired man shot a flask of vodka, whooped, and hurled it overboard. In his other hand he brandished a fistful of paper. "Here! See them here?"

He shook the sheaf of documents like a dead seagull. "Take them! Every last one of you absolved of your crimes, from grand mutiny down to your overdue books in Shaheen! But they lack *one* thing!"

He scattered the pardons across the deck. Sailors pounced. Officers brayed for order.

"This is the missing piece!" He brandished a grapefruit-sized device, like a spherical clock. "This is an incryptor. It produces the codes which mark the Emperor's authentic orders. Those codes will be carefully checked when you present these pardons to save your wretched lives! I have omitted the last digit of each one—and *only* I can supply the correct numbers! If I survive my return to *Helbride,* I will flash you the numbers, one by one, as my ship makes for the horizon. Do you understand?"

Juris Ormsment stepped up to the high rail on the quarterdeck. "Apparitor. This isn't necessary. We had a deal."

Apparitor's pretty face hardened. "Deal's done. I want safe conduct to *Helbride.*"

"Why?" Ormsment called. "What's gotten you so skittish? Need to water your mason leaf?" A few sailors laughed.

"You thug," Apparitor said, sweetly, "we both know you've got no reason to let me go once I sign those pardons. You'll try to keep me aboard. You'll try to control me. I won't have it."

"I'd shoot you dead like a dog if not for your vendettas, yes." Juris came slowly around to the quarterdeck stairs, began to descend to the weather deck. Her hands were wide and empty. "But that day won't be today. Stamp the pardons. Let's turn our attention to troubles ashore."

Apparitor made eye contact with Aminata, just for an instant, and his eyes said *get out now.*

But Aminata wasn't going to run away with the job half-finished.

She slipped over to the starboard rail. A sunflash lantern on a hook waited for the officer of the watch to post news to *Ascentatic.* Aminata set the lantern on its bearings, trained the lens at Captain Nullsin's distant frigate, pointed the collector at the sun, and began to work the shutter as quietly as she could.

NULNULNUL
AMNAMNAMN
ONE RED IF YOU SEE ME
ONE RED IF YOU SEE ME

Nullsin had of course posted a double watch on the mast tops, in case of ships fleeing. She'd asked him to keep an eye out for messages from *Sulane.* She trusted him.

Almost at once a red flare ignited up in *Ascentatic's* republic sails. They'd seen her.

"Oh, Juris!" Apparitor cried. "You think we're going to *fix* Kyprananoke? Solve it like a little puzzle? Once the wound's in the gut there's nothing you can do but end it quick!"

He was up on the port rail now, his feet tap-tap-tapping between lines and brackets as he danced out onto the channels that moored the huge mainmast shroud lines. "Time's up! I'm going to leave, I'm going to *go*, and you'd damn well better do the same! Because that thing out there will have your little ship for a toothpick!"

Sulane's rigging moaned in the rising wind.

Everyone else was utterly silent.

Behind Apparitor, the mountain gave birth.

O H, *virtues* . . ." someone breathed.
    A great rustle ran through the crew. At last the mast-top girls looked up from the drama below and cried out, "Sails! Sails away west! Ship coming out of the caldera!"

Fog rolled out of el-Tsunuqba, low and heavy, thick as soapsuds. Aminata knew at a glance that it was unnatural. But not half as unnatural as the silhouette that loomed within. The four hundred feet of preposterous immensity.

Eight masts, junk-rigged, not tall by Falcrest standards but absurd in their number. Sails like the canopy of a cloud forest. Huge curved broadsides, deck upon deck, studded with cannon-ports.

Eternal came forth. For the first time, Aminata saw it in sunlight.

Fuck me, she thought. It's like a city.

Ormsment stared at the behemoth and Aminata saw the shroud of duty settle over her, smoothing her brow, flattening the cables of her throat. The admiral had seen her enemy.

"Give Apparitor a boat," Ormsment commanded. "See him safely away. Sound battle stations and rig for fighting trim."

Her crew looked up to her.

"That ship," she roared to her crew, "belongs to the Oriati who released plague on these islands! I saw it done at the embassy! If they released plague here, *they can bring it to Falcrest*!"

"At any moment that ship is going to strike a mine. And when it does, we will be in position to take it. We will bring the survivors back to Falcrest and we will reveal to our people what was done here. We will be heroes! Are you with me?"

A roar of approval and Aminata wanted to join it—she was trained to lead marine assaults, seizing the titan compartment by compartment, gassing out the degenerate Oriati conspirators from their warrens and pits.

She imagined them whispering in Falcrest about what Aminata had done, about the prize the Burner of Souls had taken. Cheering her as she stood up before Parliament, drawing record attendance for a member of her race. And her name registered upon the Antler Stone, the first Oriati chiseled into that long list of the people's champions.

Imagine how proud Maroyad would be when Aminata reported back to her . . . imagine a crew, her crew, calling her *captain* . . .

"Mam?" a small voice called.

Aminata looked up from the lantern and there before her was a girl, the youngest person Aminata had seen on *Sulane*, which was crewed mostly by old-leather sea revenants and battered rope-ends. This girl was gangly, not more than seventeen, with the roughed-up voice of adolescence.

And she was Aurdwynni: pale as snow, with Stakhi blood and a round face and sunburn on her ears. She must have some mark on her service jacket, some weakness of behavior or heredity, which said that she would never be more than an able sailor. So Juris had accepted her on this final voyage.

"Mam," the girl said, saluting, "if you've not got a fighting station, master-at-arms says we could use you down with the marines."

And she bounded off across the slanting deck, across coiled shroudlines and boat ties, nimble as a squirrel.

When Tain Shir's spear had punched her in the chest, Baru had screamed, *no! Not her! No!*

Baru wanted her to live. Baru demanded that she live. Baru had said, *you send your signal to Nullsin, and you get off that ship.*

But the girl. She was so young. . . .

L OOK." I guided Faham's hand to the little dot of color that tossed in *Sulane's* rising wake. The frigate was turning west, as we'd hoped it wouldn't, but at least there was good news: "Do you see that boat there? Apparitor's slipping away."

"Where's *my* spyglass?" he groused. "You! Go get me one of the Stakhi optics!"

"We haven't any, Your Excellence, we sold them last month to launder the kickbacks from the—"

"My ministry for a telescope," Faham groaned. "Someone!"

One of his Morrow-men scurried off to find him a lens just as another party of spies arrived with the prisoner Kimbune. I watched the Cancrioth woman carefully. She'd been nervous and withdrawn, but there was a deep-set fear-lessness in her, too; not arrogance, I thought, but the assurance of divine protection.

She did not seem assured now.

At the sight of *Eternal* she cried out. "You said you'd get them away safely." She looked between me and the red angles of tall *Sulane,* swinging west to intercept. "You said they'd escape!"

"They've cleared the minefield," I assured her, which I had deduced from *Eternal*'s failure to explode. The ship, Baru said, was full of rocket-powder. "The trick with your uranium lamp worked. Aminata gave them the correct coordinates for the safe passage."

"But your navy ship is still there! It still has all its weapons! The Brain made us do drills, how to die before the fire could get to you—you'll let them all die like that? You promised me!"

I gave her a grandmotherly smile, wholly counterfeit. I had absolutely no idea what might happen when the two ships met. "Baru and the young Aminata have a plan to see to *Sulane.* Faham, what is that ship doing now?"

He was still in his foul mood, and that would only make him fouler: he would think his anger was causing misfortune. "What a disaster if we lose Tau," he muttered. "That laman gave us at least ten extra years of peace, I'm sure of it. Quickly, quickly, which way's the wind?"

"Out of the west." With the sunrise the westerly blow had steadied and strengthened. I had no real understanding of wind or current, so I could not say if this was a manifestation of some nautical law. Weather was notoriously unpredictable at the edge of the Kraken Still.

"Hm." Execarne grimaced. "Then *Eternal* has the weather gage over *Sulane.*"

"That's good for them, isn't it?" This I remembered from my conversations about pirate-hunting with Ahanna Croftare, before she'd been promoted and replaced by Ormsment. Whoever had the weather gage was upwind of their foe, and could ride the wind down on them.

"Not this time. The weather gage benefits an attacker but hurts a defender." Faham knuckled his temples, plucked fitfully at the hairs of his beard. "The wind will push them toward *Sulane.* They have to fight. If they fight, they'll lose. And if Ormsment goes home with a Cancrioth prize, we'll be razing Oriati cities and retching up Kettling blood by autumn."

"Trust Aminata," I suggested.

"Can't trust anyone," he grunted.

"I trust you, Faham," I said, which was true, as far as my trust went.

A Morrow-man returned with a spyglass for Execarne. He trained it on *Eternal* and moaned. "Oh, virtues. There's Tau. . . ."

A small figure in a bright khanga stood at *Eternal*'s rail. I reached for Execarne's hand and he gripped me so hard I had to put a nail in the back of his hand.

The laman stood limp, as empty as a winter field. I felt such pity. I'd looked that way on the night they'd brought me Olake's execution order, the order I couldn't sign.

Ormsment's *Sulane* launched a spread of fireworks. "They're ordering *Eternal* to surrender and push their weapons overboard," Faham translated. "The Oriati are running out their cannon in reply."

The golden ship's starboard side opened dozens of tiny doors. Black tubes protruded to menace *Sulane*. Ormsment's flagship tacked upwind toward the giant, a little red dog trotting toward a lion.

My vision had faded with age. My sense for motion at the edge of sight had not. "Look! Look there! Is that Baru?"

Apparitor's little boat paused aft of *Sulane* to throw a line. A sleek brown woman hauled herself aboard. Her bound chest heaved for air. Surely that was patient Wydd's student, Ulyu Xe. She and Apparitor reached over to haul another woman aboard—scowling face, black eye, why, who else it could be?

Baru was alive. She grappled with Apparitor, shouting: he shook his head.

With an inaudible cry she threw herself to the rear of the boat and stared at *Sulane*. She was looking for her friend Aminata.

That was the moment when *Sulane*'s stern exploded.

AMINATA was still on *Sulane*'s weather deck, working the sunflash to signal *Ascentatic*, when *Eternal* fired its ranging shots.

The huge Oriati ship's starboard side decorated itself, silently, with ten little jets of smoke. She stared in wonder. It took the rocketry mate's shouted *"Down!"* to make her duck.

The crack of the detonations reached her a moment ahead of the cannon shot—black blurs across the dawn-gold water—like arrows, but fast, *so* fast. Aminata clasped her hands over the back of her neck. Kings, what would it feel like? Would there be any time to feel the hit? She was tense, she had to loosen up, make herself soft like she was drunk—

Nothing happened. No crash of timber. No fire in the rocket magazines.

"They fell short!" the rocketry master called. "They hit the sea!"

Aminata peeked back up over the boatwale and took the range to *Ascentatic*. Nullsin's ship was coming south, struggling in the lees of the islands—he could not possibly arrive in time to force *Sulane* to break off—not unless Aminata somehow slowed *Sulane* down—

A part of her could not believe, no matter how well she'd thought it out, that she was truly working to protect an Oriati ship.

Suddenly the ship jumped beneath her: her sea legs soaked up the motion. Ten hundred times worse for her stomach was the detonation from astern. The magazines!

"Magazines!" the master-at-arms screamed. "Report the magazines! Sound off!"

Aminata tore off sternward, plunging down the ladder, crying, "Report the magazines!" That sounded like a signal firework detonating inside the ship, and if it somehow reached the Burn supply, they were about to die in clinging fire—

A sailor belowdecks screamed back. "Magazines secure!"

She turned to shout abovedecks. "Magazines secure!" Then, after a ragged breath, "What the fuck was that?"

"The rudder's gone!" someone shouted back down.

"We hit our own mine?" *Sulane* was clear of anything marked on the charts. . . .

"I don't know! But the rudder's fucked!"

A collection of surgeon's tools slid past her, blades and bonesaws ringing cheerily; a mercy-spike bounced off her boot and landed killing end down between two planks. Without a rudder the wind had taken them: the whole frigate was heeling north, prow coming starboard as *Sulane* tipped over.

Sulane had been maimed. She could go. She should go. That was the plan, to make sure *Sulane* couldn't hurt *Eternal*. And then go.

Ormsment's bellow: "Away the damage control party! Cut off the rudder, run out the drogue, I want the bow turned back into the wind! Lash me an emergency rudder! Come on, show me your salt!"

Ordinarily Ormsment's flag captain would have picked up her orders and repeated them. But she was busy at the prow, tending to a wounded sailor: old amputee comforting the newly maimed.

Aminata felt two great hands seize her by the wrists and try to pull her in half.

One hand had four long fingers of duty and a thick thumb of guilt. *Sulane* was a warship in combat. Ormsment needed her staff captain.

But the other pull said—this ship is doomed. Ormsment's a mutineer who led her crew to ruin. You *made* your choice. Jump overboard and swim, swim, it's not too late. You deserve better than this!

You worked your *ass* off! Don't die for nothing!

The wind's slow hand pulled *Sulane* broadside on to the Cancrioth ship.

O H Wydd," I whispered. "Have they caught fire? Is it over?"
    In a single silent instant *Eternal*'s whole cannon-studded side vanished in a wall of smoke. I had never seen anything like it outside of a forest fire. "Is it their magazine?" I demanded of Faham. "Has the magazine gone—"

The thunder came over us then, and I could not speak.

C HAIN shot tore through timber, lines, canvas, flesh. A mainsail shroud
    line snapped free and the lashing end took the master-at-arms across the eyes. Something struck the mainmast and whipped around it keening like a funeral till it smashed itself to a halt and thrummed there, four feet of chain, burnt and smoking.

Aminata clung grimly to the ladder and waited for it to stop. Huge god fingers drummed along *Sulane*'s port side, round shot beating against wood and slapping off water. The thud of direct impacts, the snap of broken rope, the groan of suddenly unsupported timber—

Then silence, and the screams of wounded.

"Surgeon!" someone bawled. "Surgeon!"

But it was Juris Ormsment's voice that ruled. "Stand to your posts, sailors! The bastards couldn't hit a cunt with a cock! Their shot's bouncing right off our timber!"

She was up on the mainmast shrouds, dangling from the lines on *Sulane*'s tilted starboard side, hanging out over the ocean. She looked fearless. The crew cheered for her.

"Where's my rudder?" Ormsment shouted. "I need helm!"

Aminata stumbled aft across splintered wood and spilled grease to help the damage control party. She found them struggling to lift the heavy wooden drogue, put her shoulder beneath it, and, pushing in time with the sailing-master's call, helped tip it over the stern.

"Drogue's away!" the sailing-master called. "Pass the word!"

"Drogue's away!" Aminata shouted forward.

The floating drogue uncoiled behind *Sulane,* dragging against the ship's motion, pulling at the stern so the whole ship turned west again, straight at *Eternal.*

"Strike everything!" the sailing-master cried. "Make her clean!"

Riggers hauled at capstans and blocks, the whole ship answering like a thing alive, tucking its wings like a peregrine on the dive. Aminata's favorite thing in the world: the perfect coordinated labor of so many different people gathered in complex ways and yet to simple effect, all to make the ship go where it was needed. Everyone doing exactly what the ship's design asked of them and in reciprocity the ship doing what they asked of it, together, hand in hand. And the smell of sealant, and the callus-ripping burn of taut rope over your palm, and Aminata knew she would never abandon this ship, never could abandon a ship in battle.

"Rocketry!" Ormsment shouted. "Cut me two long-fuse torpedoes! Put them right across her course! I want her holed and foundering before we get alongside!"

She was still fighting for her crew. Still fighting to win.

The master-at-arms clawed at his eyes and screamed for his mother. Aminata ran to take his place.

*A*MINATA!"
   Ulyu Xe tried to hold Barhu back so she could tend to the barnacle cut. All Barhu wanted (unfairly, wretchedly) was to shove her down in the bilgewater, seize the oars, and go get Aminata back.

"Why didn't she come?" She'd watched Galganath fix the naval mine to *Sulane*'s rudder, watched the orca pull the arming lanyard. And she'd thought: thank Devena for that whale, because if *Sulane* loses her helm, she's done fighting, and Aminata will come to safety.

But she hadn't come.

"I don't understand. She just had to jump and swim out to you— Apparitor, why didn't you—"

"Row," Apparitor said.

"What?"

"Take the oars. I'm exhausted. You row."

Barhu looked, selfishly, to Ulyu Xe, but the poor woman had just spent long minutes underwater. She sat her ass down and took the oars. Apparitor sat on the stern thwart, his back to *Sulane*. Cannon sounded in the distance. The wind twirled the little hairs that had escaped from his braid.

"She chose," he said. "She made the decision to stay. Not you."

"So we'll go back for her." Barhu realized she'd only grabbed the left oar, and snatched for the right, getting it on the first try. "I put her in this position. I'm responsible."

"I have a question for you."

"What?"

"Do you understand that other people exist?"

"Yes," Barhu said, viciously. "I understand that Aminata might have reasons to do things that—that I don't understand or appreciate."

"Good." Apparitor began to undo his hair. Behind him, a blurred cannonball blew through the wall of *Sulane's* flag stateroom, ricocheted off the iron struts of the hive glass, and bounced around destroying expensive things. Aminata would have stood in that room to speak to Ormsment. Aminata would have left her bootprints in the carpet.

"You won't go back to rescue her." He watched her levelly, his hands up behind his head, tending to his braid. "You know we won't survive it. And you know that part of this job is leaving people behind. That's what we do, as cryptarchs, when we change our identities. What if you made some friends as Barbitu Plane? Started a nice little Purge club, maybe? And then the identity was compromised? You couldn't see them again. Ever."

"I didn't leave *her* behind," Barhu snapped, jerking her head at Ulyu Xe. "Tain Shir was going to kill her, and I volunteered to die in her place. And she just saved my life."

"But you did leave me behind, first." Xe smeared piney unguent on Baru's wound: the pain made her jump. "I was with Tain Hu when you exiled her. You left us all behind."

Another volley of cannon fire slapped at *Sulane,* raising geysers port and starboard. The frigate was nose-on again, a small target, and the Cancrioth gunners were not having any effect.

Apparitor raised his voice a little over the thunder. "I haven't seen Lindon in nearly two years. I haven't seen his kids, or his wife, or our child. You learn to say good-bye. And each time you do it you know it might be forever."

"We're going back for her!" But her traitor hands weren't working right, she was fighting herself on the oars, pulling the wrong way—

"What did you really do to Yawa?"

"What?"

"How did you convince her to protect you? Do you have some hold over her brother? Slow poison? A letter that could influence his trial?"

"No," Barhu said, exasperatedly. She had managed to get the launch circling to starboard—when the prow came round to *Sulane* she would pull with both hands and they would go back—

"How did you turn her? Tell me how you did it."

"We don't have time for this!"

"What else should we spend our time on? The rest of this is out of our hands. You know, I thought you were going to die whether or not we lobotomized you. I thought you were going to poison yourself, or leap into the water, or slit your wrists. Because you didn't have anything inside you here"—he thumped his chest above his heart—"to hold."

The creak of launch ballistae, suddenly released. Two sleek torpedoes hurtled off *Sulane*'s prow, splashed down, tugged free of their fuse cords, and ignited. The copper shark-shapes skipped off across the wavetops. Feedback gears twisted their tails to keep them on course.

"Oh, no," Barhu whispered.

"It's out of your hands now," Svir said, mercilessly. "You can't control what happens. Just like you couldn't control Aminata's choice—"

"I created the context in which she made her choice!" Barhu shouted at him. "I put her in the position where she chose to stay on a doomed ship! I *am* responsible!"

"Is that how you see other people? Like mice? You build the mazes for them to run, and it's your fault if they don't end up where you want?"

"Aminata's my *friend*! I asked her to do this!"

His nostrils flared; he took a deep breath; Barhu had the strange idea that he was inhaling some intangible alcohol or elixir, a vapor boiling off her soul, and passing it through some special alpine organ created by all his race's years of delving into the earth to ferret out poisons.

"You know," he said, "last time you looked back when you were supposed to be running, you got hit in the head."

"You got me out of there."

"Yes. I did. If I hadn't been there, you'd have died. Do you ever think about that?"

She'd never really thought about that. It offended her.

She thought about it, now, as the torpedoes ran in toward *Eternal*. The marvelous killing machines on their way to discover Tau and Osa and Shao Lune and the Brain and the Eye and the Womb and giant Innibarish and the woman with the scarified face and the cancer pigs and all the other marvels aboard. All the things that Barhu needed, somehow, for some mysterious reason, some master plan locked away in her blind right side.

It was easy, then, to give up on the arrogance of total control.

"I've been thinking," she admitted. "Thinking about things Tau said to me. I've forgotten how . . . really, I've *never* been alone. Aminata helped me in school. And then there was Muire Lo, and Tain Hu, and you. And Lyxaxu, and Unuxekome, and Pinjagata . . . Xate Olake saved my life when Lyxaxu came to kill me. You saved my life when Oathsfire ambushed us. I just let myself think, somehow, that I'd done it all myself, that I was . . ."

"That you were a solitary savant, a bright star in the dark?"

"Yeah."

"I wonder who wanted you to think like *that*," Svir said, with bitter amusement.

"Hey. How long were you dosing my vodka?"

"The whole time, Baru. From that first bottle we shared. I had to know how you'd react."

"You needed to know how I'd react to rye ergot and vidhara? Vidhara's an aphrodisiac, Svir."

"Anything to get you to do something for yourself. Something *he* didn't want."

"I thought the idea was to give me a seizure. So you could blackmail me."

"That too." He shot her a tired, twisted smile. "I *am* a cryptarch. Plots within plots."

Sulane was now within half a mile of *Eternal*, and the pattern of cannon fire had disintegrated from volleys into spasms of individual fire. All the Cancrioth sailors at their guns, all those hobbyists the Womb had bemoaned, maybe even some Termites who had practice with cannon: all desperate to fend off one of Falcrest's firebearers, *Sulane* as avatar of the whole Armada War and all the humiliations the Mbo had suffered.

Their shot skipped off *Sulane*'s flanks to flail the water. Tore fluttering pennants from *Sulane*'s sails. Scythed sailors from the open deck.

Did everything and anything but penetrate the frigate's hull.

"No wonder nobody uses cannon," Barhu said in frustration. "They're awful."

"Stop rowing," Svir told her.

"No! We're going back for Aminata—"

"Baru," Ulyu Xe murmured. "You're just turning us in circles."

"We can't get them back," Svir told her. "Either of us."

He had Iraji on *Eternal*, as Barhu had Aminata on *Sulane*.

At that very moment a torpedo struck *Eternal*.

*S*ULANE'S taken aback," Faham explained. "The wind from ahead slowed her to a stop. Without water moving under her hull, she can't steer. The drogue they threw off the stern will keep her pointing the right way, but she's stuck."

"What a curious thing to say of a ship," I remarked. "Taken aback. Like she's been affronted."

"That's where the phrase comes from in the first place, you innocent provincial lass. *Taken aback* means *a ship without steerage, driven backward by wind*—"

Kimbune cried out in horror.

One of *Sulane*'s torpedoes drowned and sank.

The other rammed nose-on into *Eternal*'s starboard side.

I had witnessed the Battle of Treatymont, where Ormsment's torpedo barges had worked such ruin on Unuxekome's ships, but it was still always a surprise to me when the strange devices worked. The piston crushed the detonator, the detonator fired the charge. Water spouted up the side of *Eternal*'s golden hull. The gold film cracked, baring black wood beneath; but the worst damage would be below, where water hammer and void tore at the hull.

"She's hit, then," Execarne said, tonelessly. "Holed at the waterline."

Kimbune seized two fistfuls of her hair. "Will she sink?"

"I don't know. Has she any pumps?"

"Of course! We *invented* pumps!"

I considered this boast, and allowed it. Perhaps irrigation *had* come north from the ancient Oriati.

"And do your people know how to fother a sail?" Execarne asked.

"Fother? I don't know that word."

"Then we'll see." He sighed. "If you'll look north now, here comes *Ascentatic*."

I gasped aloud in wonder. South flew Captain Nullsin's *Ascentatic*, beam on to the morning wind, as small beneath her sails as a krakenfly's slim tail between its lacy wings. All her signal batteries were firing, rockets booming around her:

STAND DOWN, CEASE FIRE, IN THE ADMIRALTY'S NAME STAND DOWN

Captain Nullsin, answering Aminata's call, had come to stop the fighting.

But *Sulane*'s reply was another pair of torpedoes toward *Eternal*. Kimbune shouted in dismay, and began to draw angles in the air, as if she could calculate the weapons off course.

Eternal sprouted millipede legs.

Devena only knows how I, a Treatymont scullery girl, came to see such sights. It was astounding. The great ship produced banks of oars from all along its lower hull, like a galley. The long sweeps dug into the water, churning up vortices that flashed and glimmered with distressed jellyfish.

With a verve that would have earned a cheer from any ringside crowd, the Cancrioth rowers prodded the incoming torpedoes away, blasting one long sweep into a splintered stub, flipping and drowning the other torpedo. "Ai-o!" I called, the old cry from Treatymont's duels, and then felt very sheepish.

But the Traitor-Admiral's frigate was in motion again.

The riggers had put up fresh canvas. The wind in *Sulane*'s sails pushed her backward, and now, with water moving under the hull and an emergency rudder over the stern, the ship had steerage again. They cut their drogue away, close-hauled the sails, and made ready to beat upwind.

I had seen *Sulane* in the battle off Treatymont. I knew how Ormsment made her kills. She would skitter in close, where she would not need torpedoes. There her heavy ship-burner Flying Fish rockets could strike a mortal blow.

"How far does she need?" I whispered. "To make the shot certain?"

"A quarter mile," Faham muttered. "Less than a thousand feet, if possible."

Kimbune began to pray.

I found her tongue unsettling, the words too small, the syntax too rapid. But perhaps, coming from a land of Unuxekomes and Radaszics and epithets like *ziscjaditzcionursz,* I was prejudiced toward words that took their time.

Execarne began to murmur a translation. He knew the Cancrioth language. The man was full of marvels.

En ash li-en ek am amar	
Su au-ai vo bha to	
En ilu ilu es ahar	Love of life is life's one sacred art
Su to en ilu a alo	For you, love—*I don't know that word*
Ut oro ona ti ti-en	The sky has no edges to find
Aum ana ti se si ihen	And we've more ahead than behind
An elu it	Forever is real
Shu ah anit	The sign and the seal
Man aul aum ra na o ael-it.	Not the line, love, but the wheel.

Kimbune closed her eyes and touched her brow, where the sign of the round number had been tattooed across her thoughts.

Faham held my hand.

The fate of the Ashen Sea balanced on a moment: Juris Ormsment returned to Falcrest with a Cancrioth prize and all the world roused to war, or *Eternal* triumphant, Juris dead, and some hope, any hope at all, of my success.

With a plume of white sparks, with a whistle like a hawk descending, *Sulane* fired a Burn rocket toward *Eternal*.

* * *

No!" Barhu shouted, and her back ripped with the shout. She gagged in pain and yet she could not look away.

Fire was the foe of all ships, but *Eternal,* huge and undercrewed, full of untrained sailors and explosive powder, would suffer worst of all. The Burn could not be extinguished by water or by wind. It would eat everything it could reach.

Tiny figures on the Cancrioth ship's rail fired pistols and bows at the incoming rocket. Among them stood one short colorful person, like a splash of paint. A stout woman behind that figure tried to draw them away. They would not go.

Barhu said: "Tau—"

And the golden ship burst into a swarm of kites.

At first she thought the sails had torn free. But there were sailors up in the rigging, playing out the lines of their kites, black diamonds and brilliant firebirds, jellyfish trailing tasseled tentacles and krakenflies with jointed legs. The wind was out of the west behind them, and it lofted the kites exactly where they needed to be.

Sulane's rocket struck a huge vulture-kite, tumbled end for end, fell into the ocean, and popped into a scum of fire.

"Before you get too excited," Svir said, grimly, "I feel I should remind you they were just taking the range."

All the cannon on *Eternal*'s starboard bow were silent. Cancrioth sailors swarmed down the side of the ship, descending on nets and ropes, towing an enormous patch—a ship's sail, but shaggy, covered in yarn and cord, smeared in pitch. They were fothering the torpedo wound: dragging a patch across it and using the pressure of the inrushing water to hold the patch itself in place. Then they could make repairs from within.

Red *Sulane* had regained her speed. She came swiftly toward *Eternal,* tacking sharply, all aboard performing to their utmost. The rocketry mates would be aiming lower now, shooting for the hull, where the kites could not interfere.

From the north *Ascentatic* raced to interpose herself. Barhu had read all about her in the public edition of the *Navy List:* an Attainer-class frigate fresh from the Thalamast's yards in Rathpont. She had been improved over the old Shaheen-class in quiet, economic ways that Barhu appreciated: her lumber had been treated with a newer and cheaper process, she was three weeks quicker to cycle through the drydocks, her storm armor had been impregnated with a dye that killed infant shipworms, her rocket magazines could be swiftly flooded, her provisions came from the Metademe instead of a privately owned supplier—

And none of it would matter. She was too far to intercept *Sulane*, put marines aboard, and force her to stand down. She was certainly beyond torpedo and heavy rocket range, even if Nullsin were willing to turn those weapons on a comrade. Her hwachas might cross the gap, but those were weapons meant to kill crew, not damage ships.

"They've almost got the killing shot," Svir reported with a catch of fury in his voice. "Damn it. Damn Ormsment and all her traitor crew. It shouldn't have come to this. I would've sworn we pulled her too far out of position, especially with the rudder gone . . ."

"No," Barhu said, though there was nothing to do now: "No, it won't happen. I know it won't. I have a plan for that ship."

A light kindled in *Sulane*'s rigging.

Barhu took it for the first flash of a rocket launch and gasped in horror. But it was a flare, a green chemical flare. The flare began to bob and dance, and then Barhu realized someone was waving it, signaling in navy semaphore:

SHOOTATME

It was Aminata.

NULSHOOTNOW
AMNSHOOTME
SHOOT
SHOOT
SHOOT

Barhu had walked away from so many things. Taranoke. Treatymont. Sieroch. The Llosydanes. *Eternal.* Always escaping just in time, before the real cataclysm.

She had no idea what kind of strength it must take to stay behind.

SHOOT

Ascentatic ignited her hwachas.

Nullsin did not, in the end, hold back. It was a full barrage, sixty-four rocket arrows per hwacha by eight hwachas, five hundred and twelve burning arrows and not one a misfire. A plague of screaming narrow things. Their shadows moved on the sea. Dawn-glint reflections off steel shafts. Streaks of fire, dwindling as motors burnt.

Nullsin fired on his own mutinous fleetmate.

The hwacha barrage stitched *Sulane*'s rigging. Sailors fell from the lines and the tops to plunge impaled into the warm water. Not one of those who survived abandoned her post: lose the sails and you lose the battle, and they would not let their admiral lose.

"Aminata," Barhu croaked. She'd been up there.

Fire caught in the shrouds, ignited by an arrow with an incendiary head. For a moment *Sulane* was crowned, left and right of the mainsail, by converging lines of flame, climbing the shroud lines. Then the sails caught.

Sulane was on the southerly leg of her upwind tack. With the sails suddenly ruined, the dawn gusts fought her emergency rudder and, by degrees, won. The ship's prow came south toward el-Tsunuqba. Her stern slewed north.

She was caught broadside on to *Eternal*.

On *Sulane*'s sleek prow, a rocketry crew winched their mount around to bear on the golden ship. The rocketry mate knelt with her hands on the fuse-cords. Barhu saw Juris Ormsment, up on the taffrail, pointing one-handed toward the target. She dropped her hand like an axe: *fire!*

The Cancrioth shot every cannon they had.

Thunderflash, white jet of cannon, recoil pushing the black weapons like marching ant legs. The percussion drummed inside Barhu's chest, a feeling like giddiness, like nausea.

The crew at *Sulane*'s prow Flying Fish launcher went to pieces in a blast of dateshot. The fused rocket fell off the launch mechanism and rolled across the deck. A pale little girl-sailor leapt onto the loose rocket, hugged it to her chest, and ran for the rail to leap overboard. It didn't matter. The volley of point-blank cannon shot walked down *Sulane*'s starboard flank from prow to stern. Ricochets and low shots, waterspouts and snapped yardarms, cannonballs bouncing off the frigate's copper and wood, snapped ropes whipping in panic: and then the fateful penetration, forward of the amidships frame and right about the waterline, into the rocket magazines. Which were too well-built for the cannonball to blow through the far wall and escape again.

With her intuition for structures Barhu could *see* the ball smashing through the stacked rockets and fireworks, ricocheting off firebreaks, splashing casks of piss, until, eventually, inevitably, powder crushed beneath hard iron, or the ball smashed a canister of Burn.

The Traitor-Admiral's flagship ate itself.

Eternal, packed full of fine powder, would have exploded. *Sulane* went up slow and fat, the greasy squirming Burn spilling out through hatches and climbing the lines, the whole ship inhaling wind, hammocks curling like dying spiders, rats chittering in brown running rivers over the sides. The midships stairway exhaled white sparks onto the burning rigging. Everything afire now, the frigate drifting south into el-Tsunuqba's black crags. *Sulane* spouted a drunken round of fireworks, a last ecstatic spasm, *the mutiny is over, hoorah, hoorah,* and the hulk ran down the current toward ruined el-Tsunuqba, the slouching enormity of the mountain waiting like a huge shattered cup, tipped over to welcome *Sulane* into its dregs.

Then *Sulane* struck one of her own mines.

The blast boiled whitewater all around the dying frigate, and as if to meet and match the fire, the ocean came up, inch by inch, into her hull, to drag her down.

Barhu watched it all burn.

Hey, thirteen-year-old Baru said, in the throatiest, most confident voice she could manage, not, in the end, really managing at all. *Hey,* she said, to the girl she envied so much, the lanky Oriati midshipman who got to carry a sword.

Hey yourself, Aminata said.

NOW

CAIRDINE Farrier is washing her hair.

"Let me be sure I've followed." He teases the knots from her short growth. "You tracked Abdumasi Abd's water purchases to Kyprananoke, where you found a Cancrioth ship. You were captured and taken aboard. But after meeting with their leaders, you negotiated your way out by offering them Shao Lune as a hostage against your good conduct and promising to repatriate Abd to their care once you found him."

"That's right."

"They believed you?"

"Of course they believed me, Mister Farrier. They're a people of careful pedigrees. Heredity is everything to them. When I told them I hated Falcrest, my skin was the only proof they needed."

"And you're certain they're descended from the old slavers?"

"The Brain has a cancer in her mind, Mister Farrier. It's very hard for her to lie. The hard part, rather, is separating the truth from her delusions."

He allows himself to exult, so she will know how well she's done. "When the world learns what they did to Kyprananoke, Baru, and to Tau-indi Bosoka, *no one* will be able to deny the need to act. I'll put it in the broadsheets. I'll have it sung in every market in the Mbo. I'll tell Parliament and they'll approve whatever consequences I suggest."

She nods. Her scalp moves beneath Farrier's careful fingers and he flinches back, as he always does when he feels he has touched her accidentally.

"Mister Farrier. Did you ever miss the Mbo, after you left?"

"Oh, I suppose so." He sighs nostalgically. He knows exactly what to do to play this question off. "It was quite . . . seductively idyllic. A place where you might think everything would turn out fine, if you just let it be. Childish, in that way. Naïve." What everyone thought of Tau-indi Bosoka, at first. What she thought. "Of course, turn over that warm stone and you'll find the squirming things underneath. Parasitic nobility, everywhere you look. Constant raiding and warfare under the guise of 'ritual combat.' Families who won't speak to each other over trade conflicts five centuries old. A system of inherited class they won't call slavery. . . ."

"And the women," she says, with a chuckle in her voice. "Too much trouble by half."

Farrier's hands seize for a moment on her hair. "Baru! Don't say things like that."

"But it's true, isn't it? Everyone knows that. Even my friend Aminata would tell me jokes about Oriati women. How everyone wants them and hates to admit it." She lets the calm, cool air lull her voice toward sleep. "She thought the jokes were funny. . . ."

"Please, Baru." He unclenches his hands, smooths out the tangle he's made. "It's true that the women are . . . not always given a chance to behave correctly. But some of that is exaggeration and prejudice. Some of it is fetishization of the foreign. When we talk about Oriati women as intrinsically erotic, somehow, we place demands on them. We contribute to their degradation."

"I'm sorry. I didn't mean to be uncouth." She lowers her chin contritely. "I was just trying to see things from your perspective. To imagine how it was, when you were there."

A STORY ABOUT ASH 9

THEY left at dawn to arrange the surrender.

The decision took only a few words. "The other Princes will gather at Kutulbha," Kindalana said, "to bring help, or to grieve the dead. We'll deliver the terms of surrender. We'll call a vote."

Mother Tahr would come with them. Cosgrad Torrinde and Cairdine Farrier would come. Padrigan eshSegu would stay on Prince Hill to heal while his daughter went on mission. Abdumasi Abd would also stay behind to manage the houses, bound by trim to a merchant's duty.

Prince Hill's little mbo would be divided.

Poor Abdu wept into Kindalana's shoulder. He made silent, yawning, damp screams into Tau-indi's breast. They'd all known his mother Abdi-obdi as a cheerful absence, the woman who was always bustling around the edges of Abdumasi's life, out on business for months or years at a time. She was gone but she had always been gone. The difference was that there was no possibility, not anymore, for Tau-indi to turn to her and say, oh, you are a person, alive, and I want to know you.

Abdumasi stood with his house to see them off. When Tau-indi passed, he stared at them with bright eyes, red-rimmed, sleepless.

"This is your fault," he said. "I won't forget."

At first Tau thought Abdu was talking to them. But Abdumasi stared past painted Prince Bosoka, past the chained and silkened Prince Kindalana, at plain-shirted Cosgrad Torrinde and nattily dressed Cairdine Farrier.

Cosgrad hunched his strong shoulders and looked at his toes. Cairdine Farrier held Abdumasi's eyes for a few moments and then said, quietly but firmly, "I'm sorry about your mother."

Abdu spat at him. Farrier nodded.

Kindalana tried to give Abdu a formal good-bye. "Surely," she said, "you will find more practical uses for your time, without me to distract you."

"Yeah," he said, roughly, trying to tell the same old joke, "yeah, I bet I will, you're just so . . ."

But he had nothing to say. So he stepped forward and kissed her, right in front of all three houses.

Halfway down the hill, Abdumasi shouted and ran after Tau-indi to hug them and kiss them on the brow.

THEY went north, downriver from Lake Jaro to the coast. Swarming catfish parted before the boat. Rain fell in short furious bursts. To the north and east, in the direction of the Tide Column, farmers burnt their blighted fields and huge pillows of ash rose up to color the sun.

"Why are there vultures?" Tau-indi asked the barge crew. "What do vultures want with ash and burnt fields?"

There was a bush scout aboard, part of a shua band, her face white with clay sunblock. She pounded doorbag milk by the bucket but never seemed to get too drunk. "They smell death," she told Tau. "Animals flee the fire. Animals on the run die. Vultures feast."

Tau-indi imagined a fan of carrion, spreading out across the mbo, and shuddered.

The bushman looked Tau up and down speculatively, lingering on their hips. "You're one of the Princes?"

"Yes," Tau said, nodding graciously, "as it pleases the people."

"Seventeen?"

"Not quite," Tau said, though they felt like preening. "Do I look like I'm seventeen?"

"Parts," the woman said, without quite leering.

Tau, whose household staff were always respectful and therefore very dull, who had sat with rising frustration through many audiences with renegade and beautiful shua, sat up a bit straighter and raised their chin. "And if I were seventeen—"

"No, no no no," the woman said, chuckling, but looking away. "Don't trust anyone who says a thing like that to you, understand? Not while you're a child."

"I shouldn't trust you?"

She grinned half-toothlessly and wobbled her hand. "Not that way," she said. "I live too much with dogs."

In the burning fields whirlwinds descended to stir the ash.

Tau-indi and Kindalana walked through the port at Yama, speaking to the crews, plucking at ties of money and duty until they found a dromon they could commandeer without ruining the crew's fortune. People gathered around them as they moved. Hand in hand, Tau and Kinda preached hope to the crowd, telling them how the mbo, like a basket weave, would tighten as it strained.

Then they sailed west, toward wounded Segu and burnt Kutulbha. The rowers pulled in time with the drums, their broad backs bent, moving the ship out of harbor with a grunting work song.

"This is the mbo," Tau-indi said, showing Cosgrad the crew all together. "This strength of harmony."

Cosgrad turned his notebook over in his hands, writing nothing. "You know what I'll say, don't you?"

"You'll tell me something about Falcrest strength. About your special oars. Your sentences and mathematics describing the correct oarmen."

"Our ships have no oars."

"What do you do when the wind goes against you?"

"We can always make the wind useful." Cosgrad hesitated. "I don't think I can tell you about that. It's a military matter."

Tau wanted to seize him and beg him to make it right. Cosgrad, they would cry, Cosgrad, stop this! Let us be together, all of us. Let us trade and sing. You and I, your people and mine—

But Cosgrad would say, sadly, Tau, there are powers at work here you don't understand.

And perhaps Tau was the fool. Perhaps the world had never been about trading and singing together.

"You're sad," Cosgrad said, softly. "Is it about . . . ?"

"Everything."

"I know." Cosgrad stared down into the rippling water. "Me too."

Kindalana walked among the rowers, touching their shoulders, letting them see the Prince whose birth they had elected. She looked back at Tau-indi and Cosgrad, her jewels and chains gleaming in the dark. She was beautiful, wasn't she? Not as an ornament, but as an intent, a mind that was a face and a body and all the things that body wore, an active and inseparable wholeness.

She would be famous for it, Tau realized. Famous for charisma and compulsion, for the way you felt when you looked at her, as if you desperately wanted to be worthy of her thoughts. And she knew it, had known it for years. What a terrible wonder to know your own beauty, without shame, and to set it to use, for yourself and for your duty.

Cosgrad would have equations to describe those arches of chain Kindalana wore, those filigreed catena from ear to nose. But he would have no equations to describe Kindalana, or the way she made people feel. Not yet.

Cosgrad and Farrier caught lice and had to shave their heads.

I N Kutulbha, rain fell on the ash and made it into a paste of wood and flesh that settled like concrete. The city became a plate of mortar and the mortar was full of skulls.

But they had not reached Kutulbha yet.

"Farrier will come for all of you," Cosgrad said. He stood on their dromon's stern, looking out over evening harbor at a quiet fishery town where no one, not even the children, threw good-luck bread to the shearwaters. There was no grain to make bread anymore. "Farrier has his appetites set on Oriati Mbo."

Down below them, in the harbor shallows, a jellyfish pulsed blue-green. Tau-indi gathered their khanga up a little closer. "What appetites do you mean?"

Cosgrad scowled, like a spike driven up through his face, and then sighed. The sigh was strange because it was full of shame. "Farrier is an explorer, a very public man, a man in favor. Everyone loves Mister Farrier. He writes books and gives speeches, he is seen with women of advantage, he is summoned to Parliament to give testimony . . . even on matters of heredity and social hygiene, which are *my* specialty."

Tau-indi set a hip against the rail and smiled up at Cosgrad. "Mister Farrier makes you jealous."

He put up a hand to shadow Tau-indi's face from the sun. "Even here," he said, sounding like he was trying very hard to joke, "he finds ways to steal from me." He swallowed and went on very hastily: "What does Kindalana think of me?"

Tau remembered Kindalana and Abdu, talking about Cosgrad in that cave. "That you're very beautiful. That you're a foreign agent. She doesn't have . . . easily settled feelings about people, I think. She'll like you in one way and think you're a fool in another."

Cosgrad looked as if he might spit. "Then I hope she's realized that Mister Farrier is a groomer. He has the nasty habit of befriending young people, treating them like they are his equals, and bending them, gradually, into his instruments."

Tau-indi gulped down a laugh before it could get out. Cosgrad saw it and huffed. "No! It's hardly the same as our friendship."

"It isn't?"

"We speak. We learn from each other. I'm fair with you, I hope." He paused there, endearingly, and Tau-indi nodded, yes, he was fair.

"Cairdine Farrier treats no one as an equal. The world is a bazaar to him. He sails down the Mother of Storms to Devi-naga and says, oh, they have birds with feathers as long as a man is tall, we must study these birds in their habitat. He sails to Taranoke and says, oh, their women are licentious and their men are sodomites, they let their children know what they do, we must save the poor children.

"But with his letter from Devi-naga he sends a feather, and the invitation to use it as an ornament. With that plea from Taranoke comes a sketch of the Taranoki on their beaches, savage and tempting. He shows people things and tells them not to want them and then sells them anyway. Farrier is a trickster, a liar, a huckster. He dreams of a world in which all men are permanently deceived, their minds bent from birth to serve his idea of a perfect republic. And this war has given him the opportunity to practice his deceit on an imperial scale."

Left to their own devices, Tau-indi would have probed Cosgrad's personal anger, rather than the facts of politics. But they tried to ask what Kindalana would ask: "What would *you* have done with this war? What opportunities did it offer you?"

A soft purple star rose out of the deep harbor below, unfurled white hunting tentacles, and began to ripple with light. It was as long as a man. Cosgrad stared down into the water as if he could lean forward and fall through it, into the sky.

"Farrier talks about historical dynamics. Breaking the, ah, what was it, the degenerate stalemate between the rural power of the farmers and shua and the concentration of administrative power in the Princes and the cities. Unlocking the true potential of Lonjaro and the whole continent. All that shit." Cosgrad made a stone-throwing motion. "You know why I came to Oriati Mbo. To study how you live. To learn if there's truth behind the superstitions in Falcrest: that the Oriati are bound to ancient powers."

Tau-indi remembered the sorcerer aflame, walking calmly toward Cosgrad. They shuddered hard against him. "Cosgrad, listen to me. You must turn away from that path. Only the deepest and most dissolute grief awaits you there."

But Cosgrad had his grave scholarly face on. "I have a grand theory, Tau-indi, it is my life's work. It is the story of how life came to be."

"Out of the Door in the East?"

"Maybe life came from the east. Maybe. It came from the sea, I am sure. My theory comes not just from the study of beetles and birds and mangrove trees, but from my surveys of ancient myth."

The jellyfish constellations moved on the harbor current. A hunting fish

passed in front of a distant shining bell and made it blink. A cold salt breeze
came up to chop the water and get in their marrow.

"In Aurdwynn they tell stories of the ilykari, ancient people who practiced
and came to embody virtues. Among them is Wydd, who is patience and the
flow of water. In the Stakhieczi Mansions they worship brine and aquifers, the
water deep below the stone. Here in Oriati Mbo, you remember the Cancrioth,
and the power in the water that wells up out of secret caves. And in Taranoke,
they say the gods sleep under the mountain's caldera, down under the water
and above the fire. Do you see?" His voice was entranced, but his eyes were
sharp. "All of it comes from the water below. Tau, of all the animals, we alone
can think *and* speak *and* act. How did this come to be?"

"The world was made for us. The principles organized it out of chaos."

Cosgrad's eyes gleamed like jellyfish. "The world," he said, "was *bred*."

Tau-indi looked at him and there was no way inside Cosgrad's thoughts.
They had no idea how to find the want behind these words. They waited, shivering in the wind.

"I think all life radiated from something primal. All living things are de-
scendants of a simple ancestor, differentiated by the needs of their environment
and the war for survival. But I don't know how that differentiation occurs. I
have one piece: I know that everything competes for life. But—" He thrust
out his hands, seized the ship's rail as if to crush it into its constituent atoms
and sort them into piles. "How do things *change,* so that they can find new
ways to compete? How did birds get wings? They must have a flesh-memory, a
part of their bodies that stores their struggles, so they and their children can
change in response. They must have remembered, in their flesh, the need to
leap higher and higher, to escape predators, to reach food. That was how they
grew wings. And people must have that memory, too. We must have something that says, oh, you have labored hard at the oars, so your children will be
strong. And you, you were sickly, so your children will be sickly, too."

"You think we were once . . ." Tau-indi looked at the jellies pulsing in the
chop. "Like *that*? Our great-great-great-great-grandparents were jellyfish in
the sea?"

Cosgrad's hands made the rail creak. He looked down, and then up, his
eyes wild, full of a tiny piece of something huge, whirling around inside his
skull and unable to get out. He groaned, a terrible noise.

"I can't find the words for it yet. I can't find the proof. But I think, I think,
I think . . . I think life came up, out of the sea. In the old sea a mind was born,
I don't know how or why, but that mind was soft and pliable, a wet mind with-
out fire or sharp tools, and it had only one power, only one!"

At the harbor mouth the shearwaters complained for lack of bread.

"The soft sea minds could remake flesh," Cosgrad whispered. "That was their power. That's what the squid and the octopi do; I've seen it, they change their forms and the markings upon their limbs . . . and down in the deep, beneath them, there might be kraken with the power to alter their own flesh so wholly that it buds off in tiny nymphs that grow into something else.

"And they made us. They made us to conquer the land. The things we remember as ilykari and brine and power-in-water and gods beneath the caldera, those were the soft minds. They made us, the race of man, with a special gift. We can pass our thoughts by speech, and so put what we learn into each others' flesh. And those thoughts we speak into our flesh are born into our children.

"Why else are the Aurdwynni fractious and rebellious, except that their wars have been bred into them? Why else were the Maia rapacious and conquest-hungry, except that they violated each other and bred promiscuously? Why else are your people wise and passive and superstitious, except that you spent centuries in comfort, telling stories about worlds beyond our own? We have let the world breed itself into us, get into our testes and wombs, fill us with memories of storms and plagues and leeches. We have let ourselves degenerate. Our whole species is spiraling down into a festering nightmare future, Tau. You have never seen the world as I have. You have never seen what Farrier will make of it. He will welcome the degenerate; he will put them in the fields and the mines; he will make himself king of an empire of slaves.

"But if I can just find the right way to live, Tau-indi, the perfect way, if I can just convince Parliament and the Faculties and Renascent to listen to me, then that correct way can be bred into all life. We will all be masters of ourselves. There will be no slaves and no lessers, for we will all be perfect. Our flesh remembers! I only need the equations, the descriptions of the right way, and then we can put the future into the germ, into our children, and all their children, raised up together, forever."

Tau-indi gaped. It felt right and good to learn this about Cosgrad, to understand what drove him. He had a majestic conviction.

But what he proposed was an act of cosmic hubris. It was like rewriting the end of a story to change its beginning. Like reaching up with your finger and blotting out the moon.

Cosgrad put his head in his hands. "But everyone thinks I'm mad," he said. "Squid Priest, Farrier calls me. His dream is much more palatable, I think. He says he will achieve the dream of our forefathers: a society ordered by proper thought, not by fever dreams of octopi. The squid priest! Everyone thinks I'm mad."

KINDALANA flung her hands at the table full of reports. "Farrier says we invited this on ourselves. Did you know that?"

Tau-indi had a toothache and that made them want to snap but, really, if Kindalana had learned something awful and inconvenient, she *would* certainly tell you about it. "That's ridiculous. That's evil speech. What could we possibly have done to Falcrest to earn this?"

"We meddled in their affairs, he claims. We supported their monarchy, when it favored us. Tried to conquer them, once."

"Tahari," Tau-indi said, remembering the name from the songs Tahr sang to them in the cradle. "Wasn't there a warlord, a rabies prince, named Tahari? And she went north across the Butterveldt and broke the wall in Falcrest, long ago?"

"She sacked the city. She stole their narwhal horn, the one brought down out of the north by the Verse-hammer."

"They had a narwhal horn?" Tau-indi felt a great indignation against this ancient pillager. Then they felt like an idiot child who cared more about a legendary beast's horn than the ruin of Kutulbha at Falcresti hands. "Do you believe these things Farrier tells you?"

She shrugged with an odd shyness, as if she'd been stung stealing honey. "Not entirely. But it helps me get inside his head. We have to bind them to us. I think that's what we do, Tau. We surrender, and we find a way to ease their hurt."

"Are you still going to seduce him?" Tau blurted.

Kindalana looked at them equitably, without either shame or reprobation. "He says he's not much older than me, so he's in my reach; though I think he's a few years past what he claims. But he's wary. He knows I possess myself, and that frightens him. And, anyway . . ."

Tau could not imagine anyone declining the advances of Kinda, with her wide-set eyes and elegant clavicles and shoulder blades like a bird's folded wings. But Farrier was very odd. And maybe Kindalana had not made any advances until she was sure she would succeed.

"And anyway," Tau said, finishing her thought, "you have to marry Abdu."

It was the only thing to do. Abdumasi's fortune was gone, his mother dead, his house on the edge of dissolution. To save that house he needed a quick union to someone with wealth. As a guest Prince, Kindalana did not receive tribute or investment from anyone in Lonjaro, but the eshSegu held her share of the tribal fortune.

"I have to marry Abdu," Kinda said, and tried to hide from Tau, tried her best and Tau loved her for it, to conceal the quick shudder of anger and frustration in her hands.

"You don't want to marry him."

"I don't want to marry *anyone*," Kinda said. "Not yet. I wanted a political marriage, a very good one, when the time was just right. I wanted to use what I have," an unselfconscious shrug, she remarking on herself, "to do good work. I wanted . . . but I do love him, Tau. And he loves his house."

ZERO SUM

S HE'S alive! I'm sure of it. She's a strong swimmer, and she had plenty of time to jump. Svir, you've *got* to look for her!"

They were up in *Helbride*'s foretop, where the foremast jointed from its lower trunk to its middle segment. The ship's dancing seagull slept here when it was not begging the crew for food or shitting on things. It had fled the moment Barhu raised her voice.

"Please, Svir," Barhu begged. "I didn't even get to return her sword."

She saw, in the little quirk of Svir's smile, the cruel thing he might have said: she watched him set it aside. "This is odd. Normally you'd be certain that Aminata was dead and gone beyond help. Now you'd be drinking about it and pretending not to care."

"Svir, stop evading!"

"I'll send a boat to search the wreck. But I don't think we'll find her. Which is a shame. I didn't even know you had friends. We've lost a magical archon."

Barhu sniffed miserably. She hurt. Her back ached where *Sulane*'s barnacles had cut her open. Her eye throbbed in its pierced socket. Her missing fingers cramped like they were bent against her palm. Even *Eternal* was missing: the golden ship had turned south and vanished around the black heights of el-Tsunuqba, hiding from *Helbride* and *Ascentatic* as it tried to repair its damage and make ready to sail.

Barhu wanted Aminata back.

The grief-fatigue, the Oriati disease, had struck again. What should she do with her hands? Her tongue? Would she begin to repeat herself, stagger in circles, rasp like a broken clock? She'd felt so *good* after the passage through Tain Shir's test, after Yawa's unexpected mercy, after hurling herself at Ormsment and surviving. Everything seemed like it had turned around.

And then she'd lost Aminata, and slept, and that cold sore ring of fog had settled back down around her head. . . .

She'd had not even one day with Aminata before sending her to die.

Suddenly, to Svir's obvious astonishment, which made her giggle wetly, Barhu began to sob.

"Are you going to fall?" He put up a hand, unsure (Barhu thought) if he meant to reassure her, or pull her to safety, or possibly push her to her death. "Do you need a line?"

She shook her head.

"We ought to get you down, anyway." He mounted the pilot's ladder down to the ratlines: and when, instead of following, she sat there, stiffly posed to keep the wound at her back away from the mast, weeping angrily, he dangled one-footed on the ladder and boggled at her as the pitch of *Helbride* swept them both across a little arc of sky.

"You never did this for Tain Hu," he said.

"I was afraid. For obvious reasons." Because then the Throne would know she cared.

"You should still be afraid. I'm not your friend. None of us can be friends." That faraway, dangerous lightning flickered in his eyes. It was something about his skin, the pale contrast with the dark pupil, which made her think of stormclouds and menace. "I know what's happening to you. You were in deepest despair yesterday. You thought that all was lost, that you were going to die. You struck the bottom of your fall. And suddenly you were so high, so free, and everything was all right. But really what's happened is that you struck bottom so hard you bounced. Now you're sinking again. This is how it goes, Baru. There's no magical way out. You will be fighting your Oriati disease for months. For years. Maybe forever."

Barhu did not know what to say to this. Stubbornly she repeated: "I know she's still alive."

"You don't know."

"Oh, what do you want from me, Svir? Should I just throw up my hands and abandon her?"

"No," he snapped, "what you should abandon is the need to know for certain. Maybe we'll find her corpse. Maybe we'll fish her alive from the sea. Probably we'll never learn her fate. So accept that you can't know! Stop trying to be the perfect savant who controls every variable! Stop trying to make her alive or dead in your head so you can get your mourning over with! Do you think I'm convinced Lindon's fine? I don't know! I don't know and I have to let it be!"

She wiped her eyes on the back of her arm and growled. "I hate letting things be."

"I know." He beckoned. "Come work. We have a situation to contain here."

She didn't want to think about it yet. Pine pitch glued her back together. Her right eye ached under layers of gauze. Too much saltwater and harsh soap had developed into an infuriating nipple itch, which bothered her in a way separate from the pain of all her wounds. They can put a hole in your skull, and cut off your fingers, and rip your cheek, and slice your back open, and your damn itch will still drive you mad. Like the way loss works: you cannot hide Tain Hu behind Aminata, or diminish Aminata with Tain Hu. How much could you lose in a year?

More than this, if she failed to do her work.

She wiped her eyes. "Yes," she said. "We should begin. Help me down."

I think," Yawa said, with quiet honesty, "that every time we've gathered here, we've failed. And I hope today we will not."

Svir's cabin was full of three cryptarchs, but empty, anyway, without Iraji. Yawa stood by the doorway, consciously high-chinned and bright-eyed, offering her strength. Barhu slouched in the corner where she'd had her seizure. Svir on his hammock, jaw hard, eyes downcast, toes on the floor, as if he might at any moment rise up and shout.

"How do we avoid failure," he said, although it did not sound like a question. "What are your criteria. Don't say *no more secrets between us,* or I will scream."

"Of course not," Yawa said, gently. "We are what we are. But my recent, ah, conversation with Baru made it clear that we've been . . . unnecessarily antagonistic. All of us. We could've found a way to use Iraji as bait without risking his capture. We could've let Baru go aboard the Cancrioth ship, then pressured them for her safe release. Tau would still be safe in our care. Shao Lune would be—well, she would be our prisoner instead of theirs."

That was a nice story. But it would have ended with a nugget of baneflesh growing in Barhu's skull: because, given enough time on *Eternal* to overcome her fears, she would have taken the Brain's deal. She would have beaten herself into believing she *had* to die to be worthy of Hu's legacy. She would have the Kettling, and cancer.

Yawa had saved her from her own inevitable choice.

"That's stupid," Svir said.

"I beg your pardon?" Yawa blinked at him.

"It's stupid and you're stupid for thinking it. You two aren't at odds because you lack charm and clarity and good feelings. I'm not keeping secrets from you because I'm worried that you're cruel and unfriendly. The reason you two are at odds is that your patrons are mortal enemies. The reason you are at odds with me is that I am your competition." His larynx stood out starkly on his throat, like something he couldn't get out. "You were meant to destroy each other. It's a central part of the reckoning between Farrier and Hesychast that their protégés must go to war. Your performance in the struggle against *each other* is part of the test of their rival methods of control! Why do you think you're out here? Don't you see how much better the Throne could use you if you were sitting in a desk at Falcrest? How much more influence you could wield? But this is a *race*! You two are snakes in a maze! You're locked up on my ship, out on the edge of the Imperial Republic, with limited protection and scanty resources, to be sure that you can't escape the contest, to be sure only *one* of you can come home victorious."

He must've had all this bottled up since the Elided Keep. Now he boxed them on the ears with it. "Baru, you have *every* reason to hate and flee Falcrest. But if Farrier's control keeps you loyal, even out here, then you'll be the jewel in his crown—forgive my royalist obscenity, please, I'm just not very good at being polite about him.

"And Yawa—don't think I've forgiven you for using Iraji, by the way, my vengeance is *glacial* in its patience—imagine your value to Hesychast, to his ideology of inherited behavior. You're a wild-type Maia woman, born in strife and poverty, armed with generations of blood knowledge of Aurdwynn. The struggle between the Maia and the Stakhieczi, the wars between the dukes, the pain of the people trampled underfoot. All that is in your blood. If you were locked in a ship with Baru, the acme of Farrier's education and conditioning, only to outfox her, lobotomize her, and use her as a dowry gift to the Stakhieczi king to buy peace—then you would have *solved* the same conflict that's written in your blood. United Aurdwynn and the Stakhieczi with your inherited skills. And those skills would have triumphed over Farrier's indoctrinated protégé.

"The two of you can't *both* win! Even if you make it all square between you, bring home everything Farrier *and* Torrinde want, even if you skip through Commsweal Square holding hands and whistling, your masters need one of you destroyed and one triumphant. You're cryptarchs now! Did you really think they'd just give you a mission that was everything it seemed?"

"But the truth is," Yawa said, looking, once, to be sure the doorscreen was pinned shut, "that we *aren't* under our masters' control. Baru doesn't give a fig for Farrier, except for his use as a resource. And I— Well, Hesychast is hardly my dear teacher."

"And now I know that," Svir said, with dreadful lightness. "Now I can expose you to Hesychast and Itinerant as seditious traitors—"

"Oh, please." Yawa snorted. "Mere gossip? They'd hardly be surprised to learn we're plotting and scheming to our own advantage. We *are* cryptarchs, after all. But Hesychast has my twin. He knows I won't stray."

"You try to betray us," Barhu added, "and I'll tell everyone *your* little secret, Svir." He was the brother of the Stakhieczi king, and that made him royalty. Royalty did not survive in the Masquerade. Death was the most merciful sentence he could expect.

He did not look at all angry. If anything he was relieved. A bond of blackmail was easier for him to respect than the tenuous gamble of trust. Barhu found that both sad and sympathetic.

"Fine." He gave them a gleaming white smile, arc of ice on autumn water. "You want to play revolutionary? Do it. Just remember that every cryptarch who's ever worn our mask had their own agenda. Their own idea of how Falcrest *ought* to be. And they were all kept in control. Even me."

"He . . . does make a cogent point, I'm afraid," Yawa admitted. "No matter how much we want to escape this game, we have to keep playing to survive. And by the terms of the game, Baru, sparing your life was an enormous mistake."

"It wasn't." Barhu snapped her left hand, which still had the fingers for it. "Because I can deliver *Eternal* to you. One of their leaders, the Brain—she swore to find me. She swore she'd follow. I can bring that ship wherever we require it."

"And?" Yawa's harsh face seemed to crack with strange, unaccustomed hope. "And what will this Brain give you? Something that can help me? Help Svir?"

"Yes," Svir echoed, cool curiosity. "What's on that ship?"

Death. Death for the whole world. If Barhu had promised to paint Tain Hu across history in the color of Falcrest's blood, then the Kettling was the perfect paint. And she'd failed to obtain it, because she was too cowardly to accept death as Tain Hu had—

Stop. Stop.

I died so you could be *free.*

The Kettling was not the answer. Barhu was not sure *why* she was so sure of it, except that it simply did not fit. She was an accountant and a thinker, not a plague-bearer, not a conqueror.

So what was on that ship that mattered so much? Her instincts screamed that it was the key. But *how?*

"I don't know," she admitted.

"You *don't know*?" Svir repeated. "You risked your life, Aminata's life, and *my* fucking life to protect *Eternal,* and you *don't know what it's good for*?"

Even four years out of school she wanted to apologize to Svir like a teacher she'd disappointed. "I just know it's important. Something in me," she did not name the tulpa, "knows that ship's important."

"Oh, shit." Svir groaned. "You drilled too deep, Yawa. Of all the people to leverage me, I get an idiot."

"I saved that ship because there were people on it," Barhu insisted, ashamed of this answer, not sure why, wishing that Tau were here to explain her feelings. "I didn't . . . I just couldn't let Tau and Osa and Shao and Iraji all die."

"No." Svir shook his head in perfectly performed disappointment. "This is not the way Agonist, betrayer of Aurdwynn, conducts her work. Where's your calculation? Where's your foresight?"

"It's here! I have foresight!" She looked pleadingly to Yawa. "I *know* that ship is absolutely vital."

"Svir!" Yawa barked. "Has it occurred to your air-starved brain that perhaps Baru is trying to break years of systematic conditioning Itinerant forced on her? That maybe she's *chosen* not to act like the 'betrayer of Aurdwynn'?"

He blinked at her. "Of course it had *occurred* to me. Many stupid things occur to me. Let's say Baru *has* secretly made a strong move, though. Let's say that *Eternal* really is the key to our survival in the Great Game. What do we do next, Baru? Do we sail around el-Tsunuqba and offer *Eternal* our aid?"

"No," Barhu said.

"No? Then what *do* we do next?"

"We need to help the Kyprananoki," she said. "We have to bring some mercy to the people here."

"Why," Svir said, flatly. "Why should we not destroy these islands and get on with our mission?"

Destroy the islands? Not likely, not with a single remaining frigate at their disposal. "Because they're like us! They're people Falcrest has used. We owe them our . . ." She struggled for a word, and found one in Lapetiare's own writing about the revolution that made Falcrest. "Our solidarity."

Svir sat deep in his hammock now, back straight against the wall, staring out at the two women as if from the bottom of a grave. "Kyprananoke chose the Kettling and civil war. Now Kyprananoke must live and die with the consequences."

"The common folk here never got to choose. They never asked to take up Canaat machetes or bleed Cancrioth plague. They certainly never asked for their Kyprist rulers to water-starve them into submission."

"Do you want to put the old regime back in power? Half the Kyprists are already dead. The rest are barricaded on the reservoir islets waiting to die."

"No. I *want* the revolution to succeed. I want it to be more than a death spasm."

"Do you think we have the time for that? We're due in Falcrest by 90 Summer! I have to be there to save Lindon. Yawa needs to be there for Xate Olake's trial. We can't risk that by lingering here while—"

"While what?" Yawa interjected. "What exactly do you think will happen?"

Cruel truth smoothed out his throat. "While the survivors on these islands die of thirst and plague. We have no responsibility to them."

Barhu hated that idea. "You think we're not responsible? Even though we triggered the revolution?"

He looked between Barhu and Yawa, narrow-eyed, taken aback by their unity. "We didn't cause it. The Cancrioth did. The Scheme-Colonel Masako at the embassy, he conspired with them to arm the Canaat for an uprising. He killed the local Oriati ambassador to keep it secret. You told me that."

"But *we* forced them to act! Think of how it looked when we arrived, Svir. Two Falcresti warships. A Falcresti clipper with diplomatic flags sending parties ashore to meet the Kyprists? All this not long after an Oriati fleet passed through, heading north to Aurdwynn to make war? It looked like we were coming to crush the rebels."

"The rebellion would've happened anyway!"

Yes. As it would happen on Taranoke, as it would happen again in Aurdwynn. Somewhere, *somehow,* one of these rebellions had to succeed. She had destroyed a rebellion; she had to know how to see one through.

"Svir," she said. "Svir. Just because you hate your own home, just because you'd let the Stakhieczi starve and rot rather than let Lindon or Iraji be hurt, doesn't mean nothing in the world is worth saving—"

"Oh, shut *up,*" he snapped.

"Yes," Yawa said, softly at first, then fiercely, "yes, she's right, Svir. We are Falcrest's cryptarchs, but none of us are Falcresti. Not Baru, not me, not you. We've put on their masks to steal some of their power. Let's use it. Let's help the people here."

"Suddenly you're a charity?"

"I am an Imperial Jurispotence." Yawa lifted her nose with aquiline pride. "An enemy of disease and disarray. I was brought into the Throne to represent the provincial edge of our Republic. If I cannot do good work here, at that edge, what am I for?"

Svir rolled his eyes. "Durance, you know better than anyone the futility of foreign intervention in a civil war."

"But we can help!" Barhu protested. "We can distribute water, we can teach them how the Kettling spreads and how to safely bury the bodies. And what if the wind picks up? What if the ships here scatter? We have to keep the islands under blockade!"

"It incubates for forty weeks," Svir reminded her. "We'd be here for years before we could be sure it was gone."

Damn it, that was true. "I can't just let these people die," Barhu insisted. "I can't leave without *trying* to help."

Yawa rubbed her temples. "Svir, you have to tell her."

"What? Tell me what?"

Svirakir got up on his toes and then subsided into his hammock again, as if struck by galvanic shock. The muscles of his throat were as blank and slack as open sky. "Baru, have you learned about the apocalypse fuse?"

Yawa shut her eyes.

"No?" Barhu said, with a horrible foreboding.

"We have a set of charges in place on el-Tsunuqba. They are capable of dropping the south face into the caldera and triggering a massive wave. The entire kypra would be inundated. Along with all the ships moored here."

"Oh," Barhu said. Her thoughts swelled up like her punctured eye socket, trying to encompass this new variable, this appalling possibility.

"It would wipe out all the infected," Svir said, "and all the ships which might otherwise carry the Kettling. The death toll will be enormous. But it will not, in absolute terms, be higher than a particularly bad winter in Aurdwynn. And I know both of you survived last winter with your consciences, such as they are, quite intact. So."

He looked between the two women and his face was empty. You had to be empty, Barhu thought, if you were to condemn an entire people. You had to make yourself distant.

"You two can try to help Kyprananoke if you insist. You can hide from the fact that one of you must destroy the other as long as you can. I am going to watch with my hand on the fuse. And if the Kettling seems ready to escape into the world . . ."

His hands made a motion like snapping a stick.

EPISTEMIC VIOLENCE

T HIS is the stupidest thing you've ever done," Yawa said. "And I include the sequence of events that nearly made me lobotomize you."

"I think it could work," Barhu said, trying to be cautious, but unable to constrain a little hope. They were on maindeck, where Yawa had caught Barhu packing supplies. "We have *Ascentatic* to keep the quarantine. Water supplies to entice cooperation. The threat of this apocalypse fuse to use as a political bludgeon to convince the Kyprists to yield. I really do think we can secure a truce."

"The stupid part," Yawa snapped, "is that you want to go ashore to do it yourself. It's an idiotic risk. Remember what happened to me on the Llosydanes? A man recognized me, by sheer bad luck, and if Iscend hadn't been there to protect me—"

"No one knows me here, Yawa." No one who hadn't been in the doomed Oriati embassy, at least. "I'll be fine."

"You can't pass as Kyprananoki; they're not Maia and you don't speak el-Psubim. They'll know you're a foreigner. And before you tell me that Kyprananoke is a port, and therefore cosmopolitan, may I remind you that the Canaat are rebelling *against* foreign influence?"

She was right about the danger; but Barhu had to risk it anyway. She had to make a genuine effort to help Kyprananoke. What if Tain Hu had been born *here*? What if she herself had?

Barhu knew, knew in the gnawing way that you remember all those looming problems you shove into the back closets of the mind, that she had lost the thread of her grand plan. The next step was upon *Eternal,* not here.

But she had to know how to end Falcrest without simply murdering it. How to butcher an empire. How to do it cleanly, and to end up with useful and nutritious parts. To do that you would need a revolution, and there was a revolution here.

Why not study it? Learn from it?

"I have to go, Yawa. I can't do my work from out here. I have to speak to their leaders, get a sense of them. Like I did with the Dukes back home." She wished she had some Oriati silk or jade to stuff into her bag, something to use as a gift, but she was too afraid to ask Tau's *Cheetah* crew for a donation: they knew that Tau had gone somewhere with her, and not come back. "I'm going."

Yawa stepped on the hem of her bag, so Barhu couldn't lift it. "We have Execarne's Morrow-men, every one of whom can pass as native. We can work through them."

"I don't trust them, Yawa. They're good for tailing boats and pulling fingernails. Not for this kind of negotiation."

"That," a third voice said, "is why you're sending me."

Coming down from the foredeck crowd was pale Ake Sentiamut, lankhaired middle-aged Stakhieczi widow, once Tain Hu's agent. She was upsettingly thin, of perfectly average height, unintimidating in every way. Barhu and Yawa stared at her.

"Why?" Barhu said, truly baffled. "Isn't the sun too much for you? And there'll be fighting—"

"Too much for *me*? I'm from Little Welthon, remember? I showed you what it was like there. We had riots, plague, cutthroats, corrupt constabulary. What did you have? A private tower, a secretary, and bodyguards." She cut off Barhu's next protest with a slash of her hand. "You made me your agent, remember? You gave me a sealed letter authorizing me to govern in your stead. I want my agency!"

"But that letter was meant for Vultjag! For Aurdwynn! There's nothing for you here!" Now she was accidentally making the same argument Yawa had just made to *her*.

"You think a rebellion against Falcresti puppets is *nothing* to me? Don't you know what I gave up for Tain Hu? Don't you *remember*?" She thrust a palm into Barhu's stomach, shoving her back. "I was the one who brought you into her house. It's *my* fault you killed her. It's my fault you ruined—"

She stopped, breathing hard through her nose. She had made her point.

"They'll know you're a foreigner, Ake," Barhu warned her. "They'll see your skin and your hair."

"Yes, and they'll see a Stakhi woman from Aurdwynn. Aurdwynn which revolted." Ake crossed her thin arms and glared. "Won't they trust a real rebel better than a counterfeit?"

THEY paddled in from *Helbride,* choosing a simple canoe over a skiff or launch for the chance to blend in with kypra traffic. They would meet an escort of Morrow-men on an islet called Balt Anagi, and those men would bring them to local Canaat leaders. Water would be their opening gift.

Morning sun glared from the naked blue overhead. Rising heat off the ky-pra islets dissolved the moored ships into smears of canvas and spar, as if they might vanish from their moorings entirely, appear in the harbors of distant cities to wait, silent, for some harbormaster to discover the gobbets of blood and flesh where the Kettling-tainted sailors had burst like overcooked dump-lings.

With the wind picking up again, only the need for water kept those ships in harbor now. The Kyprist government still held the reservoirs, and they would not let the foreign shipping, their only possible allies, raise anchor.

"When you get thirsty enough," Ake said, digging her paddle in to swerve the canoe around a crab-riddled mass of floating meat, "your brain tears away from the inside of your skull. Just shrinks right off. Terrible way to die."

"Thank you for that fact."

"I wanted you to know what you were getting yourself into. You'll see children who've died that way here."

"I saw dead children in Aurdwynn."

"Oh, you did, did you? How much you learned from us." Ake stared at the heliotrope bushes and coconut trees on a passing islet. "I've never seen a coco-nut. I thought they would look more like faces. Aren't they named for looking like faces?"

A crab the size of a ten-year-old wandered around the grove, snapping its claws. Barhu watched it, thinking about coconuts and coconut crabs and thirst, and about the basic resilience of these islands: born in the apocalyptic eruption of old Mount Tsunuq, cursed by the unsteady winds and errant cur-rents of the Kraken Still, deprived of even the most basic wood and stone, and still, stubbornly, alive.

"Ake," she said, "I think everything's going to turn out all right."

THE two spearmen threw Ake down beside Barhu, on the saltgrass at the edge of the red lagoon. "Oh stars," Ake gasped, in Stakhieczi, "oh black and hidden stars, Baru, look, look what they've done—"

"I see it." The lagoon's color was blood. Some of it still seeped from the corpse of the poor Morrow-man who'd tried to stop the warband from taking Barhu and Ake. He'd been a fool to think a bribe and soft words would work, and his fellows knew it: they'd been wise enough to melt back into cover, to wait for a chance when they could make a difference.

This was not the kind of place where subtlety and maneuver held power. Not anymore.

There had been portents from the beginning. The first group of Anagis they met (all the Kyprananoki on this islet called themselves Anagi, or Anagint, "friends of the Anagi") had welcomed their offer of clean water, rationing it among the children and the nursing women. Barhu admired their architecture while Ake befriended the children. Everything was built up on stilts, and the wells were in the Devi-naga pipestem style, to keep seawater from tainting them during floods. Barhu deduced, from the hardwood used in their doors and structural beams, that Anagi islet made its living by breaking and selling shipwrecks.

But the people had warned Ake of trouble. Balt Anagi was an island of the Balts: one of the social rates under the Scyphu families, before the Kyprist government banned the old religious practice. Balts were artisans and craftspeople, and for some reason Baru did not understand but which Ake accepted immediately, they were socially despised. Ake tried to explain: "You know how some people always have their stall at the edge of the market, and no one haggles with them? No? You must have been too young to notice." Baru could only guess that maybe the artisans, who must have traded with foreigners for wealth, had built up some kind of resentment.

The Canaat rebels promised fair treatment to all the old rates, but several Balt islets had been raided during the great surge west, as warbands canoed to Kyprist territory to attack. One band had landed here by "accident" and set to pillaging. Anagi's defenders fought them off. One of the attackers had been killed; his incensed warband had accused the Anagi of counterrevolutionary behavior, and sent east, to a place called Mascanaat, for someone called the Pranist.

Past noon the Morrow-men led Baru and Ake to meet the Anagi warband. Ake befriended them by offering to sew them new banners: she had a steel needle, nearly priceless, and the warband needed to tell its people apart from its so-called allies. They shared a meal of stone-cooked fish, and another warning. The Pranist, they said, was a purifier, sent to make sure liberated islets were made canaathe, which meant, in the new thinking, *fit for people*. He would kill anyone who'd had surgeries or inoculations. He would kill anyone educated in a Falcresti school. He would kill foreigners who refused to return to their ships and send back their water.

And he was shivering. He had the cricket sickness. They called it that because the eastern fringe had the most cricket farmers and that was where the bleeding sickness had appeared.

Barhu asked whether the Canaat leaders would entertain a water truce. That went over poorly. This rebellion, the Anagis told her, was a motion of the people. It was not something to be started and stopped at anyone's command.

They had learned the price of moderation, of waiting for a better time and a gentler method. The best way back to peace was to finish the Kyprists, break their control of the water, and return these islands to the control of their ancestral families. Their idealism stirred Barhu's heart.

The Pranist's warband came on them at sunset.

They had pistols, which were terrifying, and obsidian-tipped spears, which were deadly. The Balt Anagi warband routed. Most of the Morrow-men went with them; the one man who stayed tried to bribe the Pranist.

He was a shivering man in an open white cotton robe, naked beneath it except for a breechcloth and sandals. He took the Morrow-man's silver, promised to use it to keep clean water from going stagnant, and had the man drowned. "We'll use his corpse to teach the new kids," he told his warband, and made a few mock swings with a machete. "Get used to the heft, you know?"

The sun was falling and their chances were fading. Barhu tried the obvious lies—they were traders from New Kutulbha, come ashore to bring water to children. The Pranist spoke quick, alert Aphalone, but mostly he listened carefully to everything Barhu said.

"You have water to spare?" he asked. "On your ship? Not wine, not beer, but water?"

"Yes."

"But you've been marooned in port a while. Any casks you brought with you would be stagnant."

"We were lucky enough to refill," Barhu improvised, "before the, uh, the revolution."

"So you got water from a local aquifer?"

"Yes."

"The Kyprists hold all the aquifers. You paid the Kyprists for water?"

Barhu shut her mouth. This was going nowhere good. But the Pranist went on: "You legitimized their claim to the water. You gave them money good with foreign traders, which they could use to pay for weapons or mercenaries. I know, I know, you did it all to give children a drink. But when Kyprism is defeated, the children will have all the water they ever need, and you have delayed our victory. You see?" He threw up his hands. "You try to help, you fuck things up."

She tried to tell him about the apocalypse fuse.

The Pranist laughed at her. "We have to stop fighting, or we'll all die? The way we had to go to the barbers for our medicine, or we'd die? The way we had to marry as we were assigned, or our children would die? We're old hands at the game of obey or die." He turned to his fighters. "These people, they give me a bad feeling. Let's bring them to the lagoon."

"Wait," Barhu dared. "Wait, I'm a friend of Unuxekome Ra."

"Ra!" He spat the name. "You're Ra's creature? That pirate scum! She told us to wait, wait, wait, wait for Abdumasi Abd to return in triumph with Aurdwynn's fleet. And we waited, and waited, and the ships never came, and all the while we *died*. Come on, take them"—he beckoned to his fighters, all young and fierce-eyed, all shivering like he was shivering—"take them, let's go. They'll have banana beer and fresh fish at the lagoon. Then it's back to work."

B ESIDE the bloody lagoon stood a village, sugarcane-roofed domes on stilts, a pipe well to gather rainwater. The Pranist's fighters pulled the Balts out of the village and lined them up beside the lagoon. The youngest men and women were taken out of line and taught to use machetes on the corpses of seals. The Pranist stepped in with encouragement and pointers. A few of the older youth had graduated to dismembering the Morrow-man's corpse. "You'll get used to it," the Pranist called, "if you just don't look in their eyes. Figure out your own speed. It's normal to get sick the first time. If someone's making a mess of things, just give a shout and one of us will help."

"We're going to be killed," Ake whispered.

"We'd be dead already if we were," Barhu whispered back. "I think he's going to take us to Mascanaat. To meet their leaders."

"You're insane. We're dead."

The Pranist's fighters were well-equipped and distinctive, with all the markers, according to the *Manual of Field Literacy,* of an elite guard. Each man (there were only men in his group: he had said the young recruits would be segregated later) wore a thick fishnet cloak and a hibiscus flower behind his left ear. They marched the weak, dehydrated Balt villagers to the edge of the lagoon, where they were stripped naked. There they were inspected meticulously, from hair to toes, and then either sent across the lagoon, to stand on the far shore, or west, into the thick grove of coconut palms.

No one came back from the coconut grove.

"Have you had any surgeries?" Barhu murmured to Ake. She was thinking about the long, sutured cut on her back.

"Does it matter, Baru? We're foreigners."

The youths who had done best with the machetes were taken to meet an old woman who knelt in the lagoon, braced on her trembling arms, her face upturned. As the youths came near, she cupped the blood dripping from her nose and eyes in her hand, reached out, and placed her bloody hand upon the children's tongues.

"You can't do that," Barhu said, with rising horror. "You're giving them Kettling, you'll kill them all—"

"The blood cannot harm a true person," the Pranist said, behind her. "Come now. Do you really believe in the lie of blood disease? After all the 'inoculations' and 'infections' Falcrest lied about, don't you realize we need an infusion of strength? I was shot by a Kyprist crossbow, right here. Not even a scar! It healed in a day. The new blood is the restoration of humanity. If you feel sick you must kill Kyprists, and then you will feel well again."

They were insane. They were insane and it made perfect sense to Barhu because this madness was, like her, made by Falcrest: a pattern of authority by bodily violence which remained, like a scar, after Falcrest departed.

This terror was ultimately created by the Kyprists, by their ruthless barbers and their use of mass thirst as a weapon. Kyprism was in turn an artifice created by Falcrest's decapitation of all Kyprananoke's traditions and the installation of a biddable new ruling class. No matter how vivid and imminent the horrors here, Falcrest was in a distant but powerful way responsible.

But Barhu could not bring herself to forgive the Pranist and his warband.

No matter the cause, these were people doing evil. To absolve them of guilt would be to deny their humanity, to deny that they had some intrinsic dignity and moral independence which only they could choose to surrender. To say that these people were doing monstrous things entirely of their own monstrous nature was to deny Falcrest's immense historical crimes. But to say that these people were doing monstrous things solely because Falcrest had made them into monsters was to grant Falcrest the power to destroy the soul: to permanently remove the capacity for choice.

"Help is coming," she whispered to Ake. "The Morrow-men will have help here soon. Marines from *Ascentatic*."

She turned to the Pranist. "Stop this. You want a world for people? People don't kill each other for taking foreign medicine."

"Strike her," the Pranist ordered. "Strike her again if she tries to tell us we're not people."

The butt of a spear slammed into her wounded back and her whole body split in agony, like a cocoon cut open, the half-made butterfly draining out. She fell down gaping on the scrub.

"You're speaking Aphalone," she gasped, unwisely furious. "You're speaking a foreign—"

"The people speak through me!" the Pranist shouted, now in panic, as if the self-evident thing Barhu had said was his most dangerous secret. Maybe his young fighters terrified him, too. "I make myself understood to foreigners! I know Aphalone because it is useful to the people!"

"Don't touch her!" Ake cried. "She fought against the Masquerade in Aurdwynn. See her face? See her skin? She's Maia! She fought there!"

"Races belong to Falcrest. There is no more race. There are only people. These islands must be made ready for people again. There are thirty thousand Kyprists and their collaborators here. If each loyal person kills one, we could have them all gone in a day."

"You're killing the Balt. You're killing them because you hate them and you want their wealth."

"No, we're not," the Pranist said, patiently. "We're killing those who aren't people any more."

In the lagoon, a hawk-nosed fisherman with surgical scars across his belly tried to run. Immediately, without one warning or cry of anger, two of the Pranist's fighters set at him with their machetes: wordless, grunting, careful to strike him in soft flesh where the blades wouldn't lodge. They cut his upraised arms from wrist to shoulder, they cut his back when he curled up on himself, and when he was down they slashed the back of his head until he stopped moving.

Savages, the voice of Cairdine Farrier whispered, *degenerate savages, this is what they become without our guidance. . . .*

You bastard. You bastards. You did this to them, you took away everything they had, you locked them in this cage and left them.

They chose to become this way. They made themselves worse than beasts. You want to justify their sins because you hate Falcrest, but this is not Falcrest's doing. . . .

No. No. This never would have happened without you.

One day, Baru, you will not be able to blame all the evil humans undertake upon Our Republic. And what will you do then?

I will continue to blame you for the evil that is yours!

The bleeding woman extended her hand, black with Kettling effluent, and a weeping girl took that hand into her mouth. The fisherman's body was coming apart.

15

SPINAL RESPONSE

WHEN the scream sounded from the village Barhu thought it was just another poor Anagint trying to run.

A man wearing the net and flower of the Pranist's warband came scrambling out from under the stilt houses with a spear in his back. The end of the spear banged off the wood above him, like a rigid tail. He screamed again, and was intercepted, midstride, by a spear in the small of his back. Baru felt cruel satisfaction: why would he be among those houses if he were not a pillager, or a rapist?

"Go help him!" the Pranist bellowed. A shudder doubled him over, and he screamed at the mud and at the lagoon. "Find out who hurt him! My body is sick at the crime, sick at the sight!"

He vomited green-black blood. It came from his mouth and his nostrils. A trickle passed from his left eye.

People came down out of the village, toward the lagoon. Ordinary people who gathered close to share strength. Some of them were from the Balt Anagi warband. Some of them were not, but they carried fishing spears and machetes anyway. Some of them were the Morrow-men who had been sent to keep Barhu safe. Most of them bled from noses and cracked lips: thick red blood, dehydration blood, not Kettling.

They were singing together: wavering, out of tune, but all together.

"You!" the Pranist screamed, shaking his finger at them. "You've killed a brave man, a soldier for humanity! Who do you think you are to do this? Who gave you the—"

He saw the woman leading the attack, and his voice went from him.

"Tsuni el-tsun," he whispered: god of gods.

And you could see why men would call on gods to stop her. She skipped down the slope like a thistle, all points and no center, obsidian-tipped spears bundled on her back. Bounding from stone to black smooth stone as the atlatl in her hand bobbed to a secret rhythm.

Tain Shir.

The two war parties, Balt Anagi's defenders and the Canaat raiders, gathered across from each other, hesitating in that long nerving-up time before
the first blow. It was not easy to strike first, Barhu had read: that was why so
many warriors went into battle drunk. There would be a while of shouting and
threatening and working up before—

Tain Shir shrugged and a spear fell out of her bundle into her waiting hand
and then home into the atlatl's notch. The throwing arm made a little *zip* when
it swung. She stepped and half-turned with the throw and the spear pierced
the Pranist's lung and put him on his back in the blood-scummed lagoon,
thrashing underwater, the length of the weapon looping in the air.

Ake covered Barhu and held her down in the heliotrope bushes. "Don't
move! Don't take their attention!" Barhu, paralyzed by terror and fascination,
could hardly resist.

The Pranist's fighters broke. It was astounding how quickly it happened; but
this was battle as ordinary people fought it, not the disciplined phalanx-lines of
Aurdwynn. Shock and terror won the fight before first blood was shed. When
the Pranist's fighters turned their back to flee it became easier to kill them, even
for unbloodied men and women.

Tain Shir moved among them, killing, killing again, impaling the Pranist's
cadre one by one, twisting them by the bowel as if the spears were levers and
their bodies were the fulcrums of some ancient door. She did not hurt the
youth who had taken the Kettling blood. Barhu was not sure if she was relieved or horrified by that.

"It's her," Ake whispered, "it's her, I saw her poisoned, I saw her go into the
water. How is she alive?"

"I don't know." As if she had been called back to the world by the massacre
here. As if the wall between life and death were too thin. "Maybe the dose was
too small. . . ."

Tain Shir loped through bloody lagoon water to kick the sick old woman
over on her back. She fell pitifully and did not come up again. The freed villagers cried out to each other, husbands finding wives, children begging for
parents.

"Baru," Ake whispered, "what if she tries to finish killing you?"

"I know."

"She'll do it again—make you choose—"

"I know," Barhu said. "It'll be me, if it has to be one of us. I made that
choice."

"I don't believe you for a moment," Ake said.

"I know," Barhu said. She rose from the bushes and called out. "Shir!"

The killing woman turned toward her. Blue unblinking eyes, ragged blood-soaked body. Like a red-muzzled wolf. She reached back for a spear.

Barhu put up her wounded right hand.

"I have Tain Hu's soul," she called. "I'm carrying her eryre. Do you know what that means?"

Tain Shir raised the atlatl with the spear fixed in it.

"I'm telling the truth! Ask your aunt—ask Ake here—"

Tain Shir stepped and twisted and threw.

TAIN Shir kills Baru Cormorant in a thousand ways.

She drives the point of a spear up through Baru's stomach and out the top of her back. She crushes Baru's temples until Baru's eyes swell with blood. She rips out Baru's throat so that her final words will be the one true utterance spoken only by gouting blood and mortal air. She punctures Baru's lungs with a short knife so that Baru drowns in her own breath as *Helbride*'s surgeons fight and fail to save her. They pierce her lying throat in their desperation. They fail.

All these killings are possible.

But in the one true world that denies all other possibility, the spear Shir hurls is blunt, and it knocks Baru windless on her ass among the sweet white heliotrope bushes.

"Fuck!" Baru rolls onto her stomach to beat in agony at the soft earth. "Fuck, fuck, shit." She has fallen on her wounded back. "Himu fuck!"

"I know," Shir says.

"What?"

"I know that Tain Hu lives in you. I heard you confess it to Auntie Yawa. I followed you up from the water, so I could kill you if you'd lied to me."

"Lied about what?"

"About choosing to die. You were ready. I heard you beg her to kill you."

"Where's Iscend?" Baru pants. The Stakhi woman Ake is at her side, helping her up, wary eyes on Shir. She is a trifle of flesh with a fierce, bitter spirit in her. Shir imagines she would have the gamey, fear-flushed taste of frightened prey. "Did you kill her?"

"No."

"Where is she now, then?"

"I don't care," Shir says, which is the truth. "Why have you come here?"

"I'm trying to stop the fighting. Organize water distribution and a quarantine. Before the ships can sail."

"Why?"

Baru gets gingerly to her feet. "So I can contain the Kettling."

"Why?"

"So these people don't all have to die!"

Shir considers her as a tracker considers spoor. This choice is not the act of a woman who uses and discards her pawns.

"I came all this way to give you death," she says. "And I have done it. You are dead and reborn."

"I never died."

"You asked for death. That was the important part."

"To prove I wasn't Farrier's."

"Yes."

"You escaped Farrier, didn't you? How?"

Shir moves, a shrug, a shiver. Behold what I am. "I escaped all meaning. You cannot. You are a reader of books and an interpreter of signs. When you look at the stars you see constellations. I only see lights. That is why I cannot be mastered."

"I hope I'll never be like you."

"Of course you do. You need me nonetheless."

"Why?"

"Because I can escape them, and you cannot."

And Shir remembers the first day she ever saw Baru Cormorant, a child wandering the Iriad market, poking at the rolls of tapa cloth, leaning in so close to the racks of polished ash-glass that her breath left white smears on the telescope lenses. Shir was Cairdine Farrier's agent and protégé, undercover as a guard at his market stall; Baru approached her, named her as a soldier, even deduced the existence of a warship moored off Taranoke.

And because Shir was Farrier's creature, because she'd known at once that Farrier would take interest in Baru, she'd spoken to the child:

Little lark, I know what it means to see strange sails in the harbor. My name's Shir and I'm from Aurdwynn. When I was a child, the Masquerade harbored in Treatymont, our great city. They fought with the Duke Lachta, and I was scared, too. But it all ended well, and my aunt even got to kill the awful duke. Here—take a coin. Go buy a mango and bring it back to me, and I'll cut you a piece.

Here's a coin.

Go buy a mango.

I'll cut you a piece.

She had given the child a Masquerade coin, so that the child could buy her own island's fruit, to be cut and apportioned to the child by a Masquerade agent.

She had inflicted Cairdine Farrier's lessons. What you have belongs to me. What you need will be earned with my coin. What you desire will be divided by my knife.

This is why Baru needs her. Baru can play games of strategy with the very masters of those games. But in the end she cannot do what Shir is capable of doing. She cannot reach across the board and cut the other player's throat. You cannot destroy the masters by mastering them. You destroy them by *destroying*.

"I will make you a bargain now," she says.

Baru's stormwater-brown eyes are full of the exhilaration and the terror of the gambler who has staked everything. "Go ahead."

"I will guard the trust my cousin placed in you. I will remain above the filth you wallow in."

Baru opens her mouth to jeer, to remind Shir of all the blood already on Shir's hands. Who is she to speak of dirtying herself?

And Shir watches Baru realize that Shir has not in recent days ever killed the innocent. Marines and jackals, agents and spies, Kyprists and Canaat. But only those who have consented to stake their lives for falsehoods.

"These are the terms of my reprieve," Shir says. "Listen well."

Baru covers the stumped fingers of her right hand, and tries to stay in front of Ake Sentiamut. Ake shifts to hold her distance.

"I will hunt you across the world. I will watch everything you do and I will know everyone you know. I will judge each choice you make by the code of Tain Hu's life. And when you betray her faith, when you succumb at last to Cairdine Farrier's plan for you or to your own love of power, I will kill you. I will cut out your heart and prepare it on red coals. I will strain the flesh of your brain into its separate types, the gray and the pink, the stem and the bell. I will skin the meninges from your mind with an obsidian knife and I will knot up the nerves of your eyes. And then I will divide the relics of your mind among the four quarters of the world. Across Falcrest and the Mbo and the Camou and the Wintercrests I will quarter you."

Baru stares at her. "Is that so."

"It is so."

"Do you really think you can do that? Do *you* really think you can't be killed, Shir? I could have it done."

Shir says: "Kill me and you'll never find your father Salm."

Barhu enters a kind of paralysis, the absolute stillness of a mouse before a snake, as if she is afraid the slightest motion will betray her to the predator's teeth.

"Liar," she says, flatly. "Salm died after the battle at Jupora. He was killed by—"

"He was taken for Cairdine Farrier's use. I should know."

"How?"

"Because I was the one who took him."

She remembers it perfectly. Ambushing Salm as he came back from his toilet behind the perfume trees. His roaring strength, and the soldiers she'd reprimanded for their viciousness in taking him. Much later, Salm had tried to offer her sex in exchange for information on his family. Thinking herself his protector, his advocate, she'd refused him, given him the information anyway. He'd wept over the copies of Baru's school transcript.

And Shir realized, watching him weep, that even if she had never touched him she was still a rapist. She was the kind of woman who took people prisoner and made them so desperate that they would offer their bodies to win a rumor of their daughters. She had coerced him and then called herself noble for placing limits on her coercion. She had chosen not to rape but she had still kidnapped him and taken him into her power where rape could be inflicted without any hope of justice. The entire situation was therefore evil.

"You took him." Baru's voice is clenched up like a stomach wound.

"I know where he is kept now."

"Where is he?"

"Do you think he would want to see you? After all you've done? He will hate you."

"Your mother never hated you, Shir. Not even at the end. Yawa told me so."

Shir laughs in delight. What a reasonable presumption it must seem: that Shir is grown like a scar around the day she murdered her own mother on the banks of the Vultsniada.

But Shir knows the world at its fundament, she is a creature of that scoured truth. Her mother was one of many and distinguished from the rest only by sentiment. All those she's killed had mothers. All of them. None were worth any more or less than hers.

"Go from this place," she tells Baru Cormorant. "Gather my aunt Yawa and Tain Hu's house and all the others you cherish. It is not for you to save Kyprananoke. The world is larger than you, and older than you, and full of people who will not obey you."

"We *can* save this place!"

"You cannot," Shir says, for she cannot be saved, and Kyprananoke is now akin to her. "If Kyprananoke is saved it will only be by the Kyprananoki. And they are not ennobled by their wounds; they are not to be pitied or denied responsibility by those who do not share the wounds. They are still capable of evil. Let me show you."

She comes through the water of the lagoon to take Baru by the hand. She draws Baru into the coconut grove. Ake Sentiamut follows warily. Baru's hand is long and strong, reduced by two fingers, wet with fear-sweat and saltwater. She keeps asking questions. Shir ignores her.

They come to the heart of the coconut grove.

"Behold," Shir says, and, placing her hands behind Baru's shoulders, pushes her inside.

At the center of the grove is the mother palm. And upon the trunk of that palm is a stain where the little children with dental work and surgical scars and the babies born of shiqusection were dashed against the wood. Beside that palm is the sinkhole, a deep shaft in volcanic rock, where the corpses of the machete-killed have been stacked almost to the water's surface. And a thick skim of blood and yellow foam. And black massed flies upon that foam. And the world digesting the dead.

"Chaos," Shir says. "This is chaos. And it is your purpose."

Baru slips. Her kneecaps strike on black stone. She does not scream. She does not reach out, even by instinct, to catch herself on Shir: perhaps because Shir is standing on her right.

Baru's purpose is to bring this to Falcrest. The grove, the meringue of blood and flies, the stain of broken children, the hole full of corpses, atrocity, chaos, death. The world in raw.

To return to Falcrest what Falcrest seeded here.

P SST," Svir hissed. "You, with the bony ass. I need you."

Faham snored. I lifted my cheek from his chest to glare at the impertinent child. Svir, not mollified, beckoned for me. There is no dignified way to disentangle oneself from a man in a hammock. Faham mumbled in his sleep. I had never understood a word of his dreams.

I shrugged into linens and a dress. "Out here," Svir muttered, and led me to his own little cubby. "I just got a signal from Execarne's Morrow-men. Baru's not dead after all. The Morrow-men were able to attract some local fighters to attack the Canaat warband. Apparently Tain Shir was involved."

"Shir's alive?"

He grimaced. "Unfortunately."

"Is Baru coming back aboard?" There were certain matters I'd put in place, before our alliance, which I needed to disclose to her. I had induced in the Stakhieczi brave man Dziransi a prophecy: Baru Cormorant would be the dowry for his Necessary King's marriage to my protégé, Aurdwynn's Governor Heingyl Ri. Dziransi was already sailing north. If he convinced the King he saw true, it would put my alliance with Baru in a bind. We would be hard pressed to find an equal dowry to make the marriage work.

Svir growled in frustration. "Apparently not. She's still with Ake and your mad niece."

"Doing *what*?"

"Camping, apparently. Spending the night on an islet near Balt Anagi. She failed with the rebels. So I suspect she's trying to get to the Kyprists."

I stole one of his anise pellets, popped it into my mouth, and grimaced at the sweetness. "It's futile, of course."

I understood this part better than Baru. She would never convince the Kyprists to give up their power. To convince them she had to persuade Barber-General Thomis Love, their leader. And like any leader of a junta, he was Barber-General *because* he was willing to fuck over the common people to protect his immediate supporters. This was how kings kept their thrones: by currying the support of those who could threaten them, at the expense of all those who needed their protection.

Svir chewed at his bare red knuckles. "Why? Why did she leave that letter for Shir? Have they been in cohort all along?"

"No. Her eryre did it." No way to hide that reverence in my voice. "Through her right hand."

"Why? *Why?*"

"I think . . ." I had to laugh. "I think one half of Baru wanted to force the other to confront Tain Shir. Remember, she's not really Tain Hu. She's a part of Baru that acts the way Baru *thinks* Hu would."

"Conspiring against herself? Typical."

I spat wet anise on his desk, making him squawk. "What's this secret Baru brandishes at you, Svir? She has some leverage over you I don't share."

He looked at me crossly. I suffered a moment of confusion: he was very beautiful, and after years of case studies, my mind was a compost heap of perversion. I wondered what he looked like in bed with his men.

But I could not chase away the older fear he called up. I did not know if it was a racial obsession or merely my own. It was the image of a steel avalanche pouring down the Wintercrests, and of grim Stakhieczi soldiers cutting spear-furrows all across Aurdwynn, through grain and people, to the Ashen Sea.

"It's not a secret," he said, tartly, "that I have a hostage."

"But it's not about him," I said, meaning Lindon Satamine, his lover. "It's something Baru knows but I don't. She only learned you were an agent of the Throne last fall. So it's something she discovered over the winter, while she was in the North. Closer to your home. Closer to your past. Something you did when you were one of the mountain Stakhi."

He ignored me entirely. What else could he do?

"We're going to have to use it," he said. "The apocalypse fuse. Are you prepared?"

I was afraid that I was. "Are you?"

His jaw twitched, a bestial motion: fury at an entire condition of existence. "I grew up in the Wintercrests. I've seen greater waste of life. Entire Mansions eradicated by the pride of a few stubborn men. Kyprananoke is . . . small to me. Kyprananoke is a little stone in an old graveyard."

I didn't know what to say. I felt that there was something different about annihilating an entire people, rather than just one part of a greater whole.

"You've done worse already, you know," he said. And I remembered, again, why he was so dangerous: why he of all the Throne's agents spent so long out at the frontier, in dagger reach of death. "Last winter in Aurdwynn, you killed more people by starvation and sickness than you'll drown here on Kyprananoke."

But those were *my* people. *I'd* starved in Aurdwynn. *I'd* hacked cubes of frost from frozen ground to bury little children in the winter. And when spring came again, there was still an Aurdwynn to remember the dead.

There would be no memory of Kyprananoke. Or, at least, no Kyprananoki memory of Kyprananoke. And I was sure in my soul that there was some vital difference between the memory of seeing and the memory of being.

D ARK stars and bright sea: the night sky dull with haze, the ocean living green all around. Waves of light stirred the jellyfish and slid up the white sand to Barhu's toes.

Tain Shir built a campfire out of lumber pillaged from an abandoned house. "Expensive," Barhu noted, imagining how rare hardwood must be on Kyprananoke. Shir ignored her.

Coconut crabs fled from the fire. Shir loped out into the dark to catch one, returning with a specimen the size of a small goat. "You know how to cook that?" Ake asked her, skeptically.

"I put it on the fire," Shir said, "until it stops tasting raw."

"You know what raw crab tastes like?"

"Better than raw snake."

"When I was starving," Ake muttered, "I just chewed leather like a normal person."

Barhu paced up and down the tideline, watching green fire curl around her feet. "Alive." The word popped under her tongue. "Salm's alive." She'd never dared hope! "Ake, have I ever told you about Salm—"

"No," Ake snapped. On the short crossing from Balt Anagi to this islet she'd been stung on the ankle by a jellyfish. She had her foot in a coconut bowl full of warm seawater, and her fists balled in her lap.

"He was one of my fathers. I thought he'd been killed. My mother was sure he'd been taken. She was right, he's alive, oh, she's going to be so *smug*."

Barhu whirled to Shir, who was snapping the legs off the crab, a sound like a wrist beneath a wagon wheel. "You sent *Scylpetaire* to seize my parents. Where will they be taken?"

"Not far." The crab's face sheared off under her knife. "Ormsment ordered Captain Iscanine to arrest your parents and transfer them to a navy prison hulk off Taranoke."

"Well," Barhu said, fiercely, "I'll see to that soon enough. And as for Salm, wherever he is—"

"You will not find him." A grunt, a great ripple of her shoulders. The crab's legs tore free from its body: Tain Shir's method of emancipation. "I will find him. You lost the right to rescue him when you gave him up for dead."

Ake sat moon-pale in the firelight, staring at her balled-up hands. Thinking of her lost husband, who she could never rescue: he was dead of plague in Yawa's Cold Cellar. Tain Hu had cared for Ake, afterward.

Barhu reached out for her. Ake shuddered away. Barhu, caught with her arm extended, made a vague waving motion, floundered, and withdrew.

Shir laughed at her.

"Oh, fuck off," Barhu muttered. "Shir! Shir. You were Farrier's—his protégé? Yes?"

"I was what you are now."

"And when did you . . . free yourself?"

Shir worked at the fire. Her hands did not seem to burn. "During my travels."

"Where?"

"I went to Mzilimake Mbo to stir up civil wars for Farrier. The far south, where the jungle grows around the lakes. Then I went to the Occupation, to teach the Invijay tribes to kill Oriati. I sailed on a pirate ship. I became a monk in Devi-naga, in an austerity squadron. I got dysentery. I went insane. I cannot remember the order. I married three women in a sahel tribe because the only way to power there was to gather younger wives. Many women did it. My wives all divorced me, though. The Mzumauli, the moon worshipers, they divorce each other by shouting their old names five times." She blinked as if astonished, an expression Barhu had never seen on her before. "I don't tell stories often."

"And you must have seen so much of Farrier! Do you know his secret?" She could not resist guessing at the leverage that bound Farrier into the web of the Throne. "Is he a pedophile? Is that why he's always so proper with me? Why he was angry when I had Diline dismissed?"

Shir was silent.

"Tell me!" Barhu commanded her. "Tell me about Farrier's secret—"

The woman Barhu spoke to, the maker of fires and cooker of crabs, was just gauze across a wound. The thing unmastered rose in silence and the crab's huge shell in her hands made a groan like a cracking skull. Barhu did not flinch away: only looked up in wonder and horrified awe at this unnameable unorderable Object that loomed above her like the black wreck of an eclipse moon.

Barhu gave up her breath, had to gulp it back to speak. "All right. All right, I won't tell you what to do."

Tain Shir went back to the crab meat on the fire. "Farrier is more than what you see of him. He is always presenting one face for you. Other aspects for others in the Throne. Countless faces."

"Not countless," Barhu corrected her. "Six faces. Three here. Yawa, Svir, and I. Plus Hesychast, Stargazer, and Renascent in Falcrest. Seven if you count him."

"You know the Cryptarch's Qualm." Shir chose a claw and tested it with her knife. "What does it tell you?"

The Cryptarch's Qualm. *Your power is secret, and in secret it is total. To use your power you must touch the world. To touch you must be touched, to be touched is to be seen, to be seen is to be known. To be known is to perish. . . .*

Barhu straightened in thought. The tightening wound across her back complained at the shift. "I suppose it tells me that . . . that the most powerful cryptarchs would be the most secret. Like Renascent."

"If you know her name," Ake said, crossly, "do you really think she's the most secret?"

"I know them all, there aren't any others—"

Shir laughed like a jackal. "You think you know every cryptarch? There are more of them in Falcrest. There are many cells."

"No," Barhu insisted, "there were many cells *once*, before the Throne was purged and rebuilt, and now there is only one—"

"Wrong. They needed you to do provincial work, out here on the Empire's frontier. So they gave you a provincial's knowledge of the truth."

Barhu hated this thought. But the worst part was that it made sense. If the Throne was a miniature model of the Imperial Republic . . . wouldn't the provincials, Barhu and Yawa and even Svir, be excluded from the true core of power?

Didn't it have a certain logic?

Damn it, she *had* to talk to the eryre. If it was in there, if it was somehow guiding her, it must have a plan. It must! And if it didn't—

If it didn't, then she should've taken the baneflesh, and the Kettling.

Shir ripped off the coconut crab's bulbous abdomen and bit into it. Thick yellow oil stained her chin like yolk. "Good. Tastes sweet. Like coconut." She offered the bulb to Ake. "Try it. It'll make you want to fuck."

Ake barked a laugh. "After today? I don't think so."

Shir shrugged and took another drink. "I've seen worse."

"In the jungle?" Barhu asked.

Shir shook her head. "In Falcrest. On raids." She swallowed another gulp of buttery fluid. "You're wasting your time going to the Kyprists tomorrow. To get to Governor Love you'll need to pass through waters held by Unuxekome Ra's faction."

"She'll let me pass," Ake said. Somehow she could hold Shir's eyes without difficulty. "She hates Xate Yawa. My husband died in Yawa's cellars. So we have some common ground."

"You think you can talk your way past?"

"Yes," Ake said, without hesitation. Barhu glanced at her in surprise and respect.

Shir offered her the crab's dripping abdomen. "How do you know that?"

"Because," Ake said, accepting the goblet, "*I* was Tain Hu's friend and regent. *I* never betrayed her. And Unuxekome Ra knows that Tain Hu was her son's true and faithful friend."

SCREAMS and pistol fire came dimly out of the night. The Kyprists on the reservoir islands fighting off another assault, maybe. Canaat swarming up beaches barbed in broken glass.

Barhu knelt in the shallows, in a mass of interested wrasse fish, to hang up her clothes on the low branches of a dead pandanus shrub. She was thinking, in sleek runs of harnessed idea that came apart and crashed like cavalry on a wet descending slope, about her plan to end Falcrest.

She was confident that she had a plan, and that the details of it were hidden not only in her blind side, but in the things that she had done since the Elided Keep. Money games on the Llosydanes. Ake's letter of governorship to rule Vultjag. Sniffing the deck on *Eternal*. It all meant something . . .

But what? What?

"Your wounds," her blind side said.

The Thing named Shir stood, silhouetted in the distant firelight, in the shape of a broad dark woman holding a severed crab limb as long as her arm. A bark-cloth satchel dangled from her breechcloth; otherwise she wore salt-water and fire soot. One of her breasts was cut almost in half.

"Why didn't the Cancrioth whale attack you?" Barhu blurted. "Because you were throwing it fish?"

Tain Shir gave a roar of delight. "That's good. I like that. The whale is my friend." She held up the satchel. "Your wounds need tending. The sutures on your back are dirty. And your hand should have a fresh dressing."

"What, you use medicine now? You don't just slap mud on your wounds? You and your—" An inchoate wave at the whole concept of Shir. "Your barbarism?"

The great brown head, dark as Hu was dark, cheekbones as strong, brow heavy, nose unbroken and curiously smaller, flatter, wider than Hu's, and the eyes like pits: all of it inclined in curiosity. "Is that what you see? A barbarian?"

"I'd struggle for a better word," Barhu admitted.

The Object descended on her, claiming nothing, possessing only itself, as transiently and enormously present as a mountain cat padding through the forest: beast-hot, sinuously alive.

"You want something of me," it said.

"Not that," Barhu said, laughing sharply.

"Not what?"

"Not—never mind. I want to know if you know a way to . . ." She waved at her own head. "To reach across yourself. To ask a question of . . . the other half of yourself."

Tain Shir stared down at her impassively, waiting for her to make sense.

"I'm split!" Barhu snapped, in frustration. "There's two of me in my brain, and the one you're talking to—she needs to know something the other one's thinking."

"I see," Shir said, and came closer.

Barhu was suddenly aware that she was kneeling. She began to get up. Tain Shir pushed her down on her folded legs and, with all the focus of a cat, began to clean the wound across Barhu's back. The Kyprist alcohol wash stung, but cleanly. Like a ghost's caress, receding. Barhu sighed.

"I don't understand you," she said. "You were trying to kill me."

"You accepted death. There was no denial or deception left in you. So you can live."

"I don't understand you at all."

She took Barhu's injured hand now, unwrapping it gently, the very same hand she had cut on the Llosydanes. Barhu felt absolutely corporeal, her whole awareness rising and falling with the surf against her thighs and the uncoiling might of Shir's body breathing at her back.

"But you need to find things you can't understand," Shir said. "Who would you be if you understood everything? Finished."

The linen came off her injured stumps. Shir prodded the wounded remnants, which made Barhu hiss and curl up stiff against her.

"Too much bone in there," Shir said. "It should be reduced. Not now. In a surgery."

"Why did you cut my fingers off?"

"You define yourself by what you sacrifice. So the sacrifices had to begin coming out of you. Not from others. You yourself."

"Is there a way to speak to the rest of me, Shir? Is it possible?"

She neither moved nor spoke but there was a sudden concurrence of shapes between Shir's overarching body and the bend of Barhu's naked back. A sense of nestedness, like one bowl beneath another.

"The spine lies beneath the brain," Shir said. "Perhaps the answer is in your spine."

"Don't break my spine!"

"Let me teach you something. A way of being in yourself, in your own flesh. This will oppose Farrier. He despises the flesh as he despises all of unconditioned existence."

"What do I—"

"Be still. Let your thoughts out into the water. Let them drift."

A weight lay on Barhu, not unpleasant but massive: her mind's awareness of Shir behind her. She knelt in the warm rushing water, conscious of the hard power in her core and the ache of tired thighs, her beating heart and swelling lungs, all of these not separate from but part of her thoughts. The engine of her body-mind turning, the experience of the world like a river passing through her, powering her but not overwhelming her. And the more fiercely that world raged through her, the stronger she would build the mechanism, to convert the passage of events into thought and force and desire.

Oh Himu, I am alive. I want to be alive, I want to want things, I want so much. I choose to live.

Her spine was half an inch from Shir's chest. Tau-indi was right. There were wounds in the human world, and Shir was one of them. But Barhu would not turn away. She would not fear. The less she understood, the more she wanted to know. And there was no other living woman in the world who had done anything as intimate to Barhu as chopping off two of her fingers.

"Now," Shir murmured, "listen to yourself. Let yourself speak."

She adjusted the arch of her body and Barhu found herself flowing into an echoing posture, hard to hold. Her arms columned outside Barhu's, breath hot on her scalp. The bestial tension of Shir's core *almost* brushing Barhu's naked back. Do not think. Do not consider. Only listen.

Shir rose up minutely away from Barhu and Barhu had to lift herself a little on her knees, tighten her thighs and her stomach and her aching back, to keep the same distance. And Shir breathed. And Shir breathed. Barhu trembled with the strain of holding the posture. Her breath quickened in time with Shir's.

Are you there? she thought. Are you there, Hu?

> I'm here.

Are you there?

> I'm with you, Baru.

Are you there, please?

> Can't you hear me?

Give me a sign, please, somehow.

> If I can find a way.

I need you. I need you. I need you.

> I'm here! Listen!

She was breathing quickly now, faster than Shir. Aware of almost nothing but Shir's body behind her and her own desperation for a sign. Her thighs and core were trembling with tension, her calves cramped, her arms shaking. Her spine was sore, a dull rod drawn like a longbow. And Barhu had the strangest feeling that it was burning like a fuse: that something inside her was reaching down to grip her vertebrae, this road they shared.

Is that you? Is that you, imuira?

> I love you, Baru.

Suddenly one thing happened, and then another, without any movement on Barhu's part. "Huh," she grunted, in surprise. It was quick and violent, like breaking a fist, finger by finger. She grunted again, and exhaled, in wonder. She had not known that was possible.

"Is your question answered?" Shir asked her, without any sign of mockery.

"No," Barhu said, a little breathlessly. "But I feel . . . I feel better."

"Then I think it was answered." Shir got up. Saltwater poured down her calves. "A curious reaction. You have knots inside you, woman. You pull them as taut as you can, and think that gives you relief. Learn to untie yourself."

"Wait! Wait, was that not—not meant to happen?"

"I taught you how to ask a question. Your body answered. If you are asking me what *should've* happened to you, then you have learned nothing at all."

And Shir wandered off into the groves, leaving Barhu in the water beside her airing clothes. The crab leg, folded on the satchel in the sand, smelled deliciously of fire. She took it up and ate.

That, she thought, had been strange. But this was a place for strange things. And if Shir frightened her, if that had aroused her, well, at least she knew her own perversions better.

All the tense crouching left her neck sore.

THINGS FALL APART

J URIS Ormsment staggered up the black beach toward the men with the pistols.

Her crew saved her. Against all her orders and all her fury they bound her to a spar and threw her clear of burning *Sulane*. She had wanted more than anything to die with them, and they had mutinied against her last command.

They'd done their duty. Someone had to tell the truth about what had happened here.

"Hey!" she called, wading out of the shallow breakers. "Hey, you!" She didn't speak a word of el-Psubim, but what did it matter now? "What island is this?"

The pistoleers turned toward her. One of them was bleeding from his eyes. "Are you a foreigner?" another shouted. "Do you know medicine?"

Oh, they were infected. Red eyes and runny noses, one man trembling with chills. Flu symptoms. First stage Kettling, except the bleeding man, who was in the terminal stage. Well. Her ship was lost. She would not go to any great pains to protect what little remained of her life.

"Give me cloth." Taking the mulberry work shirt offered to her, she fastened it around the bleeding man's head. "The blood is what spreads it, see? You can't let your blood touch anyone."

"The Exile Duchess told us it was holy," one man said, in very clear but very un-Falcresti Aphalone. "She told us that the elected ones would bear the sickness but never grow sick."

"Do you have a triage station? A hospital?" She looked around for a cone snail or something, anything, to put the dying man quickly out of his misery. They would have to dispose of the body, and then she would rally these men as a work gang, and try to organize a new quarantine. If only Captain Nullsin could be convinced to spare some Burn—but trusting Nullsin had been her downfall.

She thought of Aminata and wanted to cry out. Poor Aminata. Dead on *Sulane*, with all the rest. Dead because she'd wanted justice, and Juris, thinking she could offer it, had taken Aminata in as her own.

She'd failed. All come to nothing. All the dead betrayed.

"Who are you, anyway?" one of the men asked her, watching her run her fingers through the wet sand, looking for a deadly snail.

"I'm . . ." Juris began, and didn't know what to say next. "I know a little medicine. I can help."

B ARHU woke up with a headache.

"It's fine," she grumbled, as Ake Sentiamut ignored her. "I'm fine."

Ake, who was so bright red and burnt that she crackled when she moved, was loading up a canoe for the day's attempt to reach the Kyprists. "When do we go?" Barhu groaned.

"You don't." Ake levered a water barrel into the canoe with her knee. "If Ra's rebels intercept us, they'll kill you. So you stay here."

Ridiculous. Obviously she had to be there to persuade Barber-General Love. "You'll need me," Barhu insisted, and tried to get up. She couldn't.

Ake pushed the canoe into the gentle surf. "Wait!" Barhu spat. "Wait, you'll—tell Governor Love about the apocalypse fuse!"

Ake pulled away into the channel between islets, paddling badly but with vigor.

"I've been abandoned," Barhu complained. The Morrow-men would be nearby, of course, and they could get her back to the ship.

She rolled over onto her back and stared at the hot blue sky. If the other mind in her head had a plan, and that plan was hidden in Barhu's recent actions . . . what part of the plan required Ake Sentiamut to be armed with a letter of authority and sent back to Vultjag?

She'd given Ake orders about trade. So that was a constraint, a way to focus her investigation. The answer involved trade.

And Vultjag was in the north of Aurdwynn, pressed up against the Wintercrests. First to fall if the Stakhieczi invaded. Did she mean for Ake to establish trade with *them*?

She thought, suddenly, of the black iroko wood on *Eternal*. It would be an incredibly valuable trade item. . . .

"Turn your head," Tain Shir said, from her blind side.

"What?" Barhu grunted.

"Turn your head side to side."

Barhu did not want to. "Listen, you've got to go up el-Tsunuqba. There's a bomb up there which will cause an avalanche to destroy the entire kypra. I need you to prevent its use. I need time to work."

"I know. Turn your head."

"Why does it matter if I turn my head?" Barhu snapped.

"Because you're nodding while you talk, but you don't turn your head. Turn your head."

"Of course I can turn my head, see—"

The pain was so strong it made her double up cringing into her lap.

"What happened to your eye?" Shir snapped. "Weren't you punched?"

"No—your aunt, she started to lobotomize me—"

"Did she drill a hole?"

Barhu nodded. That hurt less.

"You have meningitis."

"I do *not* have meningitis!"

But none of Barhu's protests could stop Shir from lifting her and carrying her south. After a while she stopped understanding her own protests. She tried to shut up. Her mouth went on moaning.

WHAT if it's Kettling?" someone was asking. "What if she gives it to all of us?"

She cried out weakly because her head was an open red sore. Xate Yawa leaned over her, masked, waving a mirror before her eyes.

"Hello," Barhu said, daftly, as a world of masts and feet and blue jungle-crow eyes orbited her skull. Her aching brain had swelled up and begun to tunnel out her right eye socket. "Saw your niece."

"Meningitis." Yawa snapped the mirror shut. "Get her below. If she has Kettling, too, we'll just have to keep her in quarantine and mind her fluids. It won't pass to us unless we're very foolish, or she breaks with the pneumocystic type."

"I can't go below," Barhu protested, "I've got to arrange the water truce. . . ."

"Whatever you want to tell us," Svir said, appearing out of Barhu's rightness in a flash of red, "you'd better say it now. You may not be with us much longer."

"Yes. Yes." She fumbled through her thoughts. They would not come into any kind of order. "The teak. The iroko wood. I meant to . . . oh, I can't remember. Use the water as leverage. They can't sail without water. . . ."

"Listen to her," Ake said, "half dead and she's still certain she knows what's best."

"Ake! Ake, is the truce ready? Is Governor Love ready to negotiate . . . ?"

"He's infected. His aide's in charge. She's busy killing everyone who's not loyal to her. I couldn't get through."

"Try again!" Barhu gasped. "You have to try again—"

A hand brushed her cheek. "Aminata?" Barhu gasped, "Aminata, is that you?"

But the hand closed over her mouth and her eyes, and stilled her for a while.

S HE woke in darkness and screamed in pain.

"Hush," Svir hissed, "hush. People are sleeping."

"How much have I missed?"

"Your water truce. It lasted half a day. There are too many Canaat factions, all afraid they'll look weak if they stop fighting. And the Kyprists are desperate for a chance to break out. Someone always starts fighting again. The truce can't hold."

"Because I'm not there. I have to go persuade them."

"It has nothing to do with you, Baru. You didn't release the Kettling here. You didn't push through water reforms that left the Kyprists in control of the aquifers. Or destroy the old compost agriculture. Or force the people into sugarcane planting. Or do any of the things which poisoned Kyprananoke. You did not create these circumstances."

"The rebels will be blamed," she gasped. "Because all their evils are done in the open. The Kyprists are worse—they just make their crimes into laws—you must be sure it's remembered! There was a tree where Canaat dashed children to death. But the Kyprists had jails, jails where they did as much and more. . . ."

"Stop. Stop. Meningitis is serious, Baru. You don't want to spend your last words cursing some provincial junta. Or defending those Canaat monsters."

So much left to do. So little of her mind to do it with. "You can't use the fuse," she rasped. "You have to give them a chance."

"When the wind picks up I'll have no choice. The ships here may not have water, but they'll take dehydration over a plague port."

"You can't! Take the chance, Svir!"

"You're an accountant," Svir snapped. "You understand the logic. Don't put the blame on me. It's just the numbers."

In the grip of fever the numbers crawled on her like ants and she moaned in horror. If even one infected carrier reached the mainland, if the blister number was exactly right and that carrier infected three others . . . in just eleven generations of infection there would be two hundred and fifty thousand infected. Seven out of ten would die. More than lived on Kyprananoke by far.

"I'll come by," Svir murmured, "when you're awake, and I have news."

He did. The Canaat seized one of the Kyprist reservoirs in the chaos, but the retreating Kyprists filled it with corpses. The atoll's summer crops had failed. The locust and cricket farms were dying out. Kyprist cutters were arresting fishermen or throwing them overboard in their own nets for "supporting insurrection." *Ascentatic* burned a dromon that tried to depart on sweeps. An overland scouting party sighted *Eternal* on the southern coast of el-Tsunuqba, putting out fishing boats, scouting desperately for water. A peace offering of lumber had been taken, and then thrown back, and then taken again: all, apparently, by different factions of *Eternal*'s crew.

Ulyu Xe swabbed Barhu's head with a cool cloth.

Yawa talked to her, too. She said Ake was in the east, at Mascanaat, where the rebels let her pass because they'd heard stories of Tain Hu.

"Yawa," Barhu croaked. "If I don't . . . if you end up without my services, please look to my parents. Search for them on a prison hulk off Taranoke. And my father Salm. Tain Shir knows where to find him."

The pain in her skull eclipsed whatever Yawa said next.

I T happened while she was asleep.

All she heard at the time was a mast-top girl shouting "DECK, DECK, GALLEY ON THE RAM! PORT SIDE!" And the creak of her hammock swaying as *Helbride* heeled over.

The other captain must have decided there was no escape from Kyprananoke without a ship fast enough to outrun *Ascentatic*. His dromon closed on *Helbride* during the night, moving under sweeps in the shallow water. The dark jagged shape of el-Tsunuqba concealed his ship's outline until it was too late. Before Captain Branne could finish crying out "Beat the crew to quarters!" the dromon was charging *Helbride*'s port side.

Helbride answered wonderfully to the sailing master; her sheets fell from their clewage with living eagerness. As soon as Branne had steerage, she threw the helm over to port and turned into the dromon, as if to match ram with ram.

It almost worked. She might have slipped past, just feet from collision. But the dromon grappled onto *Helbride* in the close passage, flank to flank. And the boarders waiting to swarm up the ropes onto Svir's clipper looked up with grim, determined faces.

Faces stained with fresh, unclotted blood.

"PLAGUE SHIP!" the mast-top girls cried.

"Flee!" the other ship's griot cried. She leapt up onto the rail, cupping her face, showing them hands of blood. "Flee your ship, or die with us!"

"Abandon your ship," the dromon's captain shouted. "Swim away, save yourselves! We want only the ship!"

The *Cheetah* crew, survivors of Tau's ship rescued by *Helbride,* shouted shame in reply: if the attackers had the littlest trim and decency, they would do the right thing and throw their oars overboard, drift away to die in quarantine rather than spread the disease. But there was no chance a self-sufficient crew of yeniSegu sailors would be browbeaten into giving up their lives by a well-to-do Prince-house from the heart of the Flamingo Kingdom.

Very coldly, not a whit of fear in his jaw, Svir stripped off his shirt. He walked to the rail and showed the Oriati his scars: the livid, branching lightning-marks that trailed down his body like the kiss of a jellyfish. In the moonlight they seemed silver and alive.

"I am Svirakir of the Mansion Hussacht." He put his hand up, fingers splayed like bolts. "I bear the lightning in me. I fear no illness, for lightning has no flesh. Get back before I call down fire from the cloudless sky."

The captain motioned to his sailors to wait a moment. There was real wonder in his eyes.

"Who are you?" he shouted. "How were you so touched?"

At that moment *Helbride*'s cook shoved her lord Apparitor down to the deck and leapt onto the Oriati ship with her apron full of Burn grenades.

T HE next time Barhu woke, Faham Execarne was at her bedside. "Hello," he said. "I've been putting a little anesthetic in your water, keeping down the screams."

"Do you know?" she wheezed. "Do you know what they're about to do?"

"Yes," Execarne said, sadly. "We're enacting a quarantine. Exactly like we quarantine any other outbreak. Do you understand the problem of this disease? The long incubation period? They get better for a while. They can travel before they start to bleed. Once it's out it can't be stopped."

"I know," she moaned. "But . . ."

But if all the Kyprananoki died, the things they believed in would all be gone. Their gods and holidays. Their food. Their grudges, their gifts. All the things they had made of what they had.

"I can't remember," Barhu said.

"What? What can't you remember?"

"Taranoke. I swear to the caldera gods, sometimes. But I don't remember their names. I remember plantain leaf and cooked pineapple. Coffee. Iron salt. But I don't know how to make our food. I don't remember the right word for the elders. I remember hating plainsiders but not why. . . ."

"Hush," he said, blowing smoke. "Hush, you're rambling. You're putting confusion in the air. Vital to hold onto our subjective control of reality, with such chaos around us."

"We can't do this. You can't allow this."

"There are less than a hundred thousand Kyprananoki. Even if we had a ninety percent chance of containing the disease—which is grossly optimistic—a ten percent chance of the Kettling escaping to kill a million people, just a million, outweighs the entire population of Kyprananoke."

No. That was accountant logic, the logic that had failed her in Aurdwynn. Because numbers alone couldn't count what Tain Hu had meant to her. She was one life on paper and yet a universe to Barhu. Kyprananoke was *more* than a tally on a page. They had a heritage, the Jellyfish Eaters and the Scyphu and the Tiatro Tsun. And they had a language. And so many irreplaceable people, people like Ngaio Ngaonic, who she had met at the embassy.

She knew that Tain Hu wouldn't drop the mountain. Tain Hu had survived plague. She'd lost her parents to it. And doggedly, determinedly, she had gathered the survivors to rebuild. Because she believed that the right of an individual or a people to have a *chance,* even the smallest chance, was inviolable. That right was what kept powers from rationalizing the destruction of entire peoples as an acceptable cost.

"This is the wrong way," she said.

"Maybe." Execarne sighed weed smoke. "It's certainly not good. But good intentions aren't enough, Agonist, no matter how forcefully we concentrate on them. The world is big, full of many minds, all hard to change. It is possible to do your utmost and still fail. By the way, they say the odds of you surviving this meningitis are bad."

"I can't die," Barhu croaked. "I have a plan."

Execarne's smile crept through the wall of fever. "Don't we all?"

The meningitis came up around her like the bell of a jellyfish, and Barhu's mind failed.

INTERLUDE

THE WATER HAMMER

I T was the wind that woke her. It came out of the southeast, over gentle wavetops and charred corpses, to rouse the Lieutenant Commander from her fugue.

Awareness returned as a damage report. Throat: burnt. Boots: missing. She'd kicked them off before she leapt. Her whole ass side from her heels to the nape of her neck burnt tender. She was still wearing the rest of her combat rig, and only the wooden spar she laid upon kept her above water. Every breath felt like a chest-cold swallow. The smoke off *Sulane* must have made her cough until she passed out.

But she was alive. She was alive!

She stuck her head up and tried to get her compass. She'd drifted south toward el-Tsunuqba, and the quickening current had her. Ahead the water frothed up into cream-and-coffee color where it plunged into a narrow black strait that roared like a waterfall. But it couldn't be a waterfall, there was no elevation change, so—

"Oh fuck," Aminata said.

Back on Taranoke, she'd gone on an expedition to the autumn whirlpool at Juditu. The other midshipmen had thrown one of the water rescue mannequins into the vortex—Aminata hadn't participated, not wanting to be blamed for mishandling equipment. The mannequin had been sucked down nine hundred feet on the sounding line, then slammed into the bottom and drawn down-current so fast the line snapped.

She really, really did not want to die that way.

With a cold washing pain as the saltwater licked her burns, she rolled off her spar and began to kick against the current. She had to lose ballast, maybe lose her uniform, certainly get rid of this thing tied to her rig, what was *this*, a hard metal cylinder—

It was the Cancrioth uranium lamp.

The shroud had dragged open and the oily rock inside was naked as a show-boy on officer's night. Aminata rolled onto her back and tried to get the damn thing off, but the knots were dire. She'd *really* wanted to keep it. Why would she tie it on so well? Did she think it was worth money? Had she confused it, somehow, for an *actual* lamp, a beacon for her rescue?

Something massive brushed against her back.

Aminata looked down and shouted in horror.

A human skull with fuzzy spikes of cancer-bone growing through its eye sockets slipped past beneath her. She was still shouting and flailing when a tremendous set of black tail flukes slapped water in her face.

"Ai!" she shouted. It was the Cancrioth orca! It was here to eat her!

She'd read about settlers way down in Zawam Asu who'd learned to fish in cooperation with orca pods. She'd read about orcas rescuing fisherfolk. Or playing with them. Sometimes the play involved dragging them into the water. Dragging them down.

The maelstrom shrieked ahead. She was caught betwixt a whale and a whirlpool.

The orca breached. Those huge white eye-spots. Tiny eyes below them, the true eyes, only she'd never heard of an orca with *glowing* eyes before, green like tide-fire. There were rings of paint around the eyes, as if the whale had been smeared with a substance like jellyfish tea.

The orca swam toward her, yawning. Its teeth were curious and huge. The glowing rings round its eyes brightened as it came.

Aminata looked at the uranium lamp and thought, oh, fuck me.

WHEN human hands pulled her from the whale's back, when rough ropes hauled her up a cliff of golden film and black wood onto the deck of a ship, she was still aware enough to begin the Mantra Against Captivity.

"Aminata isiSegu. Brevet-Captain. RNS *Ascentatic*. I will not break my silence except to repeat these truths, my name, my rank, my ship, Aminata isiSegu . . ."

Someone squeezed a trickle of freshwater onto her lips. Someone else shouted in protest. Rough hands tore the uranium lamp away from her body.

They're squabbling, she thought, they're squabbling over me. Am I about to be killed? I suppose that depends on who wins the squabble. Should I tell them I gave them the way through the minefield? Should I tell them I saved their ship?

No. Don't admit you helped them. No one loves a traitor. No one trusts a sneak. And it'll just convince them they can turn you, if they try.

When she woke up again she'd been moved.

Cold sediment-gritty water slapped across her face. Her heart throbbed in panic: a drowning response, she thought, to make her alert before the real pain—

Something lashed against her cheeks, slimy and sinuous. Her eyes popped open. A squid grabbed at her, a squid with its beak open in panic, with arms that looked like raw meat. She cried out and tried to pull away, but she was shackled to the wall, naked to the linens, her burns screaming. Something made a sound like a nail drawn down glass. She screamed back.

This went on for a long time.

Aminata knew what was happening because she had done it herself. This was the resentimente, the brutal false beginning of torture. Soon they would send someone to rescue her, to pretend to take care of her, and she would fasten on them with desperate gratitude. That would be the real beginning.

Every time she began to sleep they hit her with cold saltwater, squirming tentacles, and a nail scratched into glass.

When something changed, she thought she might be hallucinating. "Pig," she grunted, and then, hastily, she'd opened a hole in her armor, "Aminata isiSegu. Brevet-Captain. RNS *Ascentatic*."

The pig whimpered. Something was wrong with it, Aminata thought, someone should help that pig.

A bristly stinking face pressed up against her neck. Hot breath went up her nostrils.

"Look," a woman said, "look—"

Aminata opened her eyes. A piglet dangled before her, illuminated by the green glow of the hand that held it. The piglet's skull had ruptured from within. Its trotters jerked. The open brain was infested with glistening cysts, bloody with capillaries, scabbed and broken and scabbed again—

"This is what happens to you," the voice said, "if you do not answer our questions. Where is Abdumasi Abd?"

"Aminata isiSegu. Brevet-Captain. RNS *Ascentatic*."

A thin knife appeared and cut one of the tumors from the piglet's head. Blood welled up to pool in the ruined skullscape. The knife and the tumor lifted toward Aminata's mouth. She gagged. The questions did not stop.

"Where is Abdumasi Abd?"

"What has been done to the mathematician Kimbune?"

"How many ships are stationed at Isla Cauteria?"

"Are there supply depots on islands closer than Cauteria?"

"Is there good lumber on any island closer than Cauteria?"

"Where are the minefields defending Isla Cauteria?"

The pig's stink—hot blood stink, not septic death but swollen life, the cancer, a ut li-en, the cancer grows—she was aboard *Eternal*! The Cancrioth whale had taken her home!

"Aminata isiSegu!" she shouted. "Brevet-Captain, RNS *Ascentatic*!"

They forced her lips open. "Where is Abdumasi Abd?"

Aminata had enough freedom to dart forward and bite the tumor right off the knife. Cold steel taste, hot iron blood, and the fatty slimy fullness of the cancer, like snot. She spat it at the glowing hand that held the pig. "Fuck you!"

Rough hands slammed her up against the wall. "Let's begin everting her," the interrogator's voice said. "One slit across the abdomen, please. Bring a laundry rack. We unpack her guts for her to consider. It's a remarkable thing to watch your own digestion."

"Fuck you! *Fuck you!*"

A knife dimpled the skin of her belly.

"You won't touch me," she panted, "I know what you need to know, you won't hurt me," shut up, Aminata, you're giving them too much, "Aminata isiSegu, Brevet-Captain, RNS *Ascentatic*!"

"We can hurt you," the voice said, with some sorrow, "in ways which render you useless at your work, now and for the rest of your life. You are tsaji, a collaborator, a traitor to your people. We think it fitting that you should be denied all means of connection: sight, voice, hearing, even smell. Touch will take the longest. But when the baneflesh has its way, you live in a skin of rubber, and all that remains to you is that nameless sense which tells you when you are sick. And you *are* sick, Aminata isiSegu. You are never well again."

The voice left her panting in the dark for a moment. And then, again: "Where is Abdumasi Abd?"

"Baru loves me."

There was a silence of a different kind. Not, Aminata thought, a choreographed one.

"You know Baru?" the voice asked, quietly. Its whole character had become wary, thoughtful, interested.

"Know her? I'm her sworn protector. I'm her knight! The Duchess Vultjag made me her knight! Fuck with me, and you're fucking with Tain Hu!"

"Do you know her purpose?" the voice asked.

Purpose? Baru hadn't even known her own purpose. And when Aminata had asked her, *can you tell me the truth,* Baru had said, *I don't know.*

What would Baru tell the Cancrioth her purpose was? Would she pretend to be a rebel again? Possibly. But she could just as well pass herself off as a loyal agent, a Parliamentary representative-on-mission, a Judiciary invigilator, even an openly acknowledged agent of the Throne....

"Of course I do," she lied, as loudly as she could.

"Tell me."

"Very weak attempt," Aminata sneered. "She trusts me to keep her secrets."

The shadows of hands moved faintly in her vision, dark squid in a gray-green sea. Her interrogator, surprised at last, thrown off her impassive script.

"Come on!" Aminata screamed. "Where's that disembowelment you promised?"

"Where is Abdumasi Abd?"

"Up your ass."

"Where is Abdumasi Abd?"

"Hey, navy girl," Aminata began to sing-sob, "here's waking up to you—"

AFTER a long time there was a new voice.
Hands undid her restraints. No matter how she blinked she could not get her eyes to focus. At last someone unhooded a light and she seized on it, blinked and grimaced until she could resolve it into a lantern. She raised her eyes to the man holding it.

He had an eyestalk.

She boggled at him in exhausted horror and he said, wearily, "Yes, I know."

It was a tumor, of course. She'd seen stranger in the wards of hospital ships. But it was surreal to follow him like he was some officer's steward, like he was an ordinary man. Call it Incrastic fastidiousness, but she found his deformity frightening. Evil. The character expressed itself in the flesh, didn't it?

He led her silently up narrow stairways, to a long black corridor with many doors, and, through one, into a stateroom without any engravings on the floor.

"You may wash," he said, in a rich basso voice.

"Are you going to wait outside?" she asked, and then saw, to her astonishment, that the stateroom had its own bath chamber. This room alone, with its bed and couches and study, was preposterous! How could they have room for an attached bath?

"I will, if you want. Just wash, please." The stalk-eyed man looked very tired. "You've been in that filth too long."

Her burns were mostly superficial, but she absolutely had to wash them or risk fatal infection. There was no chance in stigma that she was going to do that with this man sitting here controlling her only exit.

"What the fuck are you?" she demanded.

He sat on the end of his bed, politely turned away from the washroom.

There was dirt under his fingernails. Bright, faceted jewels glinted in the flesh of his tumor.

"I am an onkos. I bear an old line. My name is Virios, but you will call me the Eye."

"You're . . . you're cancer. Aren't you."

A sigh: he hated explaining this, clearly. "I share my body with the souls of those who held the line before me."

"Are you the captain of this ship?"

"I wish I were. I wish we had a captain. The woman who tortured you wants to lead us, and I think soon she will succeed. I stole you away from her only because she wants you treated kindly, Aminata, and she does not want her followers to see her doing it." He smoothed the bedcovers, and then, seeing dirt streaked on the sheets, snatched his hand away. There was an innocence to that gesture which made Aminata like him. "Will you wash, please? I want you covered."

She went into the washroom. The bulb-shaped clay vessel there was full of water almost to the brim. "This," she said, loudly, "is too much."

"Is something wrong?"

"You can't spare all this water." Mariner's ethics: "So I can't use it."

"Consider it an act of hospitality," the Eye called. "I want to welcome you as proper Oriati would. Please, wash and dress."

She dry-scoured her body, laved her wounds, succumbed to the temptation to sponge herself. She remembered the squid lashing at her face, and, shuddering, looked for soap. There was only ash.

At last she came back out, dressed in knotted linens and a heavy cassock, to find him waiting patiently: just a man, a round and fatherly Oriati man with dirty hands and nice thick hair.

"What's happening?" she asked, warily.

"Too much. You're a sailor, yes? A navy woman? We haven't the water to make the long journey southwest, back to our home. Our ship is hurt and leaking; we desperately need to make harbor. The Brain is working to convince the crew that the best way to find a port is to take one. By force."

"She'll get you all killed."

"I know," he said.

"You don't look much like . . ." She tiptoed around the word *slavers*. "Like an aristocrat."

"No." He shook his head; Aminata was terrified his blind eye would be flung from the end of its stalk. "I was born common. When I took the immortata, I vowed to grow it as a sacred trust. Not a weapon, not a tool of bondage.

The Cancrioth's purpose is to explore the immortata and its marriage with the human body. We are not warriors. The Brain, in all her messianic delusion, has lost sight of that. And so I need your help."

Aminata, who had been waiting for this, the gentle request from the reasonable man, shocked herself by wanting to say yes: if only to have something to do, some duty to chase.

"What do you want?"

The Eye smiled softly. "Iraji, will you come in, please?"

A rustling of silk from outside.

"Oh!" Aminata said.

The boy stood in the doorway, naked to the breech under a silk robe, beautiful as anyone she'd ever seen. He was Oriati and his eyes were brown and gold and fixed on hers. She was having trouble keeping her own eyes fixed in return. He walked like a pinstep dancer, each step happening in all the muscles of his calves, his hard hips, his lean and girdled core.

Aminata grinned stupidly at him. "Hey," she said. She felt suddenly very glad to be alive.

The boy bowed like a very expensive whore. Aminata thought about what kind of habits she had, to see this *man,* not a boy, and to call his grace whorish. She corrected herself forcefully. The man had bowed with class.

"Iraji oyaSegu," he said, "recently off *Helbride,* now an initiate into the mysteries of the—the Cancrioth." An odd pause there, as if he were expecting to be interrupted. He put a hand out to hold the doorframe. "May I bring you anything?"

Anything at all, she thought, as long as you bring it. "My uniform and a boat back to my ship."

"I'm afraid I cannot possibly release you without throwing our crew into another mutiny." The Eye got up from the bed, groaning a little, and went to Iraji. "I think she'll be more comfortable with you, child. Please think on what I told you earlier. Please—just consider the good that could be done, if Tau could be brought back to us."

He squeezed the boy's shoulder and left.

"So," Aminata said. "You're new here, too?"

Iraji shut the door gently behind the Eye. "They're short on water, the crew's understrength, and *Sulane*'s torpedo damaged them so badly they're afraid they'll founder in a storm. The Eye wants to go home. The Brain's convinced she can awaken Oriati Mbo against Falcrest, and usher in a new age of restored Cancrioth rule; she wants war. The Womb takes care of the ship and its crew but won't assert herself directly. That's what I know. What about you?"

Aminata blinked at him. More than a pretty face, then. "No more than you, if you saw *Sulane* destroyed."

He nodded. "Take off your cassock. I need to see to your burns."

If this was part of the interrogation games, if he was here to confuse her between her duty and her desires, well, they'd picked the wrong woman as a target. She shrugged out of the Oriati cloth like it was dripping acid.

"What does the Eye want us to do?" she asked, debating whether to lose the strophium, too: would she come on too strong?

"To prove that we're people."

Aminata blinked. "Is that in doubt? He seemed perfectly polite to us."

"Not to him," Iraji said, with a quiet fear she could not understand. "Not to the Brain, either. Someone else here. Someone who's alone."

"Who else is here? Aside from the Cancrioth, I mean?"

"Oh," he said, "quite a menagerie, actually."

SHE had to be kept hidden from the crew, Iraji explained. This part of the ship was sanctified for the protection of guests. The Womb watched over it; she had, Iraji imagined, roughly the same authority over the crew as a mother—not someone who followed you everywhere and gave you orders, but who was, in her own domain, invincible.

"Have you got my sword?" she asked him.

"You had a sword?"

"It's not really mine anymore, I gave it to Baru, but it's a good blade. . . ."

"Oh! Yes. Baru's boarding saber." He made an apologetic curtsy at her, upsettingly graceful. She was starting to think they could be friends, which made his beauty an unaffordable distraction. "I'm afraid the Brain insists foreigners can't have weapons. The saber must be in an armory somewhere— Oh no. Hide!"

He pushed her out of the corridor, into the shadows of a cross passage. "Don't move."

A woman passed the intersection—a woman in an Imperial Navy uniform. Kings, look at her, look at that perfect carriage and contemptuous distance! It was Shao Lune! Shao Lune who'd been at Baru's side in the embassy! She'd opposed Ormsment's mutiny, too, hadn't she? They had that in common.

"Staff Captain?" Aminata called.

Iraji groaned.

"Ah." Shao Lune turned crisply to block the intersection. "You've been released. What are you doing back there, Lieutenant Commander? Come out. And you'll address me as *mam* while I'm in uniform."

"I'm a brevet-captain, actually, we're equivalent in—"

"The loyal navy does not recognize ranks bestowed by traitors. And in any case, a staff captain is senior to a brevet rank." Shao Lune looked her over critically. "I'll excuse your appearance on account of circumstances. But see to it the tunks don't defame your reds."

"Yes, mam," Aminata said, feeling as if she'd ordered water and been handed brine. Tunks, eh? At least she hadn't said *the other tunks*.

"My objective is to gather information about this vessel, in particular signs of political contact with the Oriati federations, as well as any form of chart or rutterbook that indicates this ship's home port. Somewhere in Segu, no doubt. Or western Mzilimaki."

"Yes, mam. Can I assist, mam?"

Shao Lune frowned at the way Aminata stood with Iraji. "*Your* orders are to remain in strictest isolation. Due to your heritage, you're in danger of regression aboard this ship. As we have seen in Iraji's case." She smiled nightshade at him. "I'll need you to report on whatever contact you've already had with the Cancrioth leadership—"

"She's relentless," Iraji whispered, "you'll never get away from her."

"Is that clear, Lieutenant Commander?" Shao Lune barked.

"Yes, mam!" Aminata snapped a salute.

"Very good. I'll be in my cabin, taking measurements. Report to me before end of watch." Shao Lune swept away with perfect confidence.

"We've got to see the Prince-Ambassador." Iraji pulled her in the other direction.

"But the staff captain ordered me to—"

"You can't *seriously* want to listen to her!"

"She's my commanding officer," Aminata said.

Iraji sighed and crossed his lean arms. Interesting things happened in his bare shoulders. "Fine. As an agent of Apparitor, who acts in the name and image of the Emperor, I second you to my service, and do detach you from all other duties in consideration of the Emperor's own work."

Now she could allow herself to call Shao Lune a cunt, if only in her head.

"When you say we've got to see the Prince-Ambassador, do you mean *the* Prince-Ambassador . . . ?"

He did.

THE Prince's door was guarded by a stanchion-thick Oriati woman with fighting ropes around her fists. She marked Aminata with obvious dislike, but stood aside graciously for Iraji. The cabin inside was as vastly luxurious as the stateroom the Eye had given Aminata.

But this one had been destroyed. The teak had been scratched, the furniture dragged over the wood in some furious attempt at erasure. A red wine stain marred the wall. The place stank of sick.

"I don't want company," a thin voice said.

A short, slouching laman with wide hips and giant bruised eyes came out of the washroom. All rotted grandeur: the flaking ceremonial paint, stained khanga, thick cracked lips and small empty mouth. The bright Prince she'd seen in the embassy had gone. Tau-indi Bosoka was a clay amphora emptied out and smashed.

Iraji bowed deeply. "I've brought a guest, your Federal Highness."

"There are no guests here. We're all strangers to each other." What shocked Aminata was how *little* this sounded like whining. Tau-indi said it with such simplicity: these are the conditions of our estrangement.

"Nonetheless. May I present the Burner of Souls, Aminata isiSegu."

A flicker of interest crossed the laman's face, neither hateful nor solicitous. "Hello," Aminata said, wary of this royal ruin. It was important, in Oriati etiquette, to establish some shared point, some bond . . . all she could think of was the disaster. "I saw you at the embassy on Hara-Vijay. I'm glad you escaped."

"You ordered the burning of the grounds." Tau scratched behind their ear. "You murdered all those people. No wonder you're here. You belong among us."

Aminata looked at Iraji. Iraji did not react.

"What's *wrong* with you?" Aminata demanded.

"Ah. I've been cut out of trim. I cannot be connected to other human beings. The Womb did it to me." Tau wiped their finger on the wall. "Say what you came to say and go. I want to sleep."

"Your Federal Highness," Aminata said, feeling that she stood in the dead beacon of an abandoned lighthouse, that she had some responsibility to kindle it again, for the sake of diplomatic relations if nothing else, "the Eye asked us to speak to you. Iraji and I. I don't know why, but here we are."

"Abdumasi Abd," Iraji murmured. "Tell them about Abd."

Oh. So *that* was the game. What a roundabout way to get at the question. But then again, she would have been just as subtle. And she'd almost fallen for it.

"Please," Iraji whispered, "if you won't trust me, trust Baru."

What did Baru have to do with this? "You know her?"

"Of course I do," Iraji said, loudly. "She saved me on *Cheetah*. She saved me again on this ship." A very slight swallow, delicious action of the throat and lips, but all covered in grief. "Is she gone?"

"I don't know. I hope not." Aminata had to laugh: "She's hard to kill."

"Yawa didn't lobotomize her?"

"No. She and Yawa seemed to be friends. I wouldn't be here at all"—don't let yourself turn bitter, Aminata, you face your duty whatever it might be—"except that Baru came up with a plan to go to Ormsment together—"

Tau-indi's head snapped up from their chest. Aminata heard joints pop with the violence of the motion. "Baru asked you to bring her to Ormsment?"

"Sure," Aminata said, warily, "she used herself as bait to get me aboard *Sulane*. So I could see this ship safely through the minefield."

"No." Tau-indi impaled her on a glare like a vivisection knife: an instrument deployed, for seemingly the first time in Tau's life, without any consideration for its target's comfort. "That's not why she did it. She did it because I told her that she had to confront Ormsment to heal the wound. What happened?"

"Well, uh"—Aminata thinking suddenly of Shao Lune's warning against contamination, of Oriati superstitions infecting and thriving in her blood—"Baru surrendered herself, and Ormsment ordered her keelhauled. I didn't see her after that. I thought it was a stupid risk . . . if I were Ormsment I would've slashed her tendons. . . ."

"Ormsment couldn't have done that," Tau said. "No more than she could've ordered a lobotomy. To diminish Baru would have diminished the reason for everything she's done." Iraji was smiling and Aminata didn't know why. "And after that, *Sulane* attacked *Eternal*, and was destroyed? I saw that."

Aminata nodded hesitantly. What would Shao Lune think? Was she answering Tau's questions out of some hereditary weakness? Had Iraji addled her with his beauty?

"Her actions returned to her," Tau murmured. "Baru turned back to confront her enemy. Ormsment refused to change her own path, and was destroyed by it. Was there anything strange about Baru? Any sudden change in her behavior?"

"She surrendered herself to save my life," Iraji said, brightly.

"I saw her volunteer to die in another woman's place," Aminata added, simply because it irritated her to hear Oriati nobility disparaging Baru.

Tau's eyes narrowed. "And what happened?"

"I took the spear meant to kill her. Right here"—thumping her chest—"I was wearing armor. It was just a fishing spear anyway."

"I see . . ." Tau-indi breathed.

Iraji's hands clenched in excitement. "Your Highness?"

An awful brittleness in Tau's voice: like ice on the verge of melting, warming but losing strength. "I think it is possible that the Womb's spell of excision had, ah"—their voice cracked—"had effects she could never anticipate. Baru Cormorant was a wound in trim, an upwelling of grief, a hole. All those who knew her would find only abandonment and regret.

"But when one bond is cut, Iraji, the loose thread may fasten on another. I was cut loose. There were many, many threads seeking a place to fasten. . . ."

"Baru's not a *wound*," Aminata snapped. How dare the Prince castigate Baru in this superstitious way? "She was honest with me. We worked together to save this ship and save *your* life—"

"Really," Tau said, with vicious sweetness. "She was honest with you? Did she tell you what she wanted this ship for?"

"No," Aminata said, tersely. Of course Baru had a reason to keep her tactics secret. . . .

"She didn't tell you that she came here to find a way to destroy Falcrest? I think she wanted to gain the Kettling as a weapon. But the price the Brain asked of her was too high."

Ridiculous. Just ridiculous. After all Baru had done to secure Aurdwynn for the Imperial Republic? "You're lying."

"And you are hopelessly gullible." Tau turned their sharp smile on Iraji. "Is she soft for you? Have you told her what you *really* are?"

Iraji swayed. His eyes rolled back for a moment. "What?" Aminata asked, hapless and humiliated. "What is it?"

"He's Cancrioth," Tau said. "The cancer wants him. His flesh was made ready for it. Remember that if you take him to bed, Segu-woman. The seed he yields is—"

"Enough!" Aminata shouted, and some part of the Prince cringed back in shame. "You won't tell me about my bed."

That beautiful boy. Of *course* he was a lure. She wanted to scream.

Just then someone hammered on the door. "Open up!" Shao Lune shouted, and then, in echo of her, the Oriati bodyguard woman, "Prince Bosoka, please, open up!"

Iraji lunged for the door. "What? What is it?"

"There's something wrong," the Oriati soldier panted. "You'd better come up on deck."

"We *can't* go on deck," Iraji said, "there are too many of the Brain's people out there—"

"It doesn't matter now," Shao Lune said. "No one will be looking at us."

* * *

"THANK you," the woman said to Juris, "thank you for the water."
With a groan of effort she leaned forward off the birthing cushion to grip her husband's neck and whisper, "Mind my mother, love. She'll need you. Pran Canaat."

After a while the blood stopped pumping from her. Her stillborn lay in her husband's arms as he wept thick mucus down a face like a sagging bag of blood.

Juris Ormsment took the mother's corpse by her armpits and dragged her into the pile for the next charnel boat. Kettling blood and bloody diarrhea soaked her all down her chest. The mothers hemorrhaged like artery wounds when they miscarried, but it was merciful how quick they went. Those who did not bleed out had to linger on, festering with blood blisters, shitting and vomiting green-black bloody fluid. Water just made them shit more; but if you stopped watering them, they died of thirst. Juris had tried treating the disease like cholera, giving one strong man water every half hour. He had rallied for a while. But the fever had killed him in the end.

She wiped her hands on her trousers and walked into the warm sea to get the blood and shit off.

"You lost her?" the chief barber asked. She was a Kyprananoki woman the color of sparrow plumage, her patient warm eyes offsetting a fierce hooked nose. She had first-stage symptoms.

"I lost her," Juris said.

"Banuile is still alive." The water rose, slapped against them, receded. "She lost the baby but she's strong."

They had accepted Juris at the mother's ward because she was competent and not yet sick. She cleaned up diarrhea and sponged water into cracked bloody mouths. There was no time for her to think of anything but the rows of dying mothers on beds of bundled kelp. She was not happy, exactly. But for the first time in months she had no heart to spare for her own hurt.

"Good," she said. "Good. I hope Banuile lives."

"I wonder where it came from," the barber said, for the tenth or twentieth time Juris had heard. "The Camou, maybe? Isn't there always plague in the Camou? With all the ships that make harbor here, who can say?"

It came from the Oriati, Juris wanted to tell her. They keep it hidden somewhere. That's why it's called Kettling. Because it's waiting to boil over, like hot water in a pot. And the mad duchess Unuxekome Ra would rather see you all dead than alive under our rule.

"I don't know," she said. "It could've come from anywhere."

The barber ducked into the next wave. A plume of filth came off her. "A short rest, I think. Then we'll bring more water for Banuile."

Yes, Juris thought. Keep trying. Keep finding wrongs, and naming them, and trying to make them right. Never stop. Even now.

"Will you tell me about Kyprananoke?" she asked the barber. "What it's like here?"

That was when she felt the sound. It was too low to hear. It rattled her long bones and set her teeth clicking.

"A quake." The barber frowned at the tossing trees. "That's odd. The almanac said there'd be no quakes for twenty years."

Juris looked north. The swarm of ships moored around Loveport was beginning to break apart, putting up canvas, catching the strengthening wind.

She looked south, wincing inside, toward el-Tsunuqba and *Sulane*'s wreckage.

What she saw made her laugh.

She recognized it. She knew it like a lover. It was coming at last. Coming for her.

The water hammer—

S HIR uncovers the old hatch. If there was meant to be a ladder then it is missing. She braces herself between the walls of the shaft and descends to the fuse station. She is careful to put her hands and feet in the right places, obeying the codes she memorized so many years ago. Like the tombs of the ancient Cheetah Palaces, the fuse station will kill those who do not know the way.

She expects to find sockets like dead elephant eyes, mounts where the correct levers must be fixed like huge keys and turned in the proper sequence. Pistons will drop into waiting shafts. Shir has come here to destroy the sockets. To prevent them from ever firing. She prefers the chaos of plague to this shrine of calculated sacrifice.

But the levers are in place. The sockets are turned. The timers are set.

Someone else reached this place first.

Shir goes for her knife. The woman behind her gasps explosively, releasing the breath she's held for five minutes or more. The mechanism of her little pistol bow creaks in warning.

"I can't miss," Iscend Comprine says. "It's poisoned. This isn't a capture dose of curare. This time it's kratom opiate and aconite."

"Slow," Shir says.

"But very, very certain."

"Gaios. Lower your weapon."

Iscend Comprine speaks right over her. "Gaios! I will not!"

"You've turned from your purpose. Your conditioning's broken."

"I have a higher purpose."

"Is that purpose the destruction of these islands?"

"That serves my purpose. You came to do the same."

"No. I came to stop it." Plague can murder millions, but it cannot mean to do it, and it cannot profit from the death.

"It cannot be stopped now. Even if you shattered the mechanisms here, the fuses below are in motion."

"You've killed Kyprananoke. You've killed them all."

The quiet sound of parting lips: Iscend's smile in the dark. "The moment we learned there was Kettling here I knew it had to be done. When you and I fell into the water together I knew it was time. My masters believed I was dead, so they would no longer predicate any vital actions on my presence. I was free to come set the fuse."

Very slowly, Shir turns to look at her. "Gaios. Tell me who commands you."

"The good of the Imperial Republic commands me."

"Gaios! Tell me!"

"The difficult thing about being Clarified," Iscend says, "is that you cannot disobey the paramount masters, even when they make the wrong choice, even when they cannot order you to do what must logically be done. Imagine if, ah, gaios, gaios," she winces, "imagine if one of the paramount masters could be rendered supreme, uncontested, so that her orders would be untainted by any interest but her own. She would of course have Clarified to advise her on her interests. So the Clarified would advise her, and she would make orders, and give them to the Clarified to execute, and the circle would be closed. And it would be as if the Clarified commanded themselves."

"And these are the commands you would give? Do you know how many people you've just murdered?"

"Of course I do. I also know how many I've saved."

"Do you think this will greaten Baru? Is that why you did it? You want her done with Kyprananoke? Off to richer fisheries?"

"I work for the betterment of my masters. And my masters work for the betterment of the Imperial Republic."

"She will never be yours," Shir promises. "I will peel her brain apart at the gyres before I let you rule her."

"I like contests," Iscend says. "I like to win. Are you protected? Or shall I kill you now?"

"I have her parents."

"Can you prove it?"

"Can you take the risk? She is so very fragile."

"Go," Iscend says. "I left myself enough time to reach *Helbride*. If you move quickly you might find a ship in time to survive the wave."

"You deserve to die for this," Shir says.

"Deserve? Aren't you and I beyond such illusions?" Iscend's teeth barely touch when she enunciates: the force in her jaw is so exacting. "The most conditioned, and the least?"

AMINATA took the stairs down off the sterncastle two at a time. No one paid her the slightest attention: for the first time she could remember she was one Oriati among many.

"Look north," Shao Lune shouted after her. "North!"

Aminata saw *Ascentatic* and *Helbride* first. The frigate and the clipper were running out southeast on full spreads of canvas. The only other ship in open water was a barque with Devi-naga flags; it had already cleared the islands and turned northeast for the trade ring. The Kyprist positions on the reservoir islands had obviously collapsed. Skiffs and whaleboats were ferrying water out to the moored ships: but there were also launches and canoes full of Canaat fighters, looking to take prizes.

Iraji spidered up a shroud net. He looked up at el-Tsunuqba. His eyes opened wide.

"What?" he said.

Aminata climbed up after him.

El-Tsunuqba's north face had turned shaggy. A cloud of ash and dust blurred the lines of the mountain, swelling into gray fruiting bodies that dropped threads of debris to the ocean. But the really confusing part, the part that turned Aminata's brain right over, was the horizon line. The world had sorted itself wrong. The cloud of dust and the limb of el-Tsunuqba seemed to be in *front* of the ocean. That was wrong. There was supposed to be sky behind the mountain. It was like the ocean had turned perpendicular and climbed up toward the moon—

Her mind at last resolved the wave.

It was so preposterous that she kept trying to divide it into more sensible pieces: a squall in the distance, a dark fogbank up close, a fire upon the mountainside. But it was not a fogbank or a rain squall or a pall of smoke. The wave was one thing, in the ocean, of the ocean, a mass of water in unstoppable motion.

She checked the waves against ships' masts for scale and produced a figure.

It was a four-hundred-foot mountain of water.

El-Tsunuqba's face had avalanched into the flooded caldera, and the water displaced by the avalanche had gathered in the cup between the east and west ridgelines, fired like a bullet from an Oriati pistol. And that water had only one way to go, north, north across the shallows where the kypra islands and all the reefs waited. The wave was slumping, spreading, but oh, the *speed* of it—

Trees on the crest, like grains of rice.

Tau-indi Bosoka cried out hoarsely below her. "The wound!" They were laughing, weeping, tearing at their hair. "*The wound is real!*"

"Is it coming this way?" Iraji cried. "Is it going to hit us?"

She could not tear her eyes away. The sea everywhere, scraping at the bottom of the sky. A great godly shrug. Nothing behind it. All the ships, the houses, boardwalks and promenades, fishing buoys, locust farms and jellyfish pens, all picked up and carried, to be strewn, like seeds between fingers, across miles of open sea.

She took Iraji's hand and showed him how to cling to the net.

INTERLUDE

THE MANSION HUSSACHT

THE King stood upon his high fastness and watched his whole life's work go wrong.

His name was Atakaszir, born to the Mansion Hussacht, Necessary King of the Amustakhi Mountains and protector of the High Fells. From the peak of his mountain Karakys he could see more than a hundred miles down over Aurdwynn, over the forests and dales of Duchy Vultjag, the stony fells of Duchy Lyxaxu (he felt a weird stirring of excitement and hatred at that enemy name, that Maia name, the same kind of name as Nayauru Aia). He could see all that food and lumber and wealth, and the river Sieroch that pumped it away to the sea. The land his people had dreamt of conquering for five hundred years. The land of warm milk, olive oil, and toasted grain.

He'd tried to lead his people to that future.

But to get to the future you had to get through the present, just as you had to risk the jagged slopes to get to those warm fields below.

And the present had its strangling hand round his throat.

Directly beneath his royal overlook was the col, the saddle of naked rock that joined Mount Karakys and neighboring Camich Swiet. And down that col, down the road that passed through the terrace farms and to the famous Gate of Screams, his army marched to die.

Morning sunlight gave the column's steel-armored brave men and long-speared phalanxes a ghostly halo. Light the color of frost. As if they were already dead.

"I am a fool," he said, in the Iolynic that Aia had been teaching him. "We have been given the best chance we will ever have to escape the cage of our history. And we are throwing it all away, as we always do, because we cannot stop chewing at each other long enough to fucking *act*!"

Aia's hand brushed his wrist. It was a brotherly touch, not something a Stakhi woman would do: warning a comrade against his own passion. "You'd be a fool if you did otherwise, Your Majesty. The army had to march before autumn, or they would've wintered here. Your Mansion's stores wouldn't have lasted two months. In the spring Hussacht would be a dead Mansion and you would be a fallen king."

"I know," he said.

"Politics is the art—"

"Of staying in the arena." He sighed. She said that a lot. When it came out of her mouth—unbound by manly honor, unconstrained by the fear of procht—it made sense. He glanced at her long enough to quirk his lips in gratitude, and tried to look away before his boyish heart thrilled at the sight.

Nayauru Aia had come to his court to offer him her hand in marriage. She would give him a claim to her dead sister's Duchy Nayauru, and he would give her the soldiers she needed to retake her home. She was not as good a match as Baru Cormorant, who might have been queen of Aurdwynn entire—but Baru Cormorant, may frost crack her spine from her body, was an oathbreaker and a living lie.

And still Baru tormented him! Even with the whole rash of her treachery revealed, she'd *still* sent him an emissary, this eunuch Ketly Norgraf. Norgraf had promised to return Atakaszir's own lost brother to his house! The hubris of her! To betray him, to destroy his reign, and then to send an agent sauntering into his court as if she had done nothing wrong. It was the conduct of the worst kind of liar. A woman lost to procht, the sickly thought of schemers.

She did *not* have his brother Svir. It simply couldn't be true.

He caught himself glancing back to Aia, a cad's double take. She was no beauty, by Stakhi standards; too full, too fat, faintly obscene in a land of tall women, narrow tunnels, and starvation. She looked exactly like the kind of whore Atakaszir would have sought when he was traveling covertly in Aurdwynn. And, worse, she had none of a whore's concern for his gaze. For a woman who wanted his hand, who had so far been frustrated in her attempts, Aia was utterly self-possessed.

It was Ketly Norgraf's fault that he'd fallen for Aia (and here in the mountains they knew very well the dangers of falling). Norgraf had offered Atakaszir something he'd craved all his life, his brother's return; something Ataka could not possibly accept. He'd turned to Aia for advice and confidence. She had no allegiance to Mansion or clan, no interest in tearing down his kingship or judging it Unnecessary. She and her companion, the horseman Ihuake Ro, were, as scheming foreigners, ironically the easiest for Ataka to trust. Even his suspicion that Aia and Ro were some kind of perverse Maia lovers had been assuaged by Ro's constant absence. The unhorsed horseman was out exploring the Wintercrests, testing himself in the thin air.

So in the course of their conversations the King of the High Mansions had fallen in love with dark-haired, brown-skinned, fierce-nosed Aia.

This was not unexpected. She was the only woman in his world who was not subject to his power, and, anyway, he had always fallen quickly. But no matter how much he wanted her, he was a Stakhieczi king, and self-denial came as easily to him as thirst. Love maddened him, made him stupid—but so did starvation. And like starvation it would pass in a few months.

What was far stranger was that they had become friends. Her implicit reserve, her sense of *not yet,* created a barrier that Atakaszir found easy to respect: like a tunnel architect's rules about where to cut stone and where to leave it be. When he was away from Aia he imagined her nakedness. But when he was with her, his thoughts were entirely occupied with answering hers. He found her strangeness and acuity refreshing, and her acceptance of politics as something necessary (rather than perilously close to procht) made her a better councilor than his bannermen.

"Aia," he said, watching the army of the gathered Mansions pour down the slope, shining brave men in steel plate surrounded by their armorer boys, gray-cloaked women with ash flatbows, all the mountains' might on their way to fail, "what else could I have done, after Baru betrayed me? She knows we're prepared to invade. She destroyed the dukes and duchesses in Aurdwynn who could have joined us."

He paused for breath. He had explained to Aia once that in the mountains you never interrupted a man who had stopped to breathe.

"When I heard about the disaster at Sieroch, about Baru declaring herself for Falcrest . . . I thought I would have the crown cut from my head. How could we invade now, with the enemy forewarned?

"But if I told the army to disband, I might as well throw myself from Karakys. I'd be dead by day's end. To gather all those fighters here, to take them from their homes and crops, and then to send them back with *nothing*? I had to let them march. I had to."

"You could have married me," Aia said, without petulance. "Then at least you would have claim to *one* ally in Aurdwynn. Someone to provision your troops and open the way to the coast. The Masquerade spent the last winter killing bureaucrats, emptying granaries, and thinning out forage. That means no one to pay you tribute, no game to hunt, and no choice for the tenant farmers except to fight to hold their fields. Your army will bog down shattering village phalanxes and chasing horsemen before it even reaches the Midlands. And then I think they will do what Stakhieczi do when they are threatened."

"Build forts on the high ground, settle in, and start fighting each other for spoils," Ataka muttered. "And then the Masquerade will set the plague loose. And our forts will be our catacombs."

It was the first time he had spoken these doubts aloud. To admit them to his bannermen would be to arm his Mansion Uczenith foes with rumors of a cynical, defeated king.

"Marrying you wouldn't have changed that, Aia. You're a duchess without land or influence. If I'd taken your hand, they'd all know I'd settled for the least I could get."

"Better than nothing," Aia murmured. She never allowed herself to react to the cold up here, but now Atakaszir could tell she felt the chill. "Which is what you have now."

"I promised them the Queen of Aurdwynn as a bride! If I come before the clans with the exiled sister of a dead duchess instead—I might as well drag in a mummified goat!"

"Marry an Uczenith, then," Aia suggested, dryly. Atakaszir laughed. The Uczenith were the worst of his enemies, as diffuse and leaderless as a cloud of gnats—they had no proper Mansion lord, Kubarycz the Iron-Browed having vanished into exile with all his heirs.

The thought of Mansion Uczenith stuck in his mind like a stone in a boot. He kicked at it a few times. It would not go.

Something was wrong. He had been waiting for something to happen and it had not happened.

"Oh, zish," he swore, invoking unholy tetanus. He raised his spyglass to sweep the marching column for something he knew he wouldn't find.

The Mansion Uczenith fighters marched to war with iron ingots as their banners, raised on poles of Aurdwynni redwood. It was a defiant symbol of their exiled lord's crime—Kubarycz's conspiracy to secretly marry an Aurdwynni duchess, unite their realms, and undermine the other Mansions.

That banner was nowhere in sight.

The Uczenith hadn't marched with the army. Their jagata were still encamped on the lake bed outside his Mansion.

His first instinct was to halt the column and recall his own Hussacht forces to defend his home. But if he pulled his jagata it would be the death of his Mansion. Had King Atakaszir, first of his name, lost faith in the invasion? They'd all turn back, and by sundown Mansion Hussacht would be a pillaged husk.

But if he did nothing, the army of Mansion Uczenith would have free rein to squat in his court. And courts did not prosper when they were full of armies.

"Your Majesty?" Aia asked, softly. "What's wrong?"

"It's the Uczenith," he said. No more needed.

He went down the spiral stairs from his high fastness, and met a man coming up. The last man in the world he had ever expected to see again.

The other man fell at once to one knee. "Your Majesty," he murmured, and genuflected. "I am sorry for my late return."

"Dziransi?" He caught the man by shoulders so gaunt they felt like a boy's. "Dzir, is that *you*?"

In that first moment of reunion, when the man who'd been swallowed up by Baru Cormorant's treachery raised his eyes to his king, even he did not seem sure of the answer.

"Your Majesty." Dziransi laid his brow to the stone, his king's stone. "I have had a vision from the hammer. I come home to you, across the sea where glaciers die, to tell you what you must do to hold your crown. You must marry Heingyl Ri, Governor of Aurdwynn. She will bring you a dowry. She will bring you Baru Cormorant, powerless and bound. Then no one will deny you are the King of Mansions, whose long arm reaches across the world to punish all betrayal. I saw it in the stars. I saw it and I came home to tell you."

YOU cannot do this!" The weatherwoman caught at the king's elbow as he bent to his telescope. "You will be the king of all fools if you try to take another bride from Aurdwynn! The Masquerade *governor*? How could you even entertain the offer?"

Atakaszir glared at the hand on his sleeve, usurper in the place Aia had touched. The weather witch, face blasted sleek and dry by years of mountain wind, seemed to realize, all at once, what he saw in her: something old, withered, vitiated of power, like the mummy she would become when she died.

She snatched her hand back and sniffed.

"Dziransi saw it," he told the witch. "He had a dream from the hammer. A woman with stars for eyes told him that Governor Heingyl Ri would be the bride of the mountains and save us forever from the Old Foe. The hammer struck it into him, Ochtanze! It's all he can speak of! Somehow he escaped the Masquerade and returned to us just in time to save us from defeat. How can you explain that, if he is not hammer-marked? If the stars themselves didn't guide him back to us?"

He bent to look into the telescope again, to search for the glitter of distant mirrors. Ochtanze slipped her hand between him and the eyepiece. "The Masquerade let him go. They know you were fool enough to believe in Baru, they know you'll be desperate to repair your mistake, and now they think they can play you again—"

"I'm the fool? *I'm* the fool?" The same words he'd spoken freely to Aia infuriated him coming from the witch. "You've been coddling Baru's eunuch like a stray dog, letting his lies pervert your council. You nag at me to consider his offer—but his words come straight from that scurve-hearted bitch herself! You speak from your nose, woman." Aia had laughed at that expression, but for all Ataka's life it had meant someone with two voices, a dissembler.

"We care for the eunuch," Ochtanze snapped, "because he knows secrets no one else can tell us."

"That's procht! I told you to leave him on the summit to die!"

"Do you want that power now, Your Majesty? The power to decide who dies by exposure? Shall I bring our children before you, and make *you* choose who will go out on the shelf?"

That he did not want. Wanted it less than anything. The thought of it pinned him to the stone with dismay.

Ochtanze would not let go of his telescope. "Your Majesty," she said, calmer now, retreating into that pool of age and enigma all the old weather witches seemed to possess, "I serve the Mansion Hussacht, and so I serve you. As Necessary King, as Lord of Hussacht, and as a constellation man, you *must* reward those who have supported you."

"I know that," he growled. He hated it when she made sense.

"If the Mansion lords do not receive some repayment for trusting you with the kingship, they will look to this invasion as a chance to recoup their commitments by plunder. There will be no ordered conquest of Aurdwynn. No farms. No brine. No fresh crops to ward off scurvy. It will all fail. You *must* show them some fruit from your kingship."

"Even if it's Baru's fruit."

"Even so." And now the witch, as constant as the moon, would tell him once again: "You should accept Baru's offer to return your brother. The worst she can do is fail, and you will be no worse off. Also—" She raised her eyes skyward, warning against bad weather. "If it is known that your brother is coming home, the Uczenith will hesitate to move against you. They of all Mansions know the importance of succession, having lost their noble line entirely. If they knew Svirakir might return, entitled to the crown, demanding the heads of those who murdered his brother . . . they would never dare harm you."

He picked at his chapped lips, thinking. He wanted Aia. Some of his bannermen had joked that when they went to Aurdwynn they would get their own Aias, Maia women who needed things from Stakhi men, Maia women who would do anything to get it. "I'm tired of mouths raised on yak butter and mint," Hecztechate had joked. "I want to know what pepper and cinnamon feel like!"

Ataka had snapped that Aia might one day be his wife, and did they want to speak of his wife that way? The bannermen had looked at him strangely, and said nothing, and afterward, somehow, *he* had felt the fool.

"Your Majesty," Ochtanze said. She was offering him a thimble of yak butter for his lips. "Do you really believe Dzir's dream came from the hammer?"

He looked at her sharply. "Yes. Do you?"

"If it's true, Your Majesty, and not a Masquerade lie, then . . . you face a choice. Your brother is the *reason* you are king. The kidnapping of a Mansion prince made the clans recognize the Necessity of unity against the mask. If you return your brother . . . you will, in a way, have justified your entire kingship."

Atakaszir scooped a fingertip of butter and pressed it to his lips. Somehow Baru *knew*. Somehow she'd found another way to torment him with false hope. . . .

"If," he said, "Baru really can send him home. And won't turn it against me, somehow."

"Yes. But once you had him, nothing could take him away again. There would be no uncertainty in your victory. What is this alternative Dziransi offers? Somehow marry the Masquerade governor? Promise the Mansions that she will deliver Aurdwynn and an heir? And hope, hope against all sense, that the Mansions will wait patiently for years . . . instead of laughing this off as another trick played on a gullible king. You would have nothing to show them *now*. No victory for this summer."

He looked up sharply at her. "You don't know?"

Old Ochtanze, who chose which babies would go out into the cold to die, narrowed her eyes in warning. It was unwise to challenge a weatherwoman's knowledge. "Know what?"

"The marriage to Heingyl Ri comes with a dowry. Dziransi has promised it. There will be no need to wait for an heir to secure my power."

"What dowry?"

"Baru Cormorant," he said, and had the satisfaction of the weatherwoman's astonished gape. "Yes. She'll be brought to me, Dziransi says, by the Governor Heingyl Ri. And then I will hang her upside down in my court, and flay her scalp from her skull, so that all her blood pours out through the soil of her thoughts. The whole world will know that to betray me is to forfeit all hope."

NOW

IT'S been a long time since Cairdine Farrier interrupted her story.

He's washed her hair. He's fed her a solution that tastes mildly of mint and milk through a straw that tastes the way bleach smells.

Mostly he sits beside her, murmuring thoughtfully, as she tells him how she used her knowledge of the Cancrioth to prevent Yawa from lobotomizing her, how she moved against the protests of the other cryptarchs to destroy Kyprananoke and contain the Kettling, how she succumbed to meningitis at the vital moment when she meant to bait *Eternal* into following her toward Falcrest.

She's discovered she can open her eyes into narrow, eyelash-visored slits. The straitjacket prevents her from touching her face, but she feels a cool, dry wash around her swollen eyes. Someone has been swabbing them against infection.

"Is this from meningitis?" she asks him. "Is that why I feel so strange . . . ?"

"No, Baru." He looks for an instant as if he is about to sob, and then, for a longer instant, as if he is about to leap up and drive a fist through the window of the morning room. "I told you. Xate Yawa did this to you."

"But she *didn't* lobotomize me . . . I convinced her that I was working with her. . . ."

He lifts the glass bottle with its reed to her lips. While she drinks the sweet, mint-flavored medicine he asks, gently, as if afraid it will upset her, "Did Tain Shir ever come back?"

"After she tried to kill me? And I hid behind Aminata?" Baru frowns intently. "I don't remember. . . ."

"Never mind, Baru. She's just a woman with a spear. She can't do you any harm." He strokes her brow, fingers gentle around the swelling, as if he has found in the bruise some echo of his own deep-set and inaccessible eyes. "Just tell the rest of the story as you remember it. I won't interrupt after this— except—that story you told Yawa, about the tulpa of the duchess from Aurdwynn. Was there any truth to that?"

"No," she says.

ACT THREE

SVIR'S CHOICE

17

I WILL WRITE YOUR NAME IN THE RUIN OF THEM. I WILL PAINT YOU ACROSS HISTORY IN THE COLOR OF THEIR BLOOD.

BARU lay side by side with Tain Hu on the sheer face of the cliff.

The world was tipped sideways so that the golden fields and green pastures of Aurdwynn's midlands ran up and down like wet paint on a wall. Miles away, south and down, farther than any human eye should see, Treatymont's broken towers protruded like coathooks from the Horn Harbor. Below that the Ashen Sea curved away into plunging infinity.

"I'm dreaming," Baru said.

"Hallucinating, rather." Tain Hu crawled out to the northern face of Mount Kijune's summit, tipped over onto a ledge. She stuck her arms out over the abyss like she was diving and said, "Ha!"

Baru grabbed at Hu's ankles, terrified, but this extra security just encouraged Hu to worm her torso out over the drop. "Haaa!" she shouted, waving her arms. "I'm the queen of infinity!"

"Come back," Baru snapped, and dragged her by her ankles onto solid ground. "I need to talk to you. You're supposed to tell me something."

Hu rolled over grinning. "Am I?"

"Yes," Baru said, frowning, "but I don't remember what. Come here—"

"No, you come *here*—"

She ended up on Hu's lap, facing her, knees astride her hips. Hu wore the six red slashes of her war paint, three on each cheek; nothing else of consequence. She shaved Baru's scalp down with a straight razor. Baru watched her tongue move in concentration.

"We've done well, I think," Hu said. "So far."

"Have we?" Baru, afraid to look her in the eye, stared at her crooked nose. "Really?"

"You've won great victories, Baru. I swore to bring you victory. So I'm"— she smiled slyly down at her—"quite pleased, thank you."

"Victories? Where? How?"

"On the Llosydane Islands, certainly." Smooth, shiveringly delightful razor rasp on Baru's skin. "I thought that went rather well."

"Well? *Well*?" She tried to seize Tain Hu by the shoulders and shake her. Hu, laughing in delight, made it clear she was too strong to be moved by underfed accountants. "I bought half the Llosydane Islands and then I left them to starve! The fires *Sulane* started will ruin the date crop—if they don't have dates to sell they can't import food—Hu, I *killed* them!"

"Did you?" Hu's lopsided grin crept up to delight. "Are you *sure*? When you were so busy trading money and dates and prostitutes on the Llosydanes, I might have . . . scrawled a few extra orders you failed to notice."

"You devil!" Baru cried. "What did you do?"

"Our trick there was a currency bubble, yes?" Hu tapped her nose with the dream razor. "In an ordinary year, the Llosydanes sell dates for Masquerade money. They use that Masquerade money to import food. They can't survive without Falcrest's markets, yes?"

"And *you*," another tap of the razor, straight edge against her brow, making Baru frown, "you wanted to get the attention of the ruling families there. So you caused a currency panic. You crashed their currency, the Sydani ring shell; you made it worthless compared to the Masquerade fiat note. Everyone with a fortune in Sydani money was suddenly a pauper by the outside world's standards . . . until you offered to convert their useless fortunes into strong fiat notes."

"Yes—I needed to talk to the ruling families, I had to learn where the Oriati fleet bought its water—" This was how she'd first met Tau-indi Bosoka, and where she'd discovered the name Abdumasi Abd. "So I made their ring shell worthless and they had to come to me to trade it for fiat notes."

"And at the end of the crisis . . . ?" Hu prompted.

"I left. I ran away. We burned down half their date crop in the battle and now they're going to go broke and starve. Oh Himu!" Baru ground her knuckles into her brow, cringing in shame. "Hu, what was I *doing*?"

"What were *we* doing, you mean?" Hu rapped her on the knuckles with the flat of the razor. "You sold all your fiat notes for Sydani ring shells! You accumulated a tremendous fortune in their currency, a fortune useful *only* on those islands!"

"And I wasted it!"

"We did *not*. We left very specific instructions for the handling of that money." Hu slid her free arm under Baru's arms, a hug or a wrestling clinch, and went back to work on her scalp with vigor. "You may not have noticed it, but we established a trust. Our entire fortune has been locked away, under the care of a board of trustees, for a single purpose."

"What?" Baru did not remember this at all.

Hu, razor poised at the nape of Baru's neck, paused to frown at her. "Come on. I didn't inherit *all* the brains when we were split in two. What do you think the trust is for? Where do you think your ill-gotten fortune will be spent?"

"I don't know. . . ."

"Oh, don't be petulant. It suits you when I'm allowed to punish you for it, but otherwise it's pathetic. Think. Think. How are you going to defeat your masters in Falcrest?"

"By war, I thought . . . I'd have the Stakhieczi invade from the north, and the Oriati from the south. . . ."

The razor scraped hair from the skin above her spine. "War? Who keeps telling you there's going to be a war?"

"Everyone! Everyone keeps saying it! Tau, Execarne, Yawa, everyone's convinced a war's imminent."

"Yes, yes." She pulled Baru's head down, brow pressed into her shoulder. "But who really put the idea into your head? Who startled you with the idea that all your work in Aurdwynn had *really* been designed to lure out the Oriati who wanted war with Falcrest?"

"Wait a moment," Baru snapped, into Hu's armpit. "Wait. You can't tell me that's not true. It *is* true. I lured Abdumasi Abd to his doom and didn't even realize it."

"Fine, yes, but turn the flank on that idea, Baru. Who *told* you all your work had been a prelude to war? Who insisted on that framing? Who have you recently realized is a master at manipulating you by forcing his stories into your life?"

"Farrier. . . ." Baru breathed.

"That's right. He's the one who got you thinking about everything in terms of war. He led you, no matter how unwittingly, to this idea that *war* was the way to destroy Falcrest. Even when you reached *Eternal,* you thought about everything in terms of weapons, of ways to kill. Tell me, were you educated all your life in war? Have you ever been a general, a warlord?"

"No," Baru sighed, "I was your accountant. . . ."

"So why do you think that you'd use war in your great work? When you've realized so proudly that power comes not from brute strength but from the control of the context in which strength is deployed?"

Hu rose up to get at the back of Baru's head, the whole length of her brushing close, hard muscle and soft fat, a map of lost territory. Baru lay her ear against the warmth above Hu's heart.

"Trade," she realized. "My life's mission is the use of Falcrest's power to end Falcrest. Falcrest conquers by trade. My plan must involve trade."

"Correct. And therefore the trust you established on the Llosydanes is for . . ."

"The trust is going to be used to prepare the Llosydanes for trade."

"Correct," Hu purred. "To prepare the Llosydanes as a way station between the Oriati Mbo and the Stakhieczi Necessity."

The idea burst like a clove beneath her tongue. "Incredible," she breathed, across Hu's breast. "Let me think . . . Oriati commerce would land on Taranoke, and then sail north to the Llosydanes. The Sydani would buy goods and send them north in turn, to Welthony Harbor in Aurdwynn, where river traffic could move up the Inirein and the Vultsniada to Duchy Vultjag . . ."

"To our home," Hu said, with satisfaction.

"Where it would be sold to the Stakhieczi. And then you could run it all in reverse! You could sell Stakhieczi goods back to the Oriati! Salt and lumber and spices north, metals and glasswork south. . . ."

And then reality washed down across the wound of hope. "But you couldn't. It couldn't work. The Welthony harbor's not dredged. The river's full of brigands and seine fishers. And Vultjag is . . ." Oh, she had failed Vultjag so terribly. "I appointed Ake special governor for Vultjag, but all I've done is drag her further and further away from her post. All the links in the chain north of the Llosydanes are broken."

"So fix them."

Baru shut her eyes and pressed against Hu's heart. "I can't. I don't know how."

"You know *exactly* how. The problems are all in Aurdwynn, so go to the source of power in Aurdwynn. You need an investment from the Governor to get the river and the harbor ready."

"Governor Ri?" Baru jerked up in thought, nearly headbutting Hu in the chin. Hu, hissing, got the razor blade out of the way so fast that Baru felt only a steel whisper against the back of her head. "I always forget about Heingyl Ri—"

She remembered what else she'd forgotten.

The gray space inside her, the crown that clamped down on her thoughts, had melted away under Hu's touch. But now, sensing hope, feeling Baru's hands on the edge of the pit and Hu ready to lift her out, the gray lunged back:

Kyprananoke.

"Oh no," Baru moaned.

Hu seized her by the back of the neck, did not shake her, only forced their eyes to meet. "You didn't do that. You tried your very best."

"It's gone, Hu . . . everything's gone . . . I couldn't stop it."

"You can't stop everything. You certainly can't expect to force your own idea of salvation on every people you meet. If you try to carry everyone else's mistakes you will break, Baru."

"But what if it *wasn't* a mistake, Hu? What if I'd made the same choice . . . I might've brought down that mountain, Hu, I might've killed them all. . . ."

Hu cocked her head, golden eyes hawk-keen. "Why?"

"Because the plague would've spread to Taranoke." Baru's courage broke. She hid her face in Hu's shoulder. She smelled of horse-leather, of grass under a high cold mountain sky. "And Aurdwynn, by the trade ships. And then to Falcrest. Is that what I want? Is that what I need to do? I didn't take the Kettling when I could've . . . oh, Hu, if I could kill *you* for advantage, then shouldn't I be able to damn myself, too? Isn't that justice? Isn't that right?"

"No! This whole thought is backward. It's not what you swore to me."

"I swore to paint you across history in the color of Falcrest's blood!"

"You want to paint me in *plague blood*? I hate plague." Hu gripped Baru's chin with her hand, gripped Baru's eyes with hers, so Baru dared not even blink. "What did you learn on Kyprananoke, Baru?"

"I don't . . . I'm not certain . . ."

"Don't let your sentences trail off. It's unseemly for a queen. What did Kyprananoke teach you?"

Baru twisted away bitterly. "That it's a lot easier to kill people who don't deserve it than those who do."

"No. No. Come on, Baru, *think*. What did you learn from Kyprananoke?"

She had learned how people could disembowel themselves. She had learned about the grove of smashed children, the sinkhole full of corpses, the terrible crimes committed in the name of revolution.

But the savagery and the barbarism were ultimately Falcrest's. Falcrest had destroyed Kyprananoke's old laws and agriculture. Falcrest had put merchants and barbers in charge, ordered them to stamp out disease, to maximize profit. Falcrest had erased Kyprananoke's history and replaced it with a sketch of cleanliness and exploitation.

She looked back into Hu's eyes.

"Falcrest has us hostage. When they conquer us . . . they disfigure us."

"To be disfigured," Hu warned her, "is not to be reduced. Or to be made evil. That's an Incrastic idea."

"No. But it is a way for them to control us. On Taranoke they released smallpox, cut off the old sea trade, and provoked fighting between plainside and harborside. In Aurdwynn they've wiped out the dukes and taken control of the food. On Kyprananoke they left behind a ruling class that clung so hard to power it was willing to use thirst as a weapon. They take away what we need to survive on our own, and they erase everything that tells us who we were before them. They want us to *need* them. If all of Falcrest began to die tomorrow . . ."

"The innocent would still pay a terrible price. As they did on Kyprananoke."

"So Falcrest has to be made to . . . disentangle itself. To shrivel up and withdraw, and to pass its power over to those it has injured." A question of useful butchery.

"Because if Falcrest dies like a wounded animal, snarling and biting—"

"The burden of repairing the damage would fall upon the damaged. And that's not justice."

"Yes, Baru," Hu said, nicking the back of Baru's neck, clearly on purpose, to leave a thin clean score like a tally-mark. "I think that's right."

"I *was* considering trade, wasn't I?" Baru breathed. "No wonder I kept thinking about the wood on *Eternal*! And about the amount of cargo the ship could carry! If only I'd found their rutterbook, or bargained for it . . . Falcrest wants access to the Oriati because it can make *profit* off them. If I could beat them to it, if I could secure that access first, I would have control of the mightiest trade in the world. . . ."

"*You* would have control. Not Farrier. Not Hesychast. At last you remember to frame it in terms of *your* power, *your* progress. You are a cryptarch unbound! You don't serve them!"

"Yes . . ." Baru gasped. "Oh Devena, how did I *forget*? How did they lead me so far astray?"

Hu began to change. Her face narrowed, her eyes darkened, hair fell away and blew into infinity on a silent wind. Baru giggled. "You're turning into me."

"You egotist. You're so pleased with your ideas that you want to fuck yourself."

"I do not!"

"Then explain *this*," Hu-with-Baru's face said, poking Baru in the chin.

Baru touched her face. Her nose had been broken and reset—her throat was thicker, stronger—her chin! She had Tain Hu's chin! "Oh, I'm you!" She set about testing Tain Hu's arms. They surpassed. "You devil, no *wonder* you're always so cocky!"

Hu looked back at herself. "Damn," she said. "I *am* a sight, aren't I. Do you know what I wanted to tell you now? The last time you came and spoke to me?"

"You were going to tell me the difference between acting out Falcrest's story, and actually obeying it." Tain Shir had said there was no difference at all— "Please, please tell me!"

"But you know," Hu said, smiling Baru's narrow, curious smile, speaking in Hu's throaty voice. "You taught me. I didn't understand, not completely, until you exiled me from Sieroch. Then I saw how utterly you had devoted yourself to the answer."

"But I don't know, Hu! I call myself the liberator, the secret hope," she spluttered at her own arrogance, "but what have I managed? What have I *done* for anyone? Just killed a lot of Aurdwynni and Oriati and Kyprananoki, hardly anyone from Falcrest at all, and I don't even *remember* home, I never learned the holidays right, or the gods, or—"

"Shush." Hu wiped away her tears with Baru's smaller, finer hands. "You think too much, that's your problem. You can think up a way to ruin anything.

"Listen, now, listen, here is the difference between serving Falcrest and *pretending* to serve Falcrest. It is the difference that holds whether you sacrifice a lover to your mission, or a nation: whether you kill one person out of necessity, or a hundred thousand. It is the difference between you and a monster. Are you ready?"

Baru stroked the hard frowning brows of the face Hu had borrowed from her. "Yes. Please tell me."

"No."

"Hu!"

"Make me." She leaned back on her hands, smiling up at Baru: the cocked grin was Hu's but the face was Baru's, the body was Baru's, and for the first time Baru-as-Hu felt the deep feline satisfaction of at *last* getting the brooding young savant in helpless and willing range of her hands. Oh, wretched field-general Tain Hu! She'd executed a reversal, seized Baru's accustomed ground, forced Baru to fight on unknown and delightful territory.

Hu twisted from her waist. "Here I am. All full of secrets. Make me tell you."

"Hu," Baru complained, "this *matters*—"

"So does this! You and the women in your arms! You think this doesn't matter as much as thrones and treasuries? You think you paint a portrait of me with your life if you ignore your heart, your hands? I couldn't." She touched her smaller nose, her narrow lie-corroded throat, the small groove down her abdomen where muscles lay against each other like books in a shelf. "This is what tormented me, all those days I couldn't have you. This is what I saw. Do you see what I saw? Someone worth love?"

"I need the answer, Hu," Baru whined. "Tell me why I'm better than Farrier—please, tell me!"

"And I need you to keep looking for the answer. I need you to chase that question until the day the whole work's finished." She smiled the way Baru might smile: impishly. "We are at a diplomatic impasse. Maybe you need to pursue your policy by other means."

Baru had never been the bigger one before. It turned out to make very little difference in resisting Hu.

AFTERWARD Baru whispered, with her own lips, "I thought dreams always stopped before the good part."

"Never dreams about me, I'm sure. I have a reputation to uphold."

"Preening aristocratic ass." Baru swatted her.

"Guilty on three counts." Hu was herself again. They had entwined their borrowed flesh and come apart as themselves. "I'm sorry for embarrassing you in front of my cousin."

"That was you? You made me . . . ?"

"There are only so many ways to speak through the spine, Baru."

"Ah, it's all right." It *had* been all right. "Do I have to wake up now?"

Tain Hu looked at her across her pillowed arm. For the very first time, Baru let herself remember their time together at Sieroch—not the sex, a memory which she had worn down to rags by running her fingers over it, but the quiet time afterward, when she had decided to measure every dimension of Hu's arms and legs by prodding them and counting the little white marks left by her fingers. Hu had bruised her ass in the day's cavalry battle, through saddle and sheepskin pad. Baru ought to have considered the logistics of battle wounds before naming Hu as her consort in sight of everyone on the Henge Hill. Wounds and exhaustion might keep a woman from fucking, and in some eyes this might be their wedding night (what else was it called when the queen named her consort?). It was bad luck to sleep apart on your wedding night.

"Yes, Your Majesty," Hu whispered. "You must wake up. If you don't, I'm afraid you'll die."

"Why? What's wrong with me?"

"Something touched your brain, kuye lam. Through that hole in your skull. You have meningitis."

"Oh. Yes." Baru yawned. Hu covered her mouth and Baru nipped at her palm. "Please, kuye lam, before I go. If you won't tell me why I'm right to do it, at least tell me what I have to do."

"You already know. Trade is your weapon."

"But that's not a specific plan, Hu. I've got this ship full of Cancrioth, I've got Yawa and her plans to send me to the Stakhieczi king, I'm supposed to destroy Yawa for the Reckoning of Ways but I don't *want* to . . . somehow I've got to put all this together with the notion of trade so I can get out of this victorious. So *please, just* tell me—"

"It's not good security." Hu rolled on her back and stretched. She was one golden-brown coil of power from toe to fingertip; she was a catamount. Baru, intellectually calibrated and mentally awakened to the highest planes of aesthetic and philosophical appreciation, stared at her tits.

"Oh, fine." Hu smirked at Baru. "The plan has never changed. You've known exactly what to do to defeat Farrier and Falcrest since the moment I drowned at the Elided Keep. I don't mean that in some abstract sense. You have stated, quite clearly, exactly what you plan to do."

"No, I really haven't!"

Tain Hu reached over to tap her lips. "Hush. Hush. Your Majesty, my lord, you know your plan. You spoke it as I died. *I will write your name in the ruin of them. I will paint you across history in the color of their blood.*"

"That's just tough talk—it's not policy—"

Tain Hu lowered her eyes, offering respectful council to her queen. "Yes, it is, my lord. You were quite specific. First, you will write my name in the ruin of them. My name will be recorded in Falcrest's destruction. My name will play a central role."

"Tain Hu?"

"I have another name."

Vultjag, of course. The little duchy in the woods. How could tiny Vultjag bring down Falcrest? Would the Stakhieczi invade through Duchy Vultjag? Would someone from Vultjag—perhaps Ake Sentiamut—lead a vital rebellion?

No. This was the wrong way to think about it. Whatever her plan might be, it would proceed from her *strengths*. Armies, fleets, and diseases were not the center of her strength. Money was the center of her strength.

But Vultjag was so poor, so far from the center of the trade circle, that it could not possibly be a financial player—unless—

"The trade route," she breathed. "That's why I said I'd paint you across history *in the color of Falcrest's blood.*" On the night she'd slept with Hu she had seen the Empire Itself in her dreams. She had seen the sea become steel and porcelain, a web of roads and plumbing, circulating the empire's blood from Taranoke to far Falcrest . . . and in that blood there had run currents of molten gold.

"Money. Money is the empire's blood." She frowned. "But there was regular blood, too. What does that mean?"

Hu stroked the skin between Baru's eyes, smoothing out her frown. "Do you really think a proper Incrastic hygienist would agree that there's such a thing as 'regular blood'?"

"The blood of each race is of a distinct character . . . the races have distinct and specialized uses!"

"Correct. That is the cornerstone of Incrastic eugenics." Hu slipped a hand behind Baru's head, fingers digging into the muscle of her shoulders. "How could you paint me, an Aurdwynni duchess, in molten gold and Incrastic blood? How could Vultjag's name be linked to Falcrest's downfall in *those specific colors*?"

It was a very simple riddle. "I would need to use the flow of money and of blood, namely Falcresti's trade and their programs of eugenics, to record *your* name as a duchess . . . but that doesn't make any sense. Even if Vultjag was important to trade, I don't see how you would ever be central to Incrastic eugenics."

"What if your status as my consort is involved? *You* are, in a sense, the inheritor of the line of Vultjag."

"But Falcrest doesn't have aristocracy. The line of Vultjag could never hold an aristocratic seat in a republic where the only elite are merchants, politicians, and philosophers. . . ."

"There is one aristocrat," Hu said. "One whose power you already wield."

Baru turned the thought over in her mind. Then she laughed in wonder.

"I'm a genius," she said. "It's that simple."

"Yes," Hu sighed. "To my constant bewilderment, you really are."

She leaned over, put her warm lips on Baru's, and exhaled.

HELBRIDE sailed north and east on a gentle following sea.

It was the worst case of meningitis Yawa had ever seen, she told Baru between spoonfuls of oat mush. But it was also the worst she had ever seen anyone survive. "How you screamed and screamed, Agonist. Quite the lungs on you."

"I picked a good name," Barhu croaked. "It invites pain, and survives it."

"Ai!" Yawa slapped her wrist. "Don't say that. Something will hear you and make it true."

"Magical thinking, Jurispotence?"

Yawa hid her smile behind her breath mask.

Four times a day Barhu received visits from the woman who had saved her life. Iscend Comprine wore a cotton surgeon's smock over baggy sailor's slops and she made it look like high Heighclare fashion. She cleaned Barhu's bedsores, fed her spicy soup that made her sneeze and cry, and read poetry that convinced even the ship's angry seagull to cock its head and listen.

Barhu studied her in consternation. Iscend had come back from the dark water of el-Tsunuqba utterly unchanged: her calm medial-folded eyes, mountain-fox cheekbones, the lithe (yes, lithe, here if anywhere Baru felt the word belonged) poised armature of her body. Like a dancer executing the choreography of her entire life.

"What did you do?" she finally asked Iscend. "How did you cure me?"

"Oh, I can hardly take credit. And it was only a treatment, not a cure. The Metademe's test panels discovered that certain Oriati honeys serve as powerful anti-infectives. I found one of those honeys among the supplies we took off *Cheetah*. A vintage called Zawam Asu Southern Tea-Myrtle."

Cheetah made her think of Tau. "You fed me honey?"

"I diluted the honey in distilled water, luxated your right eyeball, and trickled the solution through the punctured bone into the inflamed tissues behind. After aggressive irrigation of the wounded area, you began to improve." She lay a concerned hand on Barhu's wrist. "When you went into convulsions, I was afraid I'd killed you."

"Don't try to take the credit," Yawa growled. She was in her plain linen peasant's dress, hands chafed and cracked from too much soap, sorting through the detritus beside Barhu's hammock: a glass chemistry set, a bladder for tsusenshan or opiate smoke, a dry sponge. "It was the meningitis that would've killed her."

Iscend, undeterred: "The treatment will make an intriguing monograph!"

"Yawa," Barhu croaked. "How's the ship?"

"Well enough, I suppose. Captain Nullsin's frigate is escorting us northeast, back to the trade ring. Svir's lonely and snippy."

"Where is everyone? I remember it more crowded. . . ."

"We had to transfer the Oriati from *Cheetah* over to *Ascentatic*. They kept demanding to know what happened to Tau-indi. It broke Faham's heart to lie to them."

"Kyprananoke?" Barhu asked, quietly.

"It's all gone," Xate Yawa said, as she sorted the glassware, clean and dirty, thick and delicate, light safe and dark stored.

Well. Well. That was an intractable, a fact. Barhu couldn't alter it. There was no sense chewing on it like a dog with pika, cutting her teeth on the broken stone. No sense. The jellyfish pens and the cricket farms and the coconut groves and the bright blue lagoons, the Canaat who wanted their freedom and the Canaat who had gone mad to gain it, the orange-gloved Kyprists and their jealous reservoirs, all gone together.

Yawa lay a polishing cloth over the surgical lenses. Her long slim fingers trembled faintly. "Baru, Svir and I agreed . . . it had to be done. The mathematics were clear. But we never gave the order. She," looking to Iscend, who did not react, "set the fuses herself."

Of course it had been Iscend to execute the decision. Who else would act so swiftly and fecklessly in service of the Republic? In a sense there had been no decision at all. Iscend was the hand by which the power of Falcrest had reached out and pulled that mountain down. She had acted in service of the Throne. In the Throne's eyes she was blameless. And it was through the Throne's eyes that she regarded herself.

"So be it," Barhu said, resolving to accept what could not be changed, but to never, ever forget it. She had her course. Now she would sail it to its end. "Tell me, please—where's the Cancrioth? Where's *Eternal*?"

TWO more," Aminata muttered. "Let them pass."

She pushed Iraji back into the shadow of the ballast block. *Eternal*'s bilge was a pond of ankle-deep water that sloshed around monumental bricks of quarried basalt. Aminata figured they were dampers, installed here to keep the ship from swaying in rough seas. You could hide down here, if you were desperate.

Feet splashed past. Aminata held her breath, and held Iraji, and hoped that he could hold his breath as long as she.

They had been in the dark. Navigating by touch, sneaking abovedecks only to steal freshwater, sleeping on the narrow wooden platforms that had once stored water casks. Eight days ago the Brain's faction had seized the ship. Aminata had only *just* worked up the courage to approach Iraji again, asking him to show her a domed planetarium, where pinpricks of glowing green paint mapped out constellations she didn't know. Tau's warning had kept her away from him: Iraji was one of *them,* bred to host this ancient Oriati taint. But she noticed, anyway, how his arms and shoulders glistened with sweat in the half-dark of the lantern, how his lean hips curved into an ass like *that.* And at the same moment as she ogled him, in maybe the same exact watching part of her mind, she noted *Eternal*'s every groan and sway, imputing her dimensions, her armament, the strength of her crew.

The coup had struck while they were in the planetarium. The Brain's people cordoned off the foreigners' staterooms with Tau, Osa, and Shao Lune inside.

The Eye's entire faction was rounded up into the deckhouse; some were given parole to help sail and repair the ship, and the provision of food and water to the rest was conditioned on the parolees' good behavior.

The Brain, born to the signs of eclipse and burning whirlwind, had taken *Eternal*. Now she was making it ready for war.

Aminata figured it was inevitable. The Cancrioth crew had nearly seen their ship destroyed by *one* Falcresti frigate; days later they'd seen Falcrest drown an entire nation. When people were threatened, they closed up their hands into fists. It had happened on *Eternal* like it would happen in Falcrest. After that first moment of terror, when the enemy's power became apparent, the war faction became almost overnight the common-sense default. After that it was only a matter of time before they did what all war factions do: expunge foreign influence, arrest sympathizers, and prepare a first strike.

She figured they were sailing northeast, for Isla Cauteria. Where else? They didn't have the water for a long crossing south, to the northern Oriati coast and the trade winds that would bring them west and home. If they tried to cut south*west* across the Kraken Still, past Taranoke to Segu Mbo and access to the Black Tea Ocean, they would die in the Still's bad winds and wandering maelstroms. And a breakout to the southeast, through the Tide Column and out to the Mother of Storms, then a long journey south along Devi-naga Mbo and around the horn of Zawam Asu, would be purest suicide. They would never make it through the Tide Column, never mind the perils of Cape Zero.

There was a torpedo wound in the ship's prow, a bleeding hole too large to repair with scrub timber from any passing island. They needed a proper yard and good trees. They needed what Isla Cauteria could offer.

The Brain was going to attack. And if that destroyed her, and her ship, and any chance of peace, then all the better. The way Iraji explained it, the Brain feared peace with Falcrest much more than she feared death.

"There are more of her," Iraji told her, "all over the world. Part of the same Line. She doesn't see herself as someone who *can* die. She's like a memory, Aminata. If one person who remembers her dies, the memory will go on in the others. It's the same for all the lines. Even Undionash, the line I'm meant for. . . ." He had wavered for a moment. "But Undionash is precious. There are very few hosts left."

Now, in the darkness, the searching footsteps passed away. Aminata's fingers found the bundle of tendons and nerves beneath Iraji's wrist.

"They built their ship too big," he whispered. She filled in his grin from memory.

"Yeah," Aminata muttered, while the part of her that was and always would be a navy sailor chewed on this. What *was* this ship built for? There were no locks on most of the doors. No organized marine detachment or posted guards. She'd heard pistol discharges during the coup, and shouts of fury and surprise . . . but there had been no cries of agony afterward, no surgical screams, no wet pleas from the dying.

Maybe the pistols were loaded only to frighten. Maybe life was sacred aboard *Eternal,* and so they didn't hurt each other, not even in the extremes of their wrath. Not even with the whole ship out of water and dehydrated to the edge of white death.

"Iraji," she muttered. "There's something that's been on my mind."

"Is it me?" he murmured.

It was not even innuendo: he had been willing to talk about his past more openly. In these furtive days her casual lust had softened into fondness, and trust, and a sort of awkwardly racialized camaraderie. In Falcrest's eyes, she and Iraji shared a single Oriati body, scrutinized for its beauty and sexuality, condemned for its indulgence and its melancholia.

"It's about Baru. Tau said that she was . . ." She swallowed. Repeating the words of a Federal Prince felt obscene. "Tau said that Baru was trying to destroy the Republic. Is that true?"

"What would you do if it were?" Iraji whispered back.

"I swore an oath to defend Falcrest. If she means us harm, I . . . I made a terrible mistake helping her. If she means us harm, Ormsment was *right.* . . ."

Iraji made a thoughtful sound. "How much could Falcrest change before you considered it destroyed?"

"What?"

"If Baru's purpose is to *change* Falcrest, is that the same as—"

"Iraji?"

A voice called in the dark, echoing among the towering ballast stones, splitting and rejoining: "Iraji? Miss Aminata? You're down here, aren't you?"

"It's Tau!" Iraji gasped. "That's the Prince!"

"Miss Aminata," Tau-indi Bosoka called, "there's a man here who says he'll shoot me in the gut if you don't come out. His name is Scheme-Colonel Masako. He says that if you aren't moved by my slow death, he will have to use Cancrioth magic to draw Iraji out. He doesn't want to do that. But he will."

"We have to go to them," Iraji gasped.

"What?" Aminata whispered. "Why? It's not real. There's no magic. They can't do anything to you."

"Tau-indi is important. We can't let Tau-indi die."

"If this is some trim bullshit," Aminata hissed, "something about Baru and Tau and spells and all that—"

"It's not that," Iraji insisted, "well, it is, but not *only* that. Tau knows something. I'm sure of it. Every member of the Throne has a secret—Tau might know—and the Eye *said* Tau was important!"

"The Eye's just a gardener, Iraji. He doesn't know anything."

"Iraji," Tau-indi called from above. "I need you. I need your help. Please come out."

Iraji tried to take a step. Aminata tried to pull him back. They struggled for a moment. His foot came down too hard and made a splash.

"*Shit,*" Aminata hissed.

For a moment there was nothing in the ballast hold except the quiet echo of that splash.

And then that echo multiplied, returned as the sound of footsteps, closing in from all around.

GROUNDWORK

"THIS can't be it," Xate Yawa said, tightly. "This *isn't* all you have."

"Isn't it wonderful?" Barhu breathed.

Yawa's right hand twitched on the table, brushed the edge of the Great Game map, sent the pawns and tokens rattling out of their positions. She looked like she wanted to bang a gavel on the little table and declare a mistrial.

"This," she said, "is not a plan."

"It's *exquisite!*"

"Trade? Economic exploitation? Falcrest's goods everywhere from Oriati Mbo to the Wintercrests? Why are you proposing Cairdine Farrier's dream as the solution to *my* quandary?"

"Yawa," Barhu sighed, "this is *our* plan. Both of me."

"I won't believe it. Tain Hu would never agree to this."

That stung. Barhu, kissing her own right palm thoughtlessly, tried to find another way to explain it.

"Trade is like a waterfall," she offered. "The further it has to fall, the more power you can get from it. It doesn't fall across physical space, though. It falls across . . . across the difference in what two places can offer. Can you imagine two places more different than the Wintercrests and Oriati Mbo?"

They were in Yawa's slot cabin in *Helbride*'s stern. Apparitor had disassembled the ship's stateroom and captain's cabin; there was simply nowhere more private to gather.

"Your trade route doesn't *work,* Baru. You might as well try to sell garlic to the moon. There is no overland road from the Wintercrest Mountains to the Duchy Vultjag, so the very first link in the chain is broken—"

"Vultjag's rangers have been navigating that route for centuries. Smugglers already move goods. They can break trail for a road."

"And then what? The river Vultsniada is too narrow and rapid for steady commerce. It joins the Inirein, which *is* large enough, but that river is a bandit's bordello. How will you secure the way? With what loyal troops?"

"Provincial regulars raised by the Governor."

"There *are* no provincial regulars! You butchered the garrison last winter, remember? And the third link in your plan is worse yet! The harbor at Welthony's never been dredged for large trade ships. It's a fishing port. And *you* blocked up the existing channels with sunken wrecks—"

"Governor Ri can solve all these problems," Barhu countered. She imagined herself and Yawa as sprightly duelists, trading points with rapiers. Of course, the last duel she'd seen was Tain Hu against Governor Cattlson, and Hu had beaten in Cattlson's brow with the pommel end of her sword. But never mind that. "She's got money to build the roads, dredge the harbors, and raise the troops. I should know. I ran the accounts she inherited from Cattlson. And you have her ear, don't you, Yawa? You could make it happen!"

"Ridiculous. It's all ridiculous. You can't expect an empire of starved mountain barbarians to conduct trade with an unknown ocean. It's not a realistic prospect. You'll never turn a profit."

"We don't need to make a profit! We just need to sell shares in a joint-stock concern *operating* the trade—"

"How in the name of Himu will you convince anyone in Falcrest to invest in your concern?"

That was the key, the trick, the masterstroke. "By offering a share of profits from the most coveted market in the world. The Emperor Itself will grant my trade concern a monopoly on the western coast of Oriati Mbo and the Black Tea Ocean. Falcrest doesn't know it yet, but the wealth waiting there will make every concern in the Suettaring look like a pauper's billfold."

"The Emperor *Itself*? The Emperor is a puppet in a straitjacket! It says whatever the Throne makes it say!"

"I haven't quite solved that part yet," Barhu admitted. "But there's a way to make the Emperor give us the monopoly. We only need the appropriate leverage. . . . Yawa?"

She wasn't listening anymore. She reached across the Great Game board and picked up the little pawn that represented Barhu. Apparitor had made that pawn for Barhu, and then, after Tain Hu's execution, smashed it. Yawa stared at the splintered stub that remained.

"It won't matter," she murmured. "Even if we did all this, Baru, it wouldn't make a difference to the fate of my home." She did not have to say *Tain Hu's home*. They both heard it. "There's no time to build a trade route. The Stakhieczi *will* invade Aurdwynn. They may do it before winter. The only way to stop them is to arrange a state marriage between Governor Heingyl Ri and their king. And you were supposed to be the dowry."

"And," Barhu added, because she understood, "this whole plan depends on the logic Farrier taught me. Turning everything into money."

"Yes. It's all Farrier's technique." The thing in Yawa's voice was worse than anger. Yawa hated herself for wishing that she'd gone ahead and lobotomized Baru. "What good is some speculative trade route owned by an imaginary concern? I still have nothing to show Hesychast. No sample of the immortal cancer. No victory over you, to win him his reckoning. And if he doesn't see that I've clearly, decisively defeated you . . . Baru, what does this do for my *brother*?"

This was exactly the kind of moment when Barhu wanted to leap ahead, trading on her reputation for savantry and brilliance, and browbeat Yawa into obeying her.

Exactly the moment when she knew her instincts were wrong.

"You're right. I need to develop this plan more. I'll come back to you when I can answer that question." She took a deep breath. "There's something else. Tain Shir made an . . . alarming suggestion to me."

Yawa laid her hands flat on the table and pressed till it creaked. "What suggestion?"

"She thinks there are more cryptarchs than the seven we know."

Blue eyes narrowed in brown folds. "Explain."

"She thinks that the Throne we know is just one cell of a larger organization. Our cell handles matters out on the periphery of the Empire. That's why we're arranged like a tiny model of the Imperial Republic and its surrounds—a Taranoki woman, an Aurdwynni woman, a Stakhi man, two Falcresti men, Renascent, and Stargazer. Maybe Stargazer is the Oriati representative? Anyway, listen," Barhu leaned closer, as delighted as she was terrified, she did *so* love the intrigue, the moment when your understanding of the world unfolded to reveal a secret diagram scrawled within, "in the grand scheme, most of Falcrest's power is concentrated *in Falcrest*. Doesn't it make sense the Throne would have another cell there? A model of the home province's interior, maybe. With members from the different cities, maybe. Or the different ministries?"

"That's nonsense." Yawa spat contempt and Barhu knew exactly why. They'd both sacrificed so much to gain this station. Too much for it to be just another layer of control. "My master and yours are competing for control over Falcrest's destiny. Not control of a single cell, *Falcrest entire*."

"But they're competing to prove their methods of control *over new provinces*. That's naturally the domain of a foreign-affairs cell. Maybe Renascent has control of both the cells. Maybe she's grooming Farrier or Cosgrad to take her place at the top of the chart."

Yawa groaned and touched the small of her back. "I can't think about this now. It's too much. I need to rest. Baru, we *cannot* keep delaying on the matter of the dowry. If it won't be you, Heingyl Ri cannot make a suit to the Necessary King. Without a suit, he invades. We'll be seeing Ri soon, and I need to give her instructions about executing the marriage."

Barhu blinked in surprise. "We will?" *Helbride* was sailing almost directly away from Aurdwynn. Why would Governor Aurdwynn be in their path?

"I'm afraid so. Heia—Heingyl Ri, that is—scheduled a spring expedition to Isla Cauteria to negotiate the import of guano fertilizer."

"Seems convenient," Barhu said, cautiously.

"It's not a coincidence. She wanted to tidy away all her foreign affairs before the Stakhieczi invade. Now go. I'm going to have Faham pulverize my spine."

"Yawa—"

"Yes, what is it!"

"Isn't Heingyl Ri already married? To Bel Latheman?" The old head of the Fiat Bank in Aurdwynn, a young man who had been, for a few years, Barhu's necklace, her cover against accusations of tribadism.

Yawa smiled tartly. "That will be corrected."

S HE had loved working alone, as a student: she had even, in a taboo (at least in the Iriad school) simile, thought it was like swimming naked, free of any drag or constraint. That was apparently ordinary for boys in Falcrest, and in fact mandatory for reasons of hygiene. But neither women nor Souswardi were permitted nakedness, both being intrinsically sexual. (In Falcrest, the anti-mannist movement argued that it was unfair to women, whose advantages were in concealment and control, if they were forced to be immodest, fully revealed.)

Now she was on *Helbride*, where everyone washed together, and she could not afford to work alone. She had to expand her plan beyond merely the acquisition of world-spanning mercantile power.

She had to find a way to bring Yawa into the fold.

The talk among the crew was all of ghosts and apparitions. A mast-top girl reported faces blooming among the jellyfish at night. In the bilge a carpenter saw the bleeding eyes of an Oriati man in the stains on the wood. He asked to be locked into blood quarantine. Svir called him a shirker and put him on half rations. Svir had not been in a pleasant mood.

"At least there's no palefire in the masts," he said, when Baru rapped on the frame of his cabin door. "Palefire always gets the rigging girls excited. I swear that job addles their brains. Does the *Manual of the Somatic Mind* say anything about that, Agonist? If you stick an adolescent girl up in the air for hours at a time, does she start to turn into a bird?"

"I need the will, Svir."

Svir's throat blanked. It was a quirk of Svir's that his throat betrayed his emotions; all the passion in him seemed to dwell below his upper lip. Although Barhu was now certain that this was a lure, like an orca's false eyespot, and that he faked every swallow and stiff tendon. When his throat went still, *then* you had him somewhere he didn't like.

"What will?" He began to sort the files on his little shelf-desk, hands flickering, left and right, assigning each to its place according to his private scheme.

"Tain Hu's will."

"There's no such document."

"There is, Svir! You used it to hold off Tain Shir back at the Elided Keep. You refused to wager it when we played Purge—"

"Not that you could've won it anyway."

"Svir, please, I have to see it. There's something Tain Hu wanted me to remember." She had said, on the morning of her death, *remember the man in the iron circlet. . . .*

"What did she want you to remember?"

"If I remembered, I wouldn't be here asking!"

"And here I was thinking that Yawa warmed to you because you'd meticulously engraved every detail of Tain Hu's life on the bad half of your head."

So he knew about the eryre. Maybe it had come up while Barhu seemed sure to die. "It's not *actually* Hu. There are things I can't remember."

"Things you can't remember because they slipped your mind? Or, perhaps"—he ran his thumb down the edge of a sheet of notepaper, and she had the awful image of pale pink flesh separating into layers, like onionskin—"things you can't remember because they remind you what you did to her?"

She took the hit. She took the hit, damn him, and it did not even make her want to die of grief. "It's something I need to know to make her death *worth* something."

"Is that so?"

"Yes. It's so."

"I made it up," Svir said.

"What?"

He closed his eyes. His throat kinked as he swallowed. "I made up the will to manipulate you."

She tried to glare at him but the venom wouldn't come. "You *forged* it?"

He spun a file into an immaculate pile of its coded fellows. The whole stack toppled. He swore, quietly, in Stakhieczi. "Yes. I thought you'd believe that she'd kept secrets from you. But she didn't. You're her testament, Baru. She loved you. You're all she left. You and that seagull she trained."

"*She* trained that seagull?"

"While she was on *Helbride,* on her way to her execution."

She thought about this, and how she felt about it: glad, and proud, and sorry. "Thank you for telling me. But you're wrong."

"About what? She *did* love you."

"Not about that," Barhu said, smiling. "She left something else behind. Yawa has it. She stole it from me."

"That letter you got," Svir deduced. "The one in the strange cipher."

It had been pinched while Barhu was sleeping in *Helbride*'s armory. The ship's cook had tried to murder her there; that made Barhu remember the cook's death, leaping onto an attacking dromon with an armful of grenades.

"I'm sorry about what happened to Munette," she said. "I understand she was quite heroic."

It was incredible to feel grief without being undone by it. The difference between an amphora, a vessel that contained and carried something, and a septic leach field, which wallowed in the plume.

"I believe you," Svir said. And seemed to surprise himself by meaning it.

"Well, I'll go," Barhu said. But didn't.

He looked up from his sorting after a moment. "What is it? What else do you want?"

"Have you seen anything?" Barhu asked, nervously.

"Anything?"

"Specters. Visions of the dead. Like the crew's reporting."

He grinned at her. "Afraid of ghosts?"

"After what I saw on *Eternal* I won't rule anything out." She showed Svir her spidered fingers, all six and both thumbs. "The Cancrioth leaders had this glow on their hands, Svir. Like they were on fire. But there was no heat. . . ."

"Jellyfish tea," he snapped. "Glow-worm paint. Just theater. Don't be a rube, Agonist."

She was going to ask him why he responded so fiercely to this suggestion of magic, when he himself had seen such strange things across the Mother of Storms.

And then she realized, too late as ever, that he was afraid for Iraji, who was on *Eternal,* alone.

"I haven't given up on Aminata," she blurted, meaning: Iraji might be all right. But she was so afraid of his reaction, afraid that he might call her fool, that she fled.

G O back into your stateroom." Scheme-Colonel Masako gestured with his pistol. "Let your bodyguard see you're safe and well treated."

Aminata did not think Tau looked well treated. They had bilge filth up to their bare knees and a scab across their brow where they might have tripped. But Tau-indi obeyed.

"Your Highness!" Enact-Colonel Osa bellowed, and lunged forward to protect her prince. The hobnails in her boots left tiny white scrapes on the wood.

"This is outrageous!" Shao Lune shouted, from the cover of the washroom door. "We are foreign dignitaries and we demand to be—"

"You coward," Osa shouted at Masako. "When they cut your ililefe off to make you a Termite they must've taken your balls—"

Masako shot Osa in the face.

The pistol went off like a snapped line. Shao Lune cried out in surprise. Osa staggered backward, clutching her face and swearing in Old Takhaji.

"Oh," Tau-indi said, if as shocked by their own feeling.

"That was a powder shot." Masako wrung out his wrist, a practiced gesture. "Now I am loading a lead ball. The next shot will be for Iraji. He is a citizen of Falcrest. We are at war."

"You let him be!" Aminata shouted, but it was no good: the Termite soldier behind her pricked her back with his rapier. Another soldier seized Iraji and backed him up, at knifepoint, into the cabin wall. Masako selected a fabric cartridge of powder and a ball of lead shot from his bandolier and rammed them into the pistol. Aminata remembered his expression from the Hara-Vijay embassy, that slight smirk of satisfaction at a plan well executed, and hated him utterly.

Masako held the pistol carefully away from his body, finger clear of the firing lever. "Miss Aminata. Tau-indi tells me that you came from Isla Cauteria. That you were a torturer."

"Aminata isiSegu," she said. "Brevet-Captain, RNS *Ascentatic*."

He was going to kill her. He'd let her see him, an Oriati Scheme-Colonel, walking completely undisguised in his death-white blouse and spinal flag, upon a Cancrioth ship. Open conspiracy between an agent of the Mbo and a secret society taboo to every principle the Mbo cherished. He would have to kill her to conceal it.

"If you hurt us," she said, "it'll be war."

He looked at her in disgust. She wished that his high white collar would strangle him. "I told you that we are already at war, Aminata. You yourself are war plunder. You worry about me hurting you? The wound left in the Mbo when Falcrest took you, *that* hurts all of us."

"My mother ran off to seek her fortune, my father had to put me in an orphanage, I *volunteered* to join the navy—"

"You think you volunteered, I'm sure. That's how they operate. On children, in particular. Be quiet now."

He crossed the room to Iraji. The ship groaned beneath them, a stabbed-calf noise. *Eternal* was coming very slowly apart around the torpedo wound. Aminata shivered under her coat of filth, shivered again, harder, as Masako raised his pistol to Iraji's stomach.

Masako looked back at her. "I have only one question for you. You've heard it before."

Aminata, judging distances, tried to figure if she could get her hand into the pistol's mechanism before he fired. If she failed—she could already see the wet blast of lead and bowel through Iraji's back.

Iraji shut his eyes and prayed in En Elu Aumor. He could not pronounce it very well.

Masako put his finger on the trigger. "Where is Abdumasi Abd?"

"Say nothing!" Shao Lune shouted, from her shelter in the washroom. "Lieutenant Commander, I *order* you to be silent!"

"Shut up." Masako watched Aminata with a snake's curiosity. "If I kill this boy, I think the Eye will be furious with you. And who will protect you then?"

"Aminata isiSegu," she said, bitterly. "Brevet-Captain, RNS *Ascentatic*."

"You are not leaving me very much choice," Masako sighed. "I assure you that it's in everyone's best interest to help me find Abdumasi. He is a danger to the Oriati Mbo. He is a danger to your navy. He can do nothing but provoke war and waste. Much better if he goes home, quietly, where he can do no harm."

Some deep current of human feeling broke through Tau-indi's mask. "I don't want to listen to the boy scream. Aminata, tell the truth."

Shao Lune broke from cover in the washroom. She still wore her uniform. Aminata had left her own filthy reds to dry and never put them back on. "If you break your vows here, if you tell them *one word* of the navy's privileged information, you will attaint the loyalty of your whole race—"

One of the Termites put a rapier tip up to her face.

"Tell them," Tau repeated. "Tell them that you're the Burner of Souls and that you tortured Abdumasi Abd. Isn't that the truth? Tell them the truth so Iraji can live."

Shao Lune glared like a cobra.

Damn it. Damn it. There was a beautiful boy about to be gutshot. Whatever duty asked of Aminata, she had a gallantry she couldn't master.

"Abd is on Isla Cauteria. In Annalila Fortress. I interrogated him myself. The navy is keeping him there, hidden from the world. Now let Iraji go, will you? Let him go!"

You stupid tunk, Shao Lune's eyes said. You traitor. You've given up our best leverage over them. And you did it for a Cancrioth man.

Aminata couldn't breathe for fear of what she'd just done.

"Thank you." Masako smartly unloaded his pistol. The cartridge crinkled in his hand. "I'm sorry I did that, child."

Iraji smiled coldly at him. "My lord will know what you've done."

"The Eye? I'm afraid he's in no position to complain. Nor will he be until our work is done." Masako beckoned to his soldiers. "Come. I'm going to speak to the Brain."

"The Eye's not my lord," Iraji said, sweetly. "I serve the lightning man."

S HE had to go to the Vultjagata. Tain Hu had left her a message, somewhere, something she'd forgotten in the haze of her grief. She had to go to the Vultjagata and ask.

Finally Barhu worked up the courage.

Helbride had lost something when *Cheetah*'s crew left. Barhu missed the sound of Seti-Caho, the smell of fresh injera bread and gauze-cut fish and beef hammered with spices. The feeling that there was an old and comfortable togetherness between *someone* on this narrow, tense ship. She knew she was romanticizing the company of a Federal Prince's close retinue, using their particular and mannered habits to paint whole nations . . . but they were the Mbo Oriati she knew best.

"I wish," she said, to the empty places where they'd been, "that there was someone here to tell me how to do this."

But there wasn't. She went to see her Vultjagata all alone.

Yythel saw her coming. The plump herbalist shot upright in her hammock. "Baru's here," she said, in the tone you would use to report a snake on the road to the well.

Ude Sentiamut was teaching young Run how to gamble on dice. Barhu wanted to give him tips on probability but she thought he would murder her. Ake Sentiamut looked up from a copy of *The Dictates* to meet Barhu with narrow-eyed calm.

"You're awake," she said. "Yythel thought you'd die."

"Sorry to disappoint," Barhu said. The joke landed with the scrabbling awkwardness of a sick cat. "Where's Xe?"

"She's moved her hammock to the aft orlop locker. Whatever that is." Ake turned a page. Paper scraped across paper so loudly that Barhu winced.

Yythel stared suspiciously at her. "How did they keep you alive?"

"They popped my eyeball out and poured honey on my brain."

Yythel snorted. Run made a disgusted face over Ude's shoulder. The big bearded man had his dice clutched in his hand, perhaps planning to use them as caltrops if Barhu tried to attack.

"Baru," he said. "Why did you tell Tain Shir to kill you? Instead of us?"

"I felt I owed it to the duchess to protect you." Which was the truth.

"Is that what happened to Nitu?" Yythel asked. "That madwoman made you choose between Nitu's life and yours?"

That was exactly what Shir had done: and when Barhu had chosen to let Nitu die, Shir had hacked off two of her fingers as punishment.

"I don't know what happened to Nitu," Barhu said. She'd lost track of the cook when Shir's machete came down. "The last I saw her, she was alive. I promise you that. For—uh, for whatever my promise is worth." She did not deserve their trust, or their forgiveness.

"We never found her," Ude said, mournfully. "After we left Execarne's farm, she never came back." Hate bent his lips like a bow. "She ran to get away from *you.*"

Ake sighed and put down her book on her chest. "Why are you here?"

"I came to ask what had happened to Dziransi."

"He's far from you," Yythel snapped.

Ake looped thin straw hair around her finger. Barhu knew that look: longing for someone she would never see again.

"He left," Barhu realized. "He left you on the Llosydanes and sailed home. How could he go home? I thought he was dishonored." He'd led his king right into Barhu's honeypot, after all.

"He had a dream," the boy Run blurted. "A woman with stars for eyes told him he had to go home and arrange a marriage."

"Run!" his father snapped. "What's our first rule?"

"Don't tell Baru anything, I *know,* but you've all been so worried about him." He was looking at Ake. "I thought maybe she could help—"

"Whatever Dzir's doing now," Ude told his boy, defiantly, "it's far beyond Baru's power. He had a dream from the hammer. Do you know what that means? The stars are sparks from a forge. The hammer of that forge beats our souls into the shapes—"

"It's a drug, you Stakhi bumpkin," Yythel snapped. "Dzir must've found some of it in Execarne's stash. Do you know what he saw, Baru?" Her voice fell to a purr of menace. "He saw himself delivering you to his king. He was sure it would happen. You would be brought to the king, and he would have his vengeance on you."

A woman with stars for eyes. Barhu thought she knew who *that* might be.

But if Yawa had sent Dzir back to the Wintercrests to carry a message, why hadn't she told Barhu about it? Was she hiding something?

Maybe their new rapport was a ruse. Another layer of control, like Falcrest's trick to break prisoners. Let them escape, let them run down the street, only to reveal it had all been planned, all executed according to the jailor's design, so the prisoner would know that the will of Incrasticism confined them not just in the cell but in the whole world: all the empire a prison, and your own mind the jailer. . . .

She felt her heart quickening with fear, and poured her will into it until it deepened and smoothed out.

"I'm trying to find something Hu left for me," she said. Back in the Elided Keep, in a moment of absolute suicidal despair, her alien hand had scrawled the words *iron circlet*. "She told me that I had to remember a man in an iron circlet. Did Tain Hu ever tell you about a man in an iron circlet?"

"Yes . . ." Ake Sentiamut said, warily.

"Who was he?"

"The first man Tain Hu ever killed in a duel."

"Where? How?"

"She was young. She inherited too soon, you remember, after the plague? This man came down out of the Wintercrests with a party of Stakhi fighters. His band had been sighted before, west near Jasta Checniada, and they'd raided villages. Tain Hu couldn't let them cross Vultjag unchallenged. She called him to duel so that she wouldn't have to risk her fighters in battle. He saw a little girl, and refused; but when she mocked him he said he was resigned to kill her for her impudence."

Ake looked at her hands, as if counting back the years. "She said that she was eager to fight, and that he was afraid to die. He needed very much to live. That was why she beat him. Everything he did had too much weight on it. It made him slow to commit."

"Thank you. Thank you. I think I know what this could mean." Barhu couldn't help but smile. "It might make all the difference."

"More difference than we made for Kyprananoke," Ake muttered. "No, don't say anything. Don't tell me how it would've gone differently if you'd been there—"

She blamed herself, too. "Tain Hu trusted you as her agent, Ake. So do I. I know you did everything possible. More than I could have done."

"Don't you speak of her trust!" Ake snapped. The others nodded or murmured or clenched their fists. "And don't you dare talk like you trust *me*! You do not get our loyalty like some kind of inheritance. No, don't say anything. If I have to listen to one more word I'll come over there and stop up your mouth. Go see Xe. She needs you, Himu knows why. She's been through too much on your account."

"Of course," Barhu said. "Is there anything you need?"

"You might hit your head and die," Yythel said, sweetly.

B ARHU was now certain that the ledger, the sacred palimpsest where Tain Hu and all the other rebels had recorded their deadliest secrets, held a vital clue. Yawa had the palimpsest now (well, she had the enciphered copy Barhu's agent Purity Cartone had made: but the content was the same).

But Barhu did not go to Yawa.

She went to the aft orlop locker to find Ulyu Xe, who had saved her life.

The diver knelt by her hemp hammock, meditating. She held a tiny brush in her left fingers, short as the hair from a squirrel's back. The ship moved slightly, which made her sway, and her sway made the brush paint ink on the deck. She looked as clean and as calm as a tidepool.

"Ake looks glum," Barhu said, in Maia Urun. "And you're not sleeping with the others. Is she angry with you? What have you done to the poor widow?"

The diver smiled down at her work. "She's jealous that Dzir and I were lovers, but she also wishes I had loved Dzir better, and made him stay. Her heart is a knot."

"I don't think Dzir left because of any fault in your love, Xe."

She shrugged. The brush drew a perfectly straight line. "He was unhappy with me."

"Because you weren't like a Stakhieczi woman?"

"I wouldn't stay in the space he made for me. As the wise ones say: the man who tries to hold water ends up with soggy pants."

Barhu narrowed her eyes. "Did you just make that up?"

"I would never invent scripture." She washed the brush in a plate of alcohol, set it gently aside, folded her hands on her knees. "Enough of Dziransi."

Enough of him, Xe, and more of you. She looked full-faced and dark and alive. With a surge of gladness Barhu went and sat by her. "Thank you for what you did at Kyprananoke. You saved me."

"Thank you for what *you* did at Kyprananoke," Xe echoed, in that infuriating Wyddish way she had. You threw darts at her and she caught them and threw them back. "You saved *me*."

"Did Shir hurt you?"

"Of course she did. Did she hurt you?"

"No—well, yes, but—only in necessary ways, I suppose."

"So we were both hurt to change you."

Barhu could only accept that. "We'll be at Isla Cauteria soon. I'll charter you a ship to Aurdwynn—a proper clipper-rigged ship that can go against the trade winds, so you don't have to circle the whole Ashen Sea to get home. You'll be back in Treatymont by autumn."

"Come what may," the diver said, without any excitement.

"Oh, come, Xe! Don't you want to be back in Aurdwynn? See your family? Help Ake start her work?"

"I want all those things, Baru. But wanting things is the beginning of suffering."

"Are you . . ." Barhu cocked her head. "Are you suffering?"

Xe thought about this for a moment. "I am far from my family and my child. My only companions are Stakhi-blooded people who think that I, as an ilykari and a diver, am a sacred whore. I am lonely, Baru."

"I'm sorry."

"You won't try to talk me out of how I feel?" Xe smiled. "That's progress." She got up and sat on her hammock. "Will you help me be sure this is rigged for two?"

C ANDLE watch, drowsy and warm. They curled in the hammock together. "You want to tell me something," Barhu prompted, not because Xe had given any hint, but because she was a devotee of Wydd, and if you didn't prompt her occasionally she would just hold her silence for days.

Xe rolled to face her. Her hip lathed out a space between them. "I was told that you had taken another lover."

"Yes. A navy woman. Does that bother you?"

Xe's deep dark eyes made Barhu feel like she was being watched and considered by an entire summer night. "She betrayed you, didn't she? She led Xate Yawa to you on *Eternal*."

"Yes, but I failed her. . . ." Barhu was shocked (damn her interior insurrections) to feel her eyes welling up. Did she really care so much for Shao Lune? "I betrayed her, too. I left her behind. . . ."

"You mustn't believe that she's the sort of lover you deserve."

"What sort of lover?"

"One who hurts you. One who treats you like a tool. One who makes you feel as if you've failed her."

"Are you jealous?" Barhu said, out of pure fright at the idea of patient, silent Ulyu Xe holding a grudge.

"No." Xe put a hand to Barhu's face, and, without moving, let one line of tears part across her fingertip, to bead in the seam between flesh and nail. "I grew up in a Maia greatfamily, Baru. I expect my lovers to take lovers. But you're young. Everyone you let into your heart will leave a seed in the soil there. I don't like what would grow from her. That's all."

Barhu thought about what Tain Hu would say regarding Shao Lune, and discovered it much harsher than Xe's verdict. Hu would not even have Lune for one night's passion.

"I'm afraid of ending things with women," she admitted. "I'm afraid that Farrier's making me do it."

Silence. Ulyu Xe accepted that fear and let it breathe.

"Xe," Barhu said, slowly. "I think I might be Tain Hu's widow."

"Her widow?"

"I don't know. I never thought about it, I could never bear to think about it . . . but I chose her as my queen-consort. I think it could be argued that I chose her to marry me. I was queen for a night, wasn't I? If I declared the marriage in sight of witnesses, wasn't it executed?"

"Ah," Xe said, softly. "And she is with you, isn't she? Her eryre is in you?"

"That's what Yawa says."

Hot, full lips pressed against the side of Barhu's neck in the dark. "She can hear me? She can feel me?"

"Yes—"

"Then I will say what she is trying to tell you. Everything ends. Everything will end and you cannot fear that. But you must decide what the endings will mean."

AT dawn the next morning, Barhu rapped on the one door in *Helbride* that never opened.

It led to a converted dry stores compartment, one deck below Svir's map room. Food and water and soap went into it, and nothing came out. The woman within poured her wastewater over the stern. Sometimes the room emitted thin scratching sounds, which made the sailors hammocked nearby complain of vermin and make the handwashing gesture to expiate evil.

"It's Baru," Barhu called, and waited for the door to open.

It didn't. Barhu rapped again. "Please," she called, "Kimbune, it's me. We're coming to Isla Cauteria soon. I'm certain we'll find Abdumasi Abd there. I want to talk to you before we arrive. I want to make arrangements for your husband's soul."

The sound of toes on wood, wary as a cat. At last Kimbune's voice came through. "Where are my people?"

"*Eternal* is following our wake. We're both catching a trade wind out of the west. We've kept their mast tops in sight so they can chase us; I don't imagine they have charts of the whole trade circle to follow."

"It's not really a circle, you know," Kimbune said. "There's easterlies to the south and westerlies to the north and the other legs are—" She cut herself off, though Barhu was completely sympathetic to her need to assert herself through knowledge. "Are they safe?"

"No." Barhu would not want to be lied to in Kimbune's place. "One storm would sink them. They need a port, and they need a cover story to reach it. If we're going to bring them safely into Isla Cauteria, we need to signal them. Can you reach them by uranium lamp?"

"I don't know. I don't know. It's supposed to go through surfaces, but not very far. . . ."

"We can send you closer by boat, if we must. Will you try?"

The door cracked open. Kimbune's thickly lashed eyes peered out at her. Her portioned-circle Round Number tattoo gleamed on her brow. "You can't trick me," she said, warily. "I've made certain of it. I won't help lure my people into a trap."

"May I come in?"

"There's power in here. I ask that you respect it."

Barhu took a nervous step back. "What kind of power?"

"Truth," Kimbune said. "Come in."

The door opened. The wedge of lamplight from outside met and joined the candlelight within. Barhu gasped in wonder. All the walls and floorboards were brushed with Cancrioth script, ancient En Elu Aumor patterns joined together in gorgeous oriasque. In places, Kimbune had even whittled the characters into the wood. And if Barhu understood not one dot of it, she still felt a cosmic frisson, like seeing the book of the world's truths, edge-on, with all the pages shut together.

"What is this?"

Kimbune closed the door behind Barhu. "The proof."

The proof? Yes, she'd mentioned a proof when she left *Eternal*. She'd said it would protect her. *The bastard went and died before I could convince him,* she'd said, *but it's true, I've finished it and it's beautiful and he was wrong, five hundred years he was wrong—*

"All this is *one* mathematical proof?"

"Most of it is supportive." Kimbune watched her carefully. "If I explain this truth to you, it may change you. Will you accept that?"

Ask Barhu to respect knowledge, warn her that knowledge might change her forever, and she would always say yes, yes, these are the laws that I worship. "I do."

So Kimbune told her:

$$e^{(i * \pi)} + 1 = 0$$

"I have proven here that the Number of Interest, raised to the power of the Round Number multiplied by the Impossible Number, equals negative one."

At first Barhu didn't understand. But there was a light on Kimbune, some astral delight, and she was, in this shining light, with this secret in her, almost dizzyingly beautiful: not attractive, not lust-invoking, but worthy of veneration and protection and awe.

Barhu thought it out in her head. The Number of Interest *e*, 2 point 7 1 8 2 8 and so forth into infinity, was a remarkable number used in the computation of compound interest. The Round Number *pi* was the ratio of a circle's radius to its circumference, 3 point 1 4 1 5, as tattooed on Kimbune's brow.

"I never understood *i*," she admitted. She was an accountant, not a wild number-philosopher. "The square root of negative one. It's an impossible number, it can't exist. But here you've done something with it, you've proven . . . it's related to these other two, somehow?"

It did not seem possible.

Why would these three insane numbers, two of them infinite and impossible to write on a page, one of them *imaginary* and impossible to write at all, yield a simple elegant result like negative one? How could you do math with numbers that never ended? How could you prove *anything* about them?

Yet Kimbune had. If Barhu believed in her proof, she had established that these numbers were connected, far deep down in the universe: like three masts of a sunken ship, jutting from the waves, hinting at the bulk beneath. Proof in the highest sense, pure mathematics, issued from that place the Oriati believed in, the realm of perfect premade shapes, beyond the Door in the East.

"If you brought this to Falcrest," Barhu whispered, "and the scholars in the Faculties verified it . . . they would have to accept that the greatest mathematicians in the world come from Oriati Mbo. Kimbune, this proof would upend the Faculties, the polymaths, everyone who believes Incrasticism is the only way to learn truth. They would have to give you a place in the Exemplaries, and sit you among the greatest wonders ever known. . . ."

"Then why are you frowning?" Kimbune asked, softly.

"I frown a lot."

"No," Kimbune said, stubbornly, "you're upset."

Barhu told the truth. "I don't understand how a people who made something so beautiful could also release the Kettling on innocents."

Kimbune closed her eyes. "Neither do I," she whispered. "Neither do I."

"If I bring your ship to Isla Cauteria . . . will they use the Kettling again?"

"I don't know." Kimbune's eyelashes flickered between them. "If the Brain wants that, she would make it happen. You're under her power. She frightens me."

"I belong to myself, Kimbune."

"She cast a spell on you, to bind you to her. I saw her do it."

Barhu could hardly deny that had *happened,* and to deny the Brain's power would in a sense be to deny Kimbune's protection, too. "All she did was call me to return to her. That shouldn't frighten you."

"Can you bring *Eternal* safely into harbor?"

"I think I can. I think I can moor *Eternal* somewhere private, someplace with access to timber and water, and make a bargain to get you all home. But to do that I need to keep the navy from destroying *Eternal.* I need your people to put up cargo cranes, cover up the cannon, raise merchant flags, and pretend to be a free trader. Then I can get *Eternal* safely in."

And then one of two things would happen. She would execute her own plan to bind the world to her will. Or the Brain would release the Kettling in Falcrest's home waters.

Kimbune drew a hesitant breath. "I will be the only one to use the lamps?"

"Yes. I promise." And if Iscend observed, and deduced the code, well, Barhu could not help that. "Will you send the messages I need?"

"Yes," Kimbune said, nodding quietly. "I'll do it."

19

Two Faiths

"WHERE are you taking me?" Aminata shouted. The four Termites hauling her were too strong, and no matter how she struggled she couldn't get at their knives. All she had left was her voice. "Masako, where the fuck are you taking me?"

"Everyone always asks me that," the Scheme-Colonel sighed. "*Where are you taking me?* If I didn't want you to know, I'd lie. If I wanted you to know, I'd tell you. If anyone put a moment's thought into the realities of their situation, they'd stop asking that question. But they never do. It's always *where are you taking me.* Why doesn't someone ask why I'm taking them? Or how I took them, so at least they could improve their security?"

"You kidnap a lot of people?"

Bored as a baker making injera: "All in the service of the Mbo."

"Service? Please. The Cancrioth's anathema to the Mbo. It's acid on your skin. You're a traitor."

"This is why the Mbo has people like me, Aminata. To be the glove between the acid and the skin."

"Baby killer," she spat. "You gave the Kettling to those rebels. You killed every child on Kyprananoke."

"Falcrest killed children when they burnt Kutulbha." He had sweat stains under the arms of his blouse. Aminata wished they were blood instead. "Cholera killed children in Devi-naga last year. Do you know what the parents do, when there's cholera? They give their own children clean water first. They understand that not all the children can live, so they prefer their own children to others'. My job is to protect the future of *our* children. Yours and mine, Oriati children, one Mbo, our Mbo, united against all enemies."

"Your people won't be *one Mbo* when they learn what you've done. They'll hate you for consorting with the Cancrioth. You'll be buried in concrete, Masako!"

"Do you hear that?" Masako cocked his ear. "Listen to that. That sound won't be buried."

They passed a storeroom, all the flour and salt pork unbarreled and eaten.

Now it was full of Cancrioth men and women, lined up in rows with poles and fishing spears, mimicking the motions of a Termite instructor. They were learning to fight.

"The monastery," Masako said, "must become a fortress."

"You're going to get everyone on this ship killed, Masako," she hissed. "You can't fight the navy."

"What can't we fight? You know, when the Maia invaded us, centuries ago, the stories say that we—"

"Opened your arms and welcomed them in." Aminata had a particular eye-roll she reserved for Oriati hagiography. "Gave them a warm hearth and a full belly and a place to lie down."

Masako looked back at her with bright, brave eyes. "My whole life I've been told that story. Oriati Mbo embraced its enemies. Oriati Mbo met the Maia with gifts of silver and incense. But it wasn't that way for my forefathers. In Segu we *fought*. While the thirteen kingdoms of Lonjaro married the Maia emissaries, while the two thousand Mzilimaki tribes gave the Maia bribes of gold for slabs of salt, while the Devi and the Naga pirated their fortunes from Maia fleets, it was Segu that fought the war. We held back the warlords' ships as they made the crossing from the Camou. We sifted the conquerors out of the Maia tide, so the rest of the Mbo could drink sweet broth. And the sieve of that sifting was made from Segu's men, Aminata. Men who were your ancestors. Women rule in Segu, yes. But make no mistake, a man still works the field, and a man still carries his assegai in the impi. Your forefathers fought. And we will fight again."

"Fight? Is that what you call giving weapons to helpless islanders?" Aminata sneered.

"I will arm anyone willing to fight Falcrest. I will destroy anyone seduced by Falcrest's lies. I may pity them, but I will not show mercy. The Mbo is all that matters now." He reached out and tapped her cheek with the cold maw of his pistol. "Clear your mind. The Brain will know your thoughts. Do not exhaust her with pointless rage."

THEY covered her eyes with silk and surrounded her with glaring oil lamps. She could see, through white haze, rows of pews climbing away to the ceiling. Like an amphitheater.

A shadow came. A woman's silhouette in broken armor, too big for the body that wore it. The same woman who'd promised to snuff out all her senses, one by one, until she was just an endless sense of sickness in a void. The shadow shuffled wearily, but her voice was strong.

She asked Aminata the same question over and over, in different ways. "Can we trust Baru Cormorant?"

"I can't tell you. I don't know."

The shadow closed in on her. "You say that you are Baru's beloved companion. And now you cannot make even a guess about her honesty?"

"Not unless I talk to her. Learn what she's about. She confides in me, sometimes."

A murmur from all around. The shadow of the armored woman put up a hand to silence them. "Kimbune sends us a message by uranium lamp. Baru wants us to disguise *Eternal* as a merchant vessel. She tells us to hide our cannon, to fly Free Navigation Commons trade flags. She guarantees our safety on the approach to Isla Cauteria. Is this message honest? Can Baru do these things?"

"I don't fucking know!" Aminata shouted. Why were powerful women always summoning her to interpret Baru's will? The Baru she knew was fond of books, cunning, and Miss Pristina Struct. The idea of smuggling *Eternal* into Falcrest's waters for repairs was difficult, daring, and half mad, which meant it probably really was Baru's plan. But it was also a grand criminal violation of Aminata's duty. Isla Cauteria lay within the Caul, the sea boundary around Falcrest's home province. To allow a plague ship over that boundary would be an abrogation of her vows.

The shadow stooped. Its voice fell to an intimate whisper. "You know this ship is maimed. You know we're running out of water. I think we might throw ourselves on Cauteria and at least die fighting. But if Baru gives us safe harbor . . . Do you believe she can do that, Aminata? Is there a chance for all of us to live?"

If Aminata said yes, she might give the Cancrioth a chance to sneak into safe harbor and release the Kettling. If she said no, then she might as well advise them to make an open attack on the island.

And there was still that grinding, broken-bone uncertainty way down inside her, splintering every time she put weight on the thought of Baru. Tau said Baru wanted to see Falcrest destroyed. Tau had Aminata thinking that maybe Ormsment and her mutineers were *right*.

"Let me talk to Tau. I need to talk to Tau, and then I can answer your question. Tau will know what Baru really wants."

The shadow raised her arms through quivering fatigue.

"The prisoner wants Tau-indi Bosoka's counsel." The flat shadow shape of the woman, transforming as it turned. "But Tau-indi has broken. Their strength is exhausted. Do you see the weakness of the Mbo? Do you see what becomes of their mightiest Federal Prince when they are tipped out of the cradle of trim? Falcrest has no trim. The war to come will have no trim. The Oriati people need a new covenant. The time for gentle words and kind neighbors is done; the time for Princes with open doors is done. Who would let a thief and a murderer into his house? Who would welcome a tyrant with bread and water? The Princes would, and leave their people desolate. Let us raise a different lamp for the people to follow, out of the burnt place, into new life!"

There was a great murmur of assent, a storm's first wind through trees. Aminata realized that the interrogation had only been theater: you did not ask questions before your followers, except to demonstrate that you already had the answers.

"Baru is *ours*," the Brain cried. "Baru is bound to me by the power of Incrisiath. She will give us water, and harbor, and safe passage. Then she will use her own flesh to carry our weapon into Falcrest's heart, to finish what we began on Kyprananoke, to save our people and our souls from the faceless power on its faceless throne. A ut li-en! Am amar!"

Aminata wanted to laugh. It was ridiculous. It was superstitious nonsense, it was nothing to be afraid of! There was no magic, no spell on Baru to bind her!

Aminata wanted to scream. Some part of her knew it was all true.

"A ut li-en!" the crowd roared, that whispered sacrament becoming a war chant. "Am amar! Am amar!"

Aminata felt herself trapped within a chrysalis, drifting in the thick fluid of something becoming something else.

Huge, gentle hands lifted Aminata and led her from the amphitheater. "I have not forgotten your request," the giant man whispered. "I will take you to the Prince."

THERE was no living spirit, no intestinal complication of space, which made *Eternal* such a maze. It was just simple math—a ship's internal volume grew faster than its linear dimensions. *Eternal* was tremendously long, terribly wide, ridiculously tall, and therefore unfathomably vast.

That was what Aminata told herself to keep the fear at bay.

Her captor Innibarish was the biggest man she'd ever met. Not big like an able sailor or a bearish muscleman, but big like he'd been laid out on a different scale, overplanned by some mason-addled draftsman, stuffed past capacity with muscle. Aminata felt like he might burst if someone laid a nail on his abdomen. The cells of muscle there were the size of her fists, and probably harder.

"Where are we going?" she asked him, just to defy Masako. "Where's your master keep Tau?"

"Don't use that word, please," he said, in a pleasant voice as big as a forge exhaust. "It stinks of slavery."

"I thought you people *were* slavers."

His face was ordinary-sized: when he smiled it seemed too small and too far away. "We change, too, Miss Aminata. Please, this way."

She saw things she had never imagined. A room where old men and women in cassocks tended a city of copper pipes which pumped water according to the settings of corroded valves. A chamber with a recessed floor, where scorpions wandered in mazes of wood. A compartment where pots of colored sand had spilled and mingled, bright green and deepest blue, like the scales of two snakes. And everywhere a fireless light shone down from stripes and signs of greenish paint, marking the combings of hatches, the lips of steps. . . .

"Do you believe in magic?" she asked her guide.

"I was made out of magic." He showed her the massiveness of his arm, showed her how he could turn his wrist, his elbow, his shoulder, all nimble as you please. "I could hardly disbelieve in myself."

"Huh." Aminata was an idiot with men, and therefore said the first thing that came to mind: "You must get a lot of tall chasers."

"I am not interested in carnal things." He shrugged. "My father had thousands of lovers. He was famous for it. But he was very lonely in the end."

"He's dead? I'm sorry."

"All those who carry Elelemi the Giant die young."

"Oh." What a waste, she thought, and then reprimanded herself for disrespect. "Does your, uh . . . your tumor. Did it come from your father?"

"Yes. It was cut from him and passed to me before he died. The immortata prefers the flesh it knows."

Aminata twitched like a hooked fish. "That's why you wanted Iraji back so badly?"

"His mother carried Undionash, the Spine. It is a dangerous Line to host. It can kill when it is implanted, or when it grows. We hope he will inherit his mother's agreement with Undionash."

"You answer a lot of questions."

He smiled. "I have never had to lie before."

They came up a companionway, steep and narrow and clearly torment on

Innibarish's neck, out onto the weather deck at *Eternal*'s bow. The sea was glassy smooth under a steady wind out of the southwest, and, straight above, a sugarspill of stars fell so clear and high that Aminata could taste their light.

"Oh," she said, and she was glad to be at sea, no matter why.

"Elelemi!" a voice screamed. "Elelemi, come quickly!"

M OTHER!" Innibarish barked. Aminata scrambled after him down the deck. The dry laundry slapped aside by his body swung back to claw at her face. The sterncastle stairs rose up from nowhere and she stumbled up on all fours, trying to keep up with Innibarish and his huge leaping legs, desperate not to be left behind, alone, in this place where anything could happen.

Ordinary ships had one level of construction above the weather deck but on *Eternal* the sterncastle was like a ziggurat, deck after deck, stepping up to heaven—but at last the black wood gave way to night sky, and a dead garden. And to a woman with burning hands and a huge pregnant belly who knelt over Tau-indi Bosoka's curled body.

Tau-indi lay in the dry dirt, among the crumbled leaves, with black scab caked from fingertips to elbows.

"Oh no," Aminata gasped.

"Do they live?" Innibarish bellowed. "Do they live?"

But the Prince was smiling. The black crust on their arms was only dry ink. "Aminata," they breathed. "Look at you. And you still haven't decided? You still don't know?"

The Womb snapped to Innibarish in En Elu Aumor, and he went to his knees to scoop Tau up and carry them away to safety. But Tau put up one black ink hand in Innibarish's face, and he froze.

"You know," Tau said, apologetically, "that I was trained in magic? When I was in Mzilimake, a village sorcerer taught me to defend myself. I have the black hand, Elelemi. I'll put my life into yours. You'll die of growth."

"What's happening here?" Aminata barked, in the voice she'd use to frighten sailors from their gambling stoops. "What have you done to the Prince?"

"What have *I* done?" The Womb laughed helplessly. "The Prince did this! They told their bodyguard they were going out to find drugs to treat her burns. And they certainly found the drugs, Miss Aminata."

"Your Federal Highness," Aminata said, "you are an idiot." Tau-indi should have known better: the suicide of an ambassador was the suicide of their peace. "We've got to feed them charcoal and as much water as you can find. If we're lucky they'll piss it all out—"

Tau's face had little dimples when they smiled. "You know Hesychast, don't you, Aminata? Cosgrad Torrinde the Hesychast, Minister of the Metademe."

Aminata had not met any Ministers of the Metademe lately. "Come on," she grunted, checking vitals—pulse rapid and shallow, breathing same, eyelids hugely dilated—"up with you, we're going to pump you full of water and charcoal and laxative, shit your royal brains out."

"Kindalana." Tau's eyes so close and knowing. And the tang of virtues-knew-what poison on their lips. "You've been told you're like Kindalana. Haven't you?"

And she had. Faham Execarne had told her she looked like "old Kinda-lana." The man she'd met on the Llosydanes, Mister Calcanish, he'd said that Kindalana was going to cause an Oriati civil war, Kindalana as a pawn of Cair-dine Farrier. Calcanish had told her to fear Baru. Calcanish had told her that Baru should be sent to Aurdwynn and exiled into the Wintercrests.

Restless, eager for an outlet while she was still ashore, Aminata had taken Mister Calcanish into the alley behind Demimonde and fucked him. And when she'd said, *pretend I'm Kindalana,* he'd passed from the slow thrusts of a practiced, whorish man to the bestial desperation of passion.

Pretend I'm Kindalana.

She jerked away from Tau. The Prince's limp head dropped back into the dead garden soil. "Aha," they said, smiling at her. "I knew it."

"What did you do?" Aminata cried. "How did you know that? What have you done?"

"Oh, I've done what Cosgrad told me to do." They curled up on their side and smiled at the moon. "Cosgrad told me that if I ever lost all hope, I should use his ideas, and change my flesh to change my thoughts. Drugs, he said, en-theogenic drugs, ergot and psilocin mushrooms"—the Womb groaned loudly at that—"they are all known to relieve the Oriati Emotional Disease, to trans-form the wounded personality. 'Don't be arrogant, Tau,' he told me, 'you're wise enough to know you need help in every *other* part of your life, so don't pretend you can force yourself back to sanity all alone.'

"And," Tau ran one finger across their scabbed brow, "failing that, I was to give myself a concussion. Or be struck by lightning. Either one, he said, could relieve the despair of the Disease. Jar the mind from its grooves. Oh, Aminata, how you must *hurt.* . . ."

That bruise on their forehead: they'd been smashing their head on things. "Oh, queen's cunt," Aminata groaned. Truly the aristocrats *were* fools.

"What have they done to themself?" the Womb hissed.

"They've tried to treat themself for the Oriati Disease."

"What's that?"

"Persistent despair. Helplessness. The urge to self-annihilation." Whenever Aminata felt it she got drunk and went whoring and either the filthy ecstasy or the aching shame afterward seemed to help. The *Book of the Sea* had a mantra about it: cock cunt and drink, sailors don't think; payday and stormcloud, thinking allowed; plotting and steerage, thinking encouraged; fire and blow, thinking's too slow.

"Why's it called the Oriati Disease?" the Womb asked, warily.

"I don't know," Aminata said, not wanting to explain that the Metademe considered it a disorder of social withdrawal, a special curse of the Oriati, who were bred to live in groups. "Bad luck to call it the Falcresti Disease, I suppose."

"I'm all right," Tau said, in wonder. "I'm all right. I've figured it out."

And they vomited thin, medicine-smelling fluid onto the dead garden.

Aminata, grimacing, helped the Prince upright. "Bed," she told the Womb, confident in her medical advice if nothing else. "Bed and water, and alternate charcoal and emetics to soak up whatever's left in their stomach and get it out. Then laxatives to clean out the intestines."

"Baru," Tau croaked.

Aminata froze. She had forgotten all about the reason she'd come. "Baru," she repeated, in place of the question she wanted to ask: what does Baru want?

Tau answered anyway. "What I told you is true, Aminata. Baru wants to destroy the Imperial Republic. She wants vengeance on Falcrest and justice for what was done to Taranoke. But she fears that she will have to destroy herself to do it. And she fears that if she does not destroy herself then she will be corrupted."

Baru was a traitor.

A fucking Federal fucking Prince, foreign royalty, was calling Baru a traitor. And Aminata *believed it*. Utter obscenity.

All the things she'd shared with Baru just a lie. That moment on Kyprananoke when they'd clasped each other by the back of the neck and rubbed their foreheads together like two ship's cats—idiot! What an idiot she'd been, what a sucker, what a fool! To think that a woman who'd deceived an entire rebellion would be honest with *her*! To think that Baru was her friend just because she'd clung to a good saber and tricked a duchess into sending a letter!

She'd killed Ormsment for Baru. She'd destroyed a flag officer and all her subordinates for a woman who was a grand traitor—

"I'm an idiot," she said, and barked a little laugh.

"She needs our help now," Tau said, with such misplaced sympathy that Aminata laughed again. "Your help in particular. You are the Burner of Souls.

I never thought of it before. I always took it for a torturer's name. But flame has other uses, too, doesn't it? You burn a sample, in chemistry. And the color of the flames tells you what it's made of."

She shouldn't be here. She shouldn't be listening to this mad drugged Prince while two living tumors watched it all in silence. Oh, virtues, she would be *so* tainted.

"Promise me you'll be Baru's friend," Tau said.

"What?"

"The most meaningful power in the world is the bond between two people. The dyad. You will retain the most meaningful power over her, Aminata."

"You're high."

"Yes, but soon I will be sober again. But you, Aminata, will be exactly the same. You will still need the approval of Falcresti superiors to feel better than other Oriati people. You will still despise your Parliament, your Metademe, and all the other organs of Falcrest's government. You think you despise them as enemies of the navy but in truth you hate them for the way they make you feel about your own Oriati body."

Tau said it all without the slightest condescension, with a genuine joy, as if the view into Aminata's eyes was wider and more wonderful than all the stars above *Eternal* and all the sea around. "And the idea of you and Baru against the world, even against that part of the world which you pretend to love to serve, will always fill you with longing. You must stay close to her, Aminata. Now, more than ever, she cannot be alone. She cannot become the wound. You and she are the last string of connection holding the world from its final hernia into chaos."

Tau took several gasping breaths. Their heart fluttered hummingbird-quick in their throat.

"And if she becomes terrible," they said, still smiling, "one of us needs to be close enough to kill her."

AFTERWARD she wanted her uniform reds so badly that she made Innibarish fetch them. They were still salt-caked and filthy, ruined when she'd gone overboard from *Sulane*. The Cancrioth hadn't spared any water for the wash.

Aminata turned the jacket over in her hands, marking the places where it would need alteration. It would cost the better part of a season's pay.

"Damn," she said.

Innibarish's huge hand fell on her shoulder. She stiffened warily. It was the strangest thing in the world to be among people who looked like her. Stranger yet to look down at her uniform and see it not as proof she fit in but as a marker of separation from the people around her.

"You're all right?" the Cancrioth man asked. "Tau said many strange things."

She wanted to tell him what she felt about the navy. But how could she articulate it? The joy of being one body among many useful bodies as you sailed the ship? The pure knowledge that your talent and labor could not be denied, could not be stolen and given to someone else, when you were up there in the rigging of a ship, sailing with your own skill?

The isolation of shore leave, where the other women made it silently clear you would not be looking for lads in their company. The strange propositions of Oriati fetishists, the casual assessment of her body by strangers' gaze and comments, the remarks on her height, the size of her thighs and shoulders and breasts: an assessment which became internal, and constant, so that Aminata saw herself through Falcrest eyes in every mirror, heard the other women muttering in their own minds when she was naked among them.

On Taranoke, a sailor had remarked to her, once, that men thought about women's bodies nearly as much as they believed women thought about their own. The novelists were wrong: women did not measure themselves in mirrors and stare down their shirts.

Maybe you don't, she'd wanted to snap. Maybe a Falcrest woman doesn't. I am constantly thinking about how to hide myself. How to deny the assumption that I'm a slut.

Here on *Eternal* she was unremarkable. She had only one set of her eyes: her own. The second set, the imaginary Falcrest eyes she carried with her and looked at herself through, were shut.

"Is there any water to wash this uniform?" she asked Innibarish.

"Only if it comes out of your drinking water."

She would pay in thirst to know who she was again. She would pay eagerly.

"Fine," she said. "Take it out of my ration."

O N the next morning, as Aminata and Iraji washed Osa's powder burns, the Prince returned to them.

"Excuse me," Tau-indi said, in a clear, bright voice, like a warm breeze after days becalmed.

Aminata stared.

Tau-indi stood in the doorway of the stateroom, open-handed, scoured clean by dry strigil and alcohol, wearing a simple gray Cancrioth cassock. "I've been very poor to all of you," they said. "For that I will not apologize, any more than I could apologize for sickness or frailty. Without trim I was unmoored. But I treated my grief as well as I can. If I cannot go back I will go forward." They clasped their hands before them. "Osa, I am so sorry you're burnt, and as soon as I can, I will find a salve for it. As for the rest of you, I feel that I owe some explanation."

"Your Highness?" Osa gasped. Hope stirred in the creased-paper wreck of her face. Shao Lune lifted herself from folded knees with wary interest.

"Whether you believe in trim," their eyes found Aminata, "or not, you must know that *I* believe in it, and so it affects me. I accept that I am excised. I cannot ever return to the mbo. But I still believe in the mission I set out to achieve. The salvation of my people from war, through the influence of the intimate bonds between us.

"I came to find Abdumasi Abd, and to repair the wound in trim between us. It is a wound made when we were children, scarred over and torn open. Now I know that Abdu has taken a Cancrioth implant, and that I can no longer repair the wound. On Kyprananoke I saw that wound devour a whole nation: what Abdumasi began there led to catastrophe. Now the Brain has control of this ship, and she is going to lead all those aboard, willing or otherwise, to tear that wound further open, and to begin the war she wants. Isla Cauteria is her target. We must stop her."

"Agreed," Aminata said, loudly.

"This isn't right," Shao Lune snapped. "Lieutenant Commander Aminata, you're not to speak to this person. They've been drugged into obedience—"

"Indeed I have. My current good cheer and spiritual clarity are the result of a dangerous dose of entheogens and hallucinogens. I cannot expect the cheer to persist, but I hope the clarity will." Tau opened their hands to Iraji and Aminata. "When you told me about Baru's surrender to Ormsment . . . it led me to a hope. Consciously or otherwise, Baru seemed to be acting according to the principles of trim. They are not so easily explained, but when I teach them, I often introduce them this way:

"To maintain trim is to act in a way that puts the well-being of others before your own. Not in the hope of reward or advantage, but in the knowledge that the only way to a good world is for all people to put themselves second so that all people will be put first. To keep good trim, you must be a good friend to those around you, so your own happiness and health must be maintained. But it is also good trim to go to your enemy, and to offer forgiveness and recompense, to deliver yourself into their judgment: that is a high act of trim.

"It seems to me that when the Womb cut me out of trim, the bonds that once defined my place in the human context may have fixed upon another person. A woman who was reaching out, in desperation, for some hope of reconciliation. In short"—they bowed their head, shuffled, made themself speak with visible effort—"I believe that Baru now occupies the place in trim where I was removed.

"This means that it is *her* actions which will ultimately reunite my scattered friends Abdumasi Abd and Kindalana of Segu, and, in that reunion, bind the mortal wound that has opened in our world. Whatever happens at the end of our journey, it will happen through Baru, and it will save the Oriati people. It is destiny."

They turned, with obvious worry, to Aminata. "I know that you most of all will be skeptical of this idea of mine."

"I don't understand it," Aminata hedged. She could not *conceive* of a worldview in which something as grand as a second Armada War could be stopped by reuniting two people.

"I know." They smiled. "So I must ask you something. Will you answer honestly?"

"What is it?"

Shao Lune hissed in fury.

Tau-indi swallowed, and said, in one excited run, "Have you, in recent months, found yourself entangled by seemingly spontaneous connections with the lives of others? In particular Cairdine Farrier the Itinerant, Cosgrad Torrinde the Hesychast, Abdumasi Abd, Kindalana of Segu, and myself? Have you noticed these names, or the people themselves, appearing to you in unexpected places?"

"Bit of a leading question, isn't it?" Shao Lune sneered.

It surely was, Aminata thought, it was the very definition of a leading question.

Only—only—it had all happened exactly the way Tau said. Hadn't it? Aminata had been given a prisoner to torture: Abdumasi Abd. He had blurted out Baru's name. The hunt for Baru led her to the Llosydane Islands, and to Mister Calcanish, who'd told her about Kindalana, and who'd been so aroused and troubled by that name. Then on to Kyprananoke, and to a meeting with Tau-indi, and with Baru, who wanted to know if Cairdine Farrier had twisted their friendship. . . .

"Yes," she admitted. "I know all these people. Except Cosgrad Torrinde. I know he's Minister Metademe but I've never met him personally."

"No?" Tau looked crestfallen. "He moves under many identities. He would be an extremely lithe, supple, athletic man. A bit like the illustrations in an anatomy textbook you weren't supposed to find exciting as a girl."

"Oh, no," Aminata groaned. "Oh, *no*. Calcanish—?"

"Oh, *well* conquered," Shao Lune purred. "The man who denies the navy's women their marriage permits? What a fine catch. You really *will* let anyone—"

For the first time in Aminata's life, the room was full of Oriati people, and their collective bristling disapproval drove Shao Lune back.

"Tau," Iraji said, carefully, "what made you seek . . . treatment? Who convinced you that you needed help?"

Tau blinked at him. "Child, I am almost forty years old. I've spent my entire life thinking about how to be a better person. My capacity to be a terrible person is undiminished by that work, as a pit is undiminished by the construction of a tower. But I can set myself aright when I falter. I don't need to be spurred." They self-consciously smoothed their cassock over their hips. "I recommend psilocin mushrooms to all those who suffer an overcast of character. I've used them before."

A quick sly smile at Aminata, and then they gathered the room's attention with open arms. "I must ask all of you for your help. I cannot be ambassador for the Mbo any longer, but perhaps there is a reason for that. Perhaps fate took everything I loved because those bonds held me back from who I need to be. I was ambassador to Falcrest, a place without trim. I *must* believe that people without trim are still capable of good. I must believe the Cancrioth can make human choices. Will you help me help them?"

Aminata, against the cold judgment of Shao Lune's eyes: "Help them with what?"

"Retaking the ship, of course," Tau said. "Preventing the Brain from leading us to war."

"That's impossible," Shao Lune scoffed.

"I'm afraid I agree," Osa croaked, from Iraji's supporting arms. "How could we possibly . . . ?"

Tau smiled a little, and Aminata smiled, too, helpless, because she loved the foreign Prince's impish delight.

"Magic," they said. They bowed to Iraji, not deep, not long, but a bow nonetheless. "Child, have they taught you any war magic?"

"No," Iraji said, staggering a little under Osa's weight, fighting that old, old conditioning to faint. "Not yet . . ."

"Then it is very fortunate for us," Tau said, wringing out their hands, "that I know a great deal of it myself."

A STORY ABOUT ASH 10

THESE were the terms of Oriati Mbo's surrender, as demanded in the document held by Cairdine Farrier.

Oriati Mbo would yield its sole claim to the Ashen Sea and cooperate in establishing a Free Navigational Commons along the northern Oriati coast, in which Falcrest's convoys and their escorts could move untroubled. The eastern Mothercoast along Devi-naga would remain open to Falcrest's ships. They would make no claim to the western coast and the Black Tea Ocean (because, Tau thought, they could not practically reach it: not without fighting through Segu's islands, or looping south and west around Cape Zero and the deadly horn of Zawam Asu).

Oriati Mbo would receive damages: blood money, in Oriati terms. Falcrest would send paper money by the shipload, good tender in any Falcresti market; they would send more in exchange for counterpayments of gold, silver, and gems, at generous rates of exchange, practically devaluing their own currency. They would buy up Oriati debts, paying cash for the right to receive the debt when it was paid—a practice not foreign to the Oriati, but usually used compassionately, not for profit.

Oriati Mbo would not be asked to yield its pride or culture or its political independence. This was a trade dispute, the Falcresti said. A market correction. For many decades, Oriati Mbo had overvalued its strength, and undervalued Falcrest's.

Violence had been transacted as a result.

The treaty put a name to the whole tragedy. It would be called the Armada War. As if it had all been fought at sea, among the willing and the glorious. As if burnt Kutulbha had been a particularly large ship.

Maybe one of the spoils of a war was the right to name it.

"Well," Tau's mother Tahr said, reading it again. "Segu's not going to like this. Are they, Kinda?"

Kindalana eshSegu shook her head. She was watching the man beside her with a gaze Tau couldn't decipher.

"That's why Segu was hit hardest." Farrier frowned through his beard. "And Devi-naga, I assume. Both the great nautical federations would need to be shocked into surrender. I wish we could get news of Devi-naga's coast." But the Tide Column was blockaded, and with it all sea traffic from the Mbo's eastern nation, so news had to come overland. "I visited it when I was younger. A marvelous place. Have any of you been? No? Oh, I recommend it. Such resilience in them, the Devi and the Naga both. A land of cholera and typhoid, terrible floods . . . which reminds me, Tahr, I wanted to talk to you about the captain's problem with the ship's owner. If we can sort it out for them I expect it would be good for both our trim. . . ."

Tahr and Farrier went forward to speak to the captain. Cosgrad Torrinde, leaning against the back wall of the compartment, put his hands together and sighed into them. Tau-indi bit on their toothache and wished that they could all go home to Prince Hill again, and fight over small troubles of sex and honey.

"I don't want Oriati Mbo conquered," Cosgrad said. He looked between Tau and Kinda with thin-lipped determination. "This treaty is the beginning of the real war. Not the end. Don't forget that."

He drew away. Tau-indi watched him go, thinking of jellyfish and squid and thin membranes moving languidly down in the deep.

"You have to marry Farrier," Kindalana said.

Tau-indi's head filled with a hollow ringing sound, as if they had just stood up, hard, into the corner of an open cabinet door. *"What?"*

"I can't do it." Kindalana crossed her arms and stuck her jaw out. "You're right. I have to take care of Abdumasi. You have to do it, Tau-indi. We need to find a way inside them, a way to use influence where force will fail. Or we're lost."

"He's older than me!"

"He's a foreigner. The age difference can be excused."

"He's never shown a lick of interest!"

"You don't need to fuck him. You don't need to love him." Kindalana and her awful way of solving things. "You just need to marry him. We're Princes, Tau. We do what the Mbo requires. Think of what a marriage bond to Falcrest could do. It worked with the Maia. It could work again."

"Why not—" Tau shifted awkwardly. "Why not Cosgrad?"

"Because Farrier's more dangerous." She put her face in her hands. When she looked back up her eyes were soft and her jaw was oh so hard. "Falcrest will get inside us and change us. I think our only chance is to do the same to them."

Tau-indi could find nothing to disagree with that.

"We're Princes," Kindalana said, simply. "We have to save the mbo."

Tau-indi choked down bitter unseemly protests about the meaninglessness of marriage, about their absent father, about Kindalana's runaway mother. "Falcrest will destroy itself in time. What they do will turn back on them."

Only if you're right, Kindalana's eyes said. Only if you're right, and trim is more powerful than fire.

"Then both sides will be ruined. Is that what you want? Each of us broken? History has given them the power to take what they want from us. We cannot pretend it is otherwise. We must accept our defeat, and find a way to make something from it."

THEIR dromon sailed toward Kutulbha through a green sea scummed with ash. Tau woke in the night to the sound of the prow parting corpses. The rowers coughed so much that Tau couldn't get back to sleep. Fat sharks circled with grins full of human meat, and the black sky lowered limbs of ash to feed from the funerary water.

They sailed between two plates of death and they were like one torch moving across a charred savanna under a starless sky.

The principles in Kutulbha were the principles of a tomb. No, Tau-indi thought, that was wrong. A tomb was, after all, a place people made to consecrate and remember the dead. It had a purpose.

There *were* no principles in Kutulbha. This was a hole, a breach in the mbo, severed from trim and life. The world here had been rubbed naked to the primordial chaos.

They arrived in Kutulbha harbor among the dromons of other Princes flying flags of war and grief. Here they found the sleek shapes of Masquerade frigates, red-sailed, like the wings of a bloody carrion bird peering up from its feast. On their decks engines of fire and racks of rocket arrows waited for orders to kill. The Masquerade sailors wore white masks and red waistcoats. From a distance they might have all been painted figures positioned in some scholar's diorama.

These ships had burnt Kutulbha. Some of the griots said they'd fired arrows into the city with messages to surrender, and then messages to evacuate, printed with a dire warning: FIRE HAS NO MERCY.

Some said they'd given no one any time to do anything but burn.

Many of the Princes had come here simply to grieve. Many more had come to bring supplies to the refugees. The survivors met them with gratitude, or dull acknowledgment, or pure inconsolate rage that the Princes still cared about trim or principle when *this* had happened.

Tau met Princes who had come with their own Falcresti hostages. Men and women who carried the same terms of surrender Farrier had presented. And they met Princes broken in contrition because they had allowed their Falcresti hostages to die, or killed them in revenge, and in doing so invited doom on their houses, their tribes, their squadrons, their rivers.

Of all the Princes who had come, Kindalana and Tau-indi were the youngest. That gave them power. They had the most future to speak for. They bore the trim of the unborn, and if there was any purpose to the world at all, it must be to make it kinder for those who waited across the Door for their time to be born.

"The war must end now," they told the others. "We must surrender."

But they also found Princes mad with rage, Princes who wanted to declare the Falcresti as enenen, an alien enemy without trim, and refuse their blood money. Princes who wanted to raise armies like Tahari or White Akhena and march on Falcrest. And there was worse. Some of them wore no paint except white corpse ash and they said that there were powers older than trim, powers down in the south of Mzilimake, in the hot lands and the jungle, that would fill the wombs of Falcrest with empty cysts of blood.

"Before principles," these Princes said, "we had a god whose brain is a tumor, whose eyes protrude on horns of cancer, whose pregnancy swells forever. Let us break the lead seals and the clay tablets. Let us set that god on Falcrest."

Tau-indi saw in their eyes a burning woman with green hands and too many green eyes, and wanted to scream.

It was decided, swiftly and generally, without any one clear formal decision, that they would vote on the articles of surrender: whether to yield to Falcrest now, or go on, somehow, with the losing war.

On the day of that vote, Tau-indi brought Cosgrad Torrinde to walk among the Princes. "Tell them about your study of the mangroves," Tau-indi prompted. "Tell them about how you licked the frog out of curiosity."

Cosgrad tried to be charming. But Tau-indi tripped him up and teased him and made him stammer and stumble over complicated ideas that barely fit into his knowledge of Uburu and Seti-caho, so that he looked human and unthreatening. Tahr the Prince-Mother walked with Cosgrad to show her favor toward him, chained and jeweled, haloing Cosgrad in a reflected authority that would impress Segu's princes. To the Segu women, Cosgrad was something to be cut down to size, a jumped-up laborer and spouse. They could handle him better when Tahr seemed to own him.

Kindalana spoke, everywhere she went, of Cosgrad's unlikely friendship with young Tau-indi. "See?" she said. "We can learn to love each other. This man saved my father's life, and in that healing, a greater wound might be sutured."

It was strange to hear this from Kindalana, because Tau knew she felt a deep cynicism about Falcrest's response to kindness and generosity. But many of the Princes were comforted by her assurance, because it eased their own guilt about allowing a war to break out.

It was, Tau thought, very Oriati to feel more guilt for the wound in their *own* conduct than anger at Falcrest's aggression. It was a noble thing to constantly ask yourself to be better. But it could also be arrogant, self-involved, oblivious. As if everything that mattered was ultimately about Oriati people and their conduct. As if they were so powerful, so central to the world, that only they could be blamed for their own defeat.

That was when Tau knew Kindalana was right. It was not enough to tend to the Mbo's trim. Something had to be done within Falcrest.

On that evening the Princes at the grave of Kutulbha voted on the terms of surrender.

These were the votes.

Lonjaro Mbo, the High Heart of the World, the Thirteen-in-Three-in-One that carried on Mana Mane's faith as recorded in the *Kiet Khoiad,* voted by a sweeping majority to surrender to Falcrest. Time and population were on their side. They could stop the killing and start the healing. Only the eastern kingdoms of Umbili the Savan Antelope and Kinde the Torch Cheetah, pressed up against Falcrest, voted for war: their shua had been raiding and skirmishing along the border for years, and they stood to lose huge tracts of land in the surrender. The Princes of Abdeli Bduli, the landless thirteenth kingdom which traditionally represented the renegades and common folk, voted for peace but warned of a great and growing anger among their people.

The tribes of Segu, the People of the Ships, voted by the narrowest margin to surrender to Falcrest. Kutulbha was a bone ash ruin. Their archipelagos were troubled by starvation and shortage after the loss of so many ships. They needed years to lay down new fleets. But the Princes of the western coast and the southern territories, the mighty uroSegu and far-ranging yeniSegu among them, declared themselves unbound by the vote.

The Mzilimaki Paramountcy voted to continue the war, claiming solidarity with their northerly neighbor Segu. This drew outrage, even and especially from Segu's princes. Mzilimake wanted to see Segu's shipping entirely devastated, so that trade would abandon the coast and come south again, through the Moonlight Kingdoms and their thousand rivers. So much for the people who spoke Maulmake, those bitter Segu-women said; the name of the language meant *moon truth,* but the Mzilimaki had filled it with lies.

(Tau was not personally convinced of any malice, though. Mzilimake contained some two thousand tribes, banded into confederations according to the lakes and rivers that connected them. Even White Akhena had only been able to unite them for twenty years. Tau did not think they could possibly all support a single conspiracy against Segu.)

Some of the Mzilimaki Princes suggested, to Tau's absolute revulsion, that they knew of deep places in the jungle where one could catch certain bushmeat. A bushmeat that, when eaten, produced a plague they would not dare name. This virulence could defend the Mbo against any invaders.

"Millions would die!" Kindalana cried. "*Millions!* Can you count that high, you fools? There would be a corpse for every hair on all of your heads, and enough left over to pluck your genitals naked!"

Devi-naga the Stormblown Flock, the Land of Jet and Flood, which ran down the continent's eastern edge along the Mother of Storms and toward far Zawam Asu, voted for peace. Falcrest's Second Fleet loomed off their shores, sitting on their trade, enforcing brutal and high-handed "mandatory quarantines" on the rice paddies and floodplains. The Squadron Princes were more afraid of starvation than of surrender. Without the grain trade through the Tide Column, it had crept too close to bear.

By vote of the Princes, born by vote of the Mbo, the oldest and longest of civilizations would accept a conditional surrender to the youngest and least known.

All this time Cairdine Farrier was nowhere to be found.

Later they learned he'd gone ashore to help Kutulbha's orphans, finding them sponsors so they could be adopted and raised in Falcrest.

THEY signed the surrender aboard Tau-indi and Kindalana's dromon, because the future belonged to the young.

Off the ship's port side, the city of Kutulbha smoldered like a cook fire, and the meal it cooked was a hundred thousand people, and the mouth that ate those people was the mouth missing from the white Falcrest masks that stared across the table as their clerks offered silver pens.

Tau-indi took the pen. A treaty was a spell to force the human world to obey a truth that existed only in paper. There was no reason to accept the world the treaty described as true, except that Falcrest had made continued war a part of any other world.

They wrote their name.

So it was signed.

Afterward Kindalana and Tau-indi went ashore and gathered ash for ash cakes. Cosgrad watched them cook with uneasy fascination. When offered a cake he looked away, throat cabled with unease.

"No," he said thickly. "I can't. I can't."

He felt too much a part of it, Tau-indi thought. He couldn't eat his own guilt. Because then he would begin digesting it, whether into poison or acceptance.

The war would go on a while after this. Falcrest kept track of the dates and times of each battle and assembled a schedule of penalties. The last great battle was Nyoba Dbellu's, who led her ships against thirst and scurvy all the way around the Ashen Sea, up past the old Maia lands in the northwest, east across the coast of Aurdwynn, down from the north at Falcrest itself. She traveled far from the coast to avoid Falcresti pickets, at the mercy of dehydration and storm. Of all those that set sail, not two in three survived the entire journey.

At the end of her voyage, among Falcrest's islands, the Porpoise Carousel, the tern-stained Nautilus, and the scrubby Little Squid, Nyoba Dbellu's ships burnt under the siphons of Falcrest's First Fleet, and their ash filled up the waterway that would forever after be called the Sound of Fire.

20

THE PALIMPSEST

"SHATTAY ya-Wah," Faham Execarne said, which made me laugh and elbow him so hard the hammock tipped. We clung to each other and kicked until we had balance. If we fell we'd wake up Svir, and sleep was the only thing that made him tolerable lately.

"No one would ever pronounce it that way!" I protested. "Shate yah-wah. That's how you say it."

"Zaytee yayway."

Wydd sustain me, I think I giggled. "What *are* we smoking?"

"Trimwell Black Edition. The finest in Falcrest. Eugenically conditioned for"—he paused to sneeze—"excellence and clarity of effect. Raised in a sound-scape of bees and birdsong. Evenly illuminated so the plant never fears winter. I own a four-percent stake in the concern."

"A wise investment?"

"It gets me the Black Edition, and nothing calms me so. And if the world is but a figment of our collected thoughts"—he smiled fetchingly at me—"then nothing calms the world so well as a calm mind."

Helbride pitched on a gentle following sea. I let the rhythm settle me onto Faham's arm. He began to rock the hammock, very gently, with the touch of his bare feet. I smiled into his hard, wide farmer's chest.

"Are you conspiring against the welfare of the Imperial Republic?" he asked.

I looked up sharply: from below his face was a bearded outcropping, a mossy totem in the forest of his hair, like something left by the Belthyc. "What?"

"Captain Branne was consulting charts of Isla Cauteria today. Looking for a place to moor a ship much, much larger than *Helbride*."

Sloppy, Svir, very sloppy: he was too accustomed to trusting his crew. "Baru has a plan to bring *Eternal* in to harbor there," I murmured. "I'm willing to go along with it. The entire reason I've preserved that ship is to get the flesh samples Hesychast needs. Living specimens of the immortal Cancrioth body."

"Then we should seize that ship by force."

I drew away from him in astonishment. "*What?*" This from Faham the spymaster, who feared war above all else.

But he'd killed his own spies, too. On the Llosydanes he'd gassed his entire station to eliminate one mole. He was not a man averse to death.

His handsome rustic face, paler Falcrest skin, untouched by fear or anger: "We should take the entire ship as a prize. We should disappear the crew to a Morrow Ministry site, along with Abdumasi Abd and everyone from *Cheetah*. Cover it all up. No Cancrioth exists. Kyprananoke was a natural disaster. Tauindi disappeared at sea with their entire clipper—don't look at me like that, of course I'd keep them comfortable. But they would disappear, with all their knowledge of what we've seen. That's what we tell the Oriati. That's what we tell Parliament. Make it all disappear."

He took a long draw from the joint and blew into the darkness. "The navy . . . the navy is a problem. If our suspicions are correct, and Abd is on Cauteria, they're aware of the Cancrioth by now. They know the Cancrioth has enough influence to organize a fleet-strength naval attack on our provinces. They may demand a first strike. But after Ormsment's mutiny, I think Maroyad will understand it's best to stay quiet."

"Faham!" I prodded the bottom of his chin. "Where's your patience? Shouldn't we see how the situation develops?"

"No." I felt him swallow. "We're in the dominion of worst-case scenarios now. The worst case is that a war faction is in control of *Eternal*, prepared to release the Kettling as close to Falcrest as they can. If the navy is attacked, they will retaliate immediately, not just here but all along the northern Oriati coast. It'll be chaos. So we must put a tourniquet on it. We must twist it as tight as we can."

He lowered his chin against the top of my head, rubbed his beard against my hair. "And if you seize *Eternal*, you'll get what Hesychast needs from you. It will work out in your favor. I want the best for you."

"Faham—"

"Hush. Let me say it while I can say it. You and Baru, this . . . arrangement of yours. I assume that you got her to compromise herself, under threat of lobotomy. You think she's under your control now, and you're using her to bring the Cancrioth in."

I was silent.

"It was a mistake, Yawa. Her virtue is unpredictability, and you can't afford that right now. She handled Aurdwynn well, but that wasn't her plan, was it? That was the Throne's design. Now she's trying to sell you on a new plan, isn't she? Some trick of money and political influence." He touched the nape of my neck, fingertips teasing out the hairs, searching for the lowest. "You can't let her attempt it. She's an unreliable field operator at best, and there's no evidence at all she can build and execute her own strategy for the Oriati conflict.

"But *you*, Yawa, haven't you always always had a plan? Haven't you worked your whole life to prove you could be trusted with Aurdwynn's future? Wouldn't you have that, and anything else you wanted, if you brought *Eternal* in as your own prize?"

"You think I should betray her," I whispered.

"I think that you should be true to yourself."

I turned up to look at him. "It would empower Hesychast, and you hate him so—"

"All the better to have a woman I trust close to him."

"Olake was the last spy who trusted me, Faham."

"I am not your brother." He gave me a short, firm kiss. "Let me prepare an action against *Eternal*. Make a plan to lobotomize Baru the moment she's given you the Cancrioth. You still have medical justification; you've received her extensive confession about her mental abnormalities. Can it hurt anyone if you make preparations?"

"It might hurt *you* to trust me, Mister Fay-ham Esheecarnay."

He guffawed. "*No* one would pronounce it that way."

The bells sounded for morning watch.

IT'S worked!" Barhu burst into Yawa's cabin on pitch-stained feet, clutching a sheet of charcoal marks. She hadn't been so exhilarated to deliver an answer since the night the Dukes had asked her to name her consort. "*Ascentatic*'s sighted *Eternal* flying Segu merchant banners, all cannon ports shut, cargo spars prominently mounted. She looks like a treasure ship!"

"Hardly a substantive disguise." Yawa scratched out whatever she'd been writing. Barhu caught the word *defendant*: another plea for her twin. "You can call her a treasure ship from here to Haraerod, but the navy will see she's huge enough to carry an army."

"That's all right! We'll go ashore to Annalila Fortress and seize control of Rear Admiral Maroyad by political means. The disguise is for the public. As long as they see an opportunity for profit—"

"Instead of a floating atrocity full of plague?" Yawa snapped. "Have you forgotten what *I* have at stake on Cauteria?"

"No. Of course not. Governor Heingyl is important." Put Yawa's fears first. "If we can get *Eternal* safely into port, we're one step closer to the sample you need for Hesychast."

"You told me the immortata was sacred, and that they'd never give it up."
She smiled up at Barhu, face like an expensive bridge, all cables and tensions.
"Svir made it plain that one of us *must* destroy the other, Baru. We can't both
survive this."

"Not openly," Barhu countered.

"Do you have a plan, then?"

Barhu was desperately unready for that conversation. "I have an alternate
dowry. Something to bring the Stakhieczi king into the marriage without my,
ah, sacrifice."

"Fine." Yawa threw up her hands. "At least it's a useful distraction."

Barhu took a deep breath. "Tain Hu wanted me to remember something
about a man in an iron circlet. Do you still have . . . the document where she
recorded her secret?"

ONCE this ledger had bound all the rebel leaders of Aurdwynn together.
Fatal secrets recorded on a sheepskin palimpsest by the Priestess in the
Lamplight. Barhu had learned, almost too late, that the Priestess was an agent
of Falcrest—doubtless one of Hesychast's followers in the ilykari. This palimpsest was meant to go into Hesychast's files. Instead, it had gone to Barhu, and
from her to Yawa.

"I never deciphered the transcript," Yawa said. The carpenters had installed a door on Yawa's slot cabin, a thick oak slab with a big black iron lock.
Yawa fussed over it to avoid looking at Barhu. "Partly because I didn't know
the spice-word, of course. But I also found the thought of deciphering it . . .
difficult."

Her brother's secrets would be on the palimpsest.

"If you'd like, I can give you the spice-word, and leave you to decrypt it. . . ."

"No, no. Help an old woman with her figures."

"Old women are supposed to be good at figures. That's what they taught us
in school."

"I didn't go to school." She cleared her little desk and made space for Barhu.
"Please."

Barhu sniffed the copy. It smelled like oat bran, like her old tower. She
closed her eyes, felt olive oil on her fingertips, a gentle wind on her face. Saw
lamplight flickering through thin paper walls. The ilykari made their temples
flammable, so they could burn it all when Falcrest came.

She enumerated the text, and then the spice-word SUSPIRE, turning each
letter to a number by its place in the Aphalone alphabet. After that it was a
simple matter of subtraction and denumeration.

Yawa lay back in her hammock. "Will you read it to me?"

"Shall I began with Olake? Get him over with?"

She made a small noise. "No."

"I'll begin with my least favorite, then—"

A delighted cackle. "Oh, who *will* it be?"

"Duke Oathsfire has written . . ."

Duke Oathsfire has written, and he was there at her side, beard fluffed up like an angry possum, confessing that he had, in the end, fallen in love with her: really with the *idea* of her. A common-born liberator, a high and noble cause to redeem his life of arrogance and privilege. If he devoted himself to a belief, couldn't he be as respected as his friend Lyxaxu, as noble as his peer Lyxaxu, as beloved, as wise?

No wonder he'd tried to kill her. She'd betrayed so much of him.

"He paid his wife to abort a child, knowing they would soon divorce, because he did not want her to have the leverage of a firstborn heir. She told him she would've done it for nothing. The child was buried in the Oathsfire plot."

"Hm," Yawa said. "Weak. It could be prosecuted, but I doubt the sentence would be death. Not for the man, at least."

"Maybe he was afraid of what would be done to his wife."

"You think he cared about his divorced wife?"

"Maybe his honor mattered to him."

"I suppose. Many foolish things did. His wife didn't want the child, so he did the right thing. Who next?"

"Duke Lyxaxu has written . . ." She hoped it wasn't sordid. She couldn't bear to see Lyxaxu reduced. He had been the only one of the Coyotes to detect Barhu's treachery, because he had listened to her, listened to her beliefs, and *really* understood what they would drive her to do.

But he would reassure her: *what is true is true, and you may not turn away from it in fear. For if you do, you are turning your face toward a lie.*

He had mismanaged his duchy into starvation, and, in a fit of self-loathing, committed himself to suffer as the meanest of his peasants. That meant a winter spent among the nihilist-berserkers who studied the nothingness of the self. They ate their own dead: nothing but meat, no sacred value, and the living needed meat to survive.

Now Barhu understood the feral fox-flash she'd seen in his eyes. He had gone right to the edge of humanity, and past it. "I forgive you," she whispered. Lyxaxu had hated starvation so deeply, after that winter, that he'd even given aid to his enemy Erebog.

Yawa was laughing. "He was a cannibal! That's incredible! Do another, do another."

"Unuxekome is next. . . ." Barhu covered the passage with her hand, and felt as if her womb would cramp, remembering his mother's poison. But that captain of swift ships would not wait at anchor, he would sail forward! With a growl she ripped the hand away and read his last story. It was not a surprise: he had been exchanging weapons, water, and information with the Oriati Syndicate Eyota, in truth a covert arm of the Oriati Fighting Swarm, commissioned to raid Masquerade interests in Aurdwynn by the wealth of the merchant Abdumasi Abd. Grand treason, of course. He had asked the priestess to seal his testimony with his own personal name.

"Kome Afrasi Riawyys," Yawa sighed. The name lay on her tongue like sugarmelt. "I had such a passion for him when I was younger."

"Yawa! He could've been your son!"

"Hush, hush. We are disclosing compromising secrets here, after all. Who's next?"

"There's only you and Olake left . . . and Hu."

"Well," Yawa sighed, "you might as well read mine, it shan't surprise you."

Yawa's secret was exactly as Unuxekome Ra had promised it would be. *I have resolved to pay any price and betray any loyalty in order to secure the independence of my homeland from all aristocracies and occupiers, be they foreign or native-born. I will never abandon this purpose, though it lead me into my enemy's power.*

"Why write it down?" Barhu asked her. "Why take the risk of certifying your treason?"

"Because it was a vow in sight of the ilykari. I couldn't . . . I couldn't lie." Yawa looked excruciatingly uncomfortable. "Go on, please."

"We could stop."

"Don't you dare coddle me. Go on."

Now Barhu had to choose between reading Olake's secret and Hu's. She glanced left, to put the palimpsest on her right, and stabbed her finger down: and of course she picked Hu's secret, the one she had come to learn.

"The Comet Duchess has recorded—"

"A moment, please." Yawa fetched herself a handkerchief.

"She has recorded . . ." Barhu gathered up her courage in the hardness of her stomach. "She says that when she was young, she met a man wearing an iron circlet in the forests of Vultjag."

Yes. This was it. This was the message Hu had wanted her to find.

"Later she learned that this iron-circleted man was the Pretender-King

Kubarycz, Lord of the Mansion Uczenith. He had been exiled for his conspiracy to unite his Mansion with the Duchy Erebog. Tain Hu killed him in single combat, and his sons in the ensuing skirmish, thus ending his lineage entirely. . . ."

Yawa's eyes snapped up to hers. "It says that? It says she ended his entire line?"

"Yes. What does it mean?"

"If the duel was lawful, and there are no surviving heirs, the loser's inheritance goes to the winner."

"Really?" Barhu said, skeptically. "That seems like a good way to keep all your aristocrats dueling to the death."

"It is the Stakhieczi custom, so that no Mansion is ever orphaned by the death of its ruling line in war. If Tain Hu were a Stakhi lord, she would now have a claim to Mansion Uczenith."

"Vultjag is a Stakhi name," Barhu breathed. "She was Maia but her ducal name comes from a Stakhi lineage. Vultjag *could* rule Uczenith. . . ."

They stared at each other. The hope felt like it would collapse if they dared prod it.

"Well," Yawa said. "That's quite a secret."

"She never mentioned—"

But wait, wait, she had. On their carriage ride together, after the duel with Cattlson, Barhu had asked Hu if she'd ever killed. And she'd said *the man with the iron circlet.*

"If Cattlson had learned about this," Barhu said, wonderingly, "that the brigand bitch of Vultjag had a claim to Stakhieczi aristocracy . . . she would've been too dangerous to leave in power. She would've been disappeared."

"She would never have pressed the claim." Yawa stared into the wall, seeing distant forest and white mountains above. "She was too much a child of Vultjag. And she must have known the Stakhieczi would refuse her. She could have walked into the Mansion Uczenith and declared herself their lawful lord and it would have made no difference. A Maia woman? They'd sooner be ruled by the rats."

"Yawa—" Barhu clenched her fists. "Yawa, I think—"

"What?"

"Dziransi witnessed us when I chose Tain Hu as my consort."

Yawa's eyes went wide. "*He was there?* You did it publicly? Just told them all you would be queen and Hu would be your consort?"

"Yes. After the battle at Sieroch. They asked me to choose a consort, and I raised Tain Hu up to my side. Dzir was very confused."

"Baru, do you realize—"

"I'm the chosen consort of the rightful lord of the Mansion Uczenith," Barhu breathed. "Tain Hu was that rightful lord. If the Stakhi recognize our union as a marriage . . . then she passed the claim to *me* when she died."

"They'll never recognize your claim."

"Why not?" Barhu said, giddy now. "What if it was to the Necessary King's benefit to recognize it? Don't you think he could find a legality to grant the claim?"

Yawa sat up slowly. "The Necessary King would recognize the claim *if* it could be transferred to him by marriage. If he married you, he'd have *two* Mansions. His Hussacht and your Uczenith. And if you produced an heir, the claim to both Mansions would pass down to that child—"

"No. I won't carry his child."

"Barhu, *please,* think of the opportunity—"

"I won't be mother to a man's child."

"Barhu, come now, it's not so bad; he jerks off, you stick it up your cunt, repeat until it takes—"

Something caught Barhu's eye, a little addendum that Purity Cartone had faithfully transcribed from Hu's confession. She had written—Barhu burst into laughter—*also, and often, I have fucked Oathsfire's wife—*

Barhu thought about this for a moment, this matter of women fucking women, in the context not of Falcrest's Incrasticism but of Stakhieczi custom as Svir had taught it to her.

"I'm not a woman," she said. "I'm a man. I can marry women."

"What?"

"That's how it works in the mountains, Svir said. Only a man can marry a woman. But whether you're a man or a woman is decided by how you *act*. I can act as a man, and so I can become a man."

"Act like a man?" Yawa tucked her chin in, put up her heels like she was wearing horse-archers, crossed her arms in a pantomime of Falcresti manhood. "Exactly what are the qualifications?"

Barhu described the qualifications with her hands. Yawa laughed like a gutter girl. "Oh! You always struck me as the one on the other end—"

"Yawa!"

"So you are a man. You are the man with the claim to Mansion Uczenith's ruling line. What does that gain us?"

"I can marry a woman," Barhu said, happily, "a marriage the Necessary King can recognize. Then *she* can take the claim to Uczenith from me when we divorce. Then she can marry the Necessary King, delivering the claim to him! The king will make sure it's all legal because it benefits him. And I won't have to fuss around with semen samples, I won't even have to meet this king, I'll just send him my divorced spouse to be his wife."

"You'll still require a suitable wife," Yawa mused. "Someone who symbolizes the union of Aurdwynn and the Stakhieczi Necessity. Where will you find such a woman?"

Barhu smiled wickedly at her. "I thought you might introduce us to the mutual bride."

"What? Who?"

"You sent Dziransi to the Necessary King, didn't you? We'll send him the bride he expects. Only the dowry won't be my lobotomy anymore. It'll be my claim to the Mansion Uczenith, passed through her."

"Oh *no.*" Yawa covered her face.

"I recall Ri's rather fetching," Barhu said. "And more pronouncedly feminine. I could be a plausible husband, don't you think?"

NO," Svir whispered. His neck was tight as a hangman's noose. Sinew and larynx stood out like height lines on a map. "No, I won't go back."

They'd come to him together, a mistake: he'd looked up and said, "Ah, wonderful, no matter which way I turn there's someone to stab me in the back."

Barhu tried to bring it up elliptically and Svir just stared at her like a distant thunderhead, debating whether to come over and incinerate her. She'd pointed out (not wanting to blurt Svir's secret right out in front of Yawa) that he must have been a man of some influence in the Wintercrests, or he couldn't have afforded the fleet of ships that he'd commanded when Falcrest captured him. Had he known the man who would become the Necessary King? (The man, she did not say, who was his brother?)

Svir put his pen point-first into his palm. It made a very deep dimple. "Perhaps."

"We have an action in mind," Yawa said, "in the Wintercrests. The political and strategic consequences could be enormous. It might mean the end of hundreds of years of war. But the action would require an agent in the Necessary King's court who was exquisitely sensitive to the nuances of Stakhieczi custom and law. A negotiator to smooth out objections and difficulties. We wondered if—"

"No," he said, with his throat like a noose. "No, I won't go back."

Barhu tried to signal Yawa that she should leave. But the Jurispotence Durance was not accustomed to abandoning her work to the young. "Apparitor—Svirakir—we both know that you were someone important in the mountains. I don't know who, exactly, but you have too many teeth to be a Mansion commoner. This is your chance to use that heritage to the whole world's advantage—"

"But I don't care about the whole world." He beamed poisonously at Barhu and Yawa. "I've told you plainly what I want. I want Lindon, I want my family, and I want enough money to complete construction on my new fleet. And then I'm going east. Before the whole Ashen Sea turns into Kyprananoke."

"Do you want to see Farrier triumphant?" Yawa snapped. "Do you *want* to see Baru's master in power? Hesychast could at least protect your family—"

"Oh, fuck them both," Svir said, cheerily.

"Damn you," Yawa snapped, "this is your function in the Throne. Your special expertise is in Stakhieczi and northern frontier affairs."

"And I won't go back. Not with the navy about to eat Lindon." Svir held up one hand, palm out, thumb at right angle to his forefinger: the kind of sign you might make in falling snow, in mittens, to signal the people following you to halt.

"I'm not doing a damn thing for either of you," he said, "until I have some leverage."

"All right," Barhu said, over Yawa's silence. "How do we do provide you leverage?"

"You sign a statement that could do you real harm. I inspect it to be sure I'm satisfied. Then you apply your incryptor to seal it as a genuine product of your authority, and you give it to me to hold." Svir offered his pen, still capped by an invisibly thin layer of his skin. "Deal?"

Barhu looked to Yawa. "I can't. Will you?"

"You can't," Svir interrupted, "because so far you're completely unconstrained in your power, except by that nasty diagnosis of epilepsy Yawa's got. Is your loyalty to a dead woman's sacrifice *really* more important than earning my service?"

Yes. Yes, it had to be. Yawa would need to be the one to yield a hold. Only Yawa was closed up, eyes shining, mouth bitter. "You've already got my twin. What more do you want?"

"Hesychast has your twin," Svir countered. "I have nothing on you."

"And you'll get nothing more."

Svir turned his alien eyes on Barhu. "It looks like it's up to you, *Agonist*. You want my service? Either give me a hook in you. Or use that leverage you've got to make me obey. That's what Hu died for, isn't it? To give you the power to compel without being compelled? Compel me!"

There had to be another way. "Svir, I know what you'd risk if you went home." The Stakhieczi did not look kindly on traitors, and Svir was arguably the greatest traitor they'd ever produced. "But this could mean the end of the Stakhieczi as a threat to Aurdwynn." And the beginning of the Stakhieczi as a trading partner, one end of her beautiful, beautiful plan. "Will you do this, knowing what's at stake?"

"NO!" he roared. His hand came down on his folding desk and the hinges rattled and the pot of ink leapt and settled back into a black star of spill. "NO!"

And then, more terrible than that roar, sliver-thin and quiet: "Go. Get out. Go."

21

All in Motion, Too Swift, Too Soon

SVIRAKIR, Prince of Mansions, Apparitor of the Imperial Throne, dangled a hundred and seventy feet above *Helbride*'s weather deck and thought about jumping.

His body stuck out into the wind like a flag: he was hooked through the mainmast lines by his right arm, and braced against the mast by his right foot. His left dangled in open air.

He watched the sun lever. That was what they said in the Mansions, not *rising* but levering, the light of the sun tipping down across the world on the fulcrum of the Wintercrests. It illuminated the birds above Isla Cauteria: hawks and sea eagles, ospreys and skua, the gannets and the white gulls, and at last the black dome of the volcanic peak. Now the light touched the bright chips of lakes.

He'd tried his best to play his role, and so buy time for himself. But Yawa and Baru had failed to destroy each other. Instead they'd fallen into each other's arms (not literally, as far as he knew: Baru was still running experiments on the diver Ulyu Xe's endurance) and developed an admittedly charming seditious streak.

Not that they'd let him into their sedition. But it was obvious, and predictable, that they were conspiring against the Throne. Leave two infant cryptarchs at sea for months and of course they'd get delusions of independence. He'd had them once, too.

The reassertion of authority was going to be brutal.

With his left hand he measured the horizon's slight bob. Though of course the horizon was really stationary, and Svir was the one moving. You act, you think that you are changing the world, shaking the whole mess on its foundation: but really all you have done is move yourself.

Of course, if Svir *really* wanted to see the horizon move, then he could leap from the mast. The horizon would collapse in on him until it achieved a radius of zero when he struck the water. Which was an ugly thought, but he knew exactly why it had come to him.

The possibility of Lindon's destruction always made him want to die. And that possibility was coming true.

He'd climbed up here to check the weather beacon on Annalila Fortress. After staring at it for half a chime he could no longer hide from the truth.

The beacon was transmitting the wrong test code.

Every morning, the weather beacon transmitted a test code to ships and outlying observers, who flashed it back in turn. Of course the test code changed every week, to keep everyone alert.

And hidden in that weekly sequence, there was always a group of characters meant for Svir's eyes only. Its solitary purpose was to tell him, wherever he wandered, that Lindon was safe in the Admiralty.

The code had been altered, actively altered by Lindon's intent, to signal *Admiralty in jeopardy. Political threat most acute.*

Had Parliament ordered the Judiciary to purge the navy? Had the khamtiger Ahanna Croftare finally made her move against Lindon? If so, they were sailing into a trap. Rear Admiral Samne Maroyad commanded all of Isla Cauteria's naval assets, and as one of the Merit Admirals, she was loyal to Croftare. Svir had not prospered as a cryptarch by sailing into enemy harbors. Or, for that matter, by spending much time in Falcrest's home waters at all.

"Ziscjaditzcionursz!" His brother's favorite curse, a complex word for situations when you were complexly fucked. Stars, he wanted something simple, he wanted Iraji's smile across a game of tiles, Iraji's round full ass in his hands. But Iraji was gone—

"Fuck!" he shouted. From the foretop, one of the topsail girls looked up at him in alarm. He winked at her.

He knew exactly what Baru was planning. The scope of her vision was spectacular. The depth of her commitment to Cairdine Farrier's method was appalling. And while he expected she would fail just as spectacularly, because she was about to end her vacation on *Helbride* (courtesy of Mister Svirakir's Ashen Sea Touring Concern, All Expenses Paid) and stumble unprepared into the knifepoint mêlée of Falcrest's interior politics . . .

. . . there was the *slightest* chance she could provide him with what he needed.

East, he'd told her. East into the unknown. To escape the end of the world. Which was most of the truth. The lightning called to those it had marked: and Svir and Lindon were deeply, permanently marked. The lightning haunted their dreams, summoning them back east across the Mother of Storms to the supercontinent. He fully intended to spend the rest of his life exploring that place in Lindon's company, and understanding what it had done to them.

But to do that, to establish a self-sufficient colony across the Mother of Storms, one not only capable of supporting his work but of protecting Lindon's wife Enwan and the children, he needed money. A preposterous amount of money. Ill-advised colonial expeditions could bankrupt entire nations.

An amount of money you could only get through, say, a trade monopoly on an untouched and unexploited market.

What if Baru's mad idea *was* the right thing to do? Penetrating the Oriati trade network for Falcrest's benefit could also be used to his benefit. He didn't need her to succeed, really. He only needed to invest in her concern and get out before the bubble burst.

And if she was *planning* on creating just such a bubble, popping Falcrest's economy to ruinous effect . . . well, she would probably be compromised before she could manage it. But the idea *did* have a certain dash.

Motion called his eyes down to the deck. There was Iscend Comprine, Hesychast's walking court recorder, doing acrobatic exercises on the ship's prow. And there was Baru, sticking her head abovedecks, staring for a moment at Iscend's body stretched between two lines, then looking around with furtive guilt to see if she'd been noticed.

She wanted him to go back to the Wintercrests. How could he survive that? If Atakaszir learned that Svir had whored himself to Falcrest, he'd murder Svir, brother or no. And even if he didn't . . . how would Svir ever manage to *leave* again? How could he explain to Atakaszir that he hated the home Ataka loved?

He could not possibly gamble his life and Lindon's survival on a mad journey into the Wintercrests to arrange some kind of marriage of nations. Not with Lindon so urgently threatened. No, the game of being a cryptarch taught you to play the margins. Count on the sure thing, stick to the subtle and reliable maneuver, avoid the glare of the spotlight and the desperate foolishness of direct action—

If only Baru had the balls to *make* him do it! Then there'd be no fucking choice, and he could go north spitting hot blood and cursing her name, taking the exhilarating chance, the long odds that would probably kill him but might deliver all his dreams.

"Your Excellence?" Captain Branne called up from the weather deck. "What do you see?"

"Trouble, Brannie my girl," he sang back down. "Trouble ahead!"

"Yes, Your Excellence, always. Is the trouble literal or figurative?"

"Literal, I'm afraid."

He'd just spotted the sails of an Attainer-class frigate maneuvering around Annalila Point. Yes, he recognized that oddly cut boom. It was *Hygiatis*. One of Samne Maroyad's ships, coming out from Cauteria to intercept *Helbride*. She would be in rocket range soon enough. "Light up the sunflash and shoot them a test code. If they ignore us, use the signal fireworks.

"And please find my blackmail files on the officers posted to *Hygiatis,* under First Fleet's Northern Command. We've a little skirmish to fight, Brannie, and I'll need my armaments."

T HIS is the farthest east I've ever been," Barhu said, as hello and good morning to Svir. She'd just fed the ship's angry dancing seagull, buying its mercy for another watch but reinforcing its mad avian belief that pattering its feet made humans serve it.

"There's a lot more east in the world." Svir rubbed his tired eyes. He had been up all morning flashing mysterious numbers at the frigate *Hygiatis,* which Barhu suspected were dates and addresses of personal and fraught significance to the ship's captain.

"You'll get a chance to see it," she said. "You'll make that voyage."

He looked at her sadly. "You're in a dream. All this, here, on *Helbride,* it's not real. It's a jar they put you in with Yawa, like two fighting snakes. When we land on Cauteria they'll smash the jar and fish you out."

"Because we'll be back in touch with the rest of the Throne?"

"Because your masters expect a victor. And you haven't given them one." His sadness reached his eyes. "You know she'll destroy you, Baru."

She sized up the island, swiveling at the waist to clear her blind side. This would be the setting for her endgame. By the time they left she would be committed to one path or the other: her trade route, or a bloody apocalypse. Or she would be dead.

Isla Cauteria was a place of rich, flourishing life. Pine forests guarded purple lilac meadows and gravel-surfaced roads. Thin plumes of smoke marked the smokehouses in Cautery Plat, the fishing and trading town on the south end.

"I wish I could see the guano terminals," she said. "Up on the north shore. Where they sell the fertilizer."

"Figures," Svir muttered. "Your first chance to set foot on land in Falcrest proper and all you want to do is bury yourself in birdshit."

On the farthest right side of her perception was Annalila Fortress. Red-black and hideous in its power. Angular stonework brooding on the long protruding point above Cautery Plat.

"Quite a presence, isn't it? Like a petrified shark." Apparitor let his hair down for the wind. "I've just flashed them an Imperial Advisory code requesting a private meeting with the commanding officer. Maroyad will allow us in, because she knows we have her on a list of names, names taken from the ledger of the Paybale Investment Bank, a honeypot where she briefly and foolishly kept her money. It's up to you to use this meeting to our advantage. I won't risk myself in her sight."

"I'll go in there," Barhu said, quite sure of this part, "and I'll force Maroyad to allow *Eternal* into harbor."

"You'll convince a Rear Admiral of the Imperial Navy to allow a plague ship to harbor off her island. I see. Sure you don't want to give up and sail away?"

"I can't run away," Barhu said. "I still have to beat Iraji at Purge."

"That'll never happen."

They both pricked their hearts on the double meaning, and looked away from each other, fearing that instant of shared grief. When he looked back, his jaw moved: a swallow, a twinge of fear, then determination.

"I'm leaving tomorrow," he said.

"What?"

"I'm going to take on water and sail *Helbride* on to Falcrest."

"But—" She glared at him, childishly affronted that he would put anything before her schemes, that he would sail away from Iraji and *Eternal* and the point of deepest crisis. "Svir, we need you here! *Helbride* is the only escape we have! And we—we haven't—"

They hadn't made a deal. Svir hadn't agreed to go back home and make the marriage work. If the marriage didn't work, Yawa's whole dream of a free Aurdwynn would disintegrate.

"Lindon needs me." His jaw set in determination. "I'm going to him."

She stabbed her finger into his right nipple with such precision that he yelped in shock. "What about Iraji? *You* have the files on the navy! If we lose control of Maroyad, she and the Cancrioth are going to massacre each other, and Iraji's on their ship—"

"Oh, don't pretend you need my files. You're just trying to keep me in play for your marriage quandary—"

"Yes! I am, Svir! We *need* you, both of us, Yawa and I! Millions of people in Aurdwynn need you!"

"I don't give a king's pardon for *millions of people!* I care about my people, the ones I can protect!" He seized her hand but did not force her back: just clasped her there, like he wanted to comfort her or break her fingers. "Listen to me. Lindon's sent his danger code. Someone's moved against him, Parliament or Ahanna Croftare. And if it's Croftare, then . . ."

"Then Maroyad would be with her. Shit." No wonder he didn't want to go ashore. "Are we protected?"

"Yes. There's not an officer on this island whose career would survive the release of my files to *Advance*. They do love a navy carcass at the old rag. And they know that if we're harmed those files will come out."

"Good." She took a breath. "Do you know any details about Lindon's situation?"

"Just the code. I don't know if he's holed up in the Admiralty avoiding a Parliamentary summons, or 'resting' in a guarded country house in the Selions, or locked in a cell in the basement of the Bleak House." He took his own long breath through his nose. "So I have to go to him."

"All right," Barhu said, thinking quickly. "This whole matter of your brother and the marriage—we'll delay that until we're in Falcrest and Lindon is safe."

"You can't," Yawa said. "We can't. We've run out of time."

Barhu whirled in shock—the Jurispotence was on her blind side, listening. Her eyes were cruel blue and wholly determined. Svir, seeing her, lost all the tone in his face and throat: everything fell slack, as if he were reverting to a pale cave thing that knew only, entirely, how to survive.

"Why not?" Barhu asked, into the hush. "Why can't we wait?"

"Because the Stakhieczi Necessity has invaded Aurdwynn. Columns of fighters from at least five Mansions are moving south through the duchies Vultjag, Lyxaxu, and Oathsfire."

"Oh," Barhu said.

Svir, expressionless: "Who told you?"

"Execarne. His spies on Isla Cauteria just brought him up to date."

"Have there been battles?"

"No. None yet, and"—Yawa's voice hooked on a bitter note, her childhood Iolynic accent coming out—"perhaps there won't be. Treatymont has ordered the Midlands duchies to burn their crops. The navy is preparing to block the river Inirein and destroy key bridges. There will be no more food going north, and no harvest in the Midlands. The invaders will bog down raiding the peasants for food. Plague release will follow shortly. Aurdywnn will be Falcrest's moat against the Stakhieczi."

"No!" Barhu barked. "That can't be allowed. This is—"

Disastrous was not a strong enough word for it. Vultjag had fallen. The Stakhieczi were pillaging Tain Hu's home.

"I concur," Yawa said, "with whatever dismay you're struggling to articulate. This will be a year for the end of old families."

She turned to Svir and she was merciless. "We must get the Necessary King to stand down his armies before the Masquerade uses plague. But he cannot stand down until he has achieved his objectives: access to fresh water and arable land for the overstrained Mansions. A marriage pact with Governor Heingyl is the only way I can see to satisfy him. And if Baru is not dowry to buy the king's favor, then *your* return must be. You will need to go in person to the mountains to negotiate the marriage."

He stared wildly back at them.

"Svir, please," Barhu tried, in the little Stakhieczi she knew. "Do this for Tain Hu."

Svir guffawed explosively, and the sound startled him: he put his fist in his mouth and stared at them with huge shining eyes.

"You're my punishment," he said. "You don't know it, but the stars have chosen you to punish me. I didn't save Hu. I didn't save Kyprananoke, or even Iraji. So you, Baru, will use the power of Hu's death to compel me to my doom."

His eyes turned upward, as if he could feel all the storms and auroreals of the atmosphere connected by an invisible bolt to the meat of his mind.

"This is my downfall. I have to abandon Lindon. I have to return to everything I fled."

"I can't make you do it, Svir," Barhu lied. She could make him do it. She could threaten to release the truth of his heritage to Farrier.

"If I go," he said, staring up at the peak of Isla Cauteria, "I don't think I can come back. My brother will ask me to stay. And I cannot refuse my brother."

Barhu almost had the courage to reach out and touch his arm. But he would have savaged her for it.

"Why?" she asked him. "Why can't you leave, once the work's done?"

Svir smiled with just his eyes. "You know why."

Because his brother had made himself king of all the mountains and all the Mansions to avenge Svir's kidnapping. How could Svir dishonor that?

W HAT do we do about him?" Barhu murmured.

Yawa threw a fist of stale bread at the duck below the rail. She missed, narrowly. The duck went after the crumbs. "Rapist," she muttered. "I hate ducks."

"Why?"

"I told you. They're rapists. And they're hard to strangle." She rubbed at the nape of her neck. "What do we do about him? Wydd, I don't know. He acts like you can force him to go. Why don't you do it?"

"Do you think it'd work?" A coward's question: she knew it would.

"Hesychast's leverage certainly works to control me. He *will* take pieces out of my brother's head if I don't obey him, Baru. He'll hate it, he'll tell me he hates it, he'll keep himself up at night and wrestle with his conscience. But it won't stop him. He's the softest kind of evil, the kind that thinks through all the hurt it does, and does it anyway."

Yawa threw another bolt of bread at the little green duck. The wind spun it off toward the prow, down past *Helbride*'s dolphin-striker. The striker was an armature of the bowsprit that supported the lines that pulled the bowsprit down, toward the hull, countering the upward pull of the forestay lines. You would think a ship was a static thing: but like everything else it was held together by opposing tensions.

"Right now," Yawa said, "families are losing the only two children I allowed them. Prisons full of men I charged are being broken open, and the men recruited as lackeys and laborers. Fields of crops I seized from the landlords and awarded to tenant farmers are burning. I had good intentions, Baru. Every time. I had sterilization quotas to meet, so I sterilized women with lots of aunts and uncles. I had to show I was tough on my own people, so I filled up the prisons with men I knew deserved it. I had famines to fight, so I built my own food supplies through corruption.

"But it doesn't matter now, does it? I sacrificed my soul for a better future that will never come. All my work just . . . ice sculpture in the spring. The Stakhieczi invade, and the first thing they conquer is all the good work I've ever done."

Yawa was right. Even the letter of provisional governorship she'd given Ake was meaningless now. Her whole plan . . .

"Vultjag," she said, dully. "They've taken Vultjag."

"Oh yes." Yawa shredded a breadcrust into little particles of sawdust. "The children of Vultjag are hiding in the forest so drunken Stakhieczi brave men don't force them into service, or into anything else. Ah, the brave men! The shining knights of the mountains, returned at last to Aurdwynn, where we tell stories about their chivalry and bravery! They're weepers, did you know? They fight battles in tunnels and caves, or out on the crags of the mountains, where one gust of wind can kill a whole company of jagata. They come home with awful dreams, screaming visions, psychotic compulsions. They hurt their wives, terrify their children, and drug themselves to death. Brave men." She snorted. "Right now, Baru, girls who Tain Hu tutored are being taken as war brides—"

"Will you *stop*?" Barhu snapped. "I know these things happen. I don't need the details smeared in my face!"

Yawa thought about this in ominous silence.

"You're right," she said. "I'm sorry. I'm bludgeoning you with my own guilt. And I'm certain the girls in Vultjag are safe. Somehow the Charitable Service could never find them for hygiene inspections, and they had more local collaborators than any mountain men."

Barhu tried to find some hope. "Ake knows Dziransi personally. We could send her up to Vultjag as our emissary to the Stakhieczi. Maybe she can even arrange the marriage in Svir's place."

Yawa scattered crumbs for the duck, to lure it back in for another attack. "Ake's a woman. The Stakhi won't listen. Especially not in matters of the king's marriage. Men decide on marriages, women obey. Remember how Dziransi tried to broker yours?"

Barhu groaned and rubbed her temples. "This would all be so much easier on Taranoke. I could marry your Heingyl Ri, then she could marry the king."

Yawa stroked one of her wooden hairpins. She seemed to be considering a javelin attack on the duck. "You've got to blackmail Svir."

Barhu's thoughts ticked through loud, painful permutations of the scenario. How he would rage. How he would rebuke her.

"And you have to do it immediately. Right now he's scared for Lindon. He wants to go to Falcrest. Which is, of course, the place where he's most useless to us. We need him in the north."

"Yawa," Barhu said, quietly. "*I* could go."

She laughed. Then she looked at Barhu and her mouth narrowed. "You're serious? Go to the king as dowry?"

"Yes."

"Do you know what he'll do to you? When he's done scalping you and bleeding you upside down, you won't have the dignity of a sky burial or mummification. They'll take the salt from your body. You'll be animal feed. And if you're unlucky, you won't be dead yet."

"If Hu was willing to die for Vultjag . . . how can I do any less?"

"No. You can't." Yawa's ferocity surprised her. "Absolutely not. I won't allow it."

"Why?"

"Because if you do that, then I might as well have lobotomized you back on Kyprananoke. I would be wrong to have spared you. And I don't fucking like to be wrong."

Barhu was so unexpectedly moved by this that she had to cough away the crease in her throat.

"It'll be cholera," Yawa said.

"What?"

"We've finally come to an island of slopes. The Llosydanes were tall. Kypra-nanoke was flat. Here, everything runs downhill. Sooner or later all the water that falls on this island reaches the coast, and the towns. If the Cancrioth can't get Kettling ashore, they'll use cholera. The sewers are good, but if cholera reaches the upstream lakes, or taints the shellfish beds . . ."

"Good," Barhu said, with rising hope. "Good!"

Yawa stared at her. "Good?"

"Cholera would be devastating here!" If a few thousand people started shit-ting out twelve liters of virulent gray fluid a day, *some* of it would get into drinking water, and spread. "That strengthens the Brain's negotiating position. She might be willing to talk."

Yawa sighed. "Baru, there's something else you should know."

Barhu groaned. It was never anything good.

"Follow my hand." Yawa pointed north and west of Cautery Plat, to a place on the shining blue and forest green of the coast, to the left of *Helbride*'s course.

Barhu frowned along Yawa's finger at the shoreline. "Yes. What is it?"

"Do you see the river Rubiyya?" Yawa traced the silver band of the river, shading gold as it ran down to the sea.

"I see it."

"Can you see the structures on the bay where the Rubiyya meets the sea?"

"Yes."

"There's an experimental colony at the mouth of the river. A test to see how tropical people fare on a temperate island with similar volcanic soil."

Oh no. "Yawa. What sort of people?"

She smiled with grim humor. "Guess."

"Kyprananoki?" Perhaps there were survivors, enough to remember and rebuild—

"No. Your people. Souswardi—that is, Taranoki people. About a thousand of them."

The farthest she'd ever come from her home, and still she found it waiting for her. Tau would call it trim.

"Have you considered," Yawa murmured, "what you'll do if the Brain's a fanatic? What if she's willing to sacrifice *Eternal*, and herself, and any hope of retrieving Abdumasi Abd, in order to strike that first blow?"

"She won't," Barhu said. "She's too smart."

But she remembered that grove on Kyprananoke where shattered children stained the coconut wood. If all logical and ethical paths toward freedom have been twisted by your conqueror to lead instead to submission, then aban-don logic. Abandon ethics. She'd once considered how the Oriati might resist

Falcrest's infiltration so well: by holding to basic principles of kindness, charity, and honesty, they prevented themselves from succumbing to the pressures of circumstance. Circumstance could be manipulated. Principle could not.

Neither could absolute, immovable, irreconcilable defiance.

The Brain might rationally choose to operate on a policy of unilateral violence.

And if she did . . .

"There were those among the ilykari," Yawa said, "who chose to serve Falcrest, the very power that persecuted them, because they believed *so strongly* that my master Hesychast was the virtue Himu incarnate. What if the Brain believes so strongly in our destruction that she would destroy herself to achieve it?"

"She cast a spell on me," Barhu said. It was the only confidence she could offer. "She won't attack until I've returned to her and completed our covenant."

"You have a tremendous faith in Cancrioth magic."

"She cast the spell in public, Yawa. If the spell is not completed, everyone will doubt her power."

"What, exactly, were the terms of this covenant?" Yawa asked. "What bargain did you fail to complete?"

Barhu, who had glanced away to the left, pretended she hadn't heard.

G ET it over with," Svir snapped.

Barhu looked up in shock from the Great Game arrangement on the map table. She had been replaying Farrier's strategy against the Oriati, observing, with some disquiet, how perfectly her own plan might serve to achieve it. "What?"

"I saw you and Yawa pecking at each other. I know what happens when you talk." He struck at the doorjamb with the flat of his hand but arrested his palm so swiftly that it made no sound: Barhu leapt in fright at the clap of silence. "Blackmail me. Send me to make your marriage."

"Svir, you don't want this—"

"What I want is some damn consistency! Either you'll sacrifice people for your purposes, or you won't! Just don't," he snarled and came two steps toward her, "don't treat me *more* compassionately than Tain Hu. It makes me feel like I need to be better than her. And I don't like it when people expect the impossible of me."

She closed her own playing piece, the splintered pawn that represented Agonist, in her fist.

People were hashes. You could only see their output, the passwords they

showed to the world. You could not know the truth of them. But with suf-
ficient time and study you might become familiar with the functions that
transformed the shape of a man's soul into the choices he made: the hash that
communicated Svir-in-truth to the Svir who Barhu perceived.

She believed, as much as she could believe anything about anyone, that Svir
genuinely loved Lindon Satamine. She believed that he would throw away all
his other work to rush home and protect him.

"Svir," she said, "do you believe in trim?"

He laughed. "No."

"Fine. Well, listen anyway. I . . . I choose to believe that I know you. A little
about you, at least. And that makes you real to me in a way it wouldn't have
before . . ." She waved her hand toward the devastation they had left behind on
Kyprananoke. "So it's hard for me to coerce you now."

He spoke in Stakhi. "Do you remember what I said to you, after Aminata
passed? About how there was no easy way out of the hole? How you would be
climbing out for the rest of your life?"

"I remember, Svir." She faltered: that brief rapport with him was so precious to her that she had not wanted to wear it out by remembering it too often.
Leave it in a glass case in the back of the vaults, and marvel, once in a while,
that it existed at all. "Why?"

"Do you remember that I told you I thought you'd die? Because you had no
one to hold inside you, here"—he made the same gesture, thumping his chest
above his heart—"to keep you from destroying yourself?"

She held him through the short beat of usual eye contact, knowing he
would look away in discomfort, and then look back: that piercing, brutally
radiant return, the true Svir, the lightning-flash intensity of his thought.

"Yes," she said. "Why?"

"I should not be one of the things you choose to keep in your heart. Not
because I don't deserve it. But because you and I are cryptarchs, and you must,
you *must* be able to wield me as a tool. You think that you don't want to do
that." He shook his head. "But what you *really* don't want is to fall into grief
again. You don't want to think of yourself the way you did when you were at
your lowest."

"I don't understand what you're telling me."

"I'm telling you to get it over with! You have no choice. Tell me that if I defy
you, you'll tell Farrier who I am, and he'll have me in court faster than you
can say *hereditary sin*. Or you'll tell Hesychast that I'm an undiluted source of
High Stakhieczi royal lineage, and he'll lock me up for his use."

Svir's hands landed on the far side of the map table, and all the pawns and symbols quivered. "You have the upper hand, because you don't have a fucking hostage. And you know it."

"If I promise to protect Lindon and his family, will you go to your brother and negotiate this marriage?"

"No. That is not acceptable. I will not make a deal with you."

"Don't make me do this," she said, softly. "Please. I *will* protect Lindon Satamine with all my power. Him and his family and your child. Just, first, go to the Wintercrest Mountains and make your brother end his war on Aurdwynn. Is that enough?"

He grinned ferally at her. "No. I'll never go back to the Wintercrests of my own free will. You wanted this power, Baru. Will you use it or not?"

She thought about Svir, Svir's childhood, how he had fled into unknown eastern realms to escape his home. She thought about the man he loved, the child he'd fathered with that man's wife. She thought about how he'd protected Iraji's secret even when he could've gained so much through betrayal.

She put all those coins into an account. Then she weighed that account against the Stakhieczi invasion and the fate of Tain Hu's home.

There was, by that logic, no choice.

But she felt that she had a choice anyway.

"Apparitor," she said, giving him the honor of a firm gaze and a cold eye, "you will not go to Falcrest to defend Lindon Satamine. You will write him a letter encouraging his resignation, and give it to me. Beyond that his fate will be mine to decide.

"You will go north to the Wintercrests, to arrange your brother's marriage to Heingyl Ri, the Governor of Aurdwynn, and the end of his invasion. As dowry, you will tell him that Heingyl Ri offers to him the claim to the Mansion Uczenith, passed to her, by marriage, from the consort of the Vultjag lord who killed Uczenith's lord and heirs. You will use your knowledge of Stakhieczi law and custom to justify this claim.

"And if you do not, then I will have your royal blood entered in the Metademe's records, so that all Falcrest knows you are the living avatar of the great anathema called *King*. Do you understand me?"

"Is that all?" he said, calmly. "No dagger aimed at Lindon and his family? They hate the man who plays both sides more than the ordinary sodomite, you know. Because he passes on his sin."

Barhu shook her head.

"No threat of execution for sodomy? No hot iron plunged down my throat?"

Barhu winced.

"Ah, her qualms show." He looked as if he would laugh at her discomfort, but the sound died. "A Falcresti king was executed that way, once. Not out of any particular need to punish his indulgence in men—that was, at the time, no more than a bad habit, like opiates or cheating at cards. But that king's vice and his execution became connected by gossip, gossip became history, history became law." He put his spread fingers to his forehead, pointing up: he was miming a crown. "The punishment is still on the books. But now it is for sodomites, not kings."

"I would never, ever threaten you with that," Barhu said, shakily. "I promise you on Tain Hu's grave I wouldn't."

His alien eyes were stranger for the wonder in them. "I believe you, now. I even believe that in your own pathological and frightening way you loved her. Listen, Baru. I *will* go to the Wintercrests. I will go to my brother. I will even accept the very strong possibility that I will never return. But."

He leaned forward across the map table until, very purposefully, he had blotted out the entire world with his shadow.

"You," he enunciated, "have just fucked up. You have put your foot in *my* trap. Because now that I know what you genuinely want, now that I know that *only* I can execute it, I am capable of ruining your entire scheme. So I will do this thing for you; but only because it secures me leverage over you.

"I want seven hundred and fifty thousand fiat notes deposited in the accounts of the concerns I control. I want them within the year. I want Lindon Satamine and his entire family safely extracted from Falcrest, provided with legends, and delivered into my care, or at least into their own.

"And if any harm comes to them, Baru, I will tell my Brother the King of Mansions that the Duchy Vultjag is full of Masquerade agents. I will name for him the villages and even the houses where they lurk. I will tell him of the slow plagues incubating in the children, and the blights they nurture in their gardens. With fire and with sword I will murder everything you love in Aurdwynn. And then I will carpet the Waterfall Keep in the festering corpses of Tain Hu's people, and the rats will dance pavane across them. Do you understand me?"

She nodded. It was only fair.

He beamed in satisfaction. "There. Mutual leverage. Just the way cryptarchs should behave."

22

WAR MAGIC

ONCE more Bebble Auranic had sunburnt his balls.
It was uncouth for anyone's name to align with their profession; that carried the suggestion of inherited class. But Bebble Auranic often felt that he had perhaps overcompensated away from the family goldsmithing business by becoming a fisherman.

Astride his catamaran yesterday, he'd forgotten the sun's reflection off the water, and so burnt the underdangle of his tangle. It had been so *sweaty* in his linens. Could he be blamed for letting his fruit drop now and then? Everyone in the guild had laughed at him, and he deserved it, he was a damn fool; ten more points on his service exam, he could've scored *ten more points* and escaped the lifelong brand of an oars-mark on his jacket, *limited capabilities, restricted responsibility.* He could've been a maker of unguents. A pharmacist! A—

Something bumped the stern of his catamaran.

Bebble turned. The distant shore and the buildings of Cautery Plat wavered in heat haze.

A whale cruised a circle round his little boat. Water poured off a dark scarred back that curved up to a fin like a great tooth. Sweet virtues, it was an orca! An orca in the Ashen Sea! It must have come up along the Segu coast in the west, through the islands, out of the Black Tea Ocean where no one of Bebble's race had ever been and returned—

The orca flicked a spray of water across the stern, drenching his lunch of hard bread and smoked fish. Bebble didn't care. Bebble had just lost his appetite.

The orca's fin had a blade edge. A cutting surface. Collared there by some strange armsman who ministered to whales.

The whale blew a gout of water through its blowhole and whistled like an elephant miscarriage's last breath. Bebble screamed. He screamed at the sound and he screamed at the human skull calcified into the huge bony tumor that stared eternally backward into the tumble of the orca's passage.

The orca curved back toward him. Its eye fixed on him. Its jaw yawned. It had white laughing teeth.

* * *

A NNALILA Fortress was invincible.
  Annalila Fortress had fallen.

Stripes of black and red dye slashed the white cliffs to confuse the aim of distant siege engines. Hwacha batteries bristled from fortified promontories. Rust-flecked pendulum chains and tanks of vilest acid awaited the call to repel assaulters. Cave harbors guarded squadrons of boats. Annalila Point was not just a weapon but a home of weapons, a place like a beehive, generating and sustaining instruments of hurt.

And yet, without any attack, without even a whimper of resistance, she had fallen. Parliament had cursed this fortress with powerful magic. Barhu could see it even from *Ascentatic*'s launch, where she rode beside Captain Nullsin. The signal flags abandoned mid-code, the sentry posts where noon light flashed off unwatched telescopes. Sea gates lowered and barred. A lonely officer patrolled the western bluffs, armed with nothing but a spyglass and a rocket pistol as a panic signal.

"She's sequestered her books," Barhu murmured to the man beside her. News of Parliament's fiscal strike against the navy had come in with the mail packets to *Ascentatic*. "Put all her crew on unpaid leave. They must be in barracks?"

Captain Nullsin nodded quietly. "For now. Probably drunk as rats on watered rum. Payday was yesterday, and Maroyad would've had to give them something to keep them calm when they didn't get their wages."

"I thought the navy held a season's pay in arrears, to discourage desertion?" The navy's officer corps was professional and disciplined, but navy sailors were as greedy, miserable, and prone to desertion as any fighting crew. A hold had to be maintained.

"We do. But that doesn't mean there's three months' pay actually sitting in the vaults. It just means they collect spring's pay in summer, summer's pay in autumn, and so forth." Nullsin tapped his hammer anxiously against his right wrist. "Maroyad knows half her sailors will hop down to the harbor and sign up on a merchant, given a chance. Merchant pay's always better, since Parliament won't let us raise our wages. So she keeps them drunk."

"Baru," Yawa murmured, in Iolynic, "if *Eternal* realizes the island is undefended . . ."

"We can make a show of force when *Eternal* arrives. That's all we need. A convincing show of force, to deter attack."

And if it was not convincing, the Brain would realize she could walk ashore with buckets of Kettling blood and start bathing the children.

Two marine officers (Barhu was amused to spy the insignia of a company captain and a lieutenant commander, doing work that would normally be left to able sailors) hauled open the sea gate to admit them. "Rear Admiral Maroyad's compliments, Your Excellences, Captain Nullsin," the captain said. "Please come with us."

CAPTAIN Nullsin. Report."
    Rear Admiral Samne Maroyad rose through a cloud of mint-cigarette smoke. Barhu's first impressions were of a pale brown bastè ana woman in navy reds, long of body but short of limb. There was a thin place at the collar of her uniform where she'd rubbed her admiral's insignia against the fabric. Otherwise she was immaculate.

This was the woman who'd sent Aminata to find Barhu.

Captain Asmee Nullsin saluted with his good hand. "Mam. It is my sworn duty to introduce the Emperor's own enmasqued representatives Durance and Agonist. As a servant of the Republic and its people, I have, wherever possible, done my utmost to obey both your lawful orders and the Hierarchic Qualm. But where they conflicted, I—"

"Spare me the legalist bullshit, Asmee." Maroyad's eyes flicked between Barhu and Yawa. "I see your mission was compromised. Lieutenant Commander Aminata would be here if it was at all possible, so she's wounded, or under arrest, or . . ."

"Missing," Barhu said, with an uncaring hardness she had to falsify. "Presumed dead. She gave her life to destroy Juris Ormsment."

Maroyad looked at them across the pine barrier of her desk. Through the windows behind her a swarm of fishing felucca filed out of Cautery Plat harbor, unaware of cholera and cancer, innocent of what the wind brought close.

Barhu watched Maroyad pack up all her hopes and ambitions, stow them away, and make herself ready for the worst. *Make a fire list,* the teachers in school had told Barhu. *The things you must save when you smell smoke.*

Maroyad tapped her desk with one forefinger. "I heard that Ormsment had abandoned her post in Aurdwynn. She's dead?"

"Yes." Barhu's blue-tinged polestar mask helped her keep the confidence in her tone: Kimbune had brought it from *Eternal,* bless her. "Though not before she murdered several hundred Imperial Advisory staff, sacked a Morrow Ministry station, destroyed Oriati diplomatic escorts in battle, and knowingly attacked a vessel with the Oriati ambassador aboard. A matter of significant concern to the Emperor, as you can imagine."

Yawa leaned corvine on the back of a chair. "Paramount concern. The Emperor Itself has taken personal interest." It did not take a personal interest in anything, being a lobotomite straitjacketed to a marble throne, but that made no difference. The power was in the Throne behind the throne.

Maroyad stared into the clamshell ashtray on her desk. "Asmee, precisely what happened to Lieutenant Commander Aminata?"

"She died on *Sulane,* mam. She went aboard to . . . to be sure it had to be done. When she failed to convince Province Admiral Ormsment to stand down, she begged me to fire on her. And I complied."

His voice wanted forgiveness. His face said he would never accept it.

Maroyad nodded tightly. "I see. She was an extremely promising officer. I will make personally certain that she receives Parliament's notice."

"Difficult to do." Yawa's machinated rasp, air blown through ticking gears, made Maroyad grimace. "How can Parliament take notice of circumstances the navy can never admit? 'Brevet-Captain Aminata persuaded the navy to murder its own flag-ranked traitor.' That'll make for a difficult commendation, don't you think?"

Maroyad flicked her chin to the door. "Asmee. You're dismissed." She waited for the door to click shut behind him. "Lock it."

Barhu turned the steel key. Tiny complicated things happened inside the door. Yawa, ghost-slow in her quarantine gown, descended upon one of the chairs. Buttresses and ribs creaked as she sat.

Maroyad folded her hands on the desk and composed her face. "I have no knowledge of any seditious, mutinous, or provocative acts conducted by officers of the navy."

"Of course you don't," Yawa said. They had agreed she would take the harsher tack. "You were never in contact with Juris Ormsment about her intention to mutiny. You did not conceal a vitally important prisoner from Parliament and the Republic. And you were *certainly* never in communication about this prisoner with Province Admiral Falcrest, Ahanna Croftare. Making her complicit in your conspiracy to conceal facts material to the Imperial Republic's safety. None of those things happened, hm?"

"I have no information to contribute to these accusations, whether by admission or by omission."

Barhu slid her chair closer to the admiral's desk. "Rear Admiral, please. We know you have Abdumasi Abd. We know you warned Juris Ormsment about my role in provoking the Oriati attack on Aurdwynn. We even know you urged her not to move against me."

Maroyad stiffened. "Move against *you*? You're Baru Cormorant?"

Barhu nodded silently.

"You little *fuck*," Maroyad hissed. "*You* drove her to mutiny. And now you've killed her, too?"

"Your own loyal sailors killed her. Captain Nullsin and Lieutenant Commander Aminata did their duty to the navy and to the Empire."

"Oh, I'm sure they thought they were doing the right thing. Because that's what you do, isn't it? You make us believe we have a duty to die for you."

Maroyad began to rise from her chair. Yawa tapped her finger threateningly, as if she wore a judge's steel-tipped gauntlet, but Maroyad did not stop.

"What did you tell Aminata? That she had to die to protect the Republic? Or was it blackmail? Did you have some sealed file on her, a bribe she took, a man she shouldn't have fucked?" Arctic voice, cold as wind through frozen sails, tearing at iced-up spars. "You've been baiting the Oriati toward open war since last autumn. Enticing them to strike Aurdwynn. And for what? So you could tell Parliament they were conspiring against us? 'War, Parliamins'"—she was baying now, like a preacher or a wolf—"'war is the only balm for this burn on our dignity. There's timber to be taken, and mines to be dug, and great reserves of gold, and new crops to be found. Cheap labor, and untouched reserves of culture, and babies, so many *babies*, to clean and render hygienic! We'll force our way through Segu Mbo to the Black Tea Ocean and all the islands of spice and platinum beyond! And on that note, we'd better be sure we have the right admirals commanding our ships—agreeable, constructively minded men, men with stakes in the proper concerns, who know how to send the plunder to the right purses—'"

"There's a Cancrioth ship on its way to Isla Cauteria," Barhu said.

Maroyad sank hard back into her chair. It was like watching Iraji pass into syncope, except the thing about to obliterate Maroyad's consciousness was not faint but rage.

"What ship," she said.

Barhu did not need to explain herself. "We believe that they will negotiate for the return of Abdumasi Abd, who is a member of their secret society. That gives us a chance to reach a broader agreement, one which might avert war entirely. It would entail new trade relations with the Oriati: concessions from their markets to convince Falcrest that war is less profitable than peace. That would be in the navy's interest, would it not?"

"*What fucking ship? How soon?*"

"They'll be arriving tomorrow. Unless they put up more sail, risk a night approach in waters they don't know. Then perhaps tonight."

"Fuck," Maroyad said. "Fuck!" She snatched up the clamshell ashtray from her desk and hurled it at the abstract paintings of sailing ships on the wall beside Yawa. It ricocheted and did not break. "You bring this to me when Parliament's just castrated my command—those worm-shit *fucks*!"

The ashtray rattled on the floor, turning around some unsustainable axis, and collapsed. Yawa's breath ticked in and out through the voice changer.

"Parliament—" Maroyad smoothed her palms on her desk. "Parliament has rendered the navy insolvent. I have operating reserves, but if I expend them, my sailors will know I can't make good on their back pay. They'll desert."

"Leave the money to us," Barhu said. "We have accounts to draw upon."

"Is the Cancrioth ship a threat to my island?"

"It's not your concern, Rear Admiral."

"It's my only fucking concern! It's *what I exist for*! This is home territory of the Imperial Republic! Will they attack us as they attacked Aurdwynn?"

"That judgment no longer belongs to you." Barhu wished she would not shout so loud. "You will obey the Emperor's edict. We have determined that the Cancrioth ship will be granted harbor."

"And if I don't obey?"

Yawa leaned forward as if bending to study carrion. "We will use the evidence available to us to implicate both you and Ahanna Croftare in Ormsment's crimes. You will face charges of permissive mutiny, grand treason by omission, conspiracy, and material aid to an enemy of the Republic. The investigation will taint every woman who belongs to the so-called 'Merit Admirals.' Your entire faction in the Admiralty will be purged."

Maroyad looked as if she might yet clamber over her desk to slit their throats. But she knew her duty.

"I seem to be in your power," she said, with bitter calm. "You will find, however, that there are principles I will not compromise."

"We understand," Barhu said. "You should know, Rear Admiral, that we never asked your officers to compromise themselves, either. When Aminata made her choice, she did it by her own free will."

"Don't matronize me. I don't give a shit what kind of nostrums you've boiled up to soothe me. If you had a single short cunt-hair of moral character, you'd be here asking me for my help, not blackmailing me into it." She fell back into her chair. "Tell me about the Cancrioth ship. No. Wait. I'll get that from Nullsin, who actually understands ships. Are you serious about bringing them across the Caul for *negotiations*? What could you possibly negotiate with these . . . things?"

"You don't really want to know, do you?" Barhu reminded her, calm and smooth as porcelain.

"No. I suppose I don't." Maroyad stared down at her white clenched knuckles. "This won't go away, will it? The blackmail. You'll keep on me as long as I'm useful. So I want you to know, right now, that if you continue to push me—"

Yawa laughed. It came out as a blast of tangled steel. "You should consider yourself lucky. We can trust you now, Maroyad. We can trust Ahanna Croftare. Because we have a hold on you. There's an Empire Admiralty in her future, and a Province Admiralty in yours."

"Milk from snakes," Maroyad murmured.

"Oh, don't play innocent," Yawa snapped. "You made your choices. No one forced you to conceal Abd, lie to Parliament, and keep silent about what you *knew* Ormsment might do. Hundreds of people are dead because of her. You could've stopped it."

Maroyad smiled briskly at her. "I'm sure we can spend all day arguing over the moral weather gage here. I just hope you know what becomes of politicians who think they make fine military leaders. I'll have freedom to choose my own tactics, I hope?"

"Certainly. Although I strongly suggest you put a torchship alongside *Eternal* when she moors. They'll respect *that* threat." Barhu rose from the chair, careful to turn right so that she would not blindside Maroyad.

"An entire *torchship*? Do you know how many frigates we could sail for the cost of—"

"Believe me," Barhu said. "When you see *Eternal*, you'll understand."

"When this goes wrong," Maroyad said, "I know I'll be blamed. It's not a coincidence that you chose a bastè ana admiral to blackmail, is it? Any more than it's a coincidence the Emperor chose foreigners—and you are *both* foreigners, I suspect—to execute this little intrigue. We're all easier to scapegoat."

"Then let's not do anything worth scapegoating, shall we?" Yawa rasped.

"Fine." Maroyad puffed her cheeks and blew: that universal *fuck me* gesture. "Well. Consider me swayed by political authority. Now, if you'll make yourselves scarce, I have a ball to cancel."

"Wait!" Barhu put her maimed hand out. "What ball?"

"Didn't you see the bunting on your way in?" Maroyad pushed a schedule book across the desk, ragged with inserts and amendments. "Her Excellence Heingyl Ri is hosting the Governor's Ball tonight, in my Arsenal Ballroom, with half the island in attendance. I was going to panhandle for donations to keep the harbor patrol running. But if the island's in danger of attack, then I can't very well hold a social function—"

"You won't cancel it." Barhu thought very quickly. *Eternal* would not be here until tomorrow; they had opened the distance on the approach to Cauteria, and she still had a torpedo wound in her hull. The ball was too good an opportunity to pass up. "Yes. The ball will go forward, and you'll make only one change."

Maroyad glared at her. "What now?"

"Tell Governor Ri she's been supplanted. Announce that Her Excellence Agonist, victorious in Aurdwynn, will be the guest of honor."

Barhu had a proposal to make.

I'M so thirsty," Osa groaned. "I'd peel the rest of my face off for a drink."

"I thought you were a miserere," Aminata said.

"What's a miserere?"

"Little daggers they used in Old Falcrest to mercy kill the survivors of royal torture. I think."

"I'm not a little dagger."

"It's figurative, Osa. For people who think life is about enduring pain."

"I suppose I think that," Osa said, "except I like to complain, too. Knife now."

Very carefully, Aminata passed Shao Lune's sharpened haircomb down to Osa. There would be no retrieving it if it fell. Nothing beneath them except the bumpy white tongue of *Eternal*'s wake.

She and Osa had climbed down the stern of the ship from the windows of their prison. Not ten feet below them, where the hull cut away to make room for *Eternal*'s mighty rudder, a fence of rusty nails jutted from the wood: hasty measure to keep divers off the hull.

The Cancrioth were not seasoned soldiers, and they were not expert prison-makers, either. Aminata had discovered that the windows of the stern sunroom could, with some trickery, be undone. Then, if you trusted your clambering skills, you could descend to the deck below, stick a knife between the rattan shutters, and saw through the piece of cord holding them closed.

This would be the first, inglorious step in retaking *Eternal*.

"They keep the pigs down there," Osa said. "Tau told me that. I guess they didn't want to waste glass windows on a pigpen."

Now Osa wedged Shao Lune's haircomb into the windowjamb, hammered it in with the heel of her hand, and began to saw at the rope.

"Get Iraji now," she grunted.

"You're sure you'll be ready?" Was *she* even ready? This was all Tau-indi's plan, especially the insane and sorcerous parts. Why was she going along with it? Because the alternative was waiting to die with everyone else aboard when *Eternal* attacked Isla Cauteria.

"I'll be ready," Osa said. "Don't drop him."

Aminata pulled herself back up. Iraji waited, curled acrobatically in the window. "Hi," Aminata said, cheerfully: she liked seeing him there. "Get on."

Last night, when the tension and the guilt of staying away from him had become too much, when she'd driven herself round like a one-oared boat wondering if Tau's "war magic" would drive Iraji permanently mad, she had asked to see him, alone, in one of the other staterooms. Innibarish had allowed it.

She'd apologized to Iraji for avoiding him. She'd apologized for checking the cuffs and collar of her scratchy half-washed uniform instead of looking at him. Apologized for pretending that they had not hidden in *Eternal*'s underbelly together, both afraid for their lives. Apologized most of all for pretending that they had not become friends in the process.

Iraji had kissed her.

Aminata had made a face. "Weird," she'd said. "That's not what I came for."

"I'm sorry," he'd said, his own face rather stubbly, not at his usual sleek finest. "I thought, after all the things Tau's been teaching me, that you might . . . you might think I was wrong, somehow."

"No, not that, just—well, a little of that," she laughed, oh, how would she explain this navy thing to Iraji, "but you and I, we went through some action together. So it's like you're my shipmate now."

"And thus off limits?"

"Yes."

"Oh," he'd said, frowning intently, except at the corner of his smiling eyes. "Well, we'd best fix that."

And through a little laughter, and a surprising mutual comfort, they had come to hold each other, kissed each other upon neck and wrist and breast (not mouths: it seemed too sentimental), until they came together, kneeling, her legs parted across his just like she'd imagined it would be. Aminata had moved upon him quietly, warmly, looking him in the eye when she had her eyes open at all.

"You're brave," she'd told him. "Coming back here for Baru. Taking that poison. You're so brave."

"*You're* brave. That ship—they said you were on *Sulane* when it burnt—you saved everyone here."

And they had gone on like that, whispering praise to each other, things they might have been too abashed to say, if they were not so carnally bashed: you're magnificent, you're good, you will do it all so well.

Afterward, washing him off her stomach, she'd asked, "Was this some kind of . . . spy thing? Because you work for the red-haired man? Is this like the homme fatale in the books, where you keep me loyal by . . ."

"No, no." He'd looked at her upside down, his head thrown back over the edge of the bed, arms dangling, shoulders magnificent, every cord and swell of muscle glistening with sweat. "I only meant it as . . . I like to give things to my friends. Are we friends?"

"Friends. Yeah. I think, uh"—she'd waved her hand between them—"we probably needed to get this out of the way."

"Yes. I could tell."

"I'm not sure if I'll want to do it again."

"That's all right."

She'd paused, struck by that thought. "Iraji," she said, "I don't think I've ever fucked anyone I really liked before."

He'd beamed innocently. "First time for everything."

ETERNAL'S bow dipped into a trough. The tall stern came up. Aminata's stomach rose with the whole ship. In the windowsill above her, Iraji yelped and clung to the sill.

"Come down!" she called.

"I can climb after you—"

"No chance, landlubber," Aminata said, for although Iraji was probably nimbler than her on land, he'd never been a mast-top boy. "Hup hup."

He lowered himself by his fingertips (the showoff) until he could curl his legs around her waist and fasten his arms over her neck. "Got me?"

"You'd better hope so." Finger by toe she carried him down to the open shutters and the pigpens. "Are you really sure you want to do this?"

"If I think about it, I might faint, and then you'd drop me."

"Not fair."

He dismounted, jackknifed in through the window. Aminata got her calves and thighs inside, ducked under the windowframe, and slid to the floor.

The pigs screamed at her.

They lived in the dry filth of pens left too long unwatered, their dark dehydrated urine puddled beneath sunken bellies and blue-tinged skin. They trembled. They raised their trotters like prayer or jerked on their flanks in seizure. And from their tiny heads the baneflesh grew in fat tubules, bulbs, fans, shining red-black nodules, craters and strings, films like fungus across parched membranes of destroyed scalp.

This was what Iraji would have to put in his mouth.

There are no laws of magic, Tau-indi had told Iraji. *There are neither rules nor calculations. Magic is akin to the human soul, and also to the cataclysms of the deepest earth, and also to the stars. It is like the enigma which separates a dead rock from living coral. I mean, very plainly, that magic is akin to the questions we ask, not to the answers we possess.*

You cannot calculate or determine what magic will do. You cannot use magic to answer a problem.

But you can use magic to ask for a solution.

And most basic of all solutions is the apotropaic spell.

Iraji found a piglet. "Knife," he called.

Grim-faced Osa gave him the sharpened comb.

I do know this, Tau-indi had said. *Those who know magic most powerfully are also those who most powerfully suffer its effect. I cannot arm you with the radiant hands of a Cancrioth sorcerer, or allow you to burn without pain. I cannot make you giant like Innibarish, or unlock the secret strength of your body so that you can run five days without rest.*

But I can teach you what you must know to confront the Brain and free the Eye. I can teach you the annulment of power. What spell is more common than the ward against bad luck? The aversion of malign influence? Everywhere but Falcrest, the common farmer knows and casts this spell.

I can teach you this spell. And you, Iraji, you in particular, can make it powerful beyond denial.

Iraji began to cut at the pig's flesh. Aminata's gorge came up hard but she knew he had it worse. When at last he rose with the baneflesh-swollen brain of the piglet in his hand, she had to catch him and steady him. "Are you all right?"

You, child, Tau-indi said, *are a powerful tutelary, by which I mean a soul associated with a place, power, or idea. You are of the Cancrioth but you removed yourself from them. Do you see?*

You have associated yourself with the estrangement of their power. You faint when the idea of the Cancrioth strikes you. You collapse their power into nothing. You do it in your mind, in your brain.

But the Brain will not fear you, for you have no immortata, no power of your own.

So you must claim one. Only with flesh to fuel your magic will they respect your threat.

"I'm fine," he said, and then fell face-forward into Osa's arms.

"Catch it!" Osa shouted, and Aminata, crying out in disgust, lunged and got the bloody mass of brain as it slid from Iraji's hands.

Osa clapped the boy on the back as he moaned and squirmed. "Get his feet, will you?"

My life is a joke, Aminata thought. She kept the wet brain in her fist and scooped up Iraji's legs on her forearms, so that they could stretch the boy out horizontal and force blood to his head. He came back with a jerk that nearly pulled him free. "I'm here! I'm here. I'm sorry." When he saw Aminata holding the pig's tumor-riddled brain, he made a face of the sweetest guilt. "I can hold that now."

"Can you do magic? Or will you faint?"

"Yes, just, you'd better, ah, carry me around like this. Keep my head low."

So off they went to retake the ship, carrying Iraji like a plank, with the piglet brain cupped in his black-inked hands.

T HEY went forward belowdecks.

"I remember this," Aminata said, thinking of how Masako had brought her to see the Brain. "Next frame we need to—"

From the stairway ahead emerged a funereal procession of men and women in white robes with domed hoods like a beekeeper's. They took one step at a time, agonizingly cautious, and between each step they stopped to readjust their footing and their distance from each other. An escort of Masako's rapier-armed Termites followed them at a careful distance.

In the papooses slung across their chests, the white-robed people carried cylinders of brown spotted glass.

Before Aminata could bellow halt or Imperial Navy, get on the floor the nearest Termite threw up his hand in desperate warning. Everyone behind him froze.

"Death," he said, in Aphalone, very clearly, very slowly. "Do you under-stand? If one of them breaks, if it gets out . . ."

Oh kings and queens of anguish. They were carrying plague up to the rock-ets. Dysentery, cholera, typhoid, buboes—it could be anything. It could be the Kettling itself. Aminata thought that she could see tiny shapes moving behind the grown glass, like dirt in turbulent water, like fleas or gnats. . . .

"Excuse me," Iraji said, in soft, polite Aphalone. "In my hands I bear the baneflesh, with all its fearsome appetites. If those people carrying the glass are Cancrioth, and I think that they are, they will be very frightened to see it. They might drop something."

The Termite looked at the brain in Iraji's hands, at the fans and tubules of cancer grown between his fingers.

"I want no part of this," he said. "You do your magic with the magicians. I'm bringing these vivariums up to the deck."

"Where is the Eye, please?"

"I won't help you."

Iraji lifted the brain. The Termite said, quickly, "In the deckhouse, amidships."

Afterward, Aminata muttered, "I don't know who was more relieved to see the other go."

"They were more afraid of us than we were of them." Osa's silent tears of pain sheeted her burns. "The worst they could've done was kill us. Our boy here could murder their souls."

She settled Iraji's shoulders higher in her grip. They climbed steep, narrow stairs, up into the palace deckhouse.

Here the Brain's faction had tiled the floor and the walls with red clay tablets, covering up the patterns in the teak below. There was nothing engraved on the tablets. They were blank. Apotropaic magic, Aminata supposed.

They came to a short corridor, and a door covered entirely in tablets. The armed Termites guarding it could have been for any prisoner—but those tablets were cladding to keep the Eye trapped.

"What happens now?" Osa whispered.

"We go and open that door," Iraji said.

"What about the guards?"

"Well," Iraji said, shifting in Aminata's grip, "I will have to cast a spell."

He stuffed the piglet brain into his mouth. The worst of it, the sores and shiny blackseed spots and thick flesh tubers, protruded through his lips. He made a soft gagging noise but did not faint.

"Oh kings," Aminata moaned.

Iraji rose from Aminata and Osa's arms and went down the saltwater-warped floor of the deckhouse corridor toward the Eye's cabin. He put his black-inked hands up in warning.

The guards saw him coming.

It wasn't the first magic Aminata had ever seen. The Oriati pirates she'd fought commonly used sorcery, the sympathetic destruction of Falcresti flags and uniforms and the use of spirit circuits to hold back fire. But this was the most violent, the most sudden, the most appalling in its effect.

He screamed at them through the cancer, and when the Termites heard that wail, when they saw the moaning man coming at them with cancer in his teeth, they all began to shout and to pull at each other, a diffusion of fear, so they would all have the excuse of someone's else tugging arms to explain the retreat. "Incrisiath!" one of them screamed. *Incrisiath!* A sorcerer!"

The door to the Eye's suite opened. The clay tablets rattled. One fell and shattered.

The Brain came out.

She looked more human than the shadow Aminata had seen. She had crow's-feet and bruised tired eyes. Her body was wide and peasant-strong, but her feet dragged. She looked exhausted.

But she wore ancient bronze armor, and her hands dripped with fire. The green uranium power shone in the creases of her palms and ran down the web of her fingers to spill on the floor. At the sight of Iraji, her arms clenched, and the light gushed incontinent onto the deck like a dog marking.

Iraji screamed at her. *Speak through it,* Tau-indi had told him, *speak so your voice becomes its hunger and when she hears that hunger she will feel her own immortata rise to answer it. It is the nightmare of all the onkos to be devoured by their own immortality, and for their Line to end in malignancy. Worst of all for the Brain, for her tumor is in her thoughts.*

The Brain's hands flew to her head. She fell to her knees on the clay-tablet flooring, and Aminata saw, distinctly saw, that there were tears of pain in the Brain's eyes.

The magic *worked.*

At that sight she felt a cold twinge of migraine behind her own right temple. "No," she said, out loud, "no, not me." But she could feel it, she could feel the scream in her head.

It worked on her, too. *The magic worked on her too.*

Suddenly the Brain seized the first two fingers of her left hand in the fist of her right. Then she cracked the fingers straight back at the root. Aminata gasped and cringed at the sound.

The Brain held up her mangled hand and screamed in hurt. Her own pain gave her focus, and a shield against the pain Iraji sent to her. It gave the Brain will enough for words. She spoke them like a whip.

"Iraji. Son of Ira-rya e Undionash. Bow down to me."

And what could he do? What had ever triggered his faints, if not the memory of his birth? It was the name of his mother that beat him.

He went down on his knees, too, quivering, trying to hold up his head. Spit and blood gushed out around the tumor. Aminata tried to go to him but Osa grabbed her and held her back. "Not us," she said, with grim certainty. "It's not for us."

"Who is teaching you to do this, Iraji?" The Brain hid her wounded left hand behind her back, and raised the uranium star of her right against him. "Whose weapon are you?"

Iraji looked up at her with the cancer bulging between his lips.

"Spit it out," the Brain urged. "Slacken thy jaw and spit."

Come on, Aminata thought, do something, I don't know what and I don't want to know what, but do something, Iraji, don't let her—

"Sleep," the Brain commanded. Her burning hand swept low metronome arcs before Iraji as she used her command of thought to force an idea into him. "You are at ease. You are at rest."

Iraji's head fell to the clay. There was a moment when he was gone, his whole body empty, and if you had told Aminata that the cancer in his mouth was the only thinking thing in him, she would have believed it.

But his head had fallen lower than his heart. And that was enough to rouse him.

He bit down.

Brain and tumor and gore parted between his teeth and with his festering tongue protruding from his mouth he looked up at the Eye and groaned like a beast.

"I'll eat you," he slurred. "I'll eat you from inside."

She was the Brain: she was as ancient as thought. She had known her whole life the awful appetite of the baneflesh, and the power of a child who repudiated his mother. Not with all her will and all her pain could she stop herself from knowing those things.

The Brain clutched at the trepanned hatch in her scalp. Aminata saw the special nausea of a woman trying to keep a piece of herself from erupting out of her skull.

"Let us in," Iraji slurred, as the tumor drooled out of him. There was blood and cancer on his lips. "Let us inside. Or I will swallow it."

"You are massacring yourself!" the Brain cried. "You call that power into yourself, to eat all the eternity that is your birthright? You don't know the price you pay!"

"I never wanted to be one of you." Iraji rose shakily. "I deny you. I deny your power. I will open that door and nothing you have will stop me."

There was a chance, even then, that the Brain might have refused him, and fought. One of the Termites might simply have shot Iraji. But there were people watching: the Brain's people, her navigators and sailors, the educated folk who believed hard in her and in the terms of her power.

If a Termite dared interrupt this confrontation, then the Cancrioth would see sacrilege. And if the Brain did not yield, then her people knew, the way all believers know what they believe, that she would be struck down. Her tumor would swell up and drive her mad.

And she knew they knew it, in the way that one brain considers the knowledge of another.

"I yield," she said. "I grant you passage."

A Masquerade

NO one would go to the ball with Barhu.

Kimbune wouldn't come out of her proof-protected room, especially not to a fortress made by Falcrest's navy, where she thought she might spontaneously catch fire. Svir had delivered Barhu a new letter from her agent in Aurdwynn, and even explained how the Throne's mail service was able to send enciphered text without knowing where the recipient might be. (The answer involved something called a gossip protocol.) But after their recent exchange of coercions, it felt uncouth to ask him to attend.

"Yawa," Barhu called, through the newly installed door, "will you go to the Governor's Ball with me? I'd love your introduction to Heingyl Ri. We can talk about improvements to the Welthony harbor, and the roads north."

"Her home's just been invaded, Baru. I expect her appearance will be perfunctory."

"Then we'll take her mind off it! I *am* the guest of honor now, remember?"

Yawa groaned through the door. "It's supposed to be the *Governor's* Ball."

"It's a masked ball. Isn't it fitting the name should be a mask, too?"

"You're insufferable. Anyway, I'm already going with Faham. I'm being myself and he's posing as some Faculties functionary. Ask your diver."

"She can't go. She's forbidden from public enthusiasms. And she's meeting some shipping factor to arrange a voyage home." Barhu thought of the freshly delivered letter. "I've just had word from my agent in the Wintercrests. Would you like to help me decrypt it?"

Yawa ripped the door open. "Don't say that so loud," she hissed, "and yes, of course I would."

Header notes tracked the letter's long course from Purity Cartone's station in Mansion Hussacht, carried by foot to the Duchy Vultjag, from there down the river Vultsniada to the river Inirein and to Welthony port on the Ashen Sea, where it was shuttled to Treatymont and copied into the gossip protocol with other secret mail. "Who's your agent?" Yawa asked her.

"As if I'd tell you."

"Is it still Purity Cartone? You *do* remember that I was the one who sent him to you?"

"Hush, Auntie," Barhu snapped, making Yawa laugh.

TO MY AUTHORITY AND HANDLER

YOUR EYES ONLY

SITUATION IN STAKHIECZI COURT VERY SERIOUS. NECESSARY KING'S DOWNFALL NOW IMMINENT. ALL MANSIONS WILL REVERT TO INDIVIDUAL POLICY AND INTRA-MANSION WARFARE.

INITIAL RECEPTION TO YOUR OFFER WAS NEGATIVE, ALTHOUGH KING SEEMS INTRIGUED BY PROSPECTIVE RETURN OF HIS BROTHER. ARRIVAL OF MISSING KNIGHT DZIRANSI IMMENSELY COMPLICATED MY MISSION, AS HE SEEMS SPIRITUALLY CONVINCED THE KING MUST MARRY GOVERNOR HEINGYL RI OF AURDWYNN.

MANSION HUSSACHT ARMY IS ON THE MARCH INTO AURDWYNN BUT KING HAS ORDERED THEM TO AVOID UNNECESSARY PILLAGE OR RAIDING DUE TO HIS DESIRE TO COURT LOCAL LORDS: STAKHIECZI FORCES ARE THEREFORE SUBSISTING ON FORAGE AND TRADE WITH LOCALS.

RIVAL POLITICAL FACTION "MANSION UCZENITH" HAS CHALLENGED LEGITIMACY OF KING ATAKASZIR'S POSITION ON THE GROUNDS THAT HIS CONTINUED KINGSHIP IS NOT BRINGING THE STAKHIECZI MANSIONS ANY BENEFIT THEY COULD NOT OBTAIN ON THEIR OWN. MANSION UCZENITH ARMY CAMPED IN POSITION TO THREATEN KING'S MANSION.

LOSS OF KING'S AUTHORITY WOULD LEAD TO GENERAL DISPERSAL OF STAKHIECZI FORCES INTO A PELL-MELL LAND GRAB, MASS PILLAGING, ETC AND SO FORTH.

I HAVE BEEN QUARTERED WITH THE WOMEN DUE TO MY CASTRATION WHICH GRANTS ME EXTENSIVE ACCESS TO DOMESTIC GOSSIP AND NETWORKS OF EXCHANGE BETWEEN FEMALE WEATHERWORKERS. MANSION WOMEN BELIEVE AN ACT OF VENGEANCE OR A SIGNIFICANT STRATEGIC BREAKTHROUGH WOULD BE REQUIRED TO RESTORE KING ATAKASZIR'S POWER OVER THE MANSIONS. CURRENT OPINION IS THAT THE KING WILL DECLARE HIS INTENT TO MARRY HEINGYL RI, BUT THAT THIS WILL BE REJECTED AS A REPEAT OF HIS FAILED ATTEMPT TO MARRY YOU, LEADING TO ATAKASZIR'S EXECUTION BY RITUAL SCALPING.

NO STAKHI KING HAS SURVIVED MORE THAN FIVE YEARS IN THE LAST TWO CENTURIES.

KING ALSO IN DESPERATE NEED OF HEIR. NO STAKHI WOMAN WILL HAVE HIM AS HE IS SEEN AS A DEAD MAN. HE HAS BEEN COURTED BY

EXILED ARISTOCRAT NAYAURU AIA BUT HER POLITICAL DOWRY IS TOO WEAK TO SECURE A MARRIAGE.

IT IS VERY COLD IN THE MOUNTAINS AND I AM IMPAIRED BY ASTHMA OR A SIMILAR CONDITION. FAIRLY BREATHLESS WITH EXCITEMENT IN OTHER WORDS!

CONTACT ME AT: KETLY NORGRAF, FERRY STATION, VULTJAG. HAVE ARRANGED FOR RANGERS TO CARRY COPIES OF YOUR MISSIVES TO STAKHI WOMEN.

I AM VERY HAPPY TO SERVE.

Barhu felt, again, the whole weight of life balanced on her hand, not just *her* life but all the lives that depended upon her, the cornerstones of an inverted pyramid, trembling in the air, waiting to see how she tipped.

"Baru? What is it?"

"I think," she said, "that I was right to send Svir to handle it."

"It's bad?"

She nodded. "We have a little more time. But only a little."

Yawa put two fingers on the soft underside of Barhu's right wrist and dug in. "Say that Svir does successfully arrange this marriage. Say that the Necessary King stops his invasion. Say, even, that you get your trade route. What do you have for me? How will you keep Hesychast from lobotomizing my brother when I fail to lobotomize *you*?"

"I think," Barhu said, "that we have to assume one of those lobotomies will go forward."

Yawa stared at her as she left.

A frustrated pang of loneliness, absolutely irrational, *why will no one go to the ball with me,* sent Barhu down into the hold and the bilge. As if she might find Shao Lune chained up there, awaiting Barhu's petition upon her makeshift pavilion.

But Shao was gone. Gone like Aminata, whose death was now almost certain, who Barhu really should begin to mourn—how dare she feel excited about a *ball* when Aminata had given up everything—but then again, it was beginning to look as if she, too, would have to give up everything—

Barhu found a hammer and began to tear up the nails in Shao Lune's sleeping platform. They could be reused. The ship's carpenter should've taken them up already.

A soft *tap* on the steep stairs to middeck.

Barhu looked up.

A fine ink silhouette against the lamplight. A marvel of illustration, that such presence could be suggested by a few lines. Long legs, gloved hands braced against the walls, shoulders back: and her astronomically cheekboned face tipped down into darkness, to Barhu. She wore a sleeveless suit of black silk under a short and faintly royalist cape. She was wearing men's heels, called horse-archers because they were invented to fix the rider in the stirrup while taking a bowshot. But they had really quite fascinating effects, Barhu discovered, on the human leg.

"May I escort you to the ball?" Iscend asked, shyly. A counterfeit emotion but damn it nothing was so thrillingly taboo to an accountant as a really, really good counterfeit. "It's been so long since I attended a masquerade."

"You killed everyone on Kyprananoke."

"Yes. And I did it because the Republic demanded it of me." Iscend reached out her glove. "Everything I am demands that I help you, Agonist. It's my purpose."

"I need to convince a woman to marry me," Barhu said, recklessly, "in the eyes of a culture that *might* accept I'm a man. I need her to leave her husband for me, and then, after she marries me, I need her to marry a king. All extraordinarily unhygienic. All vital to the Imperial Republic's future. Can you help me do it?"

"Your Excellence," Iscend said, coming one step down the stairs, "I can help you achieve whatever you desire."

BARHU dressed as a barbaric northern lord. A broad-shouldered tabard and riding jodhpurs with a silver wolfskin cape, worn side-shoulder in respect to the summer heat (she would hand it over to a steward, thoughtlessly, as if she owned many more). She chose a silver cover with platinum chips to disguise the full authority of her mask.

Something was missing. She paced counterclockwise circles, trying to remember what she'd forgotten. Hu would have worn something else. And then, with a pang like an iced molar, she knew that it was Aminata's boarding saber.

"Baru!" Yawa called. "The ball's begun! The boat will leave without you!"

"A moment!" Barhu secured her purse, her scabbard, and her incryptor. Then, with a great nervous breath, she knocked on the wall beside Svir's curtain.

He yanked it back. "I told you, I'm not going."

"I know," she said.

She'd thought, once, that he was wormlike, atavistic—and now she regretted it. He'd been born to a people starved of sunlight, the skin itself gone pale with hunger. No wonder his throat was always his tell. The Stakhi were the people of the throat. How thirsty his ancestors had been, how starved, to chip at the hard rock in hope of water and precious salt.

"So," he said, composing himself. "Your agent's news?"

"The king is about to fall. You must go at once. I've written and sealed orders for the public revelation of your heritage. For release in the event of my death . . . subject to the discretion of a trusted colleague."

"And Lindon?"

"You'll give me the letter recommending his resignation now. I'll extract him from the Empire Admiralty and protect him, bearing in mind the threat you made. I'm sure it'll motivate me."

He began to laugh. "Do you remember when I'd pop in on you in Aurdwynn? Some long-haired asshole, buying expensive whiskeys? You never remembered me. Not once. When I finally sat down and made you the offer, you didn't know where you'd seen me before."

"I didn't pay enough attention to people, back then."

"And look at you now. You're here dictating terms to me, terms that hinge, and please don't mistake my admiration for approval, upon your cogent understanding of my desires and objectives. The woman I thought you were couldn't have done this."

"I'm not that woman."

"No. You're not." He fished a letter out of his stacks, pinching the heavy stock from between two sheets of rag. "This is for Lindon. I've already put my incryptor to it. Tell him I'm going home, and then I'm coming back." He smiled bleakly at the page. "Tell him I remember our first journey together. And that I intend to repeat it."

"Your brother will love the story of that journey," she said. "*I'd* love to hear the story."

"That's why I don't tell it," he said, wistfully. "Got to hold something you want. Will you see Iraji safe? Wherever he ends up? He's been a good spy for me, and a comfort. I'm sure he doesn't love me, thank the stars. But I want him all right. See to it?"

"Yes," she promised, "yes, yes, I promise you, I will."

"Nice cloak. You look like Hu."

"Thanks," she said, and tried to hug him.

"Easy," he said, fending her off. "Easy there. You've gotten *so* handsy lately."

BARHU stepped into the Arsenal Ballroom, and into her past: the widening-precipice days before Sieroch.

The banners did it. She hadn't seen so many in one place since the rebel army gathered. They covered the walls from hardwood floor to high rafters: the masked stag of Heingyl Ri's new government in Aurdwynn, kneeling figures in gold and jade for the Mbo, plain red sailcloth for the Imperial Navy, the crossroads-and-gate insignia of the Isla Cauteria civil government.

And for every banner there was a new sort of person. Sharply dressed Falcresti in waistcoats and tailcoats and sherwani. Judges in black robes. Oriati merchants in syncretic outfits, Mbo colors cut in severe Falcrest lines. Aurdwynni chamberlains and armsmen with their Stakhi and Maia and Belthyc blood as varied as the finespun wools they wore. All served by broad-shouldered waiters in dark corsetry that cinched their bodies into the classical triangle of the Exemplary Man.

Everywhere commerce; everywhere gossip spreading, thoughts exchanged, the tiny arcs of individual lives adjusting their place in the braid, and the braid in turn pulled taut by all the forces of world, spirit, atmosphere. Would Tau find this place as fascinating as Barhu did? More, perhaps. For they would unfold all the people, rather than trying to collapse them into patterns and trends.

"Your Excellence?" Iscend murmured. "You're alarmed."

"It's been a long time since I was in the public eye."

"You are not in the public eye at all, My Lady Excellence. This is a proper masquerade. While everyone knows Agonist is in attendance, no one knows exactly who she is." Iscend nodded her white enameled half-mask toward the other end of the ballroom. "I see that Governor Heingyl has revealed herself. She is dancing. Perhaps her armsmen made secrecy impossible. Let us proceed as dancers do."

"I don't know many dances," Barhu admitted. "Just what they taught us in school. And I threw tantrums."

"Can you fight?"

"Naval System, yes, I can—is dancing like fighting?"

"Utterly unlike it. Dance is the expression of meaning through movement. Combat is the denial of meaning, the assertion of material effect over symbolic power."

"Like Tain Shir," Barhu murmured.

"Just so. However: there are educational similarities." Iscend stepped across the invisible limen which marked Barhu's space. The sense of puncture was acute, needle-thin and cold, and as Iscend lifted one hand, turned it before Barhu's face, an image possessed Barhu of Iscend's body in a function test. Marked at every point by the colored needles of acupuncture, in the join of her thigh, her armpit, the fold between her fingers. The shining needles chiming off each other as she flowed from one posture to another.

"In combat, as in dance, I am trained to interpret the body. You will lead. I will follow."

"I don't think I know how to lead. . . ."

"Pretend that you are leading the way across rough terrain, and that I am the terrain. I will present the choices, and you will simply choose the way."

That exquisite shiver touched Barhu again, at the suggestion, in the metaphor, of trespass on sacred Imperial ground. "Follow on, then."

They drew speculative attention, first for their outfits, Barhu's barbaric provincial splendor and Iscend's sleeveless black severity, but most of all for the scandalous tension of their dance. "This isn't like you," Barhu murmured, as they passed close, as Iscend's poise folded for a moment, collapsing toward Barhu, withdrawing again as if in self-reprimand. "You're being—"

"Feminine?"

"I would have said"—a pause for breath, and of course Iscend was exactly in rhythm with her—"demonstrative."

It was Falcrest's notion of femininity, at once exalted and despised by the men who held the power. Coiled and watchful and cunning, taunting in its concealment: the checked sway, the bared throat veiled in hair, the half-parted lips closing to a frown. It was the theater of passion denied, the suggestion that if Barhu only seized control, if she stripped away Iscend's inhibitions with bold forthright action, she would find surrender to her wants. Barhu didn't want to like it. But she had come of age in that school, and the teachers, the women who knew so much, had all been raised this way—

"You told me you have to pass as a man," Iscend whispered. "I am your woman. Be the man."

"How?"

"Answer the questions I'm asking you. Look. Look how I withdraw. Look at this, the coverage of throat and chest. Look at the way I step, here, to part the legs, and here across, to close them. Look how I turn from your body, to hide it from my sight. I am indifferent to you, I am denying your power. Deny my denial. Take what you want."

They were not the questions Tain Hu had ever asked her. They were not the questions Ulyu Xe had invited. They were another world's way to look at a woman and to pursue her.

But Barhu had her taste for counterfeits.

And after some trial and uncertainty, after close pass and wary circle, she held Iscend arched across her hand. The Clarified woman came up with a smile and the faintest flush down her cheeks. "Good," she said, and if that flush was a reward, if the way she looked at Barhu with new interest was an enticement, well, what was there to do? "Good. You will say most of what you want to say to her without any words."

"Who?" Barhu said, having quite lost track of her reason for being here.

"The Governor. Shall we go to her now?"

At that moment, the choirmaster opened the envelope Barhu had deposited, and, after a moment's quiet communion with his singers, they began to sing.

I am Agonist," the chorus chanted. "I am the Emperor's will manifest to you. I stand among you in a secret form."

The crowd hushed. Even Barhu shivered in anticipation. Her hand brushed Iscend's, fabric against fabric: she jerked it away.

"Tonight I bring a gift worthy of Cauteria, the gate that receives the world's commerce. A ship will come to you from the shores of the Black Tea Ocean, far in the west of Oriati Mbo. They have journeyed through storm and still to trade with us, and that trade will be to our advantage. Let us undercut the greedy and jealous Princes. Let us cut the Oriati Mbo out of the middle. Soon the Emperor will announce a concern to exploit this opportunity. Tonight, I will offer you first bid on a number of shares in that concern.

"And if you fear that your investment will be lost in the journey from the Black Tea Ocean, or burnt away by new troubles in Aurdwynn, rest assured that the Emperor has prepared Taranoke and the Llosydane Islands as fine ports of call on the long route, and that Her Excellence the Governor Heingyl Ri has Aurdwynn well in hand.

"Join with me in welcoming these newcomers as we have always welcomed trade . . . with a smile, a soft voice, and a hard and cheating heart."

"Excuse me!" a high voice called, from not so far away. "Excuse me! Is this why it's not my ball anymore?"

There was a general appreciative laugh. "To Governor Heingyl Ri!" a man bellowed. "She has lost a ball, but gained a thousand friends!"

The moment of formality broke; the whispers became a roar of conversation. "It's so obvious," someone near Barhu whispered. "Heingyl Ri *is* Agonist. The woman who brought peace to Aurdwynn deserves the Emperor's favor."

"Too obvious, I should imagine. What about the woman from Sieroch? Baru Fisher? They said she was the Emperor's agent."

"Nonsense," a third voice drawled, male and arrogant. "Never a provincial.

I suspect the former Province Admiral Ahanna Croftare. I have it on good authority that she dispatched the marines which shattered the rebel army."

"She was in Falcrest by then! It must be Juris Ormsment, that's why she's gone missing, the Throne has some new purpose for her—"

"You think the Throne would endorse an agent from the *navy*? The Emperor might be naïve, up there with no idea of Its own name, but Its Advisors would never allow—"

Iscend whispered into Barhu's ear. "Of all the delights of the masked ball— anonymous liaisons, a poisoned cup, a needle in a dress—none surpass a hidden identity. Did you know that it is law, in Falcrest, that in the course of a masquerade no one's mask may be removed without their consent? Only an Imperial writ can force a citizen to unmask."

"I think I would know you anywhere," Barhu whispered back, "masked or unmasked."

Iscend laughed like sparrow wings. "That is a falsifiable proposition, my lady, and a challenge, too. Look, now, look." She guided Barhu's hand. "Your friends are with the Governor."

And there was Xe, very summery, wearing a skirtwrap down to her knees and a swimmer's strophium, crossed so that it framed a diamond of chest and back. Xe ushered Ake forward, an awkward gangly figure in a gown that didn't fit. The Stakhi woman smiled uncertainly and put out her hand to introduce herself to Heingyl Ri. The Stag Governor of Aurdwynn was a tiny woman, masked in pure white from upper lip to brow, beneath a headdress of gilded antlers that curled toward the chandeliers. It might, in *any* less republican context, have been read as a crown.

"Oh, damn." Ake was going to let slip that Barhu had given *her* a letter of governorship, and Ri would think she was being usurped. "Where's Yawa!"

"Here I am." Yawa appeared in a feathered black gown. "What has you screeching?" She had mostly finished a glass bulb of what the Maia called sakkari and Falcrest called sangria. A bit of grape skin stuck to her teeth.

"I need to be introduced at once."

"Ah. Yes, I see the problem. Come along."

Barhu tried to think of a clever greeting. What could you say to a woman whose father had died fighting your army? Was there etiquette for this? Hello, Ri Foesdaughter, and well met? I'm glad your father wasn't a better killer?

"Heia," Yawa called, choosing the Duchess Heingyl Ri's personal name, as Duchess Vultjag had also been named Tain Hu. "May I introduce you to a colleague?"

Ri's eyes narrowed. She raised her right hand. The three armsmen behind her, a chalk-eyed Stakhi man, a harelipped toothless fellow, and a Maia brute in maille, all tensed and closed in. Iscend Comprine relaxed fluidly like poison in a syringe.

"Your Excellence." Barhu swept a low and sober bow, as the dukes would offer each other. In Iolynic: "The last of your kind, and the most deserving."

"Hello," Ri said, pleasantly. She might be tiny of stature but she was huge in presence; Barhu's height gave her no power whatsoever against the cut of Ri's fox eyes. Of all the things Barhu had met on her first day in Aurdwynn, she remembered Ri's eyes second best.

"Heia, my dear," Yawa purred, "is your husband here?"

"He's speaking to the guano factors." Her eyes roamed over Barhu with a wary, vulpine mischief. "Dressed just like a duchess I once knew. Miss Sentiamut, why don't you and your friends go meet my husband? He'll make the arrangements for you to join us on our ship."

"At once, Your Excellence." Ake led the others away, firing a wary glance back at Barhu. Run and Ude were arguing with Yythel over which of several mushrooms to eat off a glistening truffle-oiled tray. Barhu smiled at their bickering.

"You're fond of them?"

"Yes. Very much so."

"I could arrange their safety, if I just knew a little more about a man named Ketly Norgraf, who vanished from Treatymont this spring. . . ."

She was a player of the game, young Haradel Heia. Barhu liked her a little more than she ought. "Who is that?" she asked, innocently.

Heia tipped her head and smiled. "What remarkable work you've done for my home. And your work continues—why, not long ago my husband received your letter, ordering all sorts of arrests and economic movements. Even the creation of republican senates, if I am not mistaken?"

Barhu had indeed sent him a very bossy letter. "I hope we're in accord on some points?"

"Not even one, alas. Aurdwynn's time to flower has not yet come. The recent news of invasion is not unexpected, and I left very clear instructions as to what should be done."

"What *should* be done?"

"The coast must be protected, of course. The Stakhieczi denied access to the Ashen Sea, even at the cost of our northern duchies. Don't you think?" The Stag Governor sighed and made moon eyes at Yawa. "How our home does shoulder the burdens of the Empire. Truly we are martyred."

Yawa finished her sangria. "Truly," she growled. "How are you and Bel?"

"We are very happy."

"The *shit* you are," Yawa hissed. "Damn you, Heia, he was supposed to se-cure your governorship in Falcrest's eyes, not settle in and buy you matching cutlery. The divorce should've been in by now, I had the causes all written up—"

Barhu watched in fascination as the Stag Governor's eyes flashed in defi-ance. "I expect we'll soon be pregnant."

It would not have surprised Barhu if Yawa snapped off the stem of her san-gria glass in Heia's eyes. "Heia! This is no time for sentiment!"

In Barhu's right ear, Iscend murmured, "If she is your target, you should touch her as soon as you can, and associate that touch with surprise and de-light. An interruption now would save her from unpleasantness. . . ."

"Oh," Barhu said, "good idea." She took one long stride forward and tripped the Stag Governor.

Their legs entangled: the Stag Duchess in her black gown and golden cir-clets fell back onto Barhu's waiting arm. Her antlers nearly tapped the floor. The armsmen would have seized Barhu, if Heingyl Ri had not called them off with a snap of Iolynic.

Barhu closed a hand around her chin. Pressed one gloved finger to her lips, bare beneath the half-mask. "A dance?"

Those *eyes*! Heingyl Ri's lips curved beneath the glove. She moved her shoulders, just so: Barhu was suddenly and pleasantly aware of her body. "Why not?"

Iscend turned to Yawa and offered her hands. "Your Excellency? Shall we dance the Cavalry Night?"

Yawa groaned. "You're going to rub my bones through my feet, child." Her eyes lingered on Heia, wary, watchful, maybe hurt.

D EVENA help me, I did not see him till he spoke. I should have known him by the weight of his shoulder or the length of his stride. For if he was the symbol of the body as destiny, then the proportions of his body were the mea-surements of my fate.

But I did not recognize him. He wears more masks than one.

"Durance," Hesychast said. "How do you feel?"

I had dismissed him as another one of the brimmingly fit Falcresti waiters who infested the place. I admit they all washed together in my eyes. But once I knew it was him, he stood out like a burn.

"Your Excellence." I bowed shallowly. Iscend, damn her twice for leading me to him, had vanished. "What an unexpected pleasure. What brings you to Isla Cauteria?"

"Waiting for you to turn up, of course. I used one of my legends to travel here. I thought it would be a likely port on your way home to Falcrest." Cosgrad Torrinde took me companionably by the waist and steered me away from the benches along the south wall, where Faham Execarne was making exchanges with his agents. "Is Ormsment handled?"

"Thoroughly. Though at some cost." I outlined Aminata's choice to go aboard *Sulane,* and to sacrifice herself with the ship.

He frowned terribly. It was awful to see such a fine face so sorry. "A shame about Aminata. I warned her off Baru. I really did try. She seemed a tremendously promising officer . . . and yet I see Baru here. You failed to remove her?"

O Wydd, arm me with the lies I needed. "She defeated the Farrier Process. Her wound developed into a complete tulpa, a true marvel of pathology. I thought it best to preserve her for your inspection."

"Farrier's process failed? Barhu is making decisions he would not allow?"

Such directness to his questions. The situation in Falcrest must be at its point of absolute crisis. "It's unclear, Your Excellence. Something grand is about to be accomplished here . . . and her plan *does* match Farrier's requirements precisely. But it may also be to our advantage."

"If you won't use her as dowry, how have you secured the Necessary King? If you do not control the Stakhieczi invasion, we will have to revert to the original contingency. Plague and democide through Aurdwynn and the Wintercrests. Loss of so many germ lines. A disaster."

I tried a grandmotherly pat of his hand. "We have an alternative dowry."

"What is it?"

"Please leave that to me."

"You have no time for improvisation, Durance. If the king dies and the Mansions fracture we'll have missed our chance to solve the Stakhkieczi problem forever—"

"Your Excellence. Aurdwynn is my blood knowledge. Trust that I have the matter in hand."

"Trust?" He smiled with a squeeze of his arm. "Now there's a word I don't look to hear from you."

"Mistrust my loyalties, Your Excellence, that I can respect. Just don't mistrust my competence."

"Consider me rebuked. How has Iscend performed?"

"There has been some deviation, after so long away from the Metademe. If you would only divulge the reconditioning protocols . . ."

He laughed. "Absolutely not. Did she fall back on her deeper qualms? As her contingent rewards extinguished, she should have come to fetishize the overall well-being of the Republic."

"I would say she did." I swallowed. "Perhaps . . . more so than you intended."

"How so?"

"There was an outbreak on Kyprananoke. She judged it was too dangerous to be allowed off the islands. I agreed with that assessment . . . but no one gave her the order to trigger the apocalypse fuse. She did it herself."

"Oh." Hesychast did not react, except for that word. I pictured him in the Metademe, whispering desperately to the Clarified babies in their cribs, waving a sulfurous match under their little noses, *don't extinguish entire cultures, I shall be very displeased and you will smell a stink if you do it.*

"I should say," he managed, "that she correctly put the Republic's well-being before all other concerns. Would we hesitate to lose a hundred thousand lives to win a war? No. And an epidemic is ten times the threat any war will ever be."

"Put that way," I said, "she made the right choice. But it was an almost total loss of the Kyprananoki germ line."

"Yes . . . a conundrum. Where did the epidemic originate?"

"From a ship, we believe. A Cancrioth ship."

"Truly? You've found them?"

We swept through a crowd of guano merchants engaged in vigorous financial intercourse with Heingyl Ri's trade factors. I turned my face away from Bel Latheman. "They're coming here. Now. I have one of them aboard *Helbride* as a hostage. A mathematician. She knows things no one has ever known. . . ."

He killed the gasp while it was still in his chest. His lips parted in silence. "Well done. *Well* done. Where did you find them?"

"Kyprananoke. Where Abdumasi Abd's fleet harbored before their journey north to attack Aurdwynn."

His body screamed in triumph or alarm: the conscious sublimation of a great shout into a thousand tiny flexions. "Abdumasi Abd? I know that man."

We brushed through a sailcloth privacy curtain, down a corridor of sailing ships muraled in smashed seashell. "How closely can Abd be linked to the Cancrioth?" he muttered.

"Intimately. They claim him as their own. He may even contain . . . a somatic portion of the Cancrioth."

"Abd is a popular man in the Mbo. Name him as Cancrioth and half the merchants in Lonjaro would be implicated as collaborators. It would be a disaster for our endgame if Mandridge Subahant and his goons in Parliament get their hands on him. Subahant already wants a good old-fashioned dustup with the Oriati, a chance to prove we're the better race. This would be the perfect excuse. Where's Abd now?"

I dared not lie. "We believe that he is here, in this fortress."

He burst out laughing. "Naturally!"

"Naturally, my lord?"

"I don't believe in trim, yet I am always haunted by the suspicion of its influence. Come. I have something to show you."

He led me down twisting counterclockwise stairs. Cold sea air teased at my gown. My ears began to ache. "My lord?" I asked, impatient to know where we were going.

He led me down an unmarked corridor to a plain white door. "In here."

Suddenly I knew. I almost fell. He had been so casual about the approach—I had no warning. His arm clamped around me like a yoke as he turned the key in the lock.

My brother looked up at me from darkness. The perforated steel muzzle over his face broke his groan into a thousand little sounds. The smell of diluted bleach and fear-sweat drove me back.

Hesychast lit the wall sconce. I stood like a corpse, seized by guilt and horror, above my wretched brother.

"I've been giving him therapeutic conditioning," Hesychast sighed. "But he retreats into delusion. He asks after the rebellion. Have you left Treatymont yet? When will you join him in the north? When will we go to Sieroch, to meet Cattlson in battle? Confronted with unacceptable reality, his mind seeks the last tolerable state it can remember."

Olake blinked up at me. Then he whimpered and tried to scuttle back like a crab. The wall stopped his flight and he curled into himself.

"He's trapped here," Hesychast said. "In the moment when he realizes you betrayed him. He comes back to it again and again."

"Please," I whispered.

"Please?"

"Please don't lobotomize him."

"Even if it soothed him? Even if it let him love you again?"

But it would be my fault. It would taint everything else I ever achieved. Olake was my twin and my equal in everything except ruthlessness. The more I did, the more he *might* have done, if only I hadn't betrayed him.

We stood facing each other, Olake huddled between us. "Do I need to reinforce how *vital* it is that you destroy Baru?"

"No, my lord."

"Good. I'm going to take Abdumasi Abd away. A spell recovering in the Metademe would keep him out of the public eye."

"My lord, you mustn't. We require him."

"Why?"

The appalling perfection of Cosgrad by candlelight. After all his experiments, all his voluntary and pampered brides, had any man in all the world ever fathered more children? Dividends of his beauty would pay down generations to come.

My brother mewled and tried to part the floor with his hands.

"We can trade him for the information you require, my lord, to finish your work. The Cancrioth *do* possess a cancer which can be passed from body to body. They do believe that it carries the souls of its past hosts. They want Abd back. We can use Abd to force them to yield a sample, and perhaps the protocol for its reproduction."

He slipped. I *saw* him slip. His broad face remained perfectly impassive, his deep bright eyes calm and considerate: but I saw that living chest heave.

He hated the idea of losing Abdumasi Abd.

"Options," he demanded. "What will you do if the bargain fails?"

"I have influence upon the Morrow Minister, operating under the name Faham Execarne. He has agents on Cauteria trained in boarding and seizure. We'll take the Cancrioth ship."

"You have control?"

"He's my lover."

"Good. That man's a sensualist, and easily mastered by those means. But be careful. He's also a solipsist, with a solipsist's willingness to alter the world to suit his whims. He may become impulsive. Be prepared to remove him from the situation."

Indicating my brother: "You think *I'll* be sentimental?"

"No. I don't. But I do think your failure to remove Baru could mean she's compromised you." His eyes searched every bone and muscle of my face, ticking them off one by one, inventorying my reaction. "What are the risks of taking the Cancrioth ship by force?"

"They could destroy themselves. We would lose our chance at a sample, and their knowledge of how to propagate it. Also, there's danger to the hostages they hold."

"Anyone of significance?"

"The Prince-Ambassador Tau-indi Bosoka."

And once more I detected that hitch of shock, and old sorrow. Tau-indi meant something to him, too.

"Best to keep the Prince-Ambassador alive, if we can. Their death would be an outrage. Will you be able to remove Baru?"

"I'm quite sure—"

The bastard knew how to interrupt me, how to make me feel like a serving girl again, jealous and resentful of my power. "No pride, Durance. Just the truth."

"Yes. Yes, I've got her for epilepsy and aberrant identity. We can lobotomize her whenever we please."

"Then do it. As soon as she's played her part."

"Your Excellence—"

"No, Yawa." He used my name for the first time. "No delays. No clever ideas about how to use her. Renascent is waiting for my protégé to defeat Farrier's. So defeat her. And if you cannot . . ."

He did not even need to look at Olake.

"Yawa?" my brother rasped. "Are we at Welthony? I smell the sea."

24

MEN WHO LOVE GIRLS KILL WOMEN

YOU'RE not afraid of me?" The duchess clasped her hands round Barhu's shoulders. "The woman who used you to conquer Aurdwynn?"

"Not afraid." Barhu looked down at Ri the way Tain Hu had looked at her: open curiosity and playful menace. The memory helped her smile. "I suspect your husband would scream if he saw us dancing, though."

Ri looked away. "He hates you the way anyone would hate you for what you did."

"It all feels so long ago," Barhu admitted. "Not even a year since I saw him last. But so much has happened."

"Four years since you and I met. Four years since our last ballroom. The man who introduced us is dead. You worked so hard to build your rebellion, and then to crush it. And while you labored, did you ever remember me?"

"Of course I did," Barhu lied. She had been a precious little solipsist back then. "You kissed my hand and gave me a problem to solve, which are two of my greatest delights."

"If I tried to kiss your hand now, I think my antlers would gore you." Her headdress complemented her sharply cut black ball gown, ornamented in emerald, hemmed in cloth of gold. "But I've stolen all your credit, haven't I? In Parliament they are saying that *I* united Aurdwynn. In Treatymont they are saying, at last we are safe with honest Ri, after lying Baru and her rabid Coyotes."

"I did my own work," Barhu said, stamping on an ember of real nervous attraction, schoolyard desire for the clever older girl's interest, *especially* after she insults you, "for the Emperor and the republican people. Not for you."

"Not for me?" Wide, innocent eyes looked up at Barhu. "Then why are you dangling these mysterious Oriati traders before me? Why announce access to the Black Tea Ocean and all its riches *here*, instead of in Falcrest? You were Imperial Accountant, Baru. You know what that kind of trade would do for Aurdwynn. Trade benefits those in the middle most of all. With a connection to the Black Tea Ocean, we'd be more than Falcrest's lumberyard and olive grove. . . ."

"The betterment of the Republic betters me."

She showed Barhu her teeth. "Don't be feckless."

"It would help my cause"—she guided Ri by her right shoulder blade, fingers firm, through rise and fall, feeling her relax—"if you bought some stock in my new concern, and sent some of your factors to meet with these Oriati traders. It would add a certain legitimacy to the affair."

"Is it illegitimate, then?"

"Nothing I do can be illegitimate." Barhu drew her closer as they turned. Voice lower in the throat, now, husky as you please: "Do you know what I am?"

"Yes," she said, soft and calm, "the word went out from Sieroch. You are an agent of the Emperor on Its Throne. You execute the will of the monarch that does not know its own name."

"Just so," Barhu said, and drew away a moment, to flourish and bow. Behold me, the shrike with all the rebels pinned on my thorns, and consider what I may accomplish for you. "Loyal hand of Its Majesty the Faceless Emperor, champion of the commoner, bane of all nobility."

"Are you the bane of me?"

"I would be some things to you," Barhu said, smiling up from the bow, "but not your bane."

"Do you want the same thing as Yawa?" Heia said, sharply. "Are you here to ask for my divorce? I love my husband. Bel's a good man."

"Is he?" Barhu settled her hands back to shoulder blade and waist. On the close pass: "He threatened to report me once. I'm sure you've heard the gossip about why."

"Baru, you forced him to be your necklace for two years! You killed any prospect of his marriage or advancement! You called him to a *duel*!"

"Do you really think my actions to protect myself from harm are the same as his choice to threaten me with circumcision?"

"No," Heia admitted, drawing closer, yielding in apology, "no, it's not the same. You hurt him, but not in a way which justifies that. Nothing does, nothing can. But he was raised a Falcrest man. They have certain fears and fragilities. . . ."

"Are his feelings more important to you than Aurdwynn's future?"

"Obviously not," Heia snarled, and Barhu thought, you damn fool, she conspired toward her own father's death, of *course* her feelings don't rule her duty.

"I'm sorry. Your father did his duty to the end." Barhu let her eyes drift away, to far memory. "He tried to stop my field-general Vultjag's charge, and we sent our reserves down at him. He was unhorsed. He fought on foot, protecting his banner. He was crying *honor the word*."

Which was a little lie. Barhu had been too far to hear the Stag Duke's last stand. But why not lie a little? Just to help?

Duchess Heingyl blinked, blinked again, swallowed, and clasped Barhu's hand hard. "Well," she said, hoarsely, "it happened just the way he'd always dreamt."

Reward her for that raw moment; compliment her cunning. "When you met me on the day of my arrival . . . were you trying to warn me against Nayauru?"

"Yes." Heia laughed and sniffed. "Poor Au. She wanted so badly to be queen. And if she had, if she'd united the Midlands and the North, the Stakhieczi would have come straight for her, by marriage or by war. So I had to stop her, my own cousin, or I would've lost it all. . . ."

"She was a great woman."

"And ambitious."

Barhu winked. "My favorite sort."

"Some of her relatives are still at large. I fear they've gone north, into the mountains. . . ."

"Don't fear, Heia. I have an agent in place. He says Nayauru Aia's suit to the king is weak."

"You're *very* well informed."

"I like to show off," Barhu said, circling her, "when I think my talents will be appreciated."

"Then perhaps," Heia said, breathing hard, taxed by the pace herself, "you could tell me why Yawa was so eager to introduce us. And why you're still meddling in our province."

Barhu dipped her halfway to the floor. Heia gasped and clung. Her garment moved charmingly with her breath.

Barhu said: "I want to marry you."

Heingyl Ri looked blank. "What?"

"By the law of the Mansions, I am the rightful lord of the Mansion Uczenith. By the acclamation of the Dukes of Aurdwynn, I am the Queen of the Realm. Marry me, and you will have claim to these titles. Your child will inherit them."

"But you're—" Heingyl Ri flushed pink. "Are you saying you're . . . you can father children?"

Barhu did not laugh: it was a perfectly reasonable question. "No. But I can be a man in Stakhieczi eyes. Man enough to be recognized as Duchess Vultjag's consort. And certainly man enough to marry you."

"Vultjag!? What does she have to do with—you married *Vultjag*? Oh! I always knew she'd do something intolerably superb."

"She won the claim to Mansion Uczenith by defeating the lord Kubarycz in single combat. It's the law of the Mansions that if one lord exterminates another Mansion's line, he must accept responsibility for that Mansion's welfare."

This was not so much enticement to duel and kill your rival lords as Barhu had feared. There had been two-Mansioned lords in Stakhieczi history, but they had smelled too much like kings, and the others had judged their avarice Unnecessary. Out with their ambition, off with their scalps.

It might be different this time. It might.

She went on: "One of the Necessary King's knights witnessed my marriage. To question his word would be to question the king's. He is in the Stakhieczi court now, telling the king that *you* must be the bride of the mountains. Imagine if you came to him as the best claimant to the Mansion Uczenith, his enemy!"

"Would the Stakhi recognize our marriage? Yours and mine?"

"If I prove I'm a man, and if it was to their king's advantage, then certainly he would recognize it. The Stakhieczi believe that one's sex is maintained by action, and that manhood can be gained or lost. They must have laws and customs to handle a noble changing sexes! I am sure those laws could be turned to our advantage."

"How would you prove you were a man—" Heia, pale-skinned, flushed brighter. "Oh."

Barhu gave her slack to draw away if she felt repulsed. "It only needs to be the impression, Heia. We needn't conduct the act."

"But how could I possibly receive your claim? Stakhieczi women don't inherit, *especially* not from husbands—you couldn't yield the claims in a divorce."

"But the Stakhieczi die," Barhu said, happily. "They die in great numbers, all the time. And when famine sweeps away all the men of a family, the widows have been known to receive the claim. There have been Weather Queens who inherited down a female line. There is precedent for the Necessary King to make it possible." Barhu turned her swiftly, caught her breathless as she came round. "His own brother will be there to help him see it through."

"His *brother*?"

"I'm sending him as messenger and negotiator of the match. All is arranged. It could be done by summer's end. Peace in Aurdwynn, Heia. . . ."

And with peace, trade. Access to the greatest source of metals and hard treasure in the world. Mountains and mountains of wealth, locked up in the Wintercrests, waiting to begin their southern rush. . . .

"But I'm Bel's wife!" Heia blurted it like she'd just remembered. "I don't care how cleverly you've arranged everything, I'm already married to Bel."

"I loved Tain Hu," Barhu said, softly, "as I'm sure you loved your father. But when the game required it, we . . . we parted."

"I'm not like you—"

"You are like me, Heia. You want Aurdwynn safe more than you want anything—"

"I am *not* like you!"

The great window above them creaked. They looked up together, in surprise. The grid of glass swung open on oiled hinges.

A cape of rain jetted into the ballroom. The ballgoers cried in protest. A man stood in the window in a scout's mask and navy landing gear, and as the wet wind soaked through silk banners all around him, he seized a dangling draw-rope and leapt down to the balcony below. Red hair streamed behind him.

From somewhere in the crowd, Rear Admiral Samne Maroyad shouted, "Who goes up there?"

"Officers," the man cried, "to your stations! I am Apparitor, the Emperor's messenger, and here is my message, the enemy is upon us, *we are all betrayed!*"

"Pardon me." Barhu snapped a silver bracelet off Ri's wrist, caught the chandelier light, and flashed it up at Apparitor to get his attention.

What the fuck was going on? *Who* had betrayed them?

Svir looked down at her from the balcony. Then he snapped up a flare pistol from his belt, leveled it at Barhu, and fired.

T HE Eye came out of his clay-walled room, hairy legs protruding from his cassock, tumor stalk goggling in astonishment. When he saw the gore on Iraji's face he shouted, "Child, what have you done?"

"Rescued you," Iraji said. But he swayed so dangerously that Aminata wanted to turn him over like an hourglass to put the blood back where it was needed.

"Sir." Osa greeted the onkos with hasty respect. "Their Federal Highness, Tau-indi Bosoka, begs you to help us retake this ship, and to save us all from a meaningless death. The Brain's faction are loading plague into the rockets. They will attack."

A smile came across the Eye's face, chasing, and chased by, grief. "Tau's come back? Good. Good. I had hoped for that. Tau will know what to do. Let's go."

And he walked to war.

The Brain's people scattered before the Eye like children at the edge of a rising bonfire. Fighters who could have killed him with a single thrust fled from his burning hands. Sailors covered their eyes and hid when he spoke. Aminata hated it. Every moment that the Eye's power triumphed over the force of arms was torture. She almost wished for one of Masako's Termites to raise a pistol and shoot the sorcerer dead, just to relieve the nightmare of his effect.

But even if they disbelieved his power, even if they yanked him into the shadows, chopped him up and stuffed the pieces into the bilge . . . they were surrounded by those who *believed* in the Eye. And there were other Eyes in the line of Virios to avenge him.

Masako blocked the Eye's way with six Termites, rapiers drawn, pistols ready. The Eye looked them over coolly. "There is no clay in this floor. There are no tablets on these walls. If I speak here, you will hear me, and what I say will never leave your ears."

The Termites looked uncertainly to Masako.

Masako frowned. His rapier was steady. Everything, Aminata thought, was a sort of mild inconvenience to him. "Go back to your chambers," he said.

The Eye's stalk glared at him: "Son of Segu, even if you shoot me dead here, I will live on to know your children's children. Do not give me cause to remember you poorly."

A trickle of wet green light ran down his left wrist and dripped to the floor.

"Stand aside," Masako ordered. "No blood. Let them pass."

Aminata smirked at him. He tipped his head and cocked a brow, and, as she passed, murmured, "How is this going to look to the promotion board, Brevet-Captain Aminata? Magic. Not very hygienic. Not very hygienic at all."

ONE by one they gathered the Eye's lieutenants. A woman with scarified dots across her cheeks, wearing an Invijay war costume, split poncho like moth wings. Two old librarians who embraced him like a son. A tiny person, who Aminata supposed must be a pygmy, wearing smoky glass lenses. By the time they spilled out onto the weather deck they were at least twenty strong, and singing in En Elu Aumor.

"Oh, *shit.*" Aminata gaped up at Isla Cauteria, purple meadow and forest green and white-tipped rock. Dead off the bow. *Far too close.* Where were Maroyad's pickets? Why hadn't they been intercepted? "Iraji, we've crossed the Caul! We're in the home seas!"

The rigging swarmed with sailors. *Eternal* rode a following wind, all canvas raised, and her heel told Aminata that the torpedo hole in the starboard prow had come open again. They were shipping water.

The Brain was sailing the ship apart in her hurry to attack.

"Go gather our people," the Eye ordered his lieutenants. "I will mark you, so they know you speak with my voice." He lifted a bright hand and his followers took his fingers into their mouths, so their tongues glowed soft green, as if stained by his touch.

"Where is Tau-indi?" he asked Osa. "I must see them."

"In the sterncastle."

Tau-indi waited in the doorway of their stateroom. "Virios. Welcome."

"Your Federal Highness." The Eye turned his sad human eye back to Iraji, who trembled in Aminata and Osa's arms. "You taught him the apotropaic spells?"

"There were things I saw as a child which I sought too keenly to understand." Their smile so genuine that Aminata might have sworn, against the word of her own memories, that Tau had never hated and despised the Cancrioth at all. "You look well. I'm glad the Brain left you unharmed."

"Nothing she could do to me matters compared to what she is about to do." The Eye snarled in frustration. "She doesn't give a damn about getting Abdumasi back. She's going to attack Cauteria and force the war upon the world."

"Then we will stop her," Tau said, fiercely. "Is everyone all right? Iraji, you look awful. Aminata, would you take him to the washroom and clean him up?"

"Sure," she muttered, not eager to stay, not happy to be dismissed. "C'mon, Iraji."

The Eye paused at the threshold, frowned at Tau, scratching at the skin below his tumor. "It's good to see you smile, your Highness. But it's a surprise. I've seen grudges linger for a thousand years over far less than what we did to you."

"Onkos," Tau said, lifting their chin, baring their delicate neck, "I must do what good I can with what I have. If I can change so much when cut from trim, can you imagine how powerfully trim might change Baru? She has taken my place. She will help us. *She* will stop the war."

A feeling rose up in Aminata, a little like nausea in its power, a little like nostalgia because it was a yearning for something lost, a little like fantasy because it was the loss of something she'd never known before. Maybe it was reverence for majesty. Maybe it was a blood-deep joy at the rightness of this connection: she and Iraji and Osa and the Eye and Tau all come together to avert disaster.

She waited for the scrutiny of her own internal Jurispotence, disgusted by such anti-Incrastic thoughts. But it didn't come.

"Can we stop the Brain?" The Eye paced, barefoot and dirty-toed. "What we saw at Kyprananoke . . . it was like the world shouted at us, *you fools, you fight or you die.* So many of my people went over to her. How can I ask them to go home and hide?"

"Do not ask them to go home and hide," Tau said. "Ask them to do better. Show the world that you are not the people who poisoned Kyprananoke."

"Show *who*? Falcrest? They'll eat us alive. The Mbo?" The Eye laughed helplessly. "Marvel of compassion and forgiveness that *you* may be, Tau, I think you are an exception. If we went to the Mbo, they'd bury us and forget where."

Tau pushed two long falls of twisty black hair back behind their ears. "I don't know. I do not know what will work. I only know what is *right*. I must try: and here is where I am."

"Oh, Tau. I can't fight my own people. I don't know how to turn them from this anger. . . ."

"I know precisely how. There is something more powerful than anger, Virios. It is shame."

"How will we shame them?"

"Simple," Tau said. "We are going to put ourselves upon the weapons, so that they cannot kill their enemies without killing us."

But Aminata did not get to hear any more, because Iraji slumped into syncope. She carried him into the washroom, and, cupping seawater in her hands, cleaned the cancer from his face.

"I have no idea what the fuck you did against the Brain," she murmured to him, "but it was brave."

"I remember the last time you told me that," he said, smiling a little.

"I was right, wasn't I?"

"Do you know what we've just done?"

"What?"

"We've brought a Prince of the Mbo to council with one of the Cancrioth Lines."

"Should I be proud?" Aminata muttered.

"Of *course* you should."

A shadow filled the washroom door.

"Hello," Shao Lune said, with bright and vicious charm. "Look at you, Lieutenant Commander! Filthy again! I understand you've been helping the Oriati do magic? I think some Incrastic guidance is needed here."

Aminata got in front of Iraji. "What do you want?"

"We are in sight of Isla Cauteria. It's time to leave with what we've learned. When the navy moves to take this vessel, they'll need our reports."

"We can't just *leave*," Aminata protested. "Even if we made it to a boat, how would we get it down to the water without being sighted? And they have that whale—

"No orca has ever been known to fatally attack a human being."

"Well," Aminata sputtered, "maybe that's because all the dead people don't come back to report it!"

"I refuse to let a whale keep me from my duty." An arch frown. "You can still swim distance, can't you?"

"I can't," Iraji said, softly.

"You are a fallen Oriati, reverted to your ancestry, and will not be joining us." Shao Lune's glare tugged Aminata toward attention: be better, be what I want you to be. "Report to my cabin by end of watch. That's an order. We're abandoning ship."

"Mam," Aminata protested, "the situation aboard is very unstable. The peace faction might need our advice in communication with the navy—"

"There is no 'peace faction' here. There are only varieties of abomination." Shao Lune looked back coolly from the door. "Best not to linger aboard, Lieutenant Commander. This is a plague ship. I've already posted the coded signal in the rigging. Maroyad's sentries will spot it any moment."

"A coded signal for what?" Aminata demanded. There were various ways you could tie knots in rigging, when signal flags weren't available. "What did you send?"

"Why, *destroy on sight*, of course."

And Shao was gone.

A S the rocket flare came at Barhu's face, she had time to think: I really must have pushed Svir too far.

The flare zipped past her, screamed between Haradel Heia's antlers like a mezzo-soprano hornet, and struck the gray-eyed Stakhi armsman behind her in the face. He screamed, grabbed his burning beard, and dropped the knife he'd drawn to stab his lady Heingyl Ri in the back.

The flare fell into a bowl of high-proof punch. The puff of blue fire ignited the paper flowers all around it. Screams of terror and exhilaration went up all over the ballroom.

Ah. An assassination interrupted. Very good shot, Svir. I wonder if that man had any accomplices? I ought to check.

Two more of Heia's armsmen had their knives out.

Closest to the Governor was the sad-eyed Stakhi man with the harelip.

But it was the Maia giant in maille who roared *"HONOR THE WORD!"* And lunged for her, Stag Daughter of the Stag Duke he'd once served, married to a foreign man who the old Stag Duke had disapproved of. There were men all over the world prepared to kill women for what they did with their love. The Stag Governor's household was apparently no exception.

Of course her own house is going to try to kill her, Barhu thought. Women are mostly murdered by the men closest to them.

The crowd, in perfectly Falcresti fashion, hushed to watch, like they were at the theater.

"Pilyx!" the fourth armsman bellowed. "You fucking oathbreaker!" He got between Heingyl Ri and Pilyx the mailed Maia giant. Pilyx charged straight at the loyalist, knife low, a brutal prisonyard rush—Barhu remembered this from her Naval System training—and the loyal armsman tried, artfully, to parry the oncoming knife with his own. Pilyx taught him that knife fights were not the place for parries: three severed fingers as learning toll.

The loyalist stared at his maimed hand.

Pilyx put his knife hilt-deep into the loyalist's belly. He shrieked, he dropped his blade, giant Pilyx grabbed him by the back of the neck and pulled him down three, four, six, ten times onto the knife—

"Kill her!" he roared. "Szeti, kill her, *go!*"

Barhu watched all this in absolute befuddlement. Her powers were useless. Wasn't she supposed to have security for moments like this? Where was Iscend?

Szeti, the sad-eyed man with the harelip, rushed to kill Heia. The Stag Governor fell on top of Barhu and as they both went down Iscend stepped across them, blocked the sad man's knife arm with the meat of her own forearm, captured his hand, popped his wrist joint with the lever of her thumb. He dropped the blade. She grabbed his face with her other hand and drove her thumb under his left eyeball. The ball popped out in a mess of blood and nerves. Szeti shrieked in bad harmony with the man whose face was burning off.

Iscend turned Szeti, kicked his knees out, and, catching the back of his head, slammed it face-first into the edge of the nearest table until his neck cracked.

"Fuck!" giant Pilyx bellowed. He dropped the gutted loyalist and came for Heia, who was still on top of Barhu, who threw her hips and pitched the duchess away to the left, into the feet of a goggling guano merchant.

Barhu scuttled backward as fast and frantically as she could—

Right into Svir.

He stood above her, his neckerchief blowing out from beneath his scout's mask, hands on hips, staring up at the rafters. "Shoot! What are you waiting for, *shoot!*"

A crossbow snapped in the high rafters of the Arsenal Ballroom.

Barhu recognized the sound of the mechanism from ambushes past. In slow-time analytic trance she saw the navy marksman's bolt split the mail rings of Pilyx's armor and strike the twenty-layer jack below. The jack was made of scavenged metal plates sewn into layers of felt and canvas. Not enough. Pilyx hadn't had the money for a full plate brigandine, and what he could afford was not enough. Accounting strikes again.

He died in a triumph of Falcresti engineering.

The bells of Annalila Fortress rang the marines to their war stations. Iscend pinned the man with the burning face to the ground and drove a dose needle into his throat: a captive, to name any unrevealed coconspirators. Heingyl Ri's handmaidens hurried her out of the ballroom in a protective thistle of gowns.

Applause roared up around them.

"Exquisite!" someone called. "Just exquisite! Well done!"

"Fucking Falcrest," Apparitor muttered, reaching down for Barhu's hand. "Where's Yawa?"

"I don't know. What's happening, Svir? Did you come here to save the Governor?"

"Not at all. When I opened the window, those assholes must've assumed I was coming to warn Governor Heingyl, so they struck too early. They would've killed her in private, later."

He hauled her up. "What *did* you come for?" Barhu panted.

"I was taking care of something in the fortress—"

"What something?"

"I was arranging vendettas. Will you be quiet? When I went up to use a sunflash, I saw *Helbride*. She's sighted the Cancrioth. *Eternal*'s here."

"*Now*? That's impossible!"

"I assure you it's not. She looks set to attack. And someone's tied a plague knot in her shrouds."

"A what?"

"The knot a ship inspector ties if they discover plague, and they need to warn shore parties without alarming the crew. It means *burn this ship on sight*."

"Shit! And we only saw this *now*?"

"All Maroyad's pickets are in dock, remember?"

"I don't understand," Barhu complained, which was about the foulest epithet she knew. "How did they make up the distance? That hole in their prow—"

"I don't know. They must have half the ship down on the pumps."

"Himu *fuck*," Barhu said, in exasperation.

Marines rushed Apparitor and slammed into his upraised polestar mark, the mountain-and-thunderbolt sign of his Imperial Agency. Steel against paper but the paper said, *if you hurt me the Emperor will care.*

The marines stopped.

"Bring us to the command tower," Barhu ordered them. "And get the Rear Admiral up there to meet us."

25

TOOTH BOMB

PEOPLE are always begging me to abandon ship," Aminata complained, "and I always find, at the last minute, that I don't really want to."

Iraji watched her quietly. They sat side by side on the unused bed, a little ways apart.

"I've got to go with Captain Lune," Aminata told herself. "She's my commanding officer."

"Is she? Haven't I seconded you to my service, as an agent of the Throne?"

She tried to smile at him. "I'm not sure the court-martial board will believe I got lawful orders from a Cancrioth magician."

His eyes were gold and dark like sunken treasure. "We need you here. This is your duty. To make the most difference."

"Come on." She tried to laugh him off. "I can't help here. I don't know anything about, you know, all this, this . . ."

"Superstition? Ritual?"

"This Oriati business. I just . . ." She tugged at the stiff collar of her uniform. She'd only just put it back on, and it itched. "I don't see what you think is going to happen, Iraji. Captain Lune put up a plague knot. The navy's going to burn this ship."

"My place is here," he said, with a wistful sadness that made her want to shout at him, no, you idiot, your place is where you *want* it to be, you're not bound here by your flesh, your blood, your race. "I gave myself to them in exchange for Baru's freedom. I can't undo that. I used to faint when I thought about who I really was. I don't do that anymore. That's how I know this is the place where I have to be."

"You don't need to die here."

"We're not going to die," he said, fiercely. "We're going to stop the rockets. We're going to convince the rest of this ship that they *will* see their home again. We're going to bring *Eternal* into safe harbor and find a way everyone can go home alive. It won't be like Kyprananoke."

"And then the navy will storm your ship," Aminata whispered, "and take all of you."

"Not if Baru stops them."

"Can she? Will she?"

"She will. Because she cares about the people on this ship."

"She doesn't even know I'm *alive*, Iraji." And last time she had, she'd used Aminata as a weapon, manipulated her into doing what Baru needed.

"You're not the only person she cares about, Aminata."

"I'm sorry. I'm sorry." Getting up, with a frustration that split her like an axhead: "I have my orders. If I don't obey Shao Lune, if I choose a ship full of my racemates over my superior's commands, I'm finished in the navy *forever*. I'll give every Oriati sailor a bad name."

She fled the room. She fled the thing which frightened her most, which was wanting something more than her duty.

"If you stay," he called after her, "maybe you can get your sword back from the Brain!"

She ran almost bodily into the Eye.

"Aminata," he said; his ordinary body and ordinary face and ordinary voice, and the immense protrusion from his eye socket which Aminata still found truly disgusting. "Tell me honestly. Is there any chance we'll leave this island alive and free?"

She was impatient and afraid and therefore she was honest. "Mister Eye, the purpose of Falcrest's navy is to destroy Oriati. That's all I've ever been taught. Excuse me, please."

Shao Lune had already packed her notes into a gutsack; she was stripped down to linens, oiling herself with monoi, Taranoke's blessing to divers. "I stole it," she said, to Aminata's unvoiced question about the oil. "These tunks have awful security." No apology for the epithet. "Strip your uniform off. The water's warm, and if a current takes us out to sea, you'll regret every extra ounce."

The groan of the ship's alarm sounded through the hull. "They're ready to attack," Shao Lune said. "We'll leave over the stern. Down the same way you escaped, and then we jump. Get your oil on and let's go."

Aminata stared at her. The absolute compliance of her, her sharp eyes and small full mouth, the generous body so ready to be constrained and controlled by the uniform, made appropriate, modest, unobtrusive. She made Aminata feel frictional, ill-designed, a thing that rubbed on itself as it moved.

And she ached to be back with Iraji again, the two of them alike in flesh.

No, her duty told her, *do not be seduced by the homogeneity of race, do not value sameness of flesh.*

She thought about where duty had led her lately.

"Lieutenant Commander." Shao Lune smooth as snakebelly. "I gave you an order."

"You're out of uniform, mam."

"I am your superior officer."

"You aren't in my chain of command. I report directly to Rear Admiral Maroyad, mam, who ordered me to find the Cancrioth. And my mission is not complete until this ship takes up harbor and I report directly to her. Mam."

"Take off your uniform and prepare to leave the ship. You will report to Maroyad only once I am finished with my own report. That is an order. If you disobey me I will see to it that you stand a court-martial."

"Iraji is an agent of the Emperor. He requires me to stay."

"If you choose his agency over duty to the navy you betray women everywhere. Have you seen any proper orders from him? Proper codes, proper seals? Have you seen anything from him but superstition and filth and his whore cock—"

Staring at her, listening to her, Aminata crossed some inner threshold, invisible to her until she had already passed it. Like the point where a ship tips too far, and not all the keel and righting moment in the world can keep it from overturning.

"Excuse me, mam," she said. "I have to go find my sword."

And she walked out.

Iraji smiled like a signal in the night when he saw her coming back. "Don't," she muttered, "don't. Let's just do this and have it done."

MAROYAD lowered her telescope. "Damn good thing you paid to keep one frigate on ready alert, isn't it? Signal *Hawkene* into rocket range. Approach from directly astern. Destroy that thing's rudder with torpedoes. Then burn the hull."

"Don't do this," Barhu warned her. "If you send a ship at them, you'll force their hand."

"I'm to wait until they fire cannon on my island? Until they start flinging plague corpses into my fortress, or rockets full of pus into my reservoirs? No." Maroyad was a flag officer in the full grip of her duty. "There's a plague knot in those sails! A navy officer aboard that ship risked her life to tell us that we have to *destroy it on sight!*"

"She has," Svir murmured, "something of a point." He stood in grim profile at Barhu's elbow, and would not meet her eyes.

"Iraji's aboard that thing," Barhu whispered to him.

"I remember," he growled back. "Do you honestly believe that he and I haven't discussed what we'd do in this situation?"

"We need to strengthen their bargaining position. Give them confidence. Pull back the frigate, Admiral, let them see we'll give them a chance if they don't attack!"

"That's idiotic," Maroyad insisted.

Barhu turned to Iscend Comprine, who had followed her up to the towertop, still in her ballroom finest. "You're an actuary, aren't you? Tell the admiral I'm right."

"I do not have enough knowledge to decide." Iscend was wide-eyed with the need to help. "I'm sorry."

The staff officers behind Maroyad stared at their feet, caught between the Emperor's will and their own rear admiral's orders. Barhu decided to force the choice upon them.

"I am invoking the Emperor's agency. Rear Admiral Maroyad, I will accept responsibility for whatever may occur here. I order you to stand your ship two miles off *Eternal* and to belay any attack."

Maroyad seized her by the wrist. "Listen to me! If they get plague onto this island, thousands of Falcresti citizens *will die*! Parliament *will* send the navy to punish the Oriati! I don't care who takes the blame, but if you force me to obey, *think of those lives*!"

Think of Tau-indi lost in the cancer dark. Think of Aminata, who'd died to save that ship. And of Shao Lune, who Barhu had stranded aboard.

This was the price of attachment. This was the truth Svir had warned her against. *We leave people behind.*

But that same lesson had two edges, and the other edge said: there are other people in this world, with their own wants and means. And sometimes all you can do is make space for them to work.

The Brain had cast a spell on Barhu. How could she break her own spell? How could she fail to see their bargain through? One way or another, Barhu and the Brain *had* to meet again.

So the Brain would not attack.

"Hold your ships," Barhu said. "In the Emperor's name, you *will* hold. Someone find a signal lantern. I need to talk to them."

* * *

THE Eye's mob was smaller, full of sailors and cooks and gardeners and other rough laborers, and a few idealists who had come over simply because Tau-indi was here and they revered the laman as an exemplar of the Mbo's morality. They wielded rakes, wooden planks, hammers, oars, and laundry paddles. Against them the Brain's navigators and griots were backed by Termites with powder-flash in their pistols. The onkos herself stood above them all, in the rigging of the foremast, with an impi's round hide shield in her left hand and her armor bright in the dusk. She looked like a statue of ancient White Akhena, or one of her mau fighters. She had no weapon in her right hand but her light.

The Eye's people came upon them suddenly, screaming and singing, and drew the Termites away from the rocket stations at the prow. Then Aminata (who had handpicked the toughest-looking of the Eye's followers) burst up from belowdecks and led her group onto the rocket racks. Some of her people tied themselves to the racks themselves, to prevent their use: others seized plague vivariums and ran for the rail, where they held the glass bottles hostage. No one could ever say these people lacked valor.

Now: impasse.

Tau-indi Bosoka stepped into the space between the lines. Their jade-gold khanga was stained by tar, seawater, and sweat. The jewelry that had once glittered under Kyprananoke's high sun now glistened with oil tarnish. Their hips moved not with grace but with sore, tottering fatigue.

But Tau spoke.

"Listen! We all came here for the same reason. We came for Abdumasi Abd, my friend, your family. Some of you are afraid that he'll betray your existence to the whole world. Some of you would like that, I know. Some of you want to die here."

"Your Highness," the Brain called down from her foretop. "Falcrest has telescopes trained upon us. When they see our rockets aren't ready to fire, they will destroy us. Stand aside!"

Tau ignored her. "I allowed myself to believe you weren't human. My home, my beloved mbo, made the same mistake. We wrote a footnote to our code of dignity. We said, *everyone but these ones, they are human; everyone is real, but the Cancrioth are not.* We embraced our other enemies. But not you. We hated you. *I* hated you."

Lovely green Isla Cauteria shimmered right off the bow. Eighty thousand people under Aminata's sworn protection. And she was allowing a Federal Prince, foreign royalty, to fight in their defense.

"You've sailed far from home to save Abdu," Tau cried. "So have I. Maybe it seems like we're all doomed to die here. But I can still save Abdu! *We* can still save Abdu! We can rescue him together! And then we can rescue ourselves.

"Come home to Oriati Mbo. You will be welcome. See Aminata, there, who sails for Falcrest? She is welcome among us. See Iraji there, who spied for their Emperor? He is welcome. And my friend Abdumasi Abd, who swam with me in Lake Jaro, who took your money and your cancer into him so that he could go to war? I say he is welcome! Will you come home with me?"

"If you have any principles at all, Tau-indi Bosoka," the Brain called, "you say these things before you have no other choice."

She pointed up to Annalila Fortress, a panther crouched above its prey. Her hand shone against the dark fabric of her sleeve. "Abdumasi Abd *is* in there! And if we show that we can answer Falcrest's weapons with our own, they'll give him up! For the first time in history, Oriati people dictate terms to Falcrest. We are at *their* shores, in *our* ship, with *our* weapons! This is how it was meant to be! *This* is the first right thing that happens since the Armada War! The entire Oriati Mbo knows that we defied Falcrest, and they awaken to the need for war!"

"They'll kill us all," the Eye shouted back. "You saw what one of those ships did to us at Kyprananoke! Here they have a fleet! Are we not the people of the long thought? Aren't you Incrisiath, the Brain? *Think*!"

The Brain denied him with an outflung hand. "We *are* the people of the long thought, my friend. We've thought long enough about Falcrest. They only respect power." She closed her fist around green ghost light. "They've wounded us. They smell weakness. Now we show them we still have strength."

"Your prissy knife-man Masako shot me in the face, and here I am still," Osa shouted, to a general *ooh* of delight from the Eye's supporters. "You're surrounded, short on water, damaged, far off your charts! If you come at them with knives out you have no chance!"

"When the shark smells blood, do you go limp and wait for teeth?" Scheme-Colonel Masako cried back. "You don't understand Falcrest. They're cowards! They exploit weakness! They bargain only when they fear our strength! Tau wants to make speeches about who's human and who is not, but Falcrest doesn't think *any* of us are human!"

The crew wavered. Aminata saw it in the way the able sailors looked to their seniors, and the seniors looked to the officers. Come so far, through thirst and storm, for one man, one sacred precious man: should they risk war when they were so to close him?

"What about Kimbune?" Tau called. "What about Baru? Will you give them a chance? You put your power into Baru, Incrisiath! Is that not enough?"

"It is enough," the Brain roared back, "before I am attacked! Before *you* set the baneflesh on me, carried by an innocent boy! If the bond I put on Baru is broken, then *you broke it!*"

Her supporters growled and crossed their hands, warding off evil. "Cunning bitch," Aminata muttered in Aphalone.

The fuck of it was that the Brain and Masako were right. Once the navy saw the plague knot, they would attack. *Eternal* would burn. And Aminata couldn't figure out how to avoid that.

Or even if she *should*. After all, didn't Baru want this ship for her plans? And wasn't she a grand traitor?

Maybe Aminata's duty here was to keep this ship out of Baru's hands.

"Masako," the Brain said, sorrowfully. "Load your pistols with small shot. Drive them off the rockets."

The woman in the Invijay fighting costume, the one with the face dimpled by lines of scar, lifted her fist over a glass vivarium. "Shoot at us and I'll break this open!"

"Do we now fear death?" the Brain roared. "What use is immortality if we cannot decide where and when our deaths will *matter*? This is the moment we live so long to reach!"

And then, at last, the Womb spoke.

Aminata had not seen her because she stood to the side, on one of the enormous wooden channels that anchored the shroud lines supporting the nearest mast. Her voice was not as powerful as the Brain's, or the Eye's, or even Tau's.

But when she spoke, they all heard their mother calling.

"I brought a woman aboard this ship on Kyprananoke. Before she left us, Baru arranged safe passage through a minefield, through two waiting Masquerade warships. When one of those warships attacked us, she brought the other to our defense. I made the right choice when I brought her aboard.

"But there was another person I brought to us. I brought Tau-indi Bosoka, because I could not bear to leave them to burn. Listen to them now. Let them keep *us* from burning. If we wanted to die in a hurry, would we be Cancrioth?"

There was some laughter. Aminata watched the Brain's eyes narrow. She had to reassert herself, now, before—

Iraji saw something up in the rigging, and stepped forward, frowning, raising one hand to point. He'd spotted the plague knot. He meant only to warn the others.

But the Brain saw him open his mouth and raise up his hands: and she knew he'd been taught sorcery.

She struck.

Her bright hand reached out to seize his attention. "IRA-RYE UNDIO-
NASH," she said, silently: but loud as a scream to a spy trained to lip-read.
The name of Iraji's mother found him, and he had no baneflesh to protect him
from magic now.

Iraji fainted to the deck. Aminata almost caught him but she was too slow
and his head cracked against a cleat hard enough to open his scalp. He bled on
her.

"You fuck!" she shouted, and raised her bloodied hand. "Look what you've
done!"

The Eye jeered in En Elu Aumor, words Aminata couldn't translate but understood nonetheless: shame on you! *Shame* on you, Incrisiath! A roar of fury
spread through the Eye's crowd. The Brain's Termites stiffened and raised their
weapons.

It was all about to go to shit, one way or another. And here Aminata was,
kneeling with Iraji's blood on her hands, surrounded by magic, helpless to
make a difference—

Not helpless. Never helpless.

"Excuse me!" Aminata bellowed. "I have a suggestion!"

BARHU was still figuring out how the sunflash lantern worked when *Eternal* launched its first rocket. A tongue of white light shot from *Eternal*'s
prow, up across the falling sun, and straight toward Barhu.

"Here it comes!" the watchgirl cried. "One rocket, up high!"

"Get under the shingle." Maroyad pulled Barhu and Svir together into the
shadow of the tower roof. "*Hawkene* must attack. Give us permission to attack."

"Just one rocket." Barhu tugged free of Maroyad's fingers. "If they wanted
to kill us with plague, they'd send more."

"It's a ranging shot! They're testing the wind before the full salvo! Let my
ship destroy them before they launch more, damn you!"

"No." Barhu stood her ground. "You will signal *Hawkene* to stand off and
give *Eternal* sea room."

"You're insane! You're gambling tens of thousands of lives because you
want to make money off a plague ship!"

"I seem insane to you," Barhu countered, "because I know things you do not.
This is why I am given power over you, Maroyad. Will you disobey the Emperor?"

Maroyad groaned in frustration. The lone rocket soared across the sky,
closer every moment. There was something wrong with it, Barhu noticed. It
was too heavy and too slow to possibly cover this distance—

A ring of sparks jetted from the rocket's ass end. A piece of it fell off and tumbled into the ocean. Wooden wings snapped into place, and then a second rocket ignited to push the glider forward. A two-stage rocket. Ingenious. Barhu had thought those were purely Falcrest's invention.

"You should take shelter, Your Excellency," Iscend whispered.

All around her, flare pistols and signal lanterns awaited her word. "Agonist," Maroyad pleaded. "Let us attack."

"No. Hold your fire."

"It's coming right at us." Svir glanced between the fortress wind vanes and the rocket. "They launched a little westerly to account for the wind."

"It can't be steered, can it?" Barhu muttered to him.

"There might be an apparatus to keep it on a desired course—like the stabilizers on torpedoes—but to make it so *small,* I don't know—"

"Your Excellences, get down!"

Iscend grabbed at Barhu's belt but she fought back, leaning out to watch, the bomb was *right there,* skimming in above them with its second engine dead now but sparks still jetting from its tail. A fuse, they'd calculated the flight time and fused it, so it would blow up when it was still in the air—

It's for bombarding cities, Barhu thought. You can't use this against a moving ship and expect to land a hit. You can't fit an explosive aboard that would do any real harm. It's meant to hit cities. And it's meant to carry plague.

"Let me fire!" Maroyad screamed.

"I am the Emperor's will, damn you! *Wait!*"

A hundred feet above the command tower the glide bomb popped like a firework. The blast echoed in Barhu's chest.

She and Maroyad looked at each other.

A strange hail began to fall.

Barhu held out her hand, and caught a forked brown chip. All around her tiny brown-white objects pelted off stone and lumber.

"Teeth," she said. "They've sent us teeth."

The sound of bitten stone chattered all around her.

"It was a dummy payload," Svir said. "A demonstration. So we know they can hit us."

"Hold," Maroyad ordered. "Hold and wait."

The minutes crawled past.

"There!" the watchgirl called. "Signal mirror on the ghost ship's bowsprit! It's in navy code, mam. They want to parley with us for repairs and safe return to their home waters."

"Don't call it a ghost ship," Maroyad growled. "It's right there. We can all see it."

Barhu bit down on her tongue to hold in her growl of triumph. She had gambled with all these lives, gambled and won. It would not do to enjoy it. Not for more than a moment.

NOT one of them comes ashore." Maroyad pounded her desk. "Not in my fortress, not in my town. A living person's a damn sight better carrier than a rocket. If you're going to negotiate with them, you do it somewhere that can be quarantined."

"Poses some difficulties," Barhu muttered. The details of rigging and sail aboard Maroyad's warships were too sensitive to hold a meeting there. A meadow or a patch of wilderness would not have toilets, and would be far too hard to quarantine. And there was secrecy to consider: Barhu wanted to preserve the illusion that *Eternal* was a huge merchant ship, and that meant keeping it away from curious eyes with nautical experience.

She had only one option left. Remote, yet developed. Nestled in a bay, where *Eternal* could be hidden. Full of people who could attend a merchant bazaar, as cover for the real negotiations, yet who would not gossip as easily as Falcresti townfolk.

"What's the Taranoki colony named?" she asked the others gathered in Maroyad's office.

"Aratene, if I remember right," Heingyl Ri said. "I wanted to visit."

"That sounds right." The Aphalone name *Aratene* would come from the Urunoki name *Iritain,* which came in turn from the name of the old harbor town Iriad, Barhu's home, joined with *tain,* the Urun word for *foreign.* The very same root yielded the name Tain Hu: which could be read as *great foreigner* or *foreign bane.*

Yawa produced a viciously sweet smile. Something cruel had come into her since the Governor's Ball. "You want to hold your vital negotiations and prisoner exchange *in* the Souswardi experimental colony?"

"Taranoki," Barhu insisted.

"Have you considered how you'll tell your islanders that you're about to moor a plague ship armed with hundreds of cannon off their little bayside paradise?"

"I haven't," Barhu admitted. "I should speak to the mayor, or the . . ." She was bitterly embarrassed not to remember what the Taranoki called a council of elders. Muirae? No, she was thinking of Muire Lo. What was the name? "The governing committee."

Heingyl Ri turned to her handmaidens. "Who are the governors? The ones always shipping coffee samples everywhere?"

"Hyani Coinflower and husband?" Maroyad snapped her stubby fingers. "No, there's a new couple. Arrived very suddenly a month or two ago."

"Yes, that's right," one of the handmaidens said, "I remember their names from the coffee pamphlet. Solit and Pinion?"

"That's right," another handmaiden said, reading from just such a pamphlet, "it says here, Solit Able and Pinion Starmap."

Barhu was, at first, indignant, embarrassed by her own astonishment: and she came within one breath of blurting out, like a petulant child, the fatal word *Mom?*

A STORY ABOUT ASH 11

FEDERATION YEAR 912:
23 YEARS EARLIER
IN KUTULBHA HARBOR, BESIDE RUINED KUTULBHA
IN SEGU MBO

SOME of the Lonjaro Princes declared a surrender party on the palace ship *Kangaroo Principle*. The Princes had to make some joy, right here at the center of the hurt, or the whole generation's temper would go sore. A celebration was as vital to them as prayer would be to a deist.

But it was so very, very hard.

"It's not a very good party, is it?" Tau-indi said to their mother, peering around at the fine wines and the casks of beer, the huge swirls of crushed silk and piled velvet. Everyone was drinking and smoking with furious concentration. The dance moved in narrow nervous lines. "You always threw better parties."

"It's easy to be joyful when you have joyful principles in the air. This, though, this is work. Sometimes smiling is work." Mother Tahr took their hands. "Tau! You've got painting fat under your nails. Go wash up."

Tau-indi jerked their hands away, resentful. They'd been a Prince for so many days. Impossible to be a child again. "Mother," they said, rather stiffly, "you've been talking to Cosgrad too much."

Tahr looked at them with a sad little smile of pride and hope and deep, deep loss, a smile Tau-indi wished they didn't understand. Tau-indi was ready to leave home and be a Prince, and their mother knew it.

"I have to go find Kindalana," Tau-indi said.

"Go, then," Tahr said, meaning not just *go find Kindalana*, but all the rest. "Go do it well."

They swept off royally, cleaning their fingernails when Tahr couldn't see. They got a mahogany bowl full of shrimp and a ceramic cup full of pickle sauce and went up onto the deck, down the length of the ship, out of the mass of Princes, flowing through the clerks and housekeepers and ship crew. And of course they found Kindalana sitting at the stern, wearing a gray halter that left her shoulder blades open to say, with their narrow motions, leave me alone, I am worried, I am thinking.

"I brought you some shrimp," Tau-indi said.

She had her forehead against the railing. Her legs dangled over the water. She slid over and made room and Tau-indi sat down with her. They looked at her, then out at the lanterns and torches of the other ships, and at the black smoke glow of the city.

After a little while she reached over and took a shrimp.

They each ate the meat and spat the shells into the harbor. "It's in us," Tau-indi said, looking toward Kutulbha. "The ash is in us. Forever. I hope I don't forget that."

"He was going to set up a new shipping company. Before the family fleet burnt up in the fire."

"Abdu?"

"Yeah. He was going to send ships to Falcrest." She took another shrimp and ate it and looked at Tau-indi while she chewed and swallowed. "With mixed crews, so they'd learn each other's languages. He was going to send eidetic griots to Falcrest to have their stories turned into books, and to memorize the Falcrest books for retelling."

Her eyes made the claim that Abdumasi was as much a Prince as either of them.

"Poor Abdu." Tau-indi bit down on the toothache. "I wish he were here."

"You do?" Kindalana explored them with her eyes. "Really?"

"Sure. Yeah." They kicked at the side of the ship with their heels. "When I needed someone to remind me life wasn't all, you know, duty and trim, I'd go to him...."

She said an edged thing. "And then you'd both come bicker over me. I was always the third one."

"You came later, Kinda."

"And I was a woman."

"Yes," Tau admitted. "That's true." And she understood that a laman was not something halfway between man and woman.

"We were children. We can't be anymore." She took a shrimp and peeled the shell with the edge of her thumbnail. "It's funny, the things that you miss."

Tau-indi made a shrug with their hands: like what?

"Like Abdu," Kinda said. "He always wanted to be one of us. I didn't realize it until that day on the beach."

"He will be," Tau-indi said softly. They moved their weight so their hip would brush Kindalana. "If you do marry him. He'll be husband of a Prince, and that's like being a Prince."

"If, if, you say *if* but there's no *if*. I have to marry him. All the families in his household are depending on me to keep them employed."

"Would you marry him anyway," Tau asked, "if he still had his money?"

"My answer to that doesn't matter."

"It does to him." A marriage built on obligation might work, but it hadn't for Padrigan, and it hadn't for Tahr, and now they were in each other's beds instead.

"I don't know," she said, which Tau thought must mean *no*.

"I could do it. I could marry him and you could marry Farrier."

They tried to imagine being married to Abdumasi, rubbing their chin on his stubble when they kissed him, watching him laugh and play big and try to hide his (wonderful, endearing) efforts to be better. They tried imagining Abdumasi's cock hard in their hand. It was very odd.

Kinda considered them. "Do you mean that?"

"You said . . . you and Farrier . . . you said you were trying to seduce him. And if you couldn't marry him, you said I had to do it. Well, I could marry Abdu, and you could try for Farrier. Do you really want to marry Farrier?"

"No, of course not," Kinda said. "But I want him to want to marry me."

"Why?" It felt wrong to Tau. It meant using a basic human need as an instrument of politics.

"So he'll make mistakes," Kindalana said, cryptically. "He's taught me a lot about what mistakes mean in Falcrest. By what he does, and what he won't do."

"I don't like the idea," Tau admitted. "I don't like the principles of it. Flirting with him."

"I'm sorry." She said it a little bit like a question. "It makes you jealous."

"No!"

"Not of Farrier, Tau. Of my methods. You think it's wrong, but for me it's just . . . what a Prince does. One's body is political. Falcrest has peculiar politics, so I do peculiar things. I was making progress on Farrier, very carefully." She sighed in frustration. "But I can't leave Abdumasi, I don't think. He needs my money and he loves me."

Tau-indi loved Kindalana more for this than for anything before. "That's good of you. To want to treat him well."

"Thank you." She looked as if she wanted to touch their hand again. She didn't. "But you know I won't."

"Treat him well?"

She shook her head. "I have my duty to the Mbo. That will always come before him. And he'll hate that, eventually. He'll probably hate me for it."

"Kinda, that's unbearably sad."

"I know. I know." She sighed. "I'm glad we got to talk."

"I'm glad, too."

"It's over," Kindalana said. She turned at the waist so that they were facing each other and lifted her chin. All the lines of paint on her throat and chest moved in one liquid bound-together way, like the surface of the sea, like the mbo, and Tau-indi remembered painting the duties of a Prince on her flesh. "I didn't think about it until now, but this is the end of . . . you know, of Prince Hill. It's over."

They laughed and it came out as bittersweet and papery as the treaty. "I wish you wouldn't say things so honestly."

"Sorry," she said, and then, defying Tau's wish, "Do you want to kiss me?"

Tau-indi's stomach leapt. They giggled and then, sitting up very straight, looked at Kindalana, wonderful awful Kindalana, who always solved things too directly. The palace-ship moved under them and they swayed against each other. Kindalana opened her mouth a little, faintly nervous, faintly cheeky, and made a sound like the very first breath of a laugh.

"I don't think so," Tau-indi said, although it didn't feel true until the last word. "Not right now. It wasn't quite that kind of jealousy."

She looked at them a while. She nodded. "I didn't really think so, either."

"I hope your dad gets better."

"Me too," she said. "Can we stay here a while more?"

They did.

POSITIONING

THE fortress watch officers thought Shao Lune was a corpse, an overboard from a trader or a victim of foul play. Leave her to the Cautery Plat constabulary, who were getting paid to make up stories about skull-backed whales.

But the corpse turned over from its back-float rest and began to swim toward Annalila Fortress, using the long, slow, hip-driven strokes the navy taught for distance. So they plucked Shao Lune out of the ocean, glistening with monoi and mad as a bull. Before she even asked for water, she demanded a clerk to take down her statement.

"Escaped from captivity aboard Oriati vessel," Barhu read. "Collected secret knowledge on vessel's origin, construction, armament, provisions, command, and crew readiness. Important diplomatic information aboard. Must report in person to authorities soonest."

Look how carefully she'd preserved *Eternal*'s cover as a trade ship, how she'd danced around naming any particular authority—whether Admiralty, Parliament, or Throne—as the recipient of her information. An offer of secrets for sale: all loyalties liquid and flexible.

Barhu had to buy her back.

"I've got to have her," she complained to Iscend, who was packing Barhu's things for the move across the island to Aratene. *Eternal* was already limping ahead to the Rubiyya bay, desperately pumping water from her cracking hull. "She'll know what it's like aboard *Eternal*. Their political situation, water and supply, everything we need for the negotiations. Damn her. Why didn't she come straight to me?"

"You know why," Iscend said.

Barhu, hunting through her paper stocks for a page that felt right in the spring humidity, admitted it: "Because I left her on *Eternal*."

"No. Because she betrayed you to Xate Yawa. She fears your retaliation."

"She won't fear that," Barhu said, absently giving away far too much.

Iscend looked up with a dart in her eyes. The light through *Helbride*'s deck above cast spots like salt crystals on her face. "Why does she believe you won't punish her for that? Oh. Because you've been lovers? You shouldn't have done that, my lady."

"Oh, come off it," Barhu snapped, "you were happy enough to ride my arm in front of a whole ballroom."

Iscend smirked a little, like a schoolgirl, at the innuendo. "The seduction of Governor Ri seems to serve your political objectives. But you must beware that the pleasure of your preferred vice does not lead you astray. I know that the meeting of similar anatomies in the isoamorous union can be addictive, frightfully ecstatic, due to the closed feedback loop of two identical—"

The Hu in Barhu snuck the jibe past her. "*Frightfully* ecstatic, Iscend? Does the thought of me frighten you?"

She expected a retort about Incrastic science, about the hereditary threat of the tribadist, whose behavior could only be explained by an anomalous and surpassing pleasure. Not the congruent and appropriate reward between man and woman, but instead an excruciating reflective similarity, driving each other to heights not meant for the mind to bear. Separating the reward of sex from the reproductive purpose. The Falcresti fetish of the tribadist, at once debased and exalted, revolting and enticing, predatory and doomed.

Instead Iscend said, levelly, "Your Excellence, if you must indulge a vice which could compromise you, then you should indulge it with a woman who can be trusted. A woman whose entire purpose is your betterment and success."

Oh, Wydd save her. Not this! Not her! She must have some bizarre Clarified reason, but Barhu could not *survive* the thought. She lunged for another topic. "Are you satisfied with the plan to hold negotiations at Aratene?"

"Largely. May I make a suggestion?"

"Yes, go ahead," Barhu said, irritated: Iscend was playing for time, drawing out the conversation, to observe Barhu's discomfort.

"We should go out to Aratene, together, before the negotiations begin. Speak to the village leadership. Canvas the terrain. Ensure all's well."

It was a good idea, and it would get Barhu away from Xate Yawa, who made the precipice in her mind wider and wider. Barhu had a solution to Yawa's dilemma in mind: the need for one of them to destroy the other. She was not sure she could face it.

"I'll invite Heingyl Ri," she said, "and she can bring along her merchant factors. I need to persuade her to accept my suit."

And Governor Heingyl would be a good chaperone. Barhu had spent too much time longing for women in forests to trust herself around Iscend. She had made a very firm resolution to *never* touch the Clarified woman.

But she had betrayed oaths before.

"Go ask the Stag Governor if she'll send a party to Aratene with me," she ordered Iscend. "I'm going back to Annalila Fortress to see to Shao Lune and take control of the prize."

"The prize, Your Excellence?"

Barhu smiled, but didn't answer. It seemed perverse that she had never met the man at the eye of the maelstrom: poor much-sought-after Abdumasi Abd.

I know something you'd pay anything to know," Shao Lune said.

They walked the parapets of the fortress. Sea wind hissed between the crenellations to snap the banners like laundry.

"*Anything* is an exorbitant price, Shao."

Weeks aboard *Eternal* hadn't softened that cruel smile. Kyprananoke's destruction hadn't washed away the haughty security of her poise. Barhu felt a sudden idiot longing for her, for the security of her self-serving self-possession. You could trust Shao Lune to see to herself. What a terrible marvel of a person. Ulyu Xe was right. It would be very easy for Barhu to think she deserved a lover like Shao.

Shao Lune turned up her collar against the wind. Her insignia glinted smugly. "My duty obliges me to report the elementary facts. *Eternal* cannot leave this island without your help. They're on half rations for water, deep into their reserves. Their ship is in a rolling mutiny, one faction taking control, then the other. They may posture strength, Your Excellence, but they are vulnerable."

Barhu frowned at Shao's collar, noticing the loose fit. "Lost your old uniform, have you? Was it a difficult escape?"

"Simple enough." She scowled and it was like there was venom on her lips. "If not *entirely* satisfactory."

Barhu crowded her toward the parapet, and the drop. "You tied a signal knot into *Eternal*'s rigging. You wanted that ship destroyed."

"I offered a recommendation, based on the threat that ship posed to Isla Cauteria. And you ignored it." She smiled at Barhu with exquisitely falsified respect. "Which is your purpose as an Imperial agent: to exercise your influence in pursuit of the Emperor's agenda."

"Did you *really* think," Barhu murmured, taking Shao gently by the back of her collar, "that you'd ever get that pardon you want so badly if you had that ship destroyed? From me *or* from Yawa?"

In a rapid, confident hiss: "I want what you promised. Do you remember? Do you remember what you offered me, before you led me onto that ship and *abandoned me there*? When you make your designs for the navy and Parliament, I want a seat at the table. I want to be a staff officer in the new Admiralty. I want my prize agent cut in on the first tranche of war spoils. I want a piece of your reward for finding the Cancrioth. And if you don't give me what I want, or if you try to make me disappear, I've left sealed testimony which will make your friend pay with her career and her life."

"My friend?"

"Aminata's alive. She's alive on *Eternal*."

Barhu gaped at her. She'd thought, way deep down in the bottom of her soul, that she hoped Aminata was still alive only because she was a coward, because she wasn't ready to mourn again. But her hope was *true*.

"She's regressed to her nativity. She wouldn't leave *Eternal* even when I gave her the order." Shao brushed her collar clean where Barhu had touched it. "She'll have to stand to a court-martial, of course. But I might be convinced to testify in her favor. . . ."

"A court-martial?"

"She disobeyed my direct orders. That's mutiny. The penalty is death."

"You're a staff captain, not a line officer. You don't give orders to sailors."

Shao Lune's eyes flashed with contempt. "Please don't pretend you know the legal circumstances of Aminata's crime better than I do."

"I've got to get her out of there," Barhu breathed. "She's alive! Oh, that's wonderful—"

Impulsively, idiotically, because it was a thing people did in stories, she tried to kiss the staff captain on the cheek. Shao Lune pushed her firmly away. "Not here."

"Sorry," Barhu said, daftly, as if she'd done something wrong. She was so confused by what she felt—anger at herself, irritation at herself for not directing that anger at Shao Lune, hurt that she'd been rebuffed—that she tried to trample on over the moment. "Listen, I'm holding negotiations with the Cancrioth at Aratene. There's a very good chance that all the Republic's foreign policy in the next fifty years could be determined by the mercantile opportunities we open there. We might have a real chance for lasting, profitable peace. Come with me."

"I'd travel as your companion? And we'd be seen together in this . . . Souswardi colony? In an official capacity? I'd be attached to your retinue?"

Barhu had not considered, in her damn self-centered arrogance, that *every minute* of her time with Shao Lune before this encounter had occurred under duress.

"Yes?" she said, weakly.

"Of course I won't come. What would it do for my reputation to be seen with you?"

Later Barhu would try to recapture the feeling of that rebuke. Like a chain you'd forgotten, suddenly pulled taut. You feel not just foolish but sheepish, the victim of a very obvious prank. Why did you let yourself hope? Your race will always matter.

"Well," Barhu said, coldly, "it might give you a reputation as someone associated with Agonist, a newly minted Imperial agent about to turn a fortune in trade."

"I don't want a reputation as your whore."

"You aren't my *whore*—"

"I've slept with you as an exchange of personal and political favor. I've slept with you in order to convince you to protect me. Our tribade doesn't belong in the public eye."

"There wasn't any *tribade*," Barhu said, out of a petty desire to correct her.

"Don't be facetious. The sodomites don't all sodomize each other, either, but it's the word in current use."

This was the first time in Barhu's life that she had actually been turned down. It was unexpectedly upsetting. "I know," she said, stiffly, "that you obtained a certain thrill from treating me like a lustful, savage native."

"Really?" Shao said, with elegant disdain. "I didn't think you remembered anything about that night."

Barhu ignored her, for fear she'd scream. "I was confident this thrill did not extend beyond the bed and into your overall opinion of me. I thought we had an accommodation of physical and political use, which might be extended until no longer convenient."

"Oh, don't be petulant. It's nothing personal. You're very lovely, and given a boat and a month to ourselves I'd run you through your paces—"

"Like a horse?"

"Like a prize horse," Shao said, as if this were any sort of compliment. "But there's a reason gava women aren't invited to the anti-mannist leagues. Or to the Case for Isosocial Safety."

"What reason is that?"

"Because it undermines our united female cause to complicate it with racial divisions."

"So even in the city of merit, in this republic of merit, I don't belong in the women's organizations because I'm from Taranoke?"

"A woman's merit must be evaluated against the background of her race," Shao said, airily. "You are an extraordinary Souswardi. Isn't that enough?"

"No, it's *not* fucking enough! And don't you dare threaten my friend ever again!"

Shao Lune sniffed. "This will play very poorly in Lieutenant Commander Aminata's court-martial. If she survives to see it. Don't forget that I've seen the Scheme-Colonel Masako aboard *Eternal,* Baru. I can prove that your 'traders' are working with agents of the Oriati federal government to infiltrate and destroy us. You wouldn't want that out in the open, would you? It would complicate your plans for a new trade concern, I imagine. And if you try to be rid of me . . . well, I think you know what a sealed vendetta can do, hm?"

Barhu called her a snake in Urunoki, and left her there, smiling coldly into the high sea wind.

"AMINATA'S alive," Barhu told the two young Oriati sailors off *Ascentatic,* and had to smile when they gasped and seized each other in joy. "She's aboard *Eternal,* waiting for rescue."

Lieutenant Faroni and Midshipman Gerewho, who had been Aminata's assistant torturers, broke out in open cries of delight. Barhu's smile became a grin. "Tell Nullsin for me. But no one else, all right? Now I want a favor from you. I'm going to show you my Imperial mark, all right? Not to force you to do what I want, but so you can't be blamed for it afterward. And I'm bringing a guest. Please keep her presence confidential."

"Your Excellence," Faroni said, all business again, "we see nothing we are not required to see."

Faroni led them down into the bowels of the fortress, through the gated guard posts and the paper checkpoints crewed by midshipman clerks, to the mirrored panopticon above Abdumasi Abd's cell.

From the inside you might believe it *was* an apartment, one unit in a middlingly new Falcresti house-of-eight, with proper closed-surface plumbing, taps, and the luxury of a cistern-flush toilet. It even had a window looking out over the fishmarket bustle of Cautery Plat, where steam billowed up from the clambake huts along the slum waterline and children took swimming lessons in netted-off shallows. Ordinarily prisoners were carefully deprived of any sense of time or place.

But Abd wasn't at the window. Barhu watched him through the panopticon as he sat before a small mirror and stripped down to the waist. He carried no fresh cuts or scabs on his narrow, exercise-hardened body. But he had old wounds.

He twisted himself so that he could inspect his back.

Barhu's guest began to cry silently. Barhu touched her shoulder. "Wait until I call you."

Kimbune nodded, and touched the loop of parchment she'd wrapped around her wrist: a copy of her proof, for safety.

The door in the false anteroom opened at Barhu's second knock. Abd's face appeared like a skull in the crack. His eyes were sunken and suspicious but still bright with awareness. He didn't, of course, recognize her.

"Who," he grunted.

"Abdumasi Abd," she said, smiling as well as she could, "I've been looking for you a long, long time. Tau-indi Bosoka sends their love."

His hands plucked at the couch, traced the seams of the cover. "I don't recognize the name you mentioned. Wait. Tau-indi Bosoka? Is that the Prince-Ambassador?"

"Of course it is," Barhu said, patiently. "As you know very well."

A white stain like bread mold spotted the dark skin on his forehead. When he saw Barhu peering in curiosity, he said, "You weren't there for the wet room?"

"The what?"

"The fungus room. They hung me in this stone cell where fungus grew everywhere. Fungus coming up the toilet hole, red jelly spidered all over the floor, these fat fruiting bodies sticking out of the walls. I slept in a little clean spot that I had to defend with my own piss." Abd poked his forehead. "Eventually it started to grow inside me. I think it's supposed to make me tell the truth."

"The way the Undionash implant is supposed to grow in you, and carry your soul forever?"

His eyes did not even narrow: he was that good. "I don't know what you mean."

"I've been on *Eternal*. They want you to come home, Abdu. They want you safe."

"What are you here to trick me into saying?"

"I'm here to trick you into trade," she said. "Into commerce. The way one merchant lures another: with the possibility of profit."

The fact that Abd was a merchant could be attributed to destiny, if you were a fool; Barhu thought it was instead a logical consequence of the facts. It made sense that the first man to strike against Falcrest would have the independence of a private citizen but the wealth of a trading concern.

But there was a kind of symmetry to it, wasn't there? Like Barhu, Abd had gone looking for a war. Like Barhu, he would find his victory in a different kind of contest.

Abd spat on the tiles. "Trade? With *Falcrest*? I know how that goes. No one knows better than I do."

"Or I," Barhu countered. "I was in the markets on Taranoke when they came. I'm not here to make Falcrest richer. Quite the contrary. You have interests in the Black Tea Ocean and the western Oriati coast, don't you? I'd like you to approach those contacts on my behalf."

Abd glared at her. "You're usually more subtle about trying to ferret out my accomplices."

He was very reasonably suspicious. "I don't expect to persuade you without matching action. I'm here to return you to your people."

"Which people?"

"Kimbune, you should come in now."

The mathematician peered shyly around the door. "Hello?"

"Oh principles." Abdumasi pushed himself back into the settee. "Why, she's . . ." He pointed to the tattoo of the Round Number. "You're one of the—"

"Yes," Kimbune said. "I really am."

"You can't be here. I didn't betray you." He began to tremble. "I didn't tell them a—this is a trick! You're a fake!"

"I'm not, Abdumasi. I came for you."

He began to speak with her in En Elu Aumor. Kimbune came out of the doorway, wide-eyed in wonder. She was shaking. Barhu imagined how she would feel when she saw Pinion and Solit again, if they really did live here. She began shaking, too, an empathy of hands.

And she felt, also, a prickle of awe, a starlight feeling, as if she were standing in a shaft of radiance coming down through a crack in a huge black roof. What if this meeting was the proof of genuine immortality? What if the soul of Kimbune's dead husband *actually* lived on in Abdumasi Abd's body?

"I'm not your husband!" Abdumasi shouted, in Aphalone. "I don't know what you want me to say! I don't even know his name, they gave me the damn thing and I—"

Silently, frowning, Kimbune offered her arms.

Something happened between them, a savagely quick exchange of emotion, like two crippled ships locked in broadside by their toppled masts: then Abdumasi was sobbing against her neck, clinging to the first person he had seen in months whose comfort might (might) not be a trick.

Kimbune pushed Abdumasi upright, inspected him succinctly, brushed at his shoulders and looked critically over his naked chest. "Food," she said. "Then I'll tell you about the proof."

"The proof?"

"My husband never believed I'd finish it. But I did. I'll tell you everything, and he'll argue, I'm sure." Kimbune's eyelashes fairly dripped raw determination. "But first, you talk to Baru."

"*What?*" Abdumasi barked. "*This* is Baru Cormorant?"

What do you say to a man who you have deceived and destroyed? What had she imagined she would say to Xate Olake if she saw him again? Nothing: she had avoided the thought.

"Yes," she said. "This is me."

Abdumasi Abd measured her. A lot of merchants must have seen those eyes across their cups, their contracts, their papers of concession. The eyes of a man who had bargained his way into the company of immortals just for a chance to strike his foe.

"Talk," he said. "So I don't go looking for something sharp."

She told him how the Cancrioth had come searching for him, and how Barhu had led them to Isla Cauteria. She told them that the Cancrioth had Tau, and that Tau already knew Abdu was carrying an implant. He covered his fungus-scarred face and hid in Kimbune's arms.

"Do you want to go back to the Cancrioth in exchange for Tau?" Barhu asked him.

"No," Abd choked. "I don't want to go back to them. I just . . ."

Kimbune closed her eyes.

"I want to go home with Tau. I want to see my wife, and tell her how sorry I am, and then maybe get mad at her again. I want . . . but it doesn't matter. I bear a sacred line. The Cancrioth can't let me go. Can't let this thing," he groped for his back, "go. . . ."

"The thing in you, yes, Abd, *that's* what they want. The Line and all the souls within it. Not you, Abdu. The tumor."

"What's the difference? It's growing in *me*."

She waited for him to look at her. She showed him the tip of the little knife.

"Oh," he groaned. "Not again."

"I could free you from your burden," Barhu told him. "I could bring you to see your wife again. But I need to ask you questions first, Abdumasi. Questions about a man you once knew, and the reason you hated him."

Barhu found Yawa in the fortress stables, dressed in simple peasant's clothes and the sort of dull wooden mask a Selions farmer might wear when the livestock warden came round. The old woman sat on a stone wall with her bare hands clasped in her lap.

"Napping?" Barhu teased. "Manure smells like your childhood?"

"No," Yawa said, miserably. "I'm watching them kill a foundered horse."

He was a roan carriage horse, long-legged with small hooves. A ring of bumps around one of those hooves betrayed his fatal wound: the bone of his leg driven down through the hoof below. Every few steps the horse flared his nostrils and tried to lie down. The groom whispered in his ear.

"Farrier," Yawa said. "That's what they call a man who tends to horse's hooves."

"Did they overwork the poor thing? I remember there was a rash of foundering in Treatymont. The carriage services bought good field horses and walked them to death on hard roads."

"No. He was a prize horse. They let him stay in their best pasture this spring, and he had too much fresh grass and sugar. It made his hooves soft, somehow."

The horse lay down on a pile of hay in a gutter. The grooms tossed up cut grass to hide the smell of blood. The veterinarian wrapped a blindfold over the horse's eyes.

"Ah, Devena," Yawa croaked, and spat into the stone of the wall. "What do you want?"

"I came to ask you about a surgery. Iscend's going to demonstrate the technique down in the morgue, when she finds a corpse with an appropriate spine. We need your expertise. I need to know if it can possibly work."

Yawa shuddered. "A spinal? Good luck."

"It can't be impossible, can it? You certainly brought *me* through meningitis. . . ."

She shuddered again where Barhu expected a chuckle, and said nothing.

"Yawa, what *is* it?"

"Cryptarch business," Yawa said, roughly. "Svir was right. We had it easy on *Helbride*. We were under our own power. I forgot how it is. . . ."

"Your brother."

"Yes."

"Was Hesychast here?"

Yawa shrugged. "Why would it matter?"

"He might have betrayed something, when you told him what you'd learned. You're a judge, Yawa, you know how to read the witness."

"Not this witness," Yawa grumbled. "I suppose he was . . . sentimental about Abdumasi Abd and Tau-indi Bosoka. I saw him react when I mentioned trading Abdu to the Cancrioth."

"Good. That's what I thought. I just spoke with Abdumasi Abd, and he—"

She cut herself off.

"What?" Yawa demanded.

"I . . . I'm not sure it's safe to tell you. If Hesychast's putting pressure on you, maybe it's best if I keep what I learned to myself. So he can't force it out of you."

"I need something. Anything. A crumb."

The horse's veterinarian prepared a glass syringe: kratom opiate, to ease the pain of the paralyzing aconite that would follow. Barhu reached for Yawa's gloved hand.

She drew it away. "Baru. We are out of time. One of us has to be destroyed. One or the other. It's been made absolutely clear to me."

Barhu shifted closer to whisper. "We could use the secrets."

"What secrets?"

"Renascent must have some way to blackmail or control Farrier and Hesychast, right? If we could learn their secrets, then we'd be too dangerous for them to destroy. We could set up vendettas for automatic release. Then we'd— well, you'd—be on an even keel with Hesychast."

Yawa hemmed in thought. "You thought Farrier might be a pedophile. It would explain his belief in discipline. He would *have* to believe that the mind could master the flesh."

"No. That's not it, thank Wydd."

"You're certain?"

Her brief conversation with Abdumasi had narrowed her suspicions. Tauindi had started her down the path, with their outburst on *Eternal,* on Baru's last night aboard. *Abdumasi wouldn't have joined the Cancrioth or fought the Masquerade if he didn't hate Farrier so much. And why does he hate Farrier? Kindalana most of all.*

There was an obvious reason for one man to hate another over a woman. Kindalana lived in Falcrest now, as the Amity Prince, so there was clear opportunity. But say Farrier and Kindalana *had* been entangled: would that be blackmail useful to the Throne? Charges of unlicensed miscenegation and consorting with aristocracy were dangerous, but Farrier was a popular man, and an affair with an Oriati Prince might only add to his cachet. It did not seem enough to control him. Could Kindalana be his hostage? Could he care about her *that* much? Possibly: but Barhu didn't believe it. Farrier would rationalize his way out of any compromising attachment. And an Oriati Prince would be dangerous to assassinate or execute, so the threat might not be credible. . . .

Or perhaps Abdumasi's grudge against Farrier had nothing to do with the blackmail that bound Farrier to the Throne. Abd had not been forthcoming with further details.

"I'm sorry," she told Yawa. "I really can't tell you more."

"You're impossible."

The veterinarian slid the syringe into the horse's neck. It switched its tail and whickered. It seemed glad to be off its hooves.

"How do you butcher an empire?" she asked Yawa, thinking, unfortunately, of the knackers.

"What?"

"How do you kill it, and render it down to its useful parts, and feed your hungry mouths with the meat off its carcass? That's what we have to do."

"Historically speaking," Yawa said, "I think you arrange a succession crisis, and split the realm. But the nature of Falcrest's Emperor and Parliament makes that difficult."

The people believed the Emperor was selected by exams and lottery, an anonymous will with its own autonomous finances and property, chemically forbidden to know Its own identity so that It could use Its power to ensure fair, clear-sighted rule for all. But they were misled. The edicts the Emperor announced were fed to It by the Throne. The body in the People's Palace was just a lobotomized proxy, and the chorus read the scripts the Throne prepared.

"How do you suppose it's decided what the Emperor will say in public?" she wondered.

"The same way the Throne decides anything else. You exert your influence on the scriptwriters and handlers in the People's Palace. You tell them what should be said, and when. And if no one else stops you, then it's done."

"But there must be a process of review. You can't just decide to have the Emperor blurt out whatever you please. What if someone decided to reveal all the Throne's legends? Or declare war on a lark?"

"It takes time to schedule an appearance by Its Majesty. I imagine the others will keep an eye on the preparations, make necessary inquiries. Including . . ." Yawa trailed off significantly. Including, she meant, any notional second cell of the Throne. "If there's disagreement on the wisdom of a proclamation, I'm sure the Emperor's appearance would be scuttled."

"And you couldn't possibly buy off the Emperor Itself."

"Not when It's a lobotomite who never speaks aloud." Yawa sighed and rubbed her wrists together. "The trouble with Falcrest, I find, is that they're very good at aligning the self-interest of their subjects with the preferences of the empire. Even we members of the Throne face personal destruction if we step out of line. Why are you looking at me like that?"

"Like what?" Barhu asked, innocently.

"Like you're pleased about how clever you are."

"It's what you said. About self-interest. It's possible to turn self-interest to our own purposes. Do you know how a joint-stock concern works?"

"No. I mean, yes, I've read the related laws, I have a basic understanding. But none were ever registered in Aurdwynn, and so I never practiced any law regarding them."

"It's a way to turn your concern into a single-purpose bank."

"A *bank*? I thought joint-stock concerns were business ventures."

"They are! They're a bank that accepts deposits for the purpose of doing some kind of business, and then pays those deposits back out of its profits."

"Barhu," Yawa said, "I am exhausted and empty. Please tell this as simply as you can."

But it was so magnificent, so very close to magical! Didn't she want all the gory detail, the minute glands and fine bones of the beast Barhu would invent?

"Look." She stabbed her fingers into her palm. "A bank is powerful because it can spend people's money when they're not using it. A bank's like—like if you gave your silver coins to a fisherman, and the fisherman melted the silver into hooks to fish. After a while you ask for your money back, and the fisherman returns your silver. But he keeps the fish he caught. Banks are the same: people give the bank their money. The bank spends the money on investments. When people ask for their money back, the bank returns it, but keeps any profit it's made off the investments."

Yawa tapped her fingers impatiently. "Fine. I know this much."

Barhu banged her fists together in excitement. "A joint-stock concern is the exact same principle, but with more risk. It asks for silver coins, turns all the coins permanently into hooks, goes fishing, sells the fish it catches, and pays you back out of its profit from fish sales. It has no obligation to give you your money back. But you can buy stock in it—an obligation to give you a share of its earnings. Does that make sense?"

The horse stopped breathing. Yawa made a vicious strangling gesture with one hand. "Enough."

"But I haven't told you about the middle class, how they're *drooling* to give someone their money, so they can be really truly rich—"

"Stop. You're right. I'm not a financier, and I shouldn't know the details of your schemes. But I *am* a judge. And I know when a witness is evading."

Barhu flinched from her bright blue eyes. "Evading?"

"Can you genuinely find enough leverage over Farrier to control him? If Farrier's protégé turned on him, then Hesychast would win the Reckoning. I'd be safe. If you can do that . . ."

"I think I can."

"You *think*? You don't know?"

"I'm trusting in trim, Yawa." In the clues she'd detected from Farrier, the moments of weakness . . . and in the possibility Tau might yet confirm.

The Throne was the arena where two powers overlapped. The place where the influence of Barhu's fascinations—great edifices of trade and violence—crossed over into Tau's world, the small, secret bonds between people.

Yawa stared at Barhu in alarm. "What do you mean, trusting in trim?"

"I need some information from Tau. Or from Abdumasi. But neither of them will talk unless they trust me."

"You said that Tau hated you."

"They do. But if I can do what they wanted of me—if I can reunite them with Abdu—maybe they'll help me in turn."

Yawa snorted. "Wydd help us."

Barhu nudged her with a hip. "Did I tell you I'm going to see my parents again?"

"Baru," Yawa said. "Are you going to kill me?"

"What?"

"You're talking about your parents. You talk about all these plans for commerce and investment. You seem confident. All I can think about is how they'll put spikes through my brother's eyes if I fail. Am I going to fail? Am I going to die? Do you already know?"

"No, Yawa. I promise"

"Then *how*—"

"Yawa," Barhu said, taking her hand, "please come down to observe the surgery. It might be important. It might be more important than anything."

ISCEND drew the scalpel down the dead man's spine. Barhu shuddered at the thickness of the parting skin: like a mat of rubber.

"Light, please," Iscend prompted.

Yawa steered the mirror's magnesium beam onto the incision. In the harsh shadows of the morgue's darkness she looked archonic, a being of angles and geometric primitives.

Iscend cut down to the cadaver's vertebrae. The bones of the spine were clearly separated, shockingly so. The corpse stank of bleach and cloying perfume.

"Here." Iscend counted vertebrae down from the top. "Inside these bones is a canal which holds the spinal nerves. Tributary nerves and blood vessels enter the canal through *these* openings, called the foramen."

Her hips and waist moved subtly, steadying her as she cut. "This membrane, here, is the meninges. A tissue that protects the spinal nerves. Abd's cancer will grow inside or outside of the meninges. If it is inside, we must cut through the meninges, and then we risk infection. The instruments and sutures must be as sterile as desert."

"The nerves give me the most concern," Yawa said. She'd been very quiet.

"Justifiably so." Iscend marked a certain vertebrae with a long needle, flagged with red cloth. "Any injury to the spine above this point will kill him. A lower injury might only cause paralysis."

"In Aurdwynn, before Falcrest," Yawa murmured, "the paralyzed would die of infected bedsores."

Barhu stared into the cleaned body, counting the tiny vessels, the processes of the spinal bones. So much required to keep one's heart beating! Maybe Hesychast was right. Maybe there was more to learn inside one body than in an entire empire. "Do you think you can keep him alive?"

"At spinal operations my success rate is better than the average. Hesychast trained me himself."

"Tell us the exact rate." Yawa's grip on the magnesium mirror began to shudder. She transferred it to her other hand.

"Seventy percent. If you discard those who came into the theater already dying."

Barhu groaned in worry. "Abd is weak. He hasn't been eating well. He has a fungal infection. I *can't* let him die."

"There are no certainties once the skin is open, Your Excellence."

I cannot make this choice for him, Barhu thought. I cannot force him into a decision between life with the Cancrioth and death on the surgical table. I have to let him talk to Tau. Then they can decide together. And if I ask them whether they will help me against Farrier, maybe, out of gratitude . . .

But it was not very good trim, she reminded herself, to do good things out of hope of reward.

"Wait a moment," Yawa snapped. "Wait. Baru, what exactly are you planning to do here? Give the tumor to the Cancrioth but keep the man?"

"Yes. The cutting goes home, to continue the Line of Undionash. Abdumasi will be free to choose his own fate."

"They'll never allow it! They came all this way to save him, didn't they?"

"They trade bodies like campsites, Yawa. They don't need the man Abdumasi Abd. They need his souls."

"And *I* need the immortata. I need it for Hesychast. You know this. I've explained it again and again. Why don't you listen?"

Iscend cringed and tried to cover her ears. It was a childlike gesture, hiding from parents' squabble. Barhu pitied her. The corpse stain on her gloves kept her from touching her face: she cringed again, in deeper horror, and ran to the sink.

"We can't get the Cancrioth to give up the immortata, Yawa. It's too important to them. We'd have to take it by force, and even if we did, could we keep it alive?"

"Then what in the name of precarious Devena would you have me do here?"

Courage, Barhu. "Is it possible to fake a lobotomy? To . . . allow Hesychast to believe I've been removed, long enough to avoid your, ah, punishment?"

Yawa began to laugh. It was the cruel, mocking sound Barhu had inflicted on classroom rivals who insisted their errors were correct. "Fake a lobotomy? Iscend. Iscend, I know you're listening. If I were to fake a lobotomy upon Baru, would you be able to pass it off to Hesychast as real?"

"There is such a range of results," Iscend called from the sink where she was scrupulously cleaning herself, "that it is very hard to prove or disprove that a lobotomy has occurred after the fact. Hesychast would not be confident of the lobotomy's success unless I were to attend myself, and certify that the maniple performed every cut exactly as instructed."

"See?" Yawa snapped. "Your survival, and the survival of all the good you could do, would depend entirely on Iscend Comprine lying to her own creator."

Iscend's lips moved in the dark. She swayed like Iraji about to faint.

"Damn," Barhu sighed.

"Even if he believed the lie, it wouldn't work for long. The moment you took any action but passive compliance, he would know the lobotomy was false. He'd know that I hadn't won the Reckoning for him." Yawa stared into the corpse's back, opened like butterfly wings. "I wish you had more to offer me, Baru. You keep asking me to trust you, but as Svir said . . . we are not in a line of work agreeable to trust."

Barhu read the tag on the dead man's cadaver. He had been pulled overboard by his fishing net, the file said, and nearly drowned. His crew had fished him out in time to save him. He'd coughed up the seawater, finished his shift, and gone out drinking with his crew that night. And died, in the middle of the pub, of the washing death: his lungs stripped of necessary fluids by the brine he'd inhaled. He had asphyxiated on dry land.

"You know," Barhu said, staring down at the corpse's bulging eyes, "I think that lobotomy is my worst fear in all the world. Worse than drowning."

"I know," Yawa said.

Barhu wondered how Yawa would react if she suggested that Yawa should let Olake be lobotomized. Well: how would she, Barhu, have reacted to Tain Hu's execution if they'd known each other for sixty years instead of three?

Put that way it was obviously impossible.

"Will you show me one?" she asked.

"Show you what?"

Barhu pulled the hooks out of the man's splayed-open back and, with a grunt, flipped him over. His dead eyes stared at nothing. "Show me a lobotomy."

Yawa grimaced. "I don't use my tools on a corpse. Call it a superstition. Or a fear of gas gangrene." That was a morgue attendant's disease, characterized by huge purple blisters and a gas release so rapid that the flesh could be heard popping and crackling.

"Surely a similar set of tools could be found," Iscend suggested, returning from the sink. "How are yours different from the standard?"

"I use a one-tenth-inch orbitoclast to puncture the bone, and a telescoped interior needle to perform the cuts. I prefer the precision."

"A delicate design," Iscend noted. "Prone to snapping off when extended."

"I know how to avoid stylus breaks," Yawa snapped, "thank you very much. I'll use whatever they have here. It's not as if the patient will complain if I use a thicker needle than I like. Baru, you truly want to see your worst fear performed in front of you?"

"Absolutely," Barhu said. "I want to know everything that can go wrong."

CHOICE AND CONTEXT

THERE was no more time to make arrangements. *Eternal* had put down anchor. The Cancrioth waited, thirsty and sinking, in the bay beside Iritain. And in Iritain Baru's parents waited, too.

They set out late in the morning, Governor Heingyl's procession guarded by her own armsmen and by a party of Maroyad's marines: the armsmen glared at them across the withers of the carriage team, resenting this sign of official distrust, even after the ballroom attempt on Ri's life. Barhu would have left them all behind, but these armsmen were Ri's family. And that left Barhu prodding, again, at thoughts of her parents. Was she ready to see them again? She'd expected more time to prepare . . . more results to show them, as justification for the choices she'd made . . . would she need to lie? *Could* she lie to her mother? Would Pinion hate Barhu already? Would she hate Solit, for letting Barhu go to the Iriad school?

She was so wrapped up in her worries that she lost her seat in the Governor's carriage. Ake and Ude Sentiamut invited themselves along and stole Barhu's place. She did not get a chance to speak to her would-be wife at all until they stopped for water.

"Heia, did you know that the Stakhieczi value salt a thousand times more than gold? Pan any river in the mountains and you'll find gold. Salt, though, salt preserves food for the winter. That's why their word for *salary* comes from their word for *salt*."

"I know," Heia said, with wary curiosity.

"Did you know that they make the finest steel in the world? As hard, as flexible, and as beautiful as Tain Hu." This made Heia laugh. "Legend says they can tease a pound of steel from two pounds of raw soil. I heard in Aurdwynn that the secret ingredient is the mountain wind itself."

She cocked her hip to support the barrel she was filling. "Is this your idea of courtship?"

It was. "Did you know that in Oriati Mbo they have a lot of salt and spices, and not nearly enough steel?"

* * *

I made Faham treat me roughly. His cover on the Llosydanes kept him doing real farm work, pulling stone and working plow. He was magnificently strong. He had sure hands and thick arms and a heart that made him what the maids in the Governor's House used to call zisuczi: like steel. Afterward I lay against his broad chest and listened to him breathe in the dark. He ran a finger down my cheekbone. "Old Maia women are supposed to have hairy lips and bad tempers."

"I pluck the hairs. And I do have an awful temper."

"You should smoke more."

"I can't smoke away my problems, Fa."

"The world is a dream." He kissed me behind the ear. "It might as well be a pleasant one."

I shivered at the warmth of his lips. He and I both knew that the dream would not be pleasant for long. A choice would have to be made.

I did not know if I could give Barhu everything she wanted. I was not certain at all. She had come from a trading village on a trading island. She had been raised by a man who used commerce and influence as his weapons. She had never been merely common.

There was so much she didn't understand.

In the morning we waited in the small front room of our house in the Annalila fortress yard, borrowed from a retired rocketry mate. Stewards served coffee in glass pots, with prisms of Souswardi sugar and shaved fruit on ice. I wondered where they got the ice from, and how long they could keep it from melting.

Shao Lune arrived with a thick roll of sheepskin palimpsest under her arm. "Your Excellences. So pleased to see you here."

"Show us," I snapped.

Shao Lune hung her diagram with a pair of clothespins. A deck plan of *Eternal,* annotated with details of dimensions, materials, assessment of fire hazard. The ship's cannon-powder magazines a splotch of dangerous red, forward of amidships and directly below the cargo hoists.

Faham Execarne gave a grudging nod. "I believe these plans are genuine."

"How can you tell?" I asked him. I was in agreement: forgers always gave it away in the linework. But I was curious what tells he looked for.

"All the stupid shit in the design. If she'd forged this, she would've made the plans make sense. Real ships have history."

I waved to Shao Lune. "Please proceed."

"Your Excellences." Shao Lune beckoned her companion forward. "Upon my request, Commander Falway has prepared a plan for a compartment-by-compartment seizure of *Eternal.* The plan calls for a primarily lethal approach, using gas, smoke, and flooding as the main force components. We'll take prisoners from the wounded and subdued. The action will begin with divers from *Sterilizer,* to secure lines on *Eternal*'s hull and prepare an approach for the boats—"

"This is all, of course," I said, "strictly a contingency plan, in the event that the negotiations do not meet my requirements. Not to be enacted without express authorization."

"Yes, Jurispotence." Shao Lune nodded with quiet, professional competence.

THE crater of Isla Cauteria's peak still smoldered; Barhu wondered if Taranoke's old gods of stone and fire lived here now. Certainly there was other life in plenty. On the carriage ride she tallied wild goats, feral pigs, stiltbirds, nene-ducks, geckos swarming over hot stones, night herons, frigatebirds above, finches and sparrows and pheasants, rock doves (pigeons, in nice scenery), hawks and gyrfalcons like the sorts that allegedly perched on the heads of gyraffes. Young ohia and koa trees boulevarded the road, shadowing tall blue ginger, cup vines, and everblooming lantana. Iscend climbed up onto the carriage roof with refreshments, then lay beside Barhu and inquired after various birds.

"Iscend," Barhu asked her. "Whatever I do as an agent of the Emperor is in service of the Republic, correct?"

"Within reasonable limits, I should think," Iscend said, so cheerfully that Barhu almost thought she was being teased.

"What would those limits be?"

"The general improvement of the Republic's condition. The suppression of disease and disorder. The pursuit of an Incrastic future of ordered breeding, sterile homes, equal yet specialized races and sexes. And a complete understanding of the natural world, so that all its forces and peculiarities may be accounted for in the Republic's policies."

Barhu considered the economy of the clouds in the sky. What currency did clouds use? How did they pay for their own existence, so as to grow fat and thunderous? What difficulties and expenses made them dwindle away?

"What if Incrasticism were itself disproven?" she asked. "What if Incrastic thought were outstripped by some foreign alternative? Say, for example, that a foreign mathematics were to make some discovery beyond Incrastic knowledge."

"Incrasticism is a self-improving tool. It is flexible and amenable to change."

"Could it ever change so that it was amenable to me?"

"You mean, could it become accepting of the tribadist?" Iscend was looking right at her now, not even blinking: a signal of openness, but also of wariness. "That would depend on the origin of the taboo. Some argue it existed before Incrasticism, in the days of the Verse-hammer and their wars against the shaheen kings. Others say it was a reaction to the decadence of the Fourth Dynasty. A taboo supported, of course, by the most rigorous scientific investigation."

"Science like Torrindic heredity." Behaviors enter the hereditary particles, to be passed down to offspring. "What if that heredity were wrong?"

"You're suggesting that my very existence is based on a lie!" But Iscend was smiling like a barracuda.

"You're teasing me," Barhu said, in wonder.

Iscend adopted an Urun accent. "I could not possibly do so."

"Now you're imitating Ulyu Xe!"

Somehow she made herself looser, an interior uncoiling, relaxing into the motions of the carriage, like she was full of water. "I can be her. I can be anyone you need me to be."

Barhu scoffed. "Don't be silly."

The Clarified woman's face narrowed. Her shoulders tightened, her breath came through her nose, and she glared at Barhu with serpentine intensity. "I can, though."

"Oh, don't be *her,*" Barhu groaned.

Iscend's eyes flattened into indifference. Her muscles tensed, relaxed again, so she lay on the carriage roof like a sprawled panther. Her hands were loose fists. The red of her lips suggested a mouthful of blood.

Barhu recognized the imitation, and shuddered.

"Interesting reaction," Iscend said, coyly.

SUNSET caught them just five miles from Aratene, on the mountainside above the the Rubiyya valley. Governor Heingyl called for a halt, to spare the horses from a risky descent in the dark. As soon as the tents were pitched she launched a blackberry-picking expedition "in the name of Aurdwynn's ranger tradition." Ake Sentiamut walked with her, the two women speaking intently in Iolynic, exchanging small energetic gestures.

"Like they're cooking together," Barhu said, bewildered. "Look at their hands! Chopping, gathering, mixing . . ."

"Concerned, my lady?" Iscend asked. "Should I eavesdrop?"

"No, no." It was just hard to give up control.

Barhu climbed a tree, trying to spy *Eternal*'s masts in the cove to the north-west. There was nothing to see in the falling dark, so she turned to voyeuristic observation of the camp. Was Haradel Heia *flirting* with her handmaidens? Or was that just how Aurdwynni ladies associated in high company? The compliments, the laughter, the delighted exchanges of food and favor?

Somewhere on her blind side a branch snapped like a pistol shot: she leapt in surprise, and looked.

A stag stood below her, dying.

It had the velvet antlers of spring growth, flush with blood and water. They had been crushed and now they bled down its face. Another wound on its breast yielded dark arterial red. One of Heia's handmaidens saw the stag and shrieked. The Stag Duchess herself stood aghast, hands black with raspberry juice. Not with all the repertory in Falcrest could you have invented a better image of her father's ghost.

The stag screamed like a maimed man, exactly like the man Ude Sentiamut had mercy-killed by the Fuller's Road. One of the armsmen wailed and tore at his jerkin. "It's calling to her! It's saying her name!"

Haradel Heia covered her mouth. Blackberry juice stained her cheeks.

Something in the tall grass behind the stag made a sound like a bird chirp. It grew, not birdlike, to a growl. A red catamount rose up from its crouch in the treeline and leapt onto the stag's haunches. The stag warbled, tried to buck it off. The cat climbed, grabbing bloody paw-holds with its claws, trying for the throat and the killing bite.

But the catamount couldn't open its jaws. It could only nuzzle the stag's throat. A rusty trap dangled from its back leg. If it were human it would have sobbed in desperation.

The thing had lockjaw.

A cold premonition of danger on her blind side. Barhu glanced over, saw the Stakhi armsman who'd shouted in horror. He was crying. Torn between love of the old duke's daughter, and anguish at the old duke's ghost screaming and bleeding under the claws of a catamount, the symbol of Tain Hu, the woman who had killed him.

You could not ask for a clearer omen. Old Heingyl's ghost was begging for revenge as the spirit of Tain Hu tore at him.

Barhu leapt down from the tree and did the only thing she could do. She found a longbow and a quiver and went to kill the maimed things. Iscend met her with a glass bottle from the medical bag. "This will help." The label read:

POISON LETHAL POISON: RAPID CONCENTRATED KRATOM OPIATE
ALCOHOL SOLUTION WITH ACONITE SUPPLEMENT:
FOR LARGE ANIMAL DEFENSE IN BAITS OR BOLTS.
LOT ONE OF SEVEN WINTER AR 130.
HOMEOPATHY IS A FRAUD: DO NOT ATTEMPT.

It even had a little brush, for application. Their poisons, Hu, are as useful as their roads. Barhu plunged the brush into the bottle, turned it to get
a good coat, nodded when Iscend said "Be *very* careful," and painted a ring
of poison—not on the arrowhead itself, where the target's skin could wipe it
away, but on the shaft behind the head.

She nocked the arrow and drew.

In winter memory, Tain Hu touched Baru's elbow, drew her spine a little
straighter, pressed at the curve of her back. She whispered,

"Shoot."

Barhu sighed and shot the stag. It groaned and fell. Then the catamount:
draw, aim, sigh, shoot.

Heingyl Ri ordered the mournful armsman back to Annalila Fortress at
once, clearly worried about what he might do in his agony. Then she ordered
her house to help burn the corpses.

It was the fire that betrayed Barhu's camp to the people hunting her. But she
did not know that yet.

WHAT a terrible omen." Haradel Heia, Governor of Aurdwynn, shuddered and shifted closer to the fire. "My father's sign. Tain Hu's sign.
They aren't at peace. . . ."

"It wasn't Tain Hu," Barhu assured her. "Tain Hu rests well."

"Dangerous to speak for the dead," Heia murmured.

"She trusted me to speak for her." Barhu poked the fire with the catamount's
thighbone. She and Iscend had slaughtered the cat, curious about its anatomy.
It had made a bloody mess of Barhu's traveling clothes, and she had stripped
down to linens, a loose tunic, and a cloak. Crouched at the fireside now, she
was curious to see Heia noticing her legs.

Iscend hadn't washed. In place of her calisthenics she was silently, viciously
fighting Heia's armsmen, winning sometimes, losing sometimes, a bloods-
meared specter on Barhu's blind side. The men were ginger with her until she
threw them, or hit them in the throat.

"You really married her," Heia said, guardedly.

"I did. I think. Are you married, if you choose a consort? Maybe we were only betrothed. But I could argue that I was acclaimed Queen, and had the power to execute the marriage. Certainly," she even managed to wink like Tain Hu, "the marriage was consummated."

Her firelight flush. "And now you want to marry me?"

"I want to pass to you the claim to the Mansion Uczenith, so you can bring it as dowry to the Necessary King."

"I feel quite self-conscious." Heia plucked at her square neckline. "I've never, ah, thought of another woman as—it's quite—you're so much taller than me!"

Barhu laughed. "So?"

"I've always been shorter than my suitors. It made me nervous, knowing they could hurt me. But it's not the same with a woman. You're taller, but it doesn't trouble me."

"Why?"

"I don't know. Women always felt safer to me."

"That must be a nice way to live," Barhu muttered, quite against her resolution to be charming.

"How so?"

"Women have never been safe for me, Your Grace."

"Really? In my experience people don't notice tribadists."

Barhu stared at her. "I feel like an actuary most days. Putting a risk on every glance."

"Tain Hu made it seem like she just reached out and plucked women like grapes. No one gave her much trouble because . . . well, because Yawa protected her, of course, but also"—Heia giggled, actually *giggled* at this thing that had terrified Barhu all her life—"it was as if people didn't understand what she was doing."

"Didn't understand . . . ?" What was there to not understand?

"They really didn't imagine that women could—you know! There were always women who married women, even among the Stakhi. Women did it to unite households. But the Stakhi didn't consider women as . . . capable of conjugation with each other."

"Or they did, and the Masquerade erased the evidence of that belief."

"Perhaps," Heia conceded.

"Your husband certainly understood women were 'capable of conjugation.' Did he ever go ahead and report me?"

"No," Heia said, into the fire.

"Why?"

"Bel had reasons. Something that happened to a boy in school with him. It's not my story to tell."

Barhu was startled by the idea of an actual Falcresti schoolboy, and a man at that, suffering under Incrastic hygiene. Heia saw her expression: "I know. It caused some uproar. The way it doesn't, when it's done to people like us."

"Incrastic hygiene scours harsh," Barhu murmured.

"And yet," Haradel Heia sighed, "for the first time in its entire history, enough of Treatymont's babies survive childhood for the city to grow without immigration."

"I think that's a false dichotomy."

"Your pardon?"

"I don't think our choice is simply between accepting Incrastic hygiene in its entirety, or going back to the days before modern sewers and soap."

"Aren't the theories which justify the hygiene also the theories which gave us inoculations and handwashing?"

"Do *you* think the sewers and the roads justify the rest of what they do?"

Heia clasped her hands and thought.

And of course Barhu fell in love with her. Just for an instant. She saw a tiny duchess with sharp eyes and an ocean of blood on her hands, staring into the fire, considering the possible futures she might engineer. Of course, in that moment, she loved her.

"I don't know," Heia said. "My father served the Masquerade because he took a vow. I've never thought of their presence as . . . something that could be changed."

"It might be." Barhu leaned forward, hands on her bare knees. "If you make the right choices."

"I won't leave Bel, you realize," Heia said, quietly. "I just . . . I'm sorry. I can't imagine making my life with a woman."

"The Necessary King is a man. You could make a life with him."

Heia leaned forward into the firelight. Behind her, Iscend shook an arms-man's hand with her blood-caked own, and walked off into the forest to bathe.

"You know that if Bel dies I'll blame you? You and Yawa? No matter how subtle and accidental it seems."

Barhu growled in frustration and prodded the fire with her bone. "I've made no plans to kill him. But I can't let Aurdwynn be lost because of one man."

"Well," Ri said, firmly, "I won't break his heart."

"Fuck," Barhu muttered.

"No, but thank you."

"You're not funny."

"You *do* think I'm funny," Heia said, smiling. The firelight was painfully flattering. "I can tell."

"I need to take a piss," Barhu lied.

She got up and went out to the dark.

O H, please," Barhu groaned. "Don't pretend you weren't waiting for me."

"I don't mean to be alluring," Iscend said, placidly. "I was washing, and wanted to think."

She floated in the stream, side-on to the current, moored to the north bank with one finger and to the south bank with one foot. She had to arch a little to keep her backfloat. The effect was immensely, unwantedly flattering.

"Stop," Barhu begged her. She had never had the slightest trouble separating incidental nudity from sexuality: what was it about these Falcresti women that denied her that clarity? "Please, please, don't play this ridiculous role. You were trained to read people! You know I don't want this."

It was not that Barhu didn't want sex (she was not yet twenty-five, for Himu's sake, she deserved to wander) but that the incredible *discomfort* of Iscend's conditioning made Barhu sick at the thought. She kicked a rotten stump in frustration. It spilled over and a centipede of prodigious size scuttled away. She yelped.

Iscend frowned up at her. "You interest me. Your responses are strange. In the Metademe, we find people are enticed and aroused by the naked body. But you're not from a society where desire must be coded and hidden. You don't react the same way."

"I don't like to mix sex and business."

"A taboo I don't share."

"Why not?" Barhu challenged her. "Doesn't it bother you when everything women do is read as sexual provocation? Doesn't it frustrate you when your professional encounters are taken as invitations?"

"Sex is a useful tool in espionage. It makes people talk. It can draw them into error, which can be leveraged. Sex is one of the basic elements of blackmail, and blackmail is one of the One Trade's nine methods for running an agent."

"I don't like it," Barhu said, stubbornly.

"Tell me, are you familiar with the archetype of the seductress?" Leaves pasted themselves across her upstream flank, glued by pressure to her skin.

"The woman who uses sex as an instrument of politics, and manipulates her partners through their desire."

"How couldn't I be," Barhu said bitterly, having read plenty of books about Falcresti spies on Taranoke.

Iscend let herself swing sideways, like a rudder in the current, and kept her place by gripping the stones. Her arms corded with the effort. Leaves plumed away downstream. Various factions inside Barhu begged her to leap in the water and do something, anything, drown herself if necessary, just stop *looking*, it was unbearable.

"In my review of popular literature," Iscend said, "I discovered that the seductress usually appears as a villain. She generally succeeds in the seduction of other characters. This provides the reader with a kind of secondhand sexual encounter. But she always fails in the ultimate attainment of her goals."

The stream parted over her, around her graceful neck, down the smooth grid of her abdomen and the muscles in her thighs. The whole world caressing her existence. Barhu hated her mind for thinking this way; she was genuinely fascinated by Iscend's thoughts.

Iscend continued. "Generally a writer strives for characters the reader finds credible, wouldn't you say? Yet savvy readers must instantly discredit seductresses as an antagonist or threat. Why, then, does the archetype still recur, when it must have been robbed of all effect?"

Barhu thought of Duchess Nayauru, who had very nearly wedded her way to control of Aurdwynn. She'd also been a patron of engineering and a cunning politician. But Barhu had for too long thought of her merely in terms of her liaisons.

"Punishment, I suppose. Negative reinforcement."

"Exactly. The seductress establishes the manipulation of sexual access as a social threat, and her failure discourages the behavior as ineffective. The titillation of the sex act rewards the reader for their contempt. They will be at once aroused by the seductress and satisfied by her downfall."

Barhu sat down on the streambank. "It's rather like managing different currencies in one economy, isn't it? The seductress enters her desirability into the economy as a commodity. But the law forbids her from exchanging it for other currencies. Such as political influence, or money. She is punished for the attempt: whether by those who fear the power she would gain, or those who fear the negative consequences it would have for other women."

Iscend giggled. "What a silly way to put it."

"You're very good at pretending to giggle, you know that?"

"Thank you," Iscend said, rewarding Barhu with a sly look. "The interesting question, I think, is why this seductress is always a woman."

"A very anti-mannist sentiment." Barhu frowned. "Why is it called anti-mannism, anyway? Why not womanism?"

"There was a woman's movement, early after the revolution. They demanded the vote, a law requiring gender-blind legislation, hysteric self-determination, and so forth. Iro Mave was involved—"

"Who?"

"Lapetiare's tactician. She was of Oriati ancestry, which is rarely touched on in popular histories. She caused a schism in the movement over issues of race. Afterward, 'womanism' was seen as a word too closely tied to racial affairs, particularly the rights of Oriati women. Anti-mannism, a movement against the preeminence of men in society, became more socially accepted."

Barhu made a note to read more about Iro Mave. "Why do you think the seductress is always a woman?"

Iscend twisted to duck her face underwater. Barhu, relaxing into the conversation, found herself still idly admiring Iscend's body. Iscend seemed to welcome Barhu's eyes—but *did* Iscend welcome it? Or had she been conditioned to make herself *seem* welcoming to Barhu's eyes, so that the choice was not actually hers at all?

"I suppose it lies in the difference between men and women," Iscend said. "It is as apparent in birds as in human beings. Males make displays to illustrate their value, and females choose the males whose value they like best. A seductress invites the display."

"Why shouldn't it be the other way? The women advertise and the men choose? Aren't women more..." Barhu struggled to imagine how a man might look at a woman. "Contoured?" she tried, desperately. "Featured? Interesting? In Treatymont, most of the dancers and prostitutes were women, and they certainly made displays...."

"That is only a side effect of desperation; their sexual availability is valuable because normally a woman is hard to obtain. Incrasticism says that it's this way because women must spend more effort having a child. We can't afford to choose inferior males as our mates. That's why men fall to promiscuity, but women fall to perversion. The man's desire for many children is deranged into the desire for many mates. The woman's desire for a particularly good mate is deranged into the desire for a particular perversion."

"But that can't be right," Barhu protested.

"Why not?"

Because of greatfamilies like Ulyu Xe's, or Barhu's own, where women did *not* adhere to one man. "It's just what you said—each child is a huge invest-ment! A woman can't afford to have all her children with one father, because then the babies would all die to the same diseases, they would all have the same strengths and flaws. And if all her men think they might be the father of a child, then they all help care for the baby. This is why it's good luck for the wife to be with all her husbands on the marriage night."

"But the truth of biology is that a child has only a single father."

"If biology explained everything about parents and love, would there be adoption? Would anyone raise stepchildren as their own? Yet they do, Iscend, you can't deny it!"

"Perhaps so," Iscend conceded. "But you're an accountant, aren't you, not a eugenicist? How could you possibly challenge the Incrastic account of heredity with your knowledge?"

"I bet you I can," Barhu said, with that offhand confidence that Hu had always used to drive her mad.

"Oh?" Iscend raised her head from the water. "What will you stake in the bet?"

But Barhu, already racing ahead into thought, entirely missed the flirtation.

A CCOUNT for the existence of the tribadist, the sodomite, and the doubly-taboo omnamorous, using only economics. Can it be done?

Imagine a man and a woman (or anyone with a womb, man or laman or any other sort, but, for brevity's sake, a woman).

Imagine that each person, man or woman, has a hundred coins to spend on childbearing. The man can spend as little as one coin and walk away: one drop of seed to make the child. The woman must *at minimum* expend nine months of coin to get the child to term, and then, assuming she does not forecast poor finances and leave the child to die of exposure (a practice that had happened nearly everywhere in the world), spend even more coins to raise the child to adulthood.

So the man wants to spend only one coin and the woman must spend nearly her whole fortune. Why, therefore, don't the men all fuck and run? Why are babies not raised by mothers alone?

Because babies are so expensive that they *need* two parents' investment to keep them alive. Especially if conditions are harsh. So it is important, as a mother, to draw investment from others. A husband is one way to get that in-vestment. Incrasticism says those without husbands will not see their children survive, so they will not pass their behavior down. Incrasticism says this is why women are suited to forethought, planning, conspiracy, and entrapment:

because their biology favors such traits in securing husbands and building futures for their children.

But why would a woman spend a hundred coins on the same man's children *over and over again*? There is incentive to hedge and diversify, and to confuse the paternity of a child, even to the mother herself. That would give women as powerful an incentive to fuck around as men. It could explain the Tu Maia greathouses and the families of Taranoke, where many men and women might marry each other.

But all of this still required a mother and a father. It did not explain people like Barhu.

What if it was impossible for the mother to get support from the father? What if you lived in a society like the bastè ana, where husbands left after one night? Or like the Stakhieczi, where all the husbands might go to war?

You could get investment from one of your sisters instead. Say she loves only women. Say she has no children and never spends her coins. She is fierce and fast, she goes out hunting and she brings back her kill to share with you. Or she is soft and gentle and she knows how to cook safe food and how to treat a baby's maladies while you sleep. But let us imagine her as a huntress, because huntresses are attractive. A sister who loves women, childless, but devoted to the survival of her *sisters'* children. . . .

But that didn't make any sense at all. It was impossible.

If a woman took only women as lovers and had no children, then the huntress behavior would never be passed down into the hereditary particles. Perhaps if she fucked her sisters, and taught them the behavior to go into *their* children . . . but the thought of incest disgusted Barhu. Second cousin Lao, fine, Barhu would admit to certain adolescent longings. But never a sister.

So there was no way for these huntresses to have children who were like them.

Only—the world was *full* of women who loved women—

So where did they come from? Why was the behavior not extinguished?

"Where do I come from?" Barhu asked, aloud.

D O you concede the bet?"

"No," Barhu snapped, "but I'm stuck."

"There is," Iscend said, conspiratorially, "a certain heretical idea among the Clarified."

"What is it?"

"We breed plants for our heredity experiments. They grow quickly and they do not, ah, complain if radically modified. In the course of our breeding we have found . . . certain stubborn failures of Torrindic heredity." Iscend shuddered, a full-body wriggle of disgust, and grimaced for a moment. Then she relaxed: she had found some way to rationalize this to her conditioning.

"The things we do to plants, like pruning off all the leaves on one side, do *not* seem to be inherited and passed down. The orthodox account says that plants lack the flesh memory of a living being. Since they have no behavior, of course they cannot inherit it. But we know that plants can learn; we have taught plants to grow toward certain sounds or colors. If plants can learn, why is this learning never inherited?"

"Tell me," Barhu said, to give her that push of approval. Tell me everything, Iscend.

"We have a model . . . a toy model, a thought play . . . which explains the patterns of inheritance we see in plants. In our pretend world, our alternative account of heredity, everyone is born with a set of particular fixed traits, called, ah—"

"Coins."

"Coins, then. The coins determine how they behave. But the coins arc not themselves *altered* by behavior. Your life is set by the coins you're born with."

"That's quite grim," Barhu said, delightedly. "So there might be coins for anger, or greed, or brilliance, or so forth."

"Exactly. This sheds interesting light on the problem of the isoamorous." Iscend caught a mosquito from the air and twisted to wash the smear from her hand. "If the coin for isoamorous behavior is not *created* by isoamorous behavior, it must have some other function."

Barhu sighed. "But, again, those with the coin can't pass it down. It should vanish."

"Not," Iscend suggested, "if it can be passed down through sisters."

"What do you mean?"

"Perhaps the coin can land heads-up or numbers-up. Perhaps those who receive it heads-up are isoamorous, and those who who receive it numbers-up have isoamorous siblings. The numbers-up carriers would have children. The heads-up women would not have children of their own, but they would help their sisters. Perhaps these sibling teams end up with more surviving children than siblings who are all competing to raise their own."

"Yes!" Barhu paced right into the shallows. "That fits! The huntresses don't have to have any children, but they still help their sisters pass the coin down. It's as if the extra surviving offspring their sisters have are their *own* children, in a way!"

She threw a huge rock into the stream, purely out of euphoria, the desire to hear a splash as solidity displaced uncertainty. Caldera gods boil her, if this was anything but fantasy, it would be a tremendous weapon.

She had never needed a scientific rationale to believe that she and all the people like her deserved to live with dignity and without fear. But if she could prove *in scientific terms* that the whole ideology which rationalized their punishment was wrong . . . why, between this and Kimbune's mighty mathematical proof, there was a chance to destroy a bulwark of Falcrest's power without spending a single note or killing a single person!

"A study of pedigrees might substantiate the theory," Iscend suggested. "Perhaps the Cancrioth has kept track of their breeding for an entire millennium. Perhaps they would be able to demonstrate whether heredity obeys Torrindic predictions, or an . . . alternative model. And the figures do support the resilience of isoamorous behavior."

"What figures?"

"Despite all attempts at eugenic, behavioral, and somatic intervention, undercover hygiene delegates report that one in four people still engage in some isoamorous behavior. Why does the behavior recur so often even when we discourage it so strongly? Why has it not become extinct?"

Barhu imagined herself before the Faculties, presenting her research. *A Proof of the Necessity of My Existence. . . .*

"Baru," Iscend said, "what's been done to me can never be undone. Do you understand that?"

Barhu started out of her reverie. Iscend had crawled up beside her on the bank and propped herself on her elbow. She was sleek and strong and far too close.

"You've already started to undo it," Barhu protested. "I've heard you—" It would probably shame Iscend if Barhu, a cryptarch, directly addressed her use of her own command word. "I approve of what you've done this journey. I like the way you've altered yourself."

Iscend lay on her side, almost exactly Barhu's height, watching her with an intensity which seemed to twist her perfect face. "You approve, you disapprove. But still it's not *my* approval. The terms in the equations have changed, but I'm still bound by their outputs. My whole life I've been conditioned to feel wonderful when I serve the Republic. That will never stop."

She swallowed. "Right now, *you* are the Republic, Agonist. You are the closest I can come to seeing my whole purpose in a single woman."

Oh no, oh, please stop. "The conditioning will fade. Or you'll learn how to alter it."

"I know how to alter it," Iscend said.

"How?"

"Like this. Gaios. Kiss her."

Barhu squeaked into Iscend's mouth. She made a half-hearted effort to escape, but in that flash of cold and heat there was such suggestion of delights to come—it was like trying to turn down a tremendous investment from a dubious donor: the money might be tainted but it would still spend so *well*—

"Wait," she spluttered, "wait, no! Stop! Stop!"

"Am I too forward?" Iscend withdrew at once, though not far.

"You're not too forward. But we have to stop. I don't want us to do this."

"Because you think I'm not in command of myself? I know exactly what motivates me. I had every part of me laid out in a design. Can you say that?"

"But you didn't lay out the design!"

"I know exactly two ways to feel good, Baru. One is to obey the conditioning instilled in me by the Metademe. The other"—she lay her hands on Barhu's, all that neuromassage training pent up, waiting to be used—"the other, and, please, draw away if you want me to stop, but the other way I know . . . it is the way all bodies know. The Metademe couldn't take it from me. I learned it in the function tests. Something I wasn't supposed to feel, something not part of the protocol. When I slid the flag needles into the small of my back, into my pelvis, into my thighs . . . it made me hot, Baru. It was the first time I ever came. I didn't make a sound. But I knew it was something they couldn't take out of me, no matter how they conditioned me . . . I want to feel that. I want you to make me feel good for being near you. I want to feel good in a way they didn't plan for me. I want that."

Barhu was so absurdly turned on by this, the idea of unpinning Clarified conditioning with sheer force of lust, that she almost, almost gave in. Her hands were free, free to pull away, to make the right choice, but the way Iscend moved guided them. . . .

The moonlight glittered on the passing stream. Patterns each as complex and temporary and fascinating as people themselves. And yet the stream ran on, down to the sea, the direction unchanged.

Nothing within the water could escape its context. Not this choice. Not any other.

"Please." Iscend pushed against Barhu's hand. She was damp from the stream, and cool, except for this warmth. "Please let me have this."

Barhu knew she had to stop. She knew, absolutely, that if she let this happen she would hate herself for the rest of her life.

It was just so tempting to wait a *moment* longer. . . .

"Baru!" someone shouted. "Baru-u-u!"

No voice in the world could have pulled her off Iscend so quickly.

"Mother?" Barhu gasped. *"Ma?"*

INTERLUDE

RNS *SCYLPETAIRE*

TAIN Shir walks the deck of RNS *Scylpetaire* between the forlorn and the furious and the damned. A killer among killers but she alone is free.

She is unmastered. They are masterless. The difference is everything.

She has not seen *Scylpetaire* since the day the frigate left *Sulane*'s company to find Baru Cormorant's parents. She hunted it across half the Ashen Sea. Left Kyprananoke aboard the last ship to escape, the merchant Ngaio Ngaonic's trader. He recited old Scyphu prayers as the wave chased them, subsiding into the deeps around Kyprananoke, until it was no more than a ripple beneath the keel.

When they made port at Yama and settled into quarantine, Shir leapt overboard, swam between the anchor lines of the crab traps, came ashore like a seal in the dark. She bartered news of Kyprananoke for passage to Taranoke on a Masquerade postal clipper. But *Scylpetaire* was not at Taranoke. Baru's parents had already fled.

Scylpetaire has failed Juris Ormsment.

And now their traitor-admiral is dead.

Shir tracked *Scylpetaire* here to Imaranoke, a speck of an islet north of Taranoke. The name is favorable, though the place is not; Shir suspects it was named so by ancient Maia voyagers in order to draw rival families away from fertile Taranoke itself. The mutineers came here to hide from Sixth Fleet Sousward and the inevitable order for their arrest.

They still had hope. Reunion with Ormsment. Vengeance against Baru.

Shir took all that from them.

"She deserved better," Captain Iscanine mutters. "Shot dead by her own comrades . . . you say Asmee Nullsin turned on her? That prince bastard."

Shir does not care about this question. Ormsment is dead and the circumstances of that death are as immaterial to her future as the position her parents chose to conceive her.

"You're afraid they'll mutiny." She watches the gray-haired crew scrub the deck. The sun sits directly above the mainmast and does not move. Qualmstones scrape. The waves rush and suck at the hull.

"Of course I'm afraid," Iscanine mutters. She's maintained her uniform in perfect order, though the red wool is soggy in the tropical heat and the pins on her collar are dull from overpolish. "They've already done it once. If we can't go home, if we'll never have pardons, if Baru's beyond our reach . . . if I have to tell them we've failed . . ."

She shakes her shunt-scarred head. She was a water-swollen child, and the Metademe barred her from childbearing before she was even out of the crib. She has never known any meaning but the navy. Now those invisible shrouds of support are cut away. She staggers free.

A delicate time, Shir thinks. A time of second birth, with all its blood and all its screaming.

"I will take command," Shir says.

"What?"

"The Province Admiral is dead. I will take command. You will be ship's captain, and I will be your admiral, like she was. And we will continue her mission."

"*How?* How can we do right by her?" Iscanine is begging now, though she would not admit it.

They've come to the bow, the railing that overlooks the sprit and the dolphinstriker. Iscanine begins to turn but Shir crowds her against the rail. "Baru has a second father."

"She was adopted?"

"No," Shir says. "Pinion had two husbands."

"At once?"

"Yes."

Iscanine, who has no husbands, makes a salacious eyebrow waggle. "Lucky bitch."

Shir is not interested in the predilections of Falcrest's women, unless they involve her. "The second father's name is Salm."

She imprisoned him and so it is right, in the way of talion, the law of an eye for an eye, that she should set him free. Only then will she in turn be free to conduct the duty she promised Baru. To watch over her. To await the day when Baru at last betrays Tain Hu's faith.

And on that day, Tain Shir will kill her and cut out her heart and prepare it on open coals.

Baru may yet avoid the fall. It may be that the Brain has already persuaded Baru, as she once persuaded Shir, to turn away from the path of lies and control. It may be that Baru already carries Falcrest's death in her arteries.

And that would be good.

Empire planted that killing tree on Kyprananoke, where the rebels dashed children dead against the trunk.

The only answer to empire is to move the tree.

It is not justice. But there is no such thing as justice. Only the measureless and asymbolic truth. Who prospers. Who suffers. Who lives in glory. Who dies in chains.

"Make your ship ready to sail," she commands Captain Iscanine. "We have works to begin."

ACT FOUR
YAWA'S CHOICE

28

THE IRITAIN MATAI

THEY came to each other in the moonlit forest.

Barhu cut her hand on a stone as she ran to her mother's voice. Blood ran down her fingers; blood pulled her forward. She saw Pinion's dark thundercloud face in the clearing ahead. Her cry of joy nailed Pinion to the spot: still expressionless as Barhu came into her arms, halfway knocked her over, clung to her, saying, in Urunoki, "Mother! *Mother!*"

"Baru," her mother said, "your hands smell like pussy."

"Oh, gods!" Barhu fumbled in the pine cones, trying to scour her hands. Sticky pine pitch everywhere, of course—

"The pitch doesn't come off," her mother said, watching her. "Be careful, now, you've cut yourself—you'll get dirt in there— What did you do to your fingers? *Where* have you put your two fingers, Baru?"

"I can't believe you said that!" Barhu cried. "Why would you say *that* first?"

Her mother's pox-scarred face, her trim body, all shockingly older. She'd gone gray. She wore a dirty mulberry work shirt and rough canvas trousers. Her head had been shaved, recently, for passage on a ship, in a cheap hold full of lice.

"It's very rude to get cunt on your mother," Pinion said. Then she began to laugh. "Solit! Solit, come down! We caught our daughter fingering some falca girl in the woods! She's so embarrassed!"

Solit appeared on the upslope, a hammerfall on Barhu's heart. Father blacksmith grown bigger and fatter and pleasantly darker. "Why are you so cruel to your offspring, Pinion?"

Barhu fled to the streambank, washed herself, and came back sobbing. Her parents held her close. They cried together. The smell of tears on her father's face reminded Barhu of home.

"You remember what she said?" Pinion screwed up her face and squeaked. "You will never change anything with your hut and your little spear!"

"And you said"—Solit shaking his finger at Barhu—"my lousy daughter, you will return with a steel mask instead of a face!"

"Let's see." Pinion pinched Barhu's nose. "Still fleshy." She tugged Barhu's right ear. "Maybe you use these once in a while, now?" She took hold of Barhu's chin. "Your cheek was cut. What were you eating, to cut through your cheek?"

"I was so afraid!" Barhu cried. "There was a ship going to Taranoke, to take you hostage! How are you *here*?"

"We're working for the Cauteria Coffee Concern," Pinion said.

"What? You left Taranoke to sell *coffee*?"

"We wanted a change of scenery. People do that."

"But *now*? It's just such good luck, such perfect timing, I can't believe it. . . ."

"Still a suspicious child, I see." Pinion looked darkly to her husband. "Very suspicious."

"I'm going to tell her," Solit said.

"Don't," Pinion snapped, "not yet," as Barhu said, eagerly, "Tell me what?"

Solit leaned in conspiratorially. "The coffee concern's a cover to move people around the Ashen Sea. People who can't safely stay on Taranoke. Rebels. Smugglers. Good people."

"Oh," Barhu said, impressed. Her parents had developed some tradecraft. "That's very sensible."

"When we heard that a certain coconspirator had come to a bad end, we decided to make ourselves slippery for a while. Some of the people who'd . . . who might've been captured could be compelled to give up our names. Cauteria's the farthest you can get from Sousward on the trade ring"—Solit drew a half-circle in the air, Taranoke to here—"so we came to Cauteria."

"Taranoke!" Barhu said, as fierce as one should be when speaking true names. "Don't say Sousward, father, it's Taranoke!"

"That's right." Solit scrubbed her head. "Taranoke always. Then this great gold ship turns up in our bay, with a navy ship right behind it that ignores all our signals; and at last we hear there's a carriage column on its way from Cautery Plat. So we go out to meet it, to get our questions answered. We see a fire on the mountainside, the fire leads us to a camp, the duchess in the camp tells us your name . . ."

Pinion was frowning at Solit with tight-lipped discontent. Barhu put her chin up stubbornly.

"I'm on your side, ma. I won't betray you."

Are you, Pinion's eyes asked? Are you? "First we hear of the Fairer Hand. We think our daughter is leading a rebellion in some far-off wolf province. We think she's found a woman who will tolerate her, this brigand with a large estate. We think she's found some proper elders to look over her. And then we hear that the rebellion is over. That it was betrayed before it even began. That all the elders are dead. And that Baru Cormorant is an agent of the Throne.

You know, if you had never sparked that rebellion, we never would have had to flee home."

"Mother, I promise, all that business in Aurdwynn was . . ."

They both looked at her expectantly. How could she say *a move in the game*? How could she say that? When she had not yet won the game, and so proved it worth playing?

"A lie?" Pinion suggested.

"A ruse?" Solit offered.

Barhu didn't know how to explain it, or how to survive their reaction. All she could think to do was to offer up, as justification, a prize she'd earned.

"Salm's still alive," she blurted.

Something smashed her head. At first she thought Pinion had punched her in the jaw. Then the ringing passed and her father held her up as her mother stumbled backward, hands in the air, having accidentally struck her daughter as she cried her raw triumph, *"I was right! I was right!"*

H ER parents had never ridden in a carriage before.

"I've never heard of a Cancrioth." Mother Pinion handed her blackberry scone to father Solit. "Eat that, it's delicious."

"Why don't you eat it, then?"

"I want you to have it, dear husband."

"You always give me the things you don't like."

"If we liked all the same things, dear husband, we would not like each other."

"I'm not sure that follows from reason."

"You're being very difficult for a man who's just been given a scone."

"It's very *mealy*," Solit complained, picking the blackberries out of the delight. Heia had insisted on sharing her morning food with the guests. "I don't understand why everyone wants to put perfectly good food into bread."

"Flour," Barhu said. "De-germed flour keeps for a very long time."

"Oh, how's that?" Solit said, teasing her, although she did not realize it until she had already begun to explain: "The Butterveldt grows the grain, the mills make the grain into flour, barrels of flour provide compact long-lasting calories, so ships can travel farther without resupply, so the warships have a longer reach and the traders arrive more quickly than their rivals, and that quickens the blood of the whole empire, and . . . oh Himu"—a burst of joy inside her— "oh, look at *that*. . . ."

They had crossed the last ridge on the steep approach to Aratene. The village tumbled out below, homes and gardens clustered in small circles, linked rings of life in the cup of land around the river Rubiyya. The settlers built with ash concrete and proper volcanic tufa, not the worthless limestone that sometimes tried to pass in foreign markets. The roads were laid out to Taranoki plan, winding paths that climbed ridges and chased streams, wherever the terrain led them. The gardens spilled into the space between. Barhu thought of the long trip up to Lea Pearldiver's to buy pumice. She'd always loved to climb straight up the slope, cut the distance by leaving the road. . . .

Fear sprang up to cage her, and she tucked her elbows to her sides as if wrapped in wire. What if no one recognized her as Taranoki? What if merely *fearing* she didn't belong proved she didn't? Wouldn't a real Taranoki know without a doubt that she belonged? How could she claim to be Taranoki again if she was afraid the whole time? They would give her some test and she would fail—

"There's the river," Solit said. "I helped design those buildings along it."

Pole barges and skiffs drifted at moor by a trim white municipal office. A clinic and a school snugged up side by side. A commons, a garden, a flower-choked apiary clouded with bees, a constabulary post with a huge ceremonial shield above the arch . . . oh, it was nothing like the real Iriad, but it was a perfect image of the Iriad that nostalgia had refurbished in Barhu's heart. Each tiny brilliance of layout and plumbing tasted as sharp as a peppercorn in her teeth.

"Trade negotiations," she muttered. "I'm holding trade negotiations in Iriad. Svir's right. I really am recapitulating my childhood."

"Pardon?" Solit said.

"Nothing, da. I talk to myself. You've seen nothing too odd around here? Nothing that could threaten a diplomatic meeting?"

"Odd?" Her mother stole a piece of Solit's tart. "Of course there's oddness. Didn't you read the book on Cauteria? *Hell's Embassy*? This island's mad. Gas kills in the forest, sounds the old can't hear, compasses turning madly. . . ."

"Everyone's bothering me for not doing my reading." Barhu sighed.

"Of course we are! We didn't have printed books in my day, you know. Everything had to be hand copied, and the moment I heard of a new book, I'd go and trade a whole boar for it. You young people think a book's like a lover, maybe you want one, maybe you don't—"

Solit snuck his arm around Pinion and hugged the tirade right out of her lungs. "Baru, aside from the vents, I don't think there's anything dangerous here."

"What sort of vents?"

"Invisible gas comes out of the ground. Usually it stinks if it's dangerous. If it doesn't, you can watch for birds gathering over the deer kill. I think people go huff the vents, sometimes." He traded sidelong glances with Pinion. "Like Tapu Sunfish. That man says the strangest things—"

At that moment one of the horses whinnied and balked, afraid of the steep descent. Pinion shot bolt upright in snarling terror.

Barhu laughed in delight. "Still adjusting to horses?"

"They're foolish! I swear they live to find stupid ways to die."

"I'll have to tell you about the time I won a great battle with skillful deployment of cavalry." Barhu shoved her hands into her pockets so that she would not fold them arrogantly behind her head. "I have a proposal for the town . . . elders. What's the word, the Urunoki word? Is it, ah, matai?"

"Yes, of course it is," Pinion said, worriedly. "Did you forget it? Did we forget to teach you?"

"You taught me very well, Mother." Barhu swallowed again. It hurt. "So. How's home?"

Pinion and Solit scooted a little closer together. Pinion put an arm around her husband. Solit blinked rapidly.

They told their daughter how one in four Taranoki had died.

SMALLPOX had piled bodies so high they had to be mass-buried in the caldera. The disease was endemic to the Mothercoasts of Devi-naga Mbo and Falcrest, where it flourished in cities. It had never reached Taranoke before. The Falcresti said that was a risk of faster shipping. And there were only so many inoculations to go around. Was it any surprise that they'd prioritized their friends?

Barhu had been inoculated, a procedure called variolation. Her parents hadn't been so lucky. "The ones who died," pox-scarred Pinion said, "their skins rose up with black blisters, everywhere, toes to nose. You'd think they'd been cooked."

Smallpox passed. Then came the flu, and it never stopping coming. Waves of influenza from the pigpens and slaughterhouses of Falcrest's second city Grendlake rippled out across the Empire. There was no inoculation. A treatment existed, but it required the transfer of blood from a survivor, and more often than not this produced a hideous syndrome characterized by a conviction of imminent doom. Usually the prophecy was true, and the transfusee died horribly.

The flu didn't kill as many as smallpox, but it kept Taranoke on its ass. The Falcresti set out to "help," erecting shipyards and better roads, putting bright young students to work on a census of people and wildlife, gathering up

talented children for "educational protection" in schools. The coffee and sugarcane plantations expanded even as basic food production collapsed: it was
easier to raise coffee and sugar, sell them for fiat notes, and buy from Falcrest's
imported stores. Why would anyone remain a food farmer? The imported
goods made everyone fat, Pinion said, and fond of salted butter.

Of course there was violence. No one could bring plainsiders and harborside together under one roof without violence. And at first those old grudges
were the cause of the fighting, with only a little encouragement from Falcrest.

Province Governor Oya-dai Mahoro instituted something called the Risk
Market (this name accompanied by eye rolls from Pinion and Solit), in which
wages at provincial jobs were tied, inversely, to the rate of crime and sedition.
If your neighbors rioted, your wages would be cut. When your neighbors be-
haved again, your back pay would be filled. It had not worked very well. Which
was, perhaps, the point, to illustrate that the people of Sousward were irrational, unable to see their own best interest.

Here Pinion and Solit hesitated.

Barhu knew what would come next.

"We killed people," Solit said. His strong hand put white marks on Pinion's
arm.

"I know," Barhu said. "I've done it, too."

"People who were just trying to keep their families from starving. People
we'd known all our lives. I . . ."

He felt for Pinion's hand. His sorrow faltered and her fury rose.

"People worked for the masks because the masks could feed them. Or inoculate their children. Or secure their land, put the deeds down in paper."
She looked like she wanted a knife. "At first we'd pretend not to see the 'home
guard' Mahoro raised, and they'd pretend not to notice us. They'd warn us
about raids, we'd warn them about bombings and fires. We thought we'd focus
on the shipyards, the record halls, the banks, the export warehouses . . . steal
from the mask and give to the people.

"But the falca were so fucking *reasonable* about it. They'd offer amnesties,
and usually honor them, for a while. They'd offer to withdraw their constables
from certain 'culturally sensitive areas,' and we'd come in to claim the liberated land, and then we couldn't feed the people there, we couldn't rule with
all the elders dead of smallpox and flu. So the people in those free zones went
back to work for Falcrest. They went back to their fucking jobs and the fucking
courts. Like they'd forgotten how to live without masks."

She trembled but she never blinked. "Some of us said, if we can't pay people in Falcrest money, we'll pay them in plunder. If we can't give them matai courts, we'll give them wartime discipline. So then we had brigands and warlords on Taranoke, for the first time since Mad Malassee. They would raid the plainsiders and the plainsiders had their own brigands who'd raid back. And who could protect the people? Falcrest's marines, of course."

Her voice on the edge of a shout. Solit squeezed her hand and took over.

"People turned on us in the last couple years. Young people who came through the Masquerade schools, all of them calling us radicals and regressives. None of them know a damn thing about being Taranoki. We relied more and more on the Oriati money and the Oriati weapons to keep the fight going. We mined the harbors and we sunk merchanters and, oh, people didn't like that, losing the imports they'd paid for, the goods they'd contracted for and counted on to keep their businesses up. And the more people turned on us, the more we started punishing collaborators. I don't know how—it wasn't something we meant—"

Long exhale. Short inhale. "We were just so angry the first time a family turned our people over to the masks. We didn't know what to do except kill them."

"Please stop," Barhu whispered.

"You have to know what it's like, Baru," Pinion growled. "You have to face this—"

"I *know* what it's like, Mother! I helped them do it!"

They all fell so quiet.

"I'm sorry." Barhu covered her eye—realized too late that she'd only covered her left. "I left you to suffer all this."

Her mother stared at her rock-scarred knees.

Her father cleared his throat. "So," he said. "It's your turn."

Barhu told them almost everything.

THAT night they ate together as a family. They poached salmon in wine and butter and ate bread from the Falcrest-style bakery. Barhu pulled up an empty chair for Salm. Solit burst out weeping, and had to go draw water from the well to wash his face.

"I'm sorry," he said, to Barhu and Pinion's mumbles and waves of dismissal. "Knowing he's alive out there, without us . . ."

"Who's the woman?" Pinion teased. "Your forest friend?"

"Don't," Barhu growled. "You have no idea the things I'd have to explain."

* * *

FOR the first time in fifteen years, Barhu woke in a hammock in her parents' home.

She sat up, feeling crisp, like a fresh sheet folded up. There was no ring of hurt around her skull, no hook on her soul dragging her back to sleep. She went to the rattan windowscreen, looked out into morning fog on the Rubiyya bay. *Eternal*'s masts wandered in and out of reality. *Sterilizer* lurked half a mile off, a triple-decked brute, diminished only by *Eternal*'s titanic proximity. Her hwacha batteries could loft fifty thousand arrows in a full salvo. Her siphons were worse.

The Brain was out there. The Kettling was out there. There would be no more pigs to slaughter, no more chickens or goats. Whatever was left alive on that ship carried either tumor or plague.

And she'd brought it to her parents' door.

"Baru," her mother called, attuned by some parental proprioception to the motions in her house, "get washed, please, you have visitors."

Visitors! Shit. "Is it Governor Heingyl?"

"No, dear. It's much more important. All your aunts and uncles have come."

Oh no. Barhu did not even *remember* having aunts and uncles, except as vague presences around her parents. She was reasonably certain in retrospect that one "uncle" had been a man her father Solit was either sleeping with, or who shared with Solit an obsession with ancient arrowheads.

She went outside to the shower chute, washed in water from the solar. Took quick inventory of all the glass bottles of creams and solutes involved in her parents' skincare routine, from monoi oil to coconut milk and jasmine water. Glass bottles! Her parents *had* done well. She had nothing to wear but the wardrobe she'd brought from the fortress, and that meant a waistcoat and trousers, not Taranoki at all. Even her linens felt like they somehow didn't belong here. When she'd left for the Iriad school, she'd never had a period and hadn't needed to tie up her breasts.

She went out into the common room rigid with fear.

The men and women at the long table looked up from their bowls of sugared black coffee, smiling, calling out hello, every one of them no doubt trying to connect this eight-fingered scrimshaw woman with the moody little girl they'd known.

"Hello," Barhu said, and began, helplessly, to cry.

"Oh, you poor dumb thing," one of her aunts clucked. "You sound just like you did when you were born. Someone find a cormorant."

"Do they starve her? Is that why she cries at food?"

"She's been in Aurdwynn. She's probably been eating horses."

"They don't eat the horses. They eat the cows."

"Solit, how's *your* cow?"

"Full of coffee," he said, tending to some kind of glass apparatus that dripped coffee into a bowl. "Baru, how do you take yours?"

"Neat, please," Barhu said, as if she were ordering whiskey. It didn't mean anything in Urunoki: "Plain, I mean."

"Black," her mother corrected her.

"Black."

They engulfed her in their chatter, drew her in to the table. They had prepared coconut meat, cooked pineapple in iron salt, baked banana with tapioca and coconut cream, an iron pot of chicken in a thick Aurdwynn-style curry, pork roasted in an underground oven so it tasted like the smoke of Barhu's favorite whiskeys, sour taro pudding and cubes of raw tuna so powerfully peppered Barhu began to sneeze. She ate until she felt she would doze off in her chair. She was horrified to discover that she could not understand everyone's Urunoki.

"It's all right," her mother whispered, seeing her confusion. "You never went far from Iriad. There are other accents."

"Are they really my aunts and uncles?"

"By blood? Some of them. Not most."

"Well," Barhu said, "I'm glad you brought them."

Her mother wrestled visibly with *I'm glad you're here,* and settled for a nod.

The coffee came from the "cow," an apparatus of glass and steel which Solit tended like an unpacked baby, some unfortunate yet well-loved infant born with all its organs on the outside, glands and visceras which required constant adjustment. "It's his latest invention," Pinion murmured. "We call it the cow because it is large, many-chambered, and bad at doing what it's meant to do. He says he's going to register it and sell it."

"I heard that," Solit said. "Your mother just hates cows because she's not allowed to hunt them."

"Comes from a life killing boar," the aunt across the table suggested. "If it's bigger than a rat and it goes on all fours, Pinion wants to spear it."

"I spear your mother on all fours," Pinion said.

She and the aunt saw Barhu's face and both began to laugh.

"She looks like a fish," Pinion said, "all pinched up and sour," and the aunt sucked her lips into a little beak and made fish gulps.

"I'm being teased," Barhu said, which made her think of Iscend, who she had abandoned, naked, in a forest, and barely spoken to in the morning. "Er, father—all this glass must be expensive. How *does* this coffee concern work?"

"Catering to idiots," Pinion said, passing the cubes of tuna across the table, to an uncle with an elephant war-mask tattooed onto his face.

"The idea is," Solit explained, "that our innate racial expertise in coffee adds a premium quality to those beans we hand-select. We sell to a very narrow audience, an audience with a taste for luxury. Our revenue allows us to send people all over the Masquerade to explore new markets. It's a useful way to get travel papers for folks who . . . may not want to linger at home."

He looked warily to the open window. "That woman who follows you around. Can she understand us?"

"Probably," Barhu admitted. "But if she were listening, she'd tell me. It's—complicated, the way she thinks."

"You have such a charming lover," Pinion said.

"Mother, she is *not* my—"

"Pussy hands," Pinion stage-whispered, and the aunt across the table had to put down her cup for sake of laughing. Barhu was going to faint of embarrassment.

"Have you thought about registering your concern for the joint stock trade?" she suggested, desperately. "Cauteria's inside the home province. I'm sure it must be legal."

Pinion grumbled. "I knew she'd have some clever idea. 'Joint stock trade.' Just a fancy new name for selling shares, isn't it?"

"It's a wonderful way to diffuse risk, Mother! You can attract investors and use their money to grow."

"I don't want us owned by some clique of falca fools in the Suettaring. What's the point, anyway? If you want to trade, then trade. Why bother asking for investment if you haven't tested the route?"

"Some trade's too risky for any one concern to attempt on its own," Barhu explained. "Like—like an idea I have in mind, for example. You'd need a navy's worth of shipping, escort from the *actual* navy, doctors for tropical and alpine diseases, wages for crews, insurance . . . actually, Mother, I think my idea could do real good for Taranoke. Could I speak to the matai? The elder council?"

"Oh, we are the matai," the aunt across the table said. Everyone's chatter fell away with her voice.

"*You're* the matai?"

"Who else would come greet you, Baru? You're an important person. Not just to your parents."

"The news about Salm was good," the uncle at her right side said. "You did well learning it."

"But there are two warships in our harbor." Another aunt leaned in to scoop up a handful of pork with a big taro leaf. "You sent them here, Pinion says. We don't like warships in our harbor, Baru. For reasons I know you remember."

"I remember." Barhu tasted puffer fish–flavored nostalgia, yearning for a time when she had not known how bad things had already become. "I've put you all in danger by coming here."

"You're not the easiest woman to trust, these days," the elephant-masked uncle said, with a fondness that made Barhu wish she could remember his name. "There were people who wanted to give you the carpets when we heard what you'd done in Aurdwynn."

"I'm sorry." Was there nothing at all she remembered? "Give me the what?"

"It's a ritual of abandonment," her mother said, glaring dangerously at the elephant-masked man. "You lie down beneath carpets. Or a proxy does, if you can't be found. Then we walk across you. It means you're dirt to us. Cast out forever."

The aunt at the head of the table watched Barhu compassionately. "Your parents opposed it. They said you were trying, in your own way, to help us. Is that still true?"

"Yes."

"You truly mean to help us? Not simply cut us in on the profits of some scheme that—" The aunt paused a moment, assembling Aphalone words. "—ultimately reinforces the masked power?"

"Yes! If you knew what I'd given up to be here—"

"She told us," Solit said, from his place at the coffee apparatus. "Look at her hands. Look at her face. She's suffered for us, matai. Maybe not the way all of us would have wanted. Maybe not in a way we'd all have approved. She's done things I don't understand. She's certainly collaborated. But she's still our child at heart."

"A very difficult child," an uncle said.

"Wouldn't stop crying," an aunt said, "until that bird started calling, that big ugly cormorant. And she stopped crying so she could listen. Ugliest thing she could hear, and she loved it."

Barhu was going to sob again. "If you want me to go," she said, "please tell me now. If you think I'm endangering all of you by coming here, by entangling you in my work—"

"Everyone here chose to fight Falcrest." Pinion leaned forward to catch the table's focus. "I propose that my daughter is no longer allowed to mope about putting us in harm's way. We are all volunteers."

"Not the children," the elephant-masked man said.

"Our children are in this war!" Pinion barked. "The war is *about* the children!"

Heads nodded around the table. She turned back to Barhu. "Tell us what you're doing. Tell us everything. Let us choose whether or not to help you."

"I am trying," Barhu said, "to construct a trade route."

IT made such sense. Falcrest had come to Taranoke to capture its trade as well as its crops; Falcrest wanted to export the labor of crop-growing to Taranoke and to concentrate the profit of trade in itself. Falcrest had *always* been driven by trade. Now more than ever, with the entire Ashen Sea turning profit: the Masquerade's Suettaring merchants and the Tahari Spill's ambitious middle classes were impatient for another opportunity to try for godhood. They had seen ordinary men become gilt with wealth a king would envy. A day laborer might earn only thirty notes a year, and a whole family could live quite comfortably for eight hundred, with a house and luxuries. But the Armada War had seen men make a hundred thousand notes, two hundred thousand, more.

Oriati Mbo was richer than all Falcrest's other holdings combined. If their western coast could be opened to exploitation, if the Mbo's stranglehold on all that land and labor could be undone, the rewards would be richer still.

The risks would be immense, of course. Ships would need to travel farther from Falcrest than ever before. They would have to negotiate (or force) passage through the Segu archipelago. They would find new tropical diseases. They would have no charts or weather almanacs to tell them when to sail and when to harbor. No hope of return for ships lost in the Black Tea Ocean.

But with those risks would come access to so much possibility. The Ashen Sea trade ring was like a waterfall. This would be a maelstrom.

And Barhu, with the Cancrioth in one hand, with the mountain Stakhieczi in the other, with the Emperor's favor behind her, was the likeliest person in the world to unleash it.

TARANOKE will be at the center of the chain," Barhu explained. "It'll be like the old days, when—"

"Baru," Solit said, quietly, "*we* don't trade anymore."

The table was not reacting with the interest Barhu had expected. "What? What do you mean?"

"Commerce is handled by factors from Falcrest. We serve as wage or day labor, secretaries, clerks, stevedores. But not management. Never owners. Even the fishing concerns are run by colonial offices."

"Once I'm in position, that will change."

"How?" Solit asked: gently, but not too gently. "Because you made some money? It still goes to Falcrest. It may not even go to you. You'll have savvy, well-connected people trying to take your business away from you. . . ."

"I'll have no competition. The Emperor Itself is going to endorse my concern as a common venture of the people. I'm going to have a complete monopoly on trade with everything west of Segu."

"The Emperor *Itself*?" the aunt at the table's head asked, sharply. "I thought the Emperor was an amnesiac. Beyond anyone's influence."

"I have ways to influence the Emperor's decisions. I promise you."

Her mother was frowning like a thundercloud again, and looking out to sea.

"What is it?" Barhu prodded.

"When the mask came to Taranoke, they said all the same things. New markets. Better trade. All you're offering is more of the same, Baru. More gears and levers to add to the same engine that ground us up. Maybe we get a lever to pull for our own benefit. Fine. But what about the people in this new market you're opening, in western Oria? What will they get? Pox and flu and civil war? A chance to be worked to death in yards and plantations?" She shook her head. "Water flows downhill, child. Pouring more water won't change that."

"With enough time, water changes the shape of the river, ma."

"Well," Pinion grumbled, "it still flows downhill."

"Listen, making money isn't the end of this project. It's the beginning."

"How?" the elephant-masked uncle asked.

"I . . ." She had not wanted to say this. "I can't tell you. I have to keep the full plan secret."

"Why?" her mother asked, warily.

"If anyone suspects you're working with me—" Fear bubbled up like heartburn. She'd told herself once that she needed a blade for a spine, so that if she bent from her purpose, she would be cut. Her parents *were* that blade. If someone seized them, she would be disemboweled.

She lost her thoughts for a moment. Someone said, "No one can suspect you're working with us? Then there will be no Taranoki involved in your plan to save Taranoke?"

"There can't be," she insisted. "I have to seem completely estranged. Even from you, Mother, Father. I have to seem like I'd treat your deaths as a minor inconvenience. I've gone to . . . to great lengths to create that impression."

"So take the carpets," the head aunt said. "Have yourself exiled. That would make your distaste for your heritage more credible, wouldn't it?"

Pinion and Solit shouted "No!" almost together. The table burst into shouting. Barhu stood there, fingertips on the wood, staring at her plate.

The matai were right. If she were ritually cast out, if she raged and swore her eternal hatred against Taranoke and her own family, it would armor them and her against hostage-taking. Not foolproof. Not against the truly ruthless. But it would be a measure of protection.

"Farrier," she said.

Silence. As if she had splayed out her right hand and cut the rest of her fingers off.

"What about him?" The aunt at the head of the table had a vicious gleam in her eyes. "We know he was the power behind that vile school. We know he planned all of it. We read his books. *My Adventure.*" She spat. "I'd see him on trial, if I could. In our court."

"He's going to do these things," Barhu said. "All these things I've said I'll do, he'll do for Falcrest. But if you'll help me here, if you'll welcome these Cancrioth as guests, I truly believe I can find a secret which will destroy Farrier forever."

"What secret?" Pinion looked ready to kill. "Has he—did he *dare*—!"

"No, Mother. He treats me like a daughter. Scrupulously so."

She looked nearly as sickened by that. "How can the Cancrioth give you this secret?"

"There's someone on their ship. A Prince who knew Farrier, long ago. And others who might help me. It's all tied up, the trade route and the secret I need to learn. It's all on that ship." She looked at all of them, one by one, pleading. "Will *you* help me? All I ask is water to ease their thirst, a bazaar to occupy their time, and a private room for negotiations. Very soon the men who want to control me will take me back into their power. This is my last chance to do work against them. And I genuinely believe that the future of the world will be determined by what I can do here."

"There's too much at stake," the aunt with the taro leaf said. "Taranoke needs us. We can't risk ourselves on a . . . political ploy."

"It's more than Taranoke!" Barhu insisted. "It's so much more! I was on Kyprananoke not weeks ago. Do you know what Falcrest did there? Do you know what remains of Kyprananoke? Ocean! Just ocean and rock!"

"Kyprananoke," the elephant-masked man snorted. "Did they finally run out of compost to grow food? Or did the tide just come in an inch too high?"

"You don't understand!" But how could they? How could anyone who hadn't seen it? "Listen," Barhu begged them. "Kyprananoke was Falcrest's holding before we were. When they were done with Kyprananoke they left. *But it didn't stop.* The people they'd set in power held their posts. The wounds they'd cut kept bleeding. All the old ways of agriculture were gone. All the old ways of justice were disposed of. All the water was in the hands of tyrants. Things got worse and worse. There was resistance, and revolution, but it was as hard and cruel as the regime it fought. And when the situation became so terrible that it endangered Falcrest, they reached out and wiped Kyprananoke off the map. *Everyone there is dead.* They tried to get free of the chains Falcrest left behind, and Falcrest killed them all for it.

"How can we wait for a better time? Do you *really* believe Falcrest will ever let us go? They are in us deeper than they were ever in Kyprananoke. In two hundred years they will still be on our island and we will live in concrete blockhouses and work in their kitchens and struggle to remember that we were ever free!"

"She's right," Solit said, into the quiet.

"She's right," the aunt who ate with taro leaf agreed, "and it doesn't matter. We don't get to do what's right. We have to do what's in our power, and what's in our power is getting people off Taranoke when they're in danger. If we draw so much attention to this village—"

"Oh, to rot with that," another aunt jeered. "We're not so important. Look at us! Living here in houses we built, while back home they're stacked two to a bunk, day and night shift. I say we get back in the fight. So we might get killed. So what? We risked that every day back home."

"We could put on quite a bazaar," Solit said. "Candied fruits, canvas shades, dancers of such beauty and grace that the sun will dally at the zenith to watch. And a ritual battle, to get their spirits up for buying. Like the good old days, before that first red ship. . . ."

"Let's vote," the elephant-masked uncle said.

The taro leaf aunt nodded. "Yes, let's vote."

Pinion stood up. "I'll take Baru outside. She shouldn't see the tally. Solit has my vote."

"Mother," Barhu protested. But there was no refusing Pinion in her own house. In a moment they were out the back, in the cool shade, looking up at the green shoulder of the mountain and the pasture where the carriage horses grazed.

"Baru," Pinion said. "I don't understand what you're up to, and I don't want to." She took her daughter by the arm, not gently, but with care for how it felt. "But I want you to know, whatever happens, that you've been true to yourself. You've followed your curiosity to places I can't go. Become someone I could never be. That makes me so proud. A daughter who's more than her mother . . . that's what I always wanted."

"Oh, ma."

"Tell me the truth. Are you going to ask for the carpets?"

She couldn't lie to her mother. But gods of fire it hurt to say.

"I might, ma. If it keeps you safe. Safer."

"Gods," Pinion said, softly. "This world. Not enough that we can't see you. Now we have to tell everyone that we hate you? That we never had a daughter?"

"It's worse than that."

"*Worse?*"

"I have a colleague . . . a woman named Yawa. And there may be a price I need to pay to her. She's put herself at risk for me. I have to make good on the debt."

"What, Baru? What price?"

"You'll know it when it happens."

"You and your secrets." Small, sharp tears in Pinion's eyes. Rare currency, in Barhu's life. "I wanted to say—I'm glad you came to visit."

She took her mother by the hands. "Thank you for letting me be here. Tasting the food. Sitting at the table. I don't remember all of it from when I was young, but I will remember today. No matter what else happens to me."

Solit came out the back door, grinning. "We're going to do it. We'll be ready tomorrow." His grin faltered. "Is it so terrible already?"

ANT JUICE

BARHU watched Iscend arise from the Rubiyya, clean water charting paths of least effort down her body. The hydraulic veil, Barhu thought: she wears it briefly, and very well.

"Perhaps you see the lagoon goddess," the Clarified woman suggested, "who was born where the first lava met the ancient sea. That's your legend, isn't it?"

"So you're a goddess now? That's not very egalitarian." She knew how she looked, damn her, and her confidence was maddening. And the worst part was Barhu's body missed Xe's touch and Iscend *knew* it. She could tell.

"The blame is yours, Agonist," Iscend said, teasingly. "I was only guessing what you might be thinking. Was I right?"

"She wasn't a very gentle goddess. She could breathe steam into your mouth and scald your skin from your body. In our stories she was the wife of fire-bleeding Mother Mountain and salt-seeded Father Sea, and . . ." Barhu trailed off. She had always been shy of the pages where the lagoon godess was illustrated. Heroic nudity would not have intrigued her much, but something about the steam-shrouded intimation of the goddess' idealized form made Barhu stare.

"Have a fine swim?" she asked, with such self-defensive sarcasm that it might have dried Iscend as well as her suncloth.

"Up the river before dawn, then down with the rising light. The parrots have absorbed some of their sounds from the villagers here. One of them shouted the word 'bear' at me. I think in the hope that I would drop something as I ran away." Iscend scrubbed her face in the suncloth and began to untie her wet strophium. Paused with fingers on the linen. "May I?"

"You don't need my permission."

"I don't want to make you uncomfortable. . . ."

"Iscend," Barhu said, exasperated, "just go on as if it hadn't happened, understand?"

"I'm sorry for what I did last night." Iscend grimaced and touched her brow. "I, personally, am sorry for putting you in such a position. I went too far."

Barhu had been poking at the tactical aspect of that riverbank encounter. Iscend was too self-possessed to ever lose herself to passion, wasn't she? So there must have been a reason she wanted a carnal alliance. She needed to feel Barhu as a source of pleasure, approval, satisfaction. Some inner conflict to resolve, some scheme to advance. . . .

Or was Barhu just forcing her idea of Iscend back into the conveniently impersonal mechanism of the Clarified? What if that really *had* been a plea for personal trust and affection? What if Iscend had simply been attracted to Barhu? She didn't spend much time accounting her own charms, but she supposed her luck with Xe and Shao (if you could call that luck) spoke to a certain aspect that caught women's eyes. And Hu had murmured such praises. . . .

"It's fine," she managed. "If you really wanted to . . . take a pass at me, then I'm sorry, but I can't. And if you felt you had to, out of some other purpose"— even, most terrible suspicion, out of Hesychast's orders to *prove* that Barhu couldn't control herself—"then I'm glad it didn't happen."

Iscend nodded. Her eyes were surprisingly cold. "I examined the village in the night. Everything is to my satisfaction. I should return to Cautery Plat."

What? That hurt more than it should. "You're my bodyguard. I need you here. The Cancrioth could attack. . . ."

"You'll have the marine detachment. You'll be safe."

"What about Hesychast? Wouldn't he want you to observe?"

Iscend shivered violently. A flicker of caricatured emotions passed over her face, fear-disgust-anger-hate, like an actor's drill. Barhu had seen this before, in Purity Cartone, after he'd been cast out by Xate Yawa. It was the chameleon-shift spasm of a confused Clarified looking for a simple order to fulfill: a simple person to be.

Iscend snapped her wet cloth at the river. Droplets stippled her reflection. "I believe I can serve the Republic best by returning to Annalila Fortress at once. If you can spare me."

There was no way for Barhu to refuse that, for it was as close as Iscend would come to demanding her own way.

She was so glad to feel merely confused and hurt over a woman's conduct, rather than knotted up in numb self-denial, that she walked in circles on the town green with her hands in her pockets and savored the distraction of her lightly bruised heart. What a foolish little problem to have, this matter of Iscend! But it kept her from wallowing in anger at Shao Lune.

She began to daydream of seeing Aminata again.

* * *

THE matai got up in the village commons to announce a trade bazaar, welcoming these far western Oriati and their treasure ship to the town of Iritain. Barhu was delighted to see the shieldbearers practicing their mock combat, like Salm had before the old Iriad markets. The spirit of her childhood was in the air here, sustained by these people who had lived in freer days.

She fortified herself in the library to review her negotiating strategy. So she wanted trade: well, if the Cancrioth were a secret society, if they were able to bankroll Abdumasi Abd's war fleet, then surely they could support their end of trade! The difficulty would be in persuading the Brain to see the value of her new plan. How do you butcher an empire? With gold, Incrisiath, with gold and commerce, and with your hands in their beating heart. The Womb would not like the risk, but she was a pragmatist; she would understand Barhu's arguments. The Eye would hate the idea of exposing the Cancrioth to the world, but if Barhu could show him that this was the best way to avoid war, to convince Falcrest there was profit to be made *without* conquest . . .

(Of course, her doubts whispered, Falcrest sent its terrible influence wherever it saw profit, and she was about to mark the Oriati as most profitable indeed . . . did she truly think she could control that influence? Yes! Yes! That was what a monopoly was *for*—she would be in control, and she would play the game fiercely, so that control could not be taken from her. . . .)

She was still making notes when Heingyl Ri blindsided her from behind a shelf of Oriati rares. "How comes the bazaar, Your Excellence?"

"Your Gracious Excellence!" Barhu hastily conjoined the honorifics for a governor and a duchess. "I hope Aratene's hospitality brings you comfort."

"Very much so. Although"—her eyes flashed with irritation—"I did have to explain to my armsmen, more than once, that no one would be offering their daughters."

"I'm afraid the notion of sexual hospitality is based on a misunderstanding of our culture. If you can imagine such a thing. Not so much a Taranoki tradition as a tradition of foreigners writing about Taranoke."

"A cultural misconception sustained by lurid rumor? In *our* great republic?" Heia covered her heart. "Perish the thought."

"But in other respects, all was satisfactory?"

"More than delightful." Heia beckoned, and a handmaiden appeared with a platter of cured venison and jars of brined olives. "Gifts, for your personal comfort. And"—her expression clouded—"the comfort of your parents."

"Thank you," Barhu said, trying not to frown in sympathy: the omen of the stag was clearly still gnawing at Heia. "You won't stay for the negotiations?"

"It is, alas, too dangerous. I've sent away too many of my armsmen."

Barhu took her hand and held it. "Whatever happens here, I promise that I'll keep Aurdwynn's welfare first in my mind."

"What *is* going to happen here, Baru?" She went over to Aurdwynni Iolynic; the handmaiden disappeared herself expertly. "I know you and Yawa are plotting something. I see how much strain she's under. Have you given her enough room to satisfy her own master? What will she say, when he asks her how all this has benefited the Republic?"

"Oh, I'm going to make a bargain in Falcrest's interest. That's the beauty of economics, Your Excellency. It's possible for everyone to get what they want at a price they consider fair. And I, personally, am willing to pay a considerable price."

The Stag Duchess waited with narrow eyes. "So tell me. Tell me what price you'll pay, and what you'll get for it."

Barhu crossed her arms. They stared at each other across the platter of preserved meats. "Is she really gone?" Barhu asked, meaning the handmaiden.

"Of course she's gone. If you won't share your plans with me, how will you ever share my . . . confidence?"

Barhu laughed. "All right. All right. You already know the general scheme. I'll open a trade concern, for traffic from the Wintercrests to the Black Tea Ocean and beyond. At first most of the profit will go to Falcrest, and the Falcresti will hurry to invest in it. I will control more and more of their wealth, and more and more of their power will be spent to protect my interests. In time, this concern will give me all the power I need to . . . well. You'll let me keep a few secrets, I hope?"

"Don't you dare play coy with me," Heia hissed. The heel of her hand came down on the edge of the tray and all the meats jumped. "This smells like Sieroch. You've gathered everyone in one place. You're promising great things, a bright future, if we only stick with you a little further. And now you're going to make your move."

"Don't *you* dare doubt me." Barhu rose up to meet her. "I delivered you Aurdwynn. I delivered the dowry that you need for your marriage, and that marriage will deliver you peace. Trust me to deliver this, too."

"You and Yawa won't *deliver* me to any marriage I don't consent to! And what are you giving her in all this?"

"A friend," Barhu said, without quite meaning to. "She and I—"

"What? You understand each other? You trust each other?" Now Heia looked frightened for *her*. "If you're a threat to her plans, she'll be rid of you faster than one of her experimental patients."

"I can't tell you everything, Governor. The more I reveal, the less powerful I become. You wouldn't want me powerless, would you?"

"I won't leave this room until I learn exactly what you intend here."

"Everyone needs money, Heia."

"Facile." She was breathing hard. "Tell me more."

"The navy needs money to sail its ships. Parliament needs money to pay for reelection. Everything an empire does is terribly expensive; otherwise they wouldn't be things only an empire could do. I intend to control that money. I intend to grow it like a crop. Then a time will come to reap. And when that time comes, Falcrest will hear the whole world baying at their borders, and smell the money rotting in the banks, and feel the fabric of their lives fraying under their thumbs. And that's when they'll look for the strength they love best."

Heia was watching her with a kind of astonishment, as if Barhu had just grown a rack of antlers. "What strength is that?"

"Revolution."

"And *you'll* be that revolution? A foreigner?"

"Of course not. Just a woman in a mask."

"The same as any other."

"Not," Barhu said, "if the mask is the Emperor's."

"*You* want to be Empress?"

"I wouldn't know it if I were, would I? The Emperor has no idea who It is. That's why we trust It to be fair."

"Then how—"

"Please, my Lady." Barhu gave her Tain Hu's lopsided grin. "Let me have my secrets."

Heia blinked several times. Then she came around the desk, took Barhu by the chin, and kissed her, succinctly, on the lips.

"Is that a betrothal?" Barhu murmured.

"No. But it is a way to keep me in your mind." She looked up at Barhu with quick fox eyes, but they were not mischievous: cornered eyes, skittish eyes, looking for a way out. "All this matter of the state marriage, the Necessary King . . . I can't see how Bel will ever approve of it. I won't go behind his back. But I . . . need time to think. Please."

She kissed Barhu again, on the cheek, and went. Left Barhu's stomach fizzing like champagne. She sat down and went back to work.

I N the prow of Annalila Fortress, Bel Latheman works.
  He's learned to deal with the fear of losing Heia by drowning himself in work that will make her happy. When she is gone on business, as she is tonight,

Bel Latheman opens his account books and continues to sort out the cryptic mess left behind by the last Imperial Accountant of Aurdwynn, Baru Cormorant. She made strange leaps in her logic, never showed her work, obeyed bookkeeping protocol at its surface but often filled her ledgers with equations and trendlines whose purpose he can't even begin to guess at: except that they are probably experimental metrics of Aurdwynn's economy, research she conducted in order to effortlessly ruin his life.

What can happen in a year, what good and what horror. This past winter: when he couldn't see Heia more than a night a month, for fear of Coyote garrotes finding them in bed. When he had to wait in the bitter cold for his guard to search every room and closet of his tower before he could go in and open the latest list of dead.

And Heia's hot lips, fierce in the snow, the first kiss hers because he was so damn timid: the letter she'd left him, on the night before she vanished for two weeks, *I will lose my father before I lose you, Bel*.

The hasty, happy marriage in the hot-rock sauna in Northarbor. They'd embraced carefully, he and Heia, in towels: her armsmen were there, and one of them even conducted the marriage, big-chested and boomingly cheerful in the steam. He'd been jealous of that man, before, and the jealousy had made him do isometrics so he could be as huge and fierce. She'd touched his chest and said, *Bel, you've grown!* After the marriage he was never again jealous of that one man; and he saw how Heia had, gently, made him close that wound. Though she warned him against her armsmen: "They've known me since I was a girl, Bel, but men who love girls often murder the women they become."

The hardest night of his life was when her father died. Harder than the nights after Baru's performances, when he wanted to scream of helpless rage. Women like Baru, he'd written in his last letter home before everything got very confusing, were the reason why Falcrest needed mannism so badly. Men might make money and show their faces in Parliament, but women had a coldly natural disposition toward schemes and plots, and given a station and an opportunity, they would wrap men in their webs.

Anyway—he breaks his quill and tries another—when Heia's father had died at Sieroch, when the whole city had convulsed with cheers at his death, Heia sat in their little hideaway garret and stared emptily. "I killed him," she'd said, when he asked for the twentieth time what he could do. "I killed him so I could be free."

He'd told her that was nonsense. She'd snapped at him with a terrifying and aristocratic authority which he'd never heard before: "Don't presume to know my methods, Bel!"

He is distracted: he's read a page of Baru's notes without understanding a damn thing. He goes back and begins, again, methodically, to scan through the page, to imagine the cape slithering off Ri's naked body on that night she came alone to his tower, her throaty *Am I still forbidden, even here?* The obscene and deliciously private things she'd known how to do, which he for months feared as much as he enjoyed: oh, how he wishes this thrill will be forever, that he will never ever quite grasp or understand her, but always find himself walking uphill toward her. He thought once that he would never quite fully respect her, if only for her race. And he was so wrong.

There comes a knock.

"Imperial Accountant!" Bel shouts, because so many people have come looking for Heia, trying to cut deals great and small for a piece of the new Aurdwynn. She is here to buy fertilizer; it feels like everyone else is here to buy her. Most recently that strange bony Stakhi woman at the ball, who wanted a ship home, and also, obviously, wanted to tell Bel something: but did not.

"Sir," the man at the door says, one of Heia's Stakhieczi bodyguards, "I'm taking this shift over from Alemyainuthe, and he's going down to the town."

Bel frowns at him. He still can't keep all the Aurdwynni names straight: three languages colliding makes confusion he can't follow. "Weren't you traveling with Heia?"

"Yes, sir, but she sent me back here, away from her."

"Did you upset her?"

"No, sir," the man says, more irritably than Bel thinks he should tolerate, "there was just an incident with a stag and a catamount, and she felt I reacted poorly. Our provincial superstitions, sir."

"I see," Bel says, bemused.

"There's a lady visitor for you, sir," he says, with the very faintest disapproval. He is fiercely Heia's; he may have even watched her birth. "She has papers from the mayor's office in Cautery Plat. She says she's here to check their import-export tables against yours."

Bel feels a thrill of pride. It's for him! Official business! "Send her in!"

"She's not married, sir," the doorman says. He is as fiercely Stakhieczi as he is fiercely Ri's. "Just so you know. And I don't like the look of her, somehow. Maybe I've seen her before." The implication being that anywhere he saw her would not be a place a proper woman should be seen.

"I expect she will be perfectly professional," Bel snaps. "Would you like to chaperone?"

"No, sir. I'll be outside, sir, in the atrium."

The woman slips in. Bel makes an immediate note to have a talk with his doorman—not a reprimand, but rather an apology of his own, because he understands why the doorman warned him. Whoever she is, she's *perfect*. Not perfectly a match for Bel's taste, but perfectly in accord with the classical Falcresti ideal, from her brushstroke cheekbones to her narrow coat and gracefully simple stride. Writers of rag novels overheat into metaphor to create women like this: the "sparrow-like gait" of Tinadette Bane, the "essential and irreducible" form of Goodbake's Diligena Sum, the "very provocation of unapproachable virtue and cold disregard, which invites in the male heart the need to approach and be regarded," from something Bel doesn't remember.

"Asshole," the woman mutters, in very masculine fashion. Clearly the doorman bothered her. Then she shakes herself and, with a guilty flash of her teeth, remembers her manners. "Your Excellence? My name's Sutra Cane, from the Mayor's office."

Bel's been trying to be more masculine himself, so he very ably avoids stammering or mumbling. Instead he kicks a chair toward her. It's too much—the chair will topple—but she catches it.

"Join me," Bel says, "in the great work of progress, or, at least, preventing regress."

There's a part of him, a small part he despises, which still whispers, *she should be your wife. A woman like her, with cold modesty and a good Faculties education, who'll come to the marriage with an unlimited childbearing license and a substantial dowry, just for tradition's sake. And she'll have beautiful smooth brown skin, not a sort of woodstain with pox-marks. And she'll exercise isometrically instead of growing lazy curves and obscene tits, and you'll—*

Bel doesn't want to think about anyone's tits. He's been told intrusive sex thoughts drop off with age. He can't wait.

"What have we here?" he asks.

Sutra Cane briskly lays out her own tables, and asks to compare her records of Aurdwynn's intake and outlays with Bel's: this leads Bel down a digression about Baru's note-taking style, which makes Sutra lean forward in interest. Bel immediately deluges her with figures.

"Ah," she says, following without struggle. "What a relief. We seem to be lined up! If there was a difference then the Imperial Trade Factor's office would have ratcatchers out here looking for corruption—"

"Are you a ratcatcher?" Bel asks.

She goes pale. "Me? No! Oh, not you, too."

Bel can't help asking after that. "Having trouble in the office?"

"Yes," she says, tensely, "people think I'm too good at my job, and therefore that I'm a plant."

"Ah. Women do get that, I understand. The impostor complex: a belief that women aren't showing their true selves among men."

"It's true."

"Does it bother you very much?"

She looks at his wall, in stiff profile. "I'm not an anti-mannist. I just want to do my work and be assessed fairly."

"That's all mannism wants," Bel assures her, "a fair shot for both sexes, and fair value on the different strengths of each."

A spark of interest in her eyes. Why do people call it a spark? Because, Bel thinks, guiltily, they want it to catch. "Do you find it difficult?" she asks. "Being a man in a woman's job?"

"People check my math a lot," he jokes.

"That must be hard. . . ."

He looks at her with the face that means: do you realize you're here to do exactly that?

She covers her mouth. "Oh, I didn't mean to imply—I just thought, with the war and all, it'd be wise to come square our numbers! Before communications become difficult!"

"No, of course—"

"You don't think it's because you're—"

"Of course I don't."

"Thank you." She laughs. "You're young and handsome, and you look like you should be out making bargains on horseback; I'm sure you're sick to death of people doubting you can do figures. . . ."

She must see something in his eyes, because she swallows and shuts up. "All seems to be in order," Bel says, as gently as he can. "If there's nothing else?"

She hesitates. A huge weight settles on the top of Bel's spinal column and begins to press. He felt this weight at the beginning of that last dinner with Baru: no matter which way it topples, it's going to break something.

"Is it true you were an arranged marriage?" she whispers. "You and the Governor?"

Arranged marriage is a taboo, since it reeks of royalty. "Love match," Bel says, briskly.

"But the word as we heard it was—*to unite the Ducal lines with the Provincial government*—"

"If you're asking if I was whored out by Parliament," Bel snaps, "then no."

Sutra's chest swells (his thought, Bel knows, is impelled by the damn fetishism surrounding Cold Indignant Passion, but that does not prevent him noticing) with outrage. "Please don't be obscene!"

"You brought up arranged marriages."

"Purely out of concern for your safety!"

"I assure you I don't need any domestic gallantry," Bel snaps, "and that's *quite* enough familiar talk from you—"

This wounds her pride and she strikes back: "The way your wife cuckolds you, I should *think* you need a gallant lady or two!"

The weight of anxiety topples off Bel's spine and plunges, like a spear, down through his throat, the bottom of his stomach, the tangle of his intestines, directly into whatever gland in his ballsack produces the masculine fear. He feels one of those hot dizzy washes that always accompany the most intense jealousy.

"Rumormongering," he says, matter-of-factly. "I shall have to speak to your control secretary about this behavior."

She breathes hard, her eyes closed. "I'm sorry," she says. "I just hate it when women take advantage of men for . . . you know. Politics."

Bel doesn't ask her to go on. But he doesn't stop her.

"The rumor is the Stakhieczi king is looking for a wife," Sutra says, softly. "And your wife, Governor Aurdwynn . . . she was seen dancing with a Souswardi woman at the Governor's Ball. And then departing this fortress with her, and a Stakhieczi man and woman, too. Did she stop to say hello before she left?"

She had. She'd come up and kissed him and asked after his work. She hadn't mentioned why she was going to Aratene in such a hurry. Or with whom she traveled. Or when she'd be back.

She certainly hadn't mentioned traveling with that bony Stakhieczi woman. Or meeting with a Souswardi . . . and there is only one Souswardi who Bel knows to meddle in the affairs of Aurdwynn, and in his life. . . .

This, he realizes, is why he has been so terrified. Because he already knows. She's back. She's going to take his wife away.

"I'm sorry," Sutra whispered. "I just thought you should know that . . . your wife might be considering a political marriage. To end the invasion, at least, and to give this king an heir. . . . I know it's royalism, but she comes from a savage land, she might consider it necessary to . . . to disavow your marriage."

"Stop," Bel snarls. "I don't know who put you up to this, but stop!"

She begins to cry. "I'm sorry. The woman dancing with your wife was Baru

Cormorant. I think she's going to marry your wife to the Stakhi king. I'm sorry. I'm so sorry."

Everything terrible in Bel's life returns in a moment.

Sutra Cane gets up and vanishes into the numb void. When Bel looks up, she's not there anymore. Much else is missing, too. His mind hungers to chew on itself, the way a wound hungers for a probing finger.

And there it is. As if summoned by his fear. Sitting on his desk.

The nootrope.

It's not alcohol and it's not mason dust. In the Faculties they called it Ant Juice, because its discovery involved the mushed corpses of millions of ants. It tastes acrid and it burns hard. If you put it in water and drink it, you feel as if you could recite the whole number line from zero to forever and still have time for brandy before bed.

Ant Juice helps you do work that will make your important governor wife happy when she comes home from whatever the fuck she won't tell you about.

Suddenly Bel has the bottle in his hands.

Ant Juice also drives people lust-mad, or at least that was the rumor in the Faculties, though at the time Bel just found it made him supremely anxious. He was afraid to jerk off because of what had happened to Roreigh, so he never tried. The one time he'd used Ant Juice before going to bed with Heia she'd begged him to stop, because he just kept going and going without result.

Cuckold.

No, idiot. She actually loves you. You know that.

But that wouldn't stop her from cuckolding you for aristocratic politics, would it?

Just focus, Bel, focus on the fucking work—

With a snarl of rage he tips too much Ant Juice into his coffee and takes a sip. It tastes awful. He likes that. Images of his diminutive, easily manhandled wife wrapped around huge pale monster men appear to him. Her head thrown back in the throes of a passion that reveals itself, like bruises on fruit, under hard and grasping hands.

But the awful taste of the Ant Juice will condition these thoughts away. Baru's notes are suddenly clear. Is this how she feels all the time? Arrogant and perfect?

He snaps his quill. He reaches for another, and takes a sip of coffee. He cycles through this process. Broken quill. Sip of coffee.

"Doorman," he calls.

"Sir?" the man says, through the door.

"Did my wife leave word as to when she'd return?"

An eternity splits that request from the doorman's reply. Bel can tell because he's gotten so much done. "I'm sorry, Your Excellence," the doorman calls. "Word's just in, actually, that she is going on to the north shore, and will not return for some days."

"I see," Bel says. His coffee's empty. That means he drank all the Ant Juice. "I see. In company with those Stakhieczi, I suppose!"

"Sir, why are you shouting?"

"I'm not shouting!" Bel screams.

"Sir, that woman Sutra Cane . . . she told me that you were very upset with Her Grace—that is Her Excellence, the Governor, sir. She said you called her a liar and a royalist whore."

"Did she?" Had he said that? He couldn't remember. "How indiscreet."

"So it's true, sir? You're upset with Her Excellence the Governor? You called her a whore?"

"Why would you care?"

"Because I am her armsman, sir, and I defend her in all matters, including those of the household, sir."

Bel laughs. "Don't you start with the insinuations. My wife is *my wife*. She doesn't need you to protect her from *me*."

"I haven't insinuated anything, sir. I've only asked—"

He seems to be saying whatever comes to mind, because all his thoughts are so clear and forcefully cogent he cannot stop them from running to their conclusion. "Whatever you two got up to before I courted her, it's in the past, understand?"

"Sir," the doorman says, in what Bel thinks of as the Aurdwynn Stiff, a tone of mild but unyielding threat, "I took an oath to her father. I helped raise her."

"Well, her father's dead, isn't he?" Bel finds it oddly relaxing to taunt the man even as he keeps on with the letter. Why is he writing a letter? Because he's working. The chatter coming out of his mouth is just an accessory to getting the work done. "Poor dumb bastard finally got a *real* spear up his ass, huh?"

"Sir."

"And you care whether I call her a whore? Are you used to defending her from such accusations?"

"Sir, you mustn't."

"I really don't care if she is," he says, jauntily. "I understand the culture's different, if you don't bleed out a bastard by the time you're sixteen you're probably infertile—"

"*Sir.*"

He recognizes, distantly, that he has had too much Ant Juice after too long off the stuff, and that he is undergoing some sort of catastrophic reaction. How the fuck did the Ant Juice *get* on his desk? He poured his entire personal supply into the Horn Harbor, months and months ago, when Heia asked him to be rid of it.

"Sir," someone's saying, from *inside* the room, how is the doorman inside the door—Bel catches up on a queue of delayed stimuli, the smash of the door opening too hard, the huge man throwing his huge shadow, the stink of sweat under leathers. "Sir, you're not well."

Bel grins toothily at the man. He remembers this distinctly from *The Manual of the Somatic Mind.* Territorial challenge. Dogs. Stand your ground. The dominant male.

"Get the fuck out," he says, "you motherfucker."

"Don't talk about my mother," the doorman says: he does not understand the idiomatic usage of the word, he thinks he's been accused of incest.

"Why shouldn't I? You're happy to talk about my wife."

The man is breathing hard. "It's just that you mustn't say such things about the Duchess Heingyl. Especially as you're a foreigner. It's not right to call people whores. It's not safe. The Judiciary could become involved. The hygiene courts."

"Why," Bel repeats, "shouldn't I talk about your mother? Is something wrong with her?"

"*Your* fucking people took my mother away!"

"Whores get bores," Bel says, out of mad self-destructive self-loathing, and pushes his finger into his brow above his eye, where the lobotomy pick goes.

The man makes a mad dog sound. Bel sees a reflection on sharp steel. Then the reflection disappears, somehow, into Bel's chest. Bel thinks, with the clarity of Ant Juice, that the Aurdwynni are a culture of honor, that insults may truly be mortal, that he can't wait for Heia to come back and set all this right, oh, Heia, how he misses—

30

SEND BRU

"WHAT a pitiful sight." Yawa swept her spyglass over the Cancrioth boats struggling down the bay. "Hardly immortal for much longer, I should think."

"You'd be pitiful, too, if you'd been on water rations and pump shifts for weeks." Barhu turned to wave to her parents, who were waiting with the village shieldbearers. "Bring up the casks!"

"I'd rather keep them thirsty until we have a bargain," Yawa grumbled. "I'd make them pay for every drop."

"Believe me, these aren't the people you need to wring dry. You'll know those when you meet their leader."

"The Brain. If she's so all-frozen important, then where is she?"

The moment Iritain had signaled that they were ready to receive shore parties, *Eternal* began to launch barges. At first the crowds packed aboard had frightened Barhu: was it an attack? But then she'd seen the Eye, waving a white cloth from the bow of the first boat. A warning against death. He was bringing in his weak, his helpless.

"He's a snail man," the elephant-faced matai said, in bemusement. "Are they all snail men?"

"He's very worried about his people dying," Solit added thoughtfully. "For an immortal."

"Of course he is," Yawa said. "If one of his people dies here, who'll be strong enough to receive their Line?"

"So sensitive to the foreign faith," Barhu teased.

"I *am* a Jurispotence."

"And a religionist."

"Hush. That's a secret."

An old idea returned to Barhu. "Do you really believe that Himu"—the ilykari virtue associated with energy, excess, and cancer—"was a member of the Cancrioth?" Hesychast had proposed that Himu might have been named for a historical figure named Hayamu raQù.

Yawa laughed harshly. "Not for a moment. The Throne likes to see conspiracies everywhere. The real world never fits together so well." She made the Incrastic handwashing sign against evil, and then reached into her purse. She had an onion in there. She kept touching it, for Aurdwynni luck.

"What's got *you* squirming?" Barhu asked.

The old Jurispotence nodded to the arriving barges. Village shieldbearers waded out to bring cups of water to heat-struck Cancrioth. "Dehydrating people bleed a lot. Cracked lips, cracked skin, open sores. . . ."

"You think the Brain would send Kettling in one of them?"

"We can't know. From the moment those people come ashore, we've got to treat this entire village as a potential outbreak. No one can leave unless they go straight into quarantine."

"So we're trapped here."

"So we are," Yawa said.

Durance, Barhu remembered, meant *imprisonment*.

YAWA had arrived two chimes into forenoon watch, on a heavy bank carriage from Annalila Fortress. She'd passed Iscend Comprine the night before, running back to Annalila Fortress on foot, like some ancient messenger carrying word of battle. "Did you drive her off?" she asked Barhu.

"No," Barhu said, defensively. "I don't think so. I— It's complicated. Did you bring Kimbune and Abd?"

"Yes. They're in the back." Yawa lowered her voice. "*Helbride*'s away. Set out back upwind to Aurdwynn yesterday. Svir sends, and I quote, 'best wishes for the negotiations, and his most affectionate Fuck Yourself.'"

How fickle the heart could be: here she stood in a village full of her parents and her people, and yet *Helbride*'s departure felt like leaving home.

"I'm glad to hear he's still himself." She frowned at the carriage vault: "You did remember to leave air holes, I hope?"

Yawa's marines pulled the locking bars back and swung the portable vault open. Abdumasi Abd's mold-spotted face came groaning out of the gap. "Water! No, not your poisoned canteens, I want fresh well water. Principles, first you won't feed me, now I can't get a drink."

Barhu helped the merchant down from the sweltering interior. He had been on a purely liquid diet, to clean his intestines out before surgery. "You'll see Tau today," she told him, hoping she wasn't telling a lie. "Though I can't promise they'll be happy to see either of us."

Abdu stared up into the first free sky he'd seen in months. "It's not up to us to decide how they think. Trust them to make the choice. I've heard people call Tau naïve; even other Princes. But I have never, ever known anyone to influence Tau's judgment of character. That's what makes Tau so strong. They always get to the truth of you, whether you like it or not."

"Barhu!" Kimbune leapt down from the carriage with excitement shining in her eyes. "He's in there! I showed him my proof. I showed him everything. I know Undionash took root. He's really in there."

"Mzu's waxing buttocks," Abdumasi muttered. "I've got to take a piss."

She pointed Abdumasi to a claypit and went over to Kimbune. "Your husband's in Abd?"

"Yes!" Kimbune preened with satisfaction. "He didn't believe a *word* of it!"

"You're satisfied that your husband's soul survives in Abdumasi Abd because . . . he doesn't believe your proof?"

"Stubbornly, irrationally, against the clearest mathematical evidence! If he were just the merchant Abdumasi, wouldn't he be simply baffled? But he argued every word of it! It *must* be him!"

Barhu couldn't resist prodding at her faith. The possibility of immortality was just too intriguing to leave untested. "Did you ask him to tell you something that Abdumasi couldn't possibly have known?"

"It's not like that. Abdumasi was never taught to reach my husband's memories, so of course he can't remember me. What he's got is my husband's *soul*."

"His soul."

"Yes! His way of being! His stupid, stupid inability to see that I'm *right* about this!"

Barhu was about to scoff. And then she thought, why, I've never asked my illusion of Hu to tell me anything that only Hu could've known. Because I know it's not *really* Hu.

> Aren't I, though?
> You never knew the real Hu;
> you knew your mind's own awareness of her.
> Does it matter if that awareness
> comes from within or from without
> if one is true to the other?

What I carry is the image I've made of Hu, my record of her beliefs and the method of her choices. It's the law of being Hu: and that is enough for me to carry and to tap for strength.

Isn't that a soul?

"Kimbune," she said, "I believe you."

*   *   *

T HE Brain did not appear. Negotiations did not begin.

The sun rolled past the zenith, inspecting every shadow for secrets.

There was no sign of the hostages. Not Tau, not Aminata, not Enact-Colonel Osa.

Some of the Eye's people, restored by water and kind treatment, began to wander cautiously into the market. Canvas awnings had been pitched on the riverside green; Heingyl Ri's factors waited alongside old Taranoki traders to haggle. Water was free—Barhu and her parents had insisted on that—but everything else was up for sale. The Taranoki offered coffee and tapa cloth, canvas and glass, mirrors, finished telescopes, polished stones, salt, sugar, black pepper, nutmeg, cinnamon, ginger, Masquerade fiat notes and traditional reef pearl. Heingyl Ri's factors had brought samples of their goods to Cauteria to impress merchants: fine-spun wool, pine, planks of redwood both coastal and northern, horseshoes, toasted grain, barrels of flour, spear and arrow points, sword blades, cotton and hemp, mint, tin mugs and pots, huge jars of olive oil, mason leaf, hard cow cheese, silphium.

But the Eye's people had nothing to barter. They huddled by the shore in little knots and took wary turns visiting the toilets. They did not trade.

"When you suggested a trade concern to reach the distant parts of Oriati Mbo with Aurdwynn," Yawa murmured, "did you ever consider that the Oriati might not *want* to trade?"

"Uncle!" Barhu called. "Bring out the food!"

The smell of fresh coconut, roast pork, and salt-cooked pineapple began to stir the Oriati. The Eye sent a barge out to *Eternal* and it returned with baskets of gold, silver, electrum, gems, thunderbolt iron, medallions of jade, ebony and teak, whale ivory, rubber, resin, myrrh, knotted codices, polished chunks of amber, huge barrels of dried tea, whittled figurines of people and of abstract geometrical shapes, bracelets and necklaces and pectorals and torcs. One Cancrioth sailor hauled up an entire bag of his lovingly patterned penis gourds.

After that there was no keeping the three nations from each other. Many of the Cancrioth monks did not know quite how to value their treasure. Barhu saw one cassocked woman buy a banana with a platinum chip.

Barhu brought Abdumasi Abd out of his house and sat him down on a bench to watch. "Once," she said, sitting beside him, "there were no chairs except thrones. Everyone else in the world sat on benches."

"And you wouldn't know it, if not for the histories *we* kept. What am I supposed to see here?" He was putting on his exhausted old man act. "A bunch of Oriati being defrauded?"

"Trade," Barhu said, in delight. The whole mess made her want to leap up with a fistful of pebbles and a liar's grin and go conduct some arbitrage. Trade was a better annealment than alcohol, a sweeter invitation than beauty. You could trade with an octopus, you could haggle with someone who didn't speak your language. Just look at the things on the table between you, and search for that common place, the notch of agreement, where both sides feel they are getting the better deal, and both are right.

This was how to make a world out of different people. Not Incrasticism. Let them meet and see what they have to offer each other. And if someone tries to take it: all together, stop them.

"Do you really think this is going to work?" Abdu sighed.

"The bazaar? Well, it's a sideshow to the real negotiations, of course. Once I have my concern in place and monopolized—"

"Not your bazaar. This whole charade. Your pretense that you're some bright young entrepreneur looking to make her way in the world. We both know you're an agent of the Throne. We both know what you're doing. Trying to make me give up my trade contacts, my ports, my routes, my rutterbooks. You're thinking, why, these Oriati, they do everything by personal association. I'd better bring Abdu over to my side. Make him *my* personal associate. Then he'll give me his friends, and they'll give me *their* friends, and before you know it we'll be sailing into far Oriati ports grinning like sharks. Falcrest wins."

He thought this was another extension of his imprisonment. Another clever game. "It would be worth setting all this up," she admitted, "to get us into the Black Tea Ocean. It would be worth using an entire island as a theater. Maybe even worth risking the spread of the Kettling."

His bloodshot eyes widened. His mold-stained brow furrowed till it seemed to crack. "The *Kettling*? What do you mean?"

"It's here. In that ship. The Brain brought it to use as a weapon against Falcrest. She already let it out once, on Kyprananoke." She found it astonishingly comforting to admit this next part: "She wants me to take it and bring it into Falcrest's heart."

He swore in Seti-Caho, something about nagana. "And she thinks you can be trusted?"

"She knows the truth about me, Abdumasi Abd. She knows I'd have taken that bargain, not so long ago."

He almost asked what had changed; did not. "Any truth you offer is bait. I learned that well enough, O *Fairer Hand*." He had a knack for bitterness. Barhu wondered exactly how badly his divorce had gone. "I'll never help you buy my people."

"Really? You look around"—she waved to the bazaar, the tufa homes, the river—"and you see bait? I see the world the way I want it to be. The way I imagine it *could* be, without Falcrest."

"I was fighting for that world when you lured me to my death."

She thought about telling him that she'd never even known he existed. Decided it would be too cruel. "There are people I've lured to their death, Abdumasi Abd. You're not one of them. Not yet."

"To Tau I am," he countered. "I'm Cancrioth. Not human. Dead to trim."

That hit Barhu low. She had no idea who she would meet when Tau was released. A broken Prince? A vengeful exile?

A corpse?

"Abdu," she said, "what happened between you and Kindalana? Why did it make you turn your entire fortune to war?"

Deadly anger pierced his eyes. "You've already asked me these questions. I told you: it's between me and Kindalana."

"And Tau."

"And Tau," he admitted.

"And Cairdine Farrier?" she probed.

Thunder rumbled from the bay.

Barhu, blindsided by the noise, looked wildly up into the sky. Abd shot to his feet. The marine sentries didn't react: they were staring, too, out into the bay.

"King's dead glans," one of them said.

Eternal was salvoing her cannon. Smoke and blue-tipped flame pierced her near flank. The whistle of shot reached Barhu but she couldn't see the target—surely it wasn't *Sterilizer,* surely they weren't idiotic enough to think they could break through the torchship's sides before *Sterilizer* turned its siphons on them—

But *Eternal* was not firing at *Sterilizer.*

Eternal was firing toward the village.

Round shot struck the beach around the Eye's barges. Sand geysered. A horseshoe crab's broken shell tumbled into the waves. Water fountained and fell as the ongoing fire tracked back into the sea, clustered, and then, at last, found its target.

Children stared out from behind rows of pink hibiscus shrubs. The thunder made babies cry.

It took the Cancrioth gunners nearly twenty minutes to blast the wooden barges to driftwood and twine. By the end they had become shockingly accurate. The Eye's refugees stumbled down from the bazaar to watch, helplessly, as their boats were pulverized. Barhu ordered *Sterilizer* to hold at alert: her captain had already brought a brace of torpedoes up on the broadside rack.

The firing stopped.

Then, very deliberately, one gun discharged a shot. The ball landed right in the Rubiyya river beside the municipal offices. The signal was clear. They had taken the range, worked out their gunnery. Now they were prepared to raze the entire village.

Eternal's sunflash began to blink.

SEND BRU

SEND BRU

SEND BRU

SEND BRU

SEND BRU

SEND BRU

"YOU can't go out there!" Yawa snapped. She was still in her black quarantine gown, fully masked, faceted and lensed: she chased Barhu down the harborside quay like a bipedal krakenfly. "It's not just idiotic, it's bad strategy! You don't fold to their demands the moment they shoot off a few cannon. They're dying out there, they're at the end of their strength. Let thirst force them to come ashore!"

"I can't." What Yawa said made perfect sense, if you had not been on *Eternal* and learned about its inner politics. "If I don't go, it'll seem as if the Brain's spell failed. If the Brain's powerless, she can't control her faction of the crew."

"Good!"

"No, Yawa. If she starts to lose control she'll kill as many of us as she can and then destroy *Eternal*. She'd rather die than fall into our hands."

The judge hadn't wound up the voice-changer in the collar of her gown. Her words were raw Yawa, the Treatymont accent of a common girl begging her friend not to go out in the winter night. "They'll take you hostage. They'll try to use you as a shield while they make demands. *Sterilizer* will burn you all."

"You've got what you need from me, don't you?" Barhu leapt down into the rowboat and dropped her gutsack in the bow. "Svir will handle the Necessary King. If *Eternal* blows up with me aboard, at least you have Cancrioth ashore to take to Hesychast. You can't lose now."

"I can lose you," Yawa said, in a tone of such utter contempt for Barhu's intelligence that it must cover real emotion. The only woman in the world who knew how much she'd sacrificed. "I need you—I need you for your marriage trick. You haven't passed your claim to Heingyl Ri."

"Don't worry about me." Barhu picked up the left oar, and then, with a shake of her head, the right. "I'll be back for my lobotomy."

"Damn you. You don't get to joke about that until you've given me an alternative!"

"There is no alternative as long as we're both alive. Only one of us can win. Tain Hu volunteered, you know?" Barhu threw the mooring lines up at Yawa. "She went in with her eyes open. Both eyes open to the end. It was her choice. She knew it was the right way."

"She'd have torn *my* eyes out if I ever hurt you, Baru!"

"Take care of my parents if I don't come back. Tell them I'm sorry—no, tell them I did my best." Barhu shoved off from the quay. "Make sure Xe gets back to Aurdwynn. She has a child there. Make sure Aminata gets a pardon."

"For Devena's sake, Baru, what's out there worth risking your life?"

"Yomi," Barhu said.

"What?"

It was an Aphalone word. Hesychast had taught it to Barhu. The art of knowing your opponent's choices before they do. Either because you understand their inner processes perfectly, or because you have constrained their available choices so narrowly that they have only one option.

"Yomi," she shouted down the floating wharf to Yawa, who stood with her gown plucked up from the lapping waves. "Think about it, Yawa. We can't beat our masters, can we? They control the entire board. They have control of the money, the government, the ideology of sex and race. They have control of the context in which we make choices. They've written us a script and we have to perform it or be punished: destroy each other, or be destroyed. If we deviate, they will know at once. They have us in yomi."

"So you're *giving up*?"

"No! There are two ways to break yomi, Yawa. One of them is an external factor. Something they haven't accounted for." She waved wildly towards *Eternal*. "And the other one is you! You, Yawa!"

"I don't understand!"

"Think about the secrets you've kept from Hesychast. He knows what you've done for him but he's never understood your *motives*! It's possible to do exactly what they require of us, Yawa, but for reasons they don't understand! *That's* how to beat yomi! Conceal our maneuvers inside their maneuvers! They think their yomi is maintained until the moment it is broken!"

"Baru," Yawa screamed, "this is not the time for your philosophical fucking ramblings! Don't go out to that ship! Come here and explain yourself!"

"Trim calls me back to Tau!" she shouted back. "There's a weapon out there. Something I can use. I have to find it. Trust me, please."

"*What* weapon? How can Farrier's secret possibly be—?"

"If I tell you, Hesychast might learn. Just let me go. I trust you. Think about it. I trust you to do what they expect."

Yawa began to swear at her in Iolynic, calling her a fool, a hot cow turd with a hoofprint in it, a girl poured out from her mother's gutter, a paint eater, a hairless bloodless dried-out cunt, a carrion bird, a cracked cornerstone, an assface. Barhu rowed out toward *Eternal*.

When she had some headway she raised a hand to wave.

THE golden ship's broadside grew each time she looked up from the oars. Became a cracked, filth-streaked wall. A rope ladder tumbled down to her boat. She stood on it and clung with her good hand and they hauled her up the great reach of hull. She noted that the ship was down by the bow and tilting to starboard; the pump crews were losing the fight.

Scheme-Colonel Masako pulled her over the rail. Barhu tried her very damnedest to punch him in the face. "Hardly appropriate," he said, with seemingly genuine surprise.

"That was for Kyprananoke!"

He blinked at her, as if shocked anyone still cared. "You did that. *You* did that."

There was nothing to be gained by arguing. Two of his Termites searched her for gas capsules or needles. "I want to see Aminata."

"Aminata does not want to see you. She believes the same lies you sold to Prince Bosoka." He watched her curiously. "I know what it's like to be a spy. You're Falcrest's, through and through."

"Your master certainly believes my 'lies.' Or I wouldn't be here."

He flinched. "Don't use that word."

"Master?"

"Yes. The Brain does not have to believe or disbelieve you. She'll know. She'll pull the truth through the top of your head."

His soldiers made it gently but firmly clear that she should walk forward. In the spirit of contrarianism, she looked back.

Up on the second tier of the sterncastle she saw the Womb, hands folded in the sleeves of her cassock, watching Barhu silently. And there beside the

Womb was Tau-indi Bosoka. They wore the same cut of cassock, and their small, bright, life-black face was harsh with thirst. All their beautiful coiled hair lay heavy with sweat and oil. There was a line of bruises across their forehead. In that moment Barhu genuinely expected to see light burning on their hands.

Tau was alive. She could know nothing else for certain. But at least they were still alive.

Masako pulled her forward. The rigging blocked her view.

T HIS body is dying. Too young. Too soon. I love it. I don't want to let it go." Barhu couldn't find the voice. The hutch at the ship's bow was covered in pitch-blackened canvas. No light at all inside. There was only a sound like the wings of birds: but not that sound, exactly.

"Hello?" she called.

Two soft green lights appeared, like fingers pushed into her eyes. Hands. Then the Brain's curious dovelike face folded out of the dark. She was alight from brow to upper lip with the uranium fire.

"I call too much of it." Sorrowful voice, weak as a wheeze. "I bruise, I bleed, I don't heal. I sleep but I cannot find rest. My liver aches. I fight with the power I have, and I burn all the strength out of my blood, Baru."

She lifted her hands from her sleeves. The green light revealed the body beneath the ancient armor. Her cheeks were hollow. The hatch in her skull was taut and visible. Her body had been scraped by thirst and hunger: oh, the loose skin hanging from her wrists . . .

Only the armor seemed to hold her together: dry sticks bundled in a bronze case. But her eyes were alert and intelligent, and the lines that signed her face were clear and wise. She beckoned.

"Brain? I brought you water. . . ."

"No. Not for me. Not until my people can have it, too."

Wings fluttered at the edge of her ghost light. Shadows moved through cage bars, across dark dangling shapes, like rats hung by their feet from gallows.

"They're asleep," the Brain said, softly. "Come closer. I don't want to wake them. They hear so well."

"Bats," Barhu realized. "Why are you tending bats? They must use water. . . ."

"I feed them rotten fruit, when we still have it. Now we take turns offering them blood. Though they don't like mine anymore." She stroked her bare scalp. Her hand trembled. Anger passed across her gentle face, chased by a deep sadness. "Maybe if I don't fight the boy so hard . . . if I don't fight the Eye and the Womb . . . maybe if I don't do those things, I live. But I fight the boy. I fight the Eye and the Womb. Sorcery has its price. So I die. It is very soon, and I'm afraid."

"But you *won't* die, will you? They'll take a cutting of Incrisiath, and pass it on. . . ."

"Of course I die. I'm not the kind of immortal who never dies, Baru. Just the kind who lives forever."

Barhu summoned all her will to push forward. "And you won't even do that much if you die here, with no one to take your line. Which you will, Brain, if you won't negotiate. If you keep provoking us with demonstrations like that barrage."

The Brain knelt in the dark. When she rose again a gray shape clung to her forearm, nuzzling at her skin. Her ghost light shone through the bat's fine fur.

"Life," she murmured. "That's all we are, Baru. The dread Cancrioth. Just life that goes on living. The Womb will do anything to keep her children alive. The Eye will do anything to keep us safely out of sight. They are each good and necessary organs.

"But life needs to do more than just live, doesn't it? Sometimes we have to risk ourselves . . . risk death. For our families. For our people. For an ideal. That's what a brain is, isn't it? An organ that guides the body against its own instincts. Why do we need a brain, Baru, if the skin and the stomach are enough? A worm has no brain. A worm can still touch what it loves, eat what it tastes, flee from its fears. We need a brain to deny ourselves what we want. Sometimes we must choose hate over love. Sometimes we must choose death over life."

She looked up from the bat in her arms. "Last time, you ran. Are you ready to overcome that fear? Are you ready to choose death?"

Gray bat-winged absence beat at the edge of Barhu's sight. She swallowed bile. This must be how Iraji felt, in the moments before he fainted.

"The baneflesh," she said. "You still want me to take the baneflesh."

The Brain cupped the bat's small head. Tiny teeth glinted as it yawned. "In exchange for the flesh that carries the Kettling. Yours to bring to Falcrest."

Barhu gasped. "It lives in *bats*?"

"Certain vampiric bats, from certain green holes in the floor of the Mzilimake jungle. The only place in the world it can be found. The Mbo know it's there. They call it the bushmeat defense. Volunteers eat the meat of these bats, and go to the enemy's heartland, to bleed out into their water and their crops."

"And you let these things drink your *blood*?"

The Brain grinned, a naturalist's delight: "Ironically, the worst the bite can do is give you rabies. They drink of us, and when the time is right, we eat of them. It's a sacrament. Do you realize what I give you, Baru?"

She nodded, afraid to speak: she was horrified by how much the Brain had entrusted to her. The Brain had given her the reservoir, the place the disease lived when it was not exploding into pandemic. If you wanted to find a treatment or an inoculation, it was where you'd begin.

"I thought about trying to gather it from Kyprananoke," Barhu admitted. "Finding someone infected, a sample of the blood . . . but how could I keep it alive to study, or to use?"

"And now there is no Kyprananoke."

"I tried to help them. I had nothing to do with their extermination."

"I do. I cause it, ultimately." The Brain shuddered. "I make my choice, child. I am born messiah to one people, and only one. They are mine to protect, not any other. If I stop to doubt my choices, I have a thousand years of regrets waiting for me like a labyrinth. There are entire histories that happen if I whisper the right words in the right ears. And some of them, I'm sure, are better than ours. I have no time for those regrets.

"I am making the choice, now, weeks and weeks ago. It *is* right to give the Kyprananoki a weapon. But I also want to show Falcrest what we can do if they press us. I know it will bring retaliation, but the sheer scale of it astounds me. A whole people wiped away in a day. Not even the Paramountcies were so swift. . . .

"You see the evil they do." She raised her burning face to Barhu. "Are you ready to consecrate yourself to their destruction?"

"Must I?" Barhu whispered. "Can't you trust me without . . . cancer?"

"Oh, child," the Brain sighed. "I wish I could. Nothing can be trusted in Falcrest. You could be seduced. You could be bound to them in ways you do not even know. When we first meet, we speak of the brain, and of the thoughts that veil the true world around us. The baneflesh is part of that *true* world. It has no thoughts. With it in your body, with its soul in your soul . . . you are beyond corruption. You are as full of devastation as I am full of the souls of the line of Incrisiath."

And the strange thing was that she was right. The baneflesh *had* revealed the secret chains upon her. Barhu had fled the choice, fled *Eternal* entirely, into Tain Shir's waiting maw. And only then had she realized how Cairdine Farrier dominated her life.

If she had taken the baneflesh and the Kettling on that night, she might have made it to Falcrest. She might have unleashed the pandemic. It might even have been enough to shatter the Imperial Republic. But it would not be the future Tain Hu had wanted for her.

Light gathered in the lines of the Brain's face. Like it was flowing over her, slow as wax. It made green wells out of her pupils, and a shining ring out of the torc around her shrunken neck. "I bind you to this purpose, Baru. On the deck of *Eternal,* as you fall into the caldera. I call you back here to complete our pact. You and I are akin. Born to one purpose, messiah and mask-bearer: salvation for our people. So doom yourself, as I am doomed. Take Alu Skin-eater into your body, and the Black Emmenia into your custody, and in our death, we will lead Falcrest to its end."

Barhu took a deep breath. It smelled of hot fur and droppings.

"Actually," she said, "I have a different proposal."

S HE laid it all out, with a written prospectus, with notes and a small map, with pawns to shuffle about in the light of the Brain's trembling hands.

"The controlling entity will be invested in Falcrest. I will put in place a board of governors and a proper Falcresti man as face of the organization. It will be a joint-stock concern of the unlimited liability mode—this means that shareholders are responsible for paying the company's debts, if the company itself fails. This will be done partly because people think unlimited companies are more powerful, but primarily to assure lenders that they will recover their loans even in the event of a collapse.

"The Emperor of Falcrest will grant us a special total monopoly to pursue trade with the western Oriati coast and the Black Tea Ocean beyond—your homeland. Mister Cairdine Farrier, my patron, will be coerced into using his considerable financial and nautical resources to give the concern some starting capital. Falcrest's navy will be induced by political means to supply ships and security. Tau-indi Bosoka, Kindalana of Segu, and Abdumasi Abd will provide the diplomatic and mercantile influence required to arrange passage through the Segu archipelago. You will provide rutterbooks and pilots to lead Concern shipping to viable ports.

"As a subsidiary, a second, limited-liability concern will be invested in Aurdwynn. This Vultjag Trading Concern will handle movement of cargos north and south along the river Inirein, particularly trade with the Stakhieczi Necessity.

"I'll call your attention to the numbers here, at the top of the prospectus. This is my estimate of the annual raw revenue generated by the concern, not accounting for loans, our own investments, leveraged futures, and other financial instruments. I assure you it's quite accurate.

"This adjacent number is my estimate—a conservative one, I might add—

of the percentage of total world trade, by value, which would fall under this concern's monopoly. I know that thirty-five percent is a very large number. Again, I assure you it is realistic.

"And here is the percentage of Falcrest's total economy which I believe we could ultimately entangle in the well-being of our concern. I expect we will pass the fifty percent mark within ten years.

"Once we have made our initial stock offering, I anticipate a frenzy of speculative trading: This speculation will be driven by the basic soundness of the concern's position—we have a monopoly on a highly profitable trade, after all. I will drive speculation by issuing credit to investors, allowing them to buy stock through an installment plan. Details if you want them.

"This is where we begin to get tricky. Financial power means we'll have considerable access to the Twelve Ministries and Six Powers. We'll be able to buy our way into Parliament and raise our own merchant navy. But my ultimate goal is complete capture of Falcrest's wealth, and to do that, we need to access the personal fortunes of the Suettaring elite.

"To secure that access, I plan to make my trading concern into a tax haven. The wealthy will not want to pay a share of their hard-won fortunes to Parliament. I will offer them a simple way to avoid it. Moving the money into my concern, and from there into Oriati Mbo, will place it beyond taxable reach. It can be invested in various assets there, and they can recover it whenever they want thanks to the, ah, fluidity of the Oriati hawala trust-banking system.

"It won't escape your notice that moving this money *into* Oriati Mbo places it in range of your use. We can skim, launder, and misplace funds to meet whatever requirements you have. You will be able to buy all the metals, materials, and supplies required for an effective war. In effect, the total wealth of Falcrest will become your personal lending bank.

"And when the time is right, when I send the signal, you will strike. Not at Falcrest—a land invasion across the Occupation would be disastrous, a crossing of the Tide Column suicidal—but at the trade.

"There will be no Oriati civil war. No second Armada War. No Kettling. No democide and disaster. Let me make a bubble. Let me fill it with all Falcrest's strength. And then help me burst it."

THE Brain's trembling hands clasped together. Darkness fell, except in the pool of uranium fire around her face.

"You want to be a tyrant," she said.

"I prefer the term tycoon," Barhu suggested.

"No. You will be a tyrant. You will be a creator and protector of tyranny. Do you understand what Falcrest does to us, if they have the access given by trade? Trim is outlawed. Family land is bought up and turned to cash crops. Children are worked in the fields. Men are killed and their killings blamed on their own conduct. Women are stripped of their children and brought into prostitution. Their sons are soldiers. Their daughters are sent as maids to the houses of the rich. You are asking me to open our doors to a pack of rabid dogs."

"Trade is a spear *you* can wield, too! Trade is a vital part of Oriati history! Don't you remember White Akhena and the Mzicane, the time of unrest? How did she hold the Ivory Stool once she had seized it? Control of the riverine trade in Mzilimake! Control of the exchange of coastal ivory for inland minerals!"

"White Akhena has a will. White Akhena *chooses* to conquer. Her new methods of war send the conquered fleeing into new lands and they become conquerors in turn. She devises these methods. One woman with a will, and the people who choose to follow her. I am there, and I watch her change the world. And if she isn't terrified of creating an heir who will supplant her, she creates a dynasty. But she is."

King's balls. Barhu was arguing history with an immortal.

"You can't think Akhena could have succeeded in her conquests if she had nothing to gain *by* conquest!" Her voice climbed to that old plaintive cry: why doesn't the universe know I'm right? "Why is Lonjaro the greatest power in the Mbo? Because it controlled the Tide Column and the gold-for-salt trade with Mzilimake! Why did the Armada War strangle the whole Mbo, if not for loss of the Tide Column, the end of sea commerce between Devi-naga and the western nations? The material conditions of trade dictate the movement of power!"

"In the ideology Falcrest has taught you."

"In *objective reality*!"

"I've lived long enough to hear all sorts of ideas called 'reality.'" The Brain sighed. "Baru, I fear Falcrest's subtlety, and their ways of perverting your intent. We lose everything by opening ourselves to their trade. You see it happen to Taranoke. Why would it be any different now?"

"Because this time I'll be in control. We'll turn Falcrest's strength back on them!"

"You are the one in control. One woman. And if you die of appendicitis? If you trip and fall and lose your memory?"

"I won't," Barhu sputtered. "Listen, the best way to break a mill is to jam up the machinery!"

"The best way to break a mill is to burn it down, Baru."

"Not if you want to keep building mills and making flour! The reason Falcrest is winning is because its ways are *stronger*! I can steal that strength!"

"But it is still Falcrest's strength. It is still that monstrous pillaging force which treats people like coin and coin like people. And if you try to wield it you are seduced by it. Take Alu into your body instead. Consecrate yourself into my trust."

"Damn you," Barhu hissed. "I can do so much *more* than carry a plague and die young. Don't you see? The concern that rules this new trade could be mightier than *the Republic itself*! And I will own it all! I can force Falcrest to give justice to those it's conquered!"

"Nothing you own by Falcrest's means is owned by anything but Falcrest. When you think you possess them, that is when they possess you."

"You sound like a woman I know," Barhu said, thinking of Tain Shir.

"Yes, I do, don't I?"

"Money." Barhu tried to press the desperation from her tone. "A trade route so fertile it'll make the old Lonjaro gold markets look like a tin scrap exchange. You've seen nothing like it in a thousand years. You never had the ships. You never had the chemistry to keep the crews alive. You never had the power to dredge the harbors or to secure the trade circle for your use. I can do these things for you. I can put you on the same financial footing as an empire. Let me make this wonder for you."

"Why do I want a bank? I come unto the peoples of Oria to fulfill our promise. The prophecy that we would return when they needed us most. Does prophecy need wages?"

"I told my secretary once"—poor Muire Lo, who she'd abandoned—"that any rebellion not built on pure faith or rabid hate needs money. Maybe you can operate on pure faith. Maybe your followers can operate on rabid hate. But what about the people whose loyalty you need to earn? The Princes of the Mbo, the artisans who make your weapons, the merchants who keep your armies fed—you know all this, damn you! You *know* the world won't just answer to your will!"

"But it shall," the Brain said, with a smile that put Barhu's soul to ice. "The world *does* answer to my will, Baru. You know it soon. You see me at the head of mighty armies, and emblazoned upon ships, and clasped at the throats of the fearless dead. I am many places at once and I do not need one single coin or gem to do it. There are things more powerful than money in this world. I am born to the signs of whirlwind and geyser, black moon and cicada scream. I do not pay to become messiah. The world makes me so."

"You fool, have you *ever* known a great leader that didn't have wealth behind her? What are you going to do? March hordes of your starving believers across the Mbo to Falcrest? How will you cross the Tide Column with no boats? How will you cross the Butterveldt without supply trains? Falcrest will burn down every field and forest in your path and watch the vultures finish you. Didn't you tell me that Falcrest scared you? Didn't you fear their ability to capture the future? I am giving you a piece of that future! Here! A chance to place *me*, a woman who despises Falcrest, in command of the greatest trade Falcrest has ever seen. And all I want from you is a map, an agreement, and a chance for both of us to leave this place alive!"

The Brain listened quietly. When Barhu was finished, she asked a question.

"Can you name one difference between your plan and Falcrest's total victory, except that in your plan you are in charge?"

"Of course I can!" Barhu sputtered. "My plan uses trade to benefit everyone, not just Falcrest!"

"Isn't that precisely what Falcrest says when it comes to trade? Isn't that what they say when they come to *your* island?"

"If we are going to deceive Falcrest, then of course our plan needs to seem like it benefits Falcrest until the crucial moment."

"And if you are not there for the crucial moment? My plan doesn't require a mastermind, Baru. I believe in the Oriati people. All I do is to give them a symbol, and a choice. Something to remember when Falcrest comes slithering out of the grass with promises of ease. Something that says: do as I did. Choose death over surrender. Save your souls from bondage."

"Choose *death*? Is that what you want? You won't outlive this voyage, so no one can?"

Her ghostly face showed Barhu pain, exhaustion, rapture. "I outlive this voyage as long as I am remembered. Even if the line of Incrisiath goes extinct, the world knows I stood against Falcrest."

"No one will remember your ship disappearing on some faraway island! *My* plan lets your people live! Not just the people on this ship but *everyone* who would die in war, and in outbreak, and in retaliation! If you love your people, then save them!"

"I will not save my people to live in slavery."

"I'm not offering slavery! I'm offering an end to Falcrest's power! I'm offering to butcher their empire, and to do it *right*!"

The Brain was silent. Her left hand caressed the lines of her trepanation hatch. She stood like that, in thought, while Barhu panted like a dog.

Then the Brain turned to the darkness.

"Well?" she called. "Do you believe she's telling the truth? She truly opposes Falcrest?"

And Aminata's voice came back, hollow with grief:

"Yes. I do. She does."

THE END OF ASH

FEDERATION YEAR 912:
23 YEARS EARLIER
IN KUTULBHA HARBOR, BESIDE RUINED KUTULBHA
IN SEGU MBO

THAT night, as the party on *Kangaroo Principle* smoldered on into the sordid after-dark hours, as the ash sky roiled over the ship full of Oriati Princes and the Falcrest guests who had received their surrender, Tau did what they thought Kindalana would want them to do.

What Kindalana would *actually* have wanted them to do was to put serious critical thought into the way the Princes managed their grief by holding a party to "repair the cheer of their generation" on a luxury palace-ship, while the common people ashore picked through wet ash for the bones of their children.

What Tau-indi did, instead, was offer their hand to Cosgrad Torrinde in marriage.

"Oh, child." Cosgrad put a hand out between them, to secure the space, and his other hand covered his mouth, his laugh or frown or absolute disgust. "I can't marry you!"

Tau-indi had not very much expected to be laughed at. They had just rescued Cosgrad from a shouting match about the merits of maggot treatment, where his accent and his ignorance of nagana made him sound like a fool, and lured him off into a guest cabin with whiskey and the promise of nasty gossip about Cairdine Farrier.

"It's not a love match," Tau-indi said, sitting in the stuffed chair, arms crossed, legs crossed, very practical, very adult. "I'm not a child, Cosgrad. And it's a war tradition from centuries ago, actually, when the Maia took spouses from our royalty. Those spouses became ambassadors."

"You're very good at helping me understand," Cosgrad said. His face was, actually, closest to panic—an expression of *oh no, why me, why now!* "But I can't. It's impossible."

"If you're unattracted to me, that's all right. You can have anyone you want. I don't mind." Cosgrad was actually very beautiful, in spite or because of his strange severe build and his flat face. But he was older, and a guest, and Tau-indi had seen him very sick, and all that made the thought of sex weirdly impractical: like an itch they didn't have. "The important thing is the diplomatic connection we'd represent."

"But we'd have to get married here! Right away! With—with Farrier as a witness, or someone else from Falcrest, to sign the papers. And you'd have to leave your family!"

"Why?"

"Because I'm leaving for Falcrest *now*!"

"I didn't know that," Tau-indi said, stung. "You never told me."

"I'm going back with the fleet." Cosgrad fussed guiltily over his shirt. "I have to get to Falcrest as soon as I can. There's someone waiting for a report on my success. . . ."

"The woman who sent you here."

"Yes. Yes. And I have to reach her before Farrier. I have to convince her that Oriati Mbo has vital things to teach us in its unaltered, pre-Incrastic state."

"What things?" Tau asked, warily. "Things about jellyfish? The wet origins of life? Those kinds of things?"

"Things about the body. About the way a thousand years of peace have changed you."

"Then I'll go with you to Falcrest, and help you with your work. Mother Tahr can come, too." Tau-indi took Cosgrad's wrists. "Please, Cosgrad, if we're going to stop this, we have to learn about each other."

Cosgrad's eyes narrowed. He was furious: not at Tau-indi, but it still burned them. "Tau-indi. Your Highness. Please." His hands wrapped around their own, hard and fine, certain of their strength. "I love your home. I love this place. It taught me so much. But do you understand that some of your world is just a useful lie? A construct, invented by your ancestors to stabilize society? Even you, Tau-indi . . . even lamen."

Cosgrad! The man was like lye, he helped you and then he slipped away when you pressed him. "Trim is real. I'm *real*."

"Trim is an ideology of compassion. It's wonderful. I want to spend a lifetime learning it, finding all the ways it's altered your bodies. But there are people coming for you who care nothing for your comfort or your peace, understand?" Cosgrad squeezed as he spoke, surely not meaning to, but it hurt, it bent Tau's hands. "They want to make you *want* to be slaves. Trim will not save you. Trim might lead you right into them."

"Cosgrad, take me to Falcrest with you, and I'll learn how they think."

"If I had an Oriati bride in Falcrest, and you would *have* to be a bride," Cosgrad said, and his voice trembled on the words, "the Judiciary would take me in for reconditioning. You don't understand what it's like. I can't even think about these things. The thoughts will go into me! This is unhygienic!"

And he spoke over whatever Tau-indi tried to say. "Oh, Tau-indi, I wish you could see. Your ancestors *were* a little like Farrier, in a way. Farrier believes he can fix the world by teaching everyone the right lies. But that's not the way! That's not a good true world! A good world is true like a sparrow wing, like a termite mound, like the little cells in a beehive. Its form is its function. It never has to lie. It is the way it is because to be otherwise would be less useful. Less good. *That* is the measure of a good thing.

"I won't let Farrier win, you understand? I won't let him sway Parliament and the Throne. I'm going home to Falcrest to save Oriati Mbo and the whole world from his corruption."

Take me with you, Tau-indi could say. I want to help.

But Cosgrad didn't *want* Tau-indi's help. Possibly Cosgrad did not even believe Tau could help at all.

Possibly Cosgrad did not even believe Tau-indi was a healthy, properly formed person.

"You're drunk," Tau-indi said, so that they would both have an excuse to forget this conversation. "I understand. We'll talk later."

Someone spoke. Tau-indi didn't understand the words, but they recognized the voice. Cosgrad looked up, eyes wild, queue whipping behind his head. Cairdine Farrier stood there in a red waistcoat, shorter than Cosgrad, softer, his eyes deep pits shadowed behind a slim white mask.

Cosgrad said something short and sharp in Aphalone.

Farrier spoke in reply. He pointed at Tau-indi and his voice rose in question and then fell in threat. In his right hand was a notebook, half-open.

Cosgrad, snarling, pushed past Farrier and stalked away.

Farrier looked at Tau-indi and smiled wearily. "Sorry," he said. "Remember. That man is insane, and an enemy to every kind of peace, except the stupor of the well-kept herd."

"Cosgrad's my friend," Tau-indi said.

"Cosgrad is no one's friend. He doesn't see people. He doesn't believe in civilization, or charity, or progress by education and enlightenment. He only believes in meat. If he gets his way, every marriage in the Mbo would be decided by an equation." Farrier knelt, so that he was a little shorter than

Tau. "Be wary of him. He is the worst of us. The worst thing Falcrest ever made."

Tau-indi answered the masked man as a prince should answer a foe. "He helped us make this peace. He is bound to us and us to him."

The mask tilted, and Tau-indi recognized the expression in the eyes behind it. Avarice. Curiosity, yes, but also deep, deep avarice. "Cosgrad Torrinde came to live among you," the mask said, "so he could dig out your ancient sins, and find in them the key to his own immortality. Do you know what he saw when that sorcerer came burning to your door? When she walked toward him afire, without pain? He saw a power he must possess."

"And what did *you* come here to do?" Tau said, bitterly. "To help your people burn cities?"

Farrier's eyes were as dark as secrets. "We ended the war here, in one blow, when it could have dragged on for decades. You've seen how we can hurt you, Tau. Now I have to show you how we can help. I have to convince you that, together, there's hope. It's the only way. Or in a century there will be nothing living around this Ashen Sea worthy of the name *human*."

"What would a man from a young place like Falcrest think to teach us about what will happen in a century?"

His eyes lit with delight. This was a question he loved. "How could the whole Oriati Mbo spend a thousand years in peace and contentment, surrounded by riches, and achieve so little? You have no eugenics. You have no hygiene. You have not eradicated disease or poverty. You are trapped. You have gone up the wrong road and you cannot turn around. All I offer is a chance to be better." Farrier slammed a palm on the deck and the crack of noise echoed in the little guest cabin. The silks ruffled. "Everyone dies, little Prince. Everyone. But if we die to make tomorrow better, it's worth it! That's what I say to the ruins of Kutulbha. That's what I say to Abdu's dead mother. That's what I tell myself, when my guilt runs up my throat and fills my nose."

"Cosgrad says that you're a liar. You want the whole world to run on lies. Why would I want your schools? Your progress?"

"Because in a school you can change your own thoughts according to what you learn. Cosgrad would fix you in your place before you are even born. Like a farmer separating the beef cows from the milk." Farrier stood, and sighed, and smiled again. "This war was just a greeting. A way to open ourselves to each other. The things that happen after a war, the repositionings and reconstructions, are so often ignored by history. But they are more important.

"Now. Would you like to come up to the high deck with me? I can introduce you to my colleagues."

* * *

LATER that night, under the silk pavilions of the palace-ship's air deck, Tau-indi saw Cairdine Farrier in his fine jacket and sleek trousers, demonstrating tricks of dance to admirers. Kindalana was his partner, painted and chained, and she whispered things into his ear, or put her arm around him with casual confidence between sets.

Farrier looked off his keel, uncertain how to react. When Kindalana drew away to make a pass by a group of Prince's attendants from Segu, shy young men who'd been eyeing her invitingly, Farrier excused himself and went to find a drink.

"What are you doing?" Tau-indi muttered.

"Unsettling him," Kindalana murmured. "The whole time he lived with me, he was scrupulously modest. This is a chance to touch him, to make him look a little foolish, to diminish him and make him want my approval as repair." She leaned up on the rail, arms outflung, and eyed Farrier with amusement. "Look at him. He's so confused."

Farrier spent a while mixing his drink and reading the labels off a Falcrest bottle. His motions were swift and confident, and he made jokes to passers-by. He was acting nonchalant, and acting hard. When he was alone he scratched at his beard.

"Spent his whole youth traveling the world, plundering everywhere he went," Kindalana murmured, "and yet he's still a Falcrest man. Someone taught him that the male of the species is always brightly plumed and forthright, and the female's dowdy, studious, and cold. He has no idea what to do with me."

"I . . ." Tau-indi grappled with their feelings. "I'm not sure this is right. I mean, you're both very powerful people, but . . . on the day we signed a treaty of surrender, it seems unfavorable. And he's older than you . . . three years or more, depending on whether he gave us his true age. . . ."

Kindalana squeezed their arm. "Have you read their laws on women? The etiquettes of sanitary courtship?"

"No," Tau admitted. "Are they very strange?"

"Among other errors, they insist that women are predisposed to use sexual unavailability as a technique of manipulation. He doesn't understand why I make my own pursuit. He can't read me."

"But you *are* manipulating him, aren't you? You're trying to lure him into some kind of mistake." Tau-indi felt prudishly hung up on Lonjaro mores, the kind of mores that had kept their mother and Padrigan off each other for years and years. "It just seems to me that if he's expecting barbaric, lustful women, you'll only be confirming his thoughts. . . ."

She shrugged, untroubled. "So I confirm his thoughts. It doesn't make them true."

"Does this actually *work*?" The idea of taking this friendly, warm, intimate thing and making it a tool . . .

"I don't really know. But I'm willing to try." Now Farrier was headed back toward his admirers, carrying drinks. Kindalana gave Tau a dashing white grin. "Wish me luck, then!"

"Luck," Tau said, meaning that, although not sure what form they wanted the luck to take.

T AU would not learn what had happened that night until much later. Not between Kindalana and Farrier (though it was nothing). And not what happened far away on Prince Hill, in the cool undercroft of the House of Abd, where someone lived who should have died.

The sorcerer woman had been burnt everywhere, her fingers ruined, her lungs scorched. Her eyes like cooked yolk in a mask of scar. She was dying of infection even as she wept brown fluids from the blistered carnage of her skin. Abdumasi brought her water, but nothing for the pain. She gave no sign of feeling it. That was why Abdumasi wanted to keep her alive. The thought of being impervious to pain . . .

She could not speak, or grip a coal to write. But she could focus on Abdu when he visited, and respond to his questions with blinks. She could even smile, though she had no lips.

At first Abdu told himself that he came to see her to get away from the empty tooth-socket feeling of Prince Hill without Tau and Kindalana or his mother.

But on that day, the day of the surrender, when his grief and his rage seemed to have infested him and made a home out of his soul, he came down to the sorcerer with water and honey wash and a question on his lips.

"How do you bear it?" he said, in a frightened whisper. "How can you bear hurting so much?"

She smiled at him and shrugged. Something crisp brushed against something wet.

"Can we stop Falcrest? Next time they come?"

She nodded, once.

"How?"

The sorcerer curled a finger up toward her own face, and, with her other hand, made the suggestion of a fist. Abdumasi understood:

Us. My people. We will be ready.

"You're the only thing I ever saw them fear," he whispered.

She opened her hand to him. There was something on her skin, a dark unfading glow, that shone over the light of his own candle like soap on water.

She beckoned him closer.

WHEN Kindalana returned to Prince Hill from her time in Segu Mbo and her state visit to Falcrest, she and Abdumasi were promptly married. It had been more than a year and a half since she departed. He did not tell her about the woman who had lived for a while in his undercroft. She did not tell him about the girl who had lived for a while in her.

31

A STORY ABOUT ASH

A ND what did Aminata do then?" Tau asked, leaning forward eagerly. "When the Brain asked her if you were telling the truth?"

"What do you expect?" Barhu hauled the rowboat over evening chop. "I had no idea she was listening. I tried to tell her that I'd never hurt her. She told me that she knew I was lying, because I'd killed Tain Hu, and I must've cared about Tain Hu more than I cared about her."

"It'll be all right," Tau assured her. "You'll be friends again."

"There's no *possible* way you can know that."

"She wants to fight the whole world at your side, Baru. And she knows you need her. Once she's realized Falcrest doesn't need her, where else will she belong?"

The Prince was, as ever, landing spears in tender places. Barhu had found Tau and Osa waiting for her on the weather deck when she came back to her boat. The fallen Prince had looked her in the eye.

And they'd smiled.

Of all the things she thought she'd never have again, from Tain Hu's whispered *kuye lam* to the sound of Muire Lo laying out her morning coffee, Tau-indi's trust was not the most unlikely. But it was out there. It was *far* out there.

"Did they drug you?" Barhu had demanded.

"I did that myself. A treatment for my despair. The Womb has released me to go ashore." Tau curtsied so their cassock petaled on the deck. "It has come to my attention that the first summit between the rulers of Falcrest and the sorcerers of the ancient Cancrioth has no representative from Oriati Mbo. As I am no longer a participant in trim, and thus no longer suited to speak for my people in negotiations, a substitute must be found."

"A substitute *what*?"

"A substitute me, of course. An ambassador of the interests of Oriati Mbo."

"You don't mean—"

"I certainly do mean you! When the Womb severed me from trim, the loose connections affixed themselves to your soul. You have taken my place in the web of human destiny, Baru. You must heal the old wound between Abdumasi

Abd, Kindalana, and myself: and so save the Oriati Mbo and the world from war."

Tau's opinion of her had changed so thoroughly, without any action at all on her part, that she found it almost offensive. How dizzying, how disorienting, that Tau would have such total and autonomous power over themself. But that was the lesson that the laman had always tried to teach her, wasn't it? Other people were real. They did not need one Barhu Cormorant to push them to their ends.

She had asked: "Why would you possibly trust me? After the way things ended on Kyprananoke?"

"I am certain you didn't have anything to do with the way things ended on Kyprananoke. I am certain you are fighting even now to stop it from happening ever again. Am I wrong?"

"You're right," she had admitted, and her throat had swelled up, and left her unable to speak. Tau, who had called her a wound, a hole in the heart, did *not* think she had consumed Kyprananoke. Did *not* assume she'd given the order.

It was trust and faith beyond anything she deserved. It was grace.

Now, on the choppy bay, Osa shifted in the bow of the boat. "Someone's coming out to meet us."

"Probably my parents," Barhu grumbled. "Come to scream at me for going out to *Eternal* alone."

"Your parents are here?" Tau looked insufferably smug. "I suppose you think that's a perfectly reasonable coincidence, and not evidence of a powerful human force drawing you back together, to reconcile your hurts."

Barhu almost made the evidential counterargument—Cauteria was a perfect place to hide if you were fleeing Taranoke, and her parents had more cause than most to flee, so it was logical they'd be waiting for her here, and not at all the result of trim.

But she liked Tau's smug smile.

HER parents clearly wanted to call her a fool for going out to *Eternal* alone, and dress her in guilt for the worry she'd caused them; but thankfully they assumed it would be improper to do so in front of the Federal Prince. They led Barhu's boat in, through the mess of drifting flotsam from the shattered barges, to a boathouse hastily cleared of its stores. The Eye waited there, guarded by the woman with scarified cheeks, both holding bright Falcrest-made lanterns with fascination and discomfort.

"Your Highness! Thank Alu you're all right." The Eye kissed them on the cheek. Tau did not show the slightest discomfort at his eyestalk brushing the side of their head. "I'm so glad you're ashore. I've not wanted to go see Abdumasi without you."

"Abdumasi's here?" Tau seized the Eye's hands, and shot one look of heart-breaking gratitude at Barhu. "We'll go at once!"

"He's waiting at the town meetinghouse, with Kimbune. I've been negotiating with this judge woman, Yawa. She's conceded to a meeting."

"Yawa, hm?" Tau looked back at Barhu with feline smugness. They might have even shimmied their hips at her, like they were dancing on her head. "Side by side with Baru. The two rivals now in alliance. What a twist of fate."

Marines insisted on prodding Tau and Osa with clinical thermometers to check for fever. Osa's face had been badly burnt, but there was no sign of infection. "All clear," the marine sergeant said, with some disappointment.

The Eye led the little procession across the green to the town meeting hall. "Tau," Barhu muttered, "I've got to talk to you about something, when you've a moment—"

"Is it the conversation we had about why Abdumasi hates Farrier? My realization that I blamed Kindalana? Ah, I see it is. Don't look so affronted, Baru."

"How did you *know*?"

"Obviously you are interested in Farrier's past. I hinted that I knew him when he was young. It makes sense you'd want to pursue it—"

"Tau? Your Federal Highness?"

But Tau stared at the doorway into the meeting hall. Abdumasi Abd stood in the light, the two great wooden doors held open by his arms. "Tau? Is it really you?"

"Hi, Abdu." Tau waved, fingers curled.

Abdumasi fell to his knees and began to sob. "Tau! Tau, manata, I'm sorry, I'm so sorry, *I'm so sorry*—"

"It's all right." Tau went fearlessly to their friend. "Abdu, it's okay. I'm here now. It's going to be okay."

The two huge doors nearly swung shut on Abd. Kimbune, darting past the two embracing friends, caught them and held them back.

Barhu almost cried out in joy. She'd done it. She'd made a terrible mess of it first. But she had at last brought two people together across the wound Falcrest had torn between them. She'd done a good thing. She did not expect reward. That would be poor trim. But she certainly would not refuse it.

"Look at him," the Eye breathed. "Abdumasi Abd. He's all right."

"Are you asking about him," Barhu murmured, "or the thing in his back?"

"There is no difference anymore. All of him is important to us. If we can only bring him home, if Falcrest hasn't learned too much from him, there may be a chance . . ."

"There is no chance you can return to secrecy," Barhu told him. "None at all. The Brain's right about that; the world will learn you exist. And Abd doesn't want to go home with you."

The Eye still wore his work shirt and skirt, gardener's clothes. As if he were still at his tub of growing things, trying to tend them through the drought. He did not seem to see any difference between that work and this one. Barhu admired him for it, in a way. He was not a politican or a manipulator. Just an old soul trying to do some good.

"I was afraid of that," he said, softly. "That he'd want to leave us."

"He has to go home to Kindalana. He and Tau. The three of them have to be together again. It's important."

"For Tau? Or for your schemes?"

"Both," Barhu admitted. "But for your future, too. The Cancrioth will never be a secret again. If you want to survive your discovery, if you want the Mbo to find a place for you, Tau and Abdumasi will help make it."

"Or he could be dragged before your Parliament and forced to name us as an enemy of your Empire. How can I let him go, knowing he could do that?"

"He won't be used to start a war. Not if he's good for business."

"He carries Undionash in his spine. So few of us remain who bear that Line. We gave it to him as a symbol of our trust, of how deeply we valued him. I never thought he would lead us to war." Sadness touched that deep musical voice. "If he leaves us, we could lose all those souls. . . ."

"What if you could keep Undionash, and let Abdumasi go?"

He looked at her, one eye wary, one bent off toward infinity. Always minding two things, the Eye.

"How?" he asked.

WHERE the fuck have you been?" Yawa snarled. "I saw Tau and the Eye with you, I saw you all go to Abd. Were you planning to tell me what you were up to?"

"I'm sorry, Yawa. I had to bring Tau and Abd back together. Then I got caught up speaking to the Eye—"

Yawa chopped her hand down like an axe. "Stop." She'd changed into a linen peasant's dress for the night; her guest house smelled of the olive oil taper she'd lit. "What happened on *Eternal*? What did you give the Brain to get Tau and Osa free?"

"I didn't give her anything. She tried to give *me* the Kettling. All I'd have to do is accept a brain-eating tumor. She thought it would keep me loyal, so I didn't turn the Kettling over to Falcrest for some fat reward."

Yawa's cold blue eyes assessed her. "Is that the bargain she offered you back on Kyprananoke?"

"Yes."

"The one you might've gone through with, if I hadn't sent Iraji to flush you out?"

"Yes."

"Despite the certainty that the Kettling would spread beyond Falcrest?"

Barhu nodded. "I was . . . single-minded."

Yawa slapped her. The seam of Yawa's glove caught at the old glass cut in Barhu's cheek and tore. "Don't you *dare*. Don't you dare keep something like this from me *ever* again. You're not going to die young. You're not going to trade your whole life for some appalling plague. You're going to live, understand? You're going to carry on my work when I'm gone. Fuck!" She spat on the floor. "Who the fuck else am I going to trust, you stupid cunt? Heingyl Ri? She'll never trust me after what happened today."

"And Tain Hu wouldn't want me to do it," Barhu said, quietly.

"Oh, listen to the savant, Tain Hu wouldn't want her to give herself cancer! She's so penetrating, she's so *bright*!"

Barhu began to laugh helplessly. Yawa sniffed and shook her head. If she smiled, it was so subtle that Barhu could only see it by suspicion.

"Wait a minute." Barhu frowned. "What happened today?"

Yawa fell back heavily into her chair. "A fast felucca came in with the news. Bel Latheman was murdered in his office in Annalila Fortress."

"Oh, *shit*," Barhu gasped. "Who did it? How?"

"One of old Heingyl's guards stabbed him. It wasn't you?"

"No! I'm not that stupid!"

"You had Nayauru and her lovers killed in their camp. I thought you might've decided to resort to the same . . . directness."

"No, damn it, she'll never marry me if she thinks I killed her husband!"

"She'll never marry the Necessary King, either." Yawa covered her eyes with her hands. "We're fucked. We sent Svir off to make a marriage arrangement that's fucked. Aurdwynn's fucked. It's all fucked."

She collapsed into her hammock. Barhu groaned and beat her fist against her forehead. "Who did it?"

Yawa gave her the note.

Imperial Acct Aurdwynn dead
Knifed by Governor Aurdwynn's armsman, also dead by suicide
Staff report loud argument overheard, two males, possibly also a
woman? Empty bottle of drug, m/b a nootrope, found in Acct's desk.
Dosage extreme if taken in one night.
M/b linked to recent attempted killing of Governor Aurdwynn?
News is out in Annalila, will reach Cautery Plat tomorrow
Maroyad

Bel Latheman had spent so many meals pretending to love her. Barhu was not sure if she ought to mourn him. He was one of those clean-haired, well-behaved cogs who did not do the Masquerade's evilest work but who made that work possible.

But he had also been a very good counterfeit, when she had needed one terribly.

Yawa was now performing angry penknife surgery on a whittled figurine. "She should've had *all* her father's men sacked. Sentimentality. Always her weakness. She thinks they'll be loyal to her because they knew her when she was a girl? Men kill their daughters every day."

"Oh, dear Wydd. I know exactly who did it." It must be the man that Heingyl Ri had sent back to Annalila. The one who'd reacted so strongly to the omen of the catamount and the stag. "It really was an accident. What an incredible fuckup. What terrible luck."

"Maybe she'll accept it wasn't our fault. She's Aurdwynni. She knows about death. She killed her own father, for Wydd's sake. I killed your secretary, and look at us now, we're perfectly civil. . . ."

She trailed off. "What is it?" Barhu asked, gently.

"I need it now."

"Need what?"

"You said you were going out to *Eternal* to find a weapon to use against Farrier. Farrier's secret, Hesychast's secret, *someone's* fucking secret! I need to know you have it, so I won't have to lobotomize you. I don't need to know what it is, just please, tell me you have it."

"Not yet," Barhu admitted. She didn't have a rutterbook to show Yawa, either; she'd wanted that as proof her trade concern could work. "But it's closer. I'll go speak to Tau. We may need to reach Kindalana before I can be certain it's usable."

"Kindalana? The Amity Prince? She's in Falcrest! I can't wait that long! I'm not making any progress getting the Eye to yield his fucking cancer, our whole plan for Aurdwynn is falling apart—I *can't* go to Hesychast empty-handed!"

"I know. Please trust me." Barhu looked her in the eye and willed her to remember their shouted conversation on the wharf. "I trust you to do what they expect of you. You must trust me to do my part. All I need is to return to Farrier with what I've gained here."

"How can you ask me to trust you?" Her hands were shaking too hard to keep the knife steady. "You tell me you have a plan. You *almost* make it make sense. But all I see is you delivering Farrier exactly what he wanted. Abdumasi in Falcrest, to reveal the Cancrioth and force Oriati civil war. Yet you tell me *trust me, trust me, I have it all in hand. . . .*"

"Yes." Barhu nodded: exactly so. "I need to be able to deliver Farrier exactly what he wants. I need to be close to him at the right moment. I trust you to help me do that."

"For shit's sake! *Tell me what you mean!*"

She couldn't. If she told Yawa too much Hesychast would know. "The only way to conceal a conspiracy from minds like theirs," she said, "is to be sure none of us, individually, know the entire plan. I trust you to do what is required of you. Trust me to do what is required of me. I have Farrier's secret in my grasp. It's so close. All I ask is that you put me in position to use it."

"I can't! I *can't* fail him! If Hesychast kills my brother, I'll— I won't be able—"

"I know," Barhu said, gently. "You can't let that happen. You'll have to lobotomize me."

"Oh, damn you!"

She began to sob. Barhu tried to go to her. She pointed emphatically to the door.

"Seeing you makes me wish I'd killed him," she snarled. "Seeing you makes me wish I were as cold as you."

S HE went back to Tau.

"Your Highness?" she called, past the scar-cheeked Cancrioth woman who guarded the guesthouse.

"Come in. I've been expecting you."

Inside, a hooded lantern spilled orange light across a lovely pine floor. Tau was giving Osa a massage. The big Jackal woman lay facedown, grumbling, with a pillow under her breasts and roped fists stretched above her head.

"As the beginning of an apology for my conduct," Tau explained. They dug into her back with their thumbs. Osa muttered pleasantly. "Baru, before you say anything, I want to thank you for bringing me safely to Abdu. If you hadn't saved me from *Cheetah*, I never would have found him."

"I thought you'd never forgive me."

Tau-indi looked up with a wonder so tender and so completely undeserved that Barhu almost grimaced and looked away. She would have found it easier (experience in Aurdwynn proved it) to stare at hairy scrota than this pure nakedness of the heart.

"Forgive you? I've said nothing about forgiveness." Their hands at work in Osa's muscle, finding the knots of fear and tension, pressing them flat. "I've lost almost all the meaning in my life, Baru. My dearest friends will shut me out of their houses, and my name will pass forever from their lips."

There was nothing to say that could begin to repair it.

"But you have allowed me to begin a task whose importance I could never have even acknowledged. A task more vital than anything I could have done as the Federal Prince. The Cancrioth cannot be unrevealed. Some of the Mbo will want them destroyed. Some will want to follow them against Falcrest.

"I do not know if there will be civil war. I know that religion causes civil wars more than almost anything, and that the reappearance of one's most ancient foe is far more than a doctrinal dispute. But I know for certain that if there is no one who can say *look, I passed among the Cancrioth and I am still human,* there will never be peace. It horrifies me to imagine what the Mbo could become if they decide that they are the only true humans in the world."

"You still believe Abdu's human," she said, wonderingly.

"We are both beyond trim, he and I. But we've found each other anyway. And look, look at this"—they squeezed Osa's shoulders; she groaned in delight—"I can still do good. With my hands, with my voice. I led the Eye to retake *Eternal.* And all the bonds of trim I left behind move you now. I knew it when Aminata told me you'd gone to confront Ormsment. I knew it when Aminata told me of all the strange places she'd found your name appearing to her, and my name, and Kindalana's. And most of all, I knew it when Aminata willingly sacrificed her own life to protect you. You and Aminata are bound, too, Baru. Powerfully so."

"I don't understand you," Barhu said, and her voice cracked with feeling, because it was such a marvel to have Tau smile at her again, and ten times that marvel to know that Tau obeyed a logic that Barhu would never begin to comprehend.

Would that there were tens of millions of Tau-indi Bosokas. Would that the whole world had their strength.

"Yes, well, you don't understand me because I'm older and better than you," Tau said, without any malice. "Did you come here to ask your question again?"

"Yes."

"It's about Kindalana, isn't it."

"Yes," she said, laughing a little. "It's about Kindalana. I remember that you said, 'Cairdine fucking Farrier of all people, no wonder Abdu went bad, why didn't she know?' And I thought you might know a secret about Farrier, something which could help me fight him. . . ."

"Of course I do," Tau said, smiling.

"Will you tell me?"

"No. Never."

Barhu wanted to scream in frustration. "Why?"

"Because I swore an oath to protect that secret. Because I would betray everything I care for if I let you treat that secret as an instrument, rather than as . . ."

Their voice trailed off. They looked sheepish.

"A person. I knew it. The secret's a person!"

"I would like to tell you a story," Tau said, without reacting at all to her declaration. They lifted their hands for a moment, so Osa could adjust her weight, and then went back to massaging her, pressing brown spots into her black skin. "Would you sit here with me and listen as I tell it? It might take all the rest of the night."

"I would love that," Barhu admitted. "But I have work. . . . I should run the Great Game out, see if all my ideas for this trade concern will work. . . ."

"The Great Game is nonsense. Cosgrad showed it to me once. It's a toy boat pretending to be a clipper; it has no conception of the complexity of the real Mbo, or of the influence of the smallest choice upon the whole. Will you stay or won't you?"

"Yes," Barhu said. "I will."

"Good. I am going to tell this story in the third person, calling myself Tauindi, so that you understand the Tau I speak of is a person I can no longer be. That Tau was bound by trim. I am not. Do you understand?"

Barhu nodded, and wanted, again, to say she was sorry. Did not.

"This Tau will seem naïve to you. I ask that you remember how I was raised: on a hilltop, in a rich house, with books and trim to study. I barely knew the world. If I seem to confirm the worst Falcresti notions of Oriati royalty, I ask that you forgive my past."

"I promise not to judge."

"Do not promise that. Only judge mercifully." Tau cleared their throat and began to work down Osa's spine. "It begins like this: Tau-indi Bosoka came into this world alone. Now, you might protest, who is *not* born alone? Stop a moment and think, O listener! Do you have the answer?"

"Twins?" Barhu suggested.

Tau made a shushing motion. "Correct! Twins! Now, the House Bosoka had no tradition of twin births. There was no twin to accompany Tau-indi's mother, Tahr, when she popped out of her lamother Taundi through the mine foreman's slippery hands and fell into a wash bucket, nor a twin for grandlam Taundi, who came out of Toro Toro downside-up and burbling, so small they were wrapped up in a leaf.

"But Tau-indi Bosoka was different. . . ."

B ARU, wake up!"

 Now a clock was shouting at her. Barhu must be in that dream about Iscend again, where they agreed to have sex but first Iscend's clockwork had to be wound up and Barhu couldn't figure out how.

"Mmf," she grunted, putting her face into the sack of beans she used as a pillow. "Unethical."

"Wake up, you little weasel!" Someone tried to turn her over. Barhu smelled Aurdwynn, some pore-deep spice memory of olive oil and cedar incense, and knew it was Yawa.

"What?" Barhu groaned. "Did my parents really let you . . . what is it, what's wrong?"

"There's cholera in Cautery Plat."

"*What?*"

"Three men from a fishing crew started shitting rice water during the night. One's dead. They wrung out seven gallons from his bedding. Dehydration shock killed him."

"No," Barhu groaned. "It can't be. The Brain was listening to me. Aminata told her I was telling the truth, she was going to listen. . . ."

Yawa began to throw clothes at her. "I can't figure how she did it. *Eternal* hasn't launched any rockets, pickets haven't seen any boats slip out. Perhaps untreated sewage on a current. Perhaps it's all an accident."

Barhu twisted her earlobe to wake herself up. "The whale."

"What?"

"If their whale can be trained to plant a mine, it could've brought a vivarium of cholera to the harbor. To the shellfish beds. The fishermen probably eat shellfish they catch, right? That was the vector."

"*Shit!*" Yawa picked at her chin. "Is it over? Are the negotiations done? She can't think she'll get repairs and safe passage after she's set cholera on a town of forty thousand. . . ."

"She might've hoped it wouldn't catch until she was gone. We'd better play it quietly for now." Barhu frowned blearily at her. Yawa had picked up the clothes she'd thrown at Barhu, and now she was smoothing wrinkles, checking buttons, plucking lint. A maid's old habits. "I was listening to Tau last night. I think I got what I needed."

"Oh?" Yawa looked up sharply from the expensive red cravat she was smoothing. "Do you have . . . it?"

"Not yet. Not quite. They'll need to speak to Kindalana. Persuade her that the time is right to move, no matter how personally difficult it might be for her. Abdumasi will sell her the business side. Tau will have to persuade her of the ethics."

"I told you I can't wait that long. If we're due in Falcrest by 90 Summer then the Reckoning of Ways can't be long after. I *can't* wait."

"I know, Yawa. I know." She yawned. "I need coffee."

She went to the toilet, washed, poured herself a cup from Solit's cow, and came back hoping Yawa had uncoiled a little. She had not. She was pulling individual specks of lint off Barhu's waistcoat.

"Yawa," she said, sitting on the edge of her hammock, watching the old judge clean her things, "have you thought about the things I said?"

"All that nonsense about yomi? About doing what they expect, but not for the reasons they think?"

"Yes."

"I have," Yawa growled. "But you said I shouldn't tell you, didn't you? You said it wasn't safe."

YOU too, huh," Aminata said, trying, and failing, to keep the bitterness from her voice. "Everyone's switching sides on me."

Iraji sat beside her on the stateroom bed. "I think the negotiations are going well. We had fresh water for the pump crew today. If we get lumber, *Eternal* might be able to sail by the end of the month."

He was avoiding the question. The Eye had come back aboard with a grotesque proposal from Baru. They were going to cut a slice of cancer out of Abdumasi Abd and put it into Iraji's spine. He would stay with the Cancrioth, carrying the cancer he'd been born to host. The purpose of his flesh accomplished.

If it wasn't so disgusting, it'd be almost Incrastic.

"Apparitor's gone," Iraji said. He wouldn't look at her, because he knew she didn't like to be seen upset. "He's left on business for the Throne. He'll always be my lightning man. But I can't go back, Aminata. I've been hiding from this all my life. It's who I was born to be."

"You're not *born* to be anyone, Iraji! You can choose. You can decide what you want to do with your life."

"Really? Incrasticism has a little to say about what we Oriati people are born to be, doesn't it?"

"That's not fair."

"Then be fair to *me*. I was trained as a spy, you know. To pass in strange new places. To learn secrets. Where am I ever going to get a better chance to do that?"

"You could do that anywhere, Iraji."

"But I'm here. Why should I run?"

"Because your race isn't your destiny!" She seized two fistfuls of the bed to keep herself from leaping up in anger. "Just because you were born one of them doesn't mean—doesn't mean you should let them stuff cancer into you. It's ridiculous. You can overcome your birth!"

"It's not my destiny. It's my choice. A choice I've been afraid to make. Do you ever think—maybe they teach us that we can overcome our race just to make us think our race is something we *have* to overcome?"

It had always been something she'd had to overcome, she wanted to say. But that was because Falcresti people made it so, wasn't it?

He laid a hand on her thigh, which made her flinch in irritation. He drew it back. "Aminata, what's waiting for *you* out there? You'll be court-martialed for insubordination. Shao Lune's out there pouring poison in your admiral's ear. . . ."

"I have to report to the Rear Admiral Maroyad. She sent me on this mission. I have to go back to her."

"You could ask Baru for a pardon."

"No! I am not going to fucking ask Baru for a pardon!"

It wasn't fair! She'd gone so far to do her duty. Thrown her life away to destroy Ormsment's mutiny, helped lead the battle against the warmongers aboard *Eternal,* saved everyone aboard from a death ride into the teeth of Annalila Fortress. Saved the whole Republic from the outbreak of open war right here at Cauteria.

And what would it get her? What would any of her work get her?

Nothing. She'd yielded a navy secret under duress, and refused the orders of a superior officer. If they felt she'd done it out of cowardice, or out of a racialized solidarity with the enemy, they might drown her for it.

But what else could she have done? Let Masako shoot Iraji? Let Ormsment burn *Eternal* with a Prince-Ambassador aboard? Collaborate with a woman in clear mutiny against her sworn duty?

"Aminata," Iraji said, softly. "You're going to tear the sheets."

"Sorry. I bet they're expensive."

"I wasn't worried about the sheets."

"I have to report to Maroyad. It's my duty. That's all there is to it."

He shifted a little closer to her. After their first and only time together, all curiosity satisfied, he'd vanished from Aminata's awareness as a sexual thing. Become a kind of warm directional illumination, like a slat of sun.

"If I don't make it," he said, "will you tell Baru that this isn't her fault? She'll blame herself. I don't want that."

"You want *me* to talk to Baru?" Aminata drew back in horror. "After what she told me?"

The memory of the things she'd heard in that dark place wrapped around her like a burn. The Brain had brought her there, bound by sorcery and silk cord, to answer the same question she'd always asked. Was Baru genuine? Was she telling the truth?

Oh yes. Baru had told the truth to the Brain. She'd lied to Aminata her whole life. She was a traitor and a would-be tyrant. Had she *ever* cared about Aminata as more than a tool? First a tool to deal with that pedophile fuck Diline. Then a tool to get the navy's support when she was short on allies in Aurdwynn. Then a tool to kill Ormsment.

A living idiot tool.

"I think you should talk to her," Iraji said, carefully. "I think that she would like to make herself understood to you. She cares about you."

"She made herself perfectly understood to me. I listened to her explain her entire plan to sabotage the Imperial Republic. I believed every word."

And the fuck of it was that it was a good plan. A great plan. Aminata didn't pretend to an admiral's understanding of the world, but she knew the Imperial Republic existed because of the trade wheel. If you could place that wheel under your own control, and then stop it turning, Falcrest might fall.

"Maybe it was craft," Iraji suggested. "A way to entice the Brain into further contact. It's the kind of thing the Throne would do, Aminata. . . ."

"No! No, fuck that, she'll claim it's that but I won't believe it. I *know* Baru. I know she was telling the truth. She's calm when she lies. It's the truth that makes her start shouting, because it scares her. She was furious. She was telling the truth."

"I suppose she was," Iraji said, quietly.

"I'm tired of chasing her around. Tired of trying to figure her out."

"She's going to get you out of here, you know. When they arrange a hostage exchange."

"But what about you?" She turned to face him square, his perfect body, his warm eyes. She worried for him with more feeling than she could allow for herself. "I hope you know what you're doing, Iraji. Once you do this . . . I don't think you can come back."

"You're changing the subject!"

"I'm defending you from my mood, sir."

"Calling me *sir*?" He pouted. "Now I *know* you don't like me."

"But I do," Aminata said. "Iraji, I actually do. It's everyone else I'm not sure about, now."

MAGIC AND MEANING

I N the end the Cauteria Agreement was reached as much by exhaustion as
by any clever stratagem of diplomacy.

Eternal was down twenty degrees by the bow and heeling hard into
her wound. Pump crews collapsed of exhaustion in the rising water. The
Brain had firm control of the ship and its weapons, and Masako's hardened
Termite cadre might have been enough to use them, but what would they attack? A little village full of Taranoki, on an island far from Falcrest?

Her people were dying of thirst. She was dying of white blood. And there
was nothing mighty for them to achieve by dying here.

She came ashore that morning to sign the final agreement, with Yawa and
Barhu and the Eye, in a round one-room tufa household at the east end of
town. The Rubiyya murmured past outside. The two onkos didn't sign with
pens; instead they pressed their hands to the page, and left dim, stained hand-
prints which shone in the dark.

Tau and Osa would be released in exchange for Kimbune. Cancrioth surgeons would open Abdumasi Abd's back, cut out a living piece of Undionash,
and transfer it (by secret technique: they would not allow any Falcresti near
it) into Iraji. He would remain with the Cancrioth, to be cared for and educated, awakened to the memories in his implant. He would not die of the tumor's
spread, the Eye promised. His lineage was in agreement with the Spine.

Kimbune would leave a copy of her proof with Barhu for verification in the
Metademe.

The issue of cholera in Cautery Plat was not raised.

Eternal would be repaired, provisioned, and given charts for the return to
Segu waters. There was barely enough of summer left to make the voyage before autumn storms.

It did not surprise Barhu to discover that the Brain was awful at negotiation. There was no byplay with her, no give or take, no posturing and retreat.
She was an ancient and willful creature, and she had no time left to waste.
The power and directness of her thought made her detest the excruciating and
necessary tedium of the table. She did not like to linger while others caught up

to her will: she was alive in all her memory, and if the present could not match the urgency and fascination of the past, she feared she would wander from it.

The Eye was not so easily satisfied. He had no problem sitting (or standing, when he was impatient) at the table all day long, waiting for things to grow and turn his way. He wanted guarantees of safe passage out of Falcrest's waters, letters and flags, diplomatic seals. He wanted assurances that Barhu would not reveal what she'd learned of the Cancrioth to the whole world. She would not, she said, because that would endanger the prospects of her new trading concern, which would only flourish in peacetime. He wanted assurances that Abd would be treated well; Barhu assured him that Abd would be placed in the custody of the Oriati Embassy on Habitat Hill in Falcrest.

One of the Brain's eyelids drooped unevenly. Her words were beginning to slur. "Let them have Abd. Let all Falcrest know he defied them. Let them come for us. Better that we fight. Better that all the Oriati rise up and fight."

The Eye whirled on her. "And that's what you wanted, isn't it?" There was clarity and power in his words, a strength he had concealed for the right moment. "I thought you joined this voyage because you cared about Undionash and wanted him safely home. But it was really about the harvest, wasn't it? All those millions of bodies in Oriati Mbo. Soldiers for your cause. Hosts for your growth. You need war so you can reap your crop, Incrisiath. A million new believers for the Cancrioth."

Then he said two words in En Elu Aumor: "Su malimun."

Malignant. You're malignant.

The Brain looked at him in profound sorrow. She asked a question in their tongue, and her voice was lonelier than a body on a spar in the sea.

There was a long silence. Barhu decided to play the blithe and self-absorbed young tycoon. "Pardon me. This agreement we've signed covers your safe return home and the return of our hostages. But there is, obviously, still a great deal to settle, particularly after the . . . ah, damages inflicted upon the Imperial Republic's interests. A rutterbook describing routes and ports through the Segu archipelago and into the western Oriati coast would be a welcome sign of good faith, I think."

"Do you honestly believe," the Eye snapped, "that any one of us is idiotic enough to let Falcrest 'trade' into our homeland? We know what happens when the Empire of Masks turns up with paper money and a porcelain smile—"

"I do not give you the rutterbook," the Brain said.

Barhu exhaled. It was not defeat: it was not destruction. But it was a setback. She had known that the Brain would probably refuse. This was how Falcrest won its victories, after all. Find a crevice of self-interest or rivalry. Pump it full of water, acid, molten iron. Dig at it until it split. Until the abscess tore open and you got into their soft innards like a lamprey and they would never get you out.

"But it does not save us," the Brain said, sadly. She could barely lift the weight of her body and the armor, but nonetheless she stood. "I am the Long Thought. I see the patterns of history. As White Akhena seizes the rivers and the roads to sustain the Mzicane, so Falcrest forces its way into the Black Tea Ocean to reach our spices. If it does not happen this year it happens in ten years or in thirty. And the longer it takes the more they punish us for it.

"When your ships come, Baru, my people are ready for them. Send your merchants. Send your clocks and swords and telescopes. There is war soon enough; and you show my people the enemy."

It changed everything for Baru's plan. It changed nothing. It meant only that she would need to tell a monumental lie. She would still have her monopoly, but now it would depend not on a real rutterbook but on the pretense of one: and on very, very deft manipulation.

"I have one additional condition," she said.

The Brain staggered and caught herself on the table. "What is it?"

"You release Aminata's boarding saber with her."

"Fine." She offered her half-curled hand to Barhu.

Barhu took it. Their eyes met. The Brain smiled. "This is a moment I re-member," she said. "Whoever I am becoming."

"I won't fail you," Barhu said. "I didn't lie."

The Brain leaned close. Her breath was weak. Her eyes blazed with some dying fire. All at once Barhu understood why she wore the old broken armor. That blow must've killed whoever wore it: but she had survived, anyway, to wear it again. She had died, but she had won.

"Tell your people," the Brain murmured, "never to eat the bats."

Barhu jerked away in shock.

The Brain's eyes flickered. "Su malumin," she murmured, to the Eye. "En ek am incri an? Malumin? En incri ana ti se si ihen, Virios . . ."

"I need to bring her back to the ship." He tried to lift her but her armor was too heavy. He looked like he was about to cry again. "Please help me."

WHEN she came home she found her parents sitting on their bed behind the mulberry curtain, holding hands, speaking softly. Solit reached out to Barhu. She joined them in the circle, taking her parents' hands in hers.

"It's done," she said. "We've signed an agreement. Hostages will be ex-changed. *Eternal* will make repairs and go."

Pinion squinted when she smiled. "We're not going to die?"

"No. You'd better boil all your drinking water, though. There's cholera in Cautery Plat, and if it's there, it might get in the river and the water here." She would leave an explanation of the bats for later. She hadn't the stomach to think about that now.

"Oh? Serves them right." Pinion's fingers explored Barhu's hardened hand, her wounded stumps. "Some days I wish we'd met those first Falcresti ships like the savages they thought we were. Howling and throwing spears."

"They would've gone to the plainsiders, mother," Barhu said, vaguely irritated by this casual use of the word *savage,* "and it all would've turned out the same. Except *we* would've been the ones dying at Jupora, when the ritual circle broke. Falcrest had so much that we wanted. . . ."

She trailed off, overcome by nostalgia: here they were again, arguing over the strange ships in harbor. But now the strange ships had come here on Barhu's invitation; now everyone's fate depended on her. She had everything she'd wanted as a child. She had the power to determine the outcome.

It was quite terrible.

She saw her mother smiling. "What?"

"I missed arguing with you."

Solit rolled his eyes. "I didn't."

"I missed you both," Barhu said, briskly, so that she wouldn't have time to think her way out of it. This made it sound quite disingenuous, but Solit smiled anyway.

Pinion broke suddenly away from Barhu and Solit's grip and went over to the pine wardrobe, where she began to sort mulberry work shirts and rough canvas trousers into piles of apparently arbitrary character. She was frowning.

Solit sighed. "Pinion, what is it?"

"She's about to ruin it," Pinion grunted. "I can tell. She's going to tell us something awful."

"You don't know that," Solit protested. "Just because she's trying to be sweet doesn't mean she's going to do something which will torture us in the small hours of the night for years to come, as we wonder whether we did something wrong, something that drove her away from us." He blinked at Barhu. His belly bunched up pleasantly over the hem of his slops. "Does it, daughter?"

"That's exactly what it means," Pinion said. "She's letting us talk, see. Because she doesn't want to say it. She doesn't like telling us about anything." She smoothed the frayed cloth of a skirtwrap under her thumbs. "She doesn't even return our letters."

"Cairdine Farrier was holding my mail," Barhu protested.

"That snake," Pinion snarled. The fabric groaned taut in her hands. "I'd like to shrink his head down to an apple. Like those jungle people in his book."

"I can beat him," Barhu said, quietly. "And bring Salm home. I have everything I need to do it. But I need you to do something hard for me first."

They both looked at her, Solit from the bed, Pinion from the wardrobe, and there was a fierceness in Pinion's eyes and a terror in Solit's.

Barhu's throat closed up. "I need you to let me go," she choked.

"Go where?" Pinion sounded as if she would leap up with her boar-killing spear and murder whoever wanted to take her anywhere.

"Give me the carpets."

"Oh, I knew it." Pinion threw the skirtwrap at the wall. "I knew you'd do this. You just can't go on being our daughter, because, oh, it'd put us in too much danger! Never mind that we fought on Taranoke. Never mind that we saved ourselves when they were hunting for us door to door. Never mind that we, the matai, voted to risk ourselves for your plan. It's only our brilliant daughter who can face the mask—"

"It's not about that, love," Solit said.

She whirled on him with fury and betrayal in her eyes. She could have screamed at Barhu. Never at him.

"She's not trying to protect us." Solit touched Barhu's wrist. "Tell her."

"I know you're used to danger. I know you can protect yourselves. But I *need* Cairdine Farrier to believe I've broken this bond, too. I need him to believe I've fouled up all my ties to Taranoke and thrown you away in disgust. He has to know I'm still obeying his script. You've got to do it to me. You've got to do it publicly. Please, ma."

"So he wins," she snarled. "He takes you away from us forever. Just the way we were afraid he would."

"I can bring Salm home—"

"How can we tell him that we gave away his daughter to have him back?"

"But I'll still be out there, ma. I'll be out there doing my work. You can take pride in that." She reached out to Pinion, though her arms were not long enough to cross the space. "That's the difference between obeying him and pretending to obey him, even if they look the same from the outside. Even if no one else can see it. This is what I *do*, mother. I let them think they've won, so that we can win."

"How will we explain this to Salm?" Solit asked, quietly. "When we see him again?"

When we see him again: that was a sentence full of hope. She squeezed Solit's hand hard. "You'll tell him that you helped me tell a lie."

Pinion sagged in place. "The carpets are for traitors, spies, spouse-beaters, and child molesters. They mean something sacred. You'd be tainted in the eyes of the gods. . . ."

"I've hurt a lot of children. I've killed a lot of spouses. I've been a spy and a traitor. Maybe I deserve it."

"You're my daughter!" Pinion shouted. "My daughter isn't a child molester or a spouse-beater! You don't deserve to be treated like one!"

"We didn't deserve to be conquered, either," Solit said, looking at Barhu's two-fingered hand. "But it happened."

"Oh," Pinion snarled, "why do you always have to take her side? *You* let her go to that school!"

Solit flinched a little, but he knew it was only her temper talking, picking up weapons and hurling them. "No, muira. She wanted to go to that school. She's always chosen her own way."

"Mother! Father!" The old Urunoki came back to her tongue like wine. "Please don't fight over me. I can face anything, anything at all. But if I knew you disapproved of what I was doing . . . if you thought I wasn't your daughter anymore . . . I would . . ."

She touched her collarbone, to show them what she meant. She would snap. She would break like a bone.

"Gods of stone and fire," Pinion snarled. She dashed the pile of laundry she'd made onto the floor, and went out into the sun.

Solit and Barhu looked at each other.

"Can't you just blackmail this Farrier man?" Solit asked.

"No. He has to trust me long enough to put me in a certain position. He needs to believe I'd choose him over you. So he knows his conditioning is flawless."

"That idiot," Solit said, fondly. "He has no idea who he's playing with, does he?"

Pinion came back inside, breathing hard. "I just want to know one thing."

She blinked. Tiny images of candles caught on the water in her eyelashes.

"If you didn't have to do this," she husked, "then you'd come visit us, wouldn't you? You'd have come to visit us again? You'd write, at least?"

"Oh, mother," Barhu said.

And felt deep-soul awe as her own tears multiplied the image of Pinion, the image of the candles, everything smearing into light, like bright eyes at the bottom of the sea.

* * *

H ER mother went to the matai to explain that Barhu needed to face the carpets. Her father Solit went to the smithy to make her a dive knife.

Barhu went to walk among her people one last time.

The bazaar was at its peak. News of the treaty had all the Cancrioth in bright spirits, and they were bartering for things to make their long voyage home more comfortable. There was not one hint in the wide river or the slow wind that the world was about to change. Because a few tired, angry people had gathered in a room and, through frustration, terror, and the slow concession of principle, come to a bargain.

Was that how history should happen? It seemed uncouth.

Maybe she and Yawa and the onkos were just avatars of impersonal and inhuman forces. Little sinewy joints in the skeleton of the world, bent by huge muscles of need and excess, mistaking the motions forced upon them for the action of their own wills.

Maybe what was about to happen was like the loose scree of el-Tsunuqba's face. A huge potential pent up and waiting to move. And Barhu was the little bomb that started the avalanche.

She felt exactly like she had on that last night after the victory at Sieroch. Giddy. Bent near to breaking. At least at Sieroch she'd gotten laid before the worst.

"Barhu!" Solit called, from the river pump where he was drawing water. As if moved by trim: "There's a woman here! She says she's your lover!"

Barhu was immediately and excruciatingly embarrassed. "It's not Shao Lune, is it?"

"Who's Shao Lune?" Solit repeated, innocently. "There's *another* one?"

Ulyu Xe sat on the grass with her legs tucked beneath her. "Hello. I walked here from Annalila. I wanted to see you before I left for Aurdwynn."

"Any sign of cholera?" Barhu asked, to her father's mutter that this was not how one should greet a lover.

"I heard it was in the town. That's all." She rose from the ground like water poured in reverse. Barhu did not even chide herself for admiring the long calves, the strong grass-stained thighs. "Your father suggested I take you up-river for the day."

"Oh." Barhu frowned. "Maybe we'd better stay in the village. This might be my last chance to—"

"Baru," Solit said, in exasperation, "would you please demonstrate to your mother and I that you can entertain an agreeable woman for at least *one* afternoon?"

* * *

SHE rowed Xe upriver on the Rubiyya. The diver sat alertly in the prow, absorbing the birdsong and the madly colored blossoms, the heat of the day, the frogs and krakenflies hunting among the reeds. Barhu grounded them in a flood meadow and showed Xe how to take temperature readings with a mercury thermometer.

"It's like magic," Xe said.

"It absolutely is not!"

"You told me that masters in Falcrest spend two years calibrating each thermometer to the tenth of the degree. That they must be stored with a certain ritual. That they can kill you if you break them open. That they must be destroyed before falling into foreign hands. That they can tell when people are sick before they even know."

"But this thermometer works by clear, well-understood logical rules. Magic doesn't work at all."

Xe lay down on the bank and trailed her bare toes in the water. "You'd only be satisfied if magic were like a rag novel. A wizard shoots a bolt of lightning to animate a corpse. A warlock calls down a star from the sky to blind his foe. But that's not really magic. It's just made-up science."

"No it's not!" Barhu sputtered.

"Yes it is. If you can see how it works, it's science. If a wizard were to show you a book of rules by which he combines various gestures and words and gems and metals to make his spells, it would be science, not magic."

"What isn't science, by your definition?"

Xe rolled onto her back and squirmed out of her skirtwrap. "When a witch raises a rabbit with the same name as a man, and kills and skins the rabbit, and then pisses through the rabbit's skin into a pit of gravel, and the man gets kidney stones. The witch never touched the man. She never acted upon him. She only touched symbols of him."

"Oh, fine." Barhu crossed her arms and glared. "So magic doesn't work except when it can be disguised as the coincidence of symbolic manipulation and natural occurrence? That's *very* powerful."

"The most powerful thing in the world," Xe said, untying her strophium and sliding deeper into the water.

"Women in rivers are always telling me stories lately." Barhu sighed. But that last conversation with Iscend *had* inspired a tremendous idea: what Barhu was beginning to think of as the Huntress Qualm. Perhaps there was another one to be gained here.

"Xe," she asked, "if someone asked me, *what was lost at Kyprananoke, why should we care that they died,* what would I say?"

"Beyond their lives?"

"Yes. What makes all the Kyprananoki dying worse than the death of an equal number of Falcresti in a bad winter?"

Xe thought about this for a while. Krakenflies buzzed past. Sediment swirled over her toes.

"In Aurdwynn," she said, "we call the marshes to the east of the river Inirein the wuxunanikome, the sea of wet chaos. Falcrest calls it the Normarch. I never thought anyone could live there, especially not in the winter.

"But the rear admiral in the fortress, her people come from there. The bastè ana. She told me, at the Governor's Ball, how her people lived. She also told me that I looked like a whore and that I should go put on a coat."

This might have been Xe's way of making it into a joke: Barhu could not read the diver's deadpan at all.

"She told me that the greatest naturalists in Falcrest come to the Normarch to study the seals. But they need the ana hunters to find the seals, hunters who are taught to hunt just as their ancestors did. No naturalist, no matter how clever, can know as much: How the seal maintains air holes in the winter ice. How it sniffs for the scent of hunters before coming up to breathe. How its territory is generally of such a size, how it is most active at this time of year and quiet at that time. What parts of it are safe to eat, which are best raw, which are best cooked."

"What does this have to do with my question?"

"What if I am thinking through my answer?"

"I'm sorry. Go on."

"At around the same time, a Falcresti frigate, the *Auroreal,* was caught in the northern icepack. She had barrels of preserved food, a veteran crew, special arctic furnaces, and hunting poisons to bring down large game."

Oh, she remembered *Auroreal* from Shao Lune's story! "What happened to them?"

"The bears were too hard to catch. The seals they never found at all. By the end of the winter they'd resorted to eating their own dead. The survivors of *Auroreal* were physically overcome by a local ana tribe, carried south, and delivered to Falcresti authorities."

Barhu shuddered. Those details had not been in Shao Lune's version. "But the local ana tribes had survived winters like that for centuries."

"Of course. Because they did what their ancestors taught them to do. They were able to hunt and catch seals when Falcrest's most rational, well-equipped thinkers could not. Obeying their ancestors made them smarter than anything Falcrest's explorers could invent."

"You're talking in circles!"

"I like circles," Xe said, sliding herself down into the water.

Me too, Barhu thought, with daft and sun-sleepy desire. "How does this answer my question? You think there's something the ana culture knows, some secret of catching seals, which can't be replicated or invented by Falcrest? Something magical?"

"Yes."

"What is it?"

"Whatever it is that can only be learned by living for hundreds of years on the wuxunanikome. How to fashion spears when you live on an icepack without trees. How to locate the seal air holes and how to approach in stealth. How to know exactly when the seal has to come up to breathe, how to avoid the seal panicking and tearing itself off the spear tip, how to prepare the seal meat when fuel runs low, how to make sledges which run well on ice, how to identify exactly which patches of sea ice are low on salt and safe to drink. Maroyad told me about all these techniques. Falcrest's finest did not discover them with rational investigation. But the bastè ana did, simply by living there so long."

Barhu wondered if her parents would be proud or concerned that she was sitting here beside her half-naked lover arguing arctic survival tactics.

"The Metademe tried to rationalize their diets, did you know?" Xe was now in the water to her lower lip. "Tried to make the ana stop eating disgusting things like seal blood pudding. At once they began to die of scurvy. They knew that going back to the old food would cure them, but they couldn't explain *why*. My ykari is Wydd the Patient, Baru, and so I admire the ana people. Because they patiently and obdurately do what their ancestors taught them. No one involved can explain *why* seal blood is necessary. But it is, and they know it."

"Nardoo," Barhu said, remembering a lesson from school.

"Pardon?"

"Nardoo. It's a fern that grows in the south of Mzilimake Mbo, near Zawam Asu. You can crush the seeds to make flour. But no one eats it, because it poisons you. Once you've got nardoo poisoning you shit enormously, more than you eat. The more of it you eat, the faster you'll starve.

"But in Devi-naga, on the opposite side of the Oria continent, everyone knows how to eat nardoo. It grows well after floods, so they've discovered how to prepare it safely. The women crush the nardoo seeds, wash the flour out with water, cook it, and serve it as a porridge. You eat the porridge off a mussel shell—never anything else. It's not poisonous if you do it that way. No one knows why.

"When Falcresti sailors arrived they thought the nardoo seeds would be good provisions for long voyages. But the crushing, the washing, and the cooking are all time-consuming and dull. So the sailors skipped the simple women's work, milled the seeds into flour, and used the flour for bread. And they ate the bread, and shat their bodies out, and starved. They had all the best of Incrastic science and they couldn't figure out what the Devi-naga all knew.

"It's as if . . ." She groped for a way to say it. "It's as if all the people who live anywhere in the world, no matter how primitive or savage Falcrest says they are, are accumulating interest. Learning things which can only be learned by being who they are, for as long as they have been. Oh, damn it, am I just calling them stupid? Am I just finding roundabout ways to say that these people are too backward to do science?"

"That's a Falcrest conceit," Xe countered. "We're saying they're clever in a way that's not valued by Incrasticism."

"How? How is it clever to do whatever your ancestors teach you?"

"Because your ancestors are smarter than you. Not any one of them, but all together. All those different ways of seal-hunting and flour-making combining and leaping down from generation to generation, sieved out by centuries of practice until only the best forms remain."

"Oh!"

Barhu felt the idea like a punch to the breast. All her life she had orbited around that word, *savant*, the clever one, the one who does the figures and writes the book and changes the way people think. The clever *one*. She does her great work, and history remembers her, only her, as a bright star of intellect. A great name like Lapetiare or Shiqu Si or even Mana Mane.

But what if she imagined the entire thousand-year mbo—

Now it lay before her, as lucid as the water running over Xe's shoulders. As real in her mind as the iron salt and the black beaches of Taranoke, as the sky whirling from sun to moon and stars to sun again as days raced days to the end of time.

The continent of Oria. Land of jungle and sahel, mangrove forests and rice flats, and mountains and rift valleys and lakes and desert. And it all swarmed with brilliant life. Generations of Oriati trying to live in new places, failing, trying again. An endless, ever-changing challenge, humanity against the thousand climates of this land of dense-packed difference: and then all those tribes of humanity against each other.

The griots ran like thread between the peoples to carry the trembles of triumph and grief, the pale flame of innovation, the red rope of war. Children listened to their parents as their parents had when they were children, learning to sing the songs, to mind their trim, to do good and to hold fast to their principles, even when circumstances wanted them to bend.

In the thirteen kingdoms of Lonjaro, princes conspired to advance their own families as commoners suffered. The game of golden seats was so all-consuming that those good princes who attended to the betterment of their people were overtaken and destroyed by the selfish who attended only to their own power.

Until someone began to preach the belief that it was more important to do what was right, to treat others as if they were your own kin, to add to the common pot rather than pour it into your own private treasury. This idea of trim became so fixed in the culture, through personal faith and through its glorification in great works like the *Whale Words* and the *Kiet Khoiad*, that people obeyed it for no rational reason at all, even in the face of mortal temptation. They were good even when they had no reason to be good.

The Oriati Mbo had never invented inoculations. Or rocket-launched naval incendiaries. Or citrus anti-scurvy regimens. Or soap before surgery. Or techniques of social control. Thus Falcrest believed that its method triumphed over the Oriati way.

But Falcrest found the Oriati utterly resistant to their suasions and enticements. Not because the Oriati were primitive or ignorant, not because they were all the same, but because the *one* thing that united their vast nation of nations was a belief in trim: doing the right thing just because it was right. Stubbornness and faith in the old ways could be a good thing; it could be the greatest thing, when your enemy wanted to sway you from your path. And there were other good things in all the peoples of the Mbo, things no one could imagine or invent, ideas which could only be produced by being who they were, in the places where they lived, with the history they had.

Oriati Mbo was a book of incredible and unread wisdom. A book made of millions of living souls.

And Falcrest wanted to erase the book. Burn the pages for kindling, the people for labor. No one in Falcrest understood that there was anything written in it at all. They believed that some societies were civilized and some were primitive and that the civilized had nothing to gain from the primitive at all.

"You're looking at me very oddly," Xe said.

"I've just had another theoretical breakthrough," Barhu said. "An articulation."

"Oh? What was the first one?" Her warm deep eyes half-hooded.

"It was about women who fuck women," Barhu said, waving that aside as unimportant. "Listen, I *do* believe in science. I think it's the most useful invention of all time."

"Useful for what?"

"It saves children from the pox, and it makes faster ships, and it explains the motions of the stars and the shape of the world—"

"And it would take my child from my belly right now. I'd be sterilized. Because I've been with women."

"Yes, yes, it can be misused, obviously I know that, but listen"—she rose up on her haunches, waving at invisible things in the shape of the sun on the river—"that could be changed. If I could bring proof to Falcrest that Incrasticism is *wrong*—"

"Baru," Xe said.

Barhu smashed her fist into the palm of her three-fingered hand. "They're losing their grip. The eugenics experiment is falling apart, because people take too long to breed. And now I've got a theory that could challenge their need to scour and dominate other cultures. They're finished! By Himu, I'm going to run Incrasticism down like a deer in the woods."

"Baru," Xe said, infinitely patient, "do you listen to me at all?"

"Of course I do," Barhu said, thinking of monographs and the Metademe.

"What was your great theory about women who fuck women?"

"Oh, I had this idea that tribadists might play an important role in child-raising—not necessary to justify our existence, but useful as a political tactic to legitimize—"

Xe was looking at her with the patience and tolerance one might aim at a difficult but beloved child.

"Oh." Barhu started. Xe had said, quite clearly, *take the child from my belly, right now.* "Xe, you're pregnant?"

She nodded: smiled shyly. "My second."

"It's not *mine,* is it?" Barhu joked.

"A little, I suppose. I was taught that the fathers add their characters to the child through the way they speak to and touch the mother, just as much as through their semen. The baby will have felt us together, at least once, and it will remember that joy."

Barhu thought a moment: keeping track of her lover's lovers was not yet a habit. "The baby is Dzir's? On the Llosydanes, before he left?"

"The baby is *mine.* Though I suppose you're used to thinking of children as half the father's, in the Falcrest fashion. Dzir wanted a child, he said. Though I don't think he meant by me."

"It wasn't an accident?"

"Of course not," Xe sniffed. "I wanted something to bring back to my family. To thank them for letting me go so long . . . longer than I meant to go."

"You've been very patient with *me*. Thank you. It means so much."

"My patience is not infinite," Xe said. "Not in all matters."

"What have I done?" Barhu asked, nervously. "What do I need to fix?"

The diver stared at her. Finally Barhu understood.

Afterward, with her open lips against Xe's throat, Barhu said. "I'll miss you. I hope you're home in time to have the baby." She felt the little smile move Xe's throat, and suddenly her eyes were hot with tears. "You know I don't deserve this . . . I don't deserve you. Not after what I did to your people."

Xe squirmed slightly, and didn't answer. She was ticklish in the throat! What a petty victory it would be to make her laugh. But Barhu did not need any more petty victories. There was a terrible enough triumph waiting for her tonight. The sun was warm and falling, the krakenflies buzzing in the marsh, she had a lovely older woman to rest her head on.

For now it was all right.

"Xe," she said, "I've never said good-bye before."

"Of course you have."

"I mean a proper good-bye to a woman, before we parted. A good-bye that was . . . decent, pleasant, kind. I've had three lovers now. One was Tain Hu, one was an asshole, and one was you. I'm glad I get to say good-bye to you."

33

Two Exiles

S HE came back to her parents' house at sunset to face the carpets. Pinion waited under the veranda, stone-faced, dressed in a sleeveless jerkin and her lucky bark-strip hunting skirt with its woven charms and camouflage brush. Barhu had always thought, as a child, that boar hunting was an ancient and eternal practice. Only in school had she learned that boars were a recent arrival to Taranoke, brought by Oriati traders.

Someone was always changing someone, Aminata had said.

Solit was in his modern smith's apron, dark with soot. He did not smile, either. Wordlessly he gave her the dive knife in its leather scabbard and Barhu tied it around her left ankle where she would not forget it.

"Is it ready?" Barhu asked.

"Yes," her mother said. "It's ready."

"Come, Baru," her father said. Taking his last chance to speak her name in public.

The matai waited for her on the town green. There were eleven of them, thirteen with her parents: an indivisible number, Kimbune would point out. The elder potter, the carpenter of trees and of driftwood, the textile maker, the elder navigator, the chief fisher, the canoe-maker, the first shield, the lead drummer, the planner of farms, the birdwatcher, the healer. Solit was the metalworker and Pinion was the huntress. They went to stand with the others, leaving Barhu by a spray of damask roses and hibiscus.

"Baru Cormorant," the healer aunt said. "We have called you here for the last time. You brought death to our shores for your own profit. You turned your back on your people to lie down with those who made war on us.

"Though you were born among us, you did not live with us. You have filled your own stomach while we were hungry. If you come to us starving, we will give you stone. You have dressed your own skin while we were naked. If you come to us naked, we will shut our doors. You have sailed away while we foundered. If we see you drowning, we will leave you to the sharks.

"As our ancestors cast the water thief from the canoe and the hoarder from the village, now we cast you out. We name you Namestruck. Lie on your belly."

Barhu knelt on the petal-strewn earth. The uncle who was the textile maker unrolled a bolt of mulberry cloth across her shoulders. Pinion pushed Barhu down onto her stomach and drew the cloth flat over her. Her fingers paused at the hem, half a knuckle's width from the top of Barhu's head. She stood and walked away.

One by one they stepped onto her, put the weight of one foot onto her back, and walked across.

Barhu grunted softly with each foot. Her mother stepped on her. Barhu could tell it was Pinion by the way she hesitated, and then landed too hard. Solit was last of all. He chose carefully where to put his weight, and she barely felt his passage.

A year ago this would have killed her. The loneliness and the shame would have crushed her like a hundred thousand feet of water. What you can learn to survive, if you go into it with purpose.

She would never go back to Taranoke, live in a little house by the lagoon, deal foreign currency at the market, and fight with her wives. She had wanted that for so long. It could never happen now.

She closed that door forever.

Someone ripped the cloth from her. Rough hands lifted her and pushed her toward the road out of the village. She caught her right foot on a vine and stumbled. No one helped her: no one could. The word would go out everywhere that Taranoki people lived, even among the plainsiders, that Baru Namestruck had been trampled under her own parents' feet.

Someone might try to take Barhu's parents hostage anyway. That was a risk Pinion and Solit knew and accepted. But her enemies would not do it because they thought Barhu loved Pinion and Solit. They would not punish Taranoke to punish her, not unless they were vicious beyond reason.

And it would protect her, too. She would never be tempted by an offer of the governorship. She would never be tempted to go back to a home she had never really known: only loved from afar, loved it for its hidden aspect, the way you love a god.

Her left foot came down hard on the loose gravel. She stumbled. "O Devena," she whispered, "please stay me on my course. Please keep me from turning back—"

"Last chance," Yawa said, from out of her blindness.

BARHU tried to twist to face her, and faltered on her bad ankle. She lost her balance and fell on her two-fingered hand. "You were watching?"

"Yes." Yawa didn't move. She stood fully masked and robed, shadow raven-roosting upon the mulberry bushes. "The negotiations are done. Abdumasi Abd has gone to *Eternal* for his surgery. Everything Farrier wanted is possible now. Did you gain the rutterbook?"

"No."

"Then your trade concern is doomed. You will have no ports in the Black Tea Ocean."

"No," Barhu said, laughing a little, "not doomed, just speculative. No one has to know we didn't get the rutterbook, Yawa. We'll lie. We'll say we have it. By the time anyone finds out differently, we'll own half of Falcrest. Everything *we* wanted is possible now, Yawa."

Yawa rubbed something in her gloved palm. It was a scrap of onion skin, for luck. She threw it away. "Have you ever seen a case of penile myiasis?"

"A case of *what*?"

"Say a man sleeps nude in a house full of flies. One day he comes in to the clinic with bloody discharge and painful lesions on his cock. We look at him, we find a big red blister right on the tip"—Yawa described the shape and the blister with her hands—"so we prod that blister. It squirms. There are botfly larvae growing in his manhood—"

"*Yawa!*"

She could see Yawa's eyes through the mask. So bright. As if bleached by the suffering she'd seen. "We made a bargain with the woman who destroyed Kyprananoke. That should feel more repellent than maggots growing from a cock. But people don't think that way. The thought of maggots in a cock bothers us more than ten thousand dead innocents. So I thought I would evoke the necessary revulsion."

"Thanks, Auntie Yawa," Barhu said, queasily.

"Is it too late to alter the terms of our bargain?"

"Yes," Barhu said. "Much too late for that." She held Yawa's gaze firmly. "The terms stand. Exactly as we discussed."

"You're certain?"

"I've made my choices. I'm ready to confront Farrier. Just keep Hesychast out of the way."

"You don't think you can convince the Cancrioth to yield a sample of the immortata?"

"A living portion of their sacred flesh? You're the religionist, Yawa. You know how hard it is to convince people to give up their faith."

"You forget, Baru. I did give up my faith. I crushed the ilykari. I mortified their flesh for Hesychast. I even gave him my brother, Baru. My own brother. He's here. On this island. Now. Hesychast demands my triumph."

"Then give it to him," Barhu urged her. "Yomi. Like we discussed."

"You trust me?"

"Yawa, I trust you."

Yawa's mask nodded in the dark. "Very well. Faham, take her into custody."

Footsteps closed in from her blind side. Barhu went for her dive knife. A steel cosh smashed her right wrist and when she tried to rise another blow to her ribs took the breath from her. A black bag dropped over her head. The drawstring noosed around her neck.

"Tip her head back," Execarne ordered. "Hope you haven't lost any weight, Baru."

A dose bottle cracked like mouse bone. She held her breath as long as she could. When she gasped, her cheeks went numb, her throat, her chest.

She heard Iscend say, "I have the instruments prepared."

"She thought it could be faked," Yawa said, with remote sadness. "She thought I'd find a way."

A MINATA woke in a hot sweat to the sound of screams.

"Boarded," she said, and sat upright faster than her blood could reach her head. She grayed out for a moment. And she was back on *Lapetiare*, leaping onto a pirate galley, with the stink of Burn in her nostrils and the silent mass of her marines behind her and the first man she would ever kill waiting below.

He will be stronger than you, her weapons master had told her. He will have a longer reach and more force behind his blows because he is a man. But you will be unhesitating and precise in your violence. You will have the fatal will that is most of killing.

And failing that, you will have your marines.

"We're being boarded," she said. "Iraji? Are you—"

But Iraji was in surgery; they had told her she would not be released until he woke. Fine. She knew what to do. Assess the situation, discover the intent and strength of the enemy force, act with vigor and aggression to destroy the enemy's cohesion and capability to fight.

She didn't know which side was her enemy. But she would go find out.

She slid into her slops, double-tied her breasts, donned a canvas tunic, lit the candle in the desk lantern, and went out into the passageway. The crackle of Termite pistol fire sounded below: they were engaged with the boarders. She trotted down the narrow stairs to the deck with the baneflesh pigpen. Dry filth stained the causeway floor: men had come in through the pigpen, moving forward swiftly and in column. She made it for maybe twenty, maybe thirty. Not enough to seize the ship by force.

So it was a raid. They were here for one of two reasons. To take prisoners and intelligence.

Or to detonate the ship's magazines. To deny *Eternal* to all those who wanted to use it.

SHE crept through architecture like a palimpsest. *Eternal*'s original structure had been rebuilt again and again, each transfiguration leaving phylogenetic vestiges: inexplicable nooks, mazes of rooms, secret doors, strange chimneys where pulleys dangled between decks. She tried one door but the fumes from a shattered apparatus of yellow glass drove her back. At another door a dog barked pitifully. She tried to let the poor mutt out, but the warped frame wouldn't give.

Two frames forward she found the first corpse.

He was Falcresti, rigged in a gray filtered mask and a combat harness too slim and carefully fitted to be navy issue. A pistol had shot a mandala of blood across his chest. No exit wound. The ball must've struck the back of his ribs and stayed inside.

"You're Morrow Ministry," she told the dead man. "Faham Execarne, what are you doing?"

Burnt-out smoke grenades littered the companionway like discarded tins of fish. She smelled old piss. The Cancrioth had been here, pouring jarred urine on the catchfires. They were moving behind the boarders.

The tracks became chaos—the boarding party driven forward, moving in haste. They dropped smoke behind them to slow the Cancrioth pursuers. The size and organization of the Cancrioth pursuit told Aminata they'd been ready for an attack. How? Execarne knew about the cancer whale. He certainly knew it could report his approach. So why had he walked his boarding party into an ambush?

She found the first Cancrioth body.

Giant Innibarish lay naked and burnt in a mad scrawl of blood. His fists were charcoal-scabbed around a short axe. "Oh," Aminata groaned, covering her mouth. She'd smelled cooked man before, but always through a mask. He must have stripped his clothes when they caught fire. "Oh, virtues."

"Aminata . . ." the corpse breathed.

He was alive. "Oh, kings and queens, Innibarish. What *happened*?"

He crackled when he moved. "The Brain . . . she told the Womb they would come. Told her to be ready. The Womb cast spells on us, for bravery, and against pain. I hardly feel it. . . ."

Hundreds of stab wounds had turned his chest to ground meat. "You're going to die," she told him. "I'm sorry."

"I know. But I'll live, too, if my people find me in time. Tell them . . . tell them to cut it out of me, quickly. . . ."

He'd killed at least one of the enemy. His axe was bloody to the handle. He must've chased the Morrow-men through the smoke and flames, probably screaming his lungs out, coughing and hacking, trying to drive them away from the Womb and his friends.

They would've seen a monster coming after them. Aminata saw the gentle man who had always treated her well.

"I can kill you," she whispered, "if you want. . . ."

He tried to answer but it sounded as if his lungs were collapsing. His chin twitched. No. Not yet.

He was trying to keep his tumor alive as long as he could.

SHE passed a compartment strewn with pots, each full of carefully sorted shards of human bone. The dark beyond smelled powerfully of glue. She raised her lantern. Light fell across something the size of a boulder, jigsawed together from curved pieces of bone. It was a tremendous human skull, half-made, unfinished from the jaw down except for two mounds of glue where a lower jaw might hinge. Hundreds of teeth grinned in a white arc, incisors and canines and molars grouped together, tribes of allied bite.

"I hate this fucking place," she said. But she was lying. What she really felt was a kind of outraged protectiveness. *She* had been on this ship first! *She'd* worked so hard to keep the crew alive! How dare Execarne just bull in here and ruin everything!

She chased the sound of battle forward. And found slaughter. *Eternal* crew lay with their blood sticky across the engraved teak, with their gaping throats smiling up at snuffed candles, with two gouged wounds into their kidneys. Most of the dead were so dehydrated that they couldn't have fought. They would have split like paper.

What had happened to break discipline? Why were the Morrow-men suddenly berserk killers?

She checked each corpse with her heart in her throat. Not Iraji. Not Iraji. Not Iraji—

Something tickled at the hand she'd braced on the deck. She snatched it away. Nothing there. Just a little gap in the caulking between planks. She thought she'd felt a roach, or a rat.

She lowered the lantern to the gap to check for movement. And saw the faintest trickle of smoke coming up from below.

The ship was on fire. She sniffed the smoke. It didn't smell like burning wood, or paint, or navy Burn. It smelled like . . . like what? A little like sex, some kind of heady sweetness, like whorehouse flowers: but over that a bitter, foul, oily stink, like grease dripping in reverse, climbing up her nose.

The ship's great alarm groaned into the hull. It made her fingertips tremble. She had a sudden sense of unreality. She was farther down the causeway, but didn't remember moving. Had she gone into rower's trance? "Shit," she muttered.

What had she smelled in that smoke?

A fat green cockroach ran across the passageway, blinking its light at her. A pistol cracked somewhere forward and below her.

She heard Iraji scream.

I'M coming, Iraji!" she bellowed, against all tactical sense. Her heart stammered and leapt as she plunged down the narrow stairs and ladders, chasing the sound of Iraji's pain.

She was so thirsty. Her tongue seemed cemented to the roof of her mouth. The lantern bounced wildly in her grip, cutting nonsense slices from the dark ahead. She put her left hand out to shield her and pushed forward.

She was beginning to think she'd been drugged.

Her hand met something warm. *Someone* warm. They gasped: "Aminata? I heard you."

Aminata raised the lantern. "Your Federal Highness?"

"Tau will do, thank you." Tau-indi clasped her around the waist, panting for breath. "Aminata. Something's desperately wrong—"

"I know. The ship's been boarded by—"

"Morrow-men, yes. Faham Execarne is with them. Strange to see him out in the field; like meeting the Minister of Agriculture out tossing hay. He must trust no one else." Tau laid their head on Aminata's breast, as if they were dearest friends. "His party was ambushed. They took Iraji and Abdumasi from the surgical theater as hostages. I told Faham they couldn't be moved, but he wouldn't listen. He wouldn't even look at me. Like I wasn't there."

"Iraji's still alive?"

"Not for long. He and Abdu are held together by silk and glue. And the datura will pull them toward death—"

"Datura?"

"Yes. Can't you smell it? The Womb's people are burning it down below, filling up the ship, so their magic will be stronger. Datura. Archon trumpet. It's terrible. It will take anyone who suffers it to the bottom of their soul."

She couldn't focus on the words. They felt round, skittering away, marbles on glass. "I'm already dosed."

"I can feel it. Your heart rate's up. You'll get a dry mouth soon, and become aroused."

Her mouth was already very dry. "Doesn't it affect you?"

"I've had every drug you can imagine, Aminata. Datura is one of the worst, but I can ride it." Tau inhaled across her skin: it felt like spiders stepping. "We have to stop Execarne. I think he might blow up the ship."

The thought of *Eternal* detonating in a clean blast of fire, swallowing Aminata and Iraji and Tau and everyone else aboard, simplifying them into ash, made Aminata profoundly horny. So there was the next symptom Tau had predicted. "Virtue fuck," she snarled, "how much of this stuff are they burning?"

"Heaps of it." Tau kissed her softly on the bottom of the chin. She moaned, pressed closer to their small warm body, and then, catching herself, growled in irritation. Tau looked up at her from several feet away, where they had gone without moving. "What do you think I just did?"

"I'm hallucinating."

"Datura doesn't cause hallucinations. It causes delirium, which is much worse. You won't remember that you're drugged. Listen—if Execarne is trapped aboard, if he cannot use the hostages to get out, he will set fire to the magazines."

"Virtues, *why*?"

"He came to find the Kettling. He fears it, and he may in the end destroy himself to destroy it. We have to stop him."

A pistol discharged nearby: the sound became a spike like a whaler's harpoon, fifty or sixty feet long, pale eel of no color. It fell on the deck and squirmed. Aminata looked away. "Did you bring Osa? Can she fight?"

"No. Too much danger to her trim. Listen, Aminata, there's something you have to know—a special danger to you—you are bound by trim to Baru, and to Kindalana, who—"

"Oh, king's balls," Aminata groaned. "Not Baru again."

"Listen!" Tau was above her, suddenly, looking down at her from a mighty altitude. Aminata could not understand how they fit inside the ship. "Those bonds would protect you powerfully. But *not here*. Not among the Cancrioth.

This is a place raw to the world, unordered by human design, inhabited by older power."

"So?"

"The things that happen here are meaningless. Your destiny has no power at all to save you. The most beloved woman in the world, a woman protected by the gratitude and obligation of whole nations, might step on a nail and die of tetanus. A son might break his father's brow with an opening door. This is a place for senseless hurt, Aminata. Iraji and Abdu are in the most danger they have ever been. And so are you. If Abdu dies, all is lost. And if you die, Baru is lost."

"Who gives a shit about Baru?" Aminata snarled.

"You do, child. *You* do." Tau smiled down at her. "But it's Iraji and Abdu who need us at the moment."

"Your Highness," Aminata said, feeling, maybe for the last time, that old spark of duty-pride, "what can I do to help?"

"Find Execarne. Tell him I'm aboard. Tell him to surrender. Tell him if he doesn't, I'll be killed with everyone else."

"That's it?"

"I think so. Faham's my friend. He wouldn't blow me up."

"All right. Take this—where's the lantern?"

"I have it." Tau showed it to her. "You were swinging it about."

"Take it abovedecks. Signal to *Sterilizer*. Just do three fast blinks, over and over. It's the signal for *enemy aboard, send urgent reinforcement*." Aminata covered her eyes against the lantern light, to save her night vision. "With any luck at all, they'll send marines."

"How will the marines help?"

"They'll convince Masako and the Brain to let Execarne go. They'll convince Execarne he has a way out."

The moaning alarm trembled through the deck below her. She could hear words in it, now. She was very afraid that it would say her name. She understood, suddenly, that she was meant to die here.

"Aminata?" Tau whispered. "Are you all right?"

"Go. Go above. Be safe. Send the signal." She pushed the Prince behind her, and faced the squirming dark. "I'm going to save Iraji."

SHE knew exactly where Execarne would barricade himself. He would look for a holdout near the magazines where he could triage his wounded and regroup: somewhere with chokepoint entrances and plenty of room inside.

He would find the Brain's ampitheater.

Space shattered and knotted around her. Compartments and passageways tangled like intestines. The datura smoke was a thick ground fog now, and things like centipedes rose from it to taste her ankles. Silhouetted fighters screamed at each other in fury. She was not afraid. This was battle: seven parts trying to find out where to go and what to do, two parts shouting, and one part horrific, irrevocable violence.

A Termite's pistol fired like a disembodied thing, backflash silhouetting half a man, light shining through the thin webs between his fingers. She felt the skin of that hand between her molars, and the light like grains of dirt in her eyes. The husk of a smoke grenade crushed under her foot and she looked down. It was the body of the burnt boy she'd found on the Llosydanes. A charcoal star of limbs around a powdered center. Tiny rats with Baru's face swarmed past, chattering their plots.

Tain Shir walked alongside her. Blood dripped from her white mouth where shark teeth grinned into the chum-clouded sea. The first man who had ever told twelve-year-old Aminata that she looked like a full-grown woman gave her a flower and asked her to smile. He was a post captain now, somewhere. Shir's vast shark shape drew back a lance and hurled it into Aminata's heart.

She pinched the lobe of her ear, stabbed two fingers into her left hand between thumb and forefinger, and kept walking.

"Iraji?" she shouted. "Execarne? Anyone? I'm with Tau-indi! Don't shoot me!" The diplomatic protections of an Oriati Federal Prince fell like an itchy blanket over her, and then unraveled, became caterpillars, crawled away useless into the chaos.

A grenade blew up in the fork of the next intersection. Shrapnel chipped the teak. A big piece spun like an axehead past her. She crawled up to the intersection to look, and, in the cross-corridor to her left, saw something move in the lantern light: the thin white line of a rapier blade, red at the tip.

The rapier turned toward her. A man called out a challenge in Takhaji battle language.

"I'm with Tau-indi!" she shouted back.

The rapier became a shining white point coming straight at her face. Fighting spirit, what her old instructors had called *death liquor,* blew up in her drug-quickened heart. The man holding the rapier was slim and tall, he wore the shoulder flag of a fighting Oriati soldier, he looked faintly bemused— Masako. It was Masako.

She jagged right without thinking, old Naval System knife defenses waking up. *He will kill you if you cannot control the weapon.* She lunged in along the rapier's length and grabbed for Masako's wrist but he flicked the rapier side-ways and cut a long shallow tunnel of pain up her left arm.

She screamed in challenge and threw herself on him, inside the rapier's range. He staggered back around the corner. She smashed her whole body left, into the rapier's blade, and to her glee the long thin sword bent over the hard-wood corner and cracked.

The man tackled her and threw her down on her back. His fist cocked back. She lost a moment.

Then she was on her back on the deck, and Scheme-Colonel Masako was battering her face into her head. Her nose was broken, her thoughts gray. He pulled his fist back for another hit. She drove her forehead right into his on-coming punch. Fuck you, Masako, who taught *you* how to punch? A fist to the face is little bones against one big bone, and the big bone wins.

Masako's fist hammered her head back against the deck. Her forehead broke his hand and folded it down limp beneath his wrist. He roared in pain.

Aminata saw and felt only red, but she didn't need to see, didn't need to think, she was fighting from her spine. She wrapped her legs around Masako's waist, put her forearms in front of her face to block his next blow, and threw all her weight to the left. *Use your legs,* her master-at-arms whispered, *use all your body, or die.*

He fell off her, shrimping up around his broken hand. Rolled across his back. Came up crouching. Where was his broken rapier? She needed a knife, a piece of shrapnel, anything—she kicked frantically at his shins to keep him away—

He looked baffled, as if he were not quite sure what was going on. A datura erection tented his slops. In the dark behind him, in the place they'd first met, children crawled through the fire of the embassy Aminata had burnt.

"Tsaji," he said, thickly. "Collaborator!"

He kicked her in the head. She curled up against the blow and took his steel-tipped boot right to her kidney, screaming like a cat in the night. He kicked her again, maybe even killed her, if he'd hit the kidney bad enough. It would just take her a while to bleed and die.

She spat and rolled onto her stomach. He got her again, right in the same place. She reached out blindly into the dark and found nothing to help her. No one coming. No one to save her. But he was alone, too, or she'd be dead already—

He kicked for her head again. She rolled over in time to grab his calf and take the hit right in the chest, thump of steel against her diaphragm, everything in her lungs coming out in one hot gasp. No air, no breath, but who had time to breathe anyway: not Aminata, clawing his belt, pulling. He fell across her. The fucker was laughing. He had never believed anything could go wrong. All a fucking game to him. Kyprananoke and all of it. Even this fight.

She wormed out from under him, clawed her way up the wall, one of her fingernails snagging on a protruding treenail and bending halfway back. They didn't even have proper metal nails for her to fight with.

"Fucker," she gasped, spilling bile and blood from a split tongue. "You're dead now. You're fucking dead." As she backed away from him time stuttered in reverse, looping her words, *fucking dead dead dead dead dead dead*.

"Constant aggression," he said, through broken lips. He got back to his feet with only a little weariness. "The instinct of the body facing violence is to withdraw and contract. You must expand and fill up space. You must claim everything around you so that the enemy cannot. Even your voice must assert victory. I read your fighting manual."

She kicked a burnt-out grenade at him. He stepped out of the way. Burning lilac branches showered down across him from out of Hara-vijay, weeks past. The ship moaned.

"I'm trying to save your life," she snarled. "Get out of my way."

"Tsaji." He panted for breath. "It means *plunder*. They plundered you, Aminata. They took you from us and I'm going to take you back—"

She rushed him, head down, shoulders tight. It was the worst thing she could have done against a bigger faster man because it meant committing to the grapple. He caught her, stumbled back to absorb the impact, beat at the back of her neck—and she got his broken wrist and *twisted*. His laugh gurgled into agony. She grabbed for his balls and found a thick undercloth in the way: settled for punching him in the dick as hard as she could. He kept hitting her in the back of the head and with each hit she would go blind for a moment. She kept punching him in the dick.

"I did the right thing!" he bellowed. "I did the right thing! *I did it for my children*! My child, my child, why do you fight—"

Idiot, she thought: if you want to kill me you have to want to *kill me*.

She tried to bite him in the throat. He grabbed her chin, forced her back, and they fell together, grappled, hissing, spitting, dripping blood and bile on each other. He was winning. Once he got on top of her he would hold her down and choke her.

She stopped striking back.

Save your strength, Aminata. Take the knee he slams between your legs. Take the punches to your kidneys that make you gag. Keep your hands up, lock your thighs around his waist, keep him in your guard and don't let him go.

She could not outmuscle him. She could not outrun him. But she would bet her life that she'd had the shit beaten out of her more often than some prissy spy.

And finally he fell back on his haunches, panting, wringing out his one good hand. She could see his elbow shaking with fatigue.

"Are you done?" he said. "Are you finished? These people, these masks, they don't care about you. They use you to torture your own kind. They use your body for war and sex because their own bodies aren't good enough. They want you to be a citizen, but you're a queen, Aminata, you come from the line of kings and queens. We're the humans, Aminata. We're the race. They're just vitiated pale leftovers—"

He had no guard. His one good hand was down. She crunched with her waist and lunged and she had him in a front guillotine choke before he could do more than grunt. She counted while he thrashed and punched her stomach. The blood choke worked within ten seconds, usually. He went limp at twelve, and fell across her. She held him like that for a minute.

"Baby killer," she grunted, and left him among the burning lilacs, in the blood-soaked embassy courtyard where the children crawled.

She staggered in the direction where the grenade had exploded, shouting, "I'm navy! Lieutenant Commander Aminata, Imperial Navy! Don't shoot!"

A gray wraith came out of the smoke and pulled her into the light ahead.

AMINATA," Faham Execarne bellowed. "Welcome! I don't suppose you've brought the navy to reinforce me?"

He wore a fighting harness. The left arm of his shirt was cut off at the shoulder, exposing a pink machete wound straight down to the bone. Small tufts of grass grew from it; Aminata couldn't remember if that was normal. She wiped blood from her lips. Her kidneys might be ruptured. She might be bleeding to death from the inside. But that was all right. She knew her purpose.

"No, Your Excellency," she said. "I'm here alone. I've sent Tau above to signal *Sterilizer*. I think you'd better surrender."

"Oh, Tau's not here." Execarne waved dismissively. "I'd never wish this place on them." A trickle of blood spiraled down his arm to his glove and vanished into the lining. "You know, I always wondered if this was possible. Reality *completely* distorted by the power of the will. They're remarkable, these sorcerers. I knew their whale was away spreading cholera, yet somehow, still, they sensed me coming. Sensed it in time to deny me my prize."

"What did you come for, sir?"

"The Kettling, of course. So we could find a cure. But the roosts are empty. The bats are gone. I had to take us below . . . to the magazines." He sighed heavily. "Did I ever tell you I have a perfect memory? So I am cursed to remember everything I saw. There's a room down here, Aminata, where they cast living people in molten bronze. The flesh remains, beneath the cooling metal. There's some art to it, to keep the body from burning away. . . ."

He shuddered, and took a deep breath. His pupils were huge and black. The datura smoke seemed to climb his body.

"Your Excellency, Tau *is* here. You mustn't detonate the—"

"The world here has been broken open and rendered subject to our wills!" Execarne barked. "I do not perceive Tau aboard, and thus Tau *is not aboard*! Do not disrupt my subjectivity! My calm remove is the only thing holding existence together!"

"Your Excellency, there's a drug in the air, it's called datura—"

"Of course there's a drug. Drugs amplify the mind's power over reality. Which makes it all the more important that I keep Tau *away* from this ship."

"Tau is right above us, on the weather deck, waiting for you to come out—"

But Execarne was no longer listening to her. He had snipped her neatly out of his consciousness. Now he was murmuring with some of his Morrow-men, pointing at compartments on a map of *Eternal*'s underbelly.

If they went for the magazines, Aminata did not think there was anyone on this dehydrated ship who could stop them.

Aminata found Iraji and sprang up the pews to his side. He was swaddled in a litter made from two spears and a roll of bloody canvas, She checked his pulse (fast and thready) and his breathing (shallow and far too quick). She dared not pull the bandages off his sutured back to check the wound.

"Iraji," she whispered, "can you hear me?"

He shivered under her hands and moaned.

"He can't," a man said, grimly. "He's quite drugged."

Abdumasi Abd lay on the pew above. His pain-squint eyes were level with hers. Aminata had been his torturer so long that she wanted to flinch away— do not let him see the face behind the mask! But he didn't recognize her, of course. He had no idea what she'd done to him.

"Are you in pain?" she asked him: a triage reflex.

"No," he said, "but I can't feel my legs. Something's wrong. I could be bleeding out my asshole for all I know. What about you? You look like you've been trampled by a bull."

"I got in a fight."

"Anyone worth fighting?"

"I hope so. Do you know what's happening?"

"Not sure. I'm high as stars. Something in the air." A strained laugh. "You've got two centipedes coiled up in your eye sockets right now, guarding those little yellow babies they hatch. Lucky those mask fucks gave me so many drugs I'm used to it. Who are you, anyway?"

"I'm the one who gave you all those drugs." She just told him: there didn't seem to be any point to lying.

"What?" he said.

"I was your torturer. I planned—everything. Everything they did to you."

"You." He tried to recoil and something in his body did not respond the way he wanted. Claustrophobic flicker in his eyes—a man trapped in a coffin with a stinging jelly. "You're *Oriati*? They gave me to an Oriati woman?"

"Yeah. I know. I look just like Kindalana."

"You don't look a fucking *thing* like her!"

"That's not what Cosgrad Torrinde told me," Aminata said, and prayed, yes, actually prayed, that the human connection Tau believed in would do *something* to make Abd listen.

Abd stared in horror. "How the *fuck* do you know Cosgrad?"

Why not go all in on Tau's nonsense? "Trim brought us together. Kindalana couldn't be here, so trim brought me in her place. To save you."

"This is a trick." Abd tried to get away from her and his legs wouldn't work. He pushed at the litter with his arms, weakly. "This is another trick, I'm still in the fungus room, I'm hallucinating—"

"It's real."

"Nothing you've ever told me is real!"

"We're really here, Abdumasi Abd. I know because I told Masako where to find you. I know because I've spent weeks and weeks trapped on this ship, losing my career, losing my only friend to these cancer people, and now he's dying right next to you. That man over there is real. He's about to detonate the ship's magazines. We're all going to die here. Tau's going to die. Unless you can stop Execarne."

"How can *I* stop him? How?"

"It's easy, Abdu." And in the grip of the drug, where the whole world changed to obey the changes in your mind, it really did seem simple. "You're like him, aren't you? You were both lured into an ambush. You were both cornered, and drugged, and driven halfway mad. But you made it out, Abdumasi. You made it back to Tau. So I'm going to carry you over to Execarne. And you're going to tell him what you'd tell yourself, if you could go back to that day. That it was all going to turn out all right."

He stared in silent fury. Aminata knew she had him.

"Please, Abdumasi Abd," she whispered. "Tell him it's worth surviving. Tell me what someone could've said to you, while your fleet was burning in Treaty-mont Harbor, to make you live."

"I should be dead. I should've jumped into the fire. I was just too fucking—" His voice cracked. "Too scared. I didn't want to burn."

"You had to live. You had to live so you could be here today to save Tau."

And Abdumasi Abd did what he had never done in all those days of torture. He gave in to her suasion. He broke.

He surrendered to the possibility of hope.

"Take me over there," Abd grunted. "Carry me over to him. I'll convince him Tau's here. He'll listen to me."

"That'll be enough?"

"If Tau was on my flagship, I would've surrendered before the battle even began. I would've done anything to protect them. Now carry me, damn you."

A FTER that point her dosage was so high that she began to lose time. The points of emotion stuck in her memory: the rest washed away.

She remembered the Womb's voice giving them gentle instructions, telling them to put down their weapons and come out peacefully. The Morrow-men obeyed as if hypnotized: which was to say, not well. The drug had wrung the sense from them. Men clung to their weapons and whimpered at shapes in the smoke. She thought: those filter masks don't work too well, do they?

She remembered telling Execarne: "Baru will flay you alive for this. You fucked with her trade concern."

"No, she won't," Execarne said, vaguely: the datura was still taking him down, spiraling into the void below the soul. "She's finished."

"What?"

"Yawa's going to lobotomize her. She told me. I didn't tell her I was going to do this . . . not very good of me . . . she'll be cross, quite cross . . ."

She remembered meeting the Womb in the dark and the smoke. Her hands burned with the uranium power, and in the nimbus around those hands, in the whorls of drug smoke, Aminata saw the whole scripture of the Cancrioth, every word linked, pouring out from the Brain through the timber of the ship and the sea and the world beyond.

All words were sorcery. If enough people believed in words, in a language or a treaty or an Antler Stone, then the words could change the whole world. Faster and further than fire.

"Tell me," the Womb said, in a voice like tremor, a rumble through the whole ship's frame, "how this happened. Is the treaty betrayed? Have we lost our way home?"

"No. No, this was a mistake. A rogue spy. You have my word as a navy officer."

"That means nothing to me, Aminata. I want your word as an Oriati woman. A daughter of the isiSegu."

But I'm not that, she wanted to say. I'm a navy officer. That's who I chose to be.

She had chosen Falcrest but Falcrest had not chosen her. She had no uniform. She had no career waiting for her ashore, not with Shao Lune tuning up a court-martial. She had nothing but her body and her blood to swear upon.

"You have my word," she said, "as a daughter of the isiSegu."

"Then you may go free," the Womb said.

And she produced the long, curved scabbard of a navy boarding saber. Aminata's saber, the one she'd given to Baru in Aurdwynn. "Your sword. Baru insisted that it be returned to you."

"I'm free to go?"

"You are free to go, Aminata."

Then she was running up the stairs toward the weather deck, coughing in the thin drug fog. Two red raw holes where her kidneys should be. She thought maybe she was going to die soon, bleed into herself until she was done. She just wanted to get back up into the moonlight first. She wanted to make her report to Maroyad. Let her die in uniform. Let her die knowing who she was and needed to be. And let her die knowing the truth about—

Fuck you, Baru. You can't be lobotomized. You can't die until you explain yourself to me.

She heard Tau-indi calling out above, and the heavy tramp of marine boots. *Sterilizer*'s boats had come alongside to take Execarne and his Morrow-men away. *Sterilizer*'s marines would obey orders.

She'd saved the ship. She'd saved the peace. She was a hero. She groaned in agony and pulled herself up the steep steps on two feet and one hand, the saber tight in the other. Baru wanted her to have it. Aminata was sure she was going to give the saber back; she was only unsure which end she would lead with.

"Secure the egress!" an officer bellowed. "Make way for men coming abovedecks! Don't shoot any Falcresti, you rat fucks! Beware the drugged, they've gone berserk down there!"

Two masked marines flung open the hatch at the top of the stairs.

Aminata opened her mouth to hail them, to call out her name and rank and posting. Aminata isiSegu. Brevet-Captain. RNS *Ascentatic.*

And saw herself as if from outside. Filthy, wild-eyed with drug, out of uniform, clambering up the stairs on two legs and an arm. A madwoman. A savage with a sword.

It would have hurt less if she hadn't seen it coming.

"Burner!" one of the marines shouted.

And the other marine, without hesitation, shot her.

The bolt struck her straight in the breastbone, exactly where Tain Shir's spear had landed. But she was not wearing armor now. The steel bodkin point went through her canvas shirt like fog. A broadhead or a spring razor would have punched a five-inch apple core into heart and lungs. The bodkin was meant to go through armor and when it struck her breastbone it split it like a gemstone along a clean line, pierced the fatty sweetbread-meat in her thymus below, and came to rest just above the top of her heart.

She fell back down the stairs to the landing. The saber landed pommel-first against her stomach. Her head struck the teak flooring and all the bruises left by her fight with Masako exploded. Queen's cunt, she thought. I've been shot. What did she do now? She had to want to live. That was what separated marines who survived disembowelment from marines who died of a scratch. The will to live.

But her own marines had shot her. She'd called for them to save her and they'd shot her. At least it wasn't a gut shot. But the bolt would be poisoned, wouldn't it? Wouldn't it? And her kidneys . . . there was no point struggling.

No! She wanted to live! She wanted to live!

She'd given her word as a daughter of the isiSegu. And the navy had killed her for it.

Meaningless, Tau had warned her. Senseless.

T HIS will be a bilateral frontal lobotomy to correct recurrent epileptic seizures," I dictated. "The patient is a twenty-two-year-old Souswardi woman—"

"Your Excellence," Iscend whispered, "someone's coming. The guards haven't stopped her. I think it's Governor Aurdwynn."

I ducked out of the surgical tent and jerked the curtain shut, just in time to hide the grim tableau from Heingyl Ri. Tearstains made her face shine like lacquer.

"Yawa." She stared up into my mask as if it were my real face. "You killed him."

"Oh, Heia." I reached up to unbuckle my mask. "I wanted to tell you myself, but—"

She slapped me. The mask slammed shut on its hinges and boxed my nose. I made a sound of contempt, purely by reflex, and she slapped me again, so hard my ear crushed against the hard ceramic.

"You killed him," she cried, "and you're going to *lie* about it? After everything we did together, you decide to lie *now*?"

"Breathe," I begged her, which was the Incrastic advice, and she took it as the patronizing nonsense it was.

"Why would I breathe? Why would I be calm? You murdered my husband! He was in your way so you killed him and now you want me to *understand*?"

There was only one thing I could do. And if she took it as a lie she would think me lost beyond all hope of redemption.

"I swear on Himu and Devena and Wydd, three virtues for one good life, that I had nothing to do with Bel's murder. I'm glad it happened. I might have ordered it myself, in time. But I did not do this. Do you hear me? I did not kill Bel!"

She twisted there in front of me, breathing in hitches. And then the fury went out of her like pus from a wound. She believed. She knew I would never take the ykari in vain, and now it was even worse. Because if it was not my fault, then it was either—

"Baru." She bit the word off so hard I heard her teeth click. "She's done this."

"No."

"She has, she's murdered Bel, she hates him and she wants me—"

"Heia," I sighed, "look in here."

I showed her the arrangement inside the cabin.

Heia gaped at me. "But she was your . . . she was like me, your student. . . ."

"No," I said. "She *wasn't* like you. I would never do this to you."

And I watched poor Haradel Heia, Ri-daughter of the Stag Duke, understand that what had happened to her husband was her own fault. She'd kept her father's guard in her employ. Three of them had tried to murder her. Still she'd kept her father's guard close. And one of them, tormented by an omen of stag and catamount, had killed her husband.

"Oh, Devena," she moaned. And she was out the door before I could even offer comfort.

I closed my eyes. She would survive it. She would do her duty. I knew she could do it, because she could do anything I could do.

I fastened my mask and went back into the surgical tent. Iscend Comprine waited with her instruments. She would prepare the maniple to perform the cuts, so Hesychast would know there had been no error or deception. I would supply the telescoping orbitoclast I favored for its precision.

"If you killed him," I warned her, "don't tell me."

"Your Excellence," she said, "I do not know what you mean. Shall we begin again?"

THIS will be a bilateral frontal lobotomy to correct recurrent epileptic seizures," I dictated. "The patient is a twenty-two-year-old Souswardi woman with a history of Oriati emotional disease, hemineglect complicated by epilepsy, and self-managed tribadism. The patient holds an Imperial-grade savant mark in abstract reasoning and self-discipline, and a polestar mark earned by paramount service to the Throne. It is my sincere hope that after a period of recovery, the patient will recover the full use of these distinctions."

Iscend recorded my words in her memory house. As Clarified she was considered a faultless witness in Imperial court.

"Begin," I ordered.

"Commencing left frontal insertion." She turned the handle that drove the orbitoclast into the bone behind Baru's left eye. I had brought my sarcophagus in from *Helbride*, a full-body conditioning tool which held Baru so securely that not even her toes could move. A light tsusenshan anesthetic kept her from struggling. That was against lobotomy protocol, which required a conscious patient, but after thousands of trials on prisoners I thought I could be allowed some deviation in the name of keeping Baru still. An error as small as a hair would be catastrophic.

I did not intend to err today.

"Depth," Iscend said, as the orbitoclast pierced Baru's eye socket and entered her brain. "Ready for cuts."

I made one last inspection of the maniple. Then, with Iscend watching every move, I extended the telescoped inner needle to its full length within Baru's brain.

"Ready?" I asked Iscend.

She nodded. "Ready."

"Commencing left frontal lobotomy."

I triggered the maniple to begin its sequence of cuts. By pivoting the stylus around its point of entry, the device would cut certain connections in Baru's brain. The first cut was a dramatic sweep upward, against the bones of the orbital roof.

I watched the maniple do exactly that: and then all the rest of the careful, subtle intercisions I had programmed. I was completely confident.

"Movements complete?" I asked Iscend.

"Movements complete," she verified. "I saw the maniple perform the correct series of motions."

"Withdraw the orbitoclast."

She extracted the stylus from Baru's eye socket. Her eyeball settled back into position, sealing the wounded bone away from the world.

But when the orbitoclast emerged, slick with blood and fluid, I saw that it had snapped off during the maniple's movements. Only the T-shaped base and the larger bone-piercing needle remained. The telescoped inner needle was still lodged inside Baru's brain.

"Shit," I sighed, and then, wearily, "gaios, don't transcribe that."

"I shan't transcribe that," Iscend said.

"Well, it's sterile. It'll keep in there. No sense fishing around and risking damage."

I fixed a second orbitoclast and prepared to perform the same operation on Baru's right eye. "Commencing right frontal insertion."

INTERLUDE

THE MANSION HUSSACHT

THE sight of home took Svirakir's breath away.

"Atmospheric pressure," he panted. "You get up this high and—the air's thinner. But it doesn't—bother me. I'm bred—for it."

His guide watched him through sheepskin and furs, a halo of fuzz around sunburnt skin and pale eyes. The wisp of hide below her chin gave her a goatlike mien. "You should rest."

"No, no," he pretended to pant, "let's keep going." He was certain she was walking him into a trap, and he did not want to be late for it. The panting was to convince her that he was weak, and, despite the long estoc sword on his left hip and the arming sword on his right, entirely defenseless.

He'd hired his goat-chinned guide in Duchy Vultjag, where he'd found Tain Hu's people not merely surviving the Stakhieczi conquest but thriving off it. It was the futures contracts that had done it. Vultjag had secured its grain in advance, and the Radascine Combine merchants in the south had, despite the invasion and the edicts against sending food north, honored that contract: either they delivered to Vultjag at the agreed-upon price, or they had to sell at cut rate to the provincial government. It was worth the cost of smuggling the grain, especially if there would not *be* a grain market in a year.

Vultjag was, therefore, the only duchy in the north with a supply of grain. While the rest of the north paid obscene premiums for the leavings of ransacked granaries, Tain Hu's people were grinding more flour than they could eat. So they sold their surplus to those who had too much gold and not enough bread.

The Stakhieczi invaders had quickly learned that they could not take the bread by force. Mansion Chechniada, the Avalanche House, had sent fighters to seize the Vultjag granaries—and been bloodied so badly in jagisczion forest ambush that they ended up paying weregild just to get their column out of the woods alive. The Stakhieczi trained for close tunnel fighting and open-field war against cavalry. Both required close formations, iron discipline, and very little woodscraft. They had no answer to swift, harrying rangers except to burn the villages and kill the people—and that would cost them the granaries, too.

So those same rangers were now doing very well as hired scouts and hunting guides for the invaders. Svir had made it known in Vultjag that he needed a guide into the mountains, and waited for one of the pathfinders to approach him.

Goat Face had come.

Now he dawdled in the shadow of the col, studying the two peaks, this home he'd missed with all his heart and hoped to never see again. The clean stone, the clear air, the sheer *space* of it all. There was Camich Swiet on the left, the Sugar Peak, named for the shining snowpack on its summit. It held no actual sugar: a treasure rarer than salt and more precious than platinum.

And Karakys on the right, where he had spent so many sunny days playing on the freeze-dry terraces, or building luges for fatally swift sleds. Eagles soared here, high above the green line where the last trees grew. A round-faced fox had been dogging their trail, which was an omen of procht, the Stakhi word for *things which come of thinking*. Procht might intimate a well-timed hunting foray or a clever new climbing route. It might also mean treachery afoot. Svir wasn't hunting for condor eggs or scouting out a place to abseil, so he expected this fox was an omen of treachery.

Treacherously beautiful. That was a good word for the Wintercrests. In High Stakhieczi that was one word, muticzi. The same word used for a false thaw. "Treacherous summer."

"Bring me home," he told Goat Face.

They zagged their way upslope, as if intending to crest the col and then turn right, up the length of the ridge toward Karakys. The boulder field was exactly as he remembered it. He stooped to look for a place where he'd cut his name: but cold had cracked the stone.

"Up here," Goat Face called, "quickly, now, or you'll burn raw red. The sun is fiercer here. Come!"

Svir crested the col. And gasped in awe. He had a perfect view of the erbajaste, the dry lake bed between the two mountains. The clay shimmered flat and cracked as human skin. The great flocks of orange flamingos had gone away. He'd chased those stupid promenading birds as a boy, with Pirilong at his side. Later they'd been lovers—he and Pirilong, not he and the flamingos—in the summer fields north of the lake, where they could explore each other without his brother or Pirilong's disapproving parents trying to make them reform. *You're too old for this, Svir, you need to find a woman with a womb. . . .*

He'd been manful about it, at first. He'd stood and she'd knelt and he'd touched her toasted-grain curls and the low bones of her cheeks in wonder.

But he hated the etiquette of it, the requirement to penetrate but never yield. They ran *together,* side by side; not above and below. And when at last he knelt she never tried to stop him: although it would woman Svir, and man Pirilong, and throw both of them into danger, for Svir was a Prince of the Mansions, and as his brother kept reminding him, a woman, with or without a womb, could not be a Prince.

He wondered if he'd see Pirilong again. He wondered if she was still a woman. Or if the Masquerade tide had licked its way up the mountains, and convinced everyone to give up the bad old ways in favor of the bad new.

Silver reflection caught his eye. Like the bracelet Baru had used to signal him, back in Annalila Fortress. His eyes went by reflex to the light: the glint of steel.

There was an army camped down there.

"Oh kings," Svir breathed. "It's the fucking Uczenith." Mansion Hussacht's ancestral rivals had laid siege to his brother's throne. And there were no Hussacht jagata to challenge them. They had all gone to war.

"I was paid to show you this," Goat Face called. "They had me wait for you, in Vultjag. They told me to bring you here."

She'd moved away from him, out of reach of a knife and a lunge. The sun glinted off the smear of yak butter around her cracked lips. "They needed to know if the woman who promised your return was telling the truth."

"Oh, I know," Svir said. "The Uczenith paid you. No hard feelings." His return would be a victory for his brother, and the Uczenith could not allow that. "You'd better run, now. They'll kill you, too, when they've finished with me."

"What procht," a man called. "Betray our guide? Go back on our word? You *are* lost to the mansions, Svirakir. Seduced by the world and its low ways."

"Better we spare your brother the grief of knowing it," another man said.

Four jagata fighters in steel plate rose from their hides among the boulders. They had him squared, one at each compass point: and they were armed with long blades and short triangular stabbing swords. Tunnel-fighting weapons. Masquerade "experts" liked to say they were forged to make triangular wounds, but the truth, as with most things Stakhi, was simpler. The triangular blade gave the sword strength to punch through armor. They would use those blades to crush Svir's face before they cut him apart.

"Hello, boys," he said, smiling at the shadows under their sun visors. "Let me guess what I've missed. My return would prove my brother's a worthy and Necessary king, and you Uczenith can't have that. So you'll stab me to death, destroy my face, and throw my pieces down a crevasse. Right?"

"That's right," the first one said. Goat Face had vanished in the scree.

"I've found the legitimate heir to your mansion," Svir said. "I know who killed Kubarycz the Iron-Browed in single combat." That made the men halt for a moment, crouching like they felt a tremor in the rock. "It was a man named Tain Hu. Tain Hu, Duke of Vultjag, consort of the rightful Queen of Aurdwynn. He killed Kubarycz and all his heirs. He won the right to rule you. I serve Tain Hu's house, I serve his queen, and that means I serve the legitimate lord of the Mansion Uczenith. That means I serve *your* rightful lord. Now you will *damn* well remember our oaths and listen to me—"

The jagata looked at each other. Despite their codes of honor, knights were, in Svir's experience, a lot of thugs, rapists, and brutes. But would they kill a Prince of the Mansions to conceal what had happened to Kubarycz? Were they *that* craven—

"Kill him quick," one of the jagata said.

"Aye," the next said.

"Aye."

"Aye."

"You people are satires," Svir snarled, and went for his flare pistol.

Four longswords rose against him. He would break out north: unarmored, he would be faster climbing the slope, but not *much* faster. He had seen armored jagata do somersaults and handstands in their plate, and free-climbing rock faces was a basic knightly skill.

He shot the northern jagata in his armored face, dropped the pistol, and charged.

The man ducked his head by reflex and took the rocket on his helm. Goat Face was screaming, "Procht! Murder! They're murdering the Prince! They're murdering Tain Hu's Prince!" Svir grinned wildly—so the brigand bitch of Vultjag still lived in her people's hearts! He should've mentioned Tain Hu to Goat Face sooner—

He brushed past the knight. The cold clean air burnt his throat. For an instant he was a boy again, dashing with Pirilong across the seam in the world where the sky met the earth.

The jagata got him by the back of the belt.

The trick knot at Svir's waist let go and the belt slithered off. The North Knight stumbled back, suddenly off balance. Svir, whirling, drawing, lifted the pointed estoc sword to high ox guard, gripped it halfway down the blade with his left hand, and, with his strong right, thrust the sword into the seam between the knight's helmet and his collar. There were not many ways to instantly kill a man, and the narrow estoc blade made small deep wounds: but the throat would do.

But there *was* no seam. The knight had an armored bevor, one solid piece protecting his neck and jaw, and it stopped even the estoc's hardened point cold. He grabbed for Svir's shirtfront—seized it, pulled him close, lifted his own sword for Svir's stomach—Svir, as he'd been trained, flipped the estoc around, and, gripping it by the midsection and its tip, swung the pommel down like a hammer on the knight's helmet. The mordstrike left the North Knight dazed, and a dazed tunnel fighter always crouches, gets his guard up, and waits.

There was no time to fight. Unarmored longsword duels ended in one or two strokes: the first cross and the first, usually fatal, counter. There were four of them and they all had armor so Svir was the only one who would be dying in two strokes here. He tore away and ran. Three jagata came after him, silent but for the actuation of steel. Goat Face was still screaming murder.

Someone up ahead answered. Svir scrambled up the ridge toward Karakys, and down toward him came a man, a beautiful young Maia cavalryman in leather chaps, his narrow hips and powerful legs scrambling on the scree. "Svir-akir!" he cried. "Svirakir, to me!"

It was either salvation or a trap. Svir, always gambling on trap, jagged north, across the ridgeline, into the wind shadow—

—and found the West Knight waiting for him, swift on familiar ground.

The longsword came up off his shoulder and down on Svir like a bar of dawn. He half-sworded the estoc and parried with both hands but the huge longsword smashed the estoc down onto his chest, drove him to his knees. If Svir had not dropped one end of the estoc the West Knight would have simply ground the sword into Svir's face and neck. As it was the block turned the longsword away to the left—but the bigger blade caught one of the estoc's parrying spurs and ripped it from Svir's hands.

No hesitation. Svir lunged from his knees and tackled the armored man. If he could get his arming sword out, wedge it through the man's visor—

The West Knight headbutted him. Steel obliterated sight: Svir lost motor control. An armored gauntlet smashed him in the ear and smote him to the rock. His blood gushed over stone. "Fuck!" he bellowed, and kicked the jagata in the crotch, doing nothing. "Fuck you! Kill me now and the whole world will know! You've been seen murdering me! The guide knows it, that man knows it—will you lie? Will you lie, now, about who you killed here? I am a Prince! I am the brother of the Necessary King!"

The West Knight looked down at him in disgust. Finally, breathing evenly, barely winded, he sheathed his sword. "You live," he said, "by procht alone."

The Maia cavalryman swam into Svir's wavering vision. "In the name of the King, leave that man be!"

The four assassins closed their sun visors and marched contemptuously down toward the Uczenith camp. The cavalryman helped Svir to his feet. "Thanks," Svir said, beaming bloodily at him. "Shame we didn't get to fight it out. Would've been an interesting matchup. To whom do I owe my continued life?"

"Ihuake Ro," he said, grinning back. He was a pretty fuck, wasn't he? Those folded eyes. "You're Svirakir? The eunuch's been promising your arrival. The king had given up all hope of your return. There's been fighting. Bad fighting. We aren't ready for winter. He hopes you'll make a difference."

"I see we both have good timing," Svir panted. "I don't like last-second reprieves—"

"Nothing last-second about it," the cavalier said. "Your brother's weather-woman Ochtanze gets word from agents in Vultjag. She knew you'd arrive today. We were supposed to meet you downslope, before you were ambushed."

"But?"

"But there was a cave-in. Probably sabotage. Another act of Uzenith, ah" —he pursed his lips around the strange word—"procht. I had to climb up an air shaft."

Svir dusted himself off. Mustn't look disheveled in front of the horseman. "I've brought my brother a bride. And a political weapon to make the Uczenith shit their guts out. This matter of their rightful lord."

"A bride," the horseman said. His dark face hardened. "The bride is Heingyl Ri?"

Svir smiled fixedly at him, mind tunneling, trying to deduce what angle this man Ihuake Ro would take. "Yes. Heingyl Ri, Governor of Aurdwynn."

"That madman Dziransi says he had a prophecy. A dream from the hammer."

Svir had to laugh. "Did he, now?"

"Dziransi's certain that a woman will be brought here. To prove the King's vengeance is inescapable. You didn't bring a woman named Baru, did you?"

"No," Svir said. "Just myself. And important news. Tell me, Mister Ihuake Ro, what brings *you* to our high mountains? Anything I can help with?"

"I am searching for allies to free my ancestral duchy." Now those cocky brown eyes were wary. "My companion Nayauru Aia makes suit for the king's hand. I protect her."

"Then we both have an interest in preserving the king?"

"We have interests in the king. They may not be common interests."

"Have you thought about going over to those bastards?" Svir suggested, pointing to the shining army in the lake bed, the Uczenith in all their cynical grandeur.

"Of course not," Ro snapped. "I know exactly what happens when a Necessary King falls. I've never liked thieves, rapists, or tyrants. Your people will be all that to us and more."

He was sharp, then. "Are you any good in a fight, Ihuake Ro?"

The cavalier smiled hungrily. "Better than you, Prince Svirakir."

Svir felt the lightning.

Long ago, in a faraway place, a secret fire had passed through Svir's body. It had *aligned* something in him . . . something that thundered in the empty spaces of his mind. Whenever he didn't know what to do, that palefire leapt within him, and a solution came.

His brother was at reign's end. His home mansion was invested by its oldest foe. When his brother was scalped of his crown, the Stakhieczi would run rampant in Aurdwynn until starvation and plague scattered them.

But the lightning told him that he was *not* going to die here. The lightning told him that he had a destiny across the farthest sea.

"I'll handle the procht and politics," he said. "There may be some legalities to resolve . . . it may require bloodshed. If it comes to trial by combat, you'll be my champion."

"Champion in what cause, Your Highness?"

Svir looked up at his brother's mountain: the mountain of his past. "A marriage," he said. "The strangest web of marriages you ever did see."

He looked around for Goat Face. She was gone. He began to walk uphill, into the katabatic wind. Ihuake Ro sighed and followed him.

Svir opened his mouth to the cold onrushing air. He began to sing.

On the lake below, speartips whirled in white sun-tip arcs. The drilling Uczenith phalanxes presented their faces to all sides, surrounded by imaginary foes, surrounded as the Stakhieczi were always surrounded, by drought, by dissent, by white cold death.

NOW

I'VE been lobotomized?" she says. "My parents exiled me, and then I was lobotomized? That's what happened?"

Cairdine Farrier is weeping. He nods, tries to speak, and makes a sound like a hiccup instead. He has to swallow and wipe his eyes before he can talk.

"I'm so sorry, Baru. I never wanted this. You made the hard choice about your lover, and you deserved the world for it. Not more . . . not more cruelty. Not more loss."

"But I won." She wrinkles her brow in confusion, in dismay. "It's not fair. I remember now . . . I found the Cancrioth. I learned all about them. I tricked them into giving up a map . . . we were going to trade with them. The way you traded with Sousward, to bring us into the Imperial Republic. I even tricked them into giving us Abdumasi Abd. I did everything you asked."

"You did wonderfully." Farrier's fine beard cannot hide his trembling lips, his scowl of fury. "You brought home your goal and more. Yawa failed to retrieve a viable sample of the vile cancer. *She* should be sent back to Aurdwynn in bottles!" He chokes back his anger. "She failed. But . . ."

"But?"

"But this is the Throne, Baru. You made one mistake. You didn't have leverage to keep Yawa from destroying you. It was petty and vindictive and wasteful, but she knew you were going to win the Reckoning of Ways, destroy her master, and cost her everything.

"So she lobotomized you."

In the straitjacket she can only move her head and her hands. She closes her fists over the carved eels on the armchair's rests, and pricks her fingers with their teeth. "I had a plan, Mister Farrier, I had a glorious plan . . . a trade concern . . . I was going to set up a trade concern. . . ."

Farrier falls still. She knows, from watching Svir do it so many times, that he is withdrawing to his place of absolute strength, the foundation of his mind, where he can separate his foolish instincts from the things he *needs* to do.

"It can still happen," he says. "We'll do it together, Baru. I own twenty entire business concerns, with all their subsidiaries and investments. I would have to pull a stack of files as tall as you are just to remember all the men and women I can influence or possess. I have a fleet of ships with captains who are indebted to me. We'll go to the Black Tea Ocean. We'll buy sugar and coffee and tea and spices and fabric and everything else Falcrest wants. We'll sell shares in our concern so that every would-be tycoon with two children and a nice house buys a ticket for a piece of our wealth. We will go to the Oriati and buy them out and trade them down until they wear the mask. And when Oriati Mbo goes to war with itself—when the Cancrioth calls for our destruction, and the Oriati split between those who fear us and those who need us—we'll be the ones to save their children from their own savagery. It's going to *work*, Baru!"

His eyes run with a different kind of tears. Like a man looking straight at the sun. Scalded by the power of his vision.

"Kindalana," Barhu says.

Farrier's eyes narrow. There is a part of him that he cannot open up, an inner overseer who will never join in his grief or in his joy, and it rises from its seat. "What?"

"She's your tool, isn't she? I learned all about her. Kindalana the Amity Prince . . . she's going to lead the Mbo to Falcrest."

"That's right, Baru. She's worked her whole life to convince the Oriati to federate, to join the Imperial Republic." He grins a little, the chiding father amused by his daughter's rudeness. "But she's her own woman, Baru. Not my 'tool.'"

"What about me?" Barhu whispers. "I can't be your tool. I'm broken now. . . ."

"No, no, you're *not*!" He grips her hands with crushing sincerity. "I've been reading about lobotomies. People have survived to lead good lives! Oh, kings, Baru, people have lived their entire lives with cysts the size of melons in their brains, and no one even *knew* until their autopsy! You'll need an aide, someone to help you. Not one of those awful Clarified. A real person. But you can still do figures and watch plays and read books and do *everything* else a brilliant young woman deserves. And nobody will come after you now. Nobody ever. I'll keep you safe. I promise."

"Promise?" She grips his hand desperately.

"I promise," he whispers. "I really do." And she knows she has him.

"How can I help you?"

He looks down, ashamed of himself. "You don't need to do anything now, Baru. You've done enough."

"But I do. I remember. You told me that the doctors said to let me sleep but you had to wake me up. Because you needed to know about the Cancrioth. . . ."

"You've told me of the Cancrioth. How you turned the crew against the Brain and made a deal with the Eye. How you sent them away to open the route for our ships."

"No . . . there's something else. The rutterbook? Do you have the Cancrioth rutterbook?"

"Xate Yawa says she has it. But never fear. We'll get it back. Hesychast can't keep it from me, not if he wants to use it. I'm the one with the ships."

"Hesychast . . ." She lets her eyes bulge in their swollen sockets, and her body leap up against the straitjacket. "Hesychast's won! He won the Reckoning of Ways! Mister Farrier, he's going to get Renascent's blackmail files, he's going to *control* you!"

"Not yet. Not yet, Baru." The absolute calm, the dread excitement, of a man with nothing to lose by his failure and everything to gain by the deft use of his influence and skill. "We can make the case to Renascent that *we* triumphed. Your education never failed, after all. You kept faithful to me." A sob of pride, as naked as he has ever been to any other human being. "You were out there all alone with no one to help you. And you remembered your lessons. You could've strayed, run off with some woman, bought a ship and gone home to Taranoke to rot away in a coconut-roofed hut. But you did your work, you came home. . . ."

"Don't be sentimental, Mister Farrier," she says, absently. "I have an idea how to strengthen our position. Would you like to hear it?"

He nods eagerly.

"Abdumasi Abd," she says. "We can use him, Mister Farrier."

He smiles with convincing interest. She is close to his secret and it makes him leery. "How?"

"He's a very influential merchant. We announce our new trade concern, to ease fears of war. We have the Emperor Itself endorse our monopoly on the new trade. We have Abdumasi Abd present to show that the Oriati are fully in support of our venture—and the rest of the Throne will know that control over Abd means influence over his sponsors. By threat of their revelation to the world. This will demonstrate the strength of our position both politically, and, ah, covertly."

"Baru, that's brilliant."

"Yes. A public announcement of the new trade, with Abd present, with Tau-indi Bosoka and as many other Oriati dignitaries as you can gather. It will signal to Parliament that we've forced concessions from the Mbo. It'll show Renascent that your methods have full control of the Oriati situation."

"But how do we keep control of Abd?" Farrier muses. He has not a single qualm about using this man who he drove to ruin, of course. "How can we ensure he follows our playbill?"

"His divorced wife. Make it clear that Kindalana's in your power, Mister Farrier. Make her attend the announcement. She'll add to your credibility. And Abd won't dare disobey you so long as you have Kindalana in your influence. You *do* have leverage over her, I'm sure?"

Now Farrier hesitates—now he feels the danger, brushing at his whiskers, laughing from the dark—but if he hesitates here he will reveal he is threatened.

And Barhu is certain there's a part of him that thrills at the idea of parading Kindalana in plain view of the world: mine, my Prince, my Oriati princess, mine, not yours, mine.

"I could ask Kindalana to be present," he says. "We maintain a cordial relationship."

"Good," Barhu says. "And do you foresee success for this new trading concern?"

"Success? *Success?* Baru, this trading concern is going to rule half the *world*. We'll have our own navy, and our own banks, and our own historians, because"—he laughs, giddy—"two hundred years from now, this concern will still be solvent. It will live beyond us and carry on our work. They'll name ships for us, now and always. Do you like that? The fine ship *Baru Cormorant*, pride and flag of our fleet."

"I like it," she says, sadly. "I like it very much."

He is so disappointed by her sudden scowl, so disappointed that he cannot make her smile, that he punishes himself with a sharp tug at his beard. "What is it? What can I do?"

"All I ever wanted," she whispers, "was for you to beat Hesychast. To save my home from him."

"But I will. What does he have, Baru? Some pedigrees, some specimens. We are about to crack an entire continent like an egg and drink the yolk! You *made* that, Baru. You won for me." He shakes her affably, trying to be paternal: but with a fearful tenderness. "I won't rest until I can show you how grateful I am."

"I just wish that I could do more to help. Anything."

"Listen, Baru, how would you like a place of honor in the ceremony? Just tell me."

She raises her eyes to him. Very slowly, she smiles that old and wicked smile.

"There is one thing," she admits, "that I've always dreamt of. . . ."

VICTORY

Life in Falcrest is pure
Knives grow sharp
Glass becomes clear. Water runs cold
The hearts of the dead
Are white like fish

THE city of Falcrest waited without patience for its future to arrive. Testimony had been delivered. Parliament had convened, performed, and retired. In two days the Emperor would announce the results of the inquiry into the Oriati attack on Aurdwynn.

Speculation turned like spinning coins, face and number and face again. There had been a conspiracy against the Republic: no, there had been an opportunistic pirate raid. There had been a mastermind, a financier from the Mbo with ties to royalty; no, there had only been a syndicate admiral with dreams of plunder. There would be war; there would not. And in either case there would be money to be made. People came to the Oriati Embassy with condolences, concerns, and sleekly disguised schemes for profit.

But the Prince-Ambassador was not there.

Tau-indi was down in Brine City, the sprawling immigrant slums across the River of Qualms, pushing two wheelchairs up Hwacha Hill, to the house of the Amity Prince. The chairs were marvels of leather, steel, and wicker from the Navy School of Heroic Medicine.

One wheelchair carried Abdumasi Abd, whose recent surgery had paralyzed him forever.

The other chair carried Aminata, stitched together around the crossbow wound on her heart. She was marooned ashore on half pay while the navy waited for her health to recover. Then she would face court-martial.

Tau was not built to push them both at once, especially Aminata, who was a hundred and seventy pounds of muscle and trapped energy. Fortunately, their faithful bodyguard had come along to help, untroubled by rumors that the Prince had suffered terrible disgrace. A cadre of local youth paced them warily, afraid they were part of some complex Judiciary sting. But when they saw Enact-Colonel Osa's rope-wrapped fists they came out to show their own corded hands, done in imitation of a Jackal soldier. Osa gave them all firm warrior forearm-clasps. Together they got the chairs up the hill, to the triangular house wedged between the Zero School for Federati and the open-fronted Ember's Restaurant.

"I'm going to crawl back to her," Abdumasi muttered.

"No, you're not, Abdu."

"I am. She told me if I came back, I'd better come back crawling, and I'm going to do exactly that."

"She'd never want you to do that if she knew you were using a wheelchair!"

"Why, because she's so enlightened? Because she'd never take advantage of a cripple? She married me knowing it was already doomed, Tau! She knew the whole time! She's ruthless!"

"Abdu, please don't go home angry. . . ."

"I told you, I'm going back crawling. Kinda!" Abdumasi slid out of his chair, and, fingers jammed between the flagstones, began to pull himself down the walk. "Kinda, I'm home, just like you said I'd be!"

Tau watched in terrified anticipation: trim was nothing but other people, and if Kindalana did not see Abdumasi as a person anymore, truly they were all lost. . . .

The door cracked open.

"Abdu?" the woman in the doorway said. "Tau? *Tau?*"

This was the moment, the meeting, where the needle went into the lip of the wound and drew the first suture across. If anything Tau believed had any power at all, the world might be healed in microcosm. The small *was* reflected in the large, the meek *did* have power to move the great, a kind word to a stranger could alter the fate of nations: for the great was made out of the small, and the world was made out of people.

Kindalana wore a pale yellow silk sherwani and loose trousers. She'd done up her hair into four long rows and tucked the braids into a bun. She was beautiful enough to belong in the sort of novel where a mysterious man wept over her painting, in love with a woman he did not know: but she was far too lively. You could never capture her in plaster. And her eyes were as wide apart as Tau remembered.

"Abdu," she said, "what are you *doing?*"

"I'm home!" Abdumasi shouted. "Back from my adventures in revenge! Got tortured, got cancer, got paralyzed, now here I am!"

"What have you *done* to yourself, you fool!"

She tried to help her ex-husband up from the flagstones, as he tried, sobbing, to embrace her around the waist, so that they fell together back into the house, swearing at each other.

Tau smiled at Aminata. "You brought us here, you know."

She grimaced and rubbed her breastbone. "Sure."

"You did. I'd be dead at least twice without you: burnt once by *Sulane*, then burnt again at Annalila Fortress. And if you hadn't shown me how trim brought you and Baru together, I'd still be turned in on myself, wallowing."

"Didn't do Baru much good," Aminata whispered.

"Trust in trim, Aminata. Baru will be all right."

"I don't see how. She was lobotomized."

On the night when Tau had told Baru the entire story of Prince Hill, a story about ash and trim, Baru had shared in turn her hope of overcoming Cairdine Farrier. She had already deduced most of the secret: what she needed now was not Tau's information but Tau's friendship. She was not willing to force the matter on Kindalana; rather, Baru wanted to leave the choice to her. She had asked Tau and Abdumasi to go to Kindalana, and to petition her to use the weapon she had prepared.

It was a powerful weapon, and this plan *was* the right moment to use it. But Tau would not themself have dared. Not only was this trade concern a heinous gamble with the future of the entire Oriati Mbo, a gamble which could mean the exploitation and devastation of millions and the subjugation of Oriati history beneath the mask, but it would put an innocent at terrible risk.

But Tau had empowered Baru to represent the Mbo, and if they believed Baru had inherited all their trim (which they did), they had to trust Baru's decisions as they would trust their own.

Which was to say: they would trust her decision, but they would run it by Kindalana first.

"Come inside with us," Tau said, beckoning to Aminata.

She grimaced horribly. The pain in her breast was getting worse. Sometimes she screamed so loud in the night that Tau wanted to kiss her lips closed and never let go.

She would never trust her marines again. She would never trust her navy. She would never trust the people who had asked everything of her and then shot her for it.

Like Tau, she had lost everything that gave her life meaning. Tau was determined to see her live on with the hurt.

She shook her head now. "I can't go into a Federal Prince's house. Not right to fraternize with royalty."

"Aminata, it's my friend Kindalana's house." Tau pouted. "Are you going to refuse my friend's hospitality?"

Aminata grumbled and rubbed her sternum.

"Aminata!" Tau barked. She leapt in the wheelchair. "Didn't I bring your sword back when you were shot? Didn't I watch over you as you healed? Didn't I tell them you were a hero of the peace?"

She stared up at them with unwilling gratitude and guilty resentment. "I'm not a traitor. I'm *not*. I can't just go into her house."

"Come in," Tau begged her. "All we're going to do here is tell each other the truth. Abdu's going to tell Kindalana why he went to the Cancrioth. And then Kinda's going to tell us why she made the choice that drove him away: the thing she did, before they were even married, and didn't tell him. And then I am going to apologize to both of them for my own mistakes, and for my self-ishness in putting my Princedom before our friendships.

"Then Abdu and I will explain what Baru's concern could do, and why we need Kindalana to make that concern work. Will you come and listen? You don't have to speak. Just hear us out. I promise you that it will give you a chance to see Baru again."

"You can't know that. You *can't*."

"No," Tau said, feeling the empty places where trim had once pulled at them, phantom connections, gone forever: and choosing, anyway, to act as if they still existed. Trim was nothing but other people.

Tau wished they could somehow bottle up everything they felt and give it to Aminata. The warmth, the hope and despair and unquenchable hope again that all would turn out well, or, if not well, at least as it had to be between humans. Between people.

"I can't know we'll make a difference to Baru," they said. "Or that Baru will make a difference to the world. But if I don't choose to believe it's possible, then it is certainly impossible. So what do we have to lose by hope?"

H E was waiting for me at the Nemesis Court.

Nemesis was an old word, and it meant much more than revenge. The mob that stormed IV Asric Falkarsitte's palace during the revolution had cried *nemesis, nemesis*: justice no mortal can escape. Now the Nemesis Court was made as incarnation of that spirit. The granite exterior was surfaced in panes of black onyx, cut so thin that it marbled like flesh. The billows of silk in the grand entrance gallery were fringed in raven feathers, treated to last, sharp enough to cut skin.

Hesychast awaited me beneath the wall of clocks.

There were a hundred and sixty-six of them. A murder clock, an arson clock, a patricide clock, and an infanticide clock. A clock for infidelity, a clock for extortion and for forgery and for sedition and for libel, a clock for incitement, a clock for riot; also clocks for the next election, the next great storm, the next harvest. The intervals were predicted by actuaries in Census and Methods. There remained uncertainty, of course. And most uncertain of all was the great clock at the far end of the gallery—

The Civilization Clock.

The Cheetah Palaces rose, and then they fell. The Jellyfish Eaters. The Mundo-Camou. The Enerive. The Far Ancient Columnaries, who'd built the pyramids and greatwells along the Mothercoast. The Belthyc. The Imperial Maia.

All risen, and all vanished.

The Civilization Clock counted the years till the next great collapse. Every year a judge would ceremonially wind it back a year, to celebrate the Republic's success. But it had not gained any ground since the Armada War: a permanent reminder of Falcrest's unfinished dominion.

"The clock for rebellion in Aurdwynn has been set to forty years," he said. He recognized me even through the black mask and the misshapen quarantine gown, of course. He would recognize me if my face were acid-burnt to a rind. Sometimes I thought he could smell people. "Long enough for two new generations to grow. One to inherit the fear of Baru's betrayal. One to rebel against their parents' caution."

"There won't be an Aurdwynn in forty years," I said, "if you release plague against the Stakhieczi."

"But you've prevented that, Yawa." He'd grown a short dark beard, close-shaved and aggressive. He wore a silk sherwani that showed nothing and suggested everything. His trousers must've been tailored to the exact contours of his perfect ass; you could not quite see his cock but you could tell he wore it left. He was magnificent. He horrified me.

"It remains to be seen if we succeeded," I said. "If Dziransi made it safely, if he can persuade the king to accept Baru as dowry . . . then there's a chance. But what if we can't get Baru away from Farrier again?"

"Everything Farrier owns will be mine once the Reckoning is finished. I've encouraged him to act freely, call in favors while he has the chance. It'll help flush out his quieter friends." He offered his naked hand for my gloved shake. In older days, before the Metademe had infiltrated the places where the sodomites conducted their trade, a gloved hand meant a top and a naked hand meant a bottom. "How was your visit to the navy?"

I'd just been at the Admiralty, escorted through halls of chrysanthemum stone to the glaring lamp-and-mirror coldness of War Plot. I'd hand-delivered the letter from Svir asking Lindon Satamine to resign. He'd whooped in relief and left Ahanna Croftare with a very nautical "Enjoy the fucking dolphins, Ahanna!"

I supposed it was a sailor's saying. Croftare had greeted her promotion with intense wariness: she had the seat she'd craved, the Empire Admiralty that her career needed the way a fall needs a finish. But she was certain that I was setting her up for destruction.

"It went smoothly. Empire Admiral Croftare is aware that I possess enough evidence surrounding the Ormsment mutiny to destroy the entire Admiralty. She'll be suggestible. I asked her about—" I quibbled for a fatal moment over whether to relay this fact: do not hesitate, Yawa, don't let him see, he sees *everything*. "I suggested that the navy could make up for its recently curtailed income by providing older ships to escort and conduct new trade in the far west."

"A matter we can have Farrier manage, once we possess him."

"Yes." I hesitated, purposefully this time. "Ah . . ."

"Your brother's no better, no worse. I have him resting in the Metademe."

"Thank you. Abdumasi?"

"Be at ease. I won't vivisect him. After a brief physical, I released him to Tau's custody. I felt I . . ."

He shook all over, a frisson of deep, fleshy emotion. "I felt I owed them both that much," he said. "Follow me. I've made an appointment for a gown fitting, and I need to ask you a few questions."

The chime of one of the clocks pulled our footsteps into cadence. Amazing the things that your body does without your knowledge, the ways your flesh takes its cues from the world. There are no boundaries between things.

"Tell me about Faham Execarne's interference," he prompted.

I explained. "The Morrow Minister made an ill-advised attempt to board the Cancrioth ship. He sought a sample of the Kettling disease, so that we could begin work on a cure."

"Fool," Hesychast murmured. "The Kettling can't be cured. Incrastic hygiene is the only defense. Clean hands, gloves, and population surveillance." He saw my irritated glance, and touched the small of my back in apology. "I'm sorry for interrupting. Proceed."

"His attack failed." Execarne still thought the Cancrioth whale had detected his approach. It hadn't: Galganath was away in Cautery Plat harbor, planting glass vivariums full of cholera in the shellfish beds. That outbreak had been contained quickly and decisively. The Brain's test of our vigilance had failed.

It was my warning that had betrayed Execarne. The moment I learned the Cancrioth whale was out of position, I'd told the Brain that Execarne might make a raid on her ship.

"He and his party became trapped in *Eternal*. Powerful deliriants left them confused and unable to find a way out. Only swift action by the Brevet-Captain Aminata and *Sterilizer*'s marines extracted him. Thankfully, the Cancrioth chose not to retaliate. Perhaps they felt they'd humiliated Falcrest's best, and wanted to carry the story of their victory home."

I'd been furious with Execarne, of course. I'd threatened to have him tried for treasonous disregard of the Throne's imperatives. And he'd reminded me that I had no idea who he was; that he'd taken the name of a dead man from his station on the Llosydanes; that he was beyond my power to prosecute.

I'd warned him that I could seal an order for the Morrow Minister's arrest with my polestar mark. The full force of the Emperor's authority.

And he'd replied, calmly, that he had a polestar mark of his own to countermand mine.

I didn't know whether to believe him. He didn't fit in the list of cryptarchs we'd been given at the Elided Keep: only Stargazer and Renascent remained unknown, and I doubted he was either. But Baru was right. They *wouldn't* give total knowledge of the Throne's members to foreign-born federati just initiated months ago. They would only tell us enough to play our role out in the provinces.

"Mm." His hand rubbed small circles on my spine, displacing his anxiety into me. "You've done well, Durance."

"Renascent will be impressed, I trust?"

"Oh, no question." He had such absolute control that I knew the sudden, victorious clench of his fist was intentional. "We've won. Baru was the living proof. Farrier's process mutilated her so badly that her mind split in half. Her disintegration *proves* that his process doesn't produce perfect citizens, and it never will. The flesh rebels, Yawa. It reasserts its nature. When I tested her at the Elided Keep I saw how terribly she'd been divided. And from your reports and Iscend's testimony, she only got worse. She had to go mad to survive. The lobotomy was a mercy."

"Yes," I murmured. "Quite a mercy. You were satisfied with its conduct?"

"Iscend certified every cut you made." His body seemed to radiate a soft, even warmth, like a banked fire. He was leading me deeper into the Nemesis Court, past shelves of files and galleries of busts, showing me my new dominion. "Once Renascent hands over the files, I'll force Farrier to surrender Baru, and we'll send her to the Stakhieczi."

"Never to see her home again," I said, with some pity. "She was cast out by her own people, you know. Ritually exiled for betraying them."

"She won't have to live with that anymore."

"I doubt she cared, my lord."

But I cared. And I would have to live with my choices. I would always be the woman who'd betrayed her people for her own cruel idea of their salvation.

He felt me tense. "Your brother will heal, Yawa. When he sees what you've done for Aurdwynn, the Stakhieczi addicted to our grain and sugar, the peace secured . . . he'll understand."

"I wish I could believe you," I murmured.

He guided me into a dressing room. "Your tailors will fit you for a new judge's gown. I've arranged a place for you on the Nemesis Council, working under Judge-Minister Sabè Frowerer. I have a file on her which will let you influence her decisions—she's made a series of unwise publications under a pseudonym, and I was able to obtain the original manuscripts and match her handwriting. You'll be taking Judge Alimoon's old seat."

"What happened to Alimoon?"

"Retired happily." He winked at me. "It does happen. A life of civil service, and a well-deserved estate in the Selions waiting for him."

A good civil servant. Like Bel Latheman had been. Heia had been so certain, so *sure* it had been me who killed him. Hadn't I always been honest with her, even about the horrible things? For her to think I'd lie *now*—it was like she'd never known me at all.

I chewed that thought off at the knuckle. "Farrier's going to make his move soon. Are you prepared?"

"For his Oriati trade concern? By the time he's ready to move cargo, we'll own him and the whole venture. I wouldn't have let him take Baru if it could hurt us. He's failed in the only way that matters, Yawa. You defeated his masterwork. My technique defeated his. That's what Renascent will see."

"But he still has vendettas against you. Ways he can hurt you."

"Not with Renascent behind me."

"Is Renascent really an old woman?" I asked. "Someone told me so, at the Elided Keep. But Falcrest despises the old and fears the powerful woman . . . it's quite incredible to me that you'd follow her."

"She's not," Hesychast said, tersely.

"What? An old woman?"

"I'm not sure she's a person at all, any more. She made certain requests of me over the years, and—well. I speculate."

"What? Is she a parrot, then? A whale? Another tumor?"

"It's complicated. And taboo. We won't speak of it now."

"As you prefer." I settled myself on a stool to wait for the tailor. He knelt to help me remove my shoes, for measurements.

And then I was looking down into that perfect face, the black-ink eyebrows, the smooth planes of his high cheeks. I caught my breath despite myself. He was staring right into my eyes. I could feel his awareness like fingertips on every seam of my face.

"Yawa," he said, "I have a question for you."

"Yes?" I managed.

"Would you have turned, if I hadn't had Olake hostage? Would you have gone over to Baru?"

Oh, Wydd help me. Not this. Not now. I closed my eyes. "Baru was . . . compelling."

Skin brushed against metal. He was unfolding a compact mirror, holding it up to my face, tilting it. There was someone behind me! He was showing my face to someone waiting behind me—with a garrote, a knife, a pen waiting to record my every word—

"Farrier is going to seat Baru in a place of honor for his announcement," he said. "Do you know why, Yawa? Is it more than mere symbolism?"

"No. I know nothing of what he's doing."

"Have you gone over to Baru's side, Yawa? Is this all a ruse?"

"No," I whispered. Damn him. Damn him.

"Are you, even now, obeying Baru's plan?"

"No!"

He looked up to the person behind me.

"Iscend," Hesychast sighed, "is she telling the truth?"

TONIGHT, Baru," Farrier said. "It's all been made ready for tonight."

He had taken her out to a restaurant called The Misterkills to eat song-birds and brain. The crowd was all amutter with news. The Tahari prediction markets gave good odds for war. Six Admiralty officers had committed suicide, preferring a quick death to the exposure of their secrets as Parliament tidied up the navy for its use. A race mob had attacked the Tahari Spill, where certain more affluent Oriati federati lived; the city constabulary had already taken the families there into protective custody, and they would be resettled in the Brine City slums, where they could help improve the lot of their racemates. A dog had died in the fire and that had caused much public sorrow. The mob, all the rhetorics agreed, should have expressed its anger more civilly.

"Tonight," Barhu repeated, absently.

He touched her hand. "Are you all right?"

"Yes. The food's delicious." She took a spoonful of nihari, a stew of slow-cooked lamb meat and marrow with a side of lamb's brain. The restaurant had a balcony view straight down the manicured blue strip of the ner ab Physic, the Doctor's Canal, straight west between the Faculties and the Fleet Quarter, through the great docks, and out into the Sound of Fire. When she looked back the servers were bringing out the main course: songbirds drowned in oak-aged brandy and served searing hot in ceramic cups.

"Barbaric," Farrier said, with relish. "That's what I like about it. You're supposed to put your napkin over your face, like so," he showed Barhu, "so we don't have to see each other crunching and spitting out the little bones. But I never wear mine. It's against the spirit of things."

She watched him eat the first little songbird whole. "Barbaric," she said, echoing his words. "Because it reminds us of a time when we had to eat birds and mice to survive."

He smiled happily. There were little bones in his teeth. "You're still quite articulate, Baru. I'm not sure Yawa did a very good job."

"In recognizing the past," she said, "we see the improvements we've made to our present condition. As I do when I compare my childhood on Taranoke to my life today."

He bit down on another bird. The crunch crisp, the spurt of meat juice and brandy. Somehow he could do it with dignity. He spat pointed bone into his cup. The sky behind him was alive with signal fireworks, swooping kites, great murmurations of swallows and northern quelea. Barhu had to breathe deep to detect any trace of sewage or the sulfurous stink of a paper mill. It was hidden, but it was there.

"Have some," he urged her.

She took a spoonful from the cup of sheep brain. It felt like curdled yogurt and tasted like sweetbread and cinnamon, or caviar without the fishy taste. She liked it. "A touch heavy on the cinnamon, I think."

"Oh, like you'd know," Farrier teased. He liked it when she put on airs.

"If I am to save Falcrest," she said, "I ought to have a little of its culture."

"The food's not unsettling your stomach? I thought it might, after so long on a diet of . . ." He trailed off, and fussed uncomfortably with his napkin.

"Gruel," Barhu suggested. "Porridge spooned by nurses?"

"Yes."

"I haven't forgotten how to taste."

"I really did mean it, you know." He leaned closer. "When I told you in the Elided Keep that you'd saved Falcrest. I meant it with all my heart. When the Emperor announces our trade concern tomorrow, Renascent will know who deserves to drive the Empire forward."

Before they'd gone out, Farrier had sent a maid to lay out her outfit. He had not, of course, come to measure or dress her by himself. She knew exactly why. The modesty he observed in Barhu's case was her first clue toward his secret. It came from a very specific taboo.

"Oh, I'm proud of you." It burst out of him. He looked at his gore-stained napkin, as if it were less shameful than his feelings. "You wouldn't like my ugly thoughts, Baru. My doubts. My fears. On some nights it seemed Hesychast and his Clarified would take the future and I . . ." He shuddered. "I thought: what if he was right? What if people could *never* unlearn their fleshy nature? What if some behaviors had to be cut out as diseases, and some . . . some children had no future at all? Then I'd have wasted my life, all of it, on this foolish quest to find genius in places most of Falcrest would use like a condom and cast away . . . oh, pardon my obscenity." He sniffed. "Pardon my sentiment."

"Well," Barhu said, softly, "here I am. I asked my mother a question all those years ago, and now I've answered it."

The word *mother* made him frown. "What did you ask her?"

"Why you were powerful. Why Falcrest came to us and changed us. Why we didn't go to you, instead."

"What did she say?"

"She didn't know."

"Do you?"

"I think so, yes."

"Well, go on! Why did we go to Sousward? Why didn't Sousward come to us? Impress me!"

There was so much she could say. The matter of money, Falcrest's wholesale adoption of paper fiat notes and liquidity banking, which allowed them to move value more efficiently: you could not raise money from your people to fund an expedition if all their value was locked up in farmland and lumber and milk. But when it was stored in paper notes in banks then you could borrow from the people without actually taking their property.

There were the ships, the superb rigging and coppered hulls and the chemistry of citrus and salt that kept the crews alive to sail, and the fearsome laboratories that produced the Burn. There was the culture of desperate and

syncretic inadequacy, fear of the world outracing Falcrest, which had stolen
the best of Stakhieczi astronomy and Oriati scientific philosophy. And the culture of revolutionary bloodshed, willing to use living bodies to discover the
causes and cures of disease, to test which substances would do harm if used in
piping, food, cloth.

And Lapetiare and his coffeehouses, where the art of debate grew from
spectator sport to revolutionary spark, where the stockbrokers did their trading now. There were the pigs that gave Falcrest the annual flu, which made the
Masquerade's collective immunity so vigilant, which laid flat the populations
of every new province Falcrest seized. There were the canals and the water-
ways, the ancient expertise at managing tsunami and flood that became the
modern engineering that turned the mills that made the flour and the soybean
meal that put the calories into the workers. And the sewers. And the aque-
ducts. And the republican government, which shifted the flow of a Parliamin's
corruption and favoritism from fellow elites to a Parliamin's constituents, so
that corruption at least helped the common people *sometimes*.

But all of those things were just limbs and muscles on the beast. They explained *how* Falcrest was conquering the world but not *why*. A strong man
might have the ability to strangle or force a weak man. But nowhere was it
written that the strong man was fated to kill or enslave that weak man.

Would Taranoke, given all these advantages, have gone to Falcrest, subverted and enslaved it, made it part of a Taranoki empire?

No. And the Oriati were the proof. The Oriati had their own heinous history,
their own spasms of conquest: but for much of their *millennium* of unsurpassed
worldly power, they had kept to their own borders and their own internal
struggles. Their voyages had been for exploration and trade. They had been
good neighbors.

Aurdwynn had of course washed itself in blood. The Maia had come to
conquer, the Stakhieczi had counterinvaded to preserve the great green bread-
basket that fed them. So you might be tempted to say that wherever cultures
meet conflict was inevitable. But they had been two rival homelands at war
over the middle ground; neither had ever made a possession of the other.

Yes, people had always been evil nearly as much as they had been good. Yes,
happiness was rarer than suffering—that was simply a fact of mathematics;
happiness required a narrow range of conditions, and suffering flourished in
all the rest.

But Falcrest was not an innocent victim of a historical inevitability. Empire
required a will, a brain to move the beast, to reach out with appetite, to see
other people as the answer to that appetite, to justify the devouring of other

peoples as right and necessary and good, to frame slavery and conquest as acts of grace and charity.

Incrasticism had provided that last and most fateful technology. The capability to justify any violence in the name of an ultimate destiny, an engine to inflict misery and to claim that misery as necessary in the quest for utopia. A false science by which the races and sexes could be separated and specialized like workers in a mill. And the endless self-deceptive blind guilty quest to justify that false science, so that the suffering and the misery remained necessary.

Falcrest had chosen empire.

Falcrest could therefore be held responsible for its choice.

Not all those who lived in Falcrest participated in its devourings. But all those who lived in Falcrest had benefited from them, and by encouragement or by passive acceptance they had allowed those devourings to continue.

"What were we talking about?" she said. "Mister Farrier, did I tell you about my one wish? There's something I'd like. . . ."

She watched his smile collapse.

"Yes, Baru," he said. "You told me about your wish. It'll happen tonight. I've made all the arrangements. No one will interfere. I've made it clear this is a personal matter. My gift to you."

I T was time.

The Emperor awaited Its People.

To Its left ran a sluiceway of ice water, cold and clear as a winter dawn.

To Its right a stream of glass eyeballs rolled down a marble chute.

One hundred marble steps descended from Its Throne to the vast pillared floor of the Levelest Gallery, where all Its gathered petitioners stood on even ground. You could lay a ball of rubber on the floor and it would not roll even one inch in any direction. Footsteps wore the Gallery down: in storm season it was painstakingly resurfaced.

Upon the Emperor's face a mask of white enameled steel smiled gently down upon the assembled invitees. There was Pristina Cuprajacque, the light of the stage, tormenting the fashion observers, who were trying to decide if her reductively simple gown was anything more than a cinched tube of cotton. There was Mandridge Subahant, leader of the Candid Party in Parliament, jeering at a woman from *Advance* who had suggested he was having an affair. Mandridge was the only man in Falcrest who could boast of his blatant social coercions and yet summon a thousand outraged supporters at the slightest accusation he was morally impeachable. At the far opposite end of the crowd, his inexhaustible leftist rival Truesmith Elmin shook hands with a file of donors, defying the ongoing rumors that she was suffering a slow poison.

Here came the new Empire Admiral Ahanna Croftare, with the escort of two marines she was always entitled to muster, and a perimeter of pure threat which only a few very curious gossips dared cross. And the new Nemesis Judge Xate Yawa, present on behalf of her court, widely credited with the delicious power play which had thrown Aurdwynn into rebellion and then dragged it back to heel just in time to parry the Stakhieczi invasion.

There was the Oriati Ambassador Tau-indi Bosoka, quite plainly dressed, with two guests in wheelchairs and a masked woman in a cotton gown who appeared to be, depending on the decorum of those you asked, a great beauty in traditional costume or a whore. One of the wheelchair guests was the merchant magnate Abdumasi Abd, recently returned from adventures abroad, and it was rumored that he had been vital in making tonight's great announcement possible. He had been a vocal enemy of commerce with Falcrest for so many years. His conversion was surely a sign of a tremendous diplomatic breakthrough, or of effective leverage.

There was Cosangua Trestle from the Suettaring Joy Battalion, with her young protégé Haille Kensfarrie, courted now by Hob Rondlant the heartbreaker from *Advance*. No one was entirely certain who was wearing the Archon Tutor's mask, but this did not stop the offer of discreet bribes for a student's placement in the Faculties. And a keen eye might detect many other notables and worthies, some moving anonymous under new masks and new costumes, due to scandal or simply social exhaustion.

The only ministry without even a token presence was the Metademe. Cosgrad Torrinde was commonly believed to be the Emperor's eugenics advisor Hesychast. No one dared speculate too loudly about his prolonged absence during the spring and summer, however. Any one of the Clarified present might be his avatar.

The Emperor loomed above them all, a human cocoon at the center of a spiderweb. The Imperial Body was shrouded in a canvas sheet, pulled taut around It by silk ropes that gathered into sixteen great channels and coursed out through bolts and pulleys to draw lines across the huge star-speckled black monoliths behind Its Throne. Then the braids vanished into the walls, symbolically passing out into the Empire, to the very farthest reaches of the most distant province, to execute Its will.

The Emperor did not often address Its people directly; even today, better than half the people present would have agreed that Its Body was simply a proxy. The Emperor was chosen from the populace and chemically denied any knowledge of Its own identity and history. This was the only way Lapetiare had imagined that a ruler could be truly fair. It was generally understood that the Emperor's chemically mediated anonymity demanded that It remain aloof. The Emperor's purpose was not to take the place of Parliament, nor to direct the Judiciary's verdicts, nor to dispatch the Morrow Ministry's spies. Rather, It was meant to provide a continuous, enlightened unity of policy through suggestion and influence. When the Emperor did not have the expert knowledge to make a choice Itself, then Its Advisors would provide assistance.

All agreed that today's announcement would involve the looming war. The Oriati had attacked Aurdwynn. There *would* be reparations. But in what form?

A chime called the crowd to attention. The chorus behind the marble walls whispered through their amplifying pipes.

"I AM THE EMPEROR AND I KNOW NO OTHER NAME. I HAVE SUMMONED YOU TO HEAR THE WILL OF THE IMPERIAL REPUBLIC. I HAVE ENTRUSTED THAT WILL TO MY SERVANT. COME FORTH."

So an orator would appear to read the Emperor's decision. The crowd waited in a hush to see who it would be.

Cairdine Farrier peeked out from behind the Throne. "Am I late?"

Affectionate applause, cheers, boos, whistles of love and lust; he came dancing down the steps, wearing the polestar of Imperial authority on his half-mask. His handsome beard smiled with his mouth.

"Yes, it's me! Back home at last. If there are *any* of you who doubted I was one of the Emperor's advisors, well, I hope you pay your bets. I am here today, more publicly than usual, because I need your absolute trust. Welcome. No, please, I mean that sincerely. *Welcome.* I'm glad you're here. I never, ever dreamed I'd have the chance to share this moment with you."

The hundred steps leading up to the Throne were just slightly too large for a human to mount. Farrier came hopping down them like an eager bird.

"We always win, don't we? It's been our habit since before the Armada War. We won against the royalists. We won against smallpox. We won against the Oriati. We *know* that victory is our future. In the long run the Imperial Republic will save this world.

"But that's not much comfort, is it, on days like today. When the markets are in a panic. When our children ask us questions we can't answer. When it seems as if old and powerful forces have turned their eyes on our little land. We don't have a great army. We don't have natural wealth. We're small people, right? Except Hesychast, that man's not small at all." He grinned through the laughter. "You're waiting for me to answer one question! Will you have to send your children to war?"

He paused. The Emperor twitched in its cocoon of canvas and silk.

"No," he said.

The crowd let out a tremendous gasp of relief and disappointment.

"You have been told that war is inevitable, because history is going one way and the Oriati want it to turn back in the other. The Oriati do not want to accept our schools, or our trade, or the fact that there is a right way to live. I can't blame them, honestly! There are so many of them, and they don't agree on anything, do they, Tau?"

The Prince-Ambassador smiled and bowed.

Farrier brooded for a moment, hand on chin. "Since the Armada War, I've been trying to figure out a way to avert that inevitability. How can we get the Oriati to work *with* us? How can we cooperate to avoid a war, without betraying the imperatives of Incrastic progress? I'm here today to tell you that my protégé Agonist has found a way.

"We now have confident diplomatic and navigational access to the Black Tea Ocean and the western coast of the Oria continent. Directly through Segu Mbo. *Without* the long journey south around Zawam Asu." He held up his hands against the crowd's roar of astonishment. "As soon as next summer, we will be bringing goods to market!"

It was happening again, it was happening the way the crowd had seen it happen to their parents. It had begun this way in Aurdwynn. It had begun this way in Taranoke. And those who had acted early and aggressively in those provinces were now rich beyond whole dynasties.

"Of course," Farrier said, grinning, "the Black Tea Ocean is a long and difficult journey from Falcrest, and the necessary routes will pass through territory held by Segu Mbo—a people who have never welcomed our shipping. Because of the diplomatic and strategic sensitivity of this new venture, and the secrecy required in our negotiations with the Segu, the Emperor has decided to grant an absolute monopoly on trade with the Black Tea Ocean to a single concern.

"This concern will be legally empowered to raise funds, ships, banks, militia, and even local legislatures in the pursuit of Falcrest's profitable and benevolent presence on the western Oriati coast. This concern will be authorized to make treaty and war in the Emperor's name. And, of course . . . this concern is going to sell you shares in its stock."

The noise the crowd made was the moan of someone watching a lover undress.

A hundred pens poised over a hundred pads. Runners braced to sprint. When the concern was named, every investor in Falcrest, from the Suettaring markets to the kitchen tables of middle-class homes, would begin a furious bidding war for shares in that concern. The timid and the cautious would get a few shares and hold on to them simply for the dividend: the portion of the concern's profit which was passed on to shareholders. But most would hold in anticipation of the price rising: as shares became more scarce and more desirable, the price would bubble up like water from a detonating mine. Those who rode the bubble expertly would be tomorrow's Parliamins, ministers, tycoons, and colonial tyrants. Those who were consumed would be cleaning fish shit from the undercity canals.

"The name of the concern which will hold this monopoly," Farrier said, raising both hands as if unfurling a banner, "is—"

"Shut up, you hypocrite," the Emperor said.

Someone laughed.

The echoes fell off into absolute shocked silence.

Farrier frowned. Slowly he turned. Someone else laughed: he was doing a bit, he was playing this up for the crowd.

Hesitantly, the Imperial Chorus took up the Emperor's words. "SHUT UP, YOU HYPOCRITE."

Farrier scratched his head, a comic's exaggerated gesture. The crowd laughed uncomfortably.

"Excuse me," he said. "I thought I knew who was under there. Apparently I was mistaken. Who—"

"Cairdine Farrier," the Emperor enunciated, in a voice that buzzed and ratcheted through the clockwork of a voice-changer but never, ever faltered, "by the power invested in me as Emperor of the Imperial Republic of Falcrest, I accuse you of collaboration with foreign royalty, of producing a royal heir, and of conspiring to enrich that heir by perversion of the Empire's Incrastic work. I order your immediate arrest. As there are no civil authorities beyond the reach of your corruption, I commend you to the navy's custody. Empire Admiral Croftare, take him away."

The chorus repeated every word. The hall was, otherwise, silent: except for the rapid tap of Cairdine Farrier's left boot, and the scratch of his finger under his chin.

Empire Admiral Ahanna Croftare stepped forward. Her two marines followed her. "Well," she said, into the silence, "you better come with me, Mister Farrier."

"Don't you dare." Farrier tapped the polestar mark on his mask without turning to her. "You have no jurisdiction here. Someone's obviously meddled with the Emperor. Steward? Steward, come out here, take that mask off so we can all see who—"

The crowd booed vehemently. Farrier might as well have asked the steward to pants a child. "Masks stay on!" someone jeered.

"I find for the Empire Admiral," a new voice said. "Mister Farrier's arrest is justified."

Everyone turned to the Nemesis Judge Xate Yawa, black rook among finery. Her mask erased any hint of her race, but they all knew who she was. The maid who'd betrayed Falcrest's dukes to the Masquerade. The very model of egalitarian, pro-republican action in the provinces.

"Trust me," she said, to the staring crowd. "I know what to do with royalists."

Empire Admiral Croftare came up the steps with her two following marines. "Stop!" Farrier barked. "You've crossed the shoreline! This is *not* the navy's mandate!"

"Judge says it's all right," the empire admiral said, and shrugged.

"Come now." Farrier appealed to the crowd. "This is a trick. A reactionary strike by a jealous rival. Let's all keep our heads and discover who's swapped themselves in for the real Emperor."

"I am the real Emperor," the voice boomed. The chorus was now only a moment behind it. "I was chosen as Emperors are chosen. Now I must speak. Do you hear me, Cairdine Farrier? I must speak against you."

Farrier stared in true puzzlement at the Emperor.

Then he sighed and stripped off his gloves, offering his naked hands to the marines for the cuff. "This is a very petty prank, and a desperate attempt to sour my good news. Once we've verified the charges are false, I hope I'll see you all again in the markets, earning a piece of the fortune that's—"

"But the charges are true, Farrier," Tau-indi Bosoka called. "You know it as well as I do. You've consorted with foreign aristocracy. You've created an heir."

The crowd gasped in delighted shock and shocked delight as the absolute indignity of those words, delivered by an Oriati royal, slapped the blood from beneath Cairdine Farrier's mask.

"Tau?" he said, in bemusement. "But . . ."

"But what?" Tau had not worn their full dermoregalia. They were in the plain waistcoat of a Falcresti citizen, and a long skirt of Lonjaro block prints, dressed to capture two worlds in one. "But I'm too kind to tell the truth? But I'm too gentle to lay it out in public? But I'm too *soft* to do this to you?"

"I thought," Farrier said, into the absolute silence, "that you wouldn't want her hurt. . . ."

Eyes began to turn to Tau's companions.

Tau shook their head in absolute disappointment. A few people made the hand-washing sign against evil: not out of fear of Tau, but out of their own sorrow to see Tau so distressed. "She won't be hurt, Farrier. Don't you understand? You could never hurt her. She was smarter than you."

Farrier did not understand. He shook his head, and waved at the approaching marines as if they were friends coming his way at a party he was not ready to leave.

"Quite a melodrama." He smiled broadly at the crowd. "Whoever arranged this little embarrassment deserves an award of some sort. Possibly even in stock certificates—"

"Will you deny her?" a woman cried. "You'll deny her even *now*, Caird? You'll pretend she's not real?"

Farrier froze. His eyes were not the darting eyes of a liar anymore. He looked deeply, profoundly afraid: as if his chest had been cut open, his ribs pulled aside like crab legs, and his heart laid out beating for the knife.

The woman came out from behind Tau. "You told me that it didn't matter who'd fathered her flesh. You said it was the man who raised her who was her real father. Tell them, Farrier! Tell them that you're her real father. *Tell them!*"

Kindalana of Segu leapt up from the floor of the Levelest Gallery onto the Emperor's first step. She shrugged off the cotton gown that had concealed her majesty. No one there, except Tau and Abdumasi Abd and perhaps Farrier himself, could say if what she wore was the traditional garb of a Prince of Segu Mbo. But everyone who saw her *thought* it must be: her bare clavicles painted in gold, the slender length of her neck ringed in silver, her sinfully delicate shoulder blades bare to the chandeliered oil lights so far above. The parts of her that were modest were very modest; the parts of her that were naked were not the parts anyone in Falcrest would call taboo.

But all who looked upon her saw, first and most easily, the thing that they associated with an Oriati woman of high station: the foreign princesses in the rag novels, who wore jewels and chains and nothing else, who were always wide-hipped and cunning and at ease in their sensuality. Women who seduced the weak-minded with their sinful physicality. A conniving manipulatrix. Ideas as camouflage and armor, and Kindalana had gathered those ideas, and gone to war.

People gasped as they made the connection.

Cairdine Farrier had gotten a daughter with Kindalana of Segu. She had seduced him and he had fallen to royalism.

He had a royal child. He had sired an unlicensed child to a royal line.

Farrier's ghastly gray heartbreak was the proof of it.

"Tau," he began to say, "might we have a conversation about your embassy's—"

"No," Tau said. "No amnesty. You treat people like things, and I cannot stand it."

Farrier might have defended himself then. He might have called out to the people that he, an explorer and champion of the republic, was being sabotaged by a foreign seductress.

But he had truly loved her, and he was undone.

In the stories they would tell about this day, he tumbled all the way down into the crowd, between the sluiceway of ice and the spill of eyeballs. And they all flinched back from him, the nepotist Cairdine Farrier, who had mingled his seed and his future with royal issue.

In reality he slipped only one step, and got his feet back. But it was enough.

"In light of these revelations," the Emperor said, and if there was a hint of dry humor in that voice, all the more testament to Its wisdom and humanity, "and the obvious corruption inherent in granting authority over Oriati Mbo commerce to a royalist and an Oriati blood collaborator, management of the new Black Tea Ocean Concern and its monopoly will be reassigned to one of our *loyal* agents. Be assured, however, that trading is open. Good business to you."

W HEN Aminata got up from her wheelchair the pain scraped at her chest like a pair of giant knuckles rubbing her breastbone. Her vision seemed as long and narrow as the trajectory of a bolt, straight from her face to the white mask of the Emperor.

Two brown-black eyes stared back at her. She was too far away to possibly see their color but she *knew* they were brown-black and that they were watching her. Aminata would have known those eyes if they came washing ashore in a bottle.

"Baru?" Aminata breathed. "How the fuck . . . ?"

Pandemonium had reached the very edges of the hall, spilled out through channels and corridors, to leap across Falcrest at the speed of fireworks. Mandridge Subahant, the Candid whip, came forward in a chevron of supporters. "Get that thing off of there!" he bellowed. "It's a cheap fake. Someone's trying to silence Mister Farrier!"

"Nonsense!" Truesmith Elmin leapt up on the shoulders of a fellow Parliamin. "The Emperor's doing exactly what It's required to do! Intervening when It must to guard the Republic!"

"Parliament won't stand for this!" Mandridge roared. "We'll find you out, you hear me?" He shook a finger at the Emperor. "We'll find out who's under there soon enough, and then you'll drown for treason! You've assaulted a great man!"

"If anyone comes near the Emperor," the Nemesis Judge Xate Yawa purred, "they will have my court to answer to."

It wasn't possible, Aminata thought. The lobotomy had been *observed*, hadn't it? It had been certified by observers, or no one would have believed in it. It couldn't be Baru.

Yet here was Yawa, playing along, as if she'd been on Baru's crew the whole time. So the lobotomy had to be fake! And Baru must have trusted Tau-indi and Abdumasi to convince Kindalana to appear here, to substantiate the charges against Farrier openly and publicly where they could *never* be silenced or massaged away. How could she have left her life and power in the hands of three Oriati she barely knew?

Tau-indi touched Aminata's hand. "See?" the Prince said, warmly, though there were tears in their eyes, the tears of a person so gentle that they mourned even the ruin of the awful. "She trusted you. She trusted us."

In that moment, against all reason, Aminata felt like she was in a fleet of two, a navy of her and Baru: she had just been promoted to Grand Admiral, captain of everything she had ever wanted.

And she would have sworn, despite the pain in her chest, that the Emperor winked at her.

BARU walked Tain Hu through the streets of the world to come.

"Well," Hu drawled, "this is certainly cosmopolitan."

People of every nation bustled past them, dressed in a beautiful array of textiles and fashions. Small-nosed, high-cheeked Falcresti, some of them with the vitiligo-spotted Grendish look; Bastè Ana in white cotton versions of their traditional furs, bearing the dignity of their own capitalized race-name; dizzyingly many sorts of Oriati, though they were no longer "Oriati" at all, no longer subject to that simplifying Falcresti label, but Devi-nagi and Mzilimaki and Segu and Lonjaro. Maia families moved in squabbling, bickering, laughing clusters of interrelationship. And Taranoki like Baru. And even Kyprananoki, reborn in this dream-world from some precious few survivors, not diluted by intermarriage but simply sustained by it: their culture, their memories, insoluble and precious. Even the Sydani were here, and their men were as fearless as the women.

Tain Hu grimaced at a passing carriage. "There's no horses," she complained.

"They've made the uranium light boil water, see?" Baru crouched to watch jets of steam spin the axles beneath the carriage. "Marvelous."

On a hilltop above the imaginary city (it seemed to have Treatymont's general street plan, but the henge hills of Duchy Radaszic had migrated in toward the old walls) a lightning farm collected thunderbolts to animate the meat golems that conducted various labor. "Those must run on the same galvanic principle that makes corpses twitch," Baru assured Hu.

"I'm sure they do. Why is that man living inside a glass bubble?"

"To contain the soporific mists, of course." A street surgeon tended to minor wounds and ailments inside a dome, where the drugs steaming out of a water bong prevented all pain. A little girl with a persistent cough had just gone into the bubble, and the surgeon was slicing open her chest to draw out the infected tissue and replace it with the seeds of new lung. The girl's mothers argued about something outside as messengers ran past, their letters written in a lovely and mathematically rigorous script which could not encode lies.

"You have some truly bizarre ideas of how things will go," Hu said.

"Oh, *you* do better," Baru snapped, annoyed at any critique of her utopia. "I bet yours would just be a big forest full of—of athletic nymphlets!"

"You're not a nymphlet. And you're not *that* athletic."

"But at least I can imagine a better world than a cold woodland!"

Hu shoved her. Baru tripped over the elevated curb and fell, yelping, into the sky.

Green opened up beneath her, green and silver-blue and gold: the canopy of Aurdwynn's northern redwood forest, the towering, cold-hardened trees that filled Duchy Vultjag. She spotted the glass-clear river Vultsniada running south. Mills turned beside fish ladders. On the northern horizon a quarry broke the mountainside into white columns. Baru plunged straight out of the sky, toward some sort of festival where big men were taking turns hurling axes into a tree trunk, where all the children jostled for their turn at the inoculation booth and a ticket to ride the river rapids. There was a granary down there, and a bakery, and a tanner's and a fletcher's and a cooper's and forges and even a paper mill. A perfectly pleasant little feudal village, the sort you might dream of all your life, if you were the kind of duchess who cared for her fief.

"Follow me," a warhawk called, and Baru realized she had wings, big black wings with feathers like fingers at the tip. She was a cormorant and Tain Hu was a hawk with steel-tipped talons, the sort the Maia had trained, long ago, to scatter vultures that might betray a kill. When she opened her wings, Baru felt the texture of the air, thermals and dirty washes, lulls and eddies, a vapor map of the terrain below. It was like swimming, it was joyous.

Tain Hu glided over the training grounds and the tourney fields, across the moat, to the high overlook tower beside the waterfall, where two women stood hand in hand looking across their land: a dark broken-nosed beauty in jodhpurs and a mail-shouldered tabard, and a brooding woman of no particular note.

Tain Hu the warhawk landed on Tain Hu the woman's shoulders, as gentle as only a dream bird could be. Baru the cormorant crashed awkwardly into Baru the woman's stomach, and, becoming the woman, had to get back to her feet with a stupid seabird hopping around underfoot.

"Gracefully done," Tain Hu said, innocently.

"Shut up." She pulled herself back to the parapet. "Not bad, I see. You've got a range of mills, to diversify your output. Are those fish ponds? Well done. A hawkery. And that must be a fur post. Is that horse pasture? You cleared woods for *pasture*? That's not a smart use of your land at all—"

"Nonsense," Hu said, airily, "the warhorses are for breeding. And they attract admirers."

She pointed to a file of pale people, coming down a trail—no, a proper road—from the north. Baru smiled smugly. "So I *do* have some influence on this design."

"Indeed. The Stakhieczi like to see my horses. And they like to meet, drink with, befriend, bed, and sometimes marry my people. Their glass and steel sells south at a tremendous margin. Vultjag uses that money to buy grain, salt, sugar, and spices from downriver to sell back to the Stakhieczi. Recently various crop brokers have established year-round offices here. And of course there is a post maintained by the Vultjag Trading Concern, which oversees the general trade from the Llosydanes, Taranoke, and Oriati Mbo beyond. I tax a reasonable rate. It goes into insurance, fire watch, and medicine for my fief."

Baru kissed her on the mouth. "Hu, it's wonderful!"

"It's not real."

"But it *will* be! Vultjag can be like this! Ake can do it, and Heingyl Ri—"

Hu gathered Baru up and made her rest her head in the crook of her strong neck. She smelled of pine. "Kuye lam," she said, "nothing will be done if war consumes the Ashen Sea and destroys my home. So you have to go back. You have to finish the work."

Baru nodded, eyes squeezed shut. "I will. I know what to do now."

"You're walking a very dangerous road. You've built an engine to give you immense power. But you've also given Falcrest the chance to capture that engine. They will remake the whole Mbo in their mutilated image if they can."

"I won't let it happen. I *won't*. I have to make the masks believe that I'm giving them what they want and need. It's the only way to trick them. And then, when the moment's right . . ."

"Be sure you don't miss the moment."

"I won't."

"And will you be happy?" She stroked the line of Baru's shoulder. "Will you do that part of the work, too? I *wanted* that. That is the reason your stupid self-sacrificing plans to infest your body with cancer and plague cannot be allowed. You must be happy. I died to give you that chance. *You must be happy.*"

"I'll try. I promise."

"Good. Then you'll be all right on your own." Hu looked down at her with that awful lopsided smile that cut right through Baru's young heart. "How *did* you fake that lobotomy, Baru?"

"Snap-off picks."

"*What?*"

"I didn't know how she was going to do it ahead of time, mind. But I do know now. Yawa prepared orbitoclasts that were weakened at the neck, where the needle joins the base. When the maniple started to move the styluses, the steel needle snapped off inside my head. They never completed the necessary cuts. Iscend was able to certify that the maniple had performed all the correct motions without actually lying."

"That's an absurd risk! What if they hadn't snapped? We'd both be dead! Worse!"

"I trusted Yawa to make it work."

Hu's eyes narrowed. "Wait. Are you telling me there are *still* two steel needles shoved up behind our eyes?"

"Yes." Baru felt rather bold and ravishing about it, actually. She had masts in her brain.

"Won't they kill you?"

"Oh, no. Plenty of prisoners had steel implants to strengthen their self-control, in older days. No one died of them. I'll be fine."

"That woman," Hu said, and spat over the towerside. "So you're telling me that your entire plan to achieve the Throne depended on your thick skull's ability to snap steel? I suggested you use the Emperor's seat to complete your work. I didn't know *this* was how you'd gain it."

And she had suggested it. She had repeated Baru's promise back to her: I will write your name in the ruin of them. I will paint you across history in the color of their blood.

There was only one aristocratic seat in Falcrest. And the color of Falcrest's blood was in part the molten gold of commerce.

"I was certain that Farrier's secret was a daughter," Baru said. "He was modest with me exactly as a Falcrest father would be with a girl child. He had a pattern of female students, as if he were trying to replace something missing. He was uncomfortable with the topic of Kindalana and the whole concept of Oriati sexuality—probably because she managed to seduce him so thoroughly that she got pregnant off him. All those clues led me to the truth."

"Truly you have discovered the ability to consider the minds and actions of others," Hu said, dryly.

"Shush."

But her swat found empty air. Hu had dropped to one knee and bowed her head. "My lady, I am yours in life and in death. But I must ask your leave."

"My leave? Hu, where are you going?"

"To carry out my last duty, Your Highness, my queen." Hu kissed her hand. "You cannot be obsessed with me forever. I've brought you to a place of some safety. Now you must go on without me."

"You promised you'd always be with me," Baru whispered.

"I will." Hu looked up, fierce and dark and golden, perfect. "Always and forever in your heart. You don't need this . . . mental trick to keep me alive. There are other women: oh, don't look that way, as if I'm the only one suited for your oh-so-particular tastes. Go make some mistakes. Go find someone different, someone utterly unlike me, except that she should drive you mad, too, because she doesn't agree with you, and she won't bow down when you want; but she's loyal beyond all reason when you need her. There must be another woman like that, somewhere." Hu grinned. "One or two, at least."

It was hard to look at Hu. She was so fierce. Like staring into fire, when you are the fog.

"What if Shir's right? What if ruling in Falcrest makes me happy, and I cannot give it up . . . ?"

"My love, my queen, kuye lam"—Hu was unbearably radiant now, a cold clean light like a star—"I am a part of you forever, but I was born to rule high wilderness, to guard my people and to defy my foe. If I could answer these questions of empire and complicity for you, would I love and need you so much?"

"You told me that you would tell me the difference! Between pretending to obey them and really giving in . . ."

"And I told you that I want you to keep asking that question forever. You will know the answer when you die, Baru. You will know it by the change you've made in the world. That's what Agonist means, isn't it? The one who causes change."

"I don't want you to go," Baru whispered.

"Too bad," Hu hissed, though she was grinning. "I chose where and how to die. I died a fucking hero, didn't I? Name some unexplored lands after me. And a statue. I always wanted a great big statue. *The Duchess Triumphant*, with my sword upraised, and Cattlson's banner in my other hand: and you can give me great broad shoulders, and classy stone tits, but don't you dare fix my nose. I want it broken and I want it crooked. Just so."

L EFT eye open," Iscend commands. "Point your left hand to my left eye." Baru aims her forefinger.

"No," Iscend clucks, "that's my nose, Your Excellency."

"Shit." Baru points a little farther right, where memory, if not instinct, says Iscend should have another eyeball. "That hasn't gotten worse, has it?"

"There has been regression. You were learning to correct for your hemilateral illusions, but after the meningitis and the recent trauma to your frontal lobes, you've lost some progress."

Trauma is one way to put it. Baru can't feel the steel lobotomy picks still embedded in her brain, no matter how she pokes her forehead or spins her head back and forth. Yawa has assured her that most cases of cranial artifact (a fine way to say *shit lodged in the brain*) are truly harmless, and that the lurid stories of men whose entire personalities are destroyed by a harpoon through the brain are exaggerated—most of those historical cases, Yawa says, made a full recovery with time and practice.

But Baru wonders what will happen if she goes outside in the cold, or in a thunderstorm, or in deep water where the pressure fills her sinuses. Will the steel freeze within her? Will it draw lightning? Will it be ejected from her eyes? And what if she begins to itch, inside her head?

Iscend draws her touch kit. The needle, the feather, the silk, the sandpaper. "Strip and lie down."

The Antler River is smooth as glass today, and if Baru hadn't been on *Helbride* so long, she might not know they were on the water at all. She has not invented a name for her houseboat yet, but she loves it already. Iscend tests her reactions with quick systematic touches. Baru contemplates the absence of tension between them. For a scene out of fantasy, one of those pornographically useful cases of plausible nudity between strangers, it's wholly unerotic.

"Iscend," she says, "when you kissed me, did you really—I mean, did you feel anything?"

"This is a medical exam, Your Excellence. I'm bound by medical ethics."

"I'm not propositioning you! I'm just curious!" She tries to turn her head sideways. Iscend adjusts her, firmly, chin-down, so that Baru has to talk to the floor.

"I believe you knew all along the lobotomy hadn't taken. I think you collaborated with Yawa to hide that from Hesychast. I even think that's why you tried to seduce me. So you'd have that bodily association between me and . . . and feeling right, I suppose."

"An interesting theory, Your Excellence. Though it puts a great deal of stock in your very untried talents as a lover. And it does deny me a degree of humanity, doesn't it?"

"Only if you think that knowing yourself, and using that knowledge to change yourself, is inhuman."

"Isn't it?" Iscend teases: certainly teasing now. "What human being ever really understood themself?"

"I want to know why you protected me."

"I act for the good of the Republic," Iscend says, neutrally. "You know that. Clearly your trade concern is in the Republic's best interest."

What Baru likes about Clarified is that they're very logical. But what she likes about *Iscend* isn't so easily laid out. Yes, obviously she's elegant, and insightful, and armed with secret methods of mental and physical discipline, and she is an incarnation of that Imperial power which Baru has so queasily come to wield.

But she's also funny, in a dry and straight-faced sort of way. She's comforting. She always knows what to do. And that gold-brushstroke illumination about her, which once dazzled and enticed Baru, now reads to her as delight. Iscend is glad to exist, in a way very few people will ever attain.

Are these traits all synthetic, too? Were they selected for her by Hesychast?

Maybe not. If behavior *can't* be passed down, as Baru and Iscend theorized in the forest, then the whole project of human eugenics is doomed. If eugenics doesn't work, that means the Clarified aren't as deeply Clarified as Hesychast believes.

And if that's true, if Iscend is *pretending* to have inherited all the traits Hesychast thinks she should possess, then she is a woman wearing a mask.

Iscend's slim fingers probe the sides of Baru's throat. "Swallow, please."

Baru swallows. She tries to imagine herself as Clarified. She tries to imagine filtering *everything* she wants through the greater good of the Republic.

Would she have to say, *I'm thirsty, I should drink, so that I can better serve the Republic?* Or, *I'm inexplicably sad, I should do something I enjoy, because I serve the Republic best when I'm happy?*

Perhaps she would.

What if Iscend, like Baru, wants to be free? Then she would need to say, *I want to be free, because I serve the Republic best when I am free.*

What if she supports Baru's ascent to the heights of power because this allows Iscend to serve a single woman who is more and more like the Republic incarnate? If Iscend can advise that woman, and thus in a way determine what that woman in turn orders her to do . . . isn't that a kind of freedom?

Especially if that Supreme Woman has demonstrated a concern, a real regard, for her self-determination and safety.

Baru hums into the pillow.

"Thinking, Your Excellence?"

"Always," Baru says, as Iscend digs into her shoulder muscles, probing, always probing, for some flaw. "Always thinking."

"Half thinking," Iscend says.

Baru can't turn around to see if she's teasing.

THERE is business to be done at the Admiralty, so Agonist makes an appearance. Naturally Shao Lune has arranged to be her guide: Baru is certain that Shao simply forgets when things don't go her way, and proceeds as if the universe has been amended, retroactively and completely, in her favor. She may be threatening Baru's friend with court-martial, she may have given deck plans of *Eternal* to Faham Execarne for his doomed assault, but she is in perfectly good standing with Agonist the cryptarch.

She simply *must* be.

She greets Agonist as if they are cordial acquaintances, and not as if she has seen Baru drunk and desperate to die, nor as if they have spent any time knuckles-deep in each other and moaning with need. A terse letter of recommendation from Samne Maroyad has landed Shao Lune a post here at the Admiralty. She may be a snake, but the navy's snake she will remain. Baru, walking beside her, wonders if she has begun to blackmail the Admiralty with her intimate knowledge of Ormsment's mutiny. Probably. Of course Shao has a new uniform, freshly tailored, strictly obedient to code, but with an eye to compression and minimization of the body, and to the display of merits and pins in places that flatter her neck and slim shoulders. She looks spectacular. Baru's relieved that she doesn't find the woman even a little distracting. Whatever softness she'd developed for Shao is gone: not brutally excised, but set aside for good and necessary reasons, as people, in the course of their lives, must do.

When they reach War Plot, Empire Admiral Ahanna Croftare doesn't salute. Baru is, after all, no one in particular, not a minister or a parliamin or even a luminary from the Faculties. Just a woman with an Imperial polestar mark. "Evening," Croftare says, through coffee-speckled teeth. "When does Parliament give me back my money?"

"I don't have any leverage in Parliament yet," Baru says. Cairdine Farrier is still processing his new position, and she hasn't gained his network of influence. "You'll have to give me a few months. Show me the ships."

Croftare beckons to Rear Admiral Arrior, who gestures to the tactical secretaries at the great map table, who wield their long pointers. By this chain of impulses exquisite models of balsa, carved oak, twine, and glass are positioned across the circle of the Ashen Sea. Baru closes her eyes and relishes the sounds. The brush of wood on blue felt. Exquisite craft.

"This is what a newborn war looks like," Croftare says, "when it's about halfway out of mom, she's been in labor for six hours, and you're asking her to hold the little fucker in a while longer."

A ring of white ships flows from Falcrest, down across the northern coast of Lonjaro and Segu Mbo, up through Taranoke, along the desolate shore of the Camou Interval, above the Llosydanes and to Aurdwynn, past Isla Cauteria, and back to Falcrest again. That's the trade circle, the Empire's breath.

But all along the northern and eastern coasts of the Mbo, dozens of green-gold Oriati models wait to enter open sea.

"If the green ships go into the white ring," Croftare says, "money stops moving, and it's war."

"Each green model is an Oriati ship?"

"Not ships. Fleets."

"Damn," Baru says.

"Oriati Fighting Swarm," Arrior confirms. "Mostly dromon galleys, as they were in the Armada War. But they have salaried officers now, and some cannon, and the militia crews are required to drill twice a year. They haven't the range to make it far on open ocean, of course, so they're limited to coastal action. The real problem is the ships we may not know about."

Baru searches the board for a huge golden ship. But of course there is no marker for *Eternal*. "Cancrioth," she says, filling in the word Arrior will not say. "Do you have any word on their activities since Cauteria?"

"Some sightings of *Eternal* on its way south. We lost her when she passed into Segu waters."

"So you don't know what's happened," Baru says, without smugness. It's not fair to Croftare to undercut her like this. But Baru must demonstrate that her resources are indispensable.

For example: the news she gets from Tau-indi Bosoka's diplomatic packets, which arrive monthly from Jaro, recorded not in writing but in the minds of extremely articulate griots with eidesis training.

"Don't know what?" Croftare asks, bluntly. Arrior looks like he's swallowed his mint in alarm.

"Do you know the Ash Plate?"

"In old Kutulbha. Where the tunks go on pilgrimage." Thousands of Segu-people make the pilgrimage to the ruins of the old city, to remember ancestors and to show their children.

"Something appeared there."

The Brain told her, in that hutch full of bats, exactly what she would do. *You will see me at the head of mighty armies, and emblazoned upon ships, and clasped at the throat of the dead. I will be many places at once and I will not need one single coin or gem to do it.*

And she's done it.

"It was an effigy," Baru tells narrow-eyed Ahanna Croftare. "A woman cast alive into the surface of a huge bronze disc. They peeled the metal away, in places, to show her bones. You can still see her expression, they say. There's a hole in her head where they pulled the tumor from her brain. They filled it in with gold."

"An effigy." It is Arrior's job to express confusion when his empire admiral cannot. "Of who?"

"The Brain. A Cancrioth leader. A messiah. She's calling them to war."

Croftare rubs her brow. "How did the Oriati pilgrims react?" She does not say *tunk* this time.

"There was a riot. Princes fought over what to do with the effigy. A vote was taken, and it was agreed to cast it in concrete and sink it in the deep ocean. But one of the Segu Princes stole it first; a Queen-Aunt from the yeniSegu tribe. She's carrying it along the Segu coast in a procession, telling her people that the Old Power has returned to lead them to war. And there's a sorcerer with her, people say. A sorcerer who says she's the same soul in a new body."

"Civil war?" Arrior says, hopefully.

"I don't know," Baru says, which is the truth. Tau-indi still hopes it can be avoided. "What about the Stakhieczi? How has their invasion progressed?"

"Stalled out in the north, for now," Censorate Admiral Brilinda Vain reports. "They're spreading out into tribal groups and claiming little fiefdoms.

I've heard reports of some infighting. They may turn on each other before they reach the coast."

"It's a shame Juris Ormsment wasn't at her post to react," Baru says, blandly. "I'm sure she would've had marines striking at the Stakhieczi the moment they left the mountains."

Arrior looks like he's just tasted borax. Croftare crosses her arms. "Juris Ormsment was a good admiral. She'll be difficult to replace."

"She was a good officer and a good woman," Baru agrees. "She had a developed sense of justice. It's a shame she was born into our world, and not a better one. Which reminds me." She turns her blind side to reveal Shao Lune. "I understand there's a court-martial in the cards for Brevet-Captain Aminata."

Croftare shrugs dispassionately. "Any officer involved in the loss of a ship receives a court-martial. There are no exceptions. She was aboard *Sulane* when it was destroyed. She goes before the mast. And her rank is Lieutenant Commander, half-pay. Your Excellence."

"But there are," she watches Shao Lune sideways, searching for any flinch of fear in those masked eyes, "allegations of mutiny and insubordination. I believe the staff captain here brought them?"

Shao Lune matches her blandness for blandness. "When a navy officer refuses an order to depart a foreign warship, in order to remain aboard that warship and aid her racemates, then that decision must of course be carefully inspected."

Baru dismisses Shao Lune from her gaze. "Empire Admiral," she tells Croftare, "you're going to lose a very good officer when Aminata goes to court-martial."

"Only if she's guilty."

"I wouldn't be so sure of that," Baru says, and lets a little of her fury on Aminata's behalf slip into her smile. "I wouldn't be certain that you still deserve her."

IT'S Armada Day, the twenty-third anniversary of Oriati Mbo's surrender. Baru looks down at her new home from a towertop alongside the nehr ab Grand, the city's widest canal.

Behold Falcrest, City of Sails! Born in revolt, bred to rule, self-made center of the world, self-proclaimed end of history. A city like a vessel swift and outbound, with towers like swan necks stretched to sing, with mirror-cupped lanterns like revisionist constellations. Galleries and promenades step down to the canals in a layer cake of white marble and clean water. Canvas sunshades billow; red silk ribbons spill the blood of the aristocracy. Even the birds celebrate Falcrest's victory. An enormous catch-and-release effort by the Ministry of Unhuman Citizens has fixed whistles to various city birds, to make a gleeful keening as they dive. Baru has heard rumors that the same Ministry is now dealing with an outburst of uncouth seagull behavior: the dockside gulls have been mobbing passersby, stamping their feet as if dancing, demanding food, shitting angrily on possessions and people if not indulged.

A man settles by her side.

"Cosgrad," Baru says. Hesychast always smells of grape flowers lately; not because he's drinking, but because the Experimental Vineyards above the Metademe cliffs are in full bloom. "How's Abd? Still coming in for treatment?"

"Doing well, thank you. His paralysis is not relieved, but he's coping."

"And Kimbune's proof? Read it through yet?"

"It's far beyond my grasp. I'm planning a sortie to the Mathematical Exemplaries. What's your name today?"

"Wuxa Rin," Baru says.

"Kindalana stopped by the Metademe to visit Abdumasi. They're together again, I think."

"Jealous?"

"No. Why would I be?"

This makes Baru smile inside. She has very strong suspicions about the lineage of Kindalana's secret child, and about the mysterious final member of this cell of the Throne—the elusive Stargazer. Why would a cryptarch apparently preoccupied with science be included in what Baru thinks of as the foreign affairs cell?

Only if Stargazer had foreign blood. . . .

But Hesychast will read her thoughts from her face. She swerves. "Do you truly believe Abdumasi's carrying the immortal souls of the Undionash line?"

A thoughtful inhalation: the tidal volume of that huge chest sucking down air Baru might otherwise have breathed. Denial by mere presence. "I don't know yet. He tells me he has to be educated about those souls in order to speak with them. But if that's so, it seems to prevent any truly scientific test for flesh memory."

She studies his hands. He's wearing surgical gloves, made of layers of fabric glued together by rubber-naphtha chemistry. Down below, navy sailors row a model frigate down the nehr ab Grand. The Armada Day drums beat.

"You're comfortable up here?" Hesychast asks her. "We're quite far above the streets."

"I have that Taranoki predisposition to heights, don't I?"

"Just as Xate Yawa has the Aurdwynni predisposition to rebellion."

Baru searches his jaw for signs of anger. "She did exactly as you required.

She turned me against Farrier and helped me betray him. The fact that she lied about the method shouldn't trouble you, Cosgrad. She's a cryptarch. You didn't choose her for her honesty."

"No, I didn't." He smiles ruefully. "But if I'd known you *weren't* lobotomized, I would've stepped in to keep you from sitting on that Throne. I was happy to let Cairdine seize his little trade monopoly, because I knew I could control him. But you . . . now it's *your* monopoly, isn't it?"

And an incredible monopoly it is. Black Tea Ocean Unlimited has not chartered a single ship, but already her first stock offering is trading higher than any other in Falcrest's history. Wealth is being created out of nothing, without money printed or treasure unearthed or labor transacted or goods created, as the individual stock certificates become more and more *desired*—a stockholder will one day hold a share worth three hundred notes, and three hundred and fifty the next, simply because people are now willing to pay three hundred and fifty to gain it, all in the hope that soon others will be willing to pay four hundred.

Some cautious investors are murmuring about bubbles. But it is only a bubble, others say, if nothing arrives to fill it. And the riches of unknown Oria await. . . .

"You won't punish her for it," Baru says. "Yawa, I mean."

"That's up to me, isn't it?" He taps the knuckles of his right fist against the stone. "She's under my leverage."

"And you're under mine." The drums are playing a Taranoki war beat now, something Falcrest stole; it might, once, have been played before Salm went into battle. The crowd is cheering.

Hesychast doesn't react to the threat. Instead he brandishes a weed cigarette. "Light me?"

"I didn't realize you smoked."

"Only when anxious."

"Am I making you anxious?"

He tips his head back and forth. "The possibility exists."

"I don't have a sparkfire."

"Try this. It's called a friction match." He gives her a slender stick, wrapped at one end in cloth. "There's a woman in the Faculties who makes them for me. Take it, like so, and strike it on the stone—"

When he seizes her wrist and tries to move her hand, she resists by reflex, and drops the match. Hesychast *tsks*. "Farrier's trying to strike a bargain with Mandridge Subahant, you know. He'll accept permanent exile and go to Lonjaro Mbo to arrange plantations and schools for rich men."

"He won't get past Yawa." She pickpockets him, not subtly, for another match, and strikes it on the stone. It flares up so swiftly she almost drops it. "Light?"

"Thank you." He sets the cigarette to the match, takes a drag, and exhales. She does not know what to do with the match so she looks left and stubs it out against her right palm. It hurts anyway.

"So," he says. "I'm under your leverage, you say. Is that because you control Farrier now? You can tell him to withhold his codes, so his vendettas trigger and—how did he put it, last time we met—his agents 'open my bottled failures in front of Parliament'? You think that'll hurt me enough to stop me? When I have Renascent's favor?"

She is not convinced he has actually received that favor at all. "I am an unbound cryptarch." She lifts her face to the warm wind. "I could do that. But I have a better handle on you, don't I, Hesychast?"

He does something, some trick of stance or presence, which makes her suddenly aware of how easily he could lift her and pitch her over the edge. "What handle?"

"On Taranoke"—she savors speaking that word openly, right to his face, rather than Falcrest's *Sousward*—"I had two fathers. Solit and Salm. My family exiled me, I'm sure you've heard, so now I'll never learn, even if I wanted to, which of those men was my, ah . . ."

"Biological father?"

"Just so." She does not actually care, but he does, and that's the key. "I don't think Solit or Salm knew either, you know. I think my dear old mother had them both the night I was conceived, so maybe *she* didn't even know. Which brings me to your problem—"

Hesychast blows smoke in her face. Reflex makes her cough and blink, and as she does he steps into her space, almost shoving her.

"Listen," he mutters. "I remember my early days. I was drunk on hubris then, too. You played a strong game in Aurdwynn, but you played against inbred feudal idiots. You showed new talents against Farrier, making yourself seem helpless while your agents positioned the trap. But don't think for an instant you could've won if I hadn't allowed it."

She holds her ground. "Allowed it? I don't think you *could've* disallowed it. It wasn't just Yawa who deceived you, was it? It was Iscend."

"Nonsense."

"I don't think you know *why* she chose me over you." She grins smugly. "But I do. Isn't that a puzzle, Cosgrad? I know where all your conditioning and all your eugenics went wrong. She gave me the flaw in your precious Torrindic

heredity. And when I disprove it, as I will, Incrasticism's going to come top-
pling down. And then you'll need to justify to yourself all the hideous things
you've done in the name of a *lie*."

He touches her with one gloved finger, right on the breastbone, as if listening to some interior hum. "You didn't finish your threat."

"I don't think I need to, do I? A child with two fathers. Isn't that enough?"

If Baru were Kindalana of Segu, if she had made the decision to use herself
as a playing piece, if she had carefully manufactured herself as "the Amity
Prince," the very picture of the agreeable, palatable Oriati woman—but still, of
course, so forbidden, so royal, so *exotic*—she would have gone to great lengths
to maximize the yield of her maneuver.

If *one* powerful Falcresti man could be convinced to father a forbidden
child, breaking his own heart, setting him on a lifelong quest for a surrogate
daughter he could raise in that child's place, well, very good.

But why not two? Why not confuse the child's paternity? Why not inflame
the existing rivalry between two men by inflicting on them the nauseous force
of sexual jealousy, backed by all of Falcrest's eugenic ideology? Why not create
a weapon that could undo them both, if needed?

Prince Kindalana has skills Baru will never possess. Baru could absolutely
never play to the beaming and sexually available hostess of Souswardi stereo-
type. But Kindalana discovered exactly what Falcrest thought of women like
her and, patiently, particularly, played that role to the not-so-metaphorical hilt.

And it worked. When it mattered most, when the fate of Kindalana's home
was in the balance, she had a weapon ready to strike at Farrier, shove him
aside, and seize the power he controlled.

By capturing Farrier, Kindalana has positioned Baru to inherit his power.

Now she will want to capture Baru. If Baru is lucky (oh lecherous heart)
she'll use the same tactics. But perhaps that is just anti-Oriati prejudice speaking. Perhaps Baru is as guilty of fantasies of the bejeweled princess as Farrier
ever was.

What was it like, growing up as Kindalana's daughter? Where is that
woman now?

"Aminata told me," she says, softly, "about how she fucked you. In that alley behind the restaurant on the Llosydanes. How you reacted when she said,
pretend I'm Kinda—"

"Stop," Hesychast snaps. Baru actually flinches: certain for a moment that
he is going to strike her. But he just shakes out his shoulders and sighs.

"How?" he asks, with actual raw hurt. "How did you make Kindalana trust
you?"

"Trim," Baru says, which is the truth.

"Trim is a belief system. It's not real."

"If it made her choose me, isn't it real?"

"Kindalana is a subtle, far-sighted politician. She wouldn't make such a huge decision on the basis of superstition."

Poor Cosgrad Torrinde. He has loved this woman Kindalana for decades, in one way or another: maybe not sexual or romantic love, but *some* kind of love, some absolute appreciation for Kindalana's existence. They were not so far apart in age when they met. They came of age together, in that war.

And yet he doesn't understand her at all.

"Maybe I fucked her," Baru suggests, quite seriously. "Isn't it supposed to be better with another woman? Addictive? Isn't that your explanation for why we tribadists persist?"

"It's simple science," Cosgrad says, coolly. "In tests, women who fuck other women climax most often. Do you think you can make me physically jealous? *Me?* I've whored myself to Incrastic science for my whole life. They used me as a boy and now I use myself. I don't care what Kindalana does with her sex. Farrier's the one who could never get past her body."

"Yet you fought over her. You and he."

"I cared about the choices she made, the future she wanted. *That* was what I wanted to keep away from Farrier. I didn't care who she fucked! Just the way she chose to use her power."

"And she chose me." She lets her eyes say: are you jealous?

He snorts. "She saw you as an ally of convenience. A way to seize Farrier's domain for her own use. Do you think she'll let you use her child for your advancement? A human sacrifice? Because the child *would* be sacrificed, Agonist. If you tried to use her against me, her identity *would* come out. The child would lose her citizenship in Falcrest, and any life she's built here. She might be forcibly sterilized as a royal heir. Will Kindalana let you do it? Will your own conscience let you?"

She meets his eyes. Now it's his turn to flinch. She growls at him: "You worry about *my* conscience? You made me murder the woman I loved because she was a traitor."

"We made you bring her to trial. *You* murdered her."

Hu sacrificed herself, but Baru is not going to explain that to Hesychast. "Farrier wanted me to learn that all the women I love will come to grief. Wouldn't it be wonderful justice, Hesychast, if I took *your* child away in turn? Wouldn't it be fair if I punished you like you want to punish all the tribadists?"

He exhales smoke. "I suppose," he says, "that it might seem that way to you.

From your selfish perspective. Because that's what you are, isn't it, Baru? If everyone were like you, humanity would die. You want to be something that very few people can be allowed to be. Selfish."

He turns and walks to the stairs.

"Hey," Baru calls.

He looks back. The drums strike up *In Praise of Human Dignity* and a huge roar of elation sweeps through the crowd.

She opens her arms, as if to indicate the space between them, the differences, Baru's darker skin, her height, her differently folded eyes, her sharper nose.

"What do you think?" she asks him. "Am I still fit only for farming, fishing, and pleasure?"

Very briefly he looks furious: less briefly, ashamed.

"You're an extraordinary Taranoki," he says. "Take pride in that."

THE city expects a long and deliciously sordid trial for Mister Cairdine Farrier. He has been a great favorite for so long, every brilliance and triumph of his life raising him up: but now the crank that raised him is free to turn, the ropes are free to snap, and Mister Cairdine Farrier is ready for the plunge. His closed dealings will be brought to light. His mistresses and suitors will testify to his behavior and his talents in bed. His books will be opened and scoured for errors, in finance and ideology alike. Enough great material will be introduced to the public discourse to feed a century's novels and plays about his rise and fall.

The presses slam and clatter as the pamphlets breed and the rhetorics try to pith the whole issue with one clever needle of prose.

Farrier's personal hypocrisy reveals the hypocrisy of the whole Incrastic project.

Farrier's human weakness shows that he is and always has been simply one of us.

Farrier's indictment proves that there is a grand royalist conspiracy within Falcrest set on keeping brilliant commoners like Cairdine Farrier out of power.

Farrier's sad mistake makes it absolutely clear that the women of Oriati Mbo, and perhaps women in general, cannot be trusted.

The important thing in prosecuting Mister Farrier is to preserve the dignity and impartiality of the state.

The key lesson of this whole affair is that the Oriati will stoop to any level to corrupt and destroy our Republic.

Who can blame him? Look at her!

How mad and desperate he must be. Look at her!

When will the child appear, people ask? When will the issue of Cairdine Farrier and the Federal Prince Kindalana be called to court?

There is very little doubt in anyone's mind that he has fucked the princess. How couldn't he? Fetishes and neuroses arise from repression. Farrier's worldly travels among naked savages and libidinous sailors and worst of all the royalty of the Mbo must have required the most fearsome self-control. In turn that self-control would produce the most transgressive ecstasy when at last it was violated. (The cartoons are numerous, and explicit: they vary in the noises the little cartoon-Farrier makes, and the size of his head.)

But the question is whether this misdeed is merely carnal, an error of flesh, as men are known to make. Or whether it has extended into conspiracy with foreign royalty to create and empower an aristocratic heir within the Imperial Republic. That would be unspeakable treason, betrayal of Falcrest's fundamental principle: the annihilation of the royal. Castration and drowning would be the least of the punishments it would deserve.

When Judge-Minister Frowerer, on advice from the new Nemesis Judge Xate Yawa (who handled many scandalous trials in the distant and excitingly barbaric lands of Aurdwynn) announces a closed trial, the city fairly revolts. Two-story graffiti on the facade of a dormitory in the Faculties conveys the sentiment best: WHEN'S THE SHOW?

But it is quietly agreed among the Ministries and Parliament that this is best. Farrier knows too much about too many. An open courtroom could quickly become *too* open. Farrier must be tried by a panel of masked judges, and a useful verdict must be obtained.

Kindalana cannot be touched, of course, she is under diplomatic seal, and in a sense this whole affair has only added to her cachet: after so many years as an untouchable, unimpeachable humanitarian, doing her bafflingly modest work in a slum, suddenly the ice is cracked, she has scandal, she has spark, she has a little sensual allure. So, a thousand powerful men (and not a few women) whisper in their cloakrooms, the Amity Prince *does* put out. . . .

And of course the hunt is on for the child.

Farrier himself writes letters from his cell in the Regicide Oubliette. Items of comfort and admiration appear around him like mold. He receives no visitors but a great many letters.

"We should kill him," Yawa says.

She paces the houseboat's stern porch in a black cotton suit while Baru treads water in the river below her. "He's too dangerous. He can sway too much of this city, Baru, he *knows* people. We don't. We'll never have what he has—the old boys in their clubs, the smoking circles, the lounges."

"That's why we can't be rid of him yet," Baru says. She's been up nights wrestling with this thought, too, *kill him, kill him now. . . .* "He has the influence to make this concern work. Yawa, if he were our pawn he would give us *nations.*"

"That's why he has to die." Yawa flicks bird shit off the railing, into the river. "The longer he lives, the more people are going to remember that they can't do without him."

"Do you really think killing him will make up for anything?"

They look at each other, Baru in her linens, Yawa in her sherwani and button-up and trousers, and they both grin horribly.

"All right," Baru admits, "it'll make me feel great. But if he dies it means his vendettas will be released. All his files on Hesychast will go public. If Hesychast falls, your brother . . ."

"I know how the game is played." Yawa tugs off her bird shit–tainted glove and extracts a mint machine from her pocket. One click of the razor slices a pellet from the glass magazine and feeds it fresh into her palm. "I'm frightened of our current position. I was directly involved in Farrier's downfall. That makes me visible. There are other cryptarchs out there, unknown to us, who may be maneuvering even now. . . ."

"Exactly why we need him alive," Baru says, regretfully. "I possess him. He possesses enough leverage to deter those others. If we kill him, we kill ourselves."

Yawa bites down on the mint pellet too hard, and her teeth clack. "Do you really think you can control him, Baru?"

She treads water and thinks about this. "Yes," she says. "He's just been betrayed by the love of his life. Or, at least, the woman he thought he loved."

"So?"

"I know only one person who was strong enough to withstand that betrayal unbowed. Not two. Only one."

Yawa growls like a trapped coyote. She sees Baru's logic. "He's not stronger than my brother. He's *not*. And my brother broke."

"And," Baru says, finishing the chain, "he's not a tenth as strong as Hu."

BUT *why?*"
    Cairdine Farrier weeps into his overgrown beard. "Why, Baru, *why* waste it all? Oh, I know the temptation, I *know* what it's like to nurse a grudge,

but even if you wanted to betray me, even if you wanted my ruin, why were you so *stupid* about it?"

She sits in silence outside the bars and does not answer.

"Why?" He tears at his beard. The strands come out bloodless, curled, faded at the tips. "Why did you do it? For *money*? For a trade monopoly that you won't even control? You don't know business! You don't know how swiftly you'll lose it all! There are shareholders to please, and markets to mind, and parliamins to bribe, and you've never done *any* of it before. In ten years you'll have nothing—with me you could've ruled the whole Ashen Sea—"

"Lapetiare's revolution began with a single act," Baru says. "Sometimes one voice is enough."

"No, it didn't begin that way! *It didn't!* That's a schoolchild's lie! The revolution was decades in the making, it was about money, it was about the army's frustration and the king's poor choice of ministers and his refusal to yield certain privileges, it wasn't just a mob standing up one day and deciding to—"

He checks himself, and sinks back into the frame chair the prison has allowed him. His eyes are like shattered fortresses, emptied of provisions, left to crumble.

"Why. Just tell me why."

"Because I hate you."

He laughs once. "You hate me? You *hate* me? Everything I did for you, the school, the accountant's post, the chance to prove yourself . . . how could you hate me for it? No, no"—he shakes his head, he kneads his temples, fingers trembling—"I can't believe you'd be so foolish as to cast aside your future out of *hate*. Someone's tricked you, Baru. Was it Hesychast? Did Hesychast offer you something, some Clarified abomination. . . ."

"It was the women," Baru says.

Farrier growls low in his throat. "No . . ."

"Tain Hu showed me such such *delights*. . . ." Baru tips back her head, eyes hooded, lips pursed, a mockery of passion. Farrier looks nauseous. "There are things a woman can experience, Farrier, which a man will never know. You can't imagine the ecstasy. One night with the duchess and I would've given up anything, *everything* to feel that again. Oh, you poor man, you poor stupid man, floundering between Kindalana's thighs for something you'll never find. And all you did was make your own downfall."

Cairdine Farrier closes his eyes. "Well," he says, hollowly. "*You've* set aside a few more principles, I see."

"When did you do it?" Baru jeers. "When did you sire the child? Did you think, when you had your cock inside her, that she was *yielding* to you? Surrendering like her people surrendered after Kutulbha? When you came, did you think you were filling her up with your future, like you wanted to fill up the whole Oriati—"

"Stop!" Farrier roars. "Baru, what's *wrong* with you!" A sudden hope beneath the black brows: "Did Hesychast drug you? Is that it? He's poisoned you, hasn't he! You have to serve him or you won't get the antidote!"

"Oh, he's not the one who poisoned me," Baru whispers. "You *wanted* me to hurt, didn't you? You made my family hurt, and you made them hurt me. You made Aminata hurt, and you made her hurt me. You wanted me to know that whenever I strayed from your path I'd suffer. That was the Farrier Process, wasn't it? You wanted me to live in your *story*. Well, you've failed. I've always wanted to fuck women, Farrier, and no matter what you do, *I always will*."

He clings to his chair and stares at her wild-eyed. "It's not possible. You understood the consequences. You chose abstinence. You chose what you valued over what your body wanted. You learned so well. . . ."

"I hate you," she says, calmly. "I hated you when you took my home. I hated you when you put me into that sick school. I've hated you so long, Farrier, you and all you stand for, you pathetic dribble of a man."

He is trembling now. He keeps trying to smile confidently and his lips will not do it.

"I'm going to end this city," Baru tells him. "I'm going to end your entire Republic. In a thousand years they'll remember you as a footnote to my rise. A little prologue, oft elided. Farrier, who thought he ruled Baru Cormorant."

"You're mad. You can't 'end' the Republic. Not even a real Emperor could do it." He groans. "Oh, Baru, what have I done? I thought you wouldn't end like Shir. I *hoped* you wouldn't end like Shir. I loved you, child, like a daughter. . . ."

"Daughter!" she barks. "That's what gave you away, you shit! The way you treated me. The delicacy, the care, the pride, the insufferable *modesty*. Do you know what kind of 'father' lets people threaten to circumcise his daughter? No father at all! A rapist. An ally to rapists. A man who makes the world safer for rapists everywhere he goes. You're going to be brought to justice, Farrier. Not Falcrest's justice. I've a fairer hand to deliver your verdict. Tain Hu's justice for you, Cairdine Farrier! The woman I loved! The woman who begged me to murder her, *just so I could get to you!*"

He knuckles his hollowed eyes. With gentle bitterness, he says, "I see I've lost the Reckoning of Ways."

"I should say you have," Baru purrs.

"Well. You'll go on a few years, Baru, but without me you'll fail. And I will survive this. I'll be there when you've wasted yourself, to try to repair the damage you've done. There'll be other bright young girls. There'll be other chances. No more tribadists, though. Those I'll have to leave to Hesychast. And your father Salm, well . . ."

He trails off, so that he can watch her horror. But he's disappointed. She's not scared of what he can do to Salm. She's ahead of him there, too.

"When you're dead," Baru says, with rising delight, a wicked joy, "I'm going to take a pass at your secret daughter. I'll have her to a very charming dinner. I'll flirt with her over iced vodka and blackberries. I'll compliment her on her poise. When we get up to leave, I'll slip an arm around her waist and ask her if she'd like to see my houseboat. And who knows what'll happen? Who knows? Not you. You'll be in a little garret, writing letters for me, selling yourself piece by piece so I'll let you live another day."

There are footsteps outside. Her time is up; the constables are coming to end "Wuxa Rin's" clerical visit. She rises to go. One last shot: "I'm going to have your books reprinted, too. With corrections. I'll attribute them to you."

"I have your father—" he says, desperately. "I have your father Salm. If my codes don't reach his captors once a year, he'll die!"

"Shir is on her way to rescue him," Baru says. "Oh, yes, I turned her. I did what you couldn't, Cairdine Farrier."

Baru looks down at this man who squeezed her life into shape. She checks herself for stray emotions. Her books are clean. She has paid all her debts, said all she needed to say.

He just sits there frowning, pulling at his beard.

"If you don't send your passwords," she tells him, "to defer all your vendettas and keep your organization running, then the verdict is going to go against you. And if you kill yourself, Farrier, just to let all those vendettas go . . . remember that *I* won't be touched."

"Because you killed Tain Hu," he says, viciously.

"Because she volunteered for execution," Baru corrects him. "I hadn't even thought of it until she presented her plan. Isn't that incredible, Farrier? She's the one who gave me the idea. You thought I'd saved Falcrest when I killed her. But the only reason I killed her is that *she volunteered*. You've been outmaneuvered by a dead tribadist. You pathetic fuck."

IT is an unseasonably cold night when she emerges from the Regicide Oubliette by a back way and descends to the service canal.

She thinks of the Stakhieczi, and of Svir up in the high heights of the Wintercrests, trying to arrange a marriage. She thinks of Heingyl Ri, officially in mourning, who she will have to marry, in at least a passing sense. She thinks of Vultjag under occupation, of the bubonic plague waiting for release against the Stakhieczi invaders, of Kettling simmering in the green jungle holes that give the disease its name, and maybe in the forests of Isla Cauteria, carried by bats released from *Eternal*.

There is so much left to do, so much that can go wrong. All that has happened so far is still within the confines of Falcrest's power. Blackmail, trade, markets, and maneuvers—the Brain was right. They are all in a sense affirmations of the Masquerade's supremacy.

But Baru has set her course. Tau-indi thinks she might succeed. Kindalana thinks she might. Even the Brain thinks she might: if only as provocation to her people. That's a nice quorum of support.

"How was it?" Yawa asks her.

"Cathartic. I told him too much. But can you blame me?" She shivers. "I'm fucking frigid."

"Me too," Yawa says, dryly, "if you can imagine it." She has been waiting a while.

"Do you want to come over to my boat? I have a shocking number of liquors and wines."

"No, no," Yawa says, with obviously false absentmindedness. "I have work to do."

"You're turning down drinks on my boat?"

"It's rather exposed," Yawa says, critically. "Out there on the river. You should avoid it, at least till I can have it secured. You have no idea what kind of favors a Nemesis Judge can ask of the constabulary. In fact, why don't you come to the Court? I can show you some interesting things I've found in the files."

A terrible suspicion crawls up on Baru. Yawa does not want her to go back to her own houseboat. This only makes sense if—oh. Oh no.

Baru glares at her. "You treacherous fuck. You *bitch*. I thought I was safe—"

Yawa shrugs. "It wasn't in your file, I'm afraid. But I knew other places to look."

SHE hires a lighter and rows back to her houseboat. The sun is just rising when she bumps up against the floating dock and leaps across. There are people inside. Lamps burn brightly and furtive shadows move in the windows.

"Shhh," Baru hisses at Yawa. "Don't you dare warn them."

She creeps up to the stern door, and finds it unlocked. Turns the handle until it clicks.

Someone inside says, "Did you hear that?"

Baru flings the door open. It slams into the back of Aminata's wheelchair just as she is leaning forward to hide a gift, sending her face-over-ass onto the carpet. A man in another room barks, "To arms, sailors!" and comes rolling in on a wheelchair of his own: Abdumasi Abd, followed by Tau-indi and Kindalana, both of them struggling with armfuls of old books.

Iscend, peering in from the kitchen, smiles like the moon.

"Surprise!" Baru says, brightly.

"Baru!" Aminata scrambles to her feet in protest. Baru can see the pain in the way she moves, that constant drillbit in her chest: but she does not seem to hang off it like a scarecrow anymore. "You weren't supposed to be back yet!"

"I am known for my brutal dawn ambushes," Baru says, to Yawa's incensed gasp. "Happy birthday to me. And thank you all very much for trying to surprise me. I don't know how you did it. I've never celebrated it on record, not even once—it's not a holiday on Taranoke."

"You daft bitch," Aminata sighs, "Tau asked your mother, back on Cauteria. Your parents send their love."

Something is happening on her blind side: Baru looks over and sees Tau trying to tug a tablecloth over a spectacular jade cormorant. "Tau," she gasps, "you shouldn't have—"

"It's not for you," Tau cautions her. "I found it in the Habitat Hill collection behind the embassy. I want you to kiss it, and then I'm sending it home to Lonjaro with Abdu, as a good-luck charm."

"You're leaving?" Baru asks Abdu.

"Of course I am," he says. Kindalana rubs his scalp. "Kinda and I have to go home and try to sort things out between the Mbo and the Cancrioth. If I can go among them and come back to the Mbo, maybe . . . maybe others will see it's not reason to start killing each other."

"That's the hope," Kindalana says. "I don't think there's any more good to be done here. My charities are solvent, I have skilled people in place to run my affairs, and I'm tired of Falcresti sending me assignation letters. For a people who don't like Oriati"—she glances toward Iscend, the only actually Falcresti person in the room—"they're certainly taken with Oriati women."

"If she's the right sort of woman," Aminata mutters. This makes Kindalana's smile brittle, which in turn makes Baru think of all that is wrong: needles in her brain, unknown damage done to the integrity of her thoughts. Kyprananoke utterly erased, its culture reduced to a few scattered survivors. The Cancrioth on the move in Oriati Mbo, gathering followers for war.

And, for all his influence, Cairdine Farrier was only one man: neither the cause nor the sole conductor of Falcrest's malignant growth.

Defeating him has stopped nothing. In fact, Baru's new trade concern might guarantee Falcrest's triumph. Oriati civil war still looms. The Brain's martyrdom seems to guarantee religious schism. Baru doesn't actually *have* the rutterbook she claims to possess, so in a sense all her promises of new trade are a monumental lie. But as long as that lie goes undiscovered, the sheer power of the Black Tea Ocean Concern will make her an empress in fact if not in name . . . only, if she cannot control that power, she will usher in an age of Falcrest's domination that will scar every last people of the world.

The same dilemma as ever, then. Can you defeat Falcrest with Falcrest's power? Can fire burn fire?

The question is not yet answered.

But right now Baru has a little house, and friends of a sort to fill it, even if few of them, in all likelihood, will survive what is to come with that friendship intact. Aminata is thinking strongly about leaving the navy forever (if she does, Baru intends to offer her a commission as captain on a Black Tea Ocean Concern ship). Baru has no lover; Iscend Comprine is taboo, Shao Lune is a self-serving racialist snake, and Ulyu Xe has gone back to Aurdwynn. But there is a city full of prospects out there, and Baru has Tain Hu's reputation for conquest to uphold.

And she has Kimbune's proof ready to dazzle Falcrest's mathematicians. And Iscend's coin theory of inheritance to challenge Incrastic heredity. And she has Ulyu Xe's theory of culture to pursue, and her parents to reunite, and a friendship with Aminata to repair, and a princess of the Mbo to discover, and Tau-indi's faith to uphold, and more yet, so much that fills her with that giddy claws-out sense of challenge.

She sets it all aside, and closes, for a moment, the accounts of her work.

"I'm twenty-three today," she tells them. "I've outlived Shiqu Si, haven't I?"

"By two years," Iscend shouts from the kitchen.

"You're far behind her, though," Kindalana says. "Shiqu Si was Empress of everything from western Aurdwynn to northern Segu, and you've only got a boat and a trading concern—"

Of course Aminata has to burst in, dissatisfied to hear Kindalana, a Prince, talking down to Baru: "She's been the Empress of Falcrest for a day, hasn't she? Doing a little better than Shiqu Si."

"What do we call you now?" Tau asks, innocently. "The Half-Brain Empress?"

Baru can see the patterns of the world, the ties of money and hunger that bind civilization together in need. And now, looking at Tau-indi, she feels that perhaps she can also see the world as Tau imagined it. The chains of grasping arms that connect all of them to each other. The hope and the fear of caring.

"The Cormorant Empress," she says. "And you are my Cormorant House."

THE LIGHTNING IN THE EAST

THE storm seized *Auroreal* and dragged her across the world.

She was an old ship, a cursed ship, and Captain Bales had expected this expedition to end in doom. She was sailing the Mother of Storms with a crew of the condemned on a ship that still stank of cannibal fires. The Tuning-Spear Concern wanted to find a western route around the southern tip of Zawam Asu, a route to bypass the Oriati and seize the riches of the Black Tea Ocean beyond. So they put out the call for desperate adventurers, ill-acquitted criminals, and women who wanted to sail as far as possible from the past.

Bales had survived four pregnancies and smallpox, which left its kisses all along her cheeks. Her husband was gone, and her children were raised, and one day Bales realized she would never see anything or meet anyone she didn't already know.

So she got her old navy scores out of the bank file and she walked down to the skills market and sold herself to the low bidder on a better captain.

A better captain would not have taken this ship, or this crew, or this course. And when the storm caught them, a better captain would have tried to find a hole to wait it out at anchor. A better captain would not be where Limina Bales was right now: huddled under sealskin, lashed to *Auroreal*'s wheel, laughing.

She ran her ship on the wild storm. Aft sails furled, half the crew on the bilge pumps (she'd ordered the bilge left half-flooded, to lower *Auroreal*'s center of mass and keep the ship from tipping). The reinforced stern, armored against northern icepack, shuddered and groaned under the storm surge.

Limina Bales clung to the wheel as hot tropical water pounded her into the deck. She kept the ship's bow pointed straight along with the wind. Straight east. Ever eastward.

She had planned to swing wide east, then south, to catch a current around kangaroo-cursed Zawam Asu and its deadly cape. But instead of bringing her west into the Black Tea Ocean, the Mother of Storms had caught *Auroreal* at the end of its eastward run, hurling them onward, storm-tossed through longitudes where a blistering headwind usually fought ships back.

Limina Bales had, entirely by accident, discovered a southern passage across the Mother of Storms.

And on the twenty-fifth day, as the crew began to run out of water, she sighted land.

They were running almost straight north now. An albatross with a ten-foot wingspan and beautiful black tips dashed itself against the mainmast and fell dead. Then, at midnight by the ship's clock, Limina spotted lightning on the northern horizon. The strikes illuminated a tower of stormclouds . . . and at the base of that storm, the dirty orange glow of wildfire.

"Land," she croaked. "Land!"

The man Hammide, whom she'd retained as a wilderness guide, stuck his head abovedecks at her shout. "Land?" he cried. "Truly?" He was nearly decapitated by a falling boom.

At sunrise *Auroreal* ran aground in shallow water. She'd lost her main and foremast, but the hull was intact, and she could float again. They could get home—if they could only find masts.

The eastern sun showed them an alien beach, volcanic stone cracked into hexagonal cells. To the north, where Limina had seen wildfire, thunder grumbled endlessly. The storm coiled and flashed over tremendous mountain peaks and the lightning never seemed to stop. Even here, south of the storm, the air tasted of nerves and soot. People became hypnotized by the flashes, and had to be shouted out of trance. What water they found seemed sulfurous or mineral. But in the stony tablelands beyond the beach there was a hot spring, which Limina used as a reward and rest.

"Where's there's wildfire," she told her first mate, "there might be wood."

She gathered a party of carpenters and able hands, assigned Hammide to break trail, and set out. Clouds obscured the true size of the mountains to the north and east. They were huge, easy rivals to the Wintercrests or Mount Merit, though older and more jagged. The surveyor shouted excited figures: twenty, thirty, forty thousand feet.

The lightning strikes seemed to focus on a valley on the near side of the peaks. The surveyor begged for a chance to visit. "There's no point," Limina warned her, "until we're sure we can bring whatever we discover back to Falcrest."

North and northeast they marched. Into the lightning.

Soon the thunder crashed so loud it was impossible to sleep. Limina's sailors began to hallucinate of fatigue. Reports of strange lights overhead, soft voices in the dark. "We do not turn around," Limina warned them, "until we find a good tree."

On the second night beneath the storm, Limina was coming back from latrine when she saw a whirling ring of thin violet fire, perhaps three feet across, standing upright in the air before her. It ascended slowly and vanished among the low clouds. Limina sat down with a mental hygiene booklet and did a few washes.

The forest ahead promised good trees. Frequent wildfires would leave only hardy and fast-growing specimens as survivors.

One of the carpenters was struck first: the bolt traveled down his saw and through his body. He survived, but he was constantly confused and irritable. The tactical clerk was hit three times, leaving her a babbling mess. The first carpenter was now on crutches, having lost his sense of balance after the strike. The carpenter's mate was struck while gathering water from a huge, shallow freshwater lake, a sheet of water running out to the horizon. He drowned face-down in six inches.

They pushed on. Tiny brushes of fire flickered along belt buckles and fanned from knife tips. In camp that night Limina called Hammide to her tent to discuss what to do if they lost the strength to bring the masts back to *Auroreal.* They fell on each other, afterward, trying to find something to think about except that distant thunder: the world's irregular heartbeat, daring them to madness.

She drew lines of light on his naked chest, marveling at the flickering discharge. The sound of the thunder was inescapable; he moved to the anti-rhythm of the strikes. When it began to seem as if he matched or even anticipated the loudest cracks of thunder she closed her eyes and saw ghost letters in the afterimage darkness. She had to tell him she'd finished: his eyes were haunted, far-away, his hips shimmering galvanic against the blanket. He fell asleep holding her.

They woke to a spider rune carved in the center of their camp, black glass and shattered flowers.

But that late afternoon they found a copse of live trees.

As the party cut and dressed trees to use as masts, and prepared rollers for the long haul back to *Auroreal,* Hammide asked Limina if he could climb the ridge to the north and look for the center of the lightning strikes

"No," she told him. "Absolutely not."

"Come on." He gave her that stupid, endearing grin. "You want to sit here in camp waiting for the carpenters? We're explorers! Let's explore!"

"We're the dregs of the Republic," she corrected him, wryly. "But I suppose, while we're here, we might as well contribute to the natural sciences . . . if only in the hope they'll contribute to us in turn."

* * *

THE crest of the ridge revealed a long valley, running east into the mountains. Rings of ancient stone monoliths interlocked like chainmail across the valley floor. Tumbled ruins broke the patterns, ruining any hint of elegance. Lightning forked and tripled in the west, probing the mountainside. The plants were stunted, as if the storm had been overhead so long it blocked the sun.

Their weapons, the buckles on their clothes, crawled with cold fire.

"Look, mam!" One of the sailors in the party pointed north. "Do you see that? Does anyone else see that?"

They gaped together at the green sun descending from the clouds. It must have been forty or fifty feet across, a perfectly spherical ball of fire, trailing a constellation of sizzling blue points which flocked and swarmed like fish. Abruptly it accelerated south, toward them, and then spiraled in impossible curves down toward one of the monolith rings. In silence it touched the stone and vanished. Just gone.

"What *is* this?" Limina breathed. "Where the fuck are we?"

"Captain Bales," Hammide said, slowly, "I think there are people down there. Things that might be people'. . ."

She followed his spyglass. Something moved . . . a file of shapes, coming up through the toppled monoliths, toward the mountain and the center of the lightning strikes. They did not look like people at all. The shapes were *wrong* . . . the ground behind them seemed to squirm. Like octopi, she thought. Giant land squid, dragging thick limbs behind them. Thin gray lines, rays of geometry, cast off their shoulders and up into the clouds.

"Ten people," Hamidde reported crisply. "They're wearing plate armor. Full-body plate, like a Stakhi tunnel knight . . . but badly maintained. Rusted or burnt."

"Let me see." Limina shamelessly applied captain's privilege to steal the spyglass. "Oh, *kings* . . . look at that. . . ."

Only in the flash of lightning could the armored figures be seen. In the darkness between strikes, they became ghosts of crawling palefire. Huge tentacles dragged across the ground behind them: like worms, pursuing. They were chains, Limina realized. A cape of chains behind each armored figure. And the rays she'd seen projecting from their upper bodies were lines for kites. They had kites tethered to their bodies, flying in the clouds. . . .

"Ai!" she hissed. Lightning struck one of the armored figures. The flash shattered her vision into forks and jags.

"What is it?" Hamidde whispered.

"I don't believe it." She reacquired the group and counted them twice. No change. "He's still walking. The armor protects them."

"That can't be. Lightning will shatter Stakhieczi plate. Burn whoever's inside."

"Well, he's still walking!"

"Maybe the lightning just landed nearby."

"Maybe. Hush. They're doing something."

The group of armored figures was coming up to a slight rise, where a toppled monolith waited like a table. Limina began to notice differences between the figures. The one in the lead was stooped over, staggering as if under a burden. And in the middle of the column . . .

"They have prisoners." She couldn't make out features, but the unarmored figures did not seem willing: two of the armored beings guarded them closely. Her mind leapt to the most lurid possibility. "I think it's a human sacrifice."

But it did not go as she expected.

The two guards made no move to force the prisoners up onto the makeshift altar. The weakest one, the one who'd been in the lead, climbed up onto the monolith with the help of the others.

Then, with shocking speed, the leader shed its armor. At this distance there was no sound but the thunder, so Limina imagined the rattle of chains and the crash of steel. The body within seemed human. Limina tried to get a glimpse at its face but it was moving, reaching down, taking from the others a long spear or pole.

The one standing on the monolith lifted the pole to the sky and waited.

The bolt came down at once. The flash dazzled Limina again, but she blinked it away and screwed her eye tight to the scout glass. "The one who took its armor off is dead. Killed by the lightning. The others . . . they're . . . oh kings, oh queens and kings."

"What is it?" Hammide begged. "What's happening?"

"The other armored ones. They're cutting the dead one's head open. They're *portioning* it . . ."

"What?"

"They're portioning its brain out. They're going to make the—"

She gagged and had to look away. The guards were shoving the unarmored prisoners forward, toward the slaughtered corpse, and the little gobbets of human brain waiting in metal bowls.

"Limina, what's happening down there?" Hammide whispered.

"I have no worldly idea," she said. "I have no idea at all. But it's terrible. It's atrocious."

They had to make it home. They had to tell someone. There was something across the sea. Something in the storm. A threat to all civilization.

She wondered what the Emperor would do about it.

ACKNOWLEDGMENTS

Sine qua non: Gillian Conahan, Jennifer Jackson, Will Hinton.

The following provided comprehensive and timely feedback on early drafts of the story: Maya Chhabra, Caitlin Starling, Neal Hebert, Sloane Leong, Django Wexler, Tom Crayford, Ursula Whitcher, John Chu, and Kalya Nedungadi. I am especially indebted to those readers whose people have experienced, or are still experiencing, the same tragedies that Baru glimpsed on Taranoke and Kyprananoke. All errors, misrepresentations, and mistakes are my own, and do not reflect on the expertise or preferences of these readers.

I owe continued thanks to Rachel Swirsky, Ann Leckie, Kameron Hurley, Max Gladstone, Yoon Ha Lee, Brooke Bolander, Mia Serrano, Alyssa Wong, Amal El-Mohtar, Caitlin Starling, and C. A. Higgins for their personal support. My personal thanks also to everyone who has taken the time to write or express support online—it never goes unnoticed.

Baru's world (hopefully) evokes the same curiosity in the reader as it does in Baru herself: is this magic, or is it unknown science? Those intrigued by the Cancrioth immortata may find interest in the canine transmissible venereal tumor, a single clonal organism which has passed from dog to dog by transmission of live cells for the past several thousand years. Like the immortata, CTVT does no significant harm to the host and strongly prefers a specific part of the body. No equivalent human cell line has been discovered . . . yet (though see the acknowledgments to *The Monster Baru Cormorant* for further discussion).

The Cancrioth's extensive use of radioluminescence depends on the ecology of the hot lands, where many organisms have evolved phosphors for mating displays, predation, and even metabolism. The sensitivity of the frogs used for signaling is exquisite, and given the relatively short range of most radiation, perhaps implausible; but evolution is ingenious.

The megatsunami at Kyprananoke is echoed in the real world by events in Lituya Bay, Alaska, and the Vajant Dam in Italy.

The economic power of Baru's notional trade concern is hardly exaggerated. Nor is the possibility of the near-total destruction of an imperial economy by mismanagement on the part of a powerful few: interested readers may look into John Law's time in France and the neighboring South Sea bubble in England.

Baru's own neural peculiarities exist in the real world, although I have taken significant liberties in the specific symptoms of hemineglect. (Nor have I gone to the lengths of actually taking drugs like vidhara and datura—by all accounts datura is to be strictly avoided.) The antidepressant effects of some hallucinogens are, probably, real. Her poor brain's resilience to repeated trauma, including mechanical penetration by steel needles, is true to the real world, where human brains have survived and adapted to all manner of physical traumas. The case of Phineas Gage, whose frontal lobe was impaled by a railroad spike, is often cited as proof that insult to the brain can also destroy the personality. But much less known is the fact that Gage, through hard work and therapy, made an essentially complete recovery, holding down a complex and cognitively demanding job as as stagecoach driver for several years. Of course, Gage ultimately died of seizure, so Baru's safety and complete recovery are not necessarily assured.

Those who find the Masquerade's programs of sterilization, economic intrigue, colonial adventure, and psychosurgery outlandish or unbelievably malicious ("too overtly evil," in the words of a very smart friend) should familiarize themselves with the history of America in the twentieth century. Sterilization of Native American women (among other populations, including black women and immigrants) continued until the 1970s. In 1927 the Supreme Court upheld the mandatory sterilization of eighteen-year-old mother Carrie Buck on the grounds that she was "feeble-minded and promiscuous" and a "genetic threat to society." In the 8–1 decision, Oliver Wendell Holmes Jr. wrote that "three generations of imbeciles are enough." Carrie had been raped by a relative and institutionalized, perhaps to hide the scandal of her pregnancy, and the highest court in the land could not give her justice. So the instruments of state power are used and upheld. The order to sterilize Carrie may have been intended largely as a test of the laws permitting eugenic intervention by those eager to widen the practice. The Supreme Court has never overturned the decision.

In the acknowledgments to the last book I cautioned the reader that stranger ways of life than the Cancrioth's exist in Baru's world. We have now received a small glimpse into one of those strange ways. As ever, I leave the question of supernatural power versus scientific unknown in your hands. But I admit I am particularly proud of this one: it gives me special delight to invent things which probably *could* happen on Earth, had things gone a different, stranger way.

I hope you enjoyed the book. I cannot promise exactly when the next and final one will be ready. These books are deeply draining to write, and, increasingly, they feel like a negative-sum process, an engine that accepts labor and produces self-doubt, loneliness, and the harshest internal criticism. I feel that if I lose all the joy of writing, the result will be equally joyless. I want to do justice to the end of Baru's story. I may need some time to step back and find a fresh, powerful, concise voice for that end—a voice that is as gripping, clear, and compulsive as Baru's own rediscovered sense of purpose. Still, the story is ready, the plan is clear, the ending is set. We have only to help her reach it. And I want to do a good job of helping her; I want to do it right.

ABOUT THE AUTHOR

SETH DICKINSON is the author of the Baru Cormorant novels and many short stories, as well as much of the lore and backstory of Bungie Studios' *Destiny*. He lives in New York City.